ALSO FROM JOE BOOKS

Disney Frozen Cinestory Comic
Disney Cinderella Cinestory Comic
Disney 101 Dalmatians Cinestory Comic
Disney Princess Comics Treasury
Disney•Pixar Comics Treasury
Disney Darkwing Duck: The Definitively Dangerous Edition
Disney Frozen: The Story of the Movie in Comics
Disney Big Hero 6 Cinestory Comic
Disney•Pixar Inside Out Cinestory Comic
Disney•Pixar Inside Out Fun Book
Disney Gravity Falls Cinestory Comic Volume One
Disney•Pixar The Good Dinosaur Cinestory Comic
Disney•Pixar The Good Dinosaur Fun Book
Disney Zootopia Cinestory Comic
Disney Winnie the Pooh Cinestory Comic
Disney Descendants Wicked World Cinestory Comic Volume One
Disney Alice in Wonderland Cinestory Comic
Disney•Pixar Finding Nemo Cinestory Comic
Disney Star vs the Forces of Evil Cinestory Comic
Disney•Pixar Cars Cinestory Comic
Marvel Thor: Dueling with Giants

Don't miss our monthly comics...
Disney Princess
Disney Darkwing Duck
Disney•Pixar Finding Dory

And Disney Frozen, launching in July!

DISNEP
DESCENDANTS
Wicked World
Cinestory Comic
Volume 2

JOE BOOKS LTD

Published simultaneously in the United States and Canada by Joe Books Ltd,
567 Queen St W, Toronto, ON M5V 2B6

www.joebooks.com

First Joe Books Edition: August 2016

ISBN 978-1-77275-328-8 (paperback edition)
ISBN 978-1-55275-350-9 (ebook edition)

"Night Is Young"
Words and Music by Lindy Robbins, Jintae Ko and Tanner Underwood
© 2015 Walt Disney Music Company (ASCAP)
All Rights Reserved. Used With Permission.

ADAPTATION, DESIGN, LETTERING, LAYOUT AND EDITING:

For Readhead Books:
Alberto Garrido, PF Ispizua, Ernesto Lovera, Ester Salguero,
Salvador Navarro, Rocío Salguero, Eduardo Alpuente, Heidi Roux,
Heather Penner and Carolynn Prior.

Library and Archives Canada Cataloguing in Publication
information is available upon request

Printed and bound in Canada
3   5   7   9   10   8   6   4   2

Disney

DESCENDANTS

Wicked World

Cinestory Comic
Volume 2

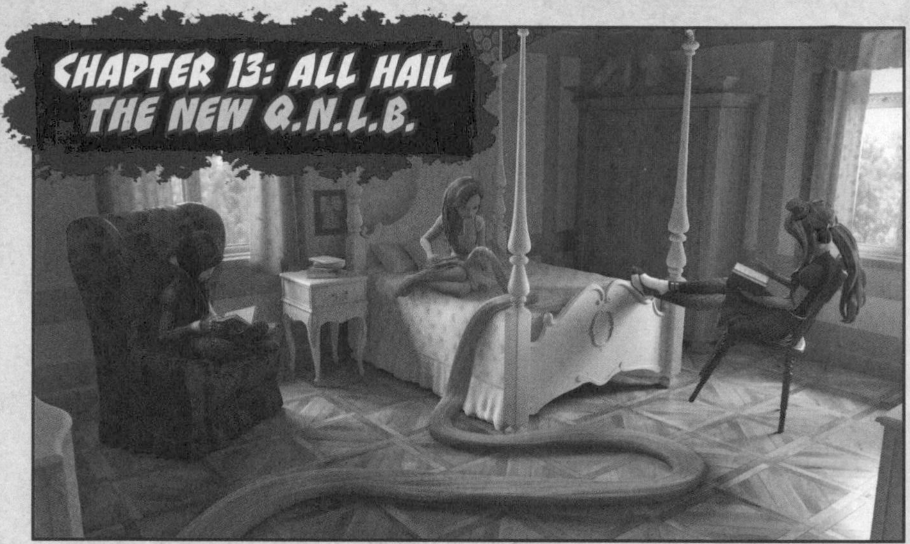
CHAPTER 13: ALL HAIL THE NEW Q.N.L.B.

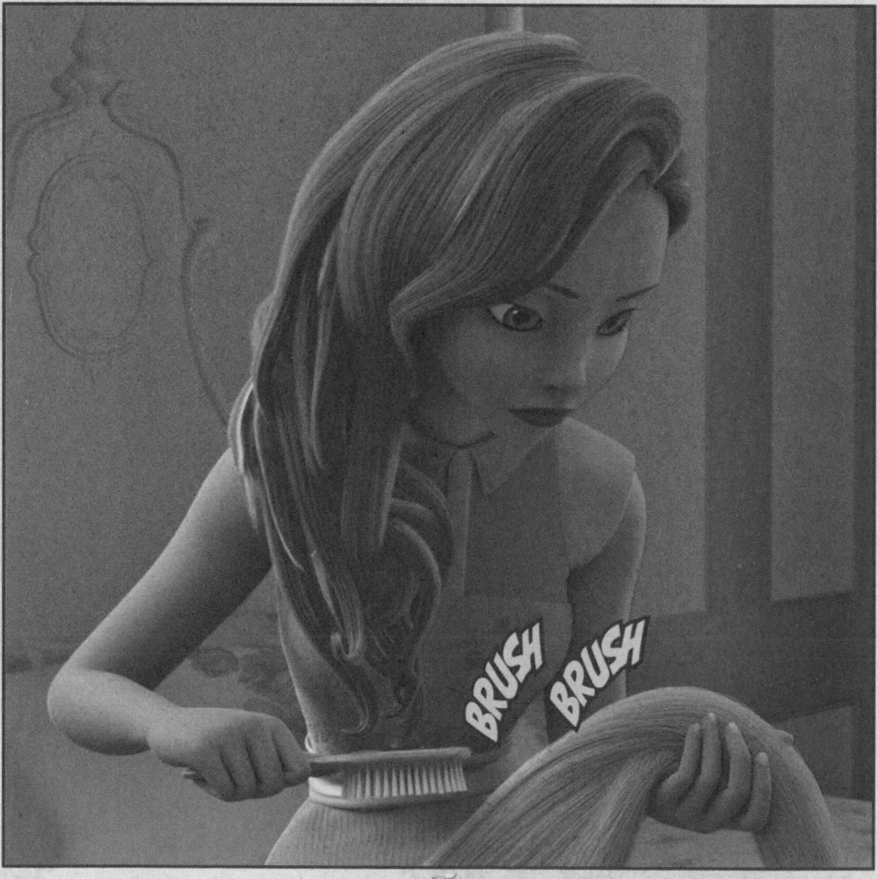
BRUSH
BRUSH

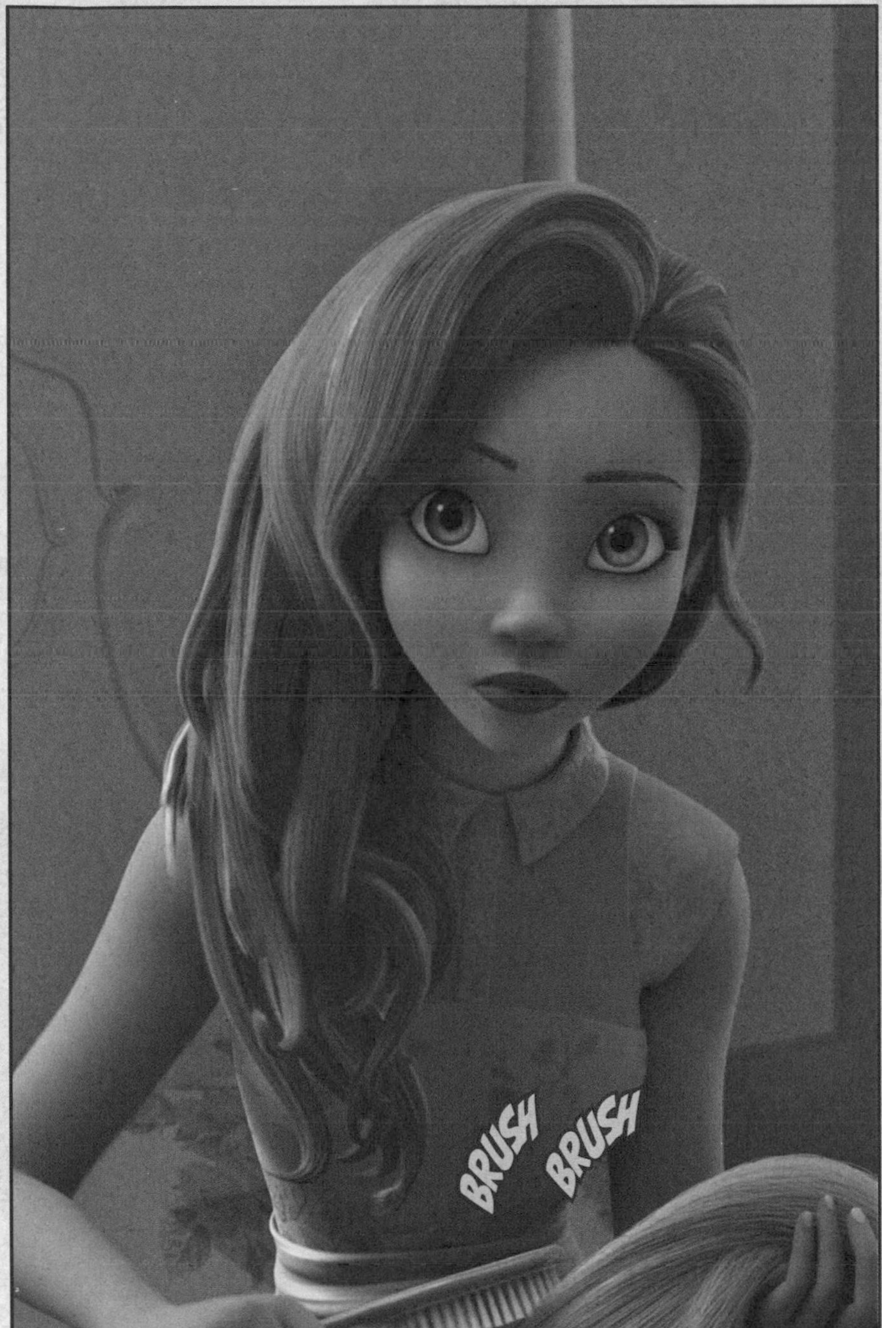
BRUSH
BRUSH

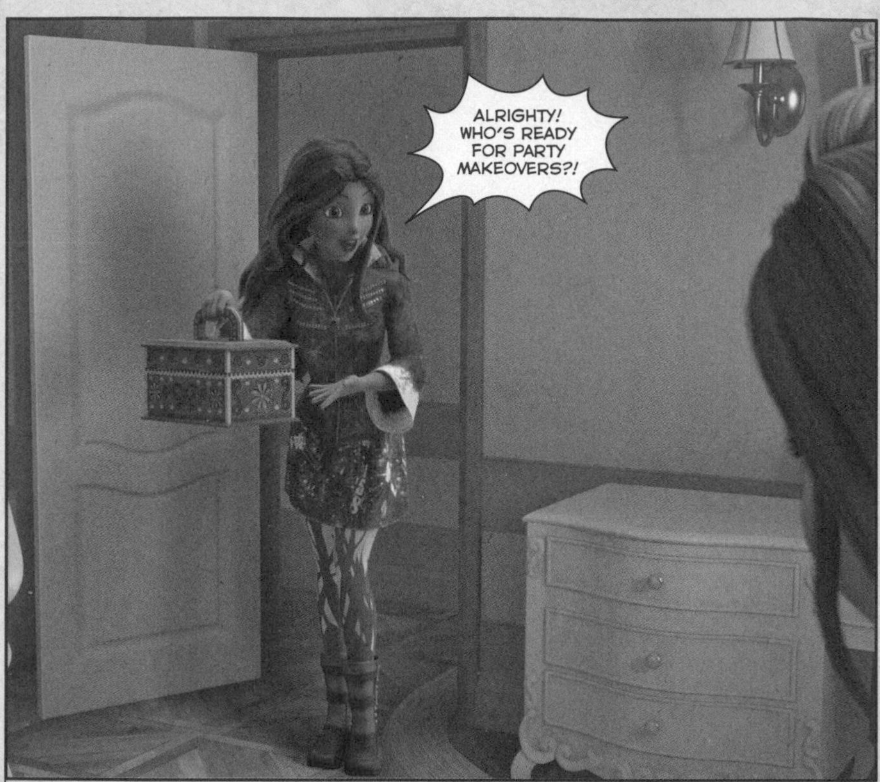
ALRIGHTY! WHO'S READY FOR PARTY MAKEOVERS?!

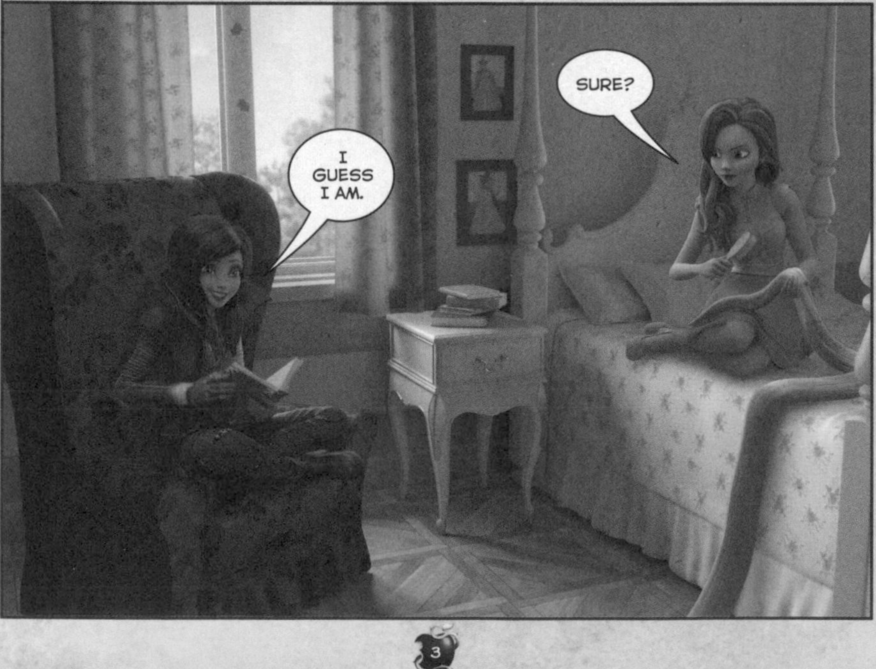
SURE?
I GUESS I AM.

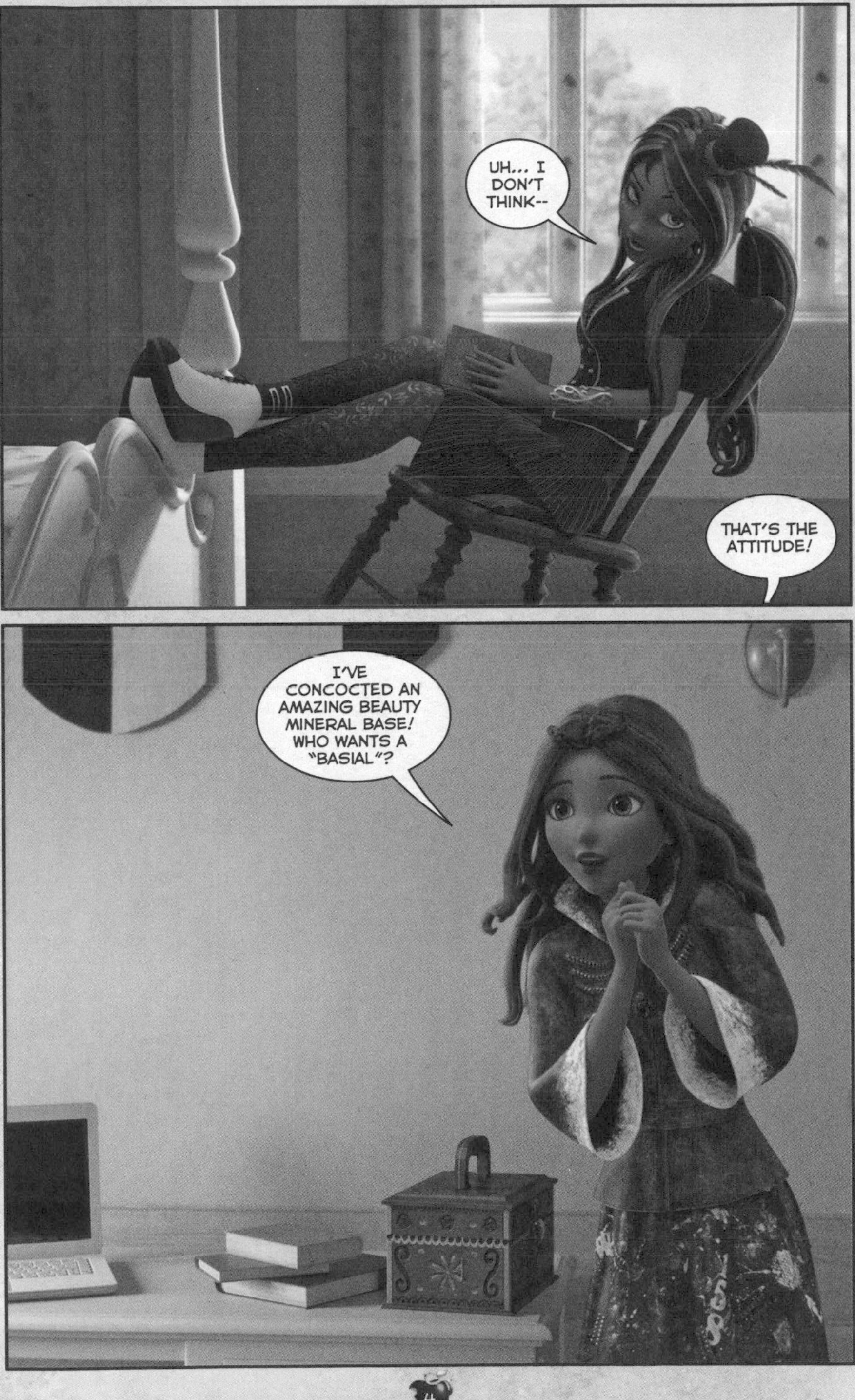
UH... I DON'T THINK--
THAT'S THE ATTITUDE!
I'VE CONCOCTED AN AMAZING BEAUTY MINERAL BASE! WHO WANTS A "BASIAL"?

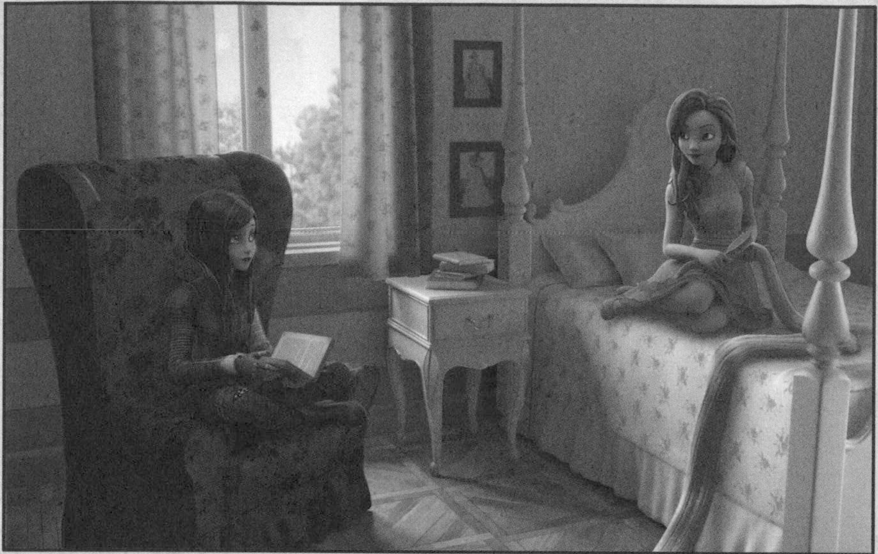

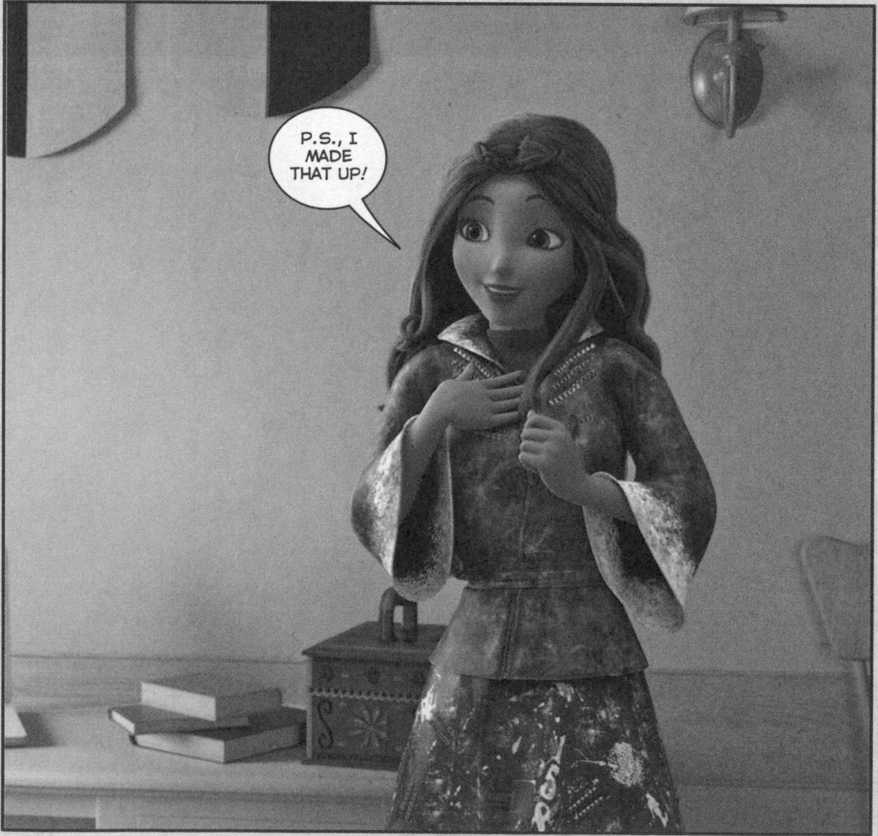
P.S., I MADE THAT UP!

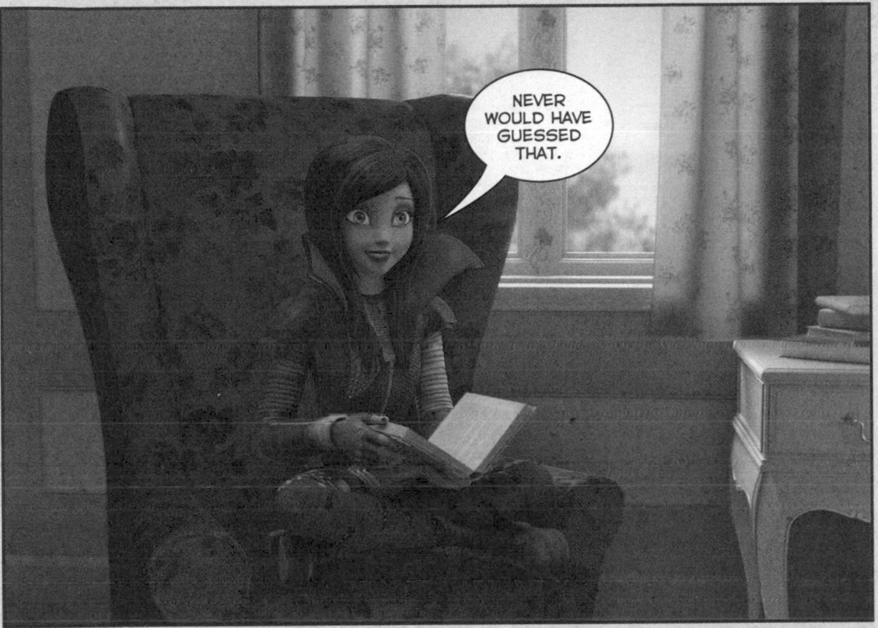
NEVER WOULD HAVE GUESSED THAT.

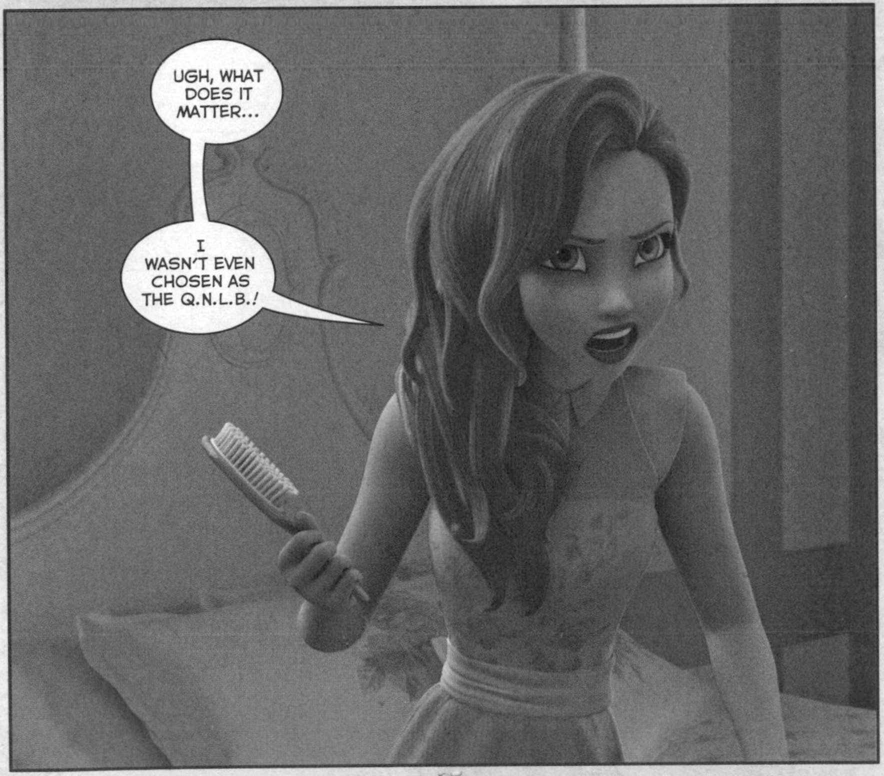
UGH, WHAT DOES IT MATTER...
I WASN'T EVEN CHOSEN AS THE Q.N.L.B.!

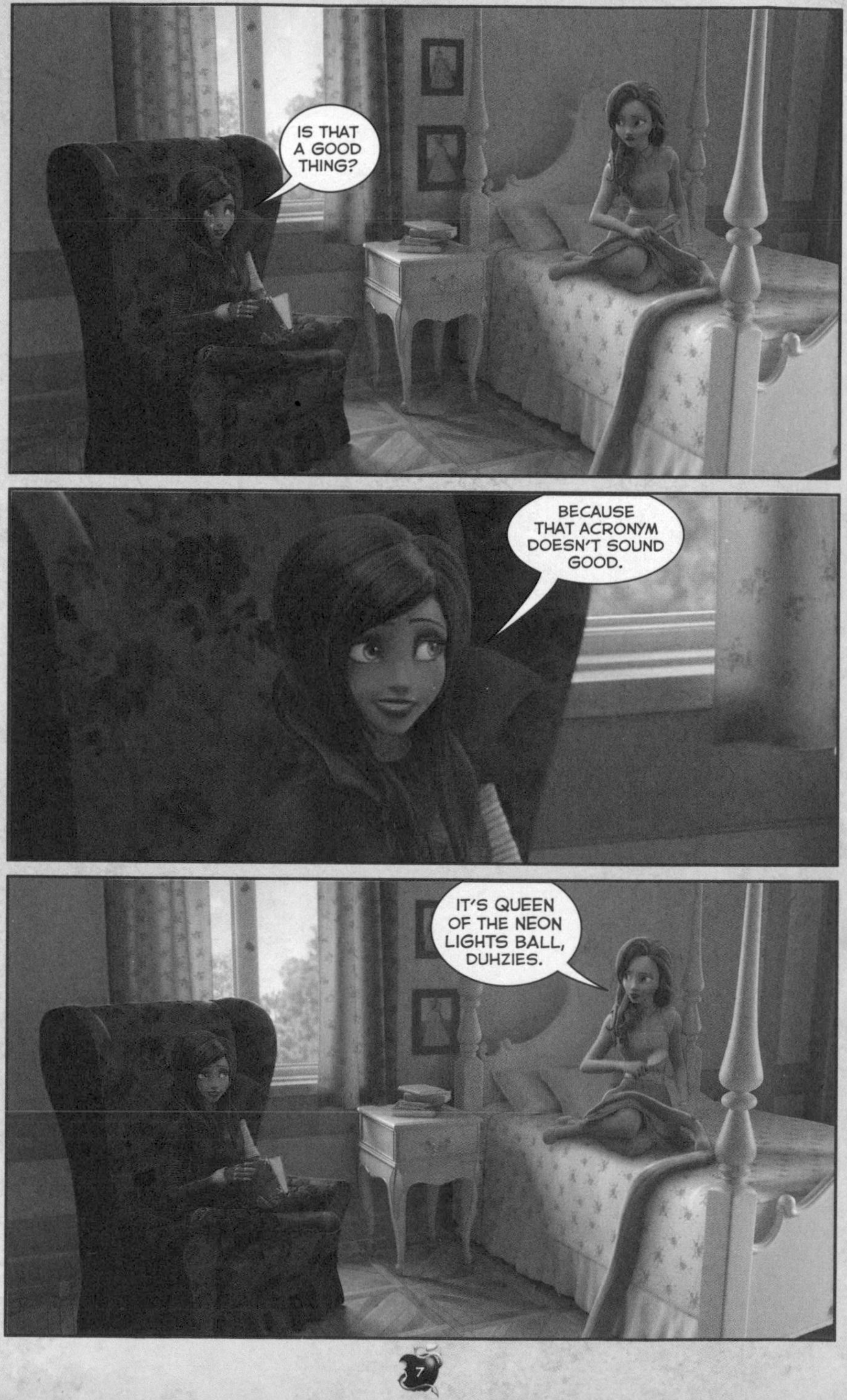
IS THAT A GOOD THING?
BECAUSE THAT ACRONYM DOESN'T SOUND GOOD.
IT'S QUEEN OF THE NEON LIGHTS BALL, DUHZIES.

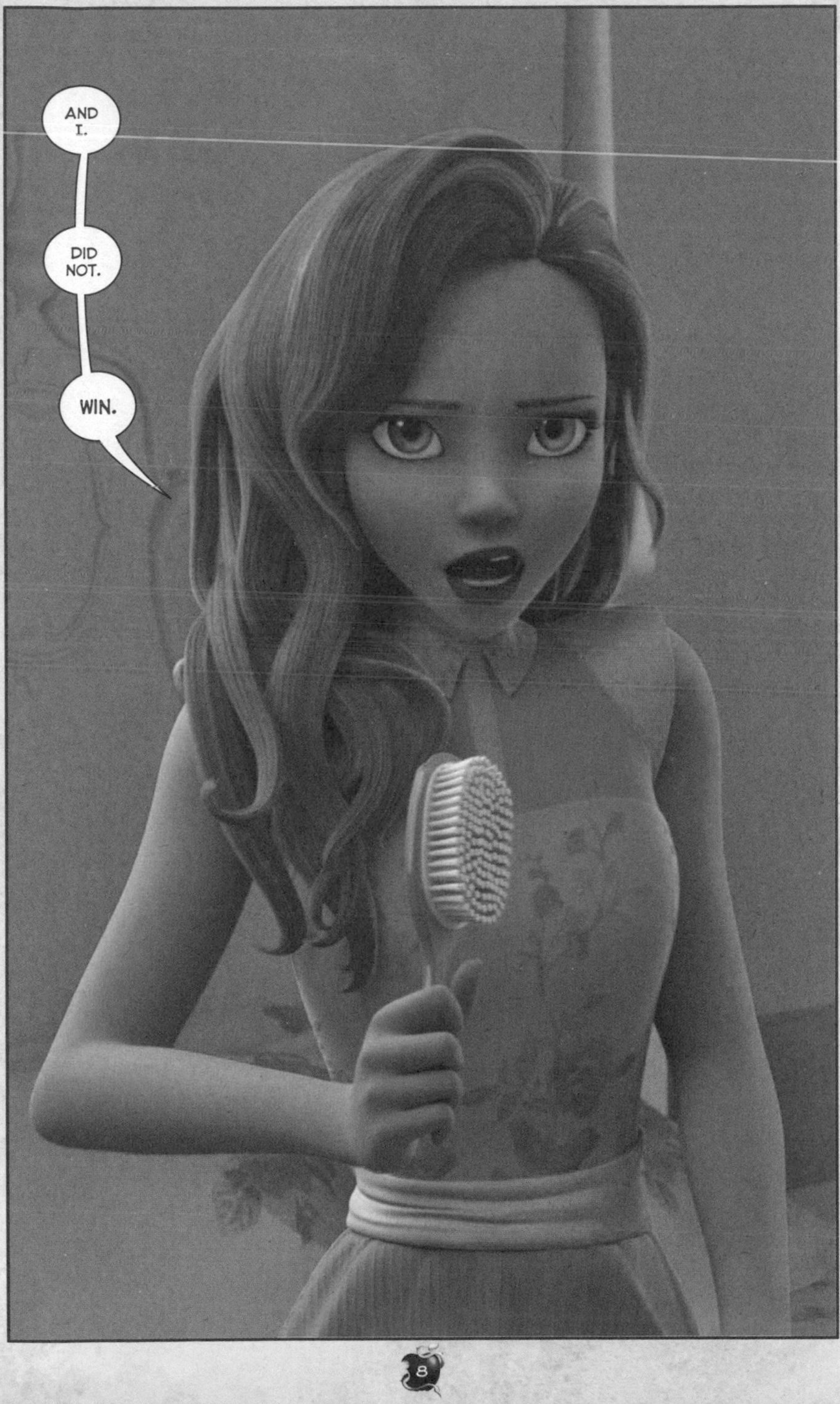
AND I.
DID NOT.
WIN.

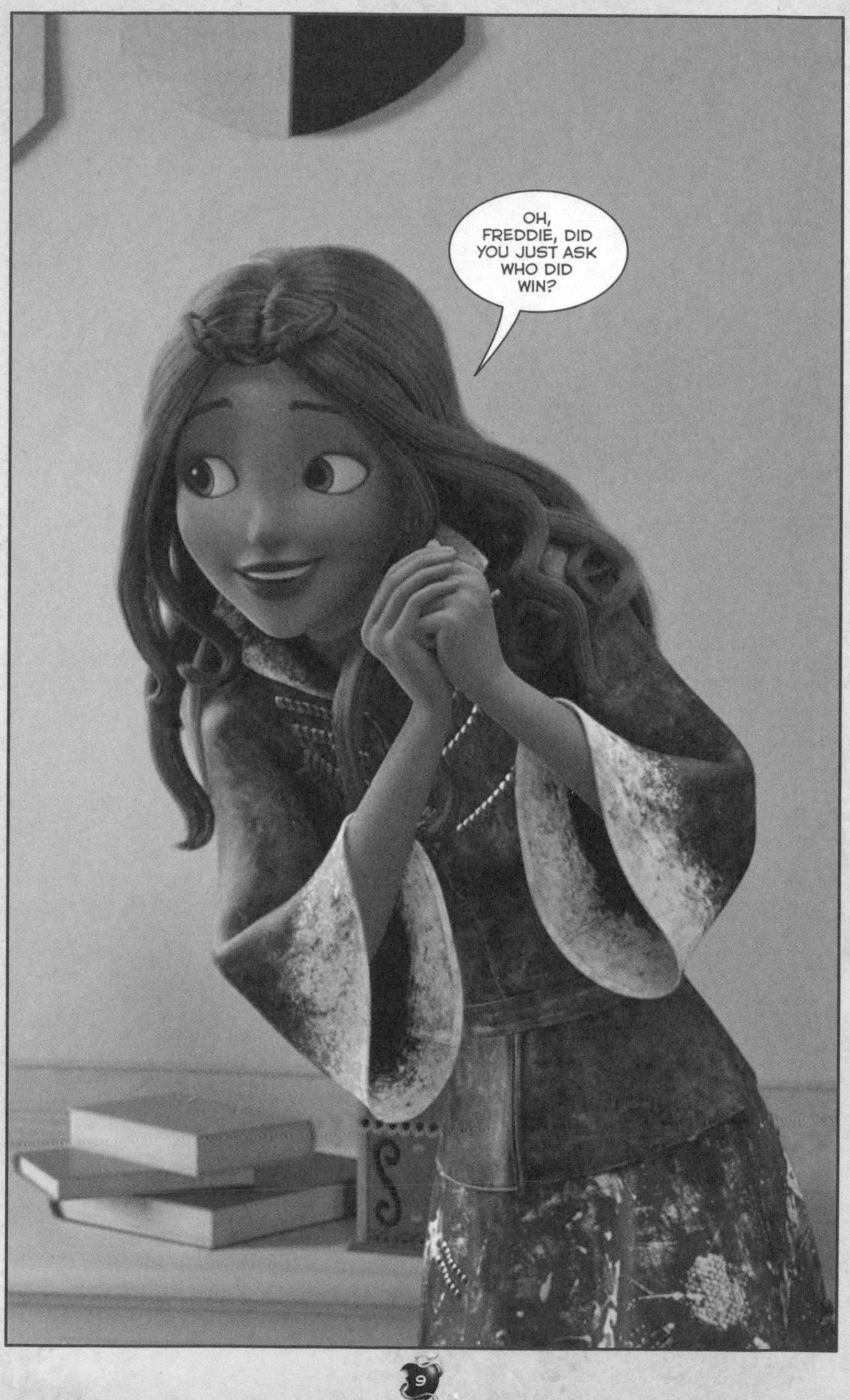
OH, FREDDIE, DID YOU JUST ASK WHO DID WIN?

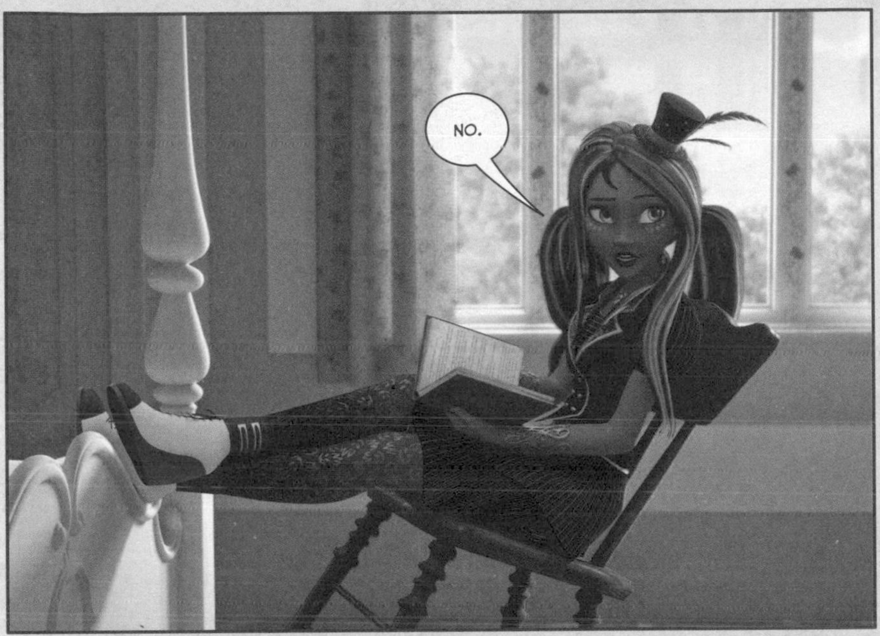
NO.

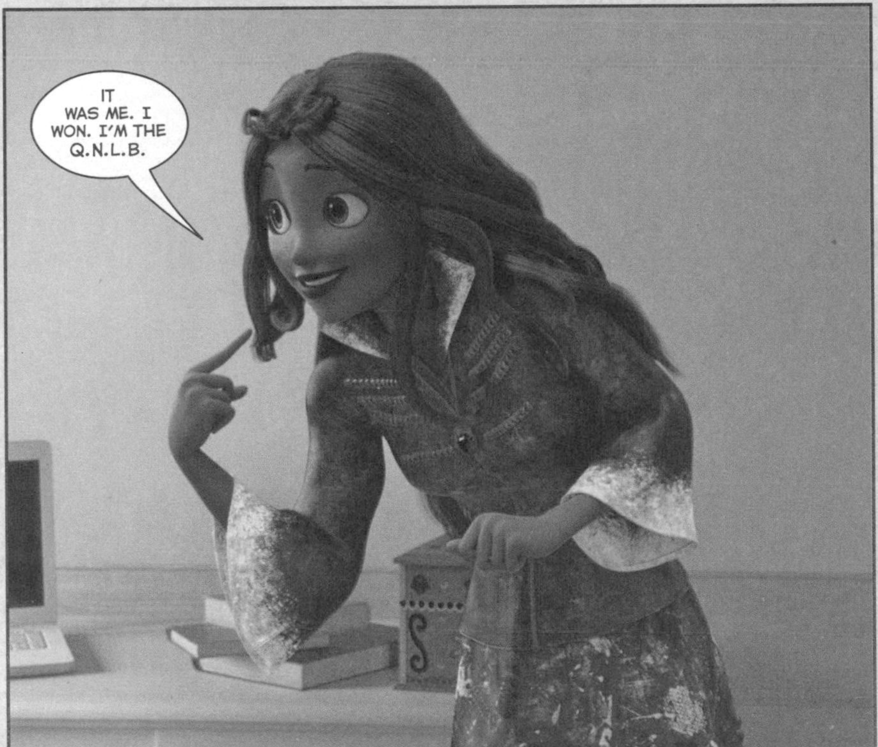
IT WAS ME. I WON. I'M THE Q.N.L.B.

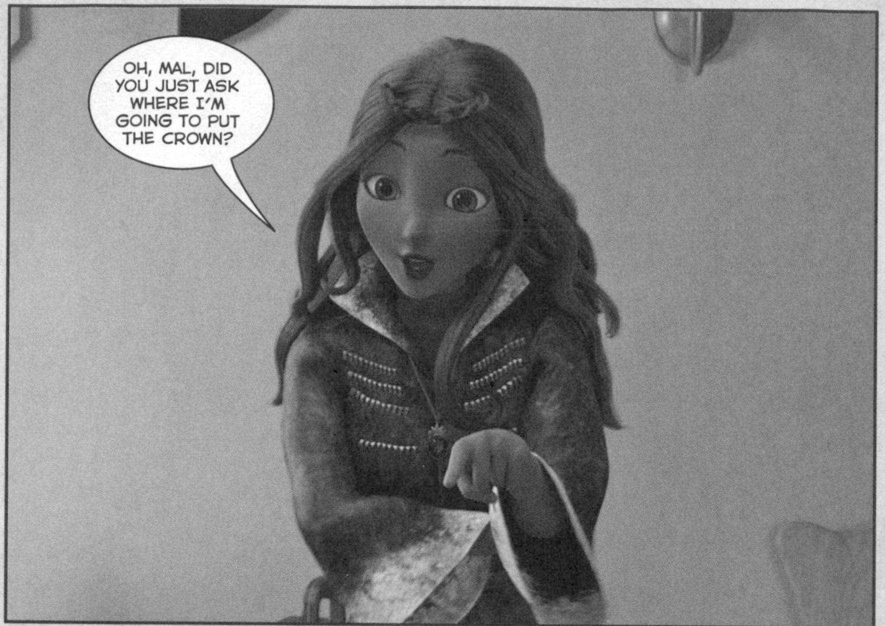
OH, MAL, DID YOU JUST ASK WHERE I'M GOING TO PUT THE CROWN?

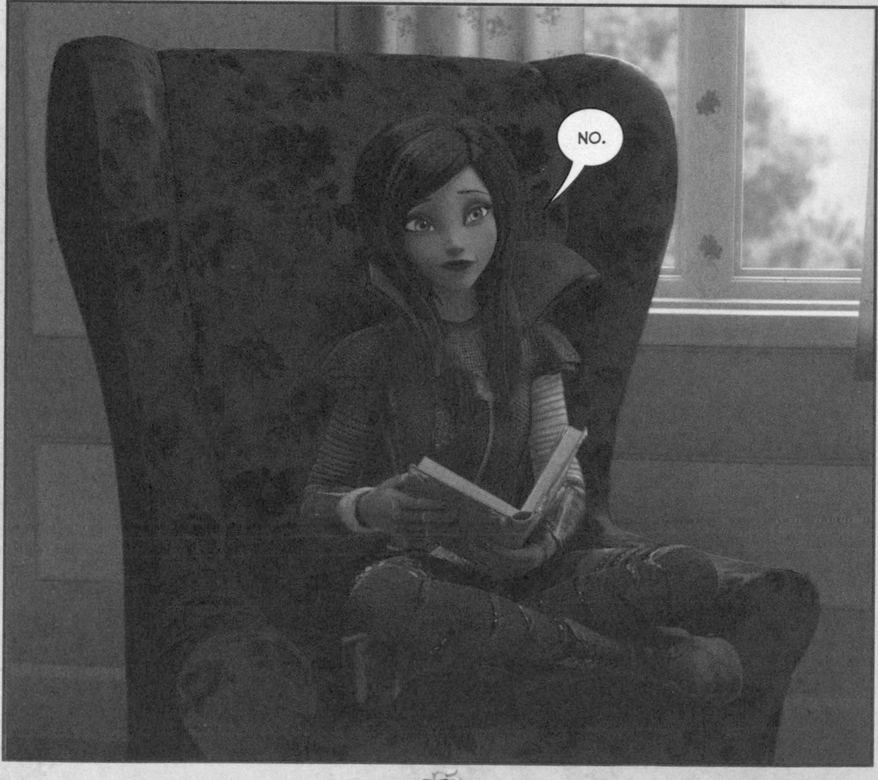
NO.

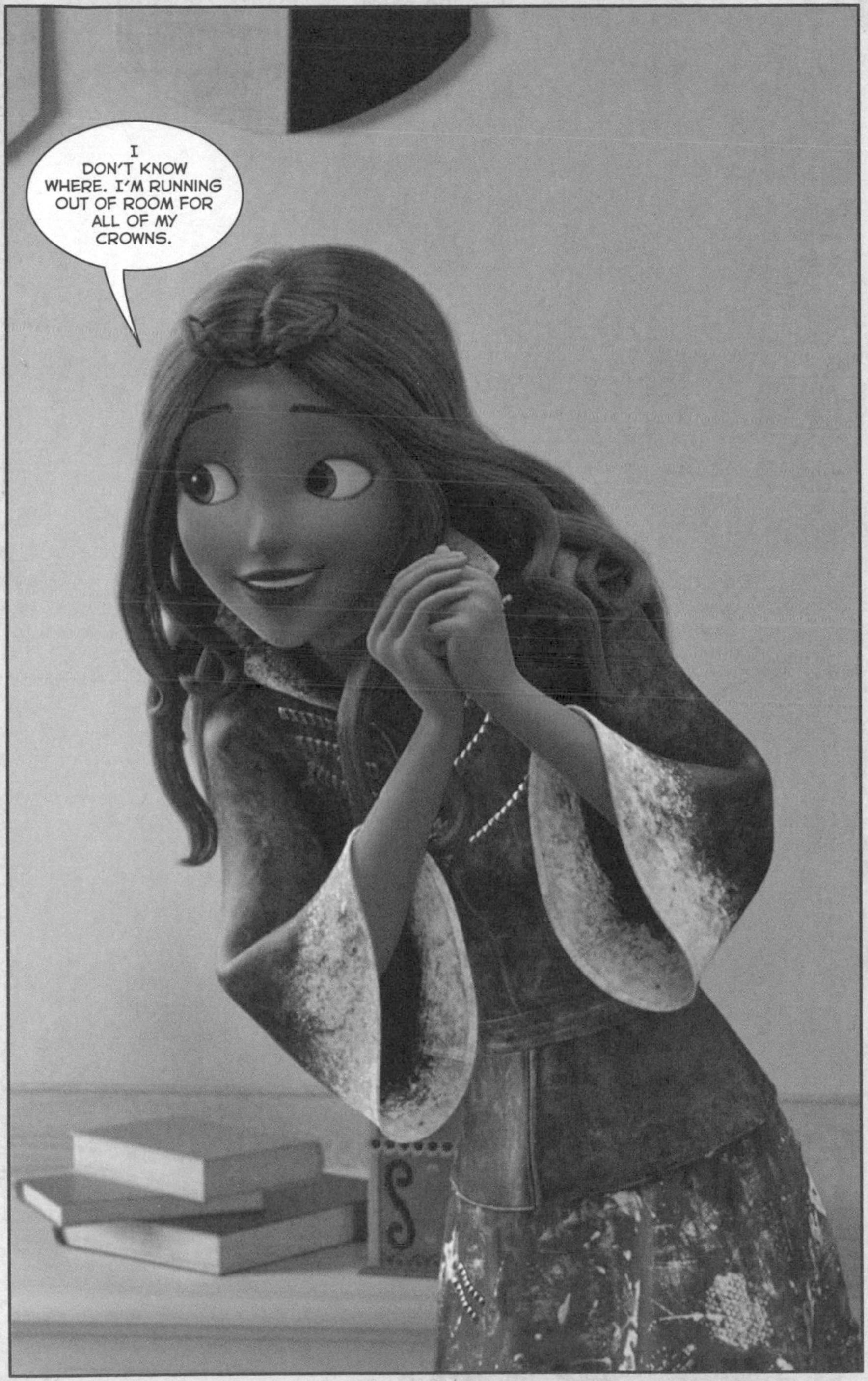
I DON'T KNOW WHERE. I'M RUNNING OUT OF ROOM FOR ALL OF MY CROWNS.

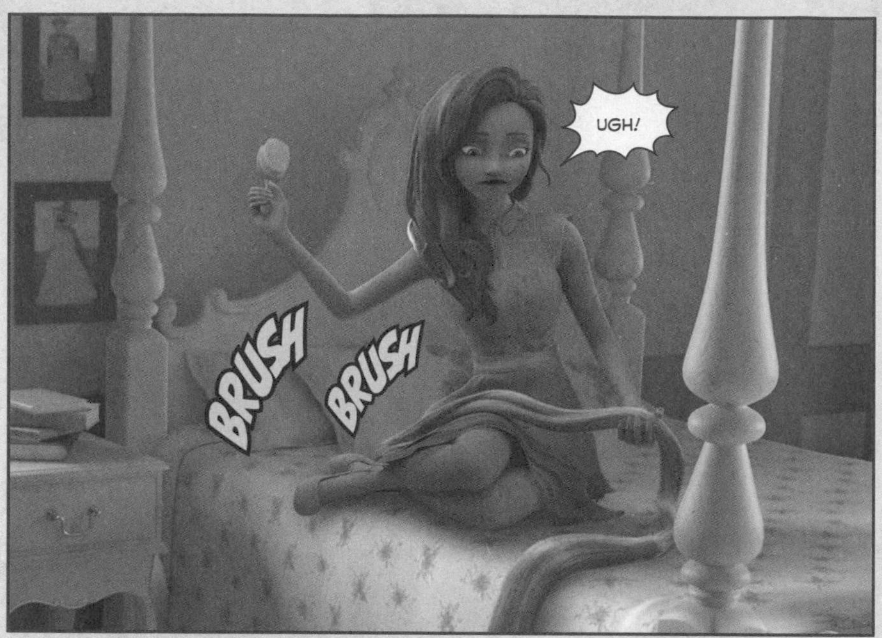
UGH!
BRUSH
BRUSH

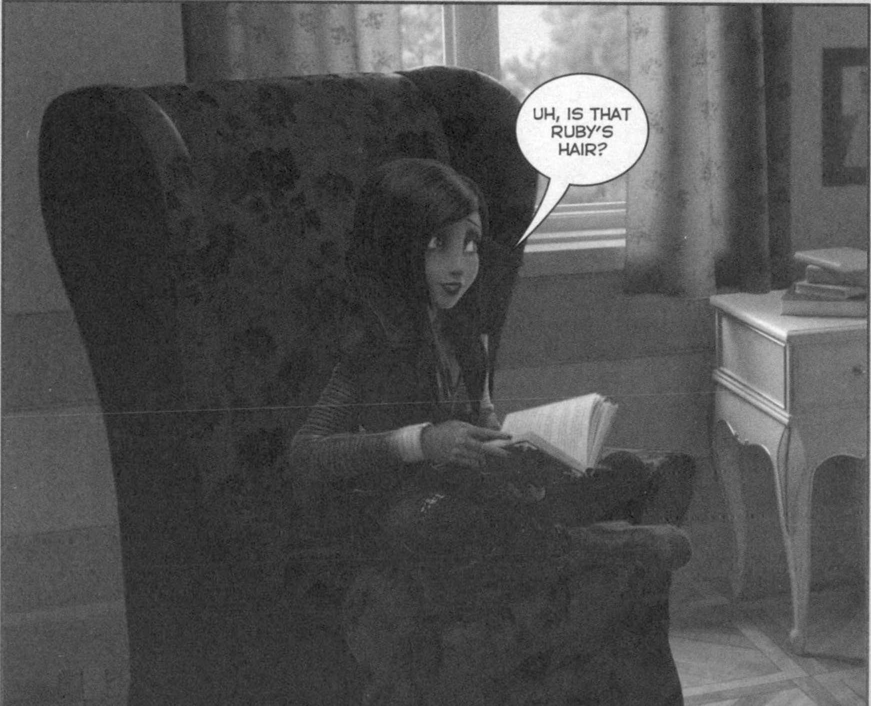
UH, IS THAT RUBY'S HAIR?

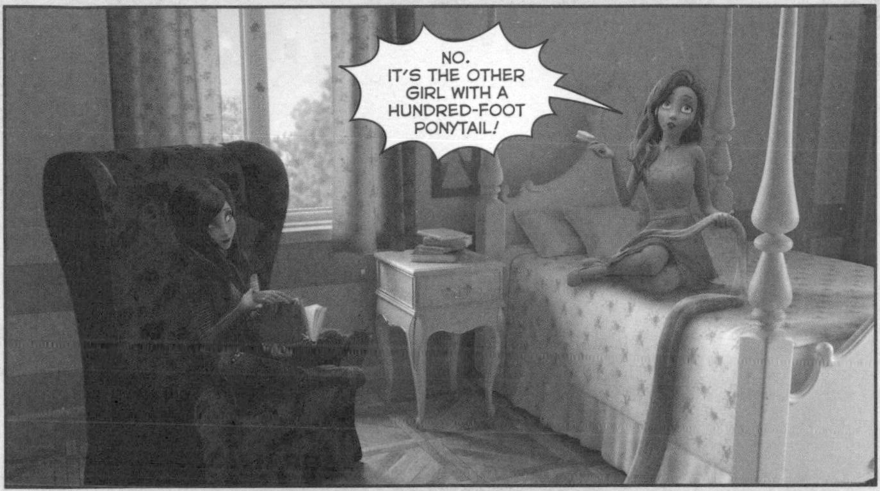
NO.
IT'S THE OTHER GIRL WITH A HUNDRED-FOOT PONYTAIL!

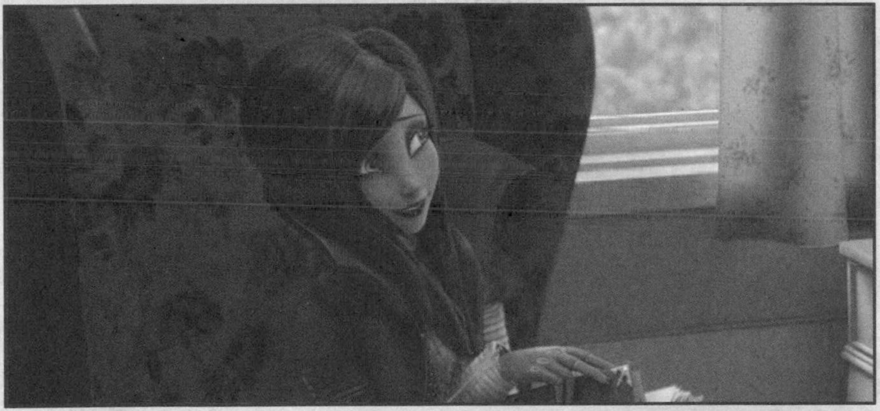

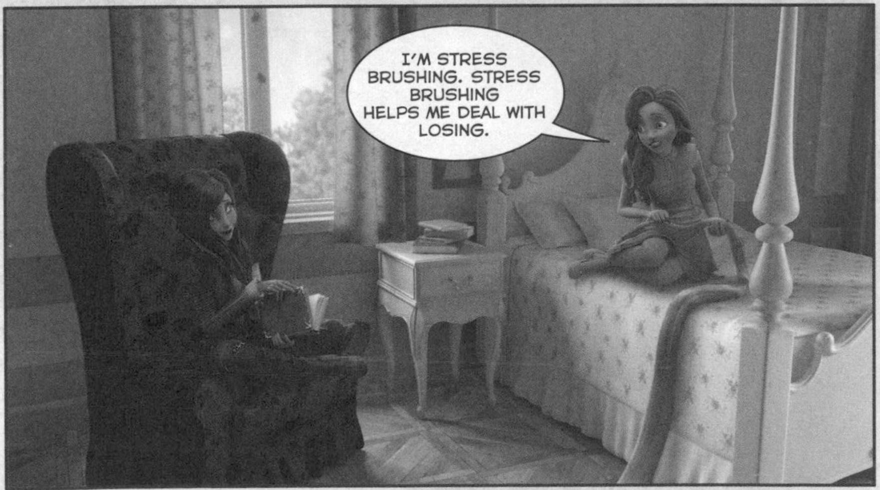
I'M STRESS BRUSHING. STRESS BRUSHING HELPS ME DEAL WITH LOSING.

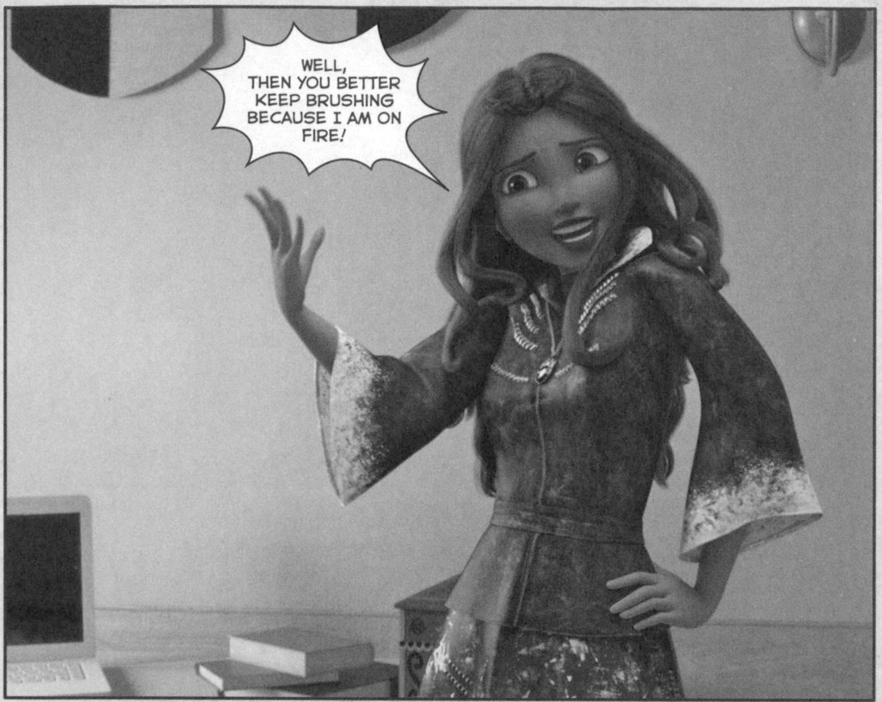
WELL, THEN YOU BETTER KEEP BRUSHING BECAUSE I AM ON FIRE!

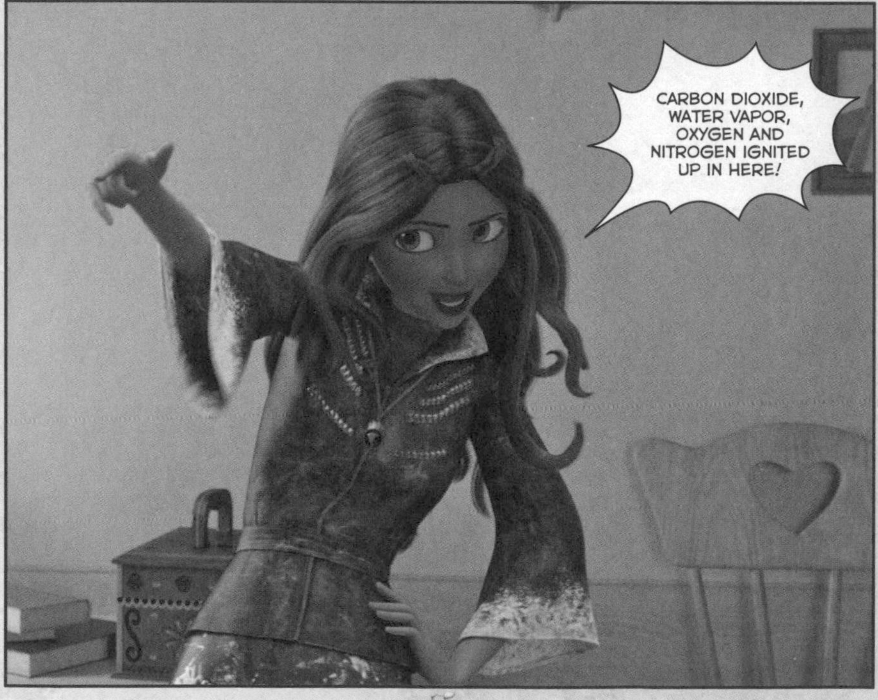
CARBON DIOXIDE, WATER VAPOR, OXYGEN AND NITROGEN IGNITED UP IN HERE!

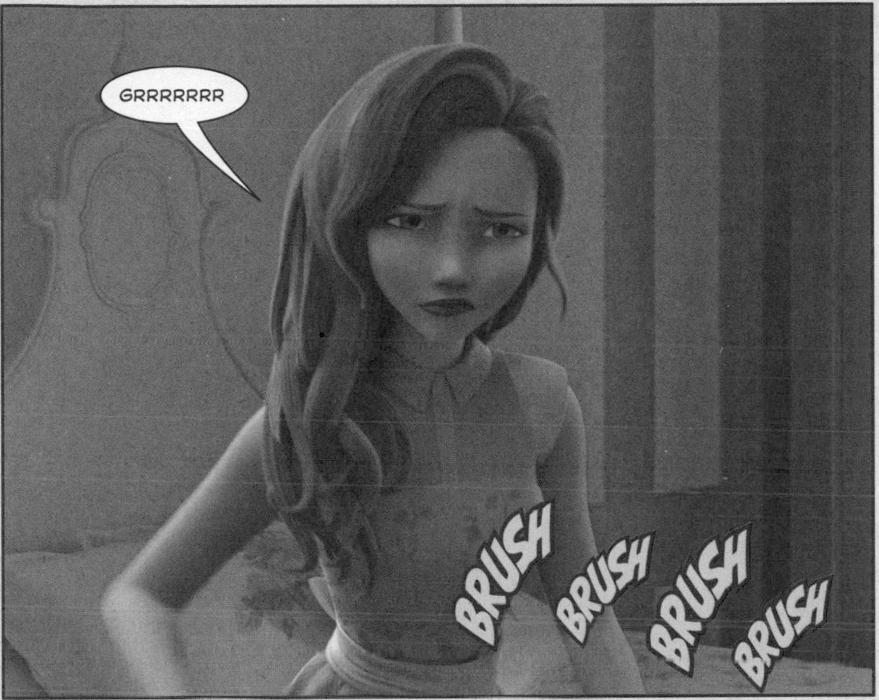
GRRRRRRR
BRUSH
BRUSH
BRUSH
BRUSH

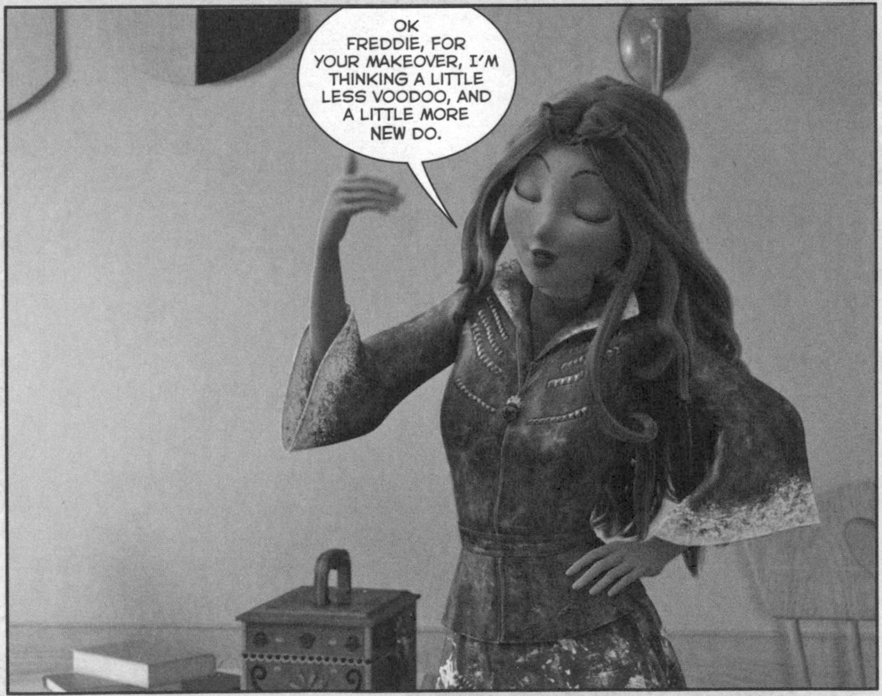
OK FREDDIE, FOR YOUR MAKEOVER, I'M THINKING A LITTLE LESS VOODOO, AND A LITTLE MORE NEW DO.

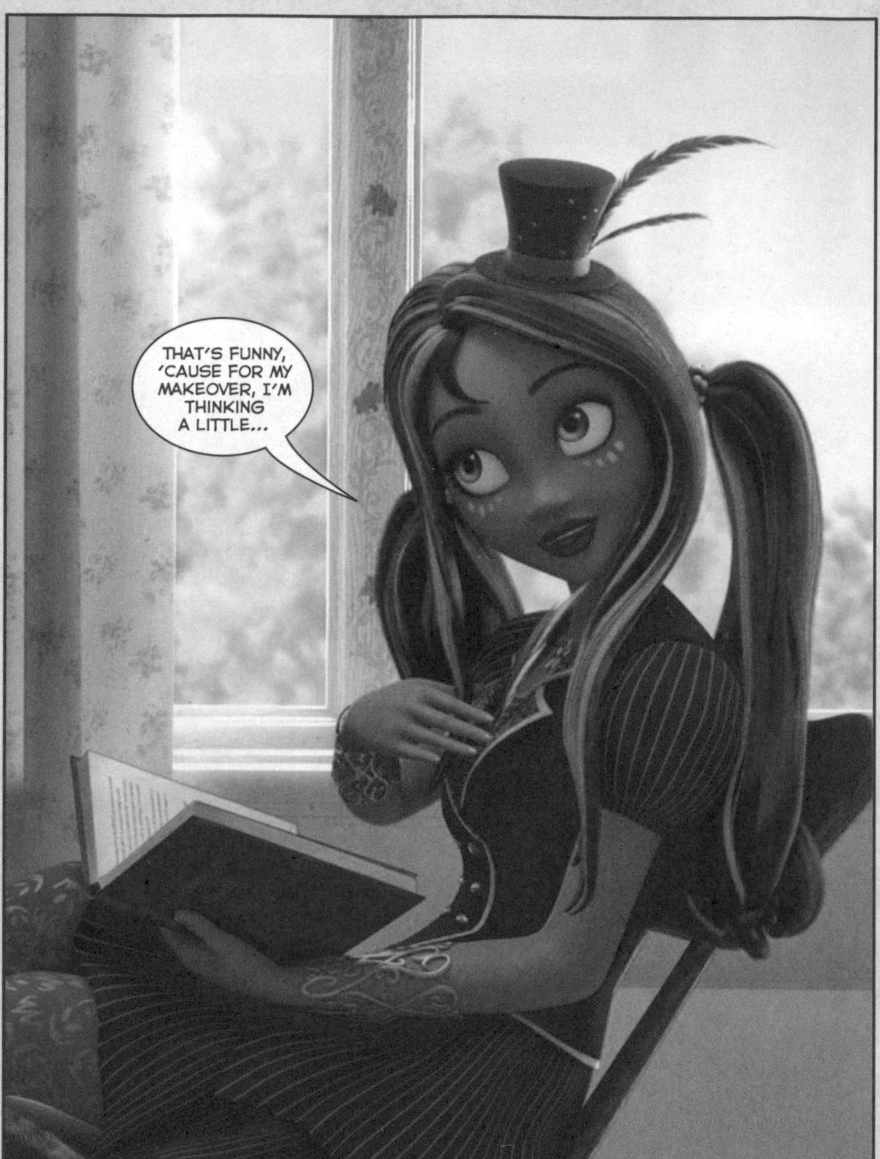
THAT'S FUNNY, 'CAUSE FOR MY MAKEOVER, I'M THINKING A LITTLE...

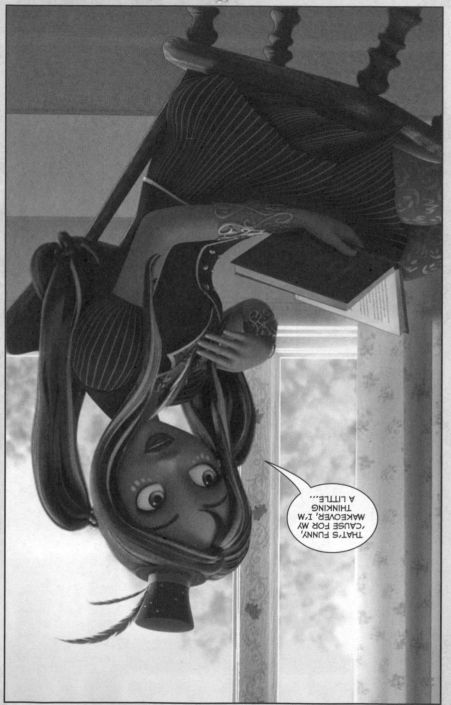

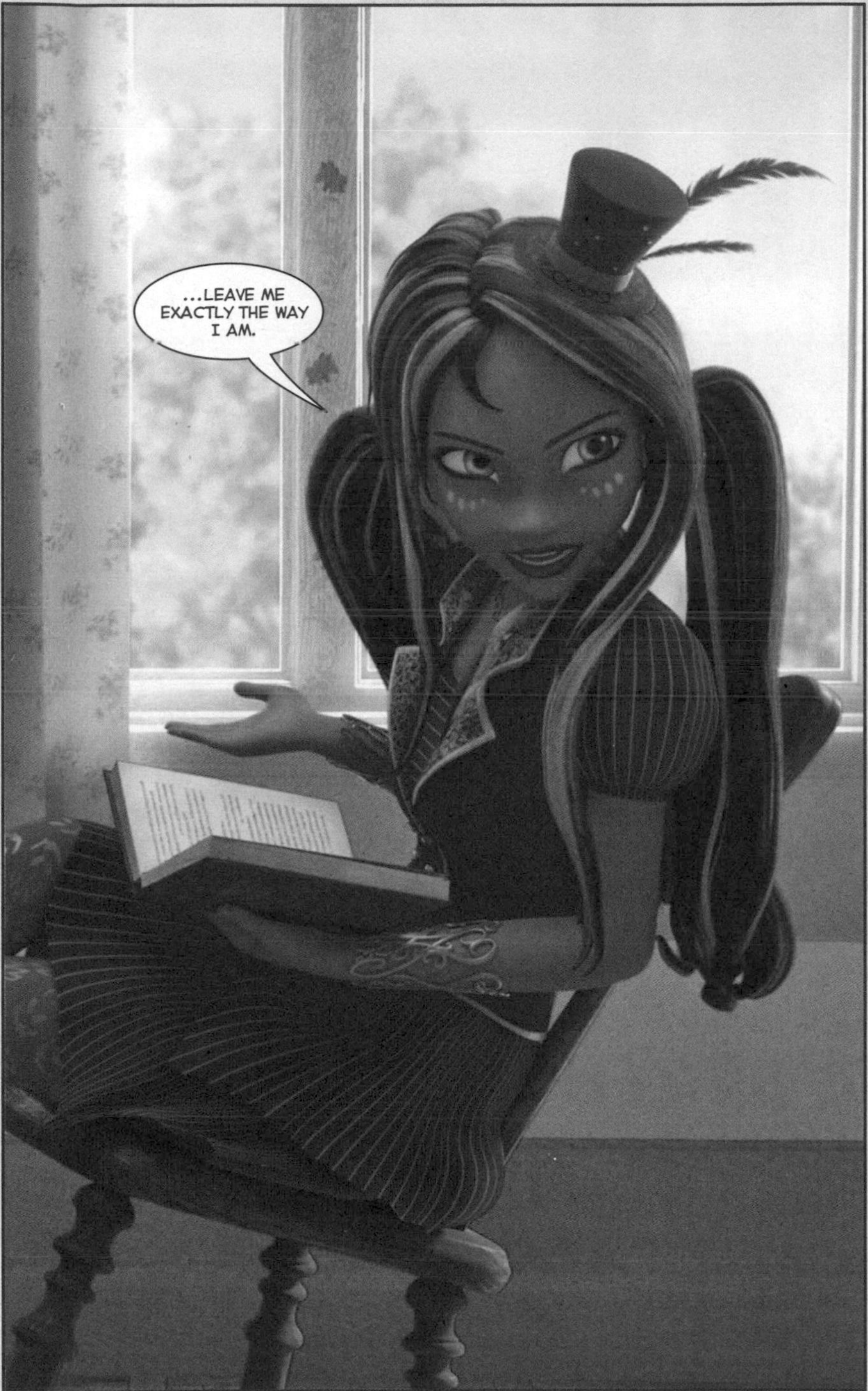
...LEAVE ME EXACTLY THE WAY I AM.

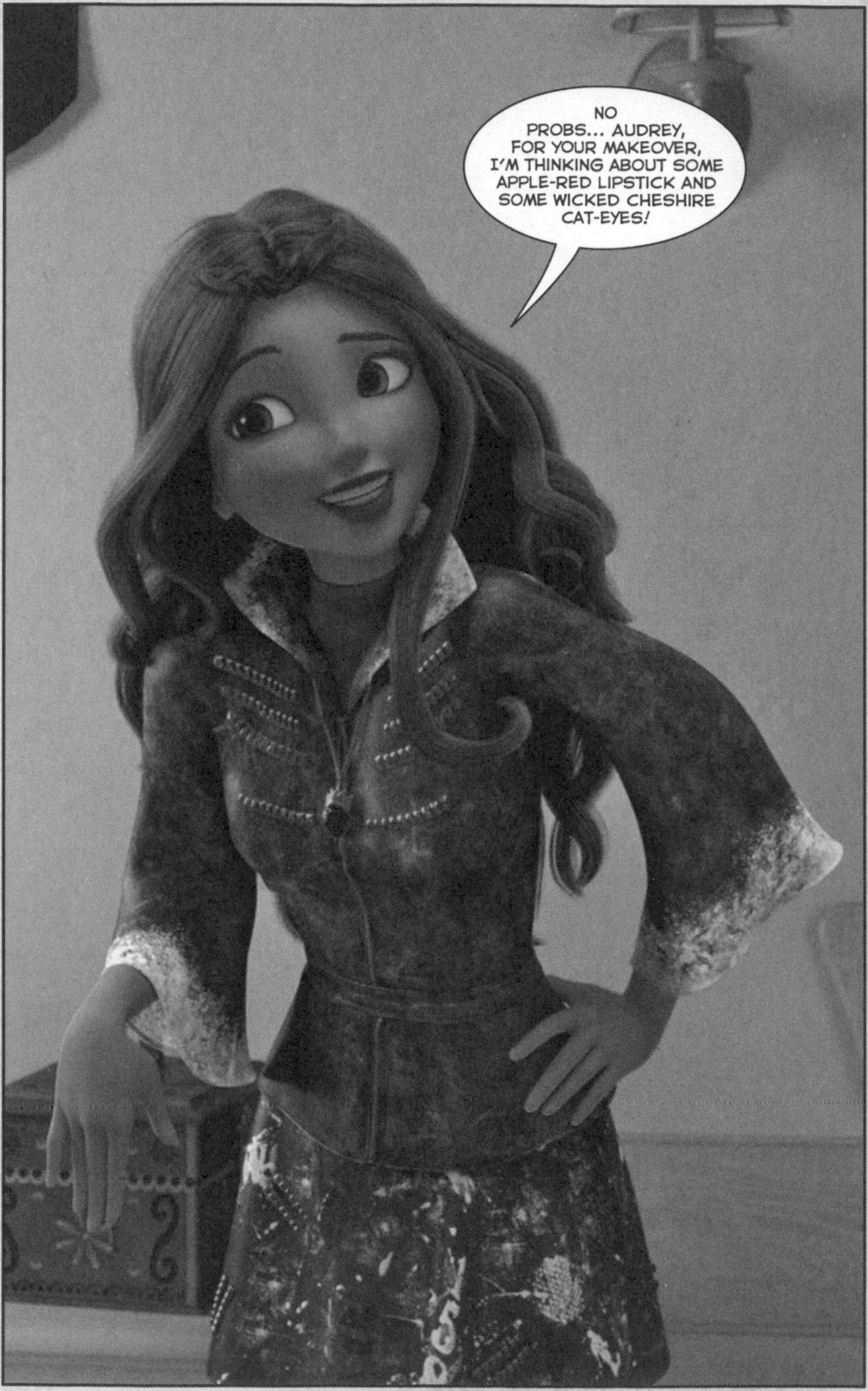
NO PROBS... AUDREY, FOR YOUR MAKEOVER, I'M THINKING ABOUT SOME APPLE-RED LIPSTICK AND SOME WICKED CHESHIRE CAT-EYES!

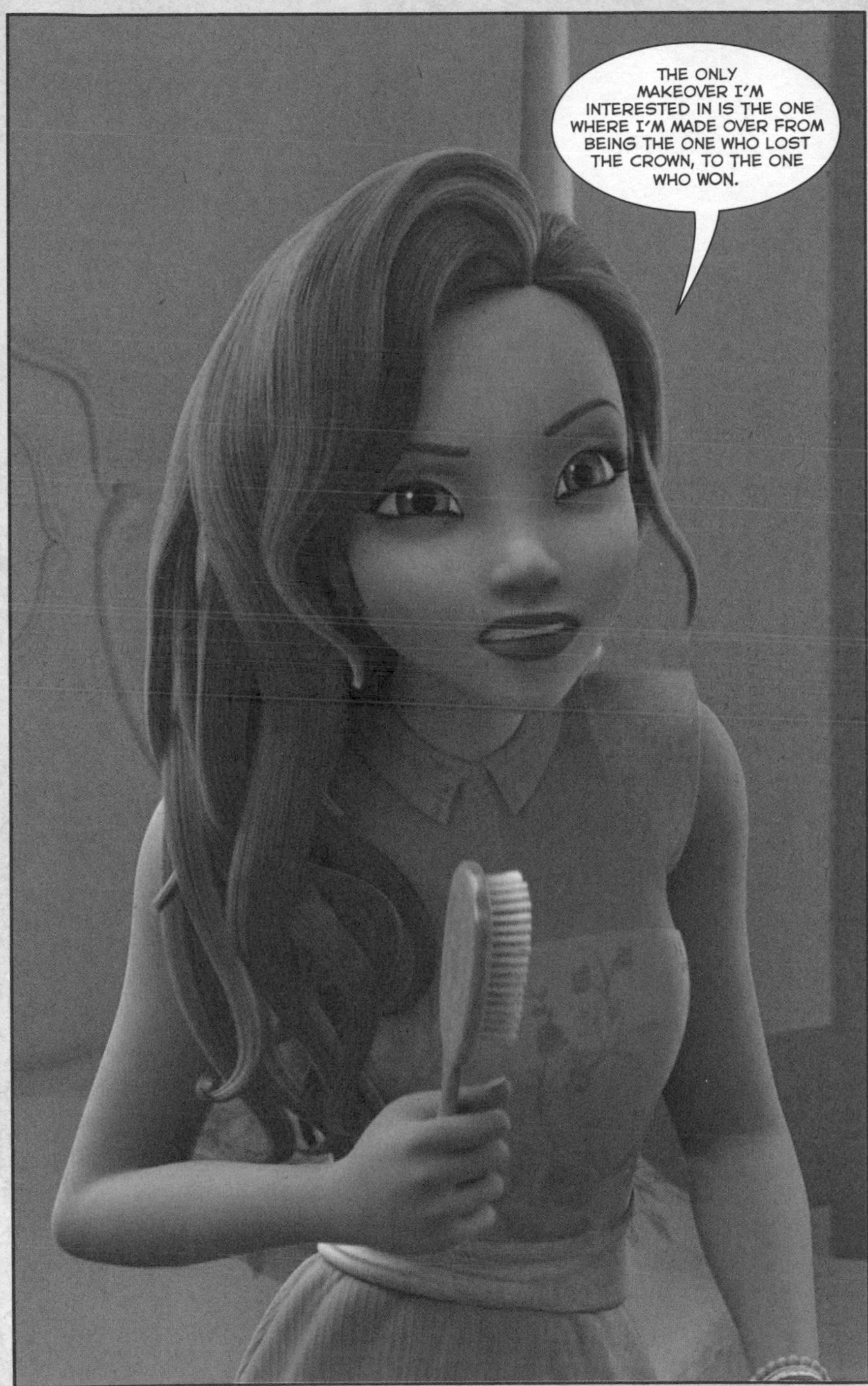
THE ONLY MAKEOVER I'M INTERESTED IN IS THE ONE WHERE I'M MADE OVER FROM BEING THE ONE WHO LOST THE CROWN, TO THE ONE WHO WON.

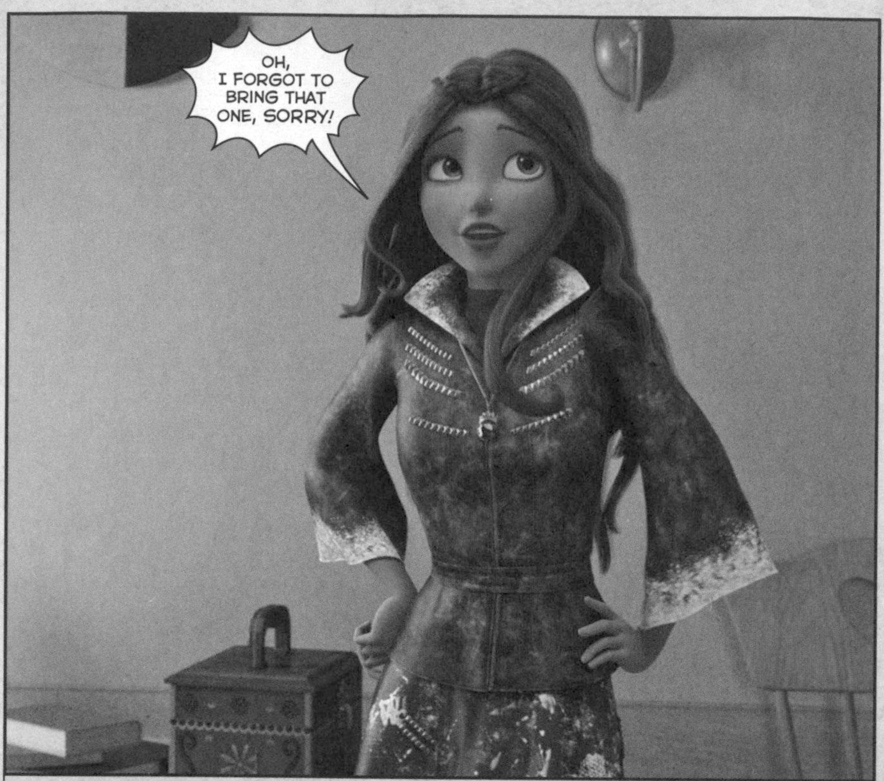
OH, I FORGOT TO BRING THAT ONE, SORRY!

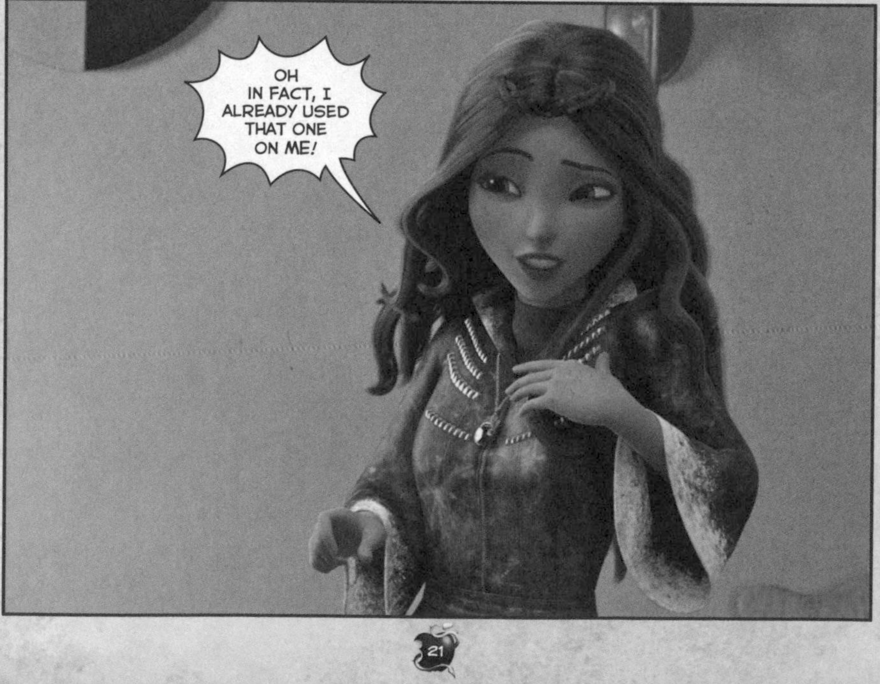
OH IN FACT, I ALREADY USED THAT ONE ON ME!

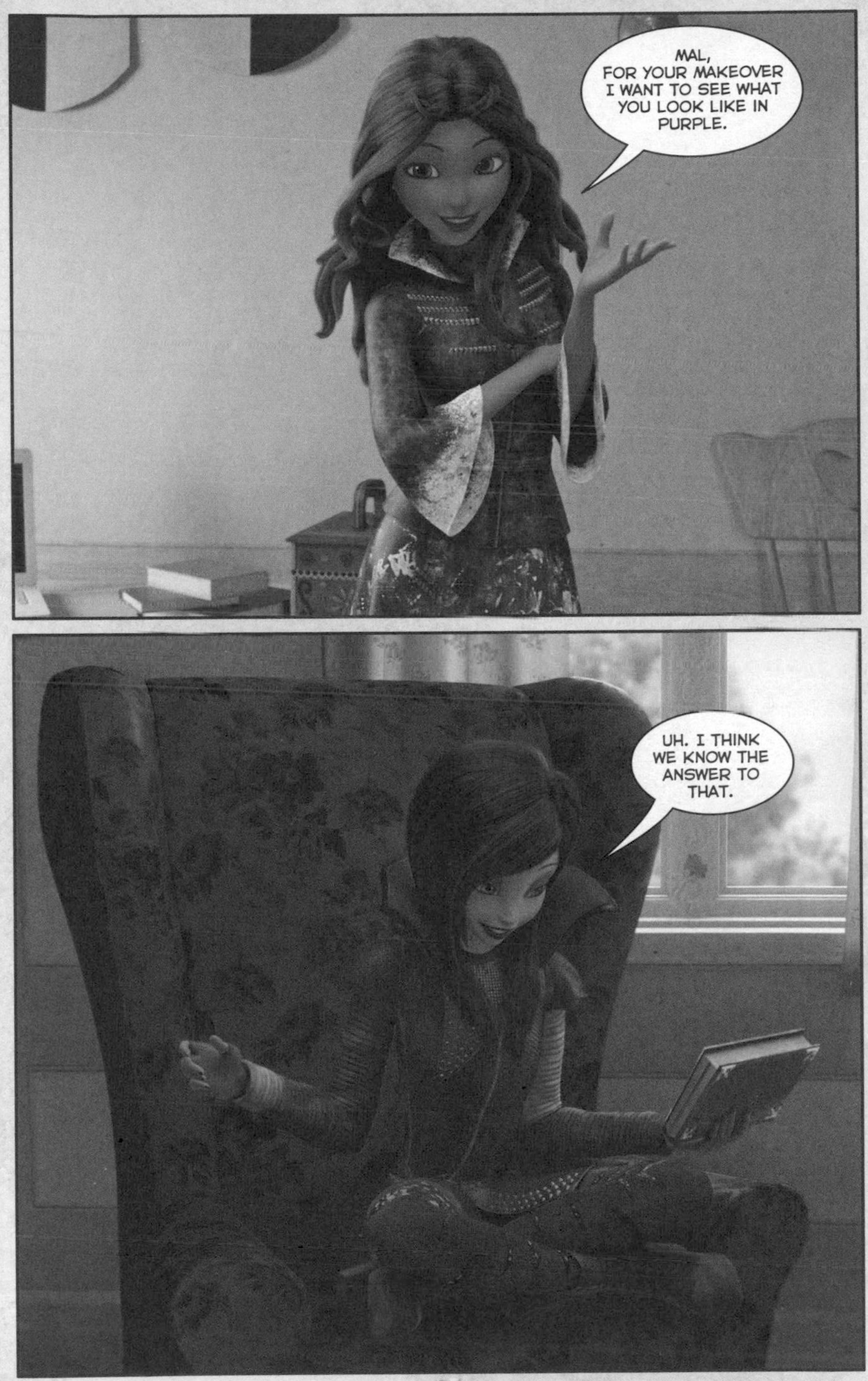
MAL, FOR YOUR MAKEOVER I WANT TO SEE WHAT YOU LOOK LIKE IN PURPLE.
UH. I THINK WE KNOW THE ANSWER TO THAT.

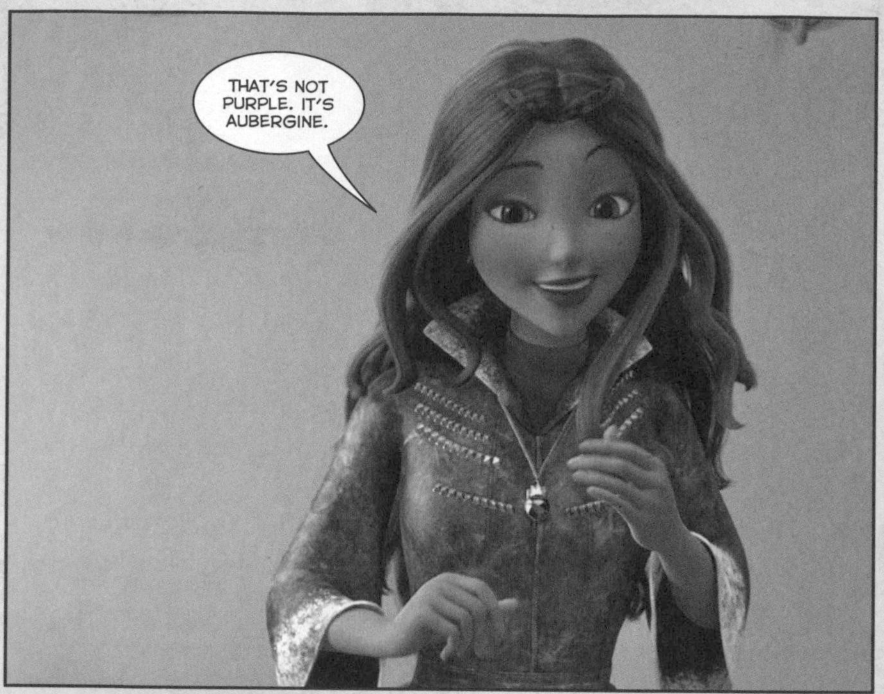
THAT'S NOT PURPLE. IT'S AUBERGINE.

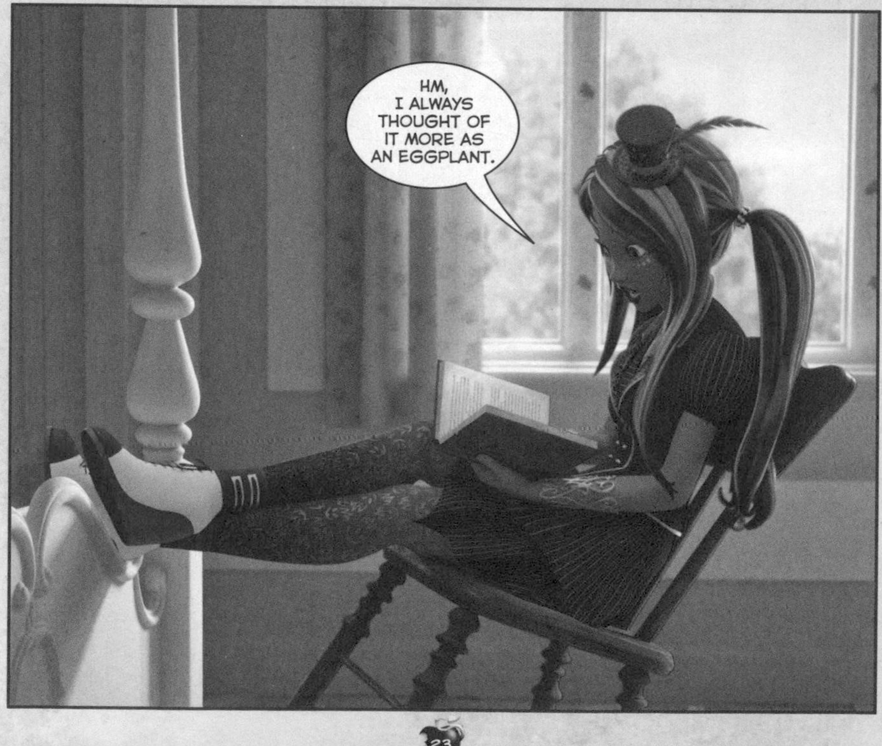
HM, I ALWAYS THOUGHT OF IT MORE AS AN EGGPLANT.

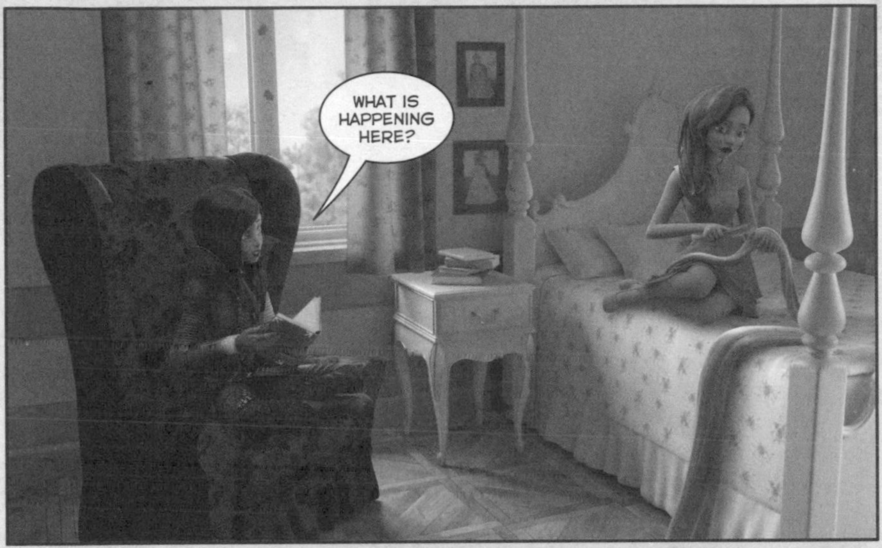
WHAT IS HAPPENING HERE?

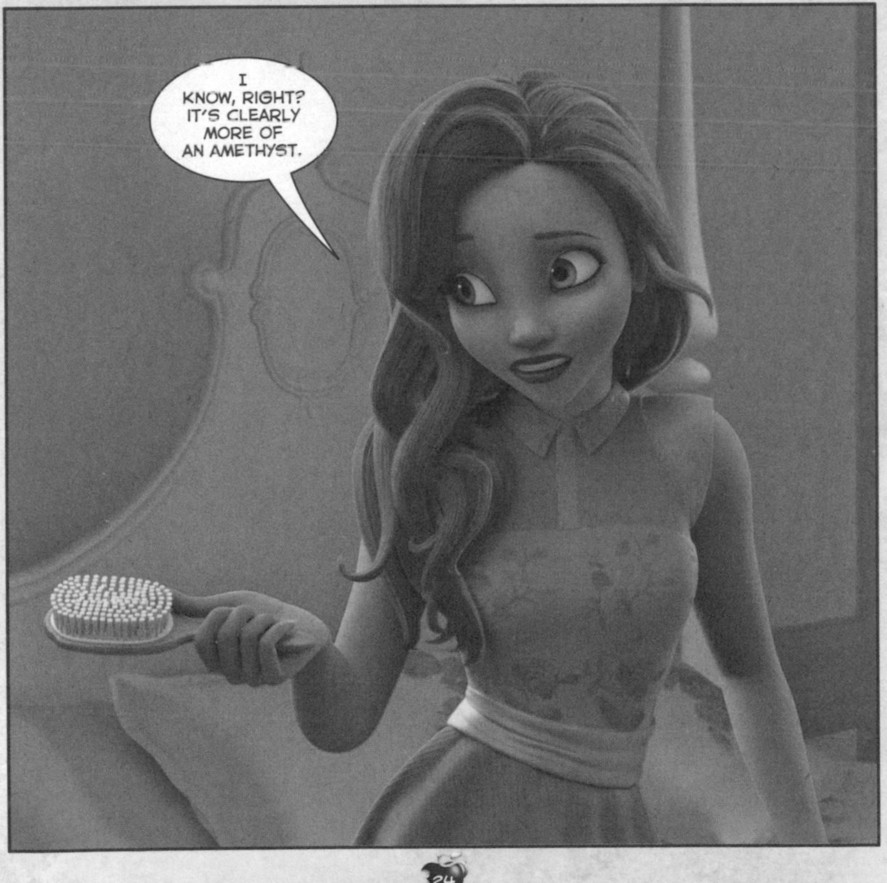
I KNOW, RIGHT? IT'S CLEARLY MORE OF AN AMETHYST.

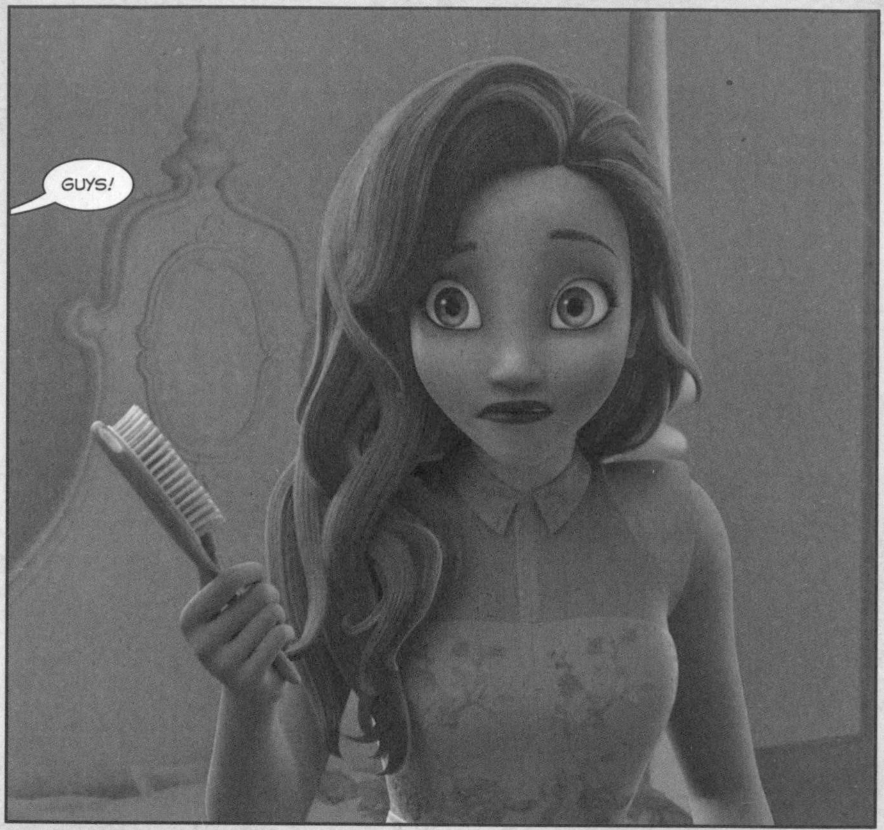
GUYS!

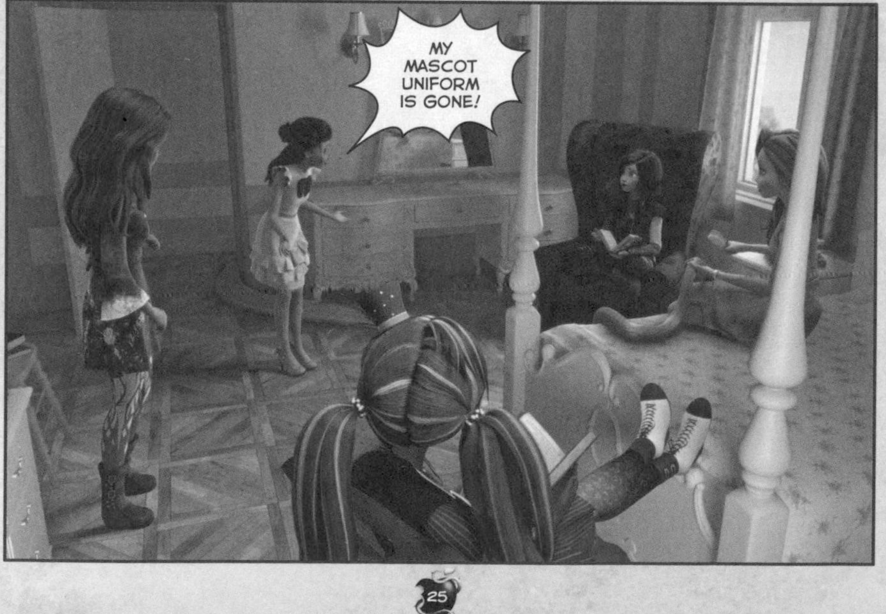
MY MASCOT UNIFORM IS GONE!

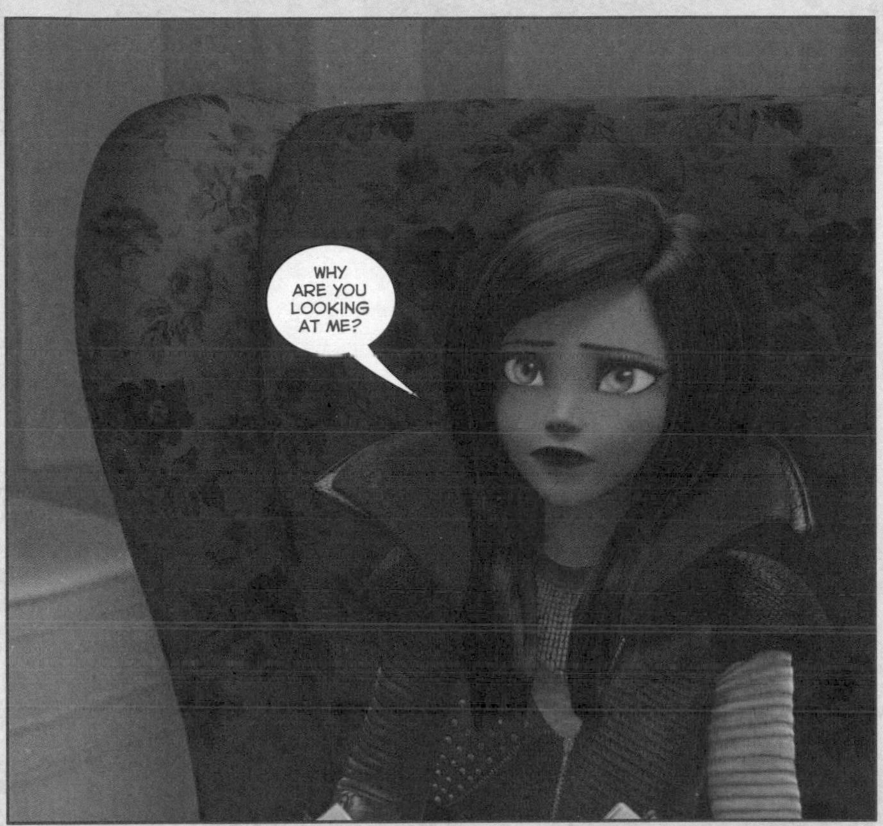
WHY ARE YOU LOOKING AT ME?

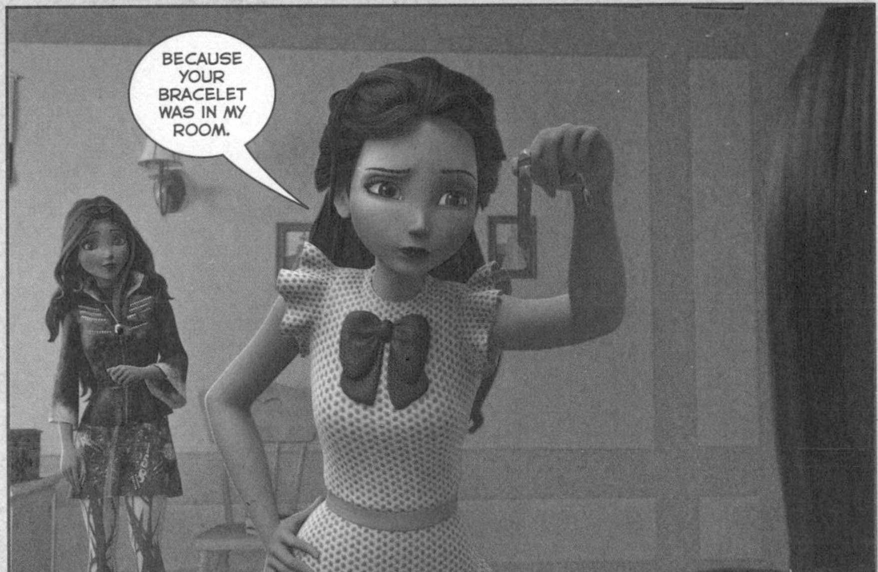
BECAUSE YOUR BRACELET WAS IN MY ROOM.

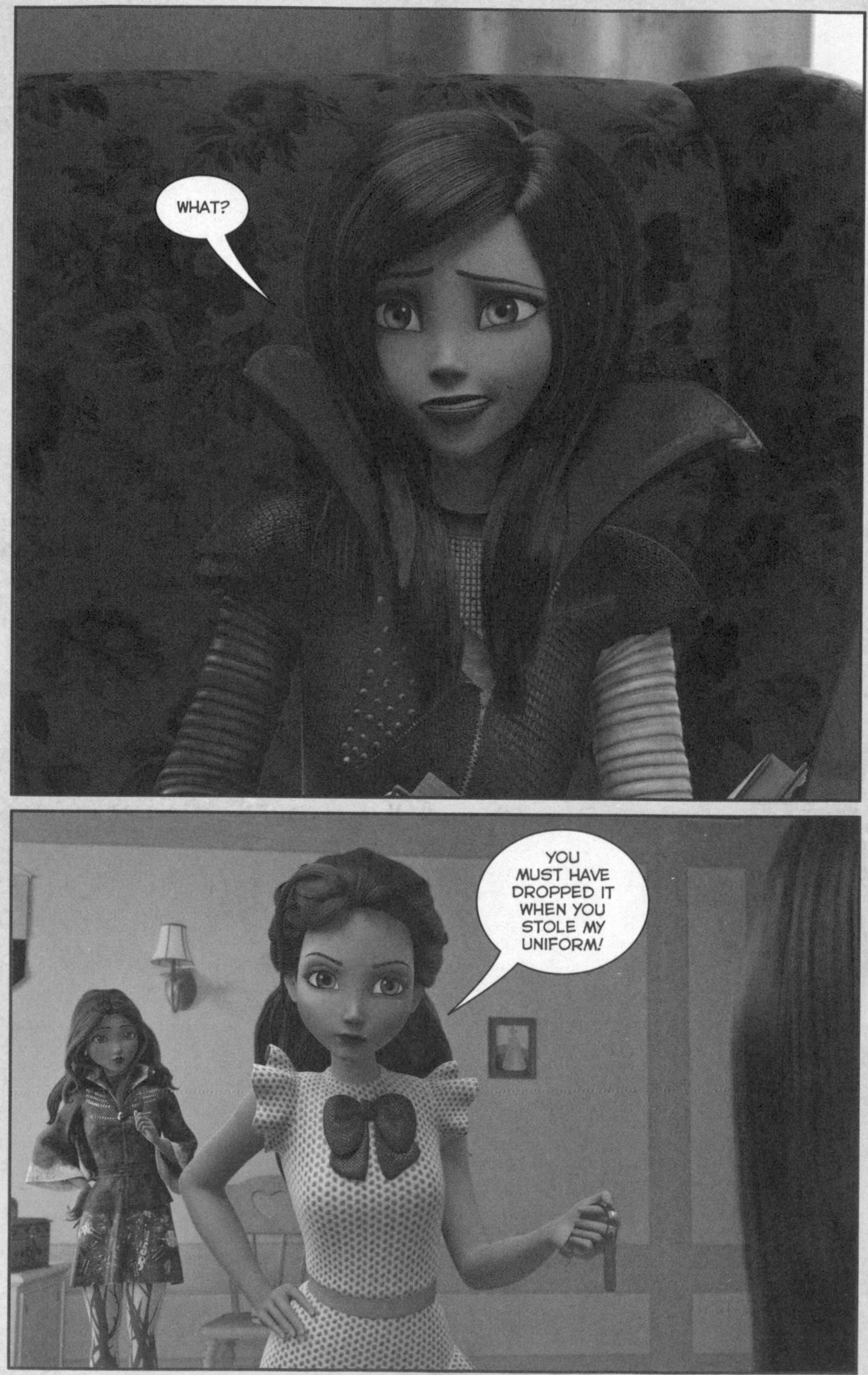
WHAT?
YOU MUST HAVE DROPPED IT WHEN YOU STOLE MY UNIFORM!

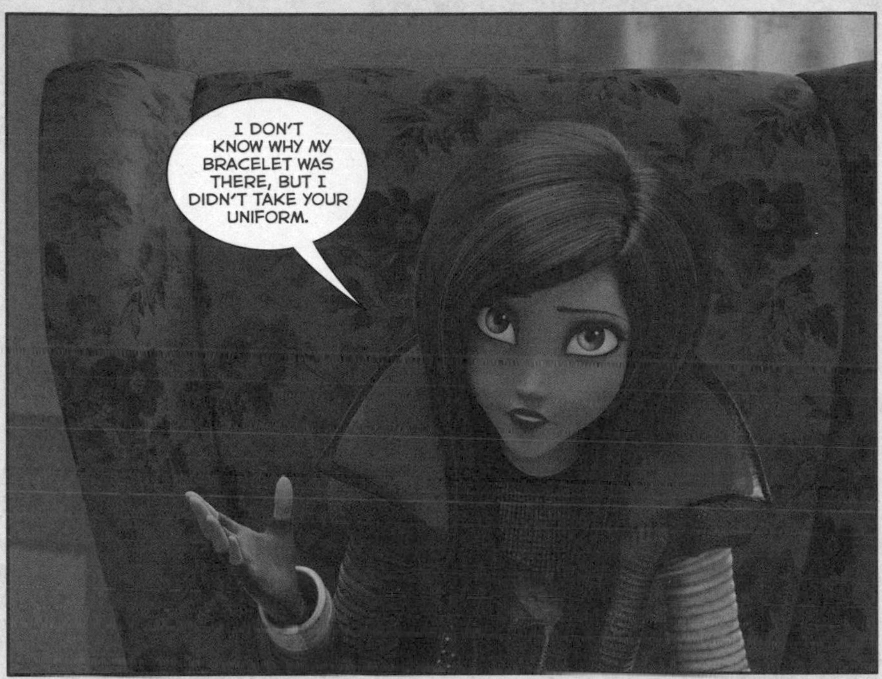
I DON'T KNOW WHY MY BRACELET WAS THERE, BUT I DIDN'T TAKE YOUR UNIFORM.

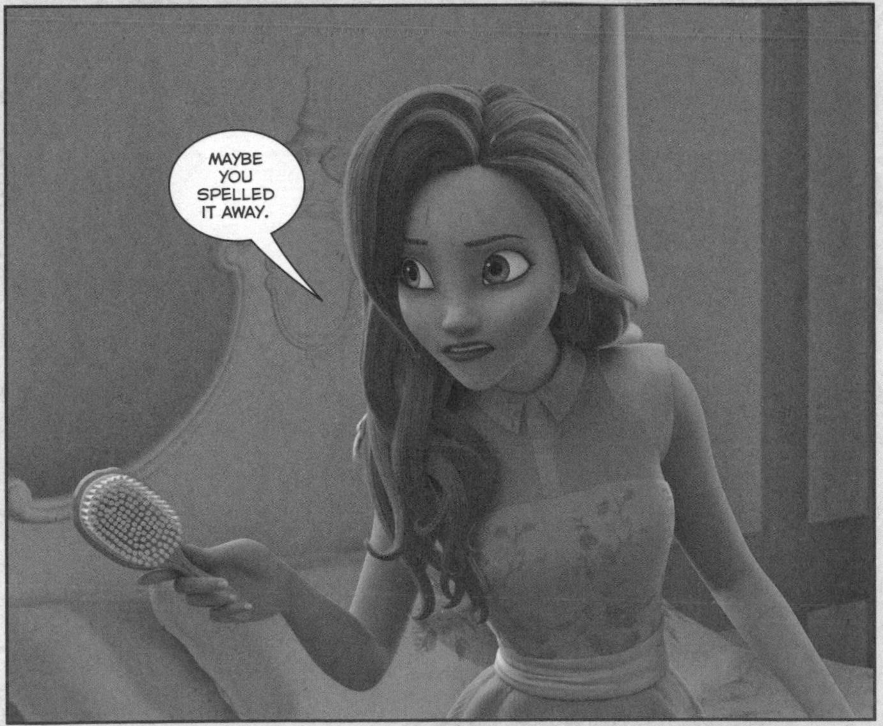
MAYBE YOU SPELLED IT AWAY.

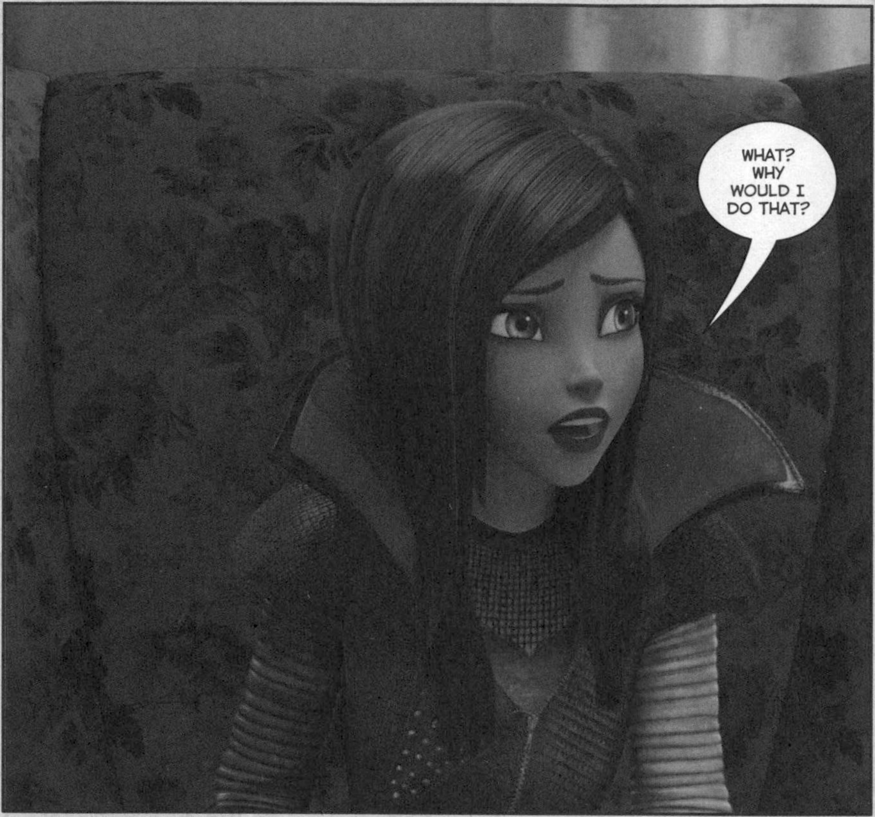
WHAT? WHY WOULD I DO THAT?

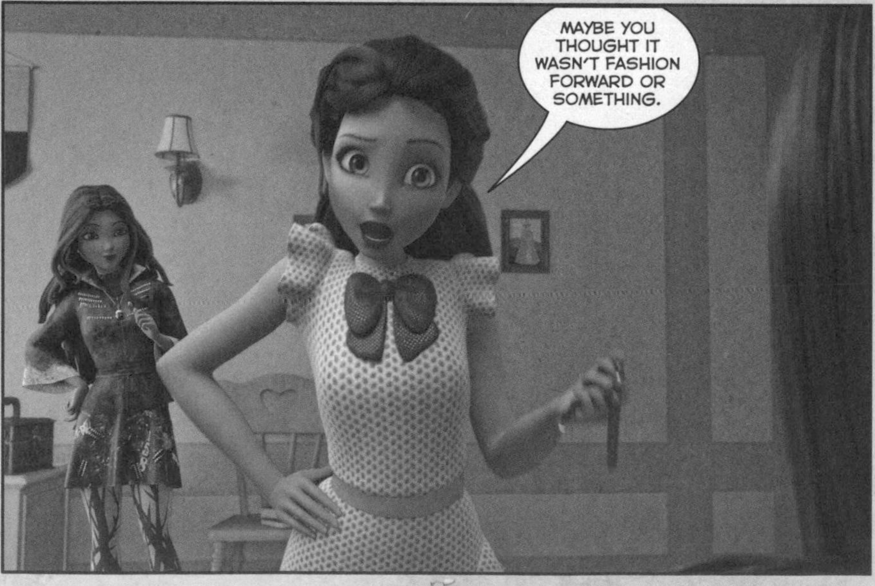
MAYBE YOU THOUGHT IT WASN'T FASHION FORWARD OR SOMETHING.

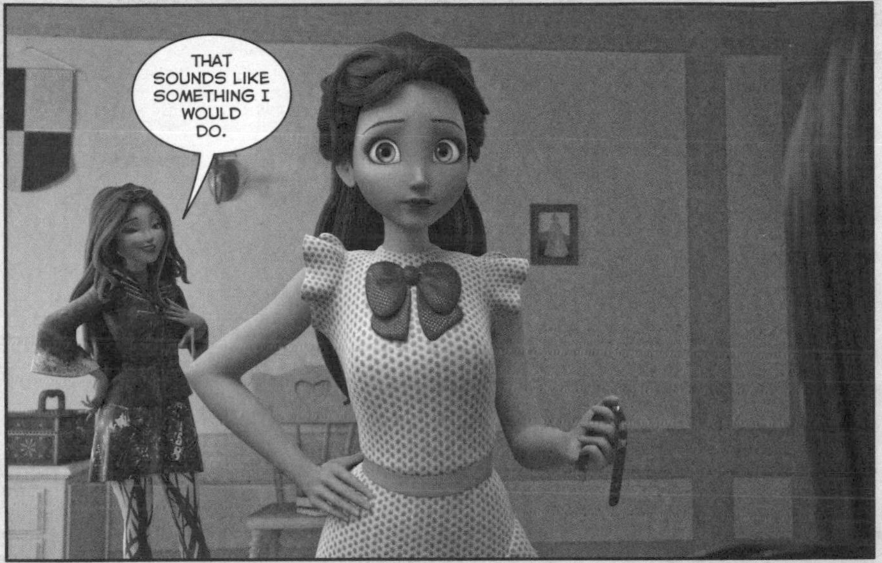
THAT SOUNDS LIKE SOMETHING I WOULD DO.

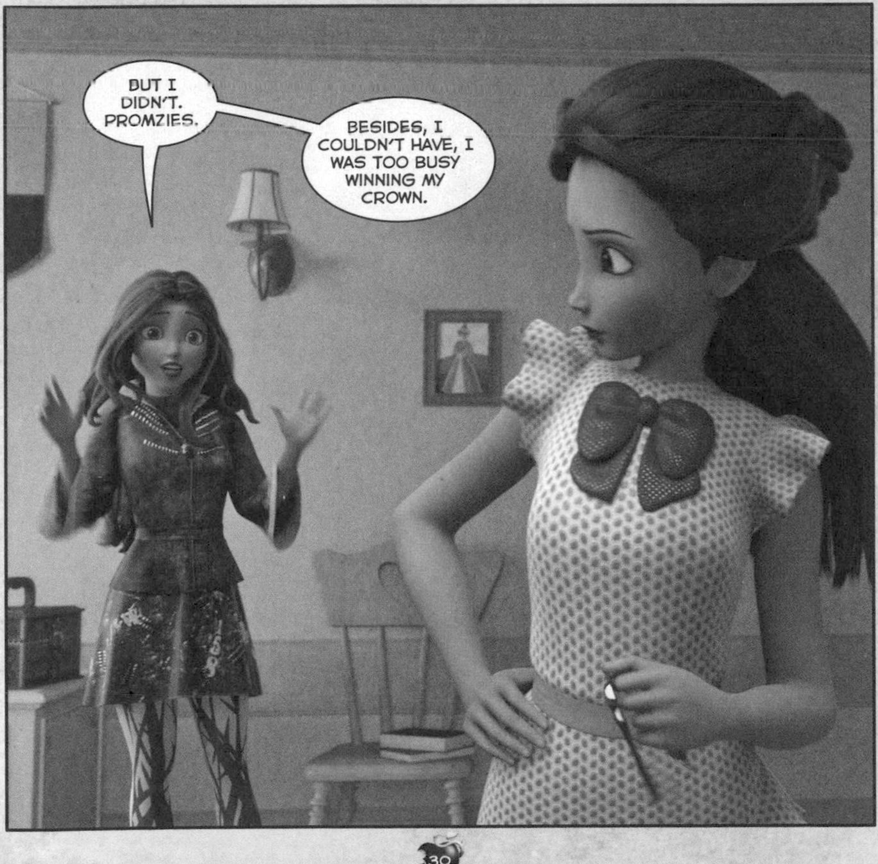
BUT I DIDN'T. PROMZIES.
BESIDES, I COULDN'T HAVE, I WAS TOO BUSY WINNING MY CROWN.

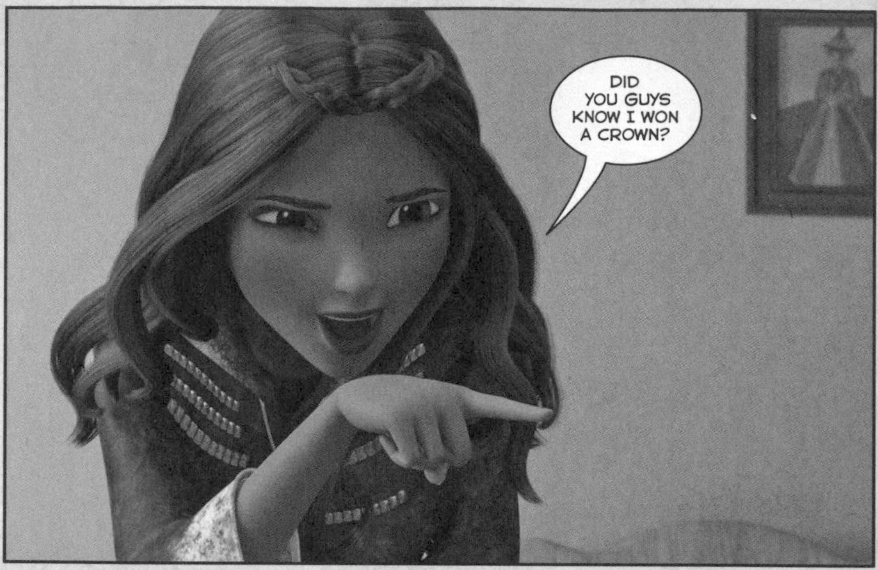
DID YOU GUYS KNOW I WON A CROWN?

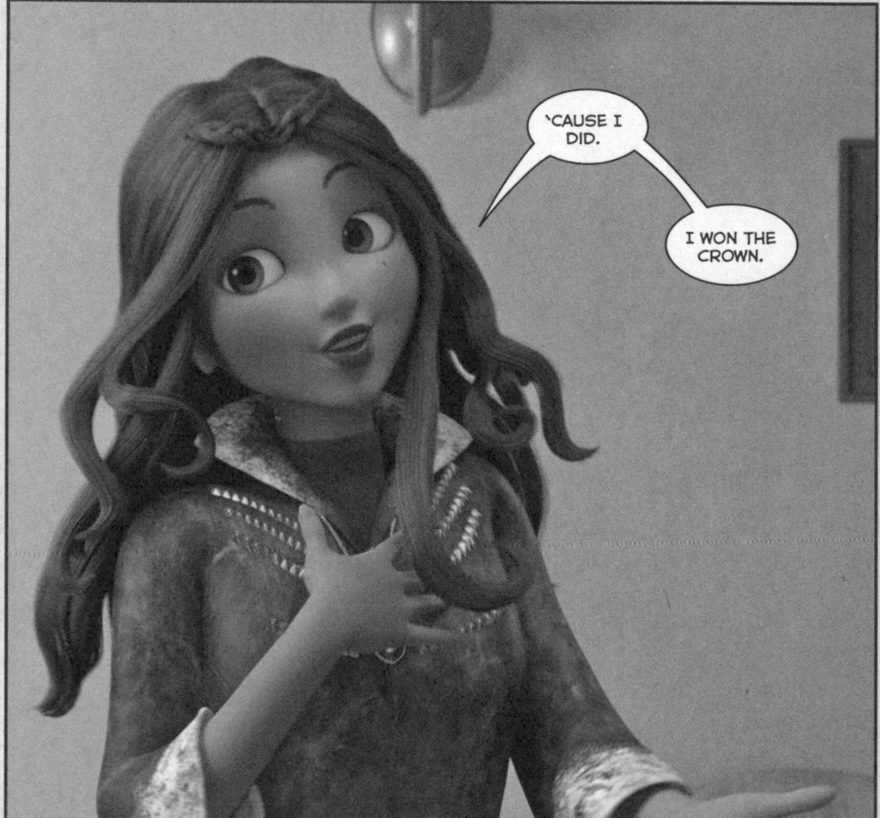
'CAUSE I DID.
I WON THE CROWN.

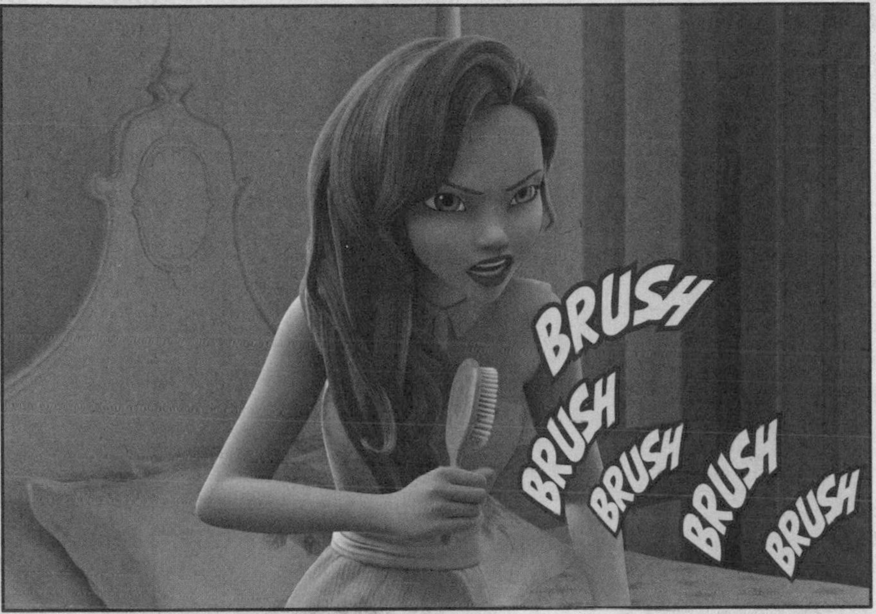
BRUSH
BRUSH
BRUSH
BRUSH
BRUSH

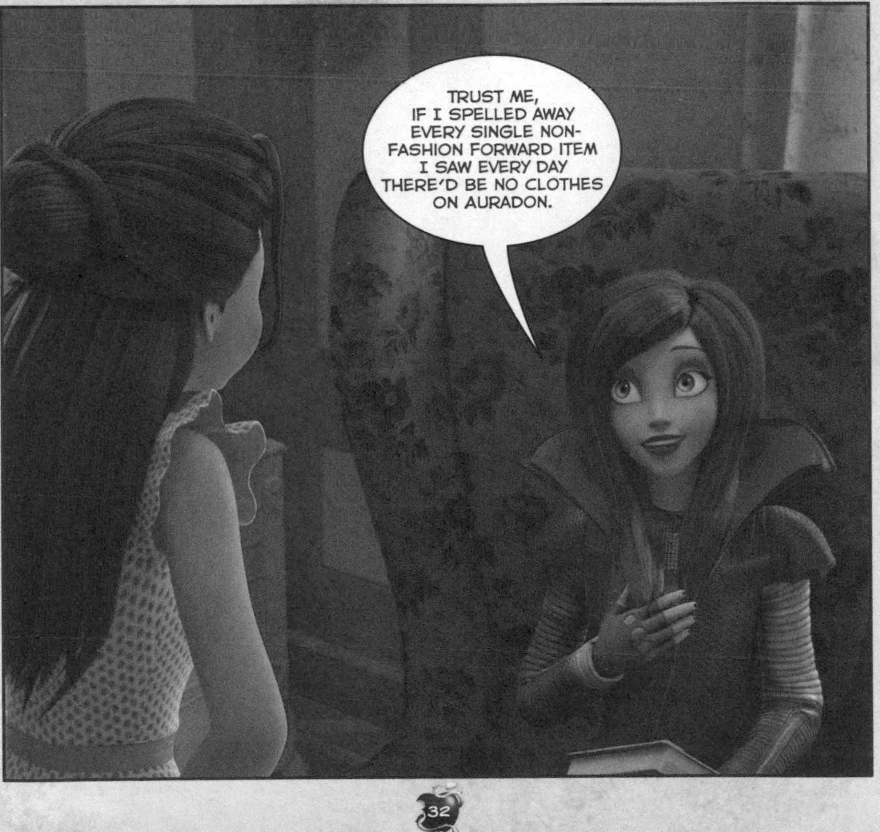
TRUST ME, IF I SPELLED AWAY EVERY SINGLE NON-FASHION FORWARD ITEM I SAW EVERY DAY THERE'D BE NO CLOTHES ON AURADON.

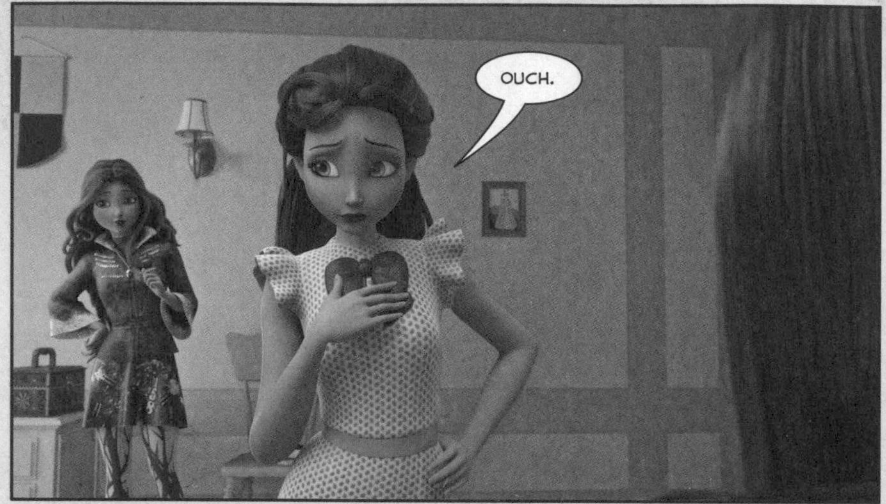
OUCH.

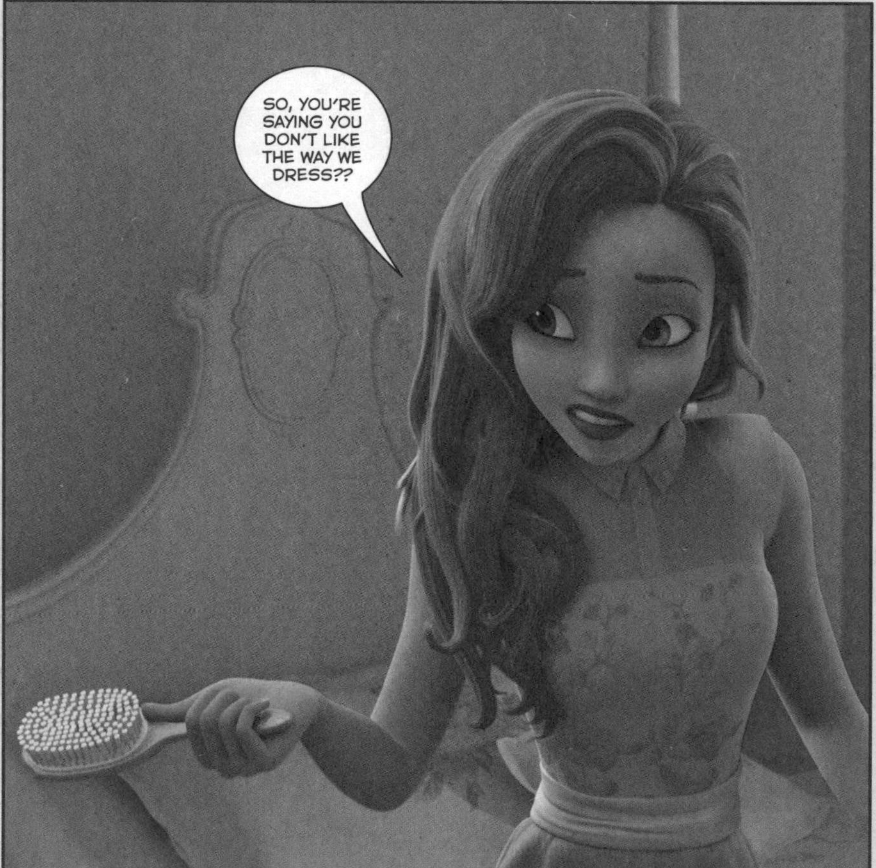
SO, YOU'RE SAYING YOU DON'T LIKE THE WAY WE DRESS??

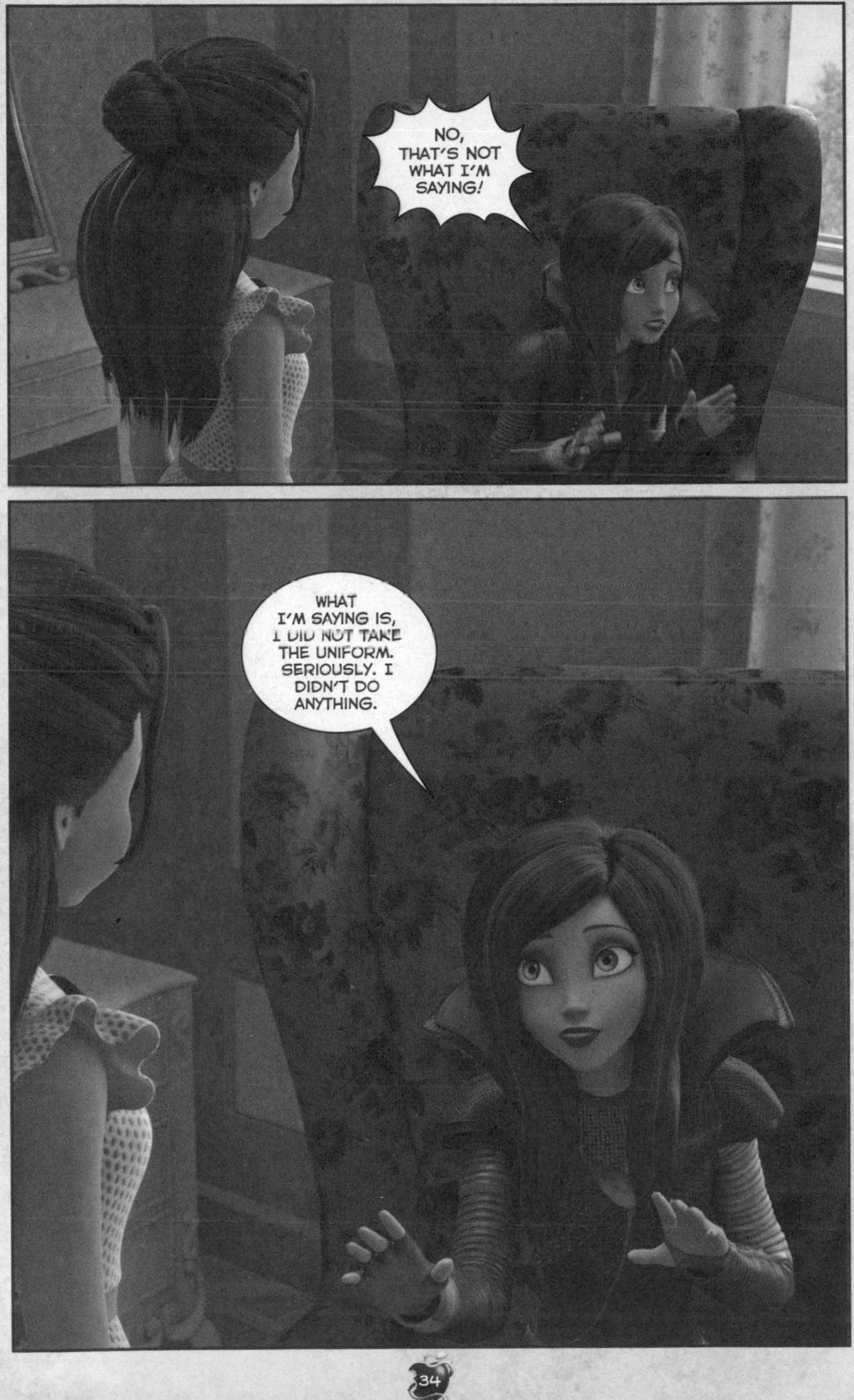
NO, THAT'S NOT WHAT I'M SAYING!
WHAT I'M SAYING IS, I DID NOT TAKE THE UNIFORM. SERIOUSLY. I DIDN'T DO ANYTHING.

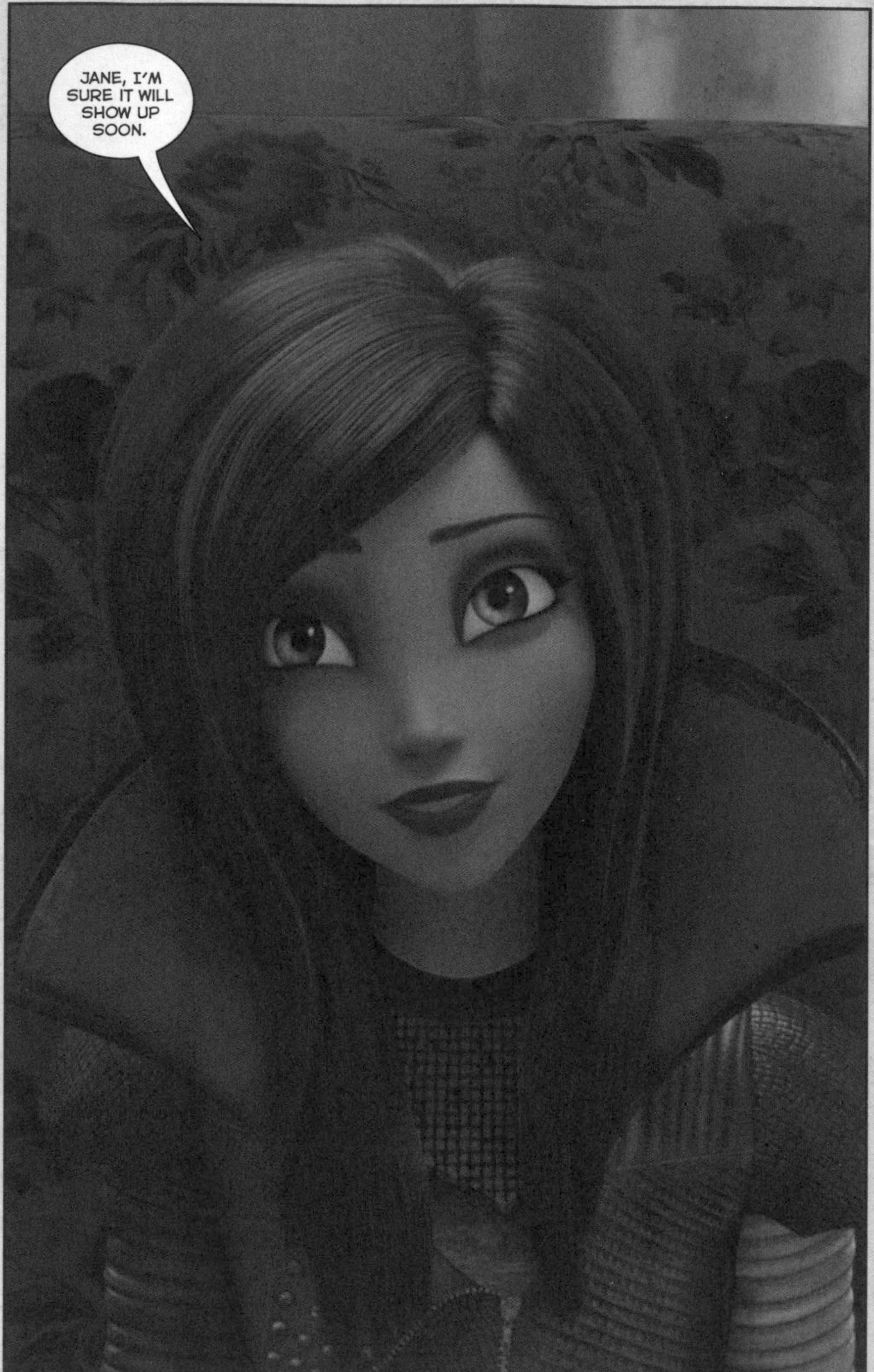
JANE, I'M SURE IT WILL SHOW UP SOON.

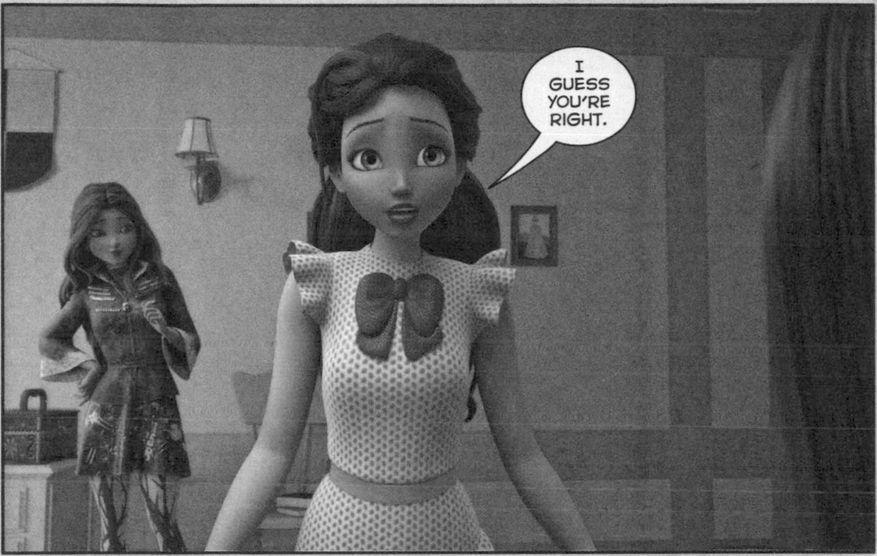
I GUESS YOU'RE RIGHT.

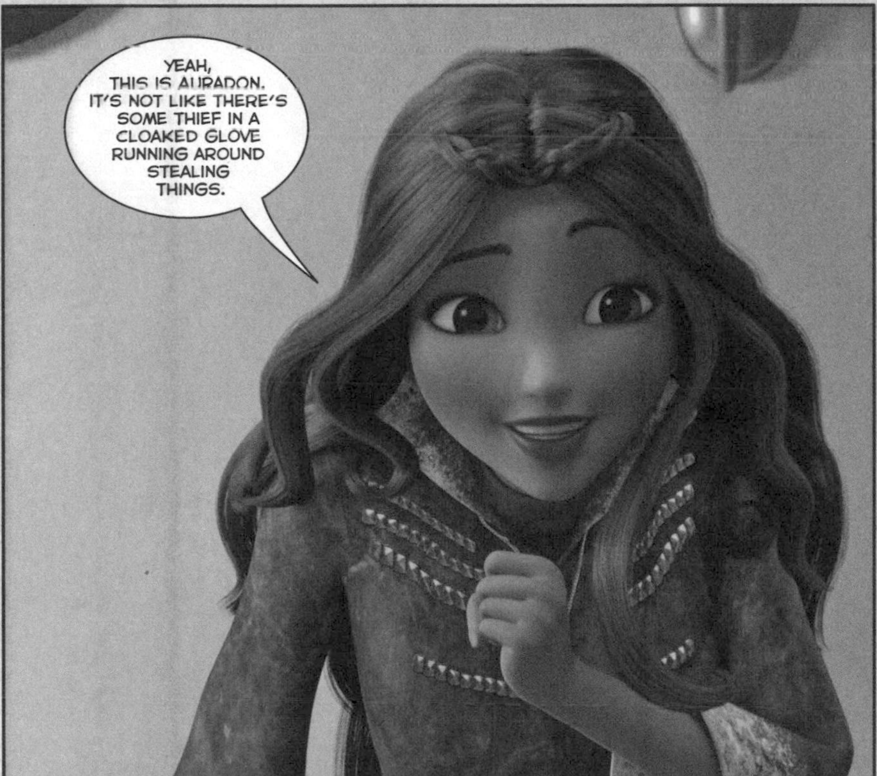
YEAH, THIS IS AURADON. IT'S NOT LIKE THERE'S SOME THIEF IN A CLOAKED GLOVE RUNNING AROUND STEALING THINGS.

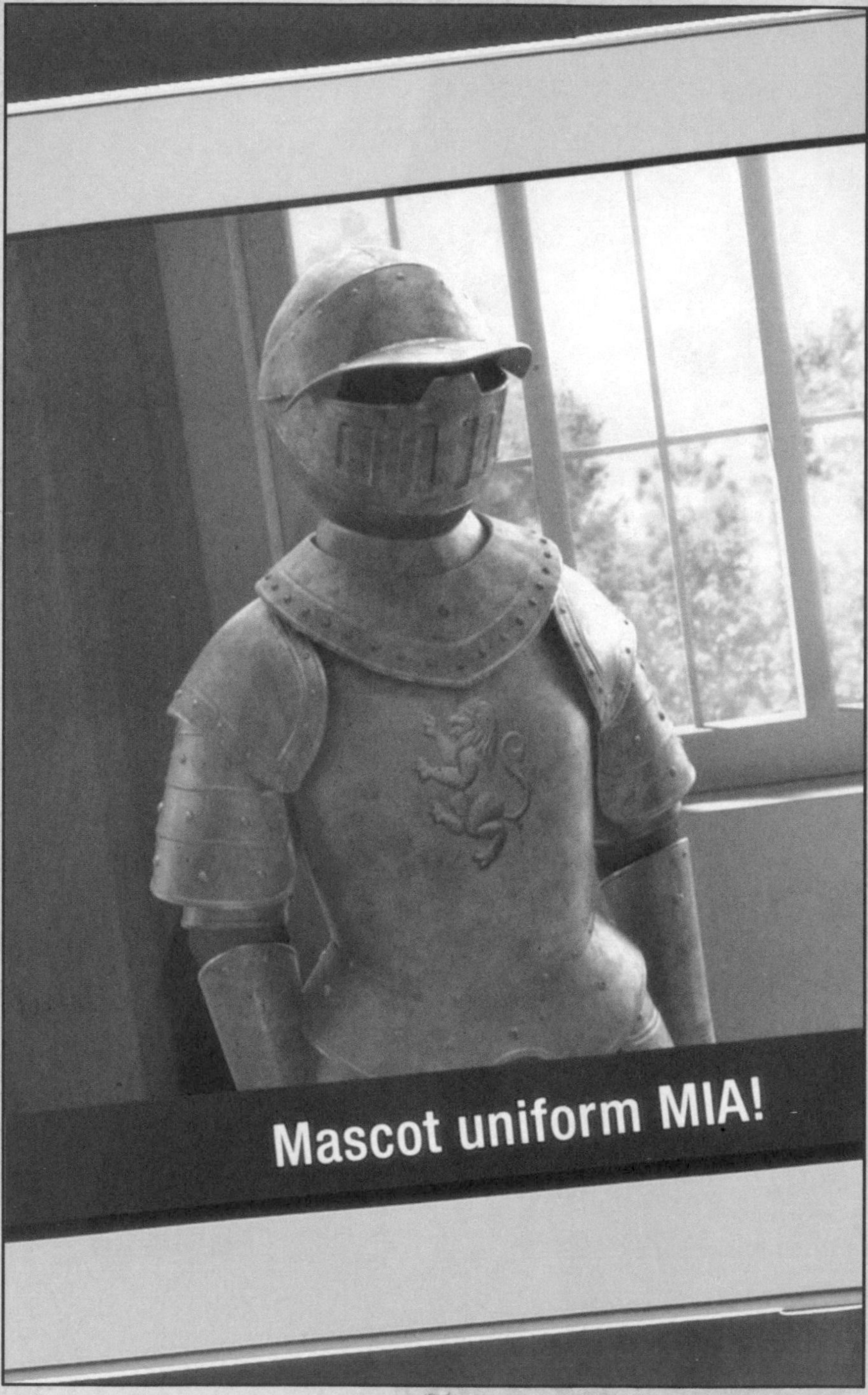
Mascot uniform MIA!

CHAPTER 14: MAD FOR TEA

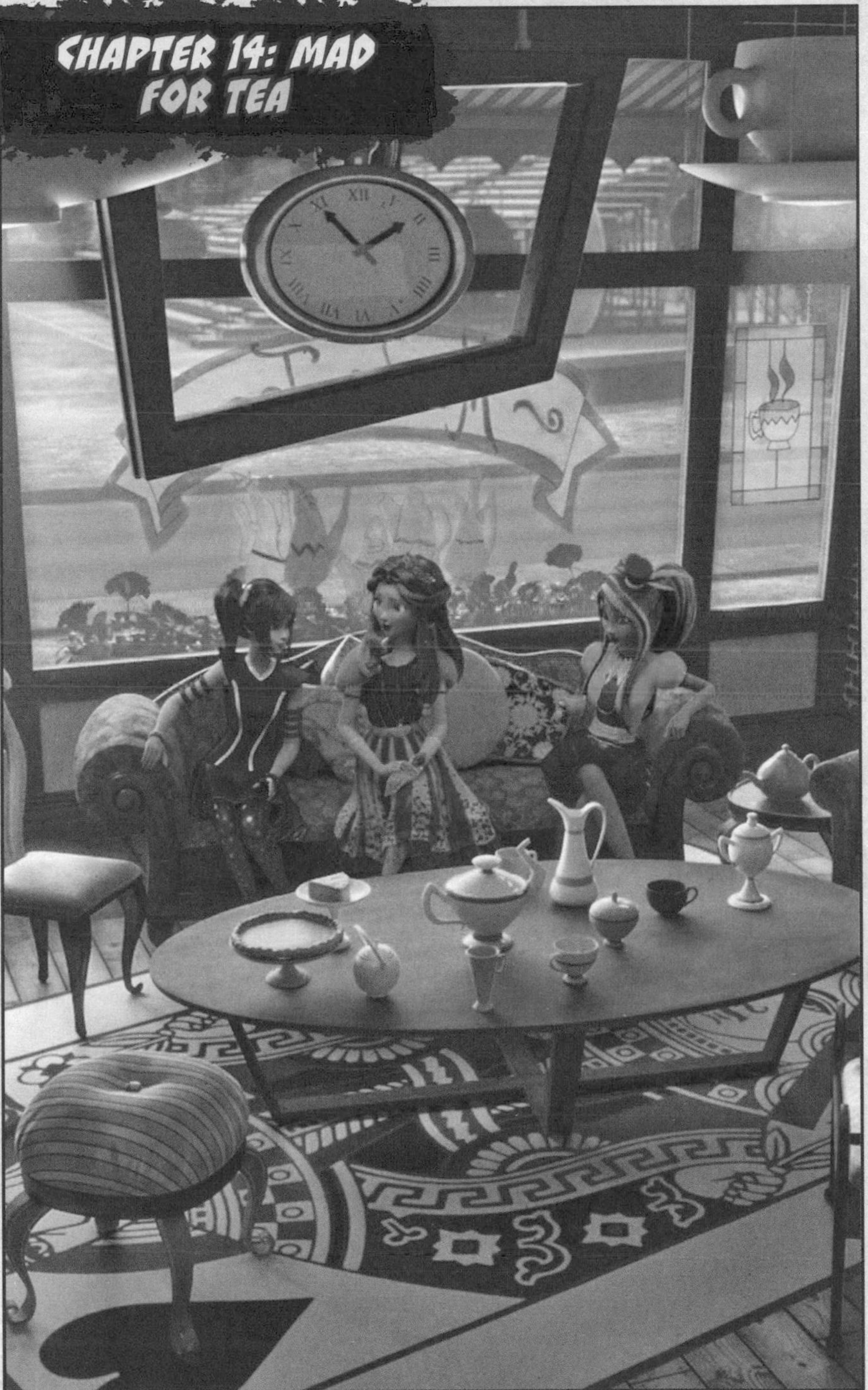

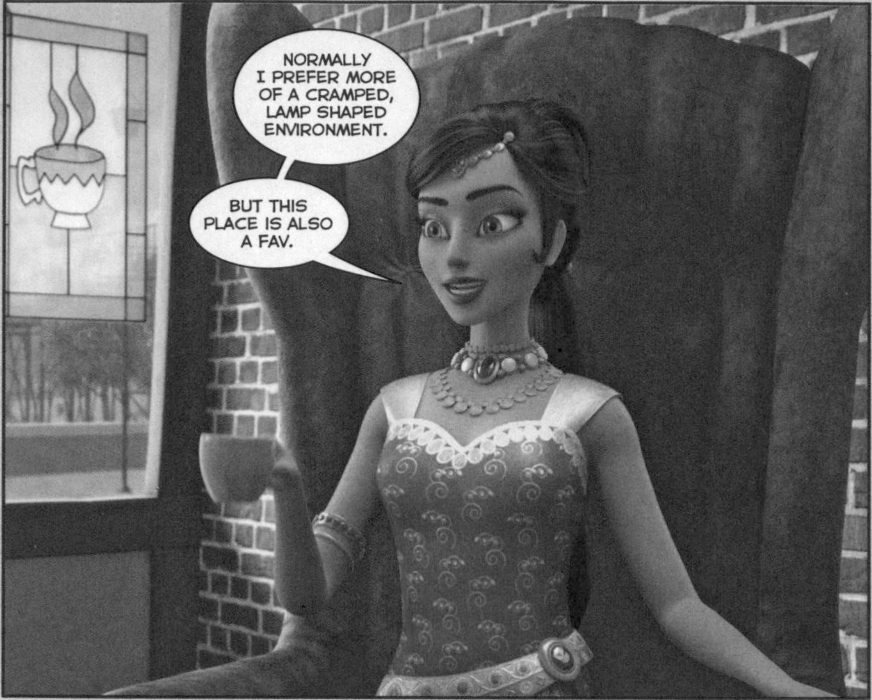
NORMALLY I PREFER MORE OF A CRAMPED, LAMP SHAPED ENVIRONMENT.
BUT THIS PLACE IS ALSO A FAV.

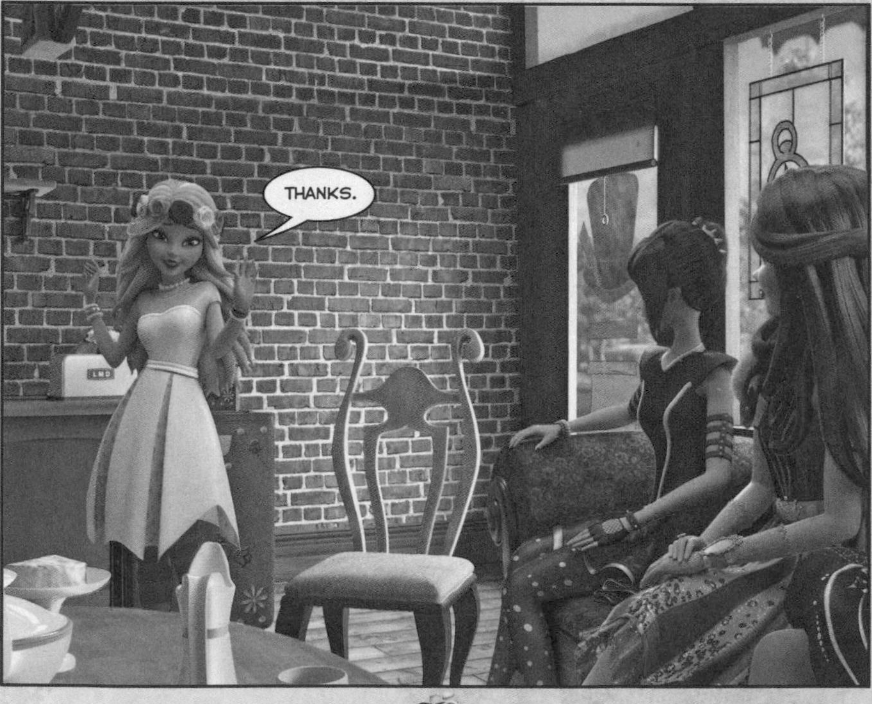
THANKS.

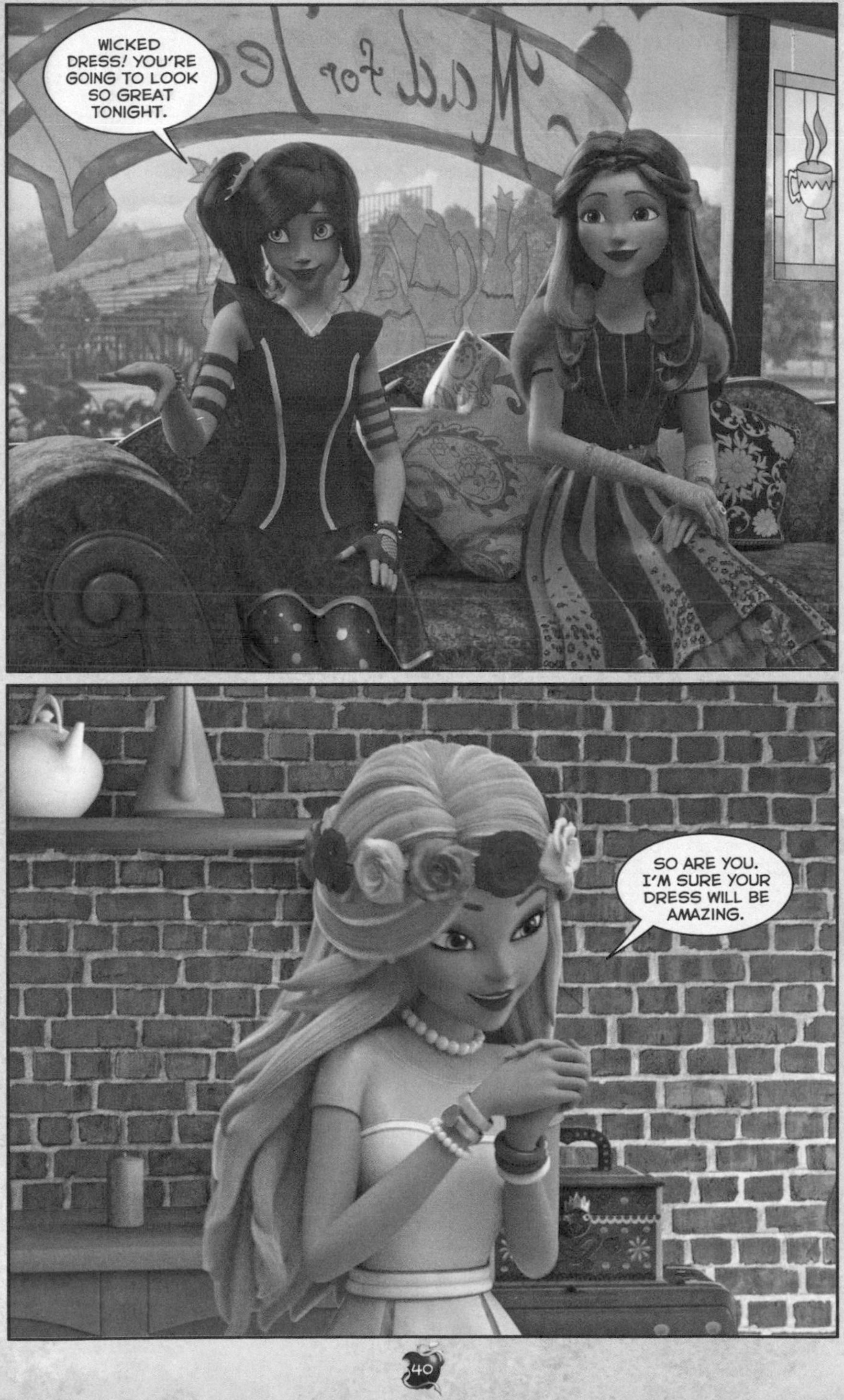
WICKED DRESS! YOU'RE GOING TO LOOK SO GREAT TONIGHT.
SO ARE YOU. I'M SURE YOUR DRESS WILL BE AMAZING.

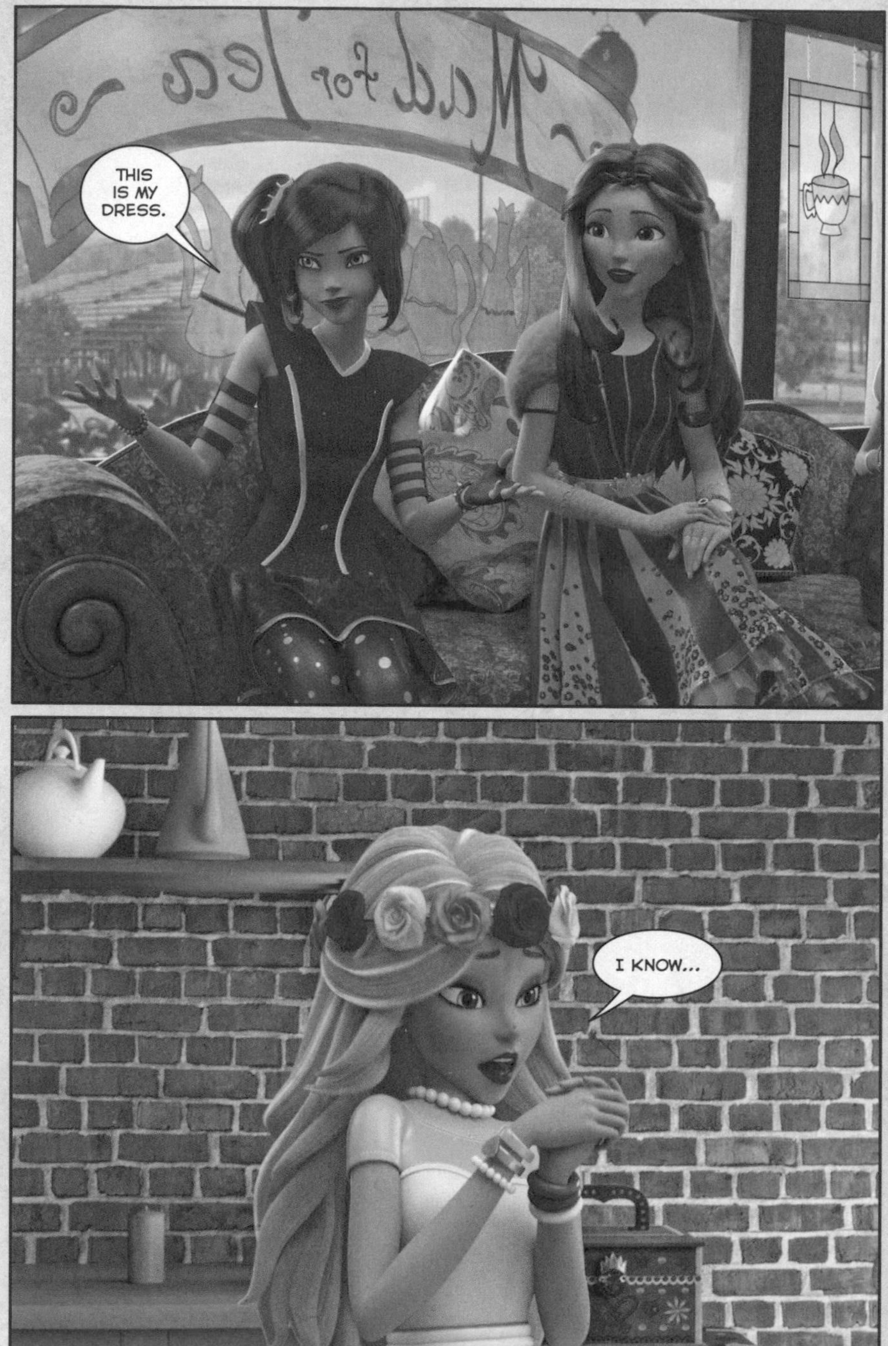
THIS IS MY DRESS.
I KNOW...

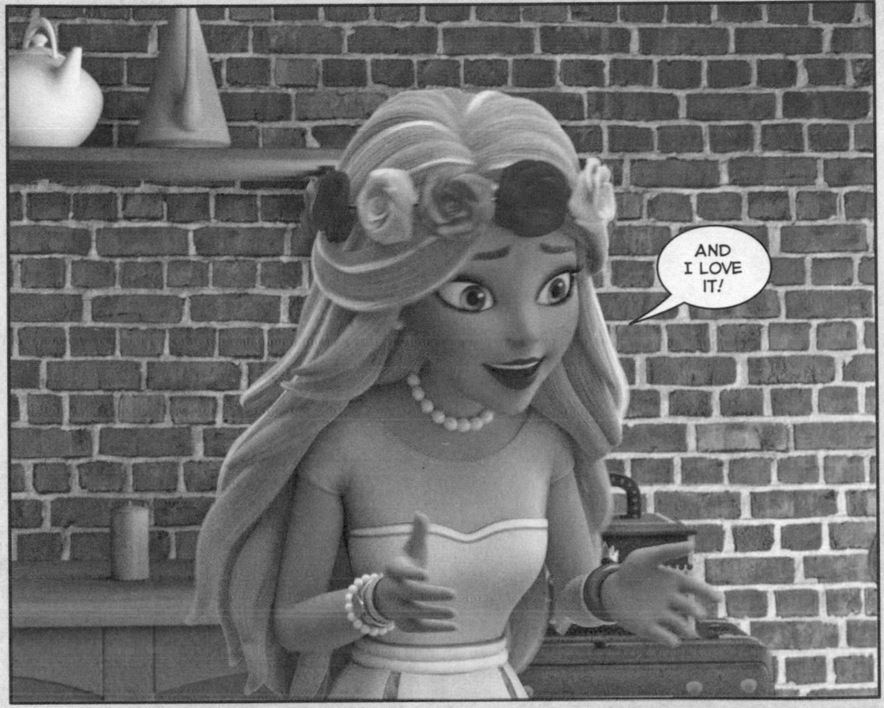
AND I LOVE IT!

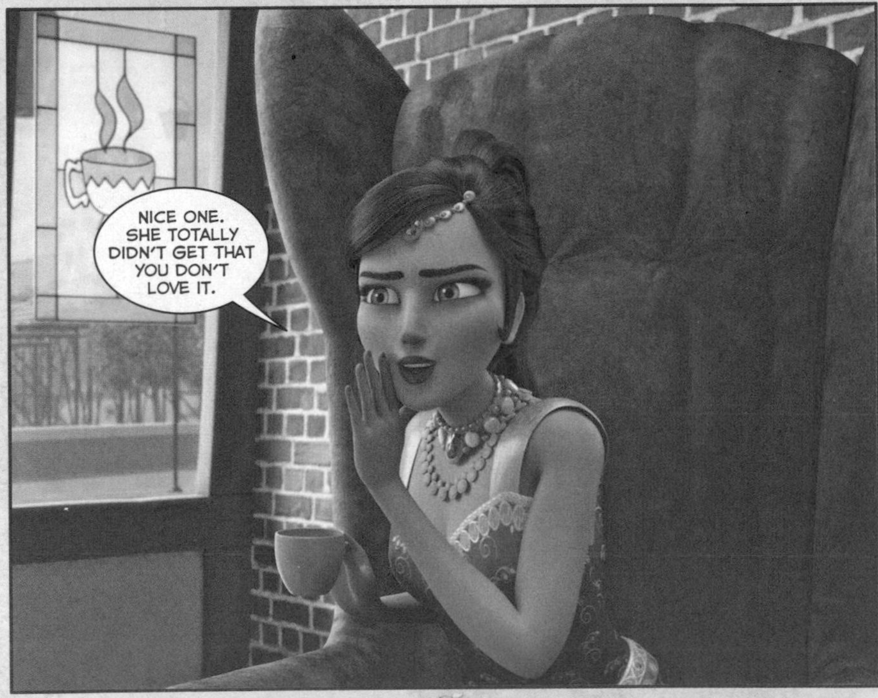
NICE ONE. SHE TOTALLY DIDN'T GET THAT YOU DON'T LOVE IT.

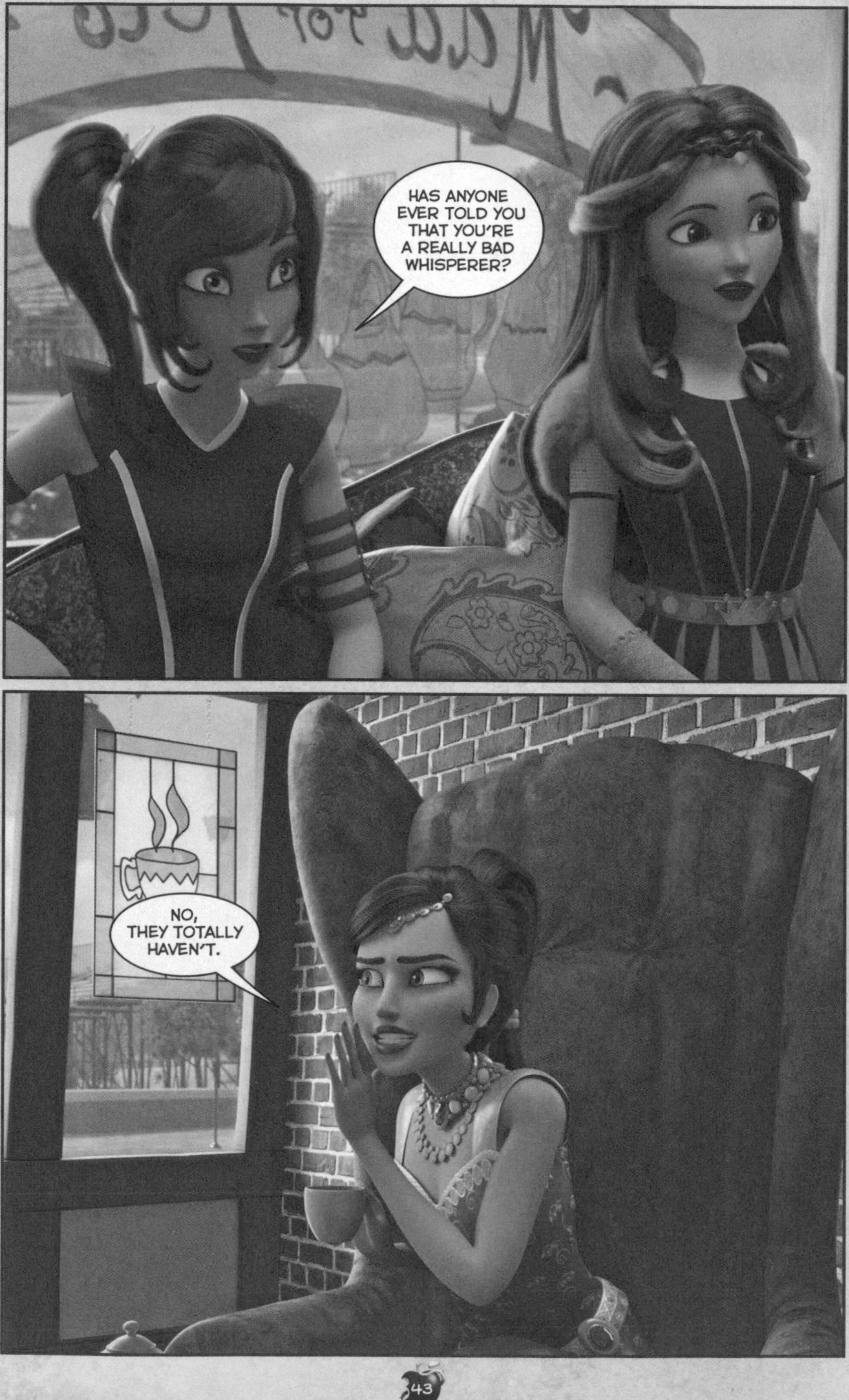
HAS ANYONE EVER TOLD YOU THAT YOU'RE A REALLY BAD WHISPERER?
NO, THEY TOTALLY HAVEN'T.

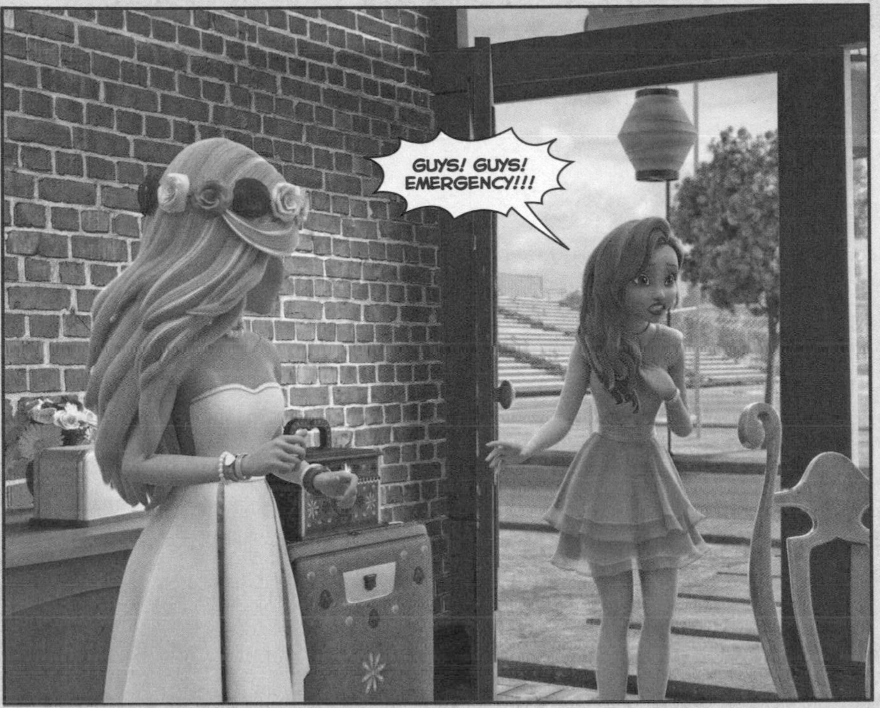
GUYS! GUYS! EMERGENCY!!!

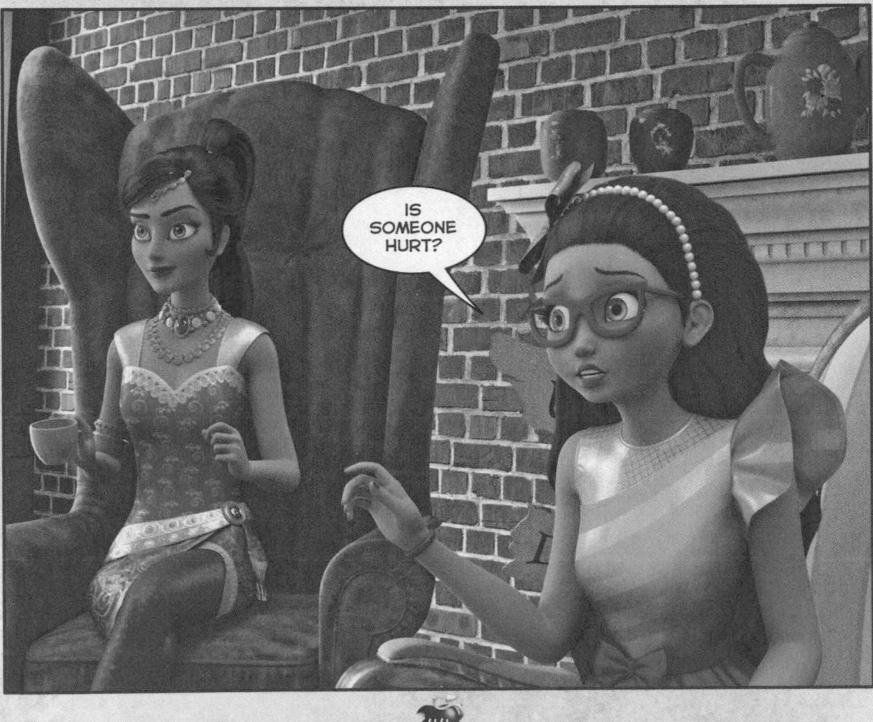
IS SOMEONE HURT?

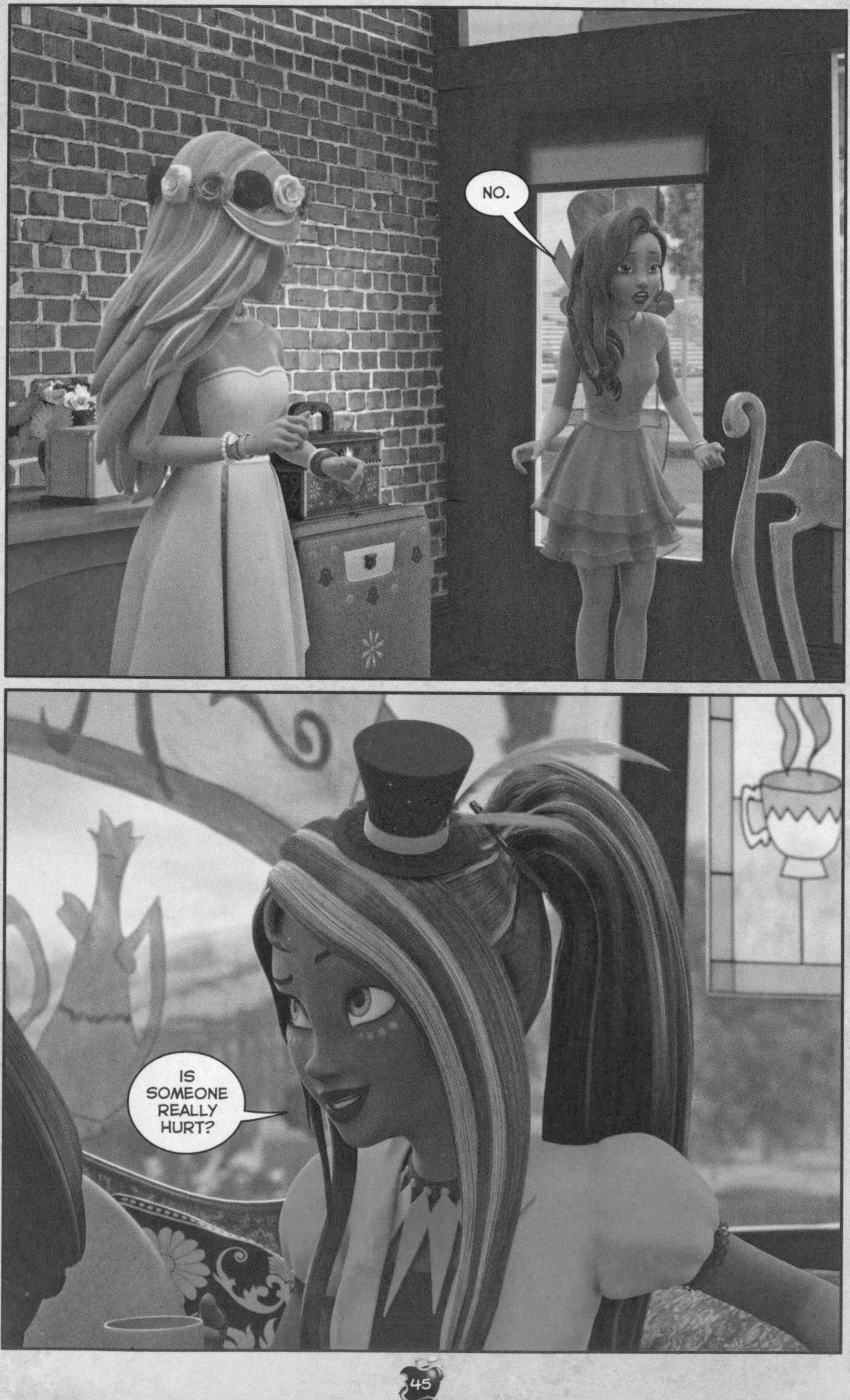
NO.
IS SOMEONE REALLY HURT?

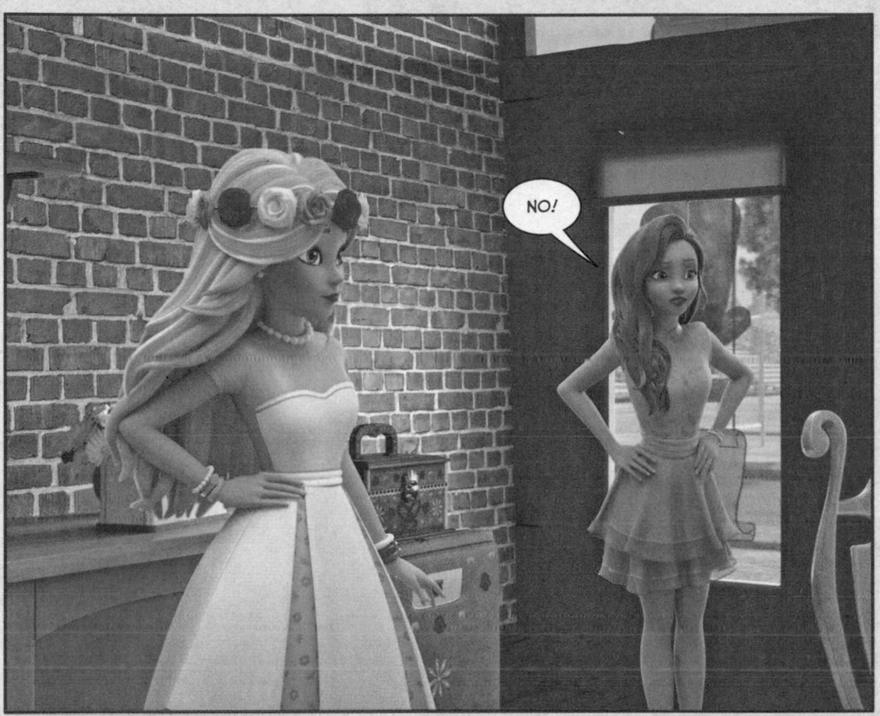
NO!

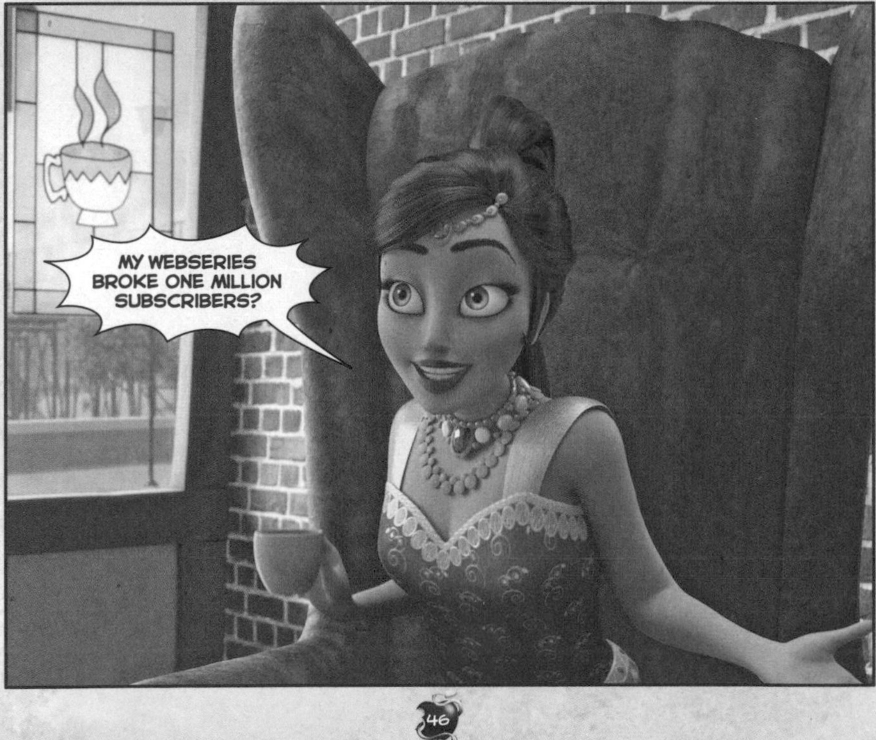
MY WEBSERIES BROKE ONE MILLION SUBSCRIBERS?

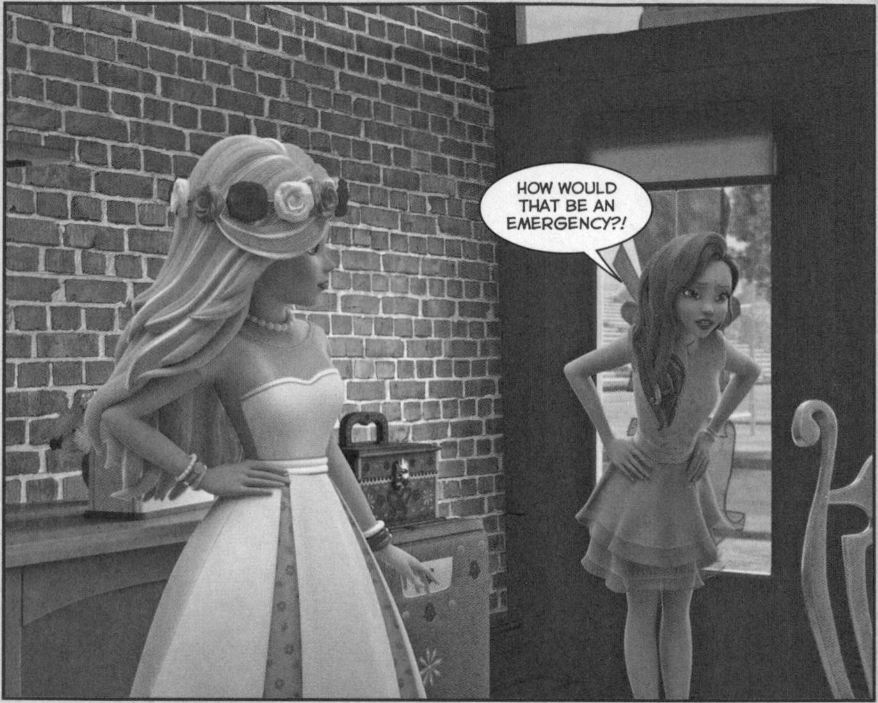
HOW WOULD THAT BE AN EMERGENCY?!
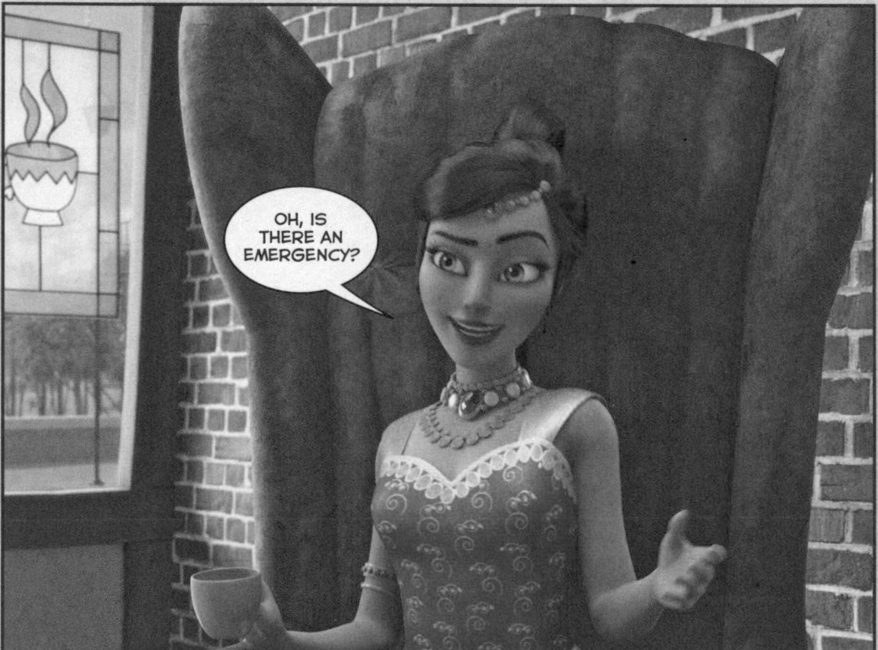
OH, IS THERE AN EMERGENCY?

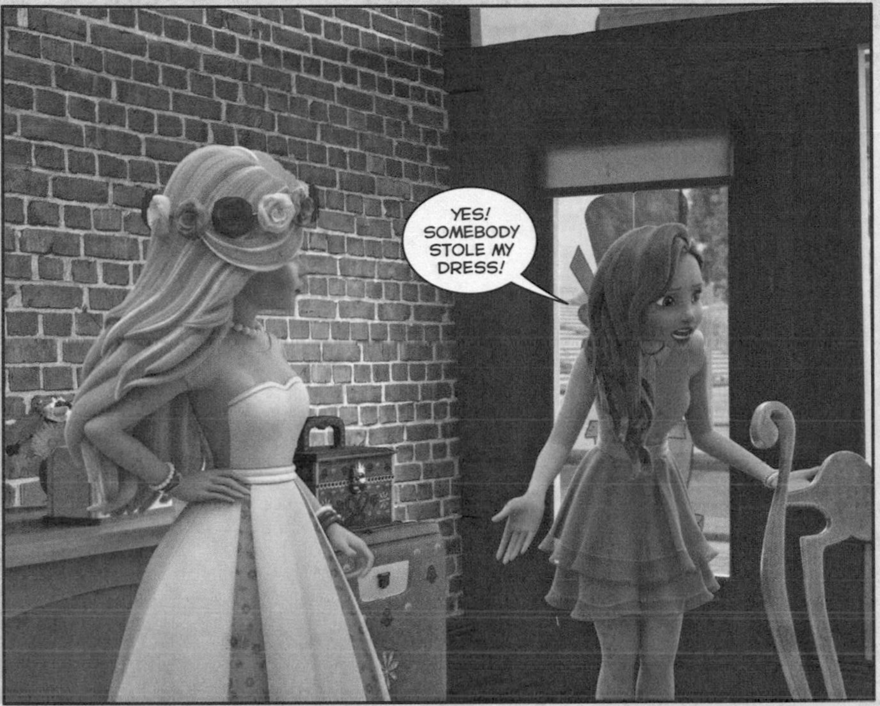
YES! SOMEBODY STOLE MY DRESS!

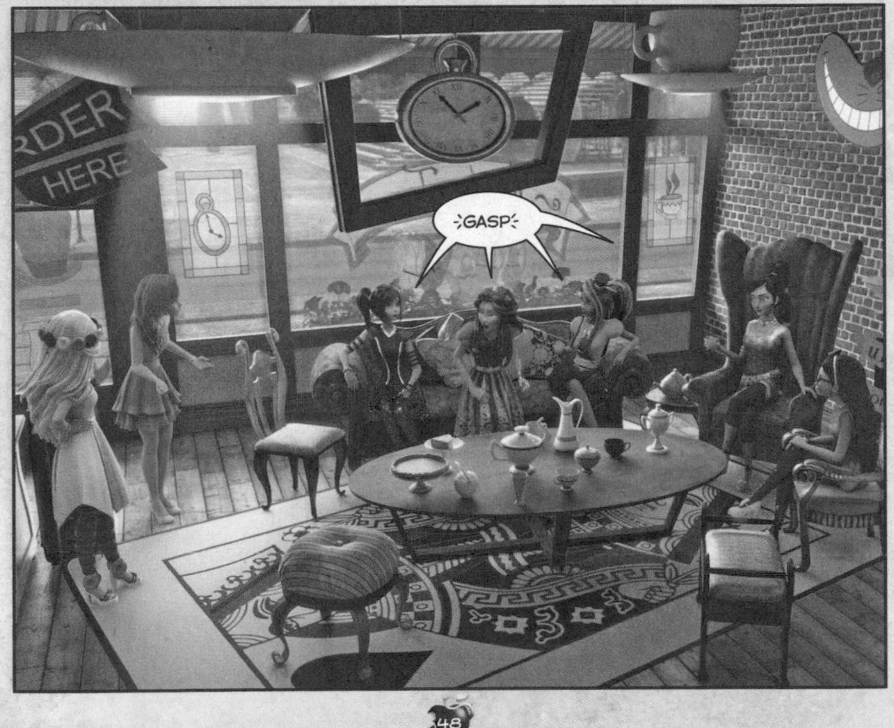
ORDER HERE
GASP

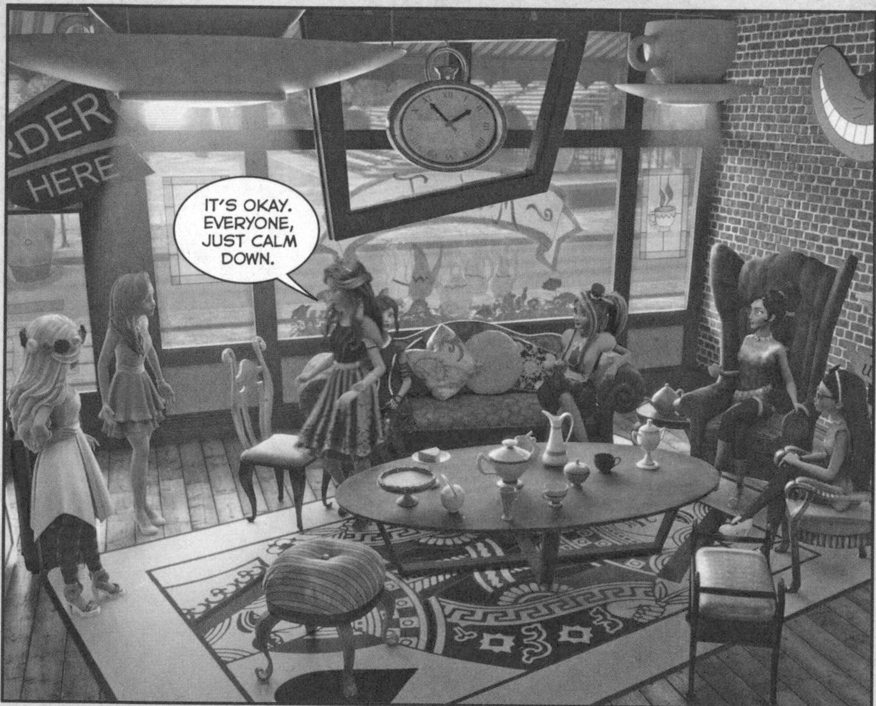
ORDER HERE
IT'S OKAY. EVERYONE, JUST CALM DOWN.

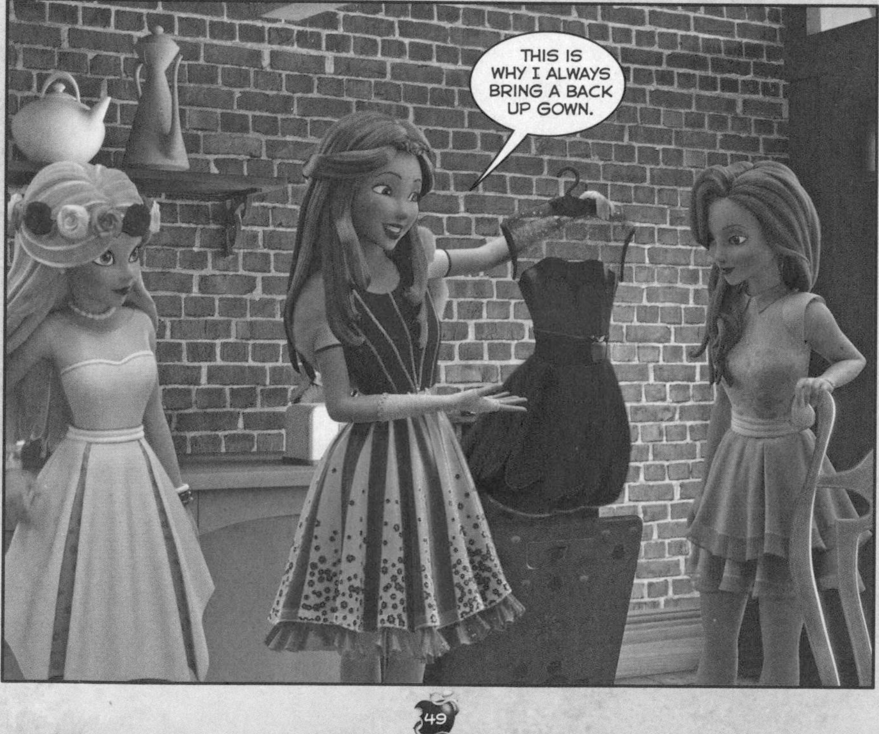
THIS IS WHY I ALWAYS BRING A BACK UP GOWN.

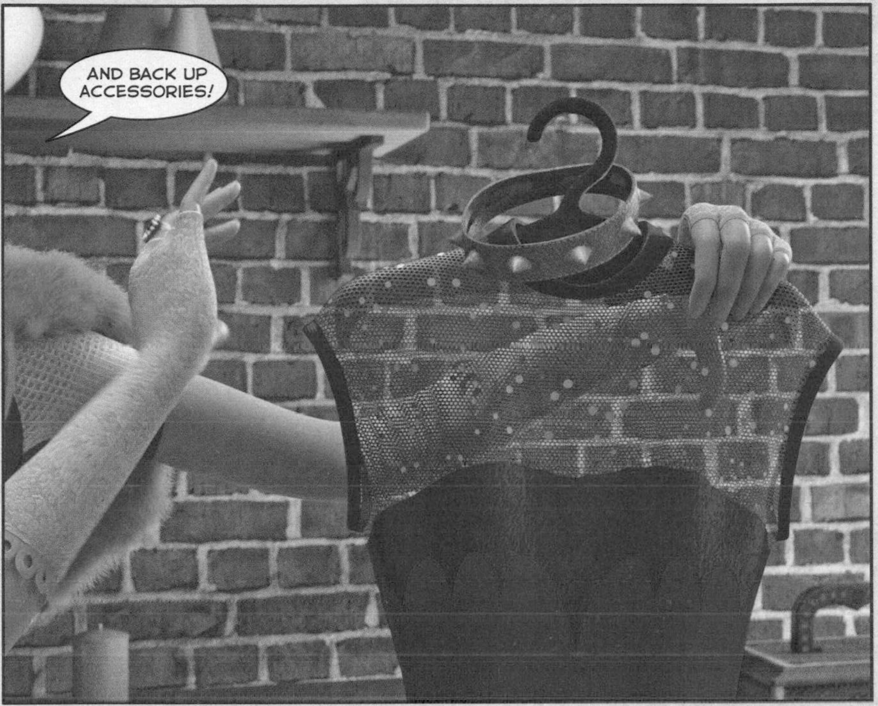
AND BACK UP ACCESSORIES!

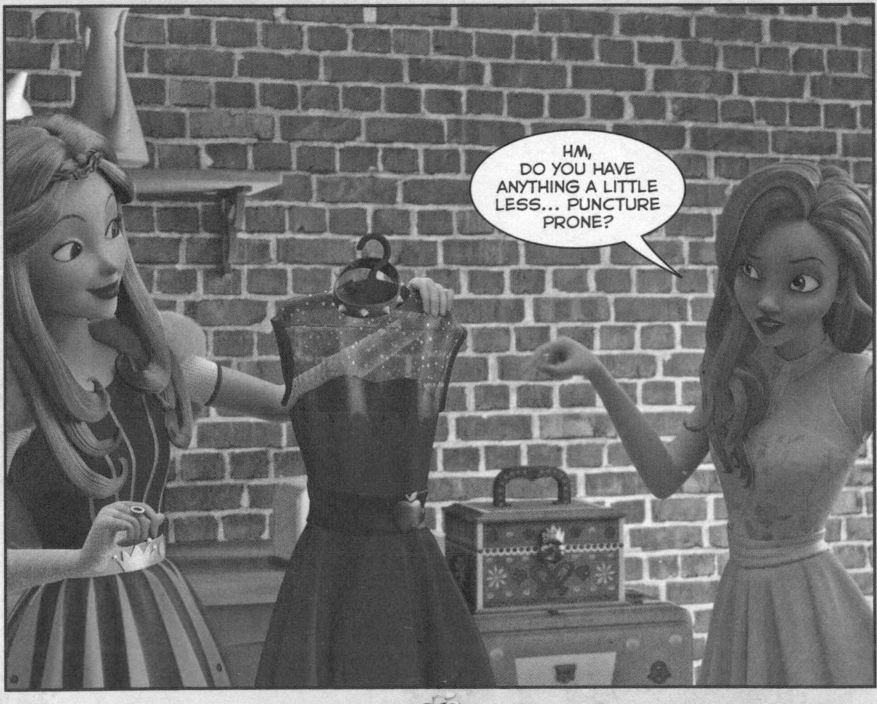
HM, DO YOU HAVE ANYTHING A LITTLE LESS... PUNCTURE PRONE?

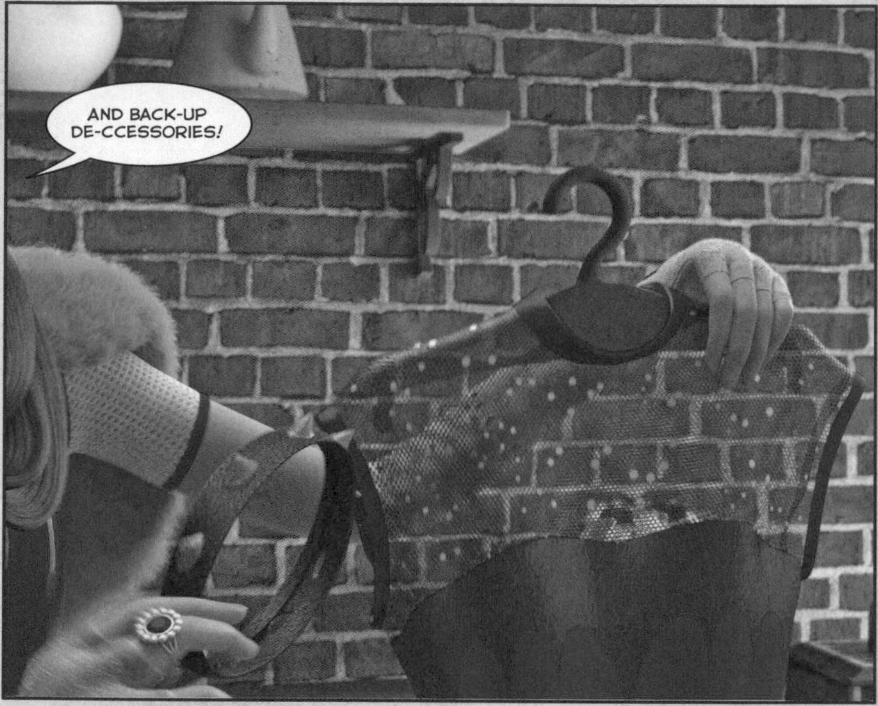
AND BACK-UP DE-CCESSORIES!

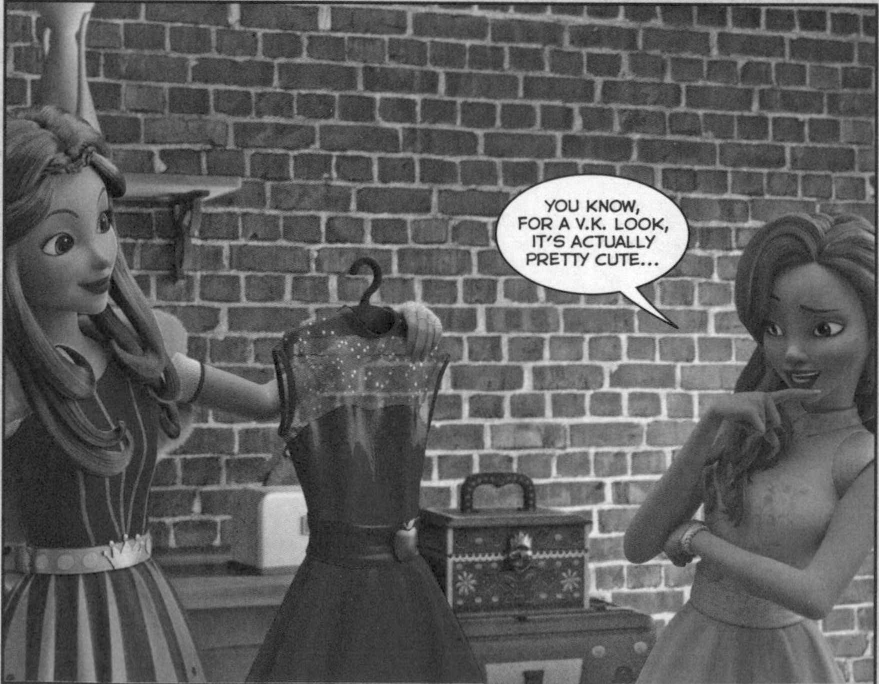
YOU KNOW, FOR A V.K. LOOK, IT'S ACTUALLY PRETTY CUTE...

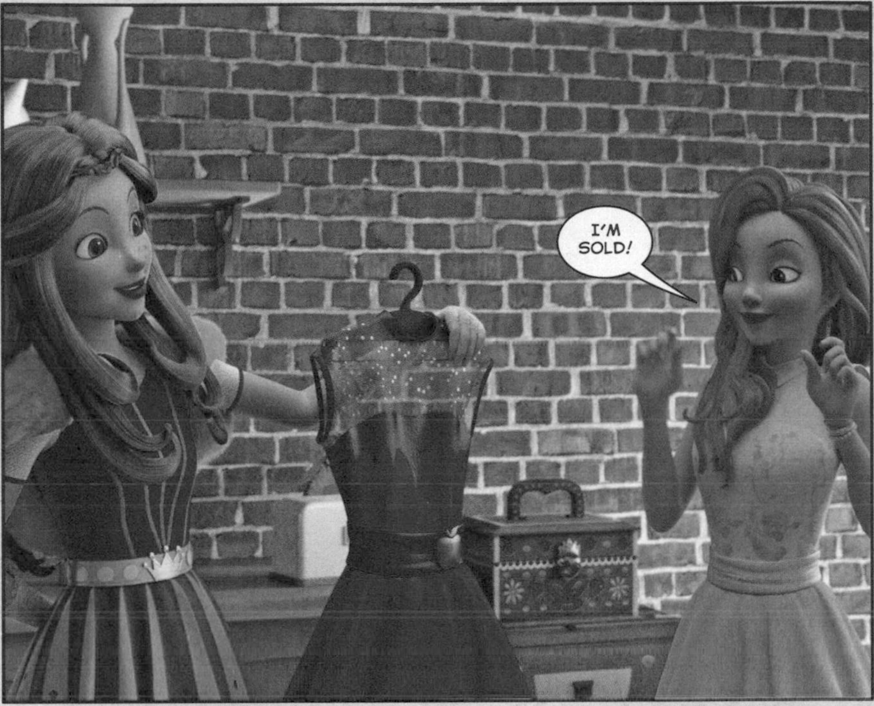
I'M SOLD!

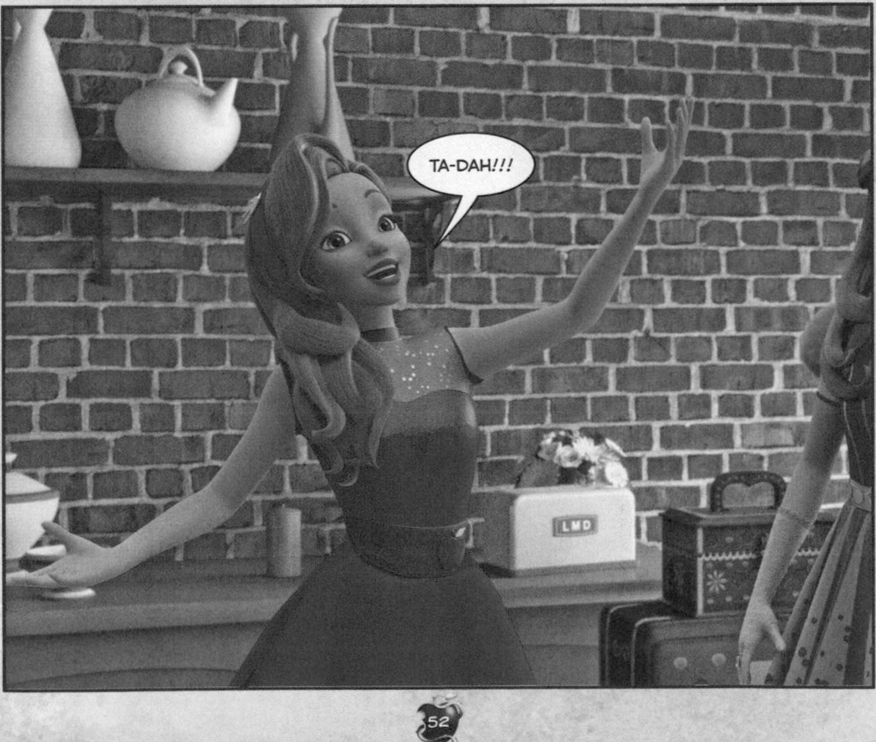
TA-DAH!!!

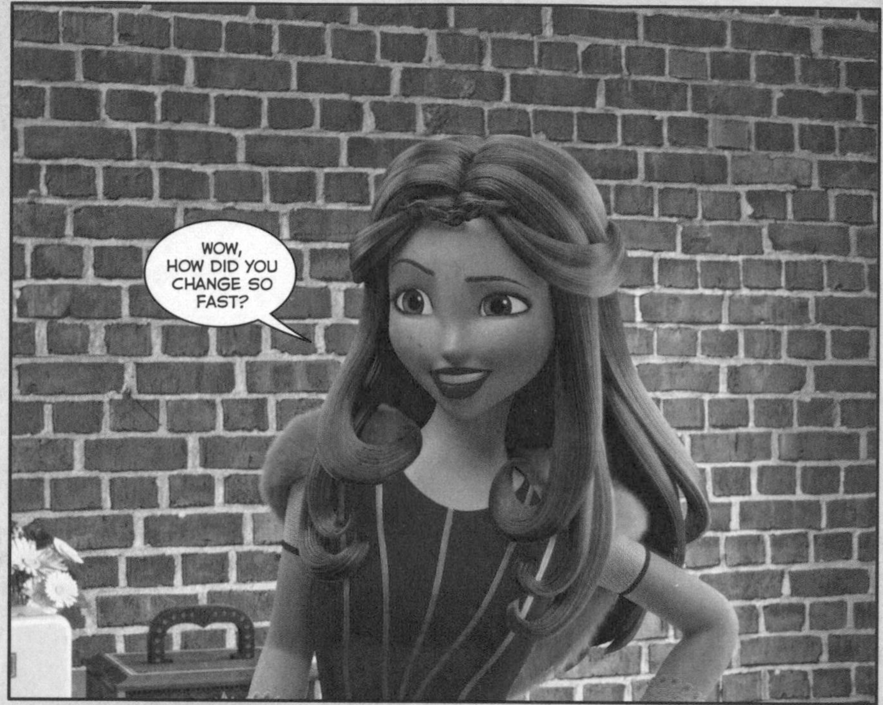
WOW, HOW DID YOU CHANGE SO FAST?

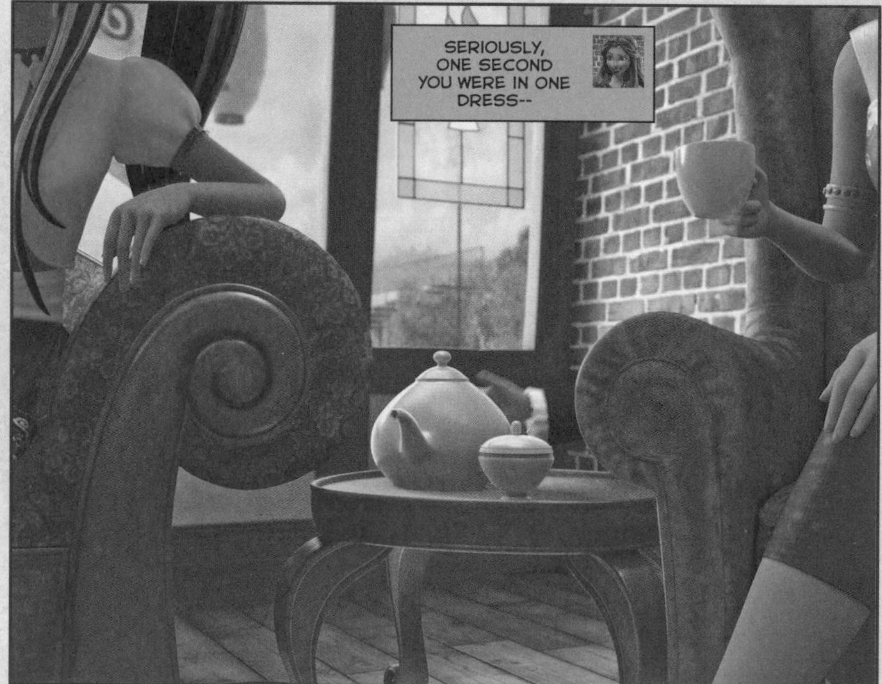
SERIOUSLY, ONE SECOND YOU WERE IN ONE DRESS--

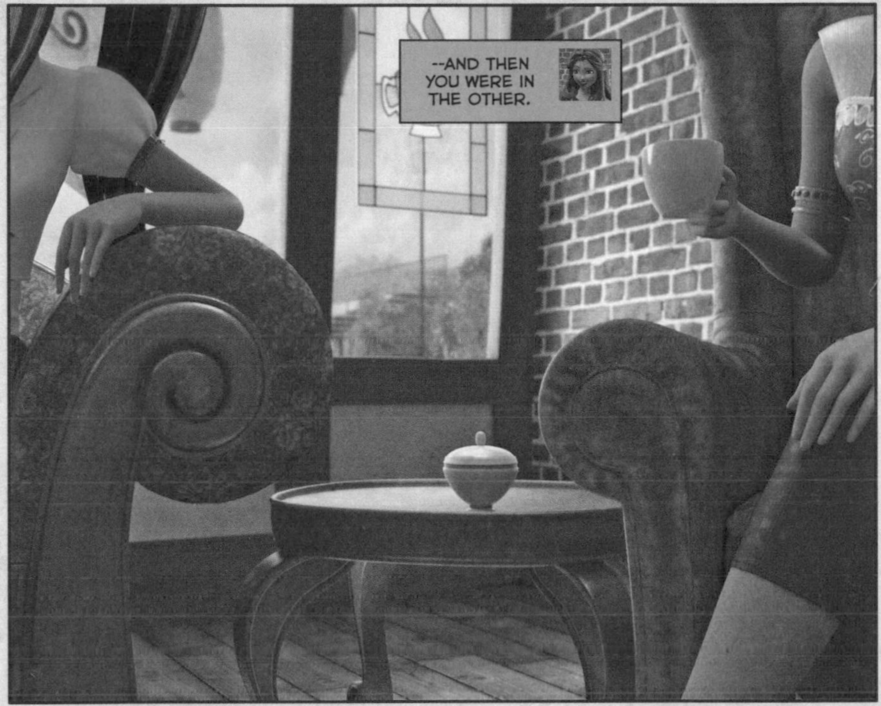
--AND THEN YOU WERE IN THE OTHER.

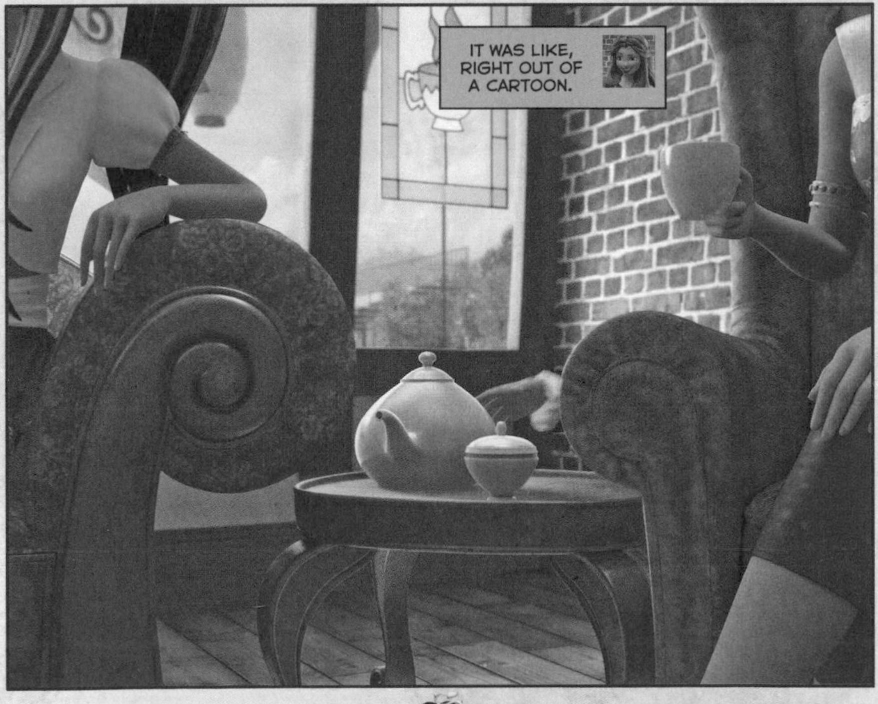
IT WAS LIKE, RIGHT OUT OF A CARTOON.

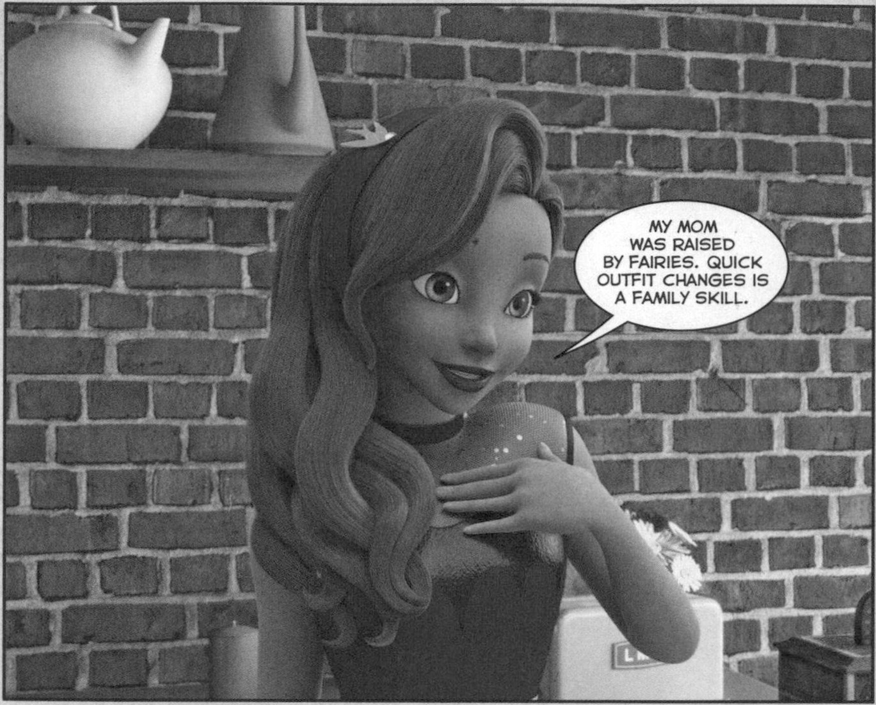
MY MOM WAS RAISED BY FAIRIES. QUICK OUTFIT CHANGES IS A FAMILY SKILL.

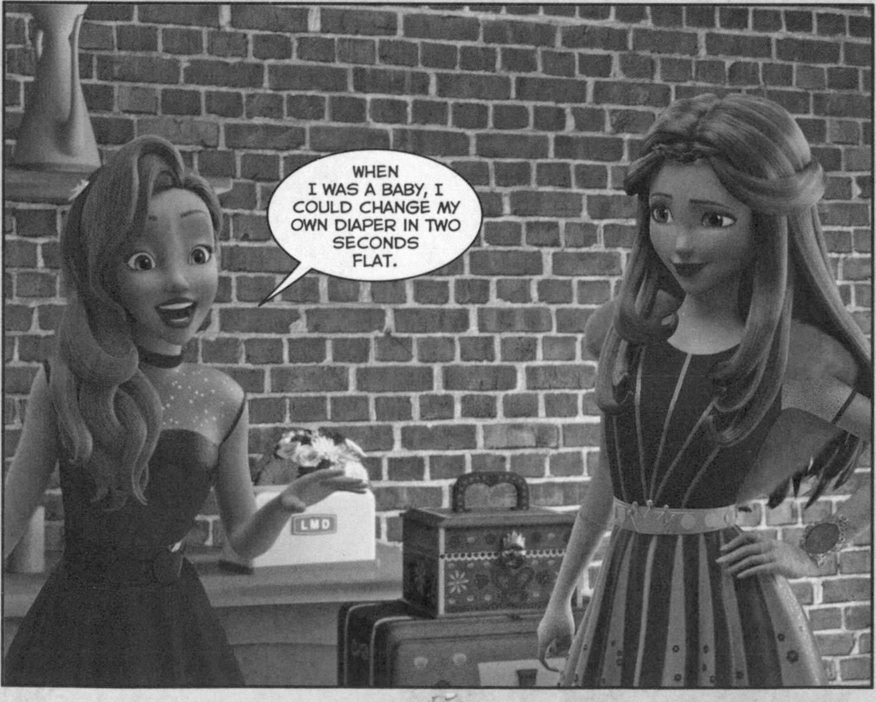
WHEN I WAS A BABY, I COULD CHANGE MY OWN DIAPER IN TWO SECONDS FLAT.
LMD

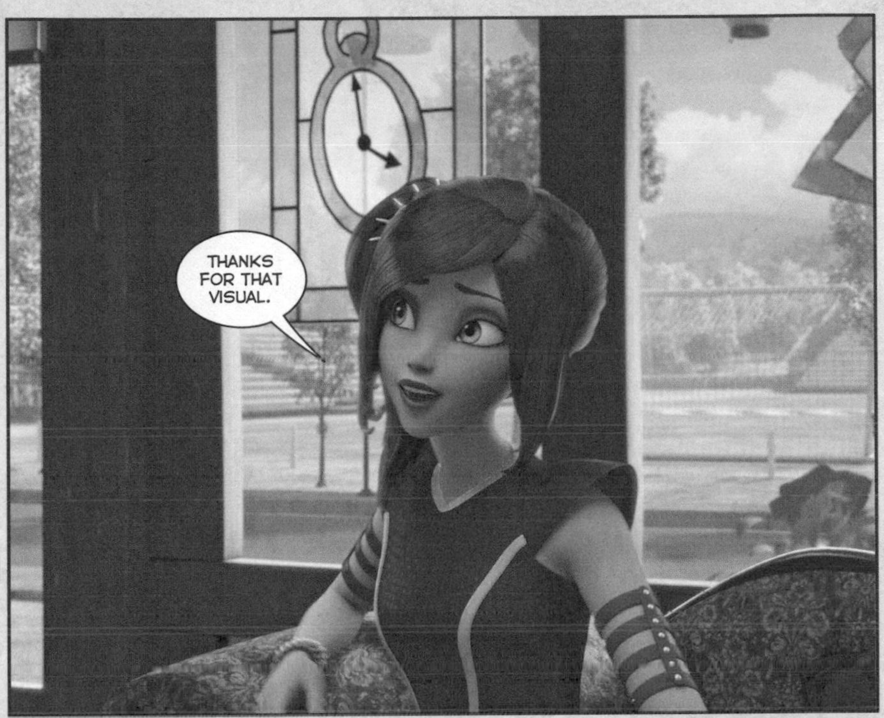
THANKS FOR THAT VISUAL.

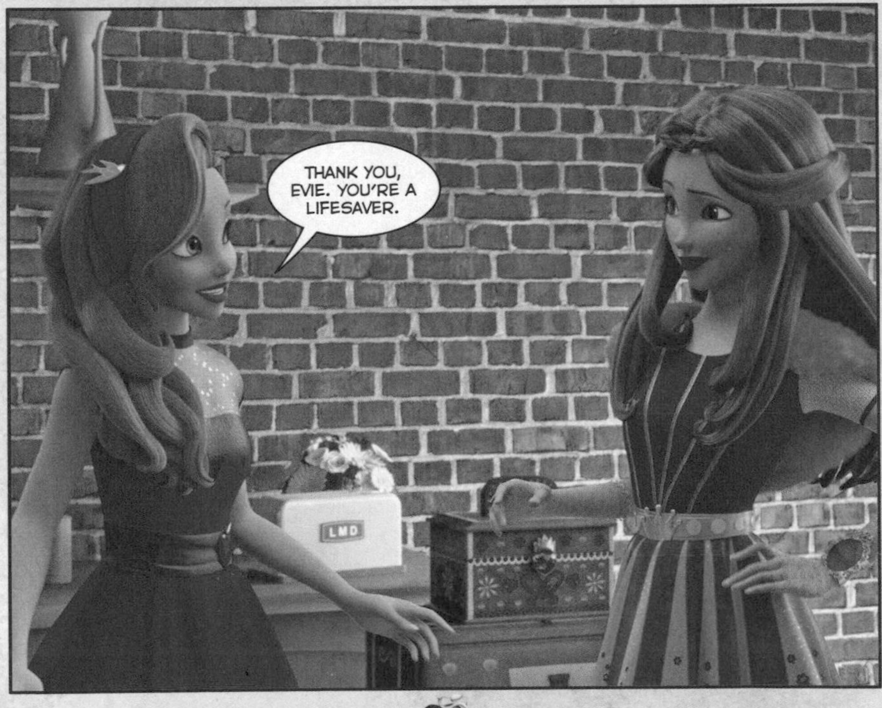
THANK YOU, EVIE. YOU'RE A LIFESAVER.

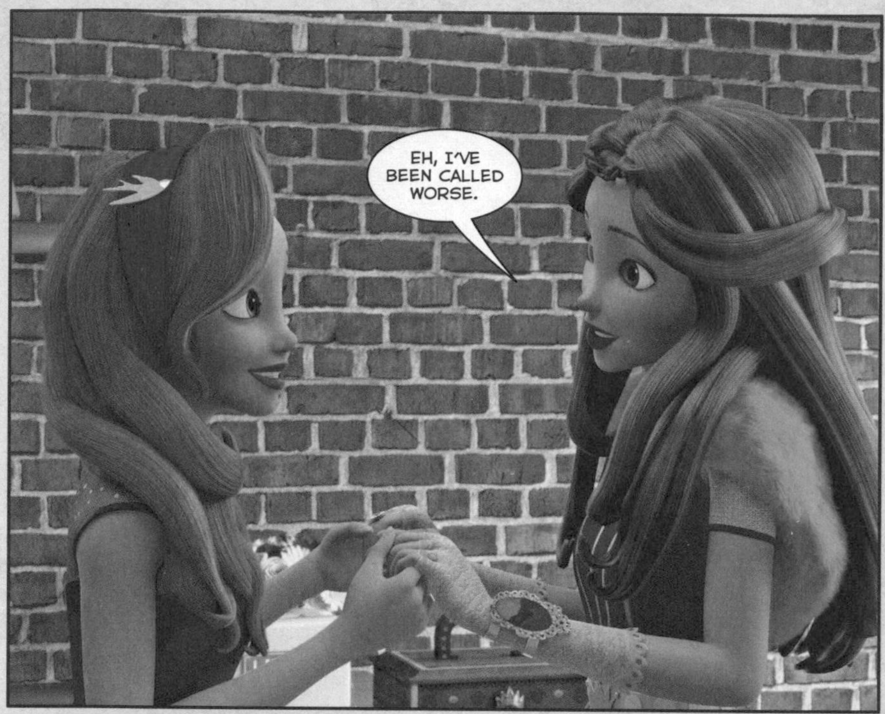
EH, I'VE BEEN CALLED WORSE.

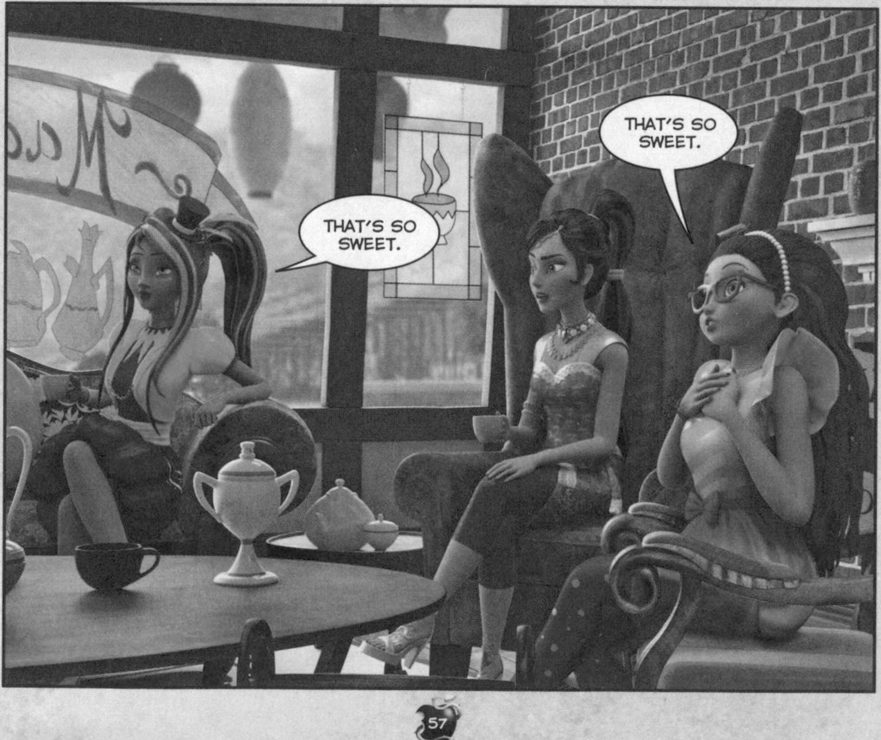
THAT'S SO SWEET.
THAT'S SO SWEET.

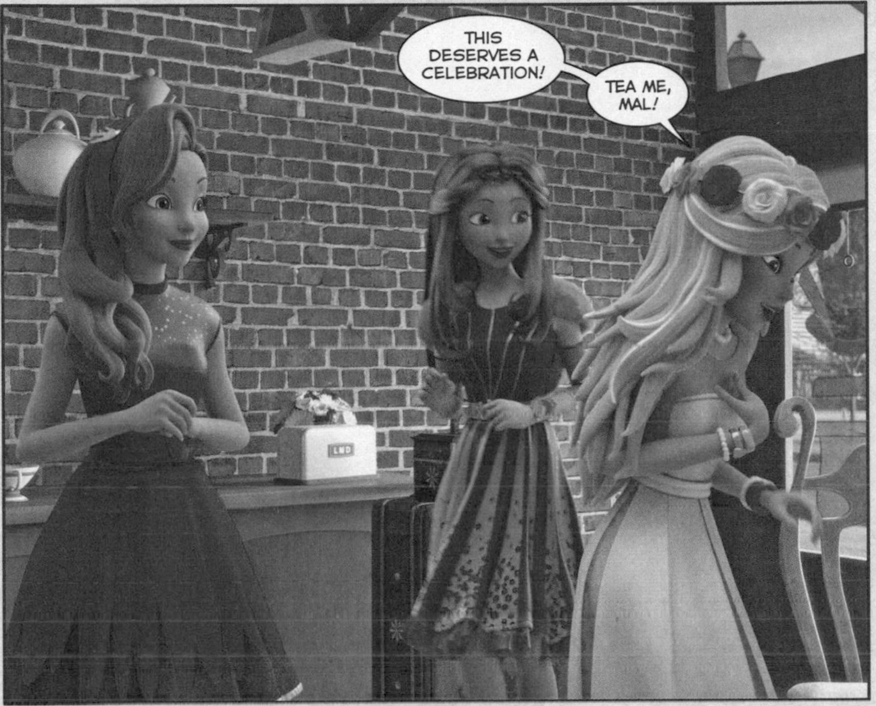
THIS DESERVES A CELEBRATION!
TEA ME, MAL!

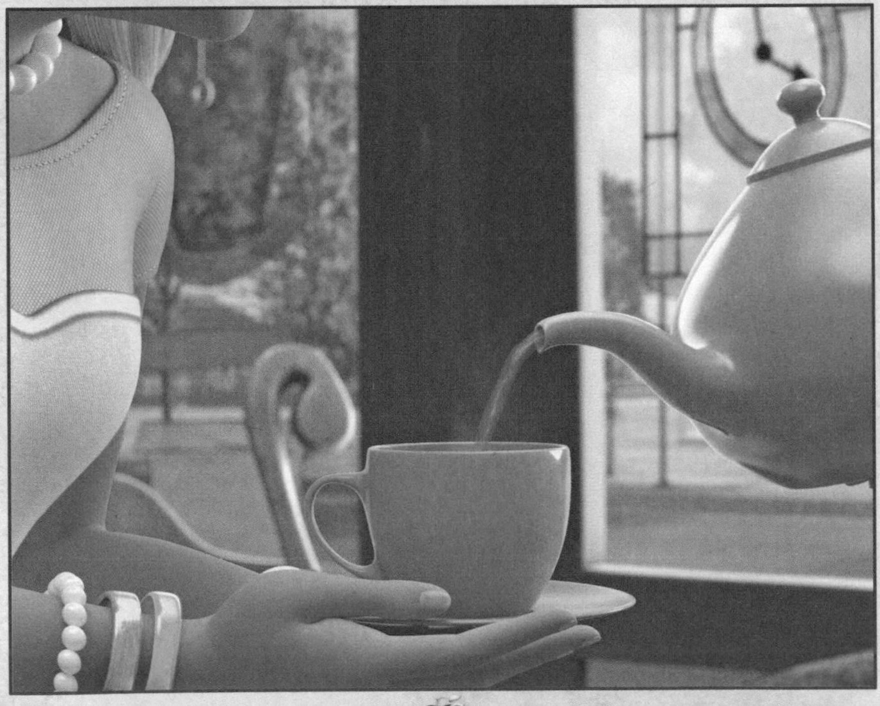

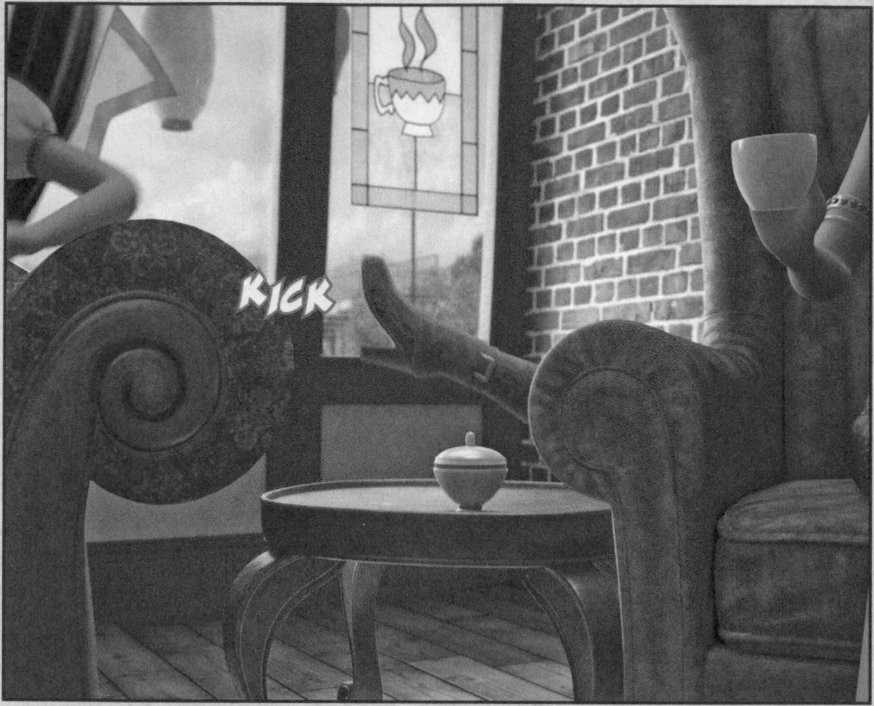
KICK

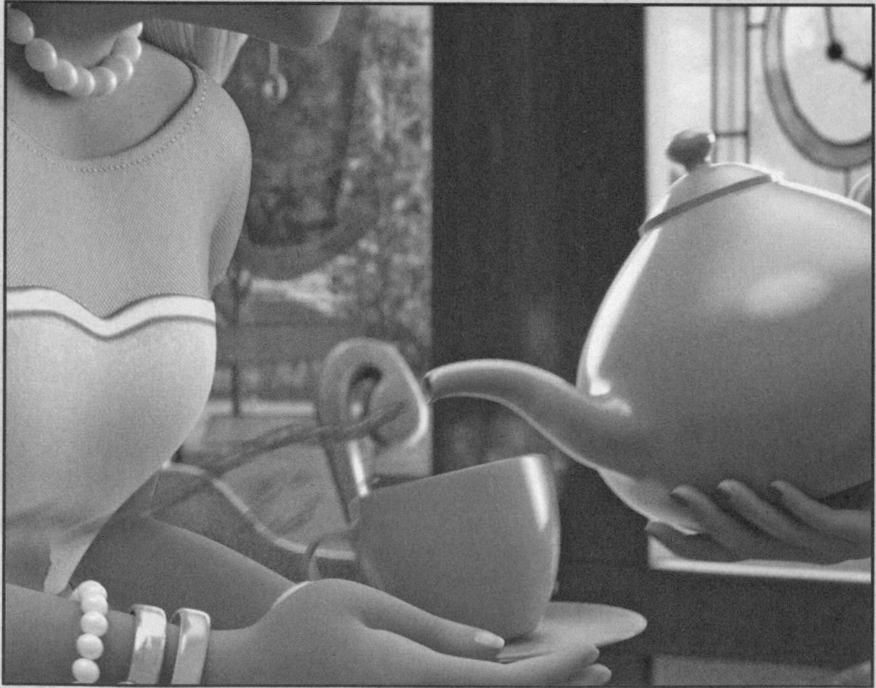

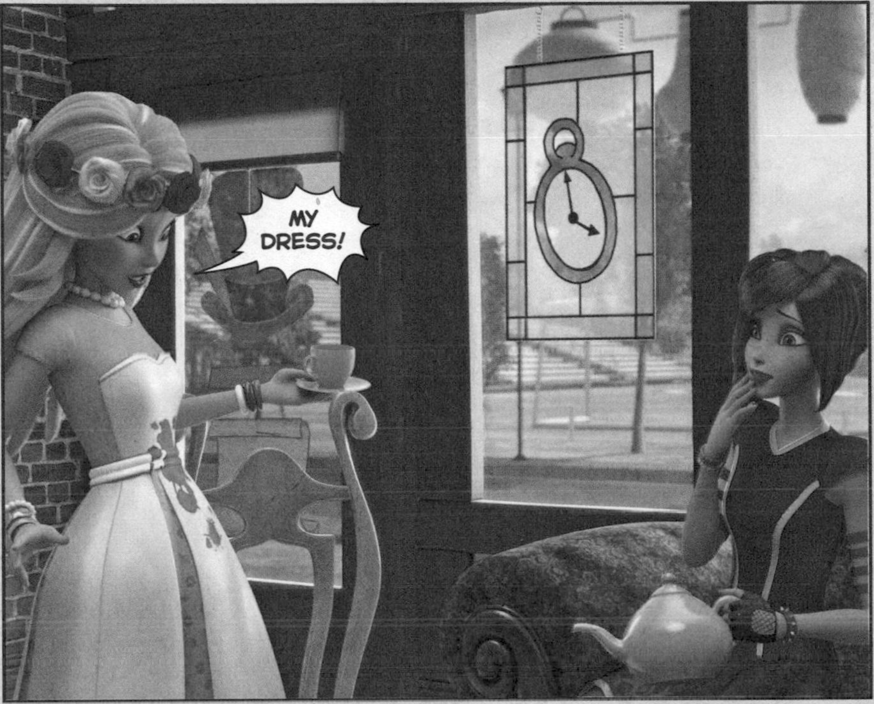
MY DRESS!

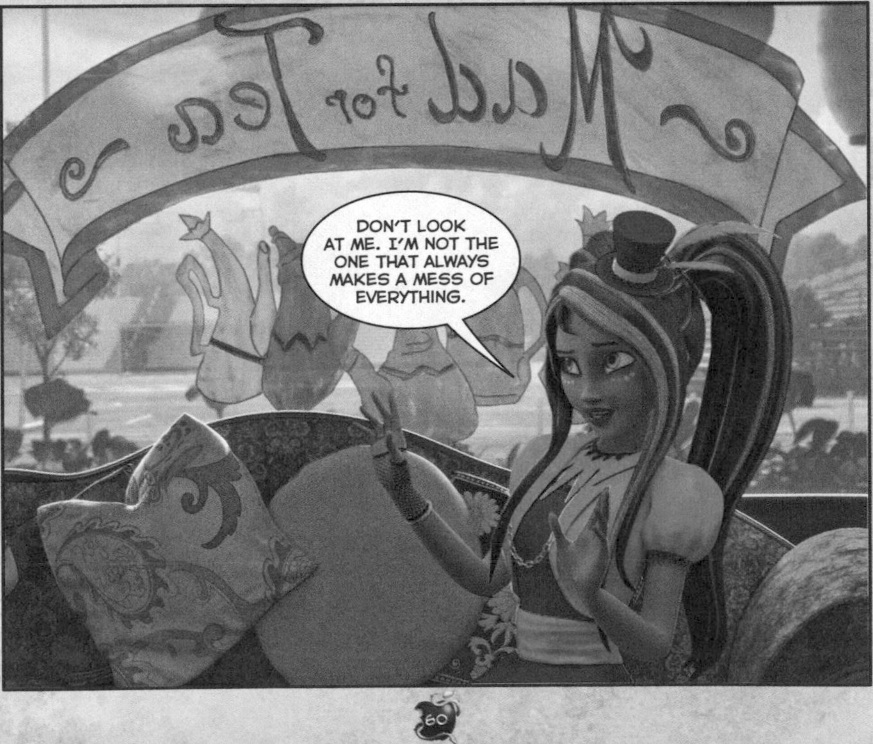
Mad for Tea
DON'T LOOK AT ME. I'M NOT THE ONE THAT ALWAYS MAKES A MESS OF EVERYTHING.

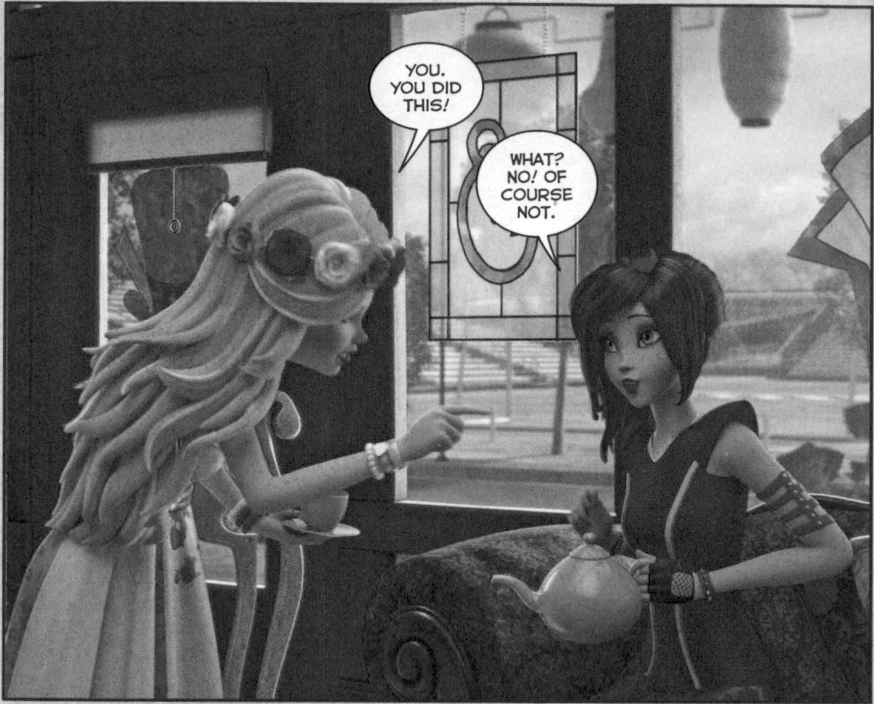
YOU. YOU DID THIS!
WHAT? NO! OF COURSE NOT.

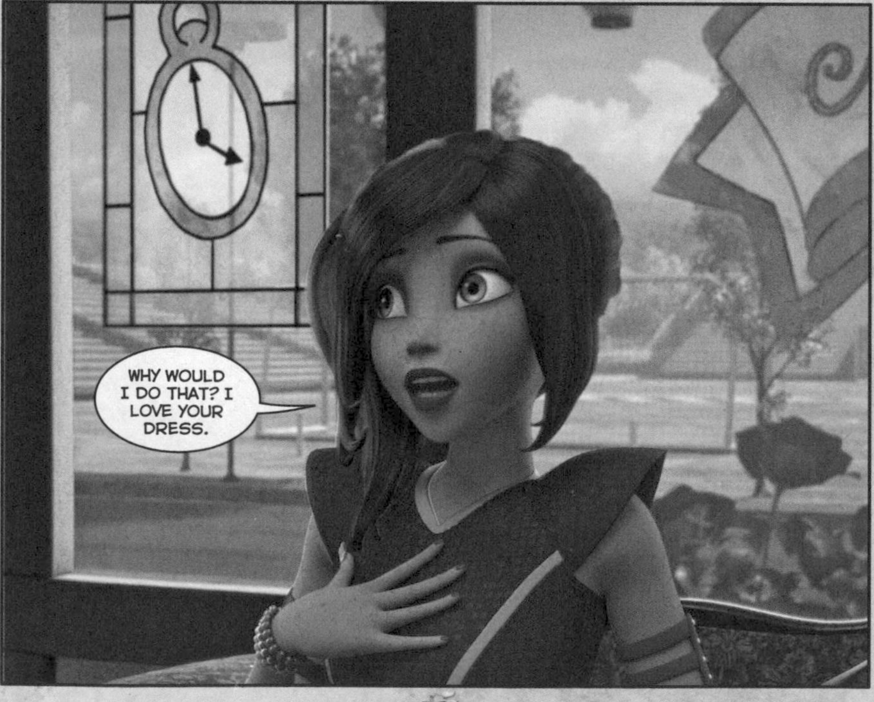
WHY WOULD I DO THAT? I LOVE YOUR DRESS.

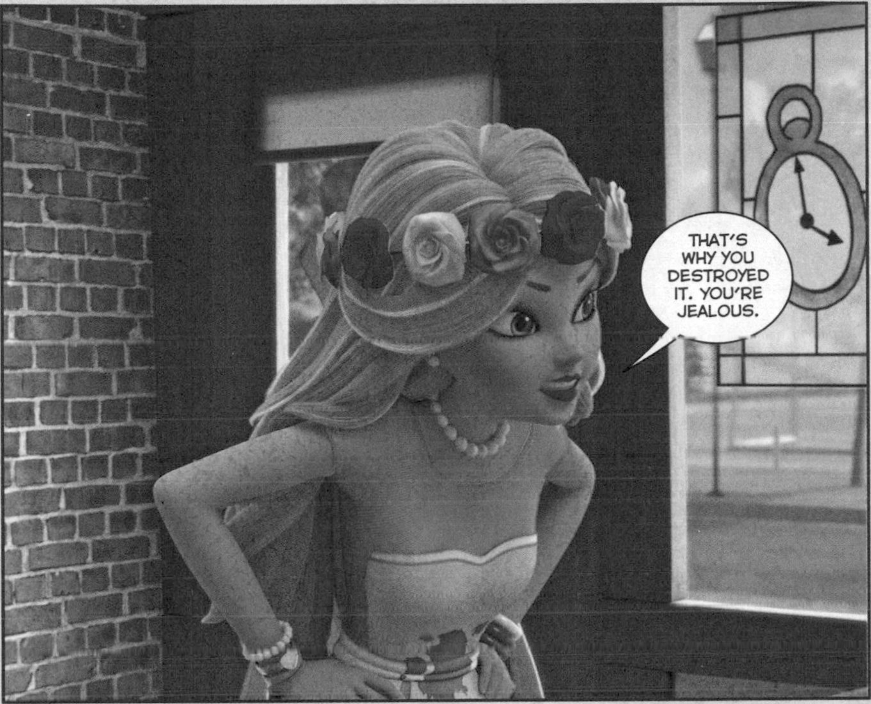
THAT'S WHY YOU DESTROYED IT. YOU'RE JEALOUS.

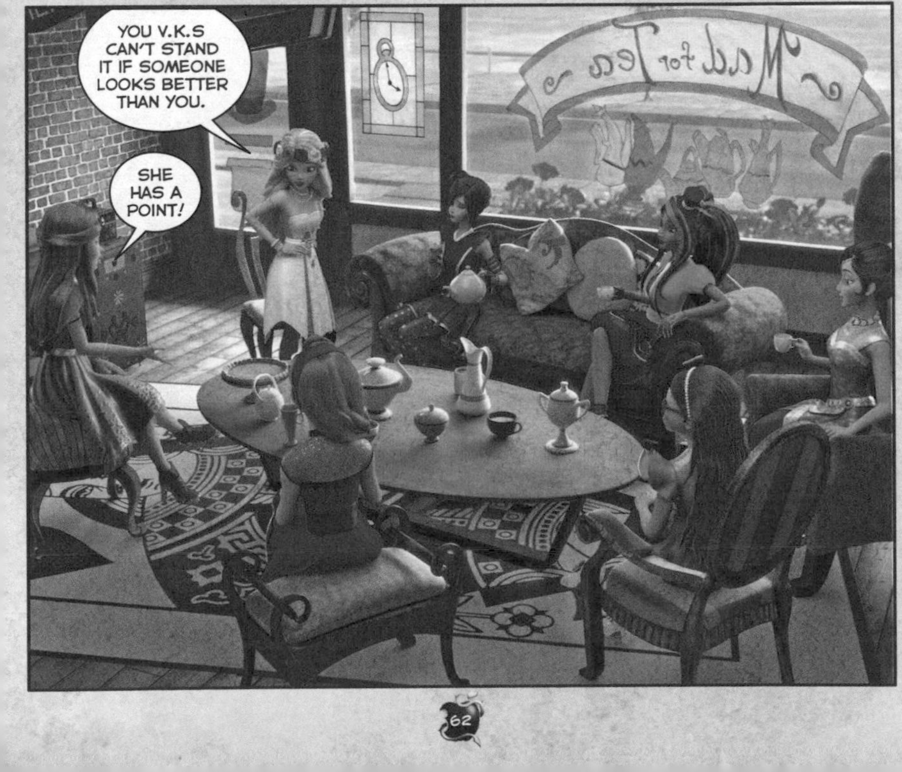
YOU V.K.S CAN'T STAND IT IF SOMEONE LOOKS BETTER THAN YOU.
SHE HAS A POINT!

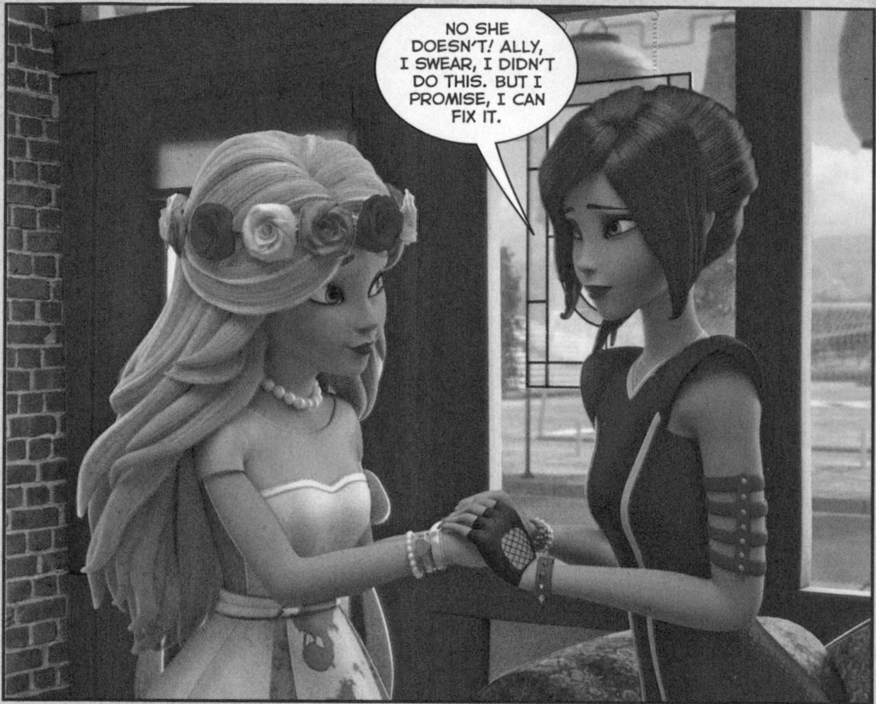
NO SHE DOESN'T! ALLY, I SWEAR, I DIDN'T DO THIS. BUT I PROMISE, I CAN FIX IT.

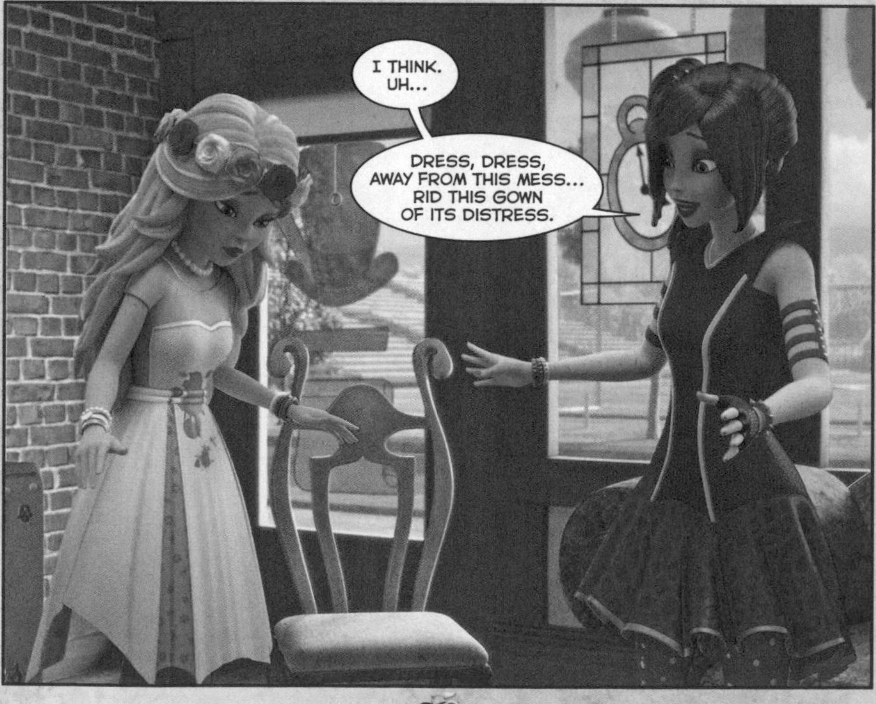
I THINK. UH...
DRESS, DRESS, AWAY FROM THIS MESS... RID THIS GOWN OF ITS DISTRESS.

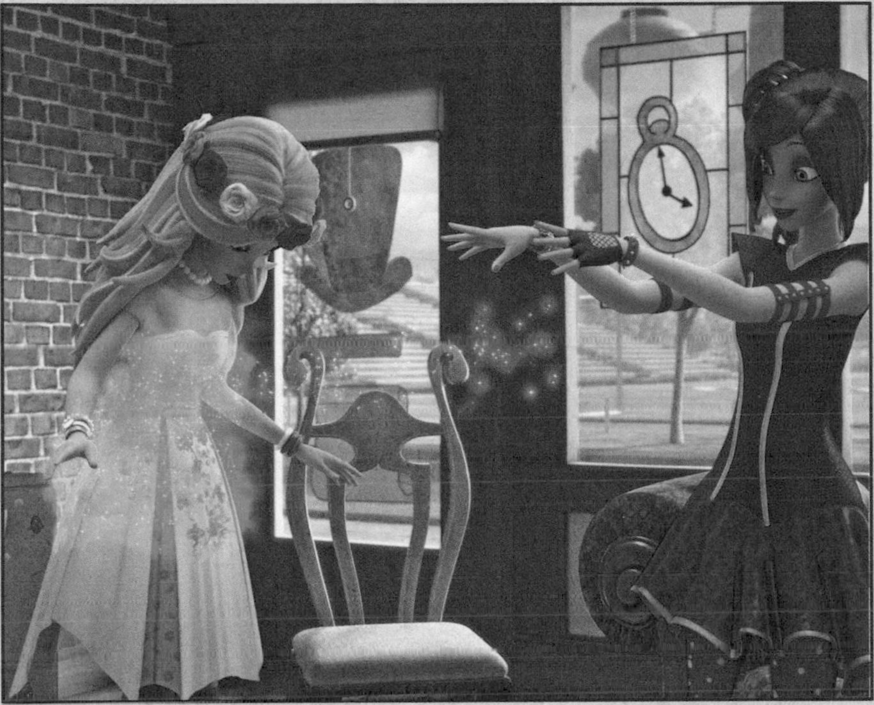

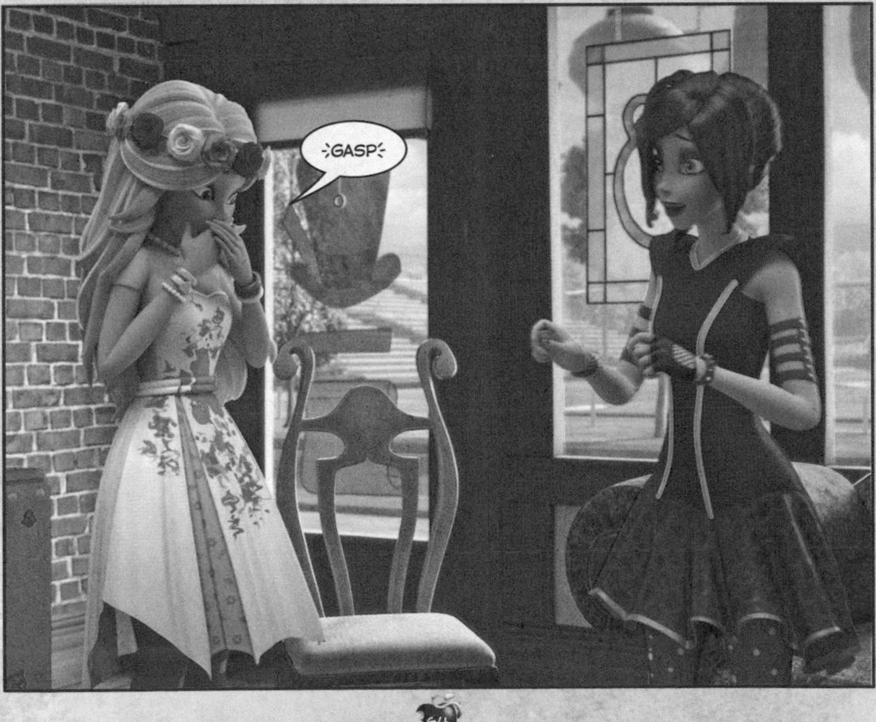
GASP

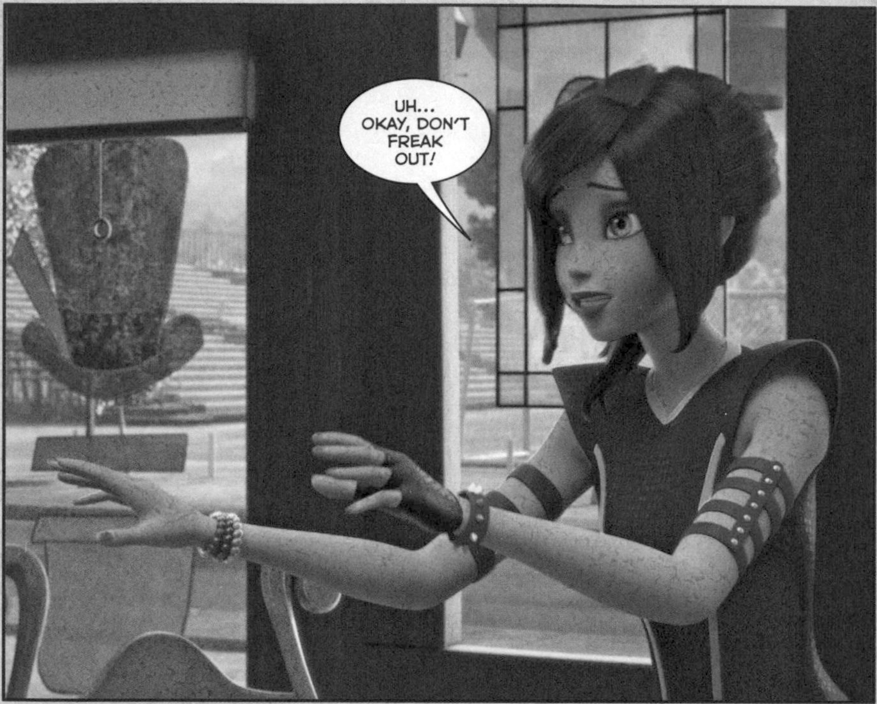
UH... OKAY, DON'T FREAK OUT!

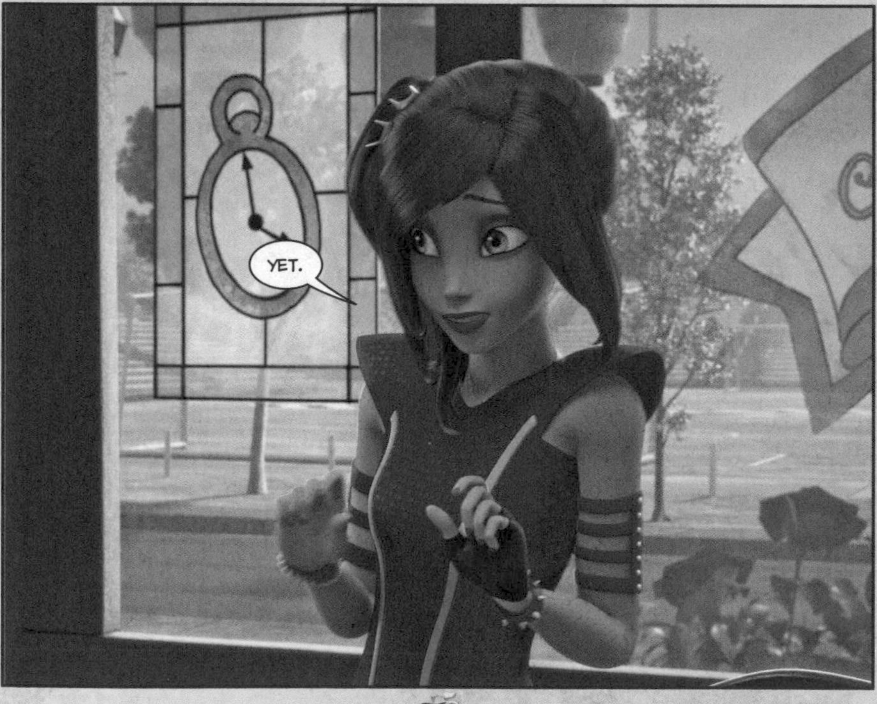
YET.

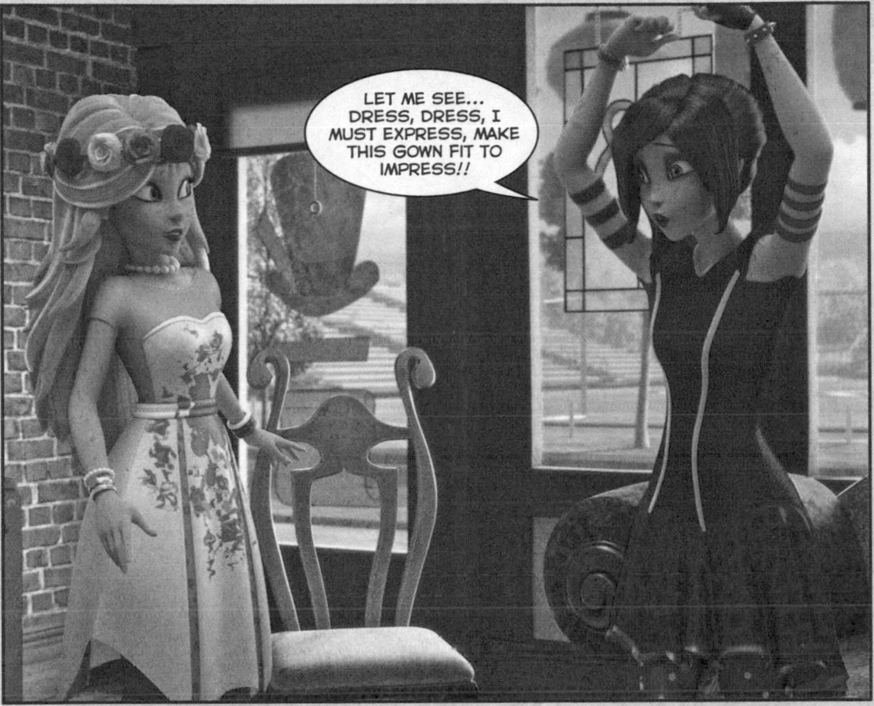
LET ME SEE... DRESS, DRESS, I MUST EXPRESS, MAKE THIS GOWN FIT TO IMPRESS!!

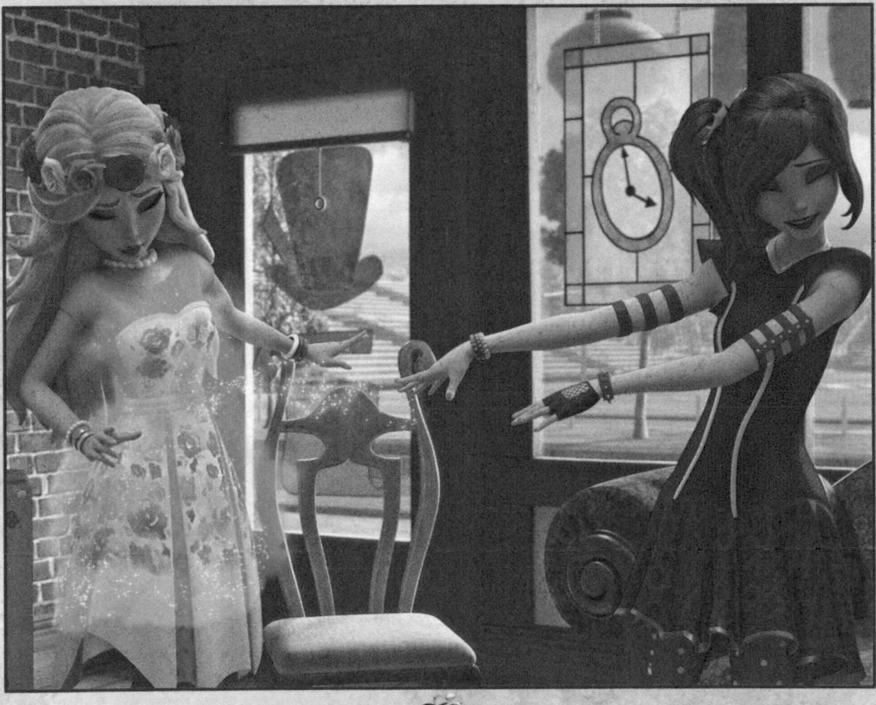

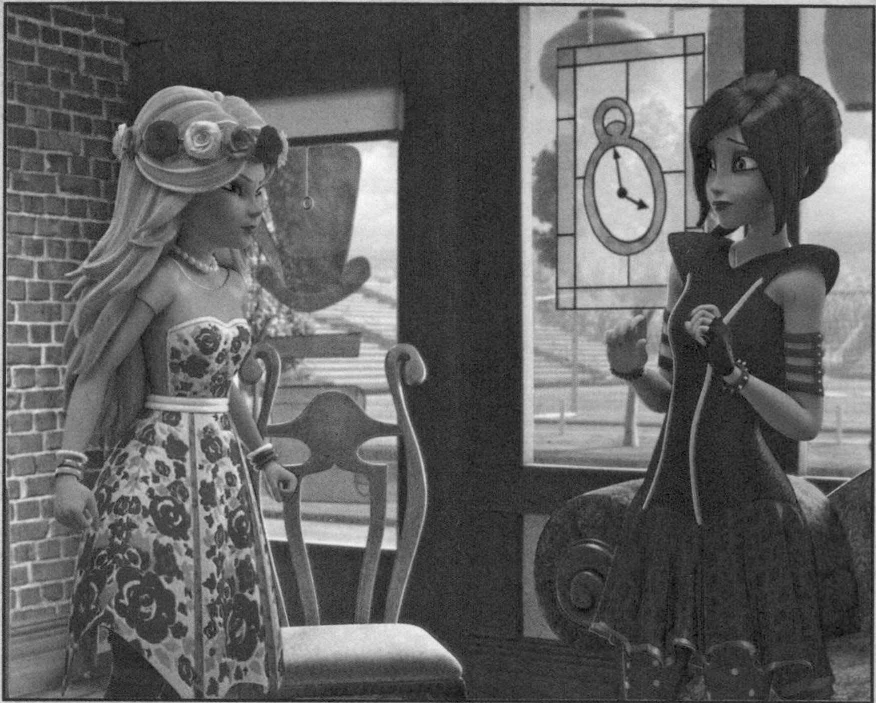

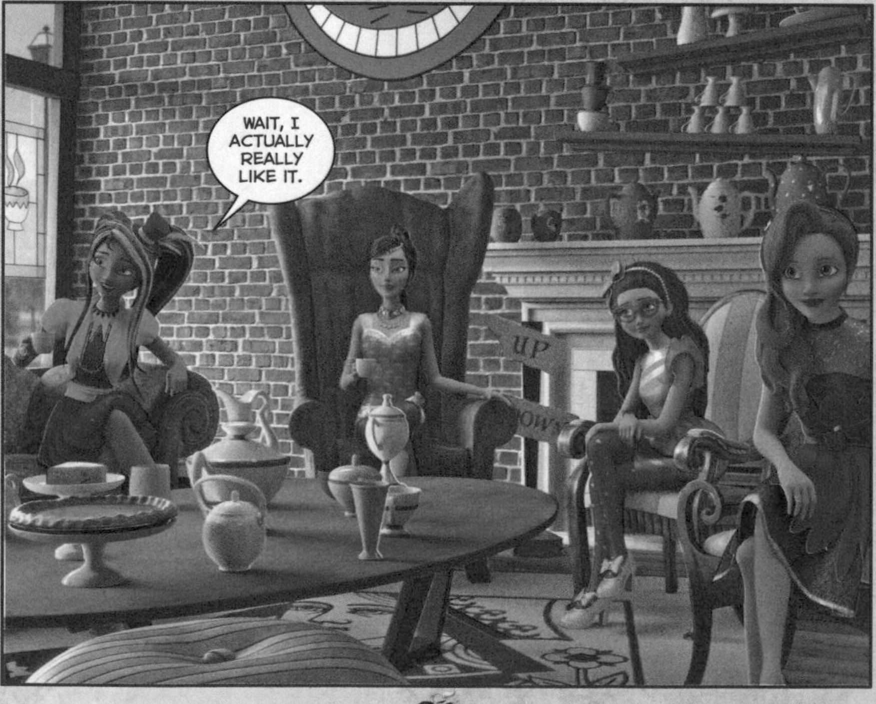
WAIT, I ACTUALLY REALLY LIKE IT.

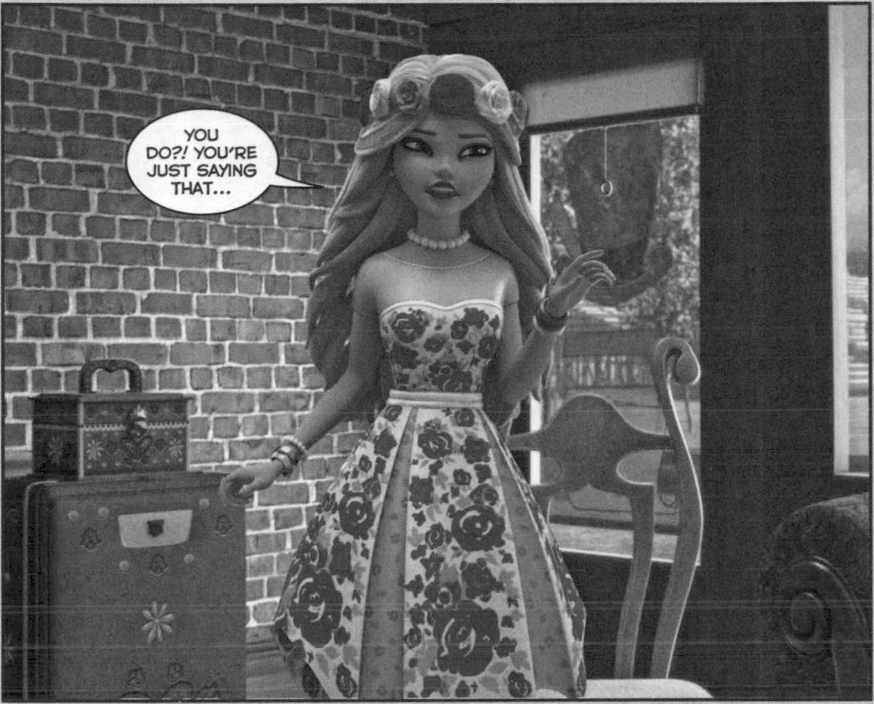
YOU DO?! YOU'RE JUST SAYING THAT...

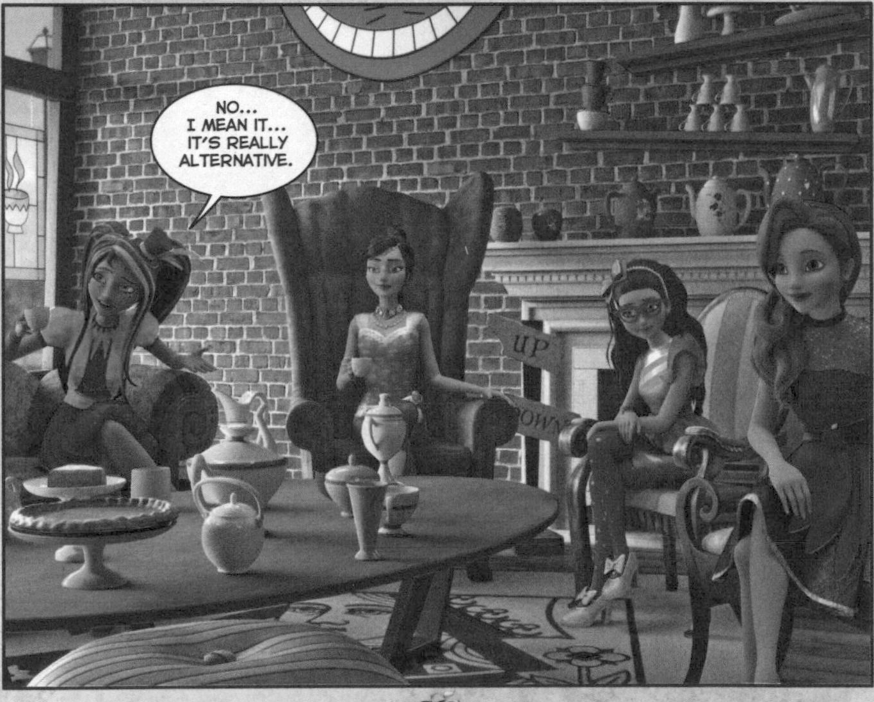
NO... I MEAN IT... IT'S REALLY ALTERNATIVE.
UP
DOWN

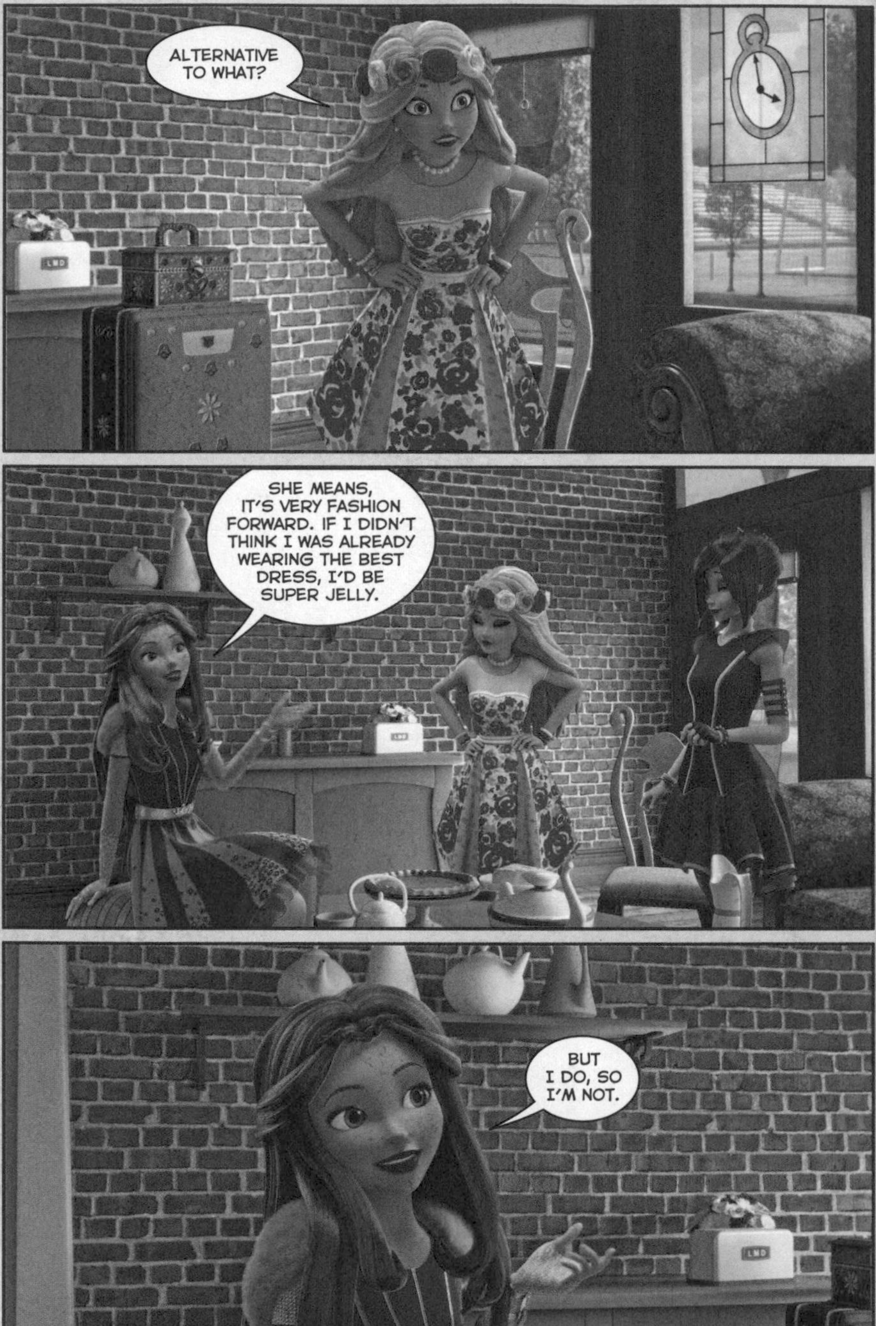
ALTERNATIVE TO WHAT?
SHE MEANS, IT'S VERY FASHION FORWARD. IF I DIDN'T THINK I WAS ALREADY WEARING THE BEST DRESS, I'D BE SUPER JELLY.
BUT I DO, SO I'M NOT.

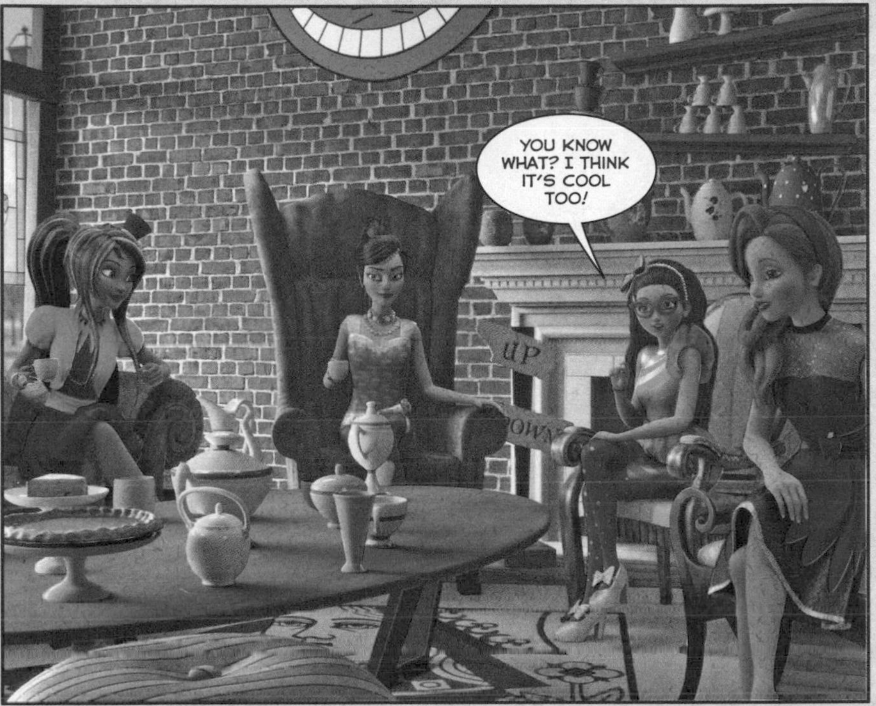
YOU KNOW WHAT? I THINK IT'S COOL TOO!
UP
DOWN

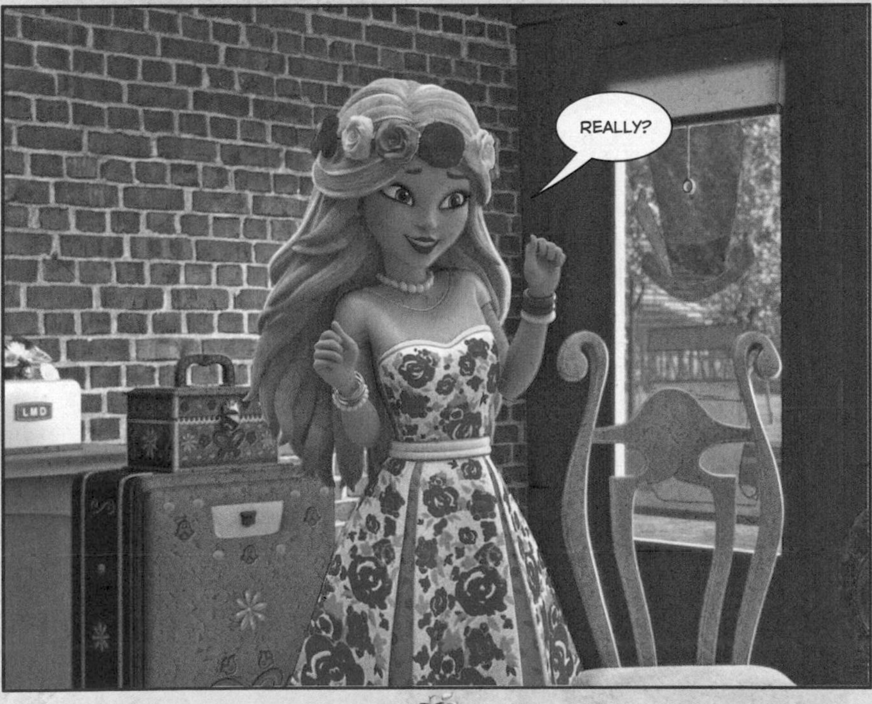
REALLY?
LMD

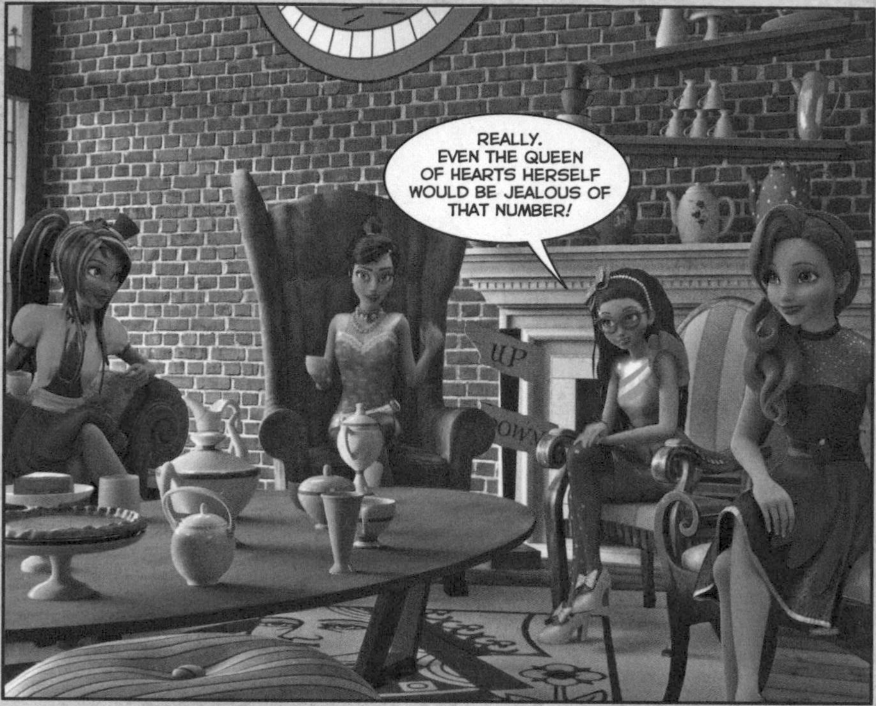
REALLY. EVEN THE QUEEN OF HEARTS HERSELF WOULD BE JEALOUS OF THAT NUMBER!
UP

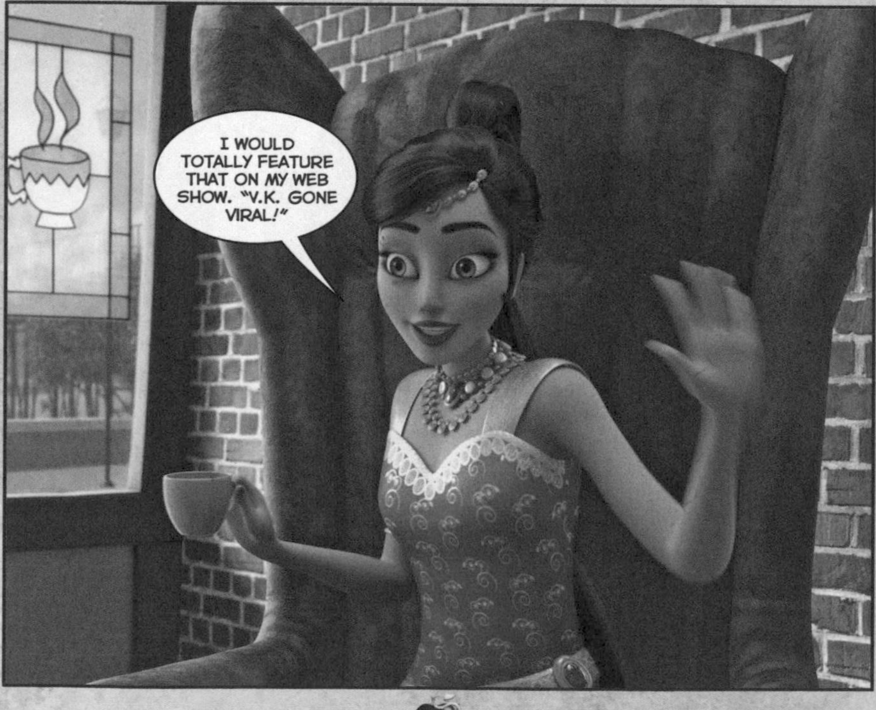
I WOULD TOTALLY FEATURE THAT ON MY WEB SHOW. "V.K. GONE VIRAL!"

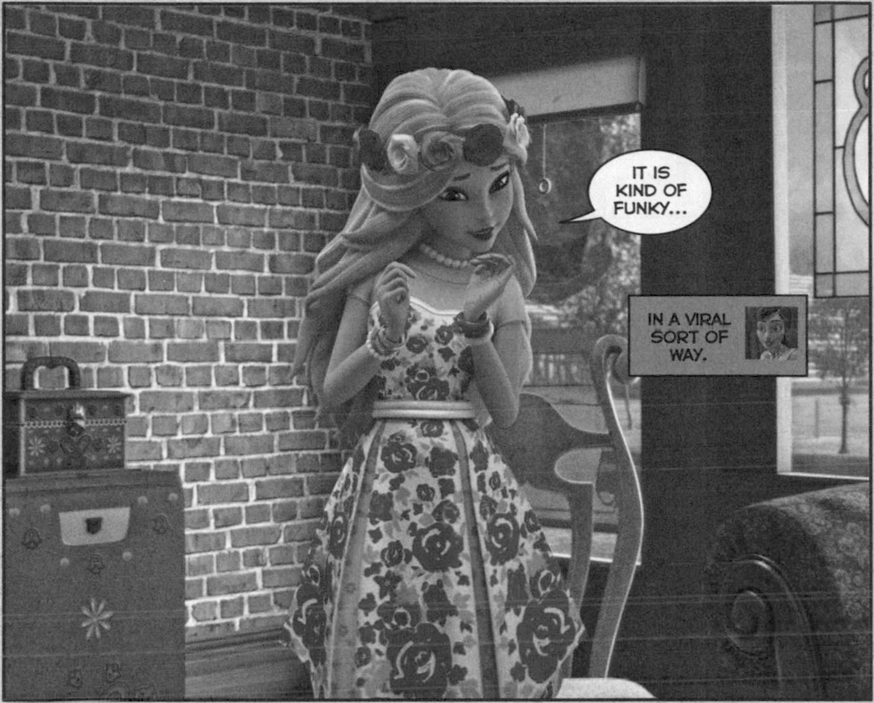
IT IS KIND OF FUNKY...
IN A VIRAL SORT OF WAY.

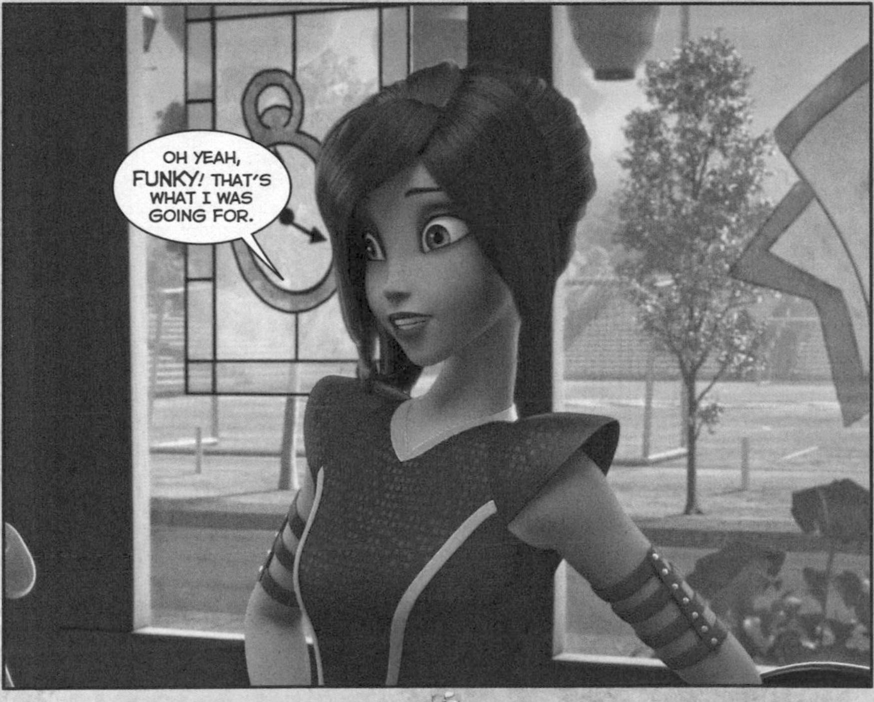
OH YEAH, FUNKY! THAT'S WHAT I WAS GOING FOR.

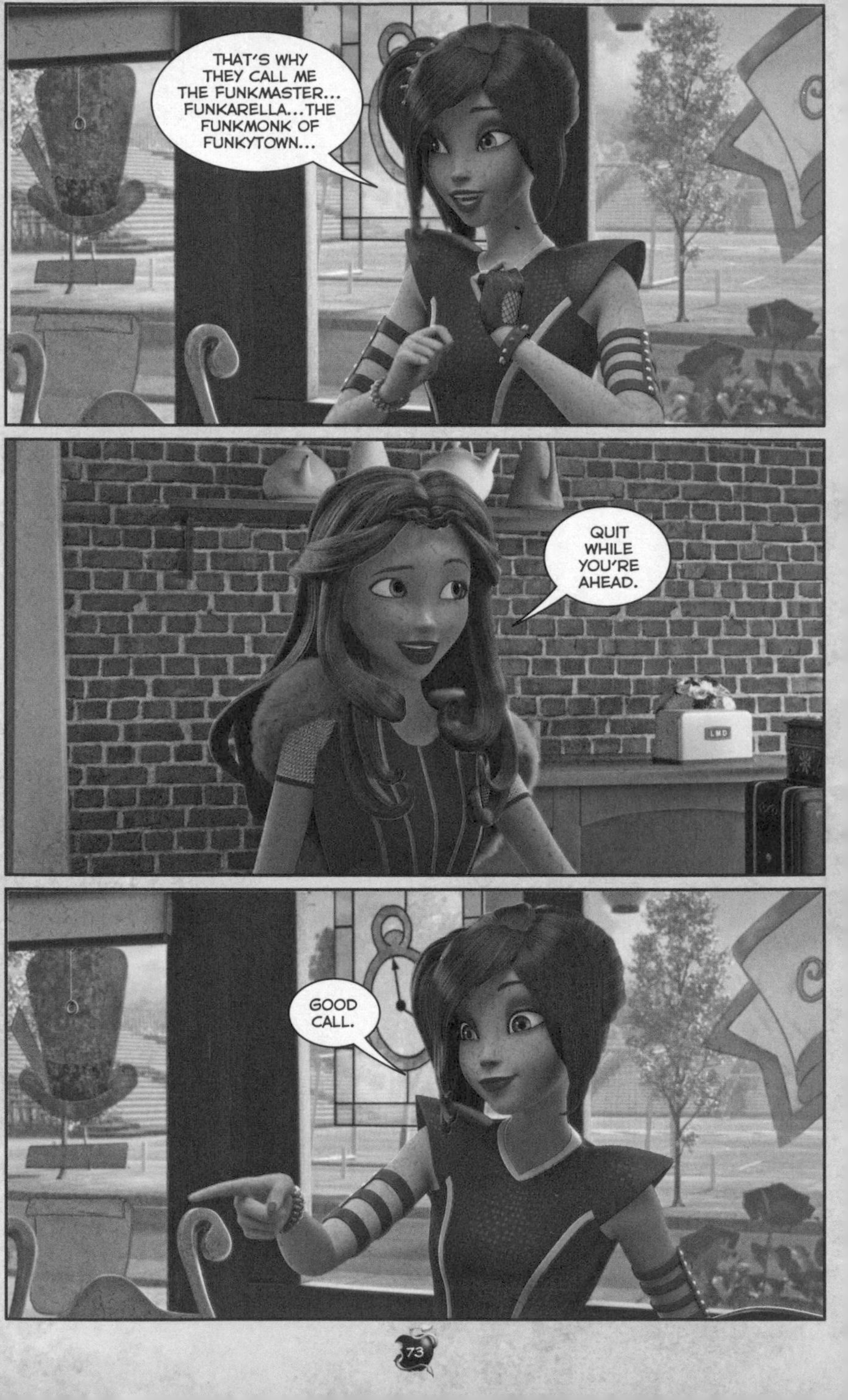
THAT'S WHY THEY CALL ME THE FUNKMASTER... FUNKARELLA...THE FUNKMONK OF FUNKYTOWN...
QUIT WHILE YOU'RE AHEAD.
GOOD CALL.

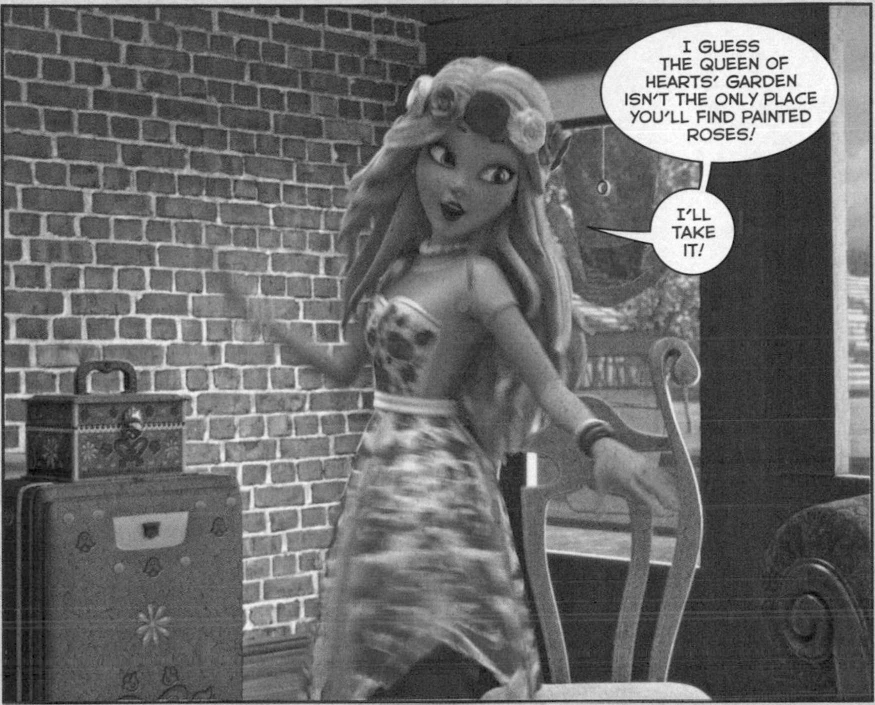
I GUESS THE QUEEN OF HEARTS' GARDEN ISN'T THE ONLY PLACE YOU'LL FIND PAINTED ROSES!
I'LL TAKE IT!

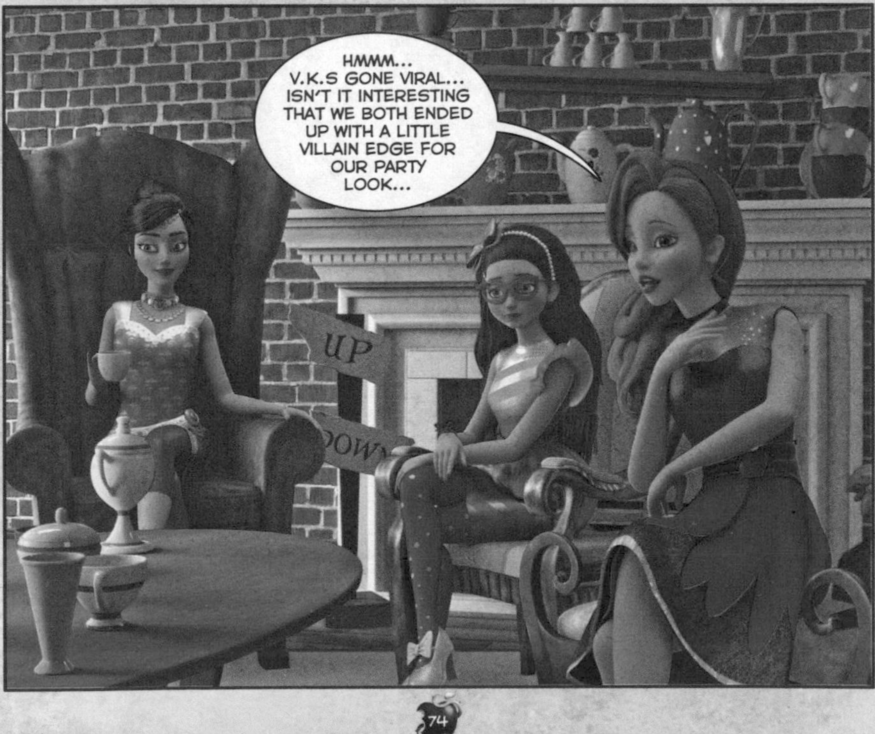
HMMM... V.K.S GONE VIRAL... ISN'T IT INTERESTING THAT WE BOTH ENDED UP WITH A LITTLE VILLAIN EDGE FOR OUR PARTY LOOK...
UP

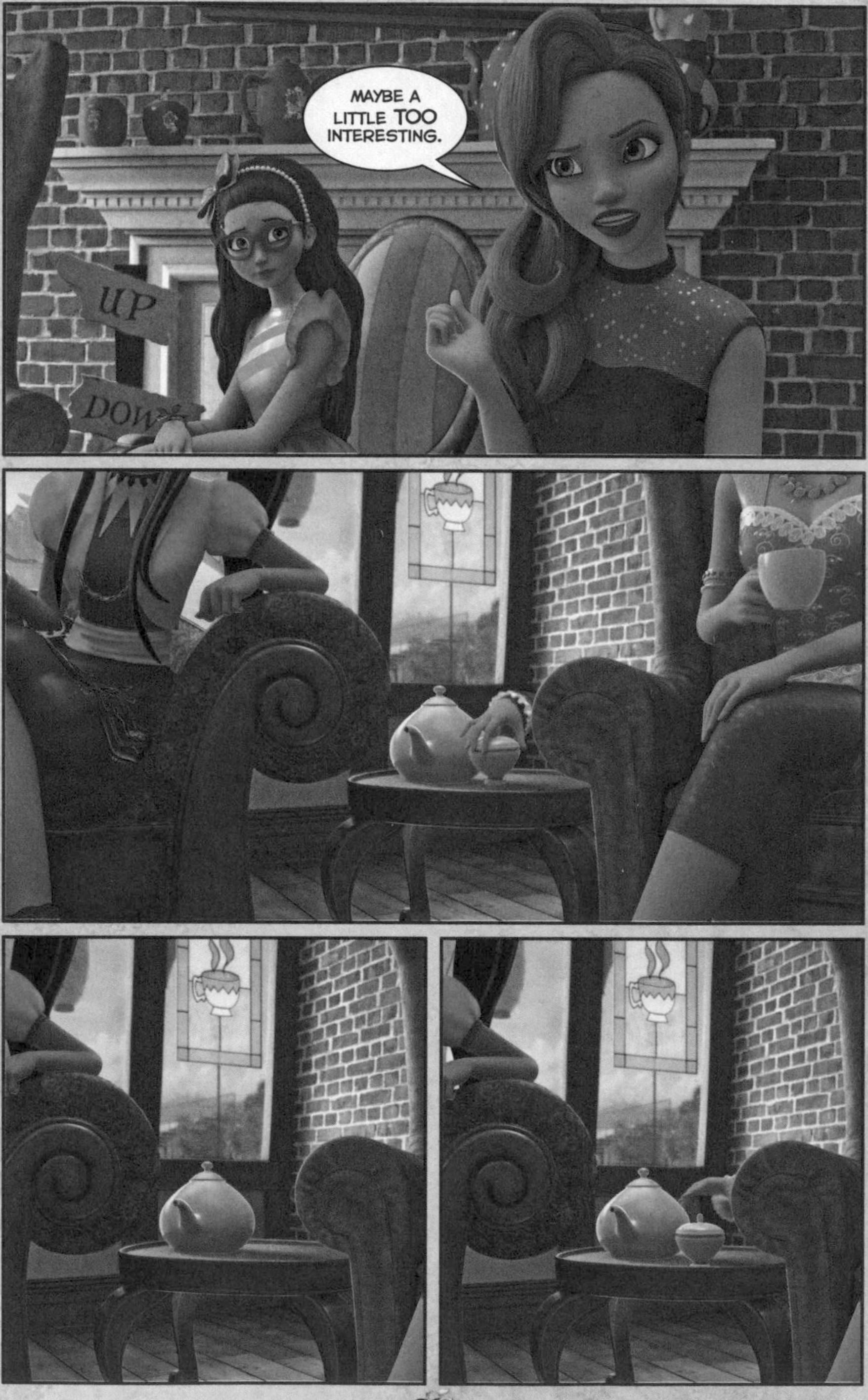
MAYBE A LITTLE TOO INTERESTING.
UP
DOW

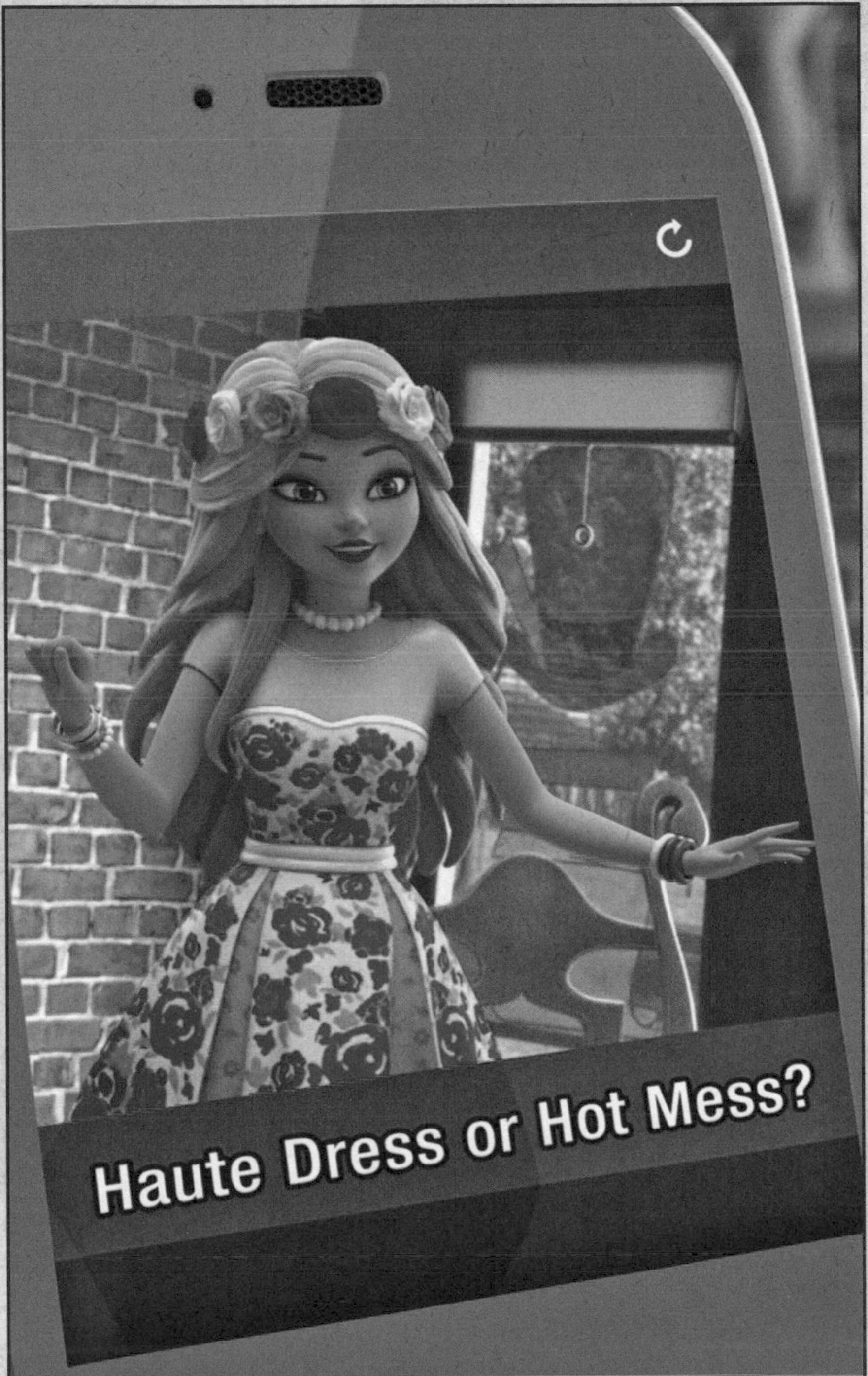
Haute Dress or Hot Mess?

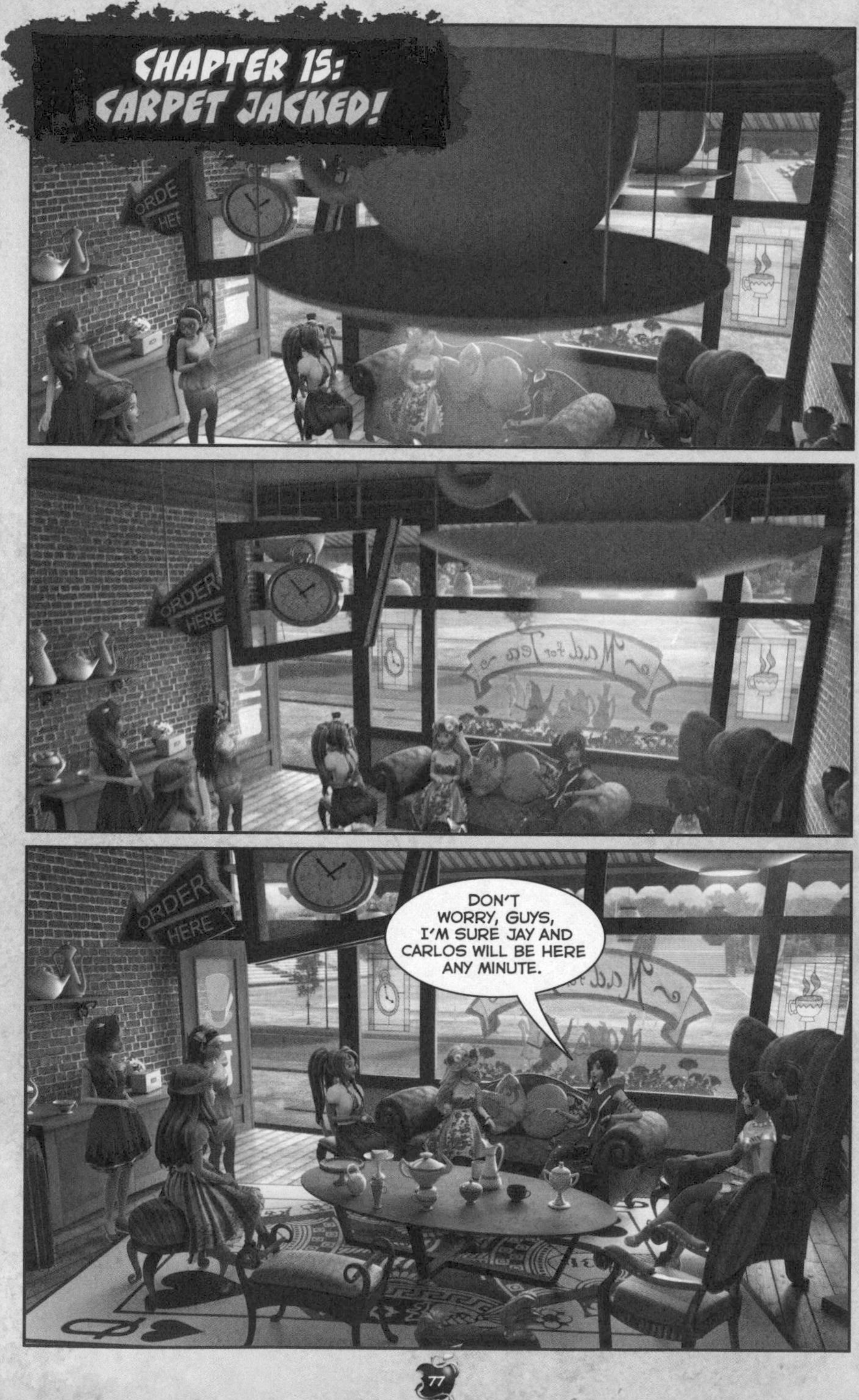
CHAPTER 15:
CARPET JACKED!
DON'T WORRY, GUYS, I'M SURE JAY AND CARLOS WILL BE HERE ANY MINUTE.

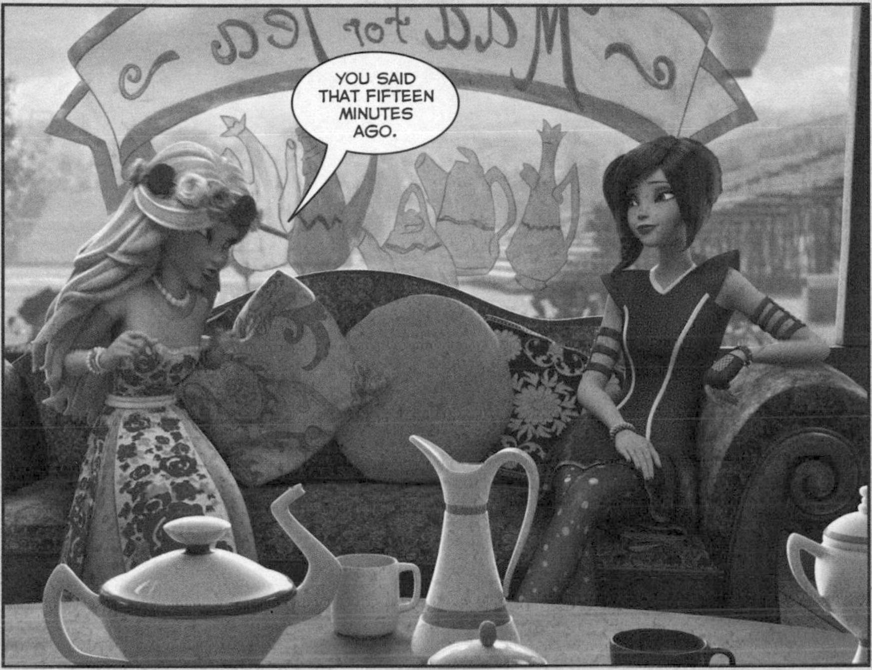
YOU SAID THAT FIFTEEN MINUTES AGO.

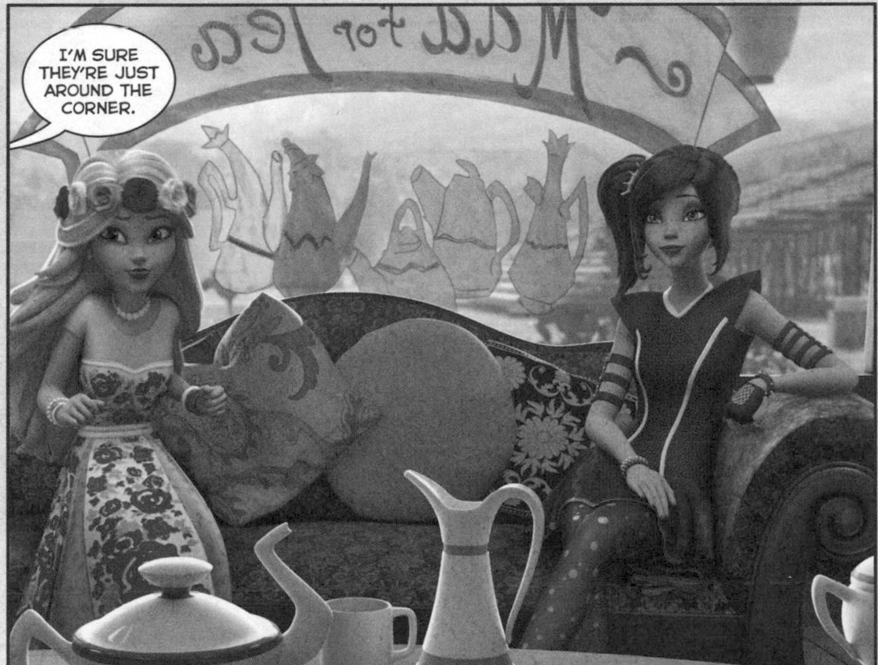
I'M SURE THEY'RE JUST AROUND THE CORNER.

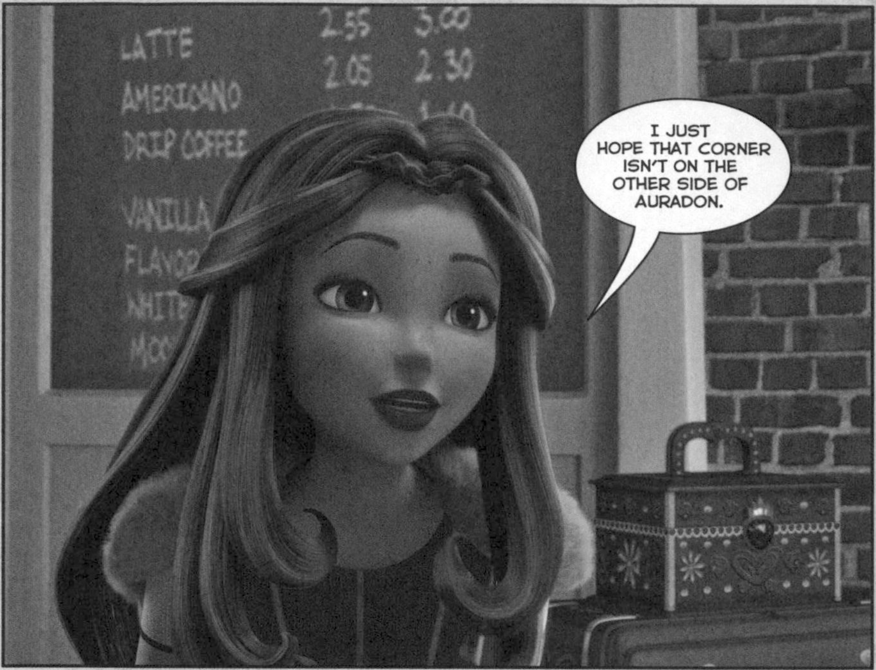
LATTE 2.55 3.00
AMERICANO 2.05 2.30
DRIP COFFEE
I JUST HOPE THAT CORNER ISN'T ON THE OTHER SIDE OF AURADON.

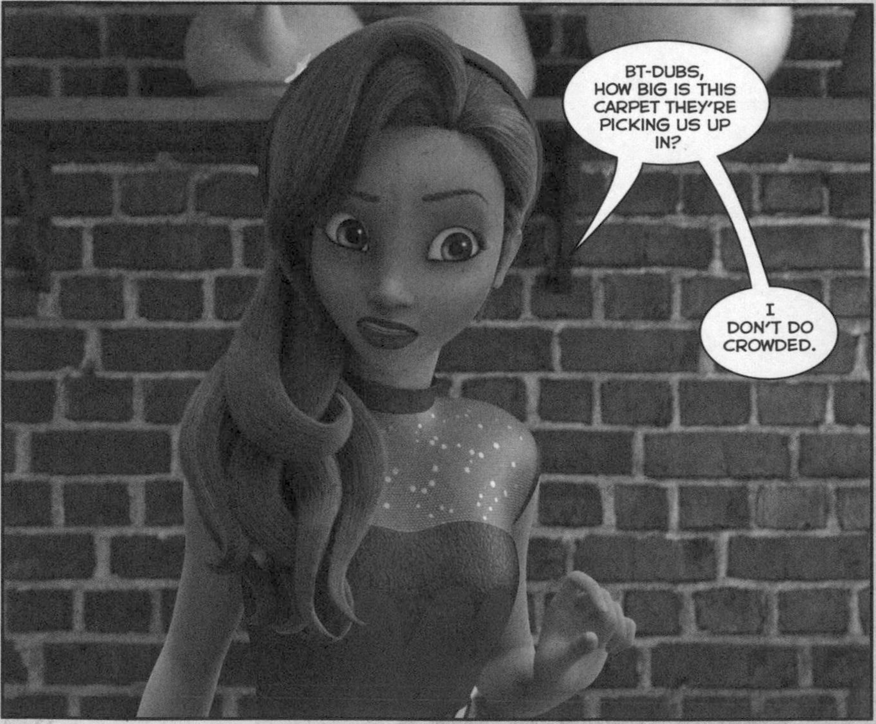
BT-DUBS, HOW BIG IS THIS CARPET THEY'RE PICKING US UP IN?
I DON'T DO CROWDED.

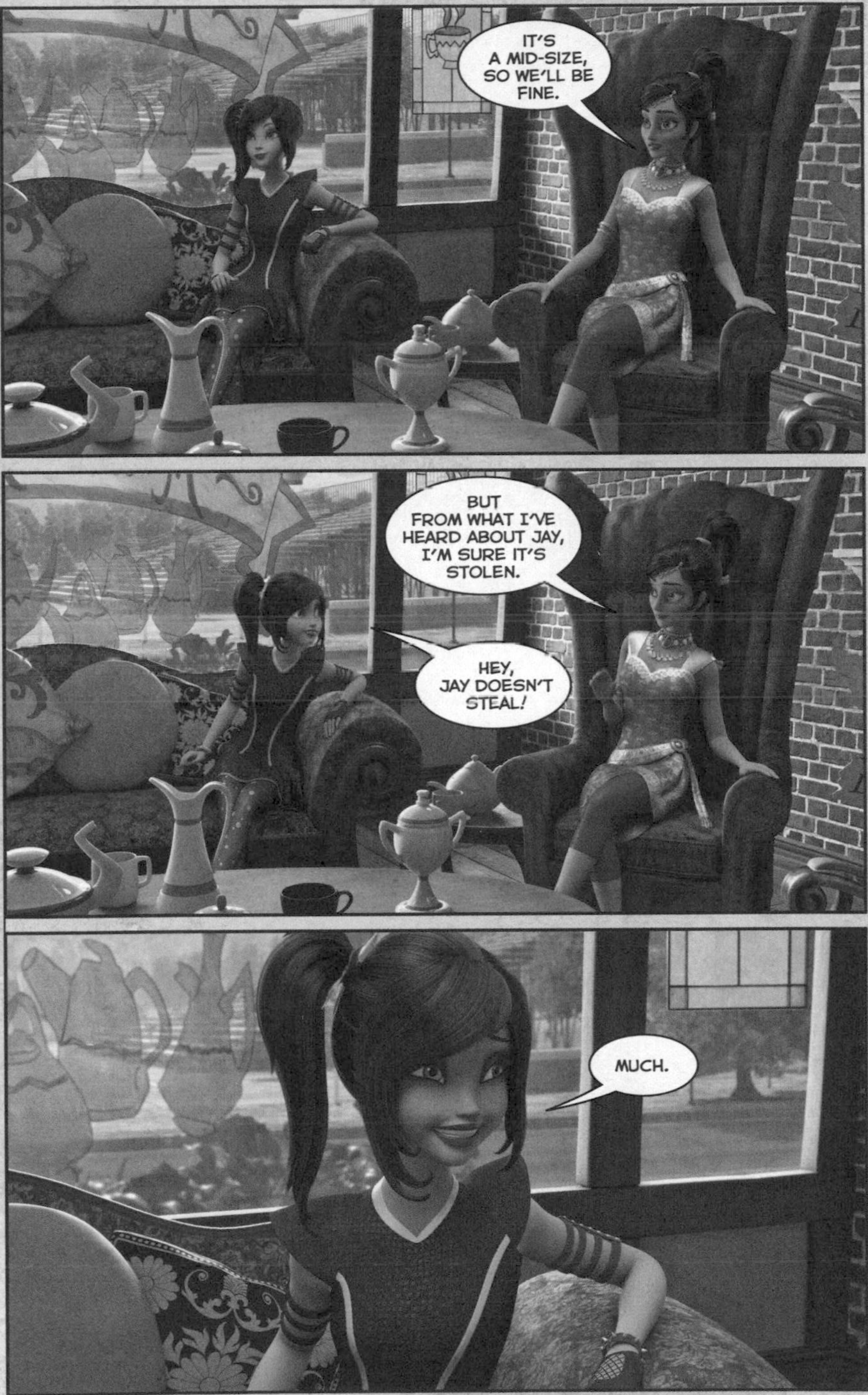
IT'S A MID-SIZE, SO WE'LL BE FINE.
BUT FROM WHAT I'VE HEARD ABOUT JAY, I'M SURE IT'S STOLEN.
HEY, JAY DOESN'T STEAL!
MUCH.

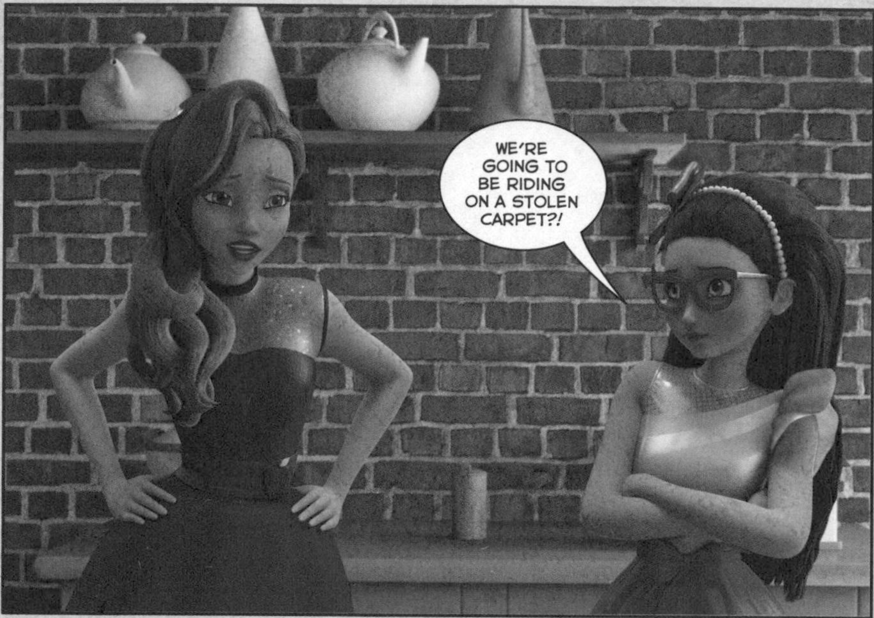
WE'RE GOING TO BE RIDING ON A STOLEN CARPET?!

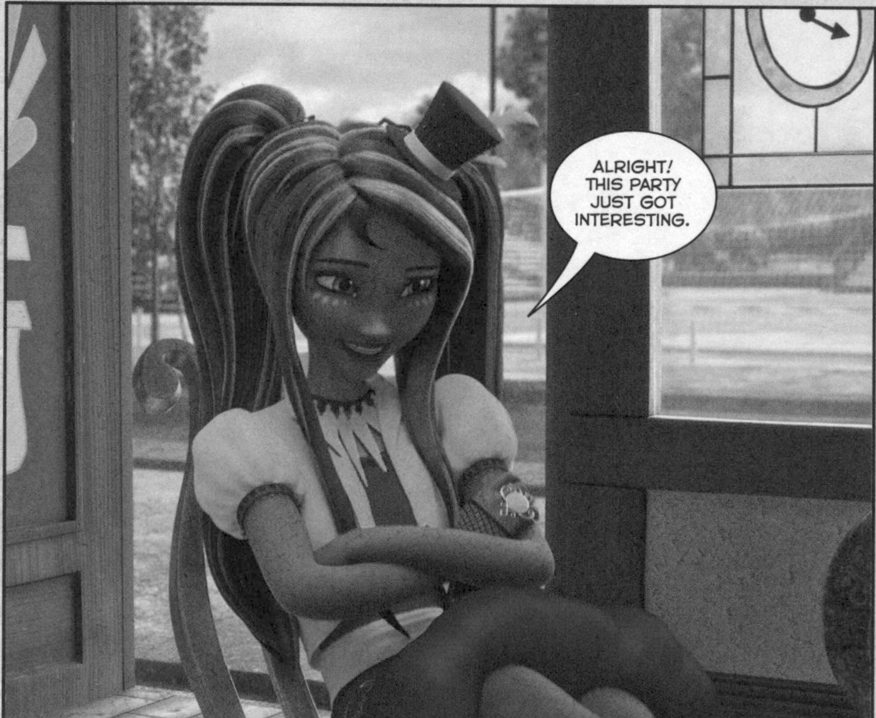
ALRIGHT! THIS PARTY JUST GOT INTERESTING.

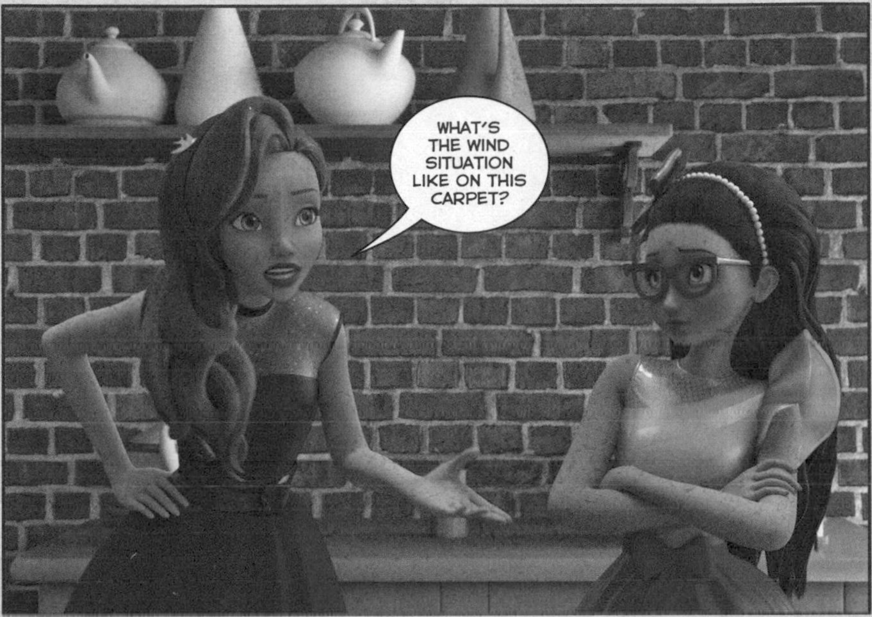
WHAT'S THE WIND SITUATION LIKE ON THIS CARPET?

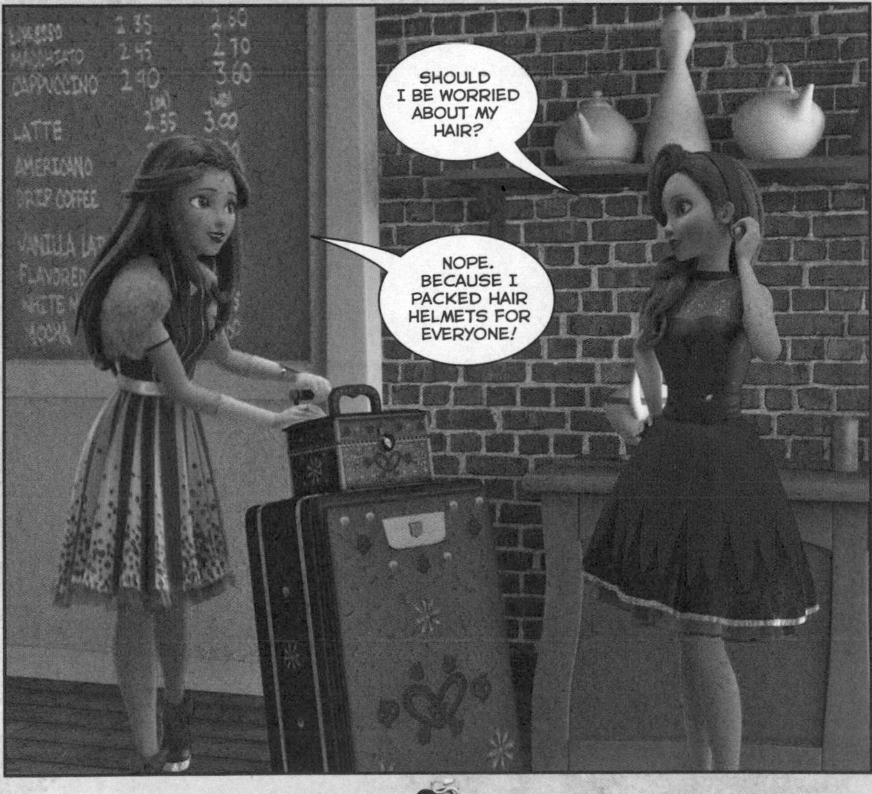
SHOULD I BE WORRIED ABOUT MY HAIR?
NOPE. BECAUSE I PACKED HAIR HELMETS FOR EVERYONE!

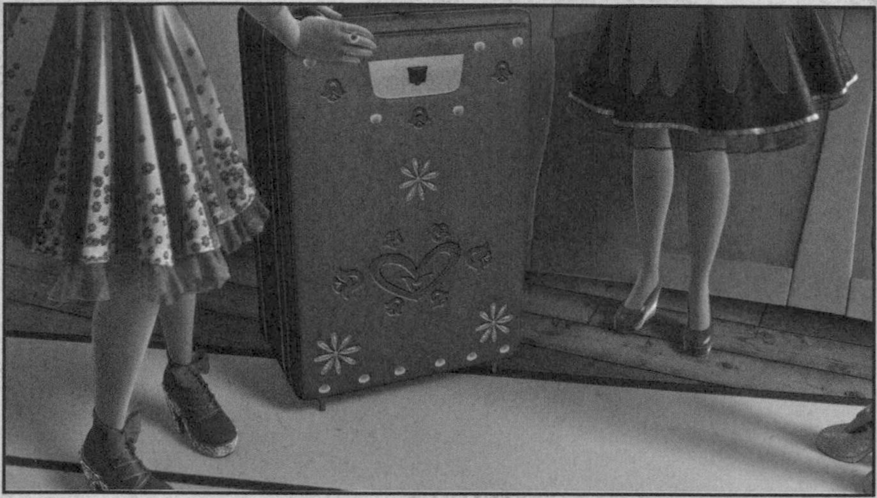

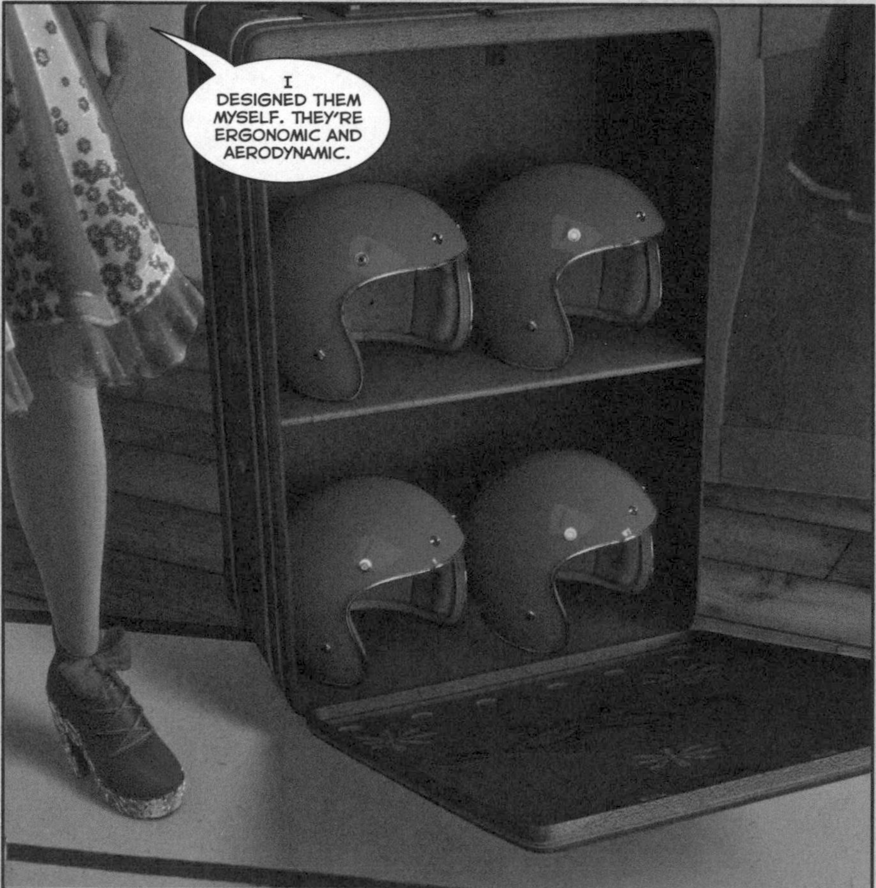
I DESIGNED THEM MYSELF. THEY'RE ERGONOMIC AND AERODYNAMIC.

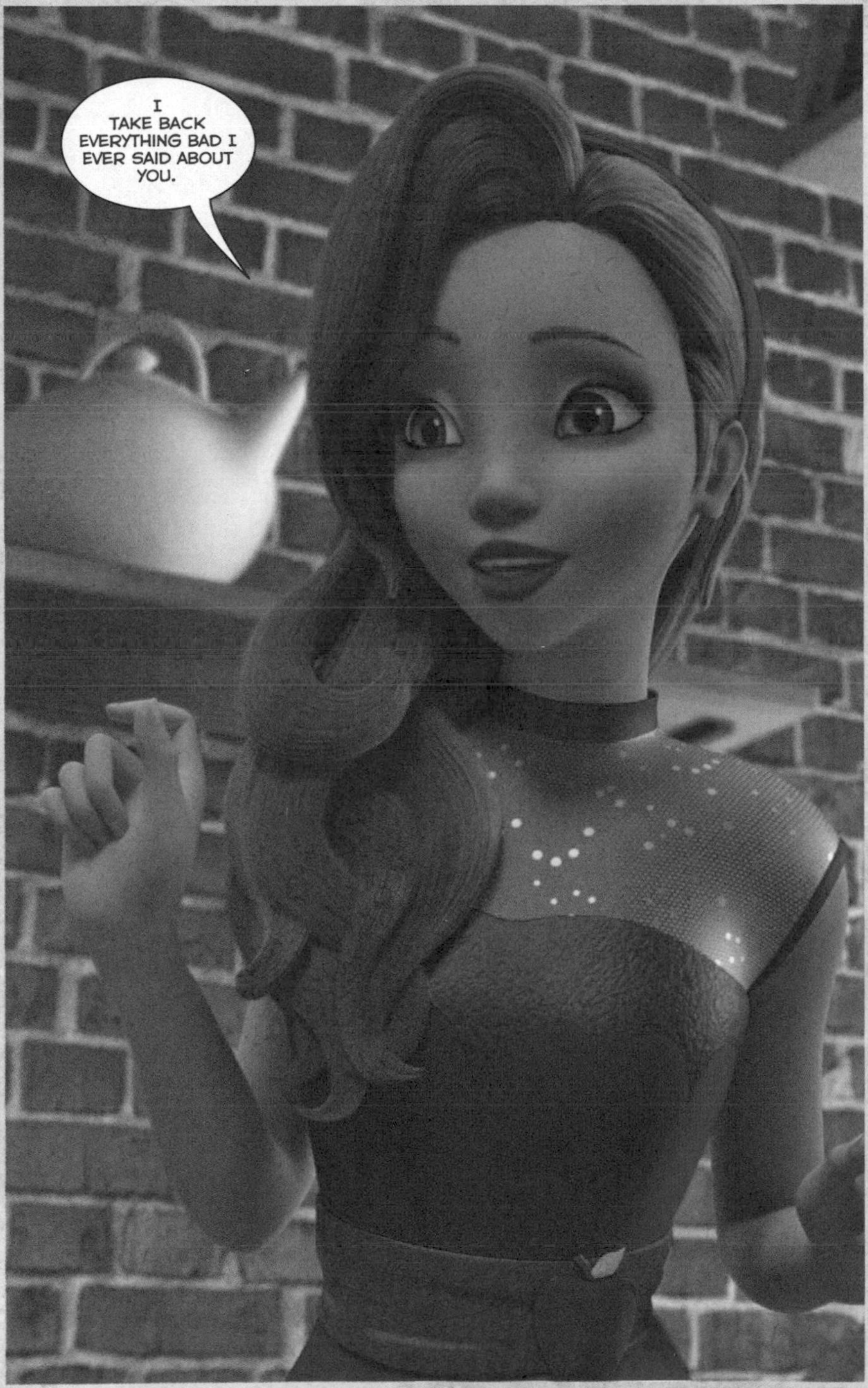
I TAKE BACK EVERYTHING BAD I EVER SAID ABOUT YOU.

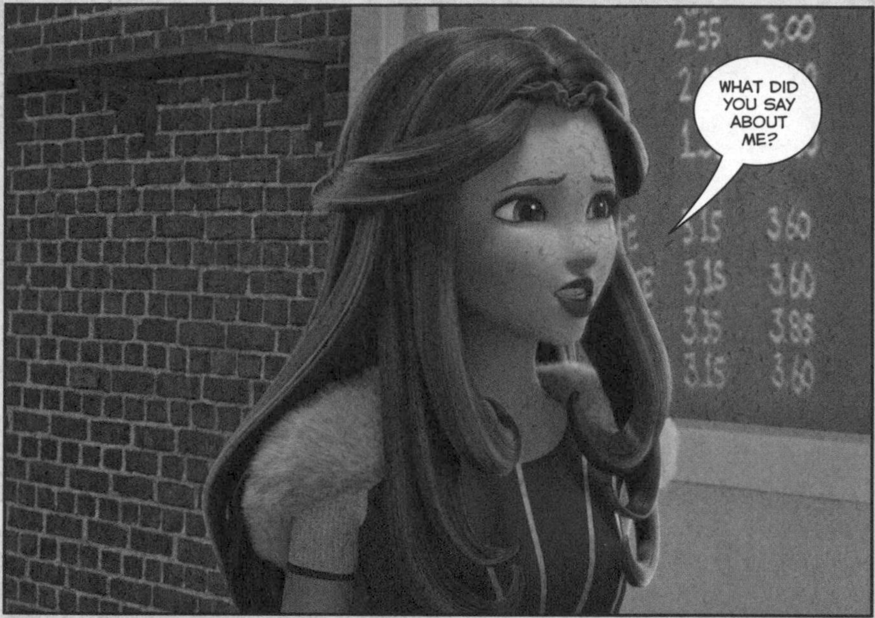
WHAT DID YOU SAY ABOUT ME?

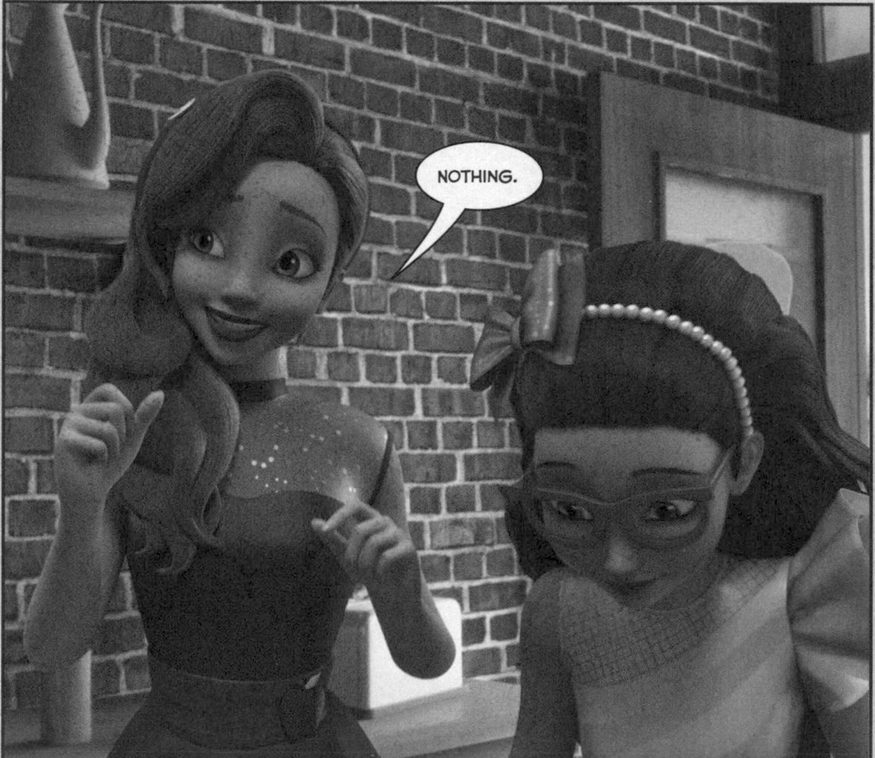
NOTHING.

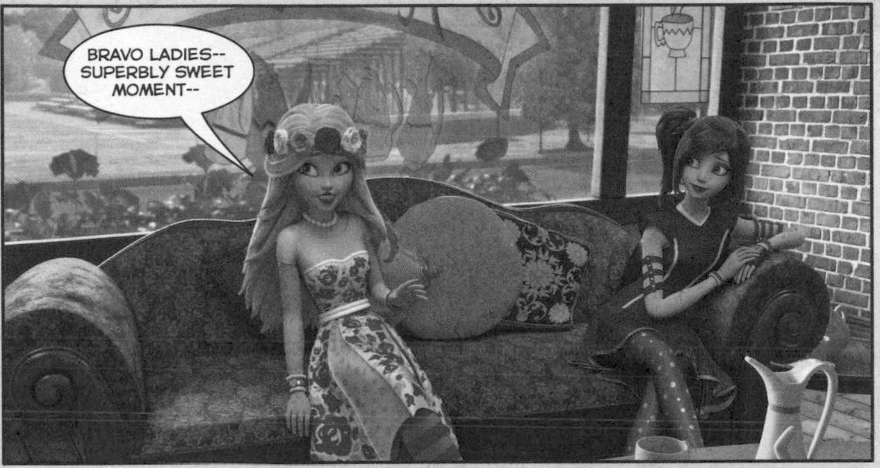
BRAVO LADIES--
SUPERBLY SWEET
MOMENT--

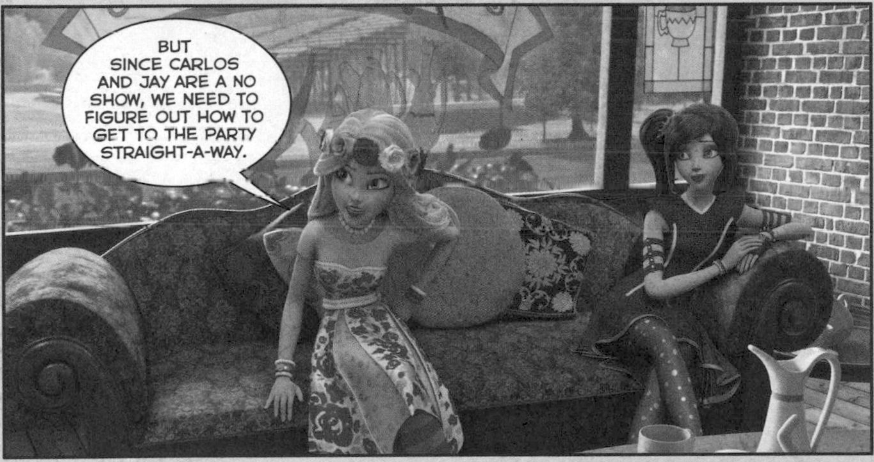
BUT SINCE CARLOS AND JAY ARE A NO SHOW, WE NEED TO FIGURE OUT HOW TO GET TO THE PARTY STRAIGHT-A-WAY.

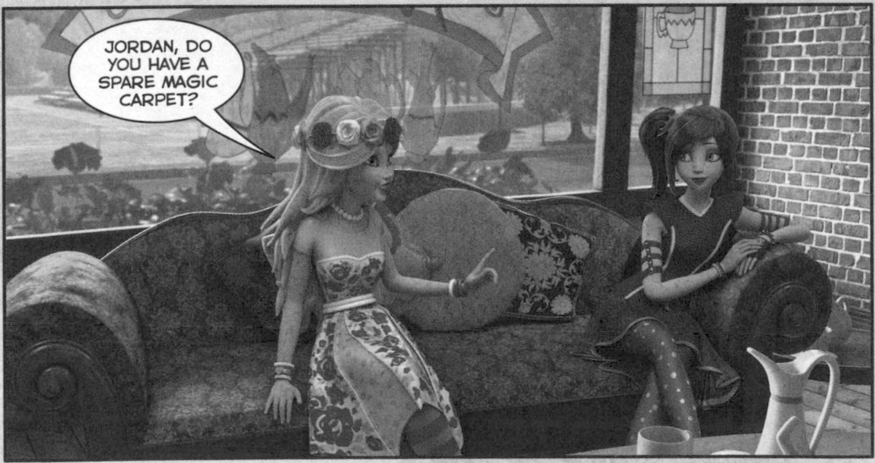
JORDAN, DO YOU HAVE A SPARE MAGIC CARPET?

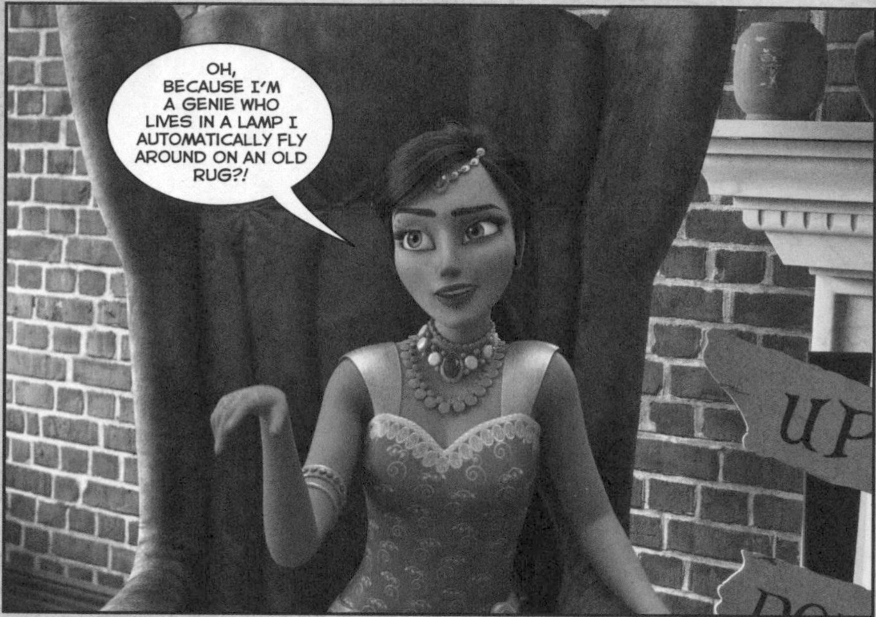
OH, BECAUSE I'M A GENIE WHO LIVES IN A LAMP I AUTOMATICALLY FLY AROUND ON AN OLD RUG?!

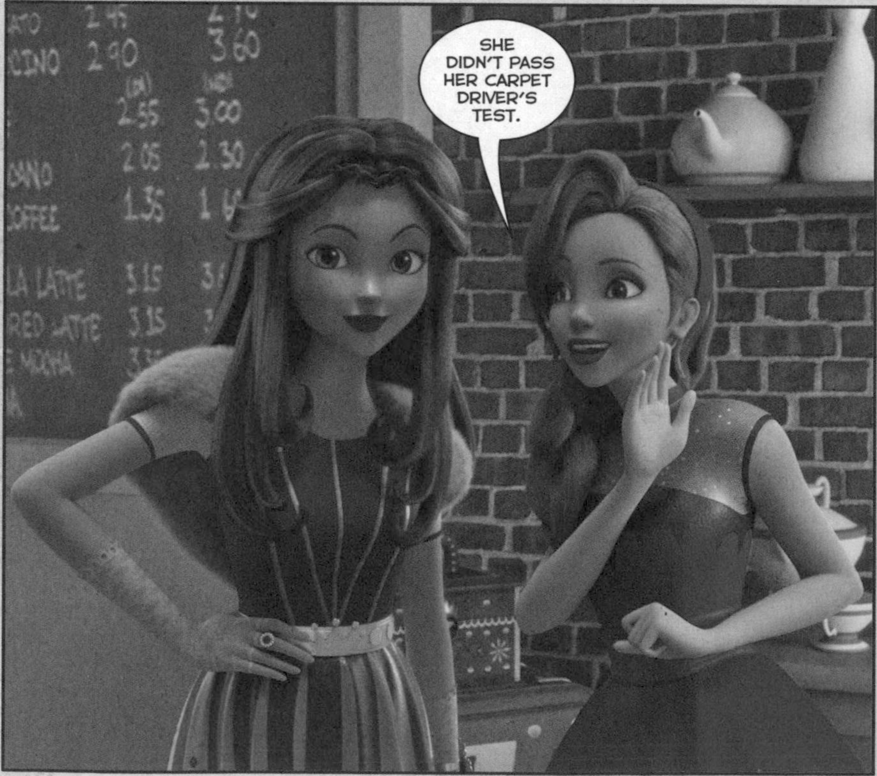
SHE DIDN'T PASS HER CARPET DRIVER'S TEST.

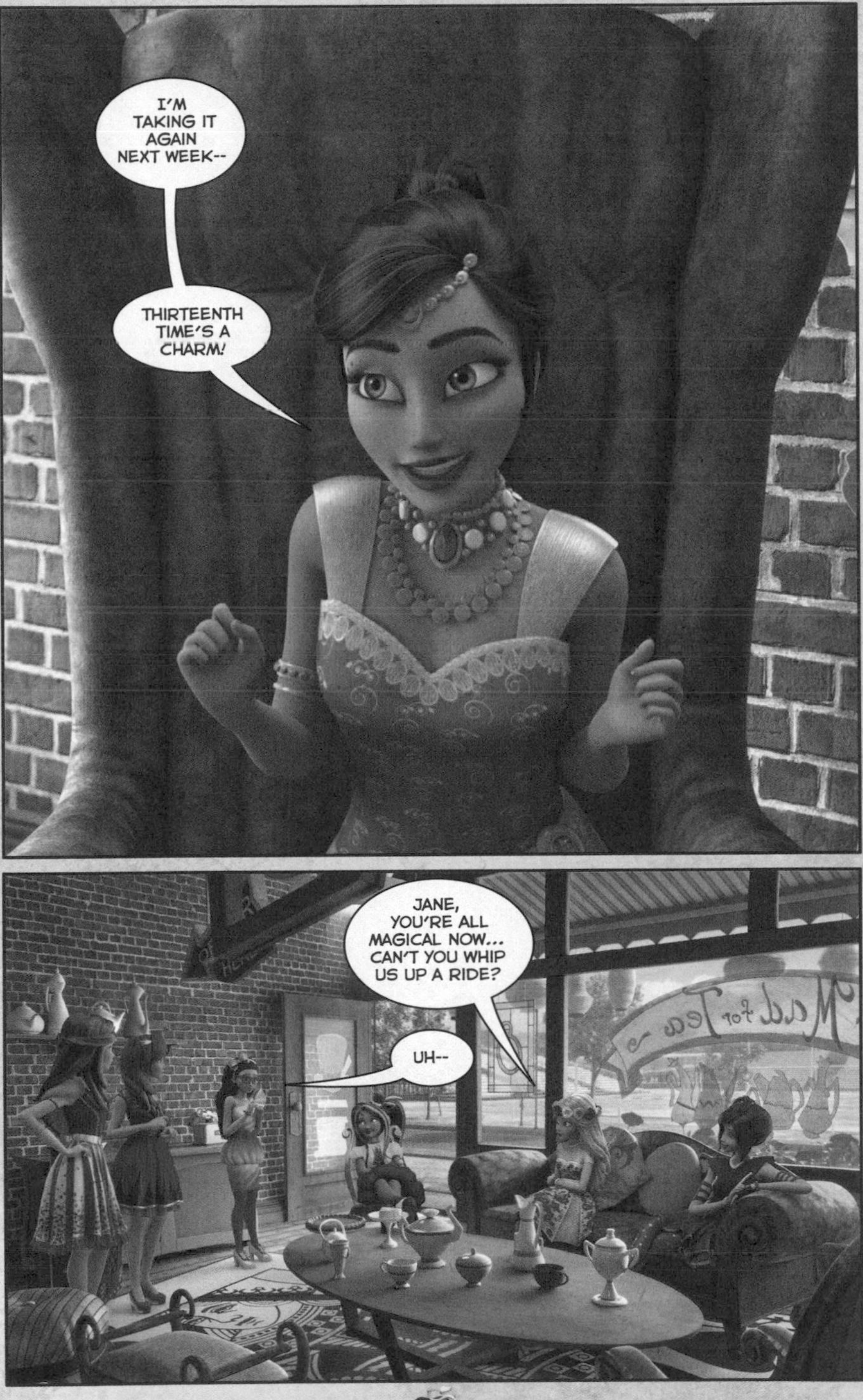
I'M TAKING IT AGAIN NEXT WEEK--
THIRTEENTH TIME'S A CHARM!
JANE, YOU'RE ALL MAGICAL NOW... CAN'T YOU WHIP US UP A RIDE?
UH--

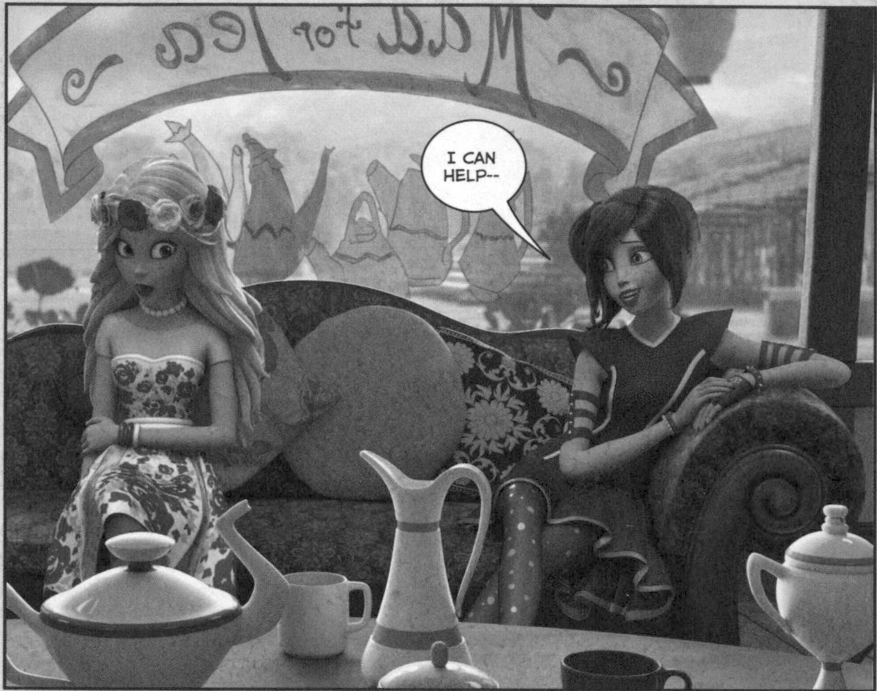
I CAN HELP--

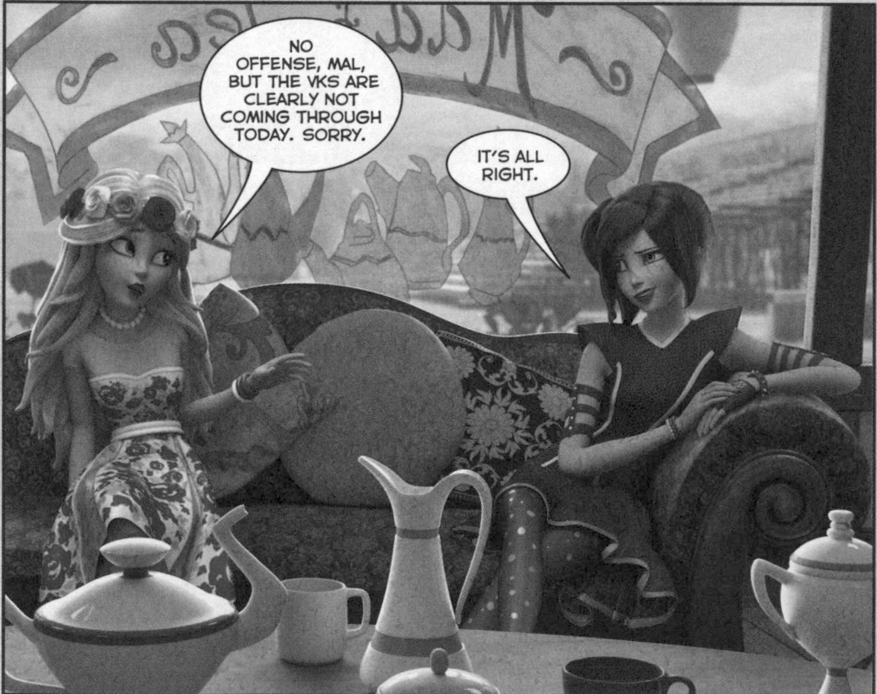
NO OFFENSE, MAL, BUT THE VKS ARE CLEARLY NOT COMING THROUGH TODAY. SORRY.
IT'S ALL RIGHT.

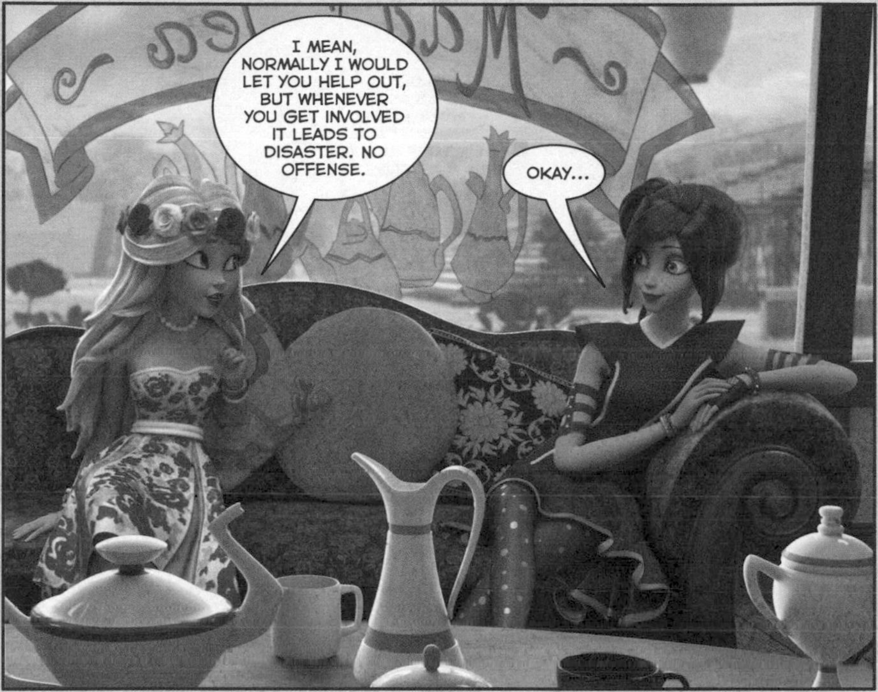
I MEAN, NORMALLY I WOULD LET YOU HELP OUT, BUT WHENEVER YOU GET INVOLVED IT LEADS TO DISASTER. NO OFFENSE.
OKAY...

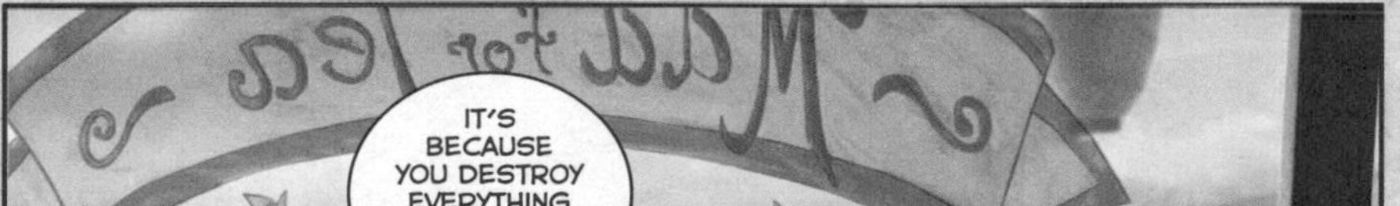
IT'S BECAUSE YOU DESTROY EVERYTHING YOU TOUCH. NO OFFENSE.

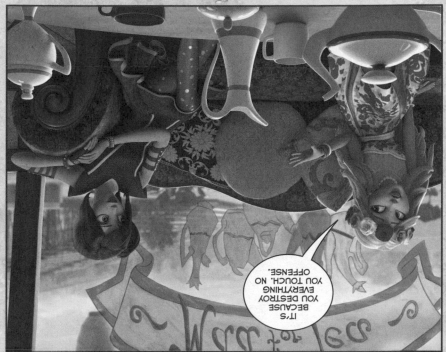

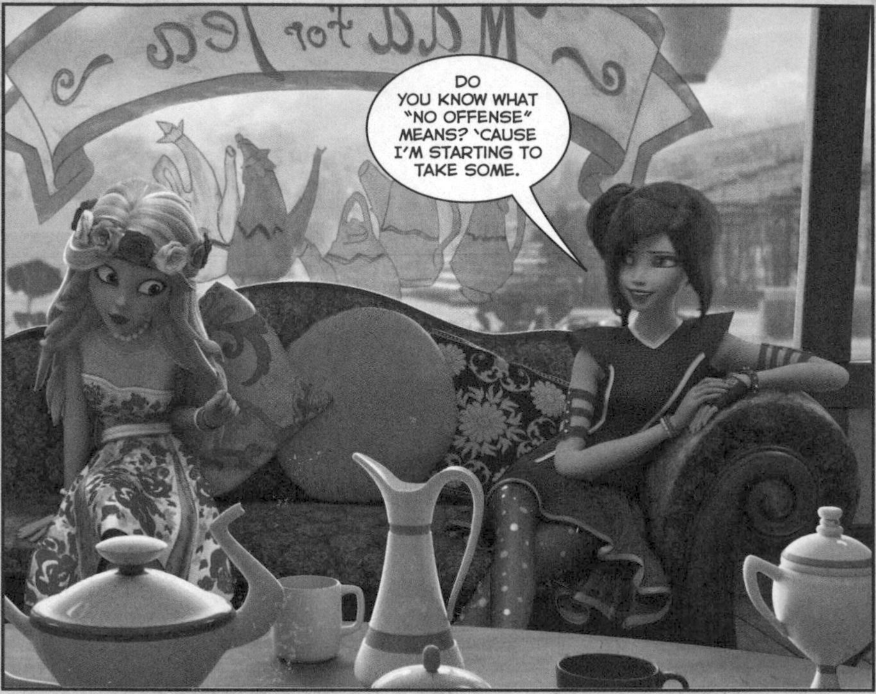
DO YOU KNOW WHAT "NO OFFENSE" MEANS? 'CAUSE I'M STARTING TO TAKE SOME.

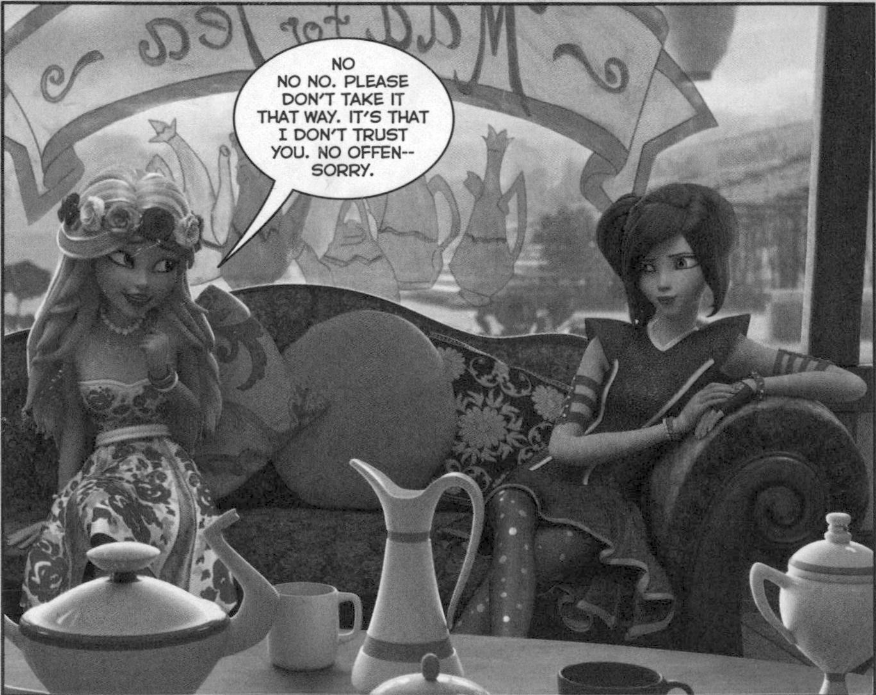
NO NO NO. PLEASE DON'T TAKE IT THAT WAY. IT'S THAT I DON'T TRUST YOU. NO OFFEN-- SORRY.

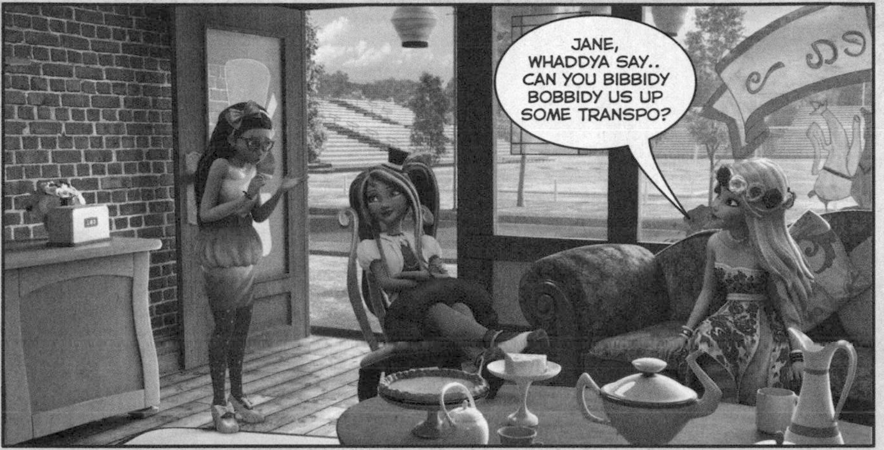
JANE, WHADDYA SAY.. CAN YOU BIBBIDY BOBBIDY US UP SOME TRANSPO?

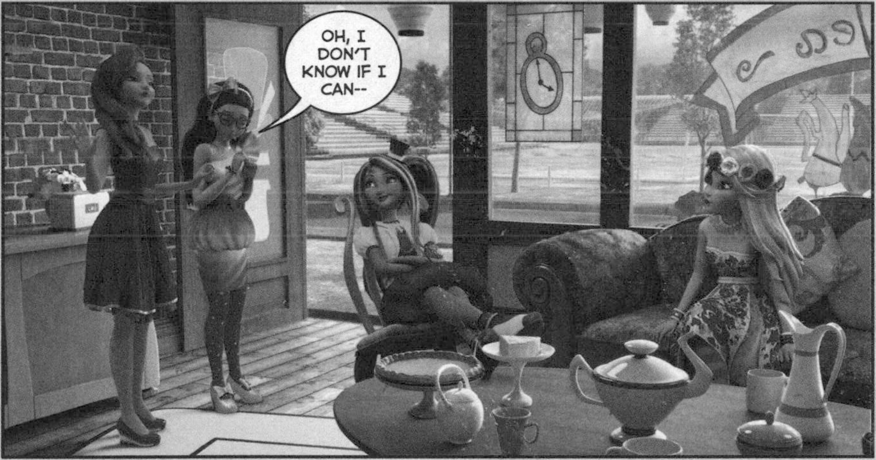
OH, I DON'T KNOW IF I CAN--

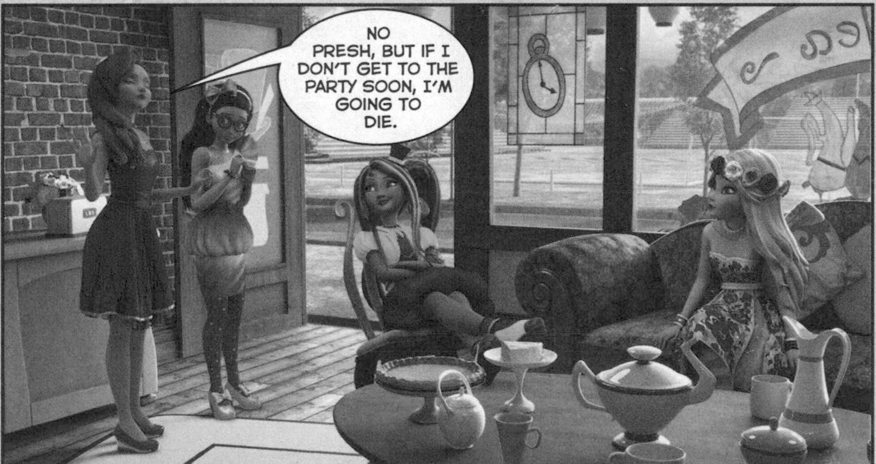
NO PRESH, BUT IF I DON'T GET TO THE PARTY SOON, I'M GOING TO DIE.

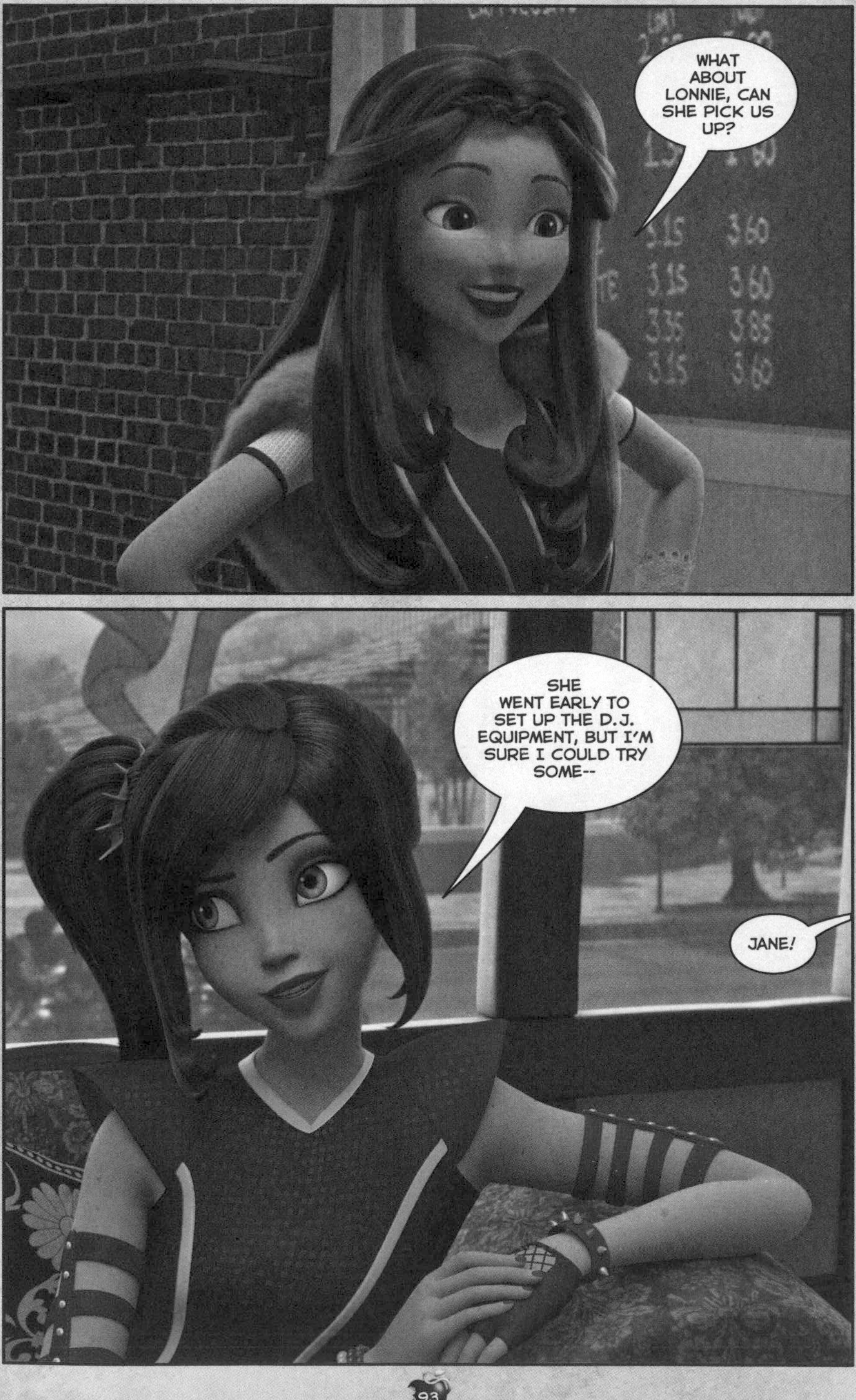
WHAT ABOUT LONNIE, CAN SHE PICK US UP?
SHE WENT EARLY TO SET UP THE D.J. EQUIPMENT, BUT I'M SURE I COULD TRY SOME--
JANE!

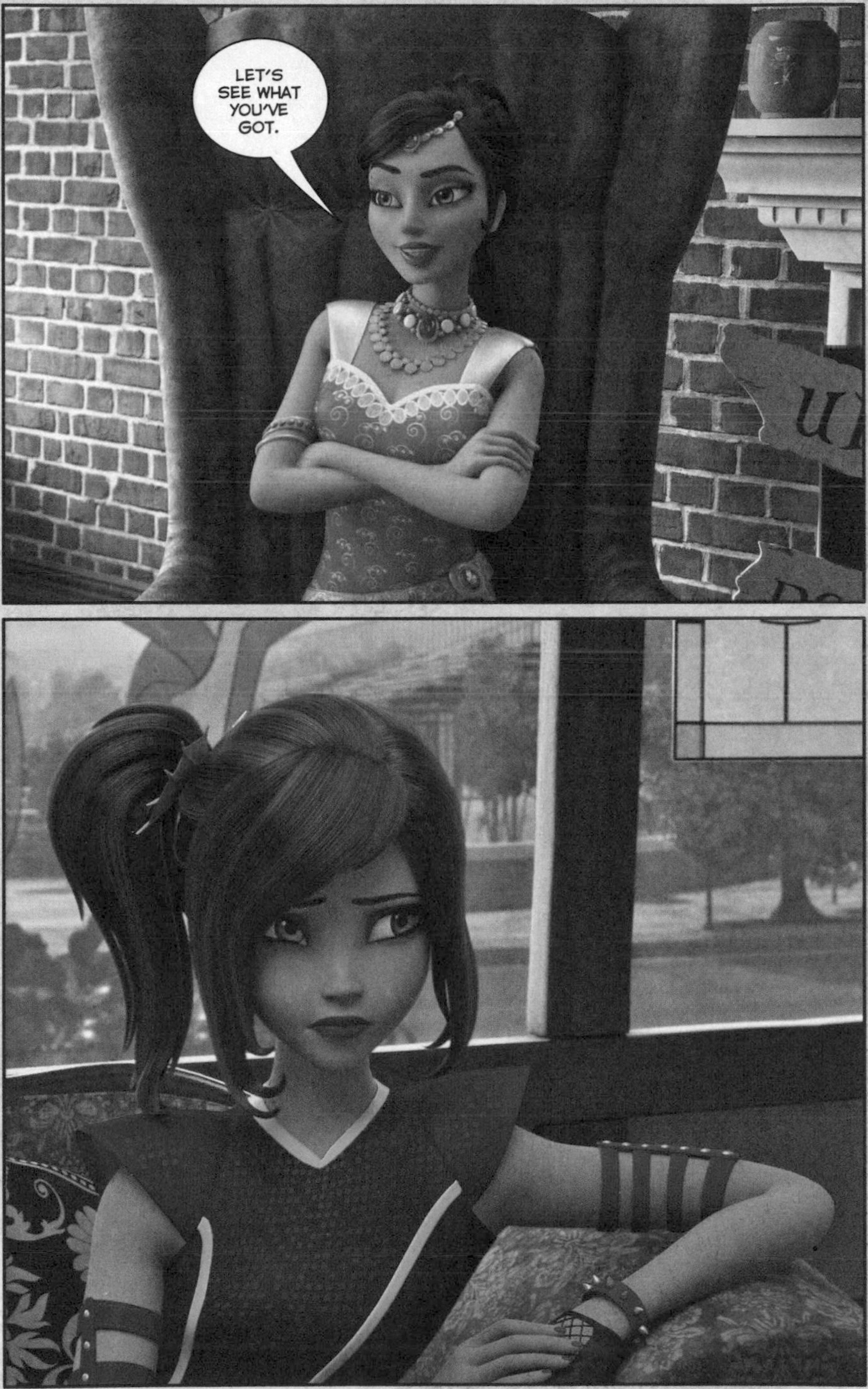
LET'S SEE WHAT YOU'VE GOT.

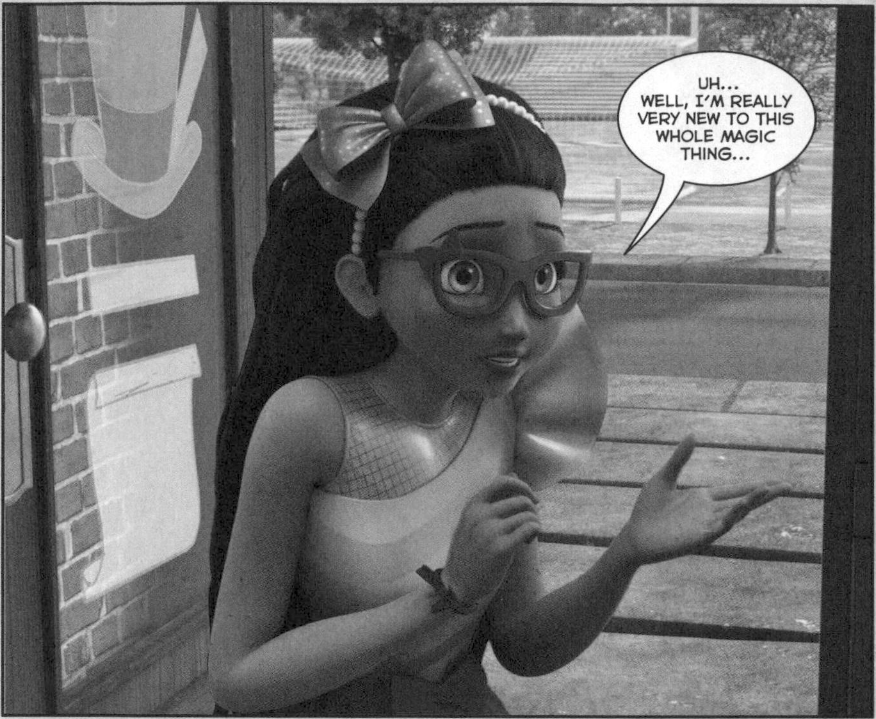
UH...
WELL, I'M REALLY VERY NEW TO THIS WHOLE MAGIC THING...

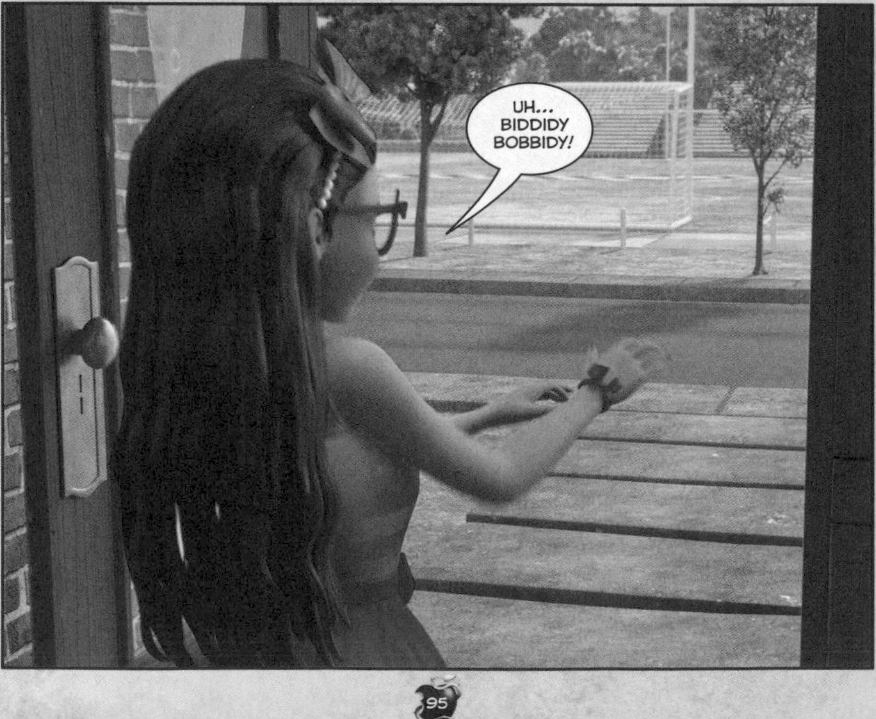
UH...
BIDDIDY BOBBIDY!

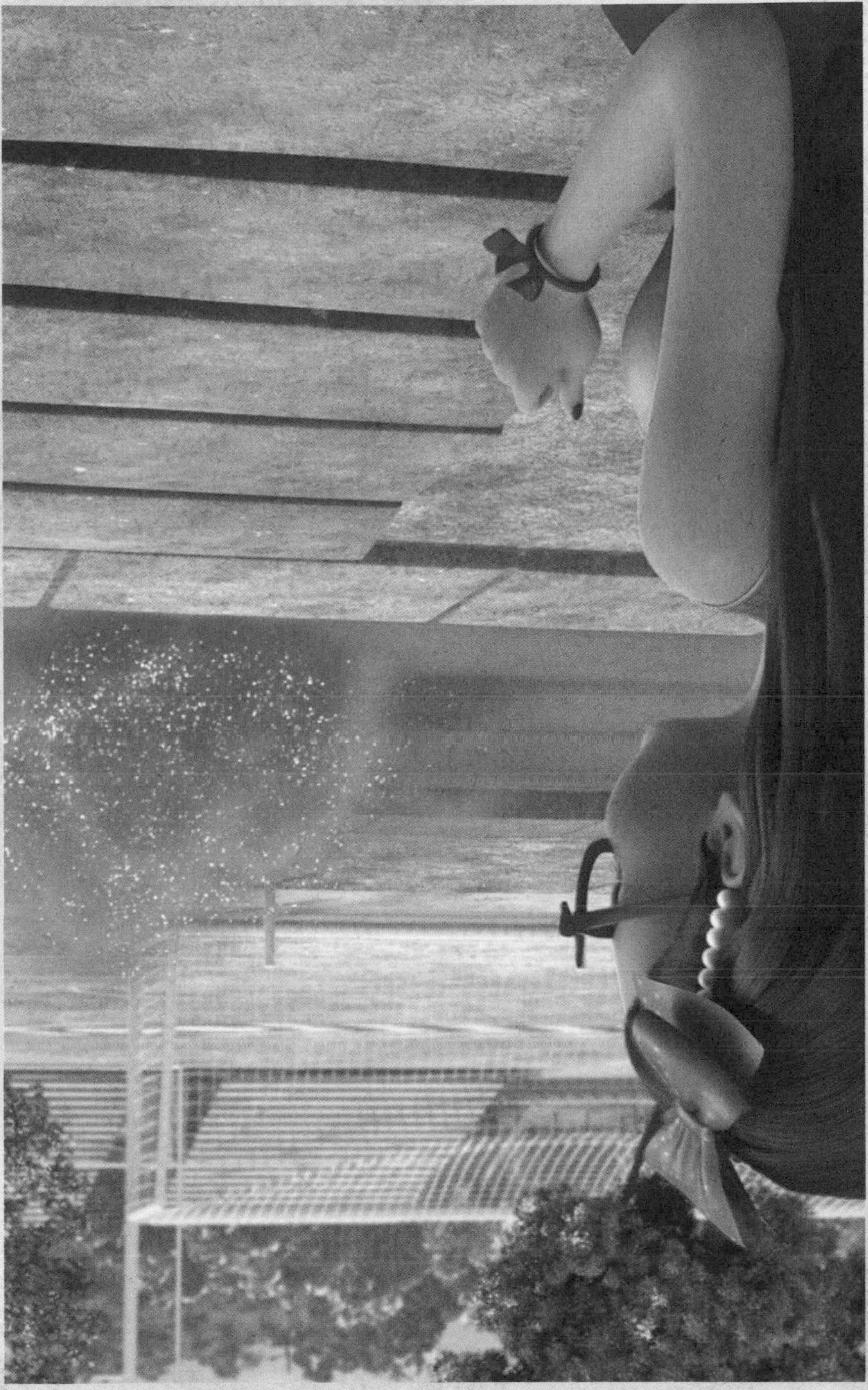

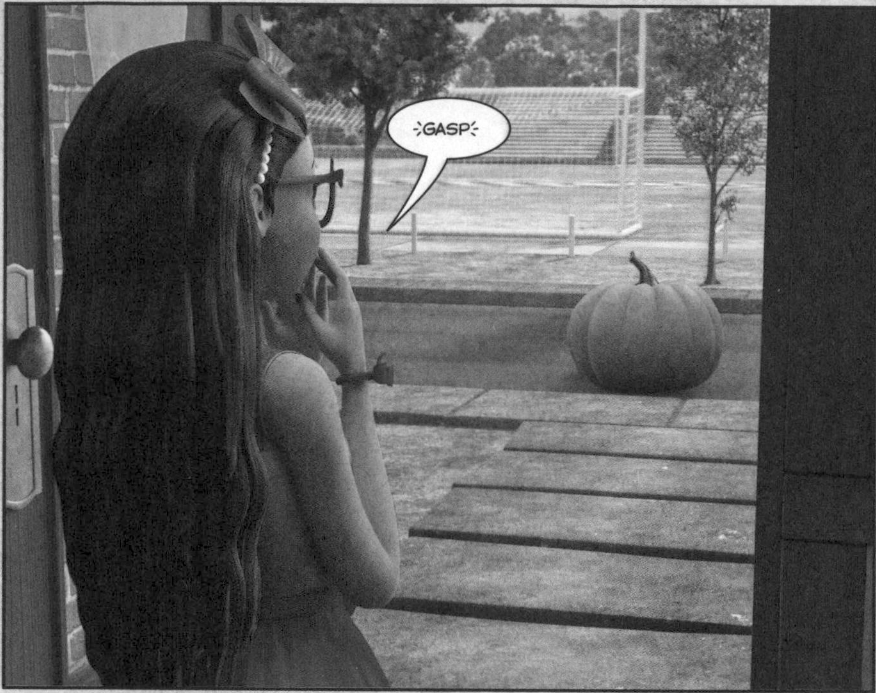
GASP

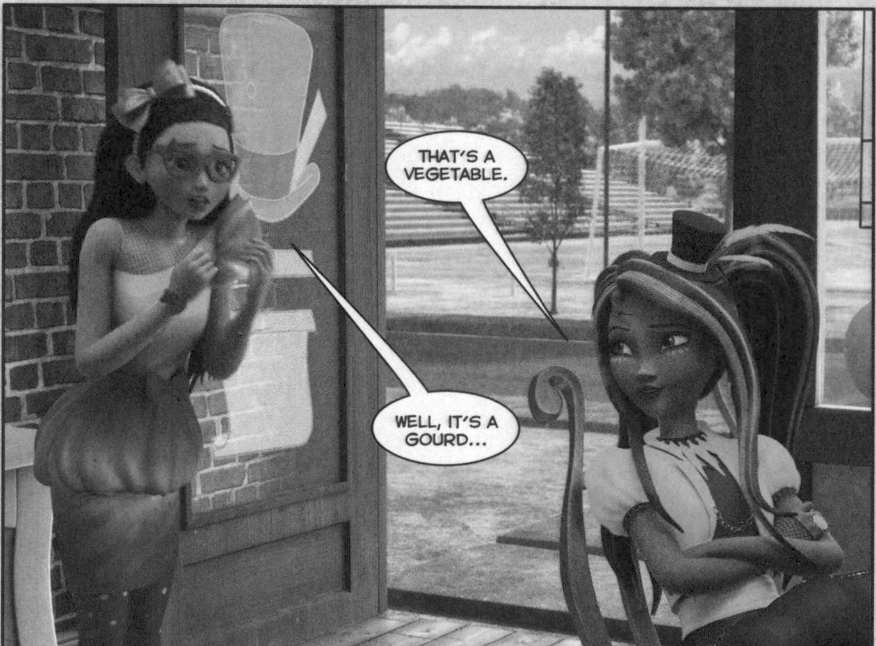
THAT'S A VEGETABLE.
WELL, IT'S A GOURD...

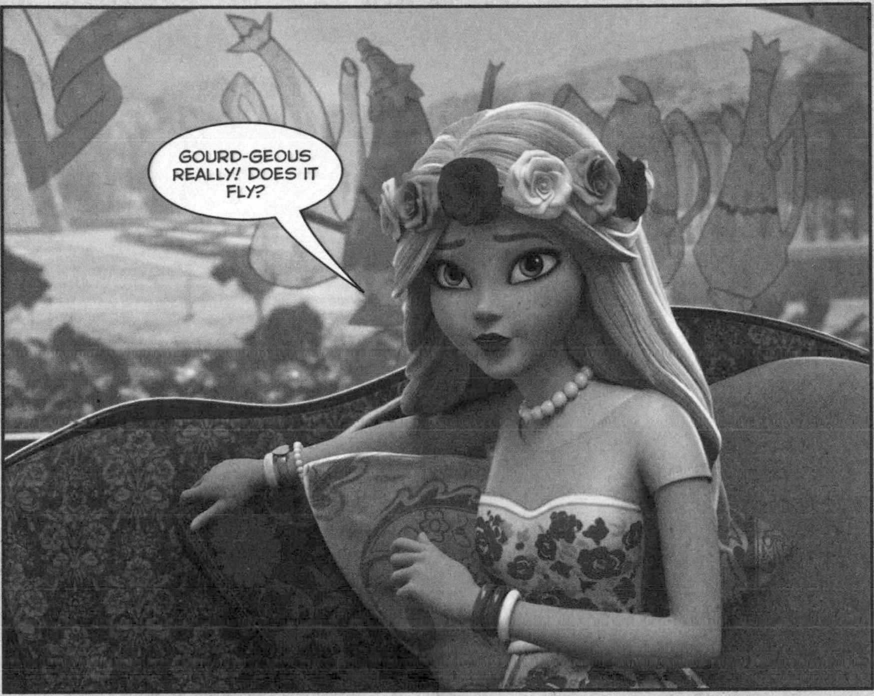
GOURD-GEOUS REALLY! DOES IT FLY?

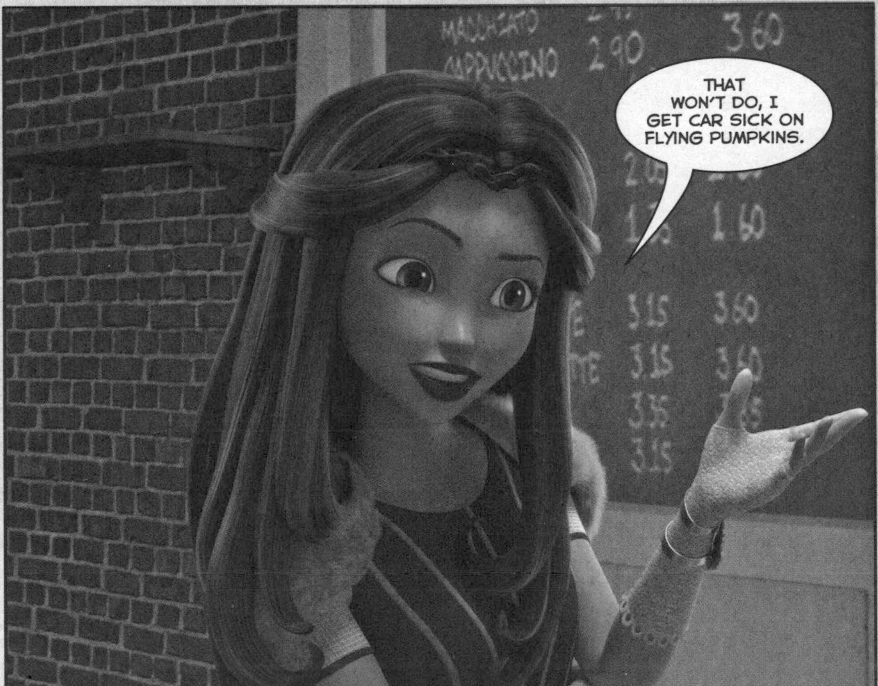
MACCHIATO
CAPPUCCINO 2.90 3.60
THAT WON'T DO, I GET CAR SICK ON FLYING PUMPKINS.

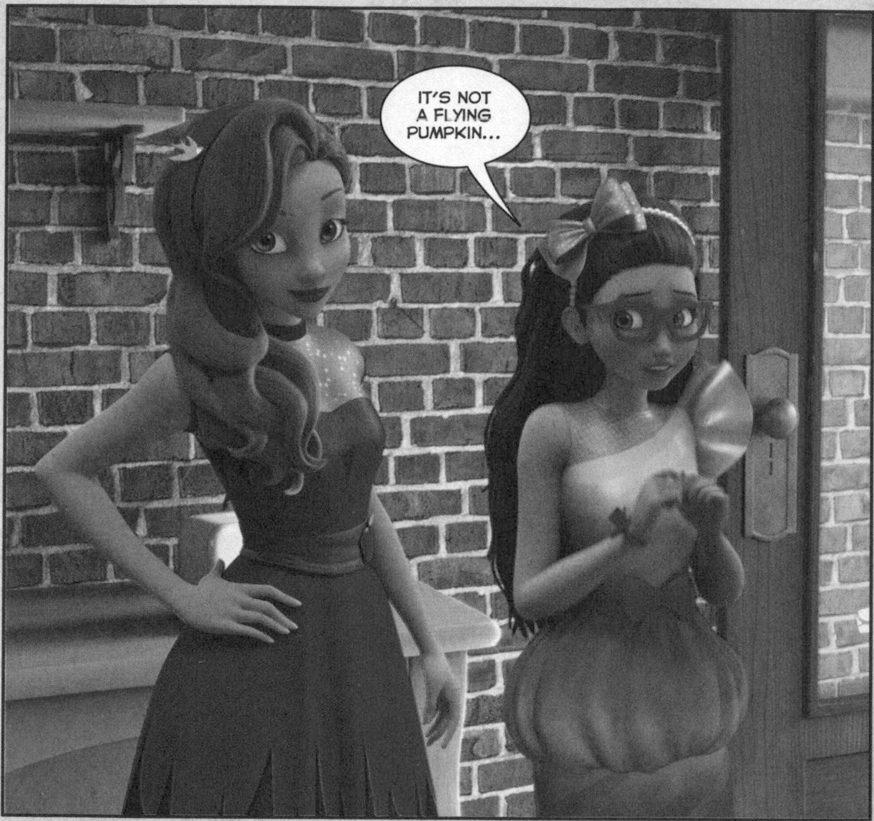
IT'S NOT A FLYING PUMPKIN...

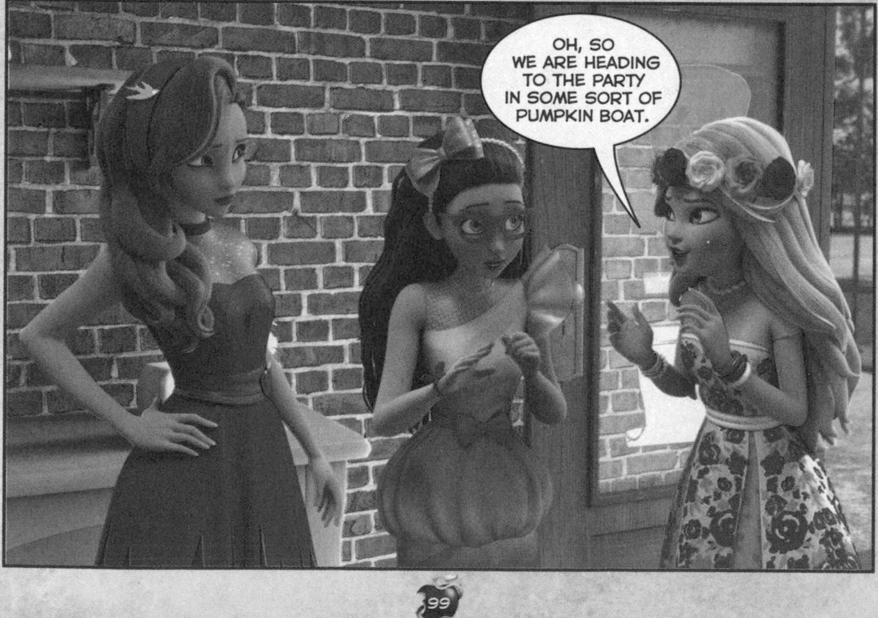
OH, SO WE ARE HEADING TO THE PARTY IN SOME SORT OF PUMPKIN BOAT.

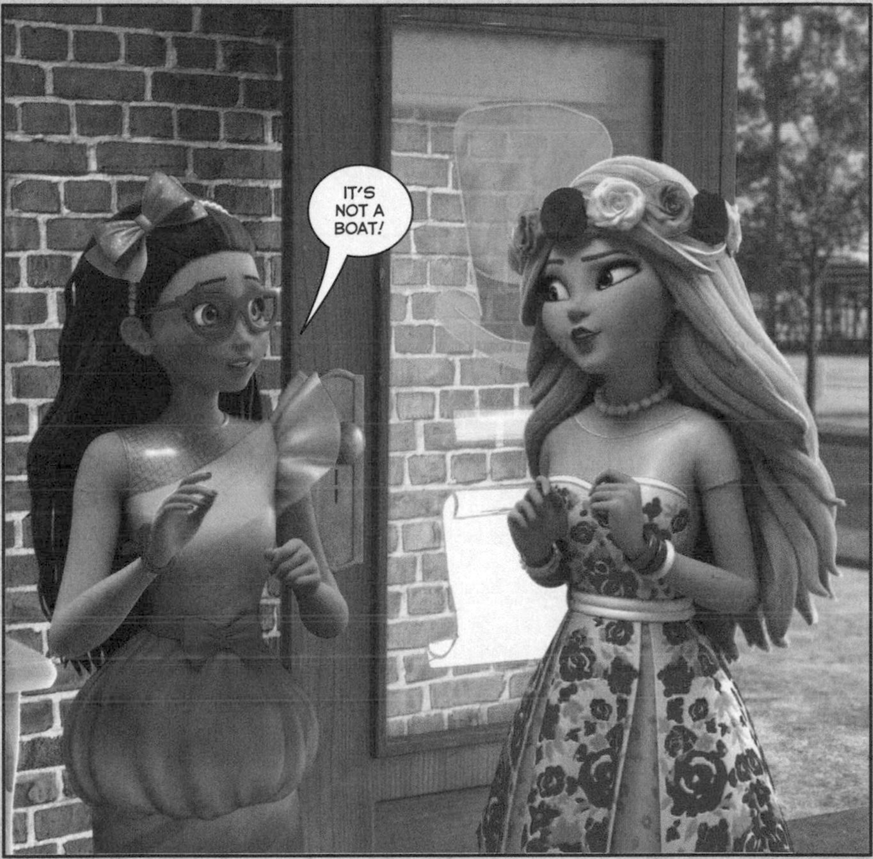
IT'S NOT A BOAT!

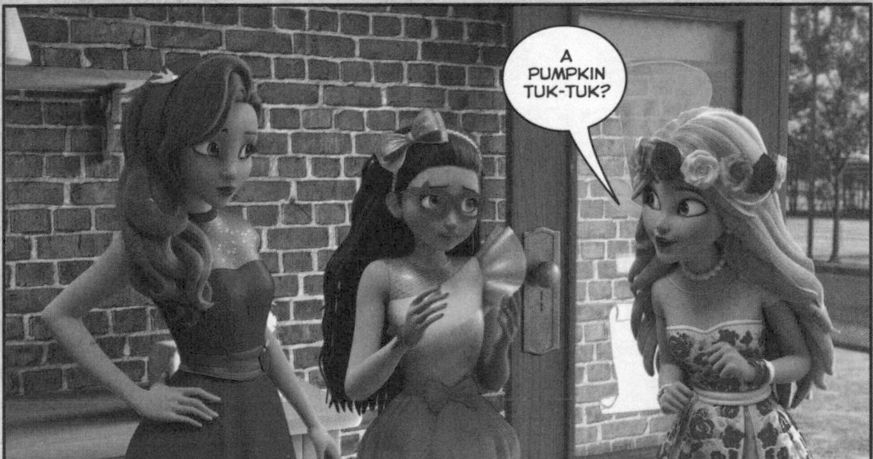
A PUMPKIN TUK-TUK?

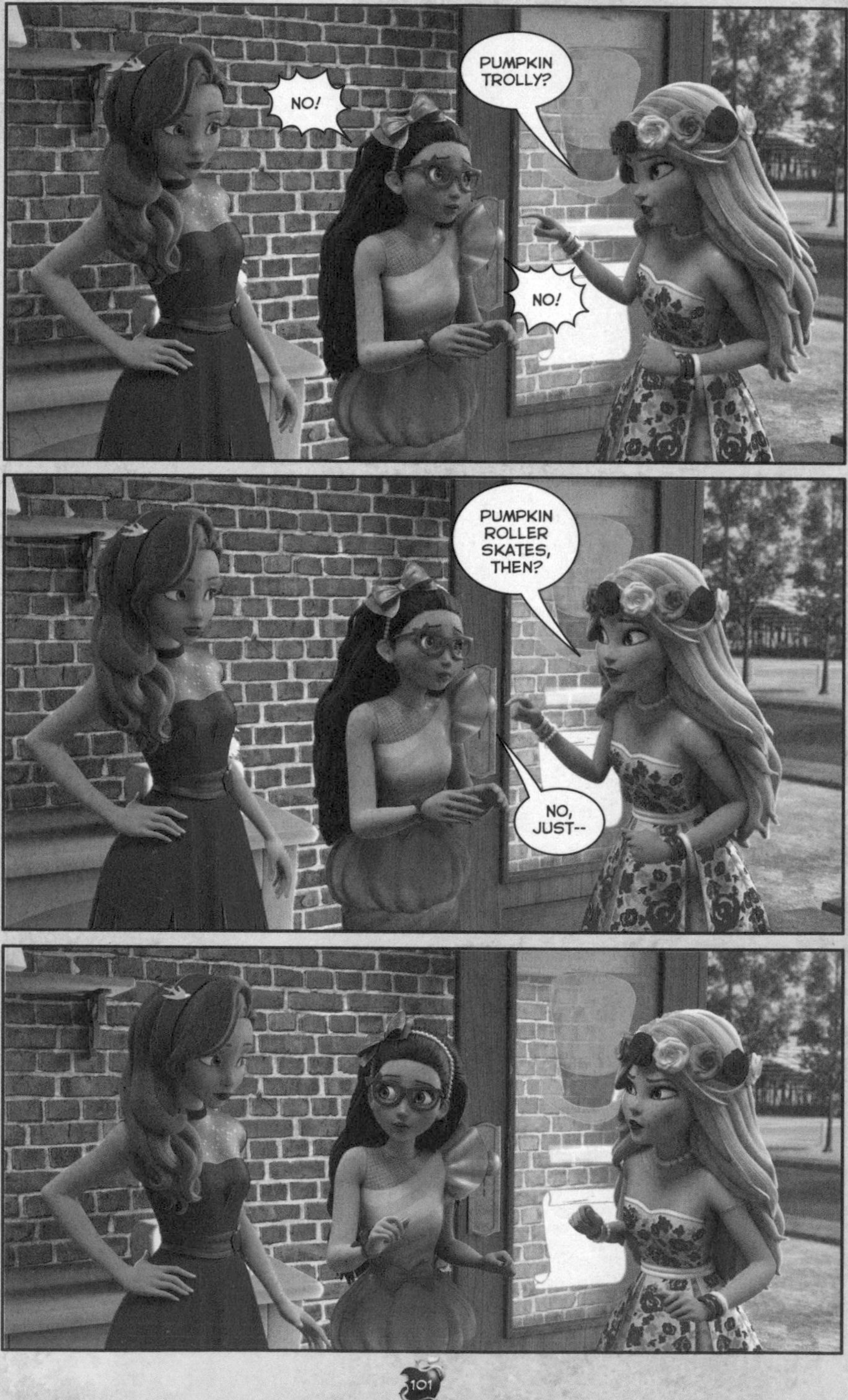
PUMPKIN TROLLY?
NO!
NO!
PUMPKIN ROLLER SKATES, THEN?
NO, JUST--

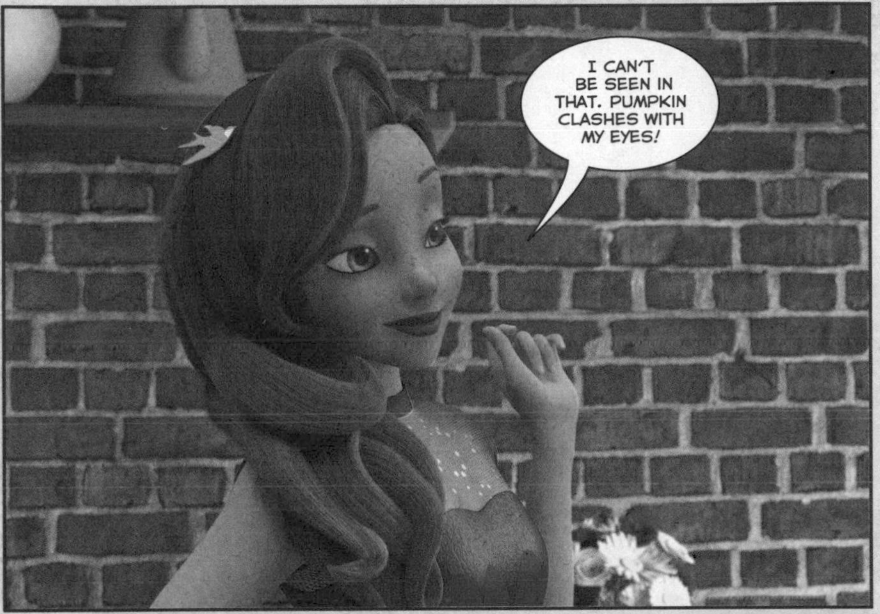
I CAN'T BE SEEN IN THAT. PUMPKIN CLASHES WITH MY EYES!

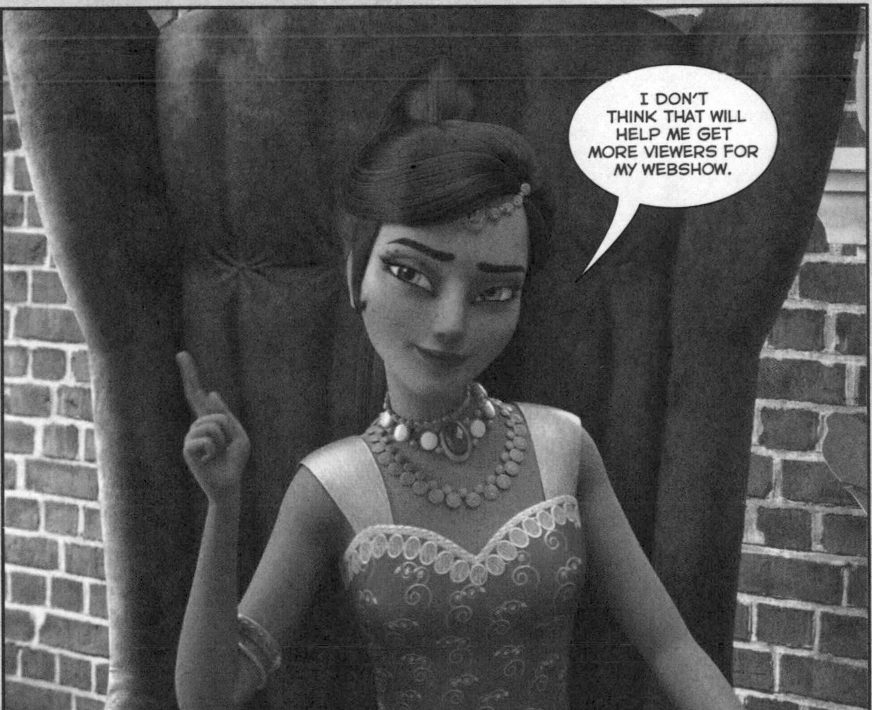
I DON'T THINK THAT WILL HELP ME GET MORE VIEWERS FOR MY WEBSHOW.

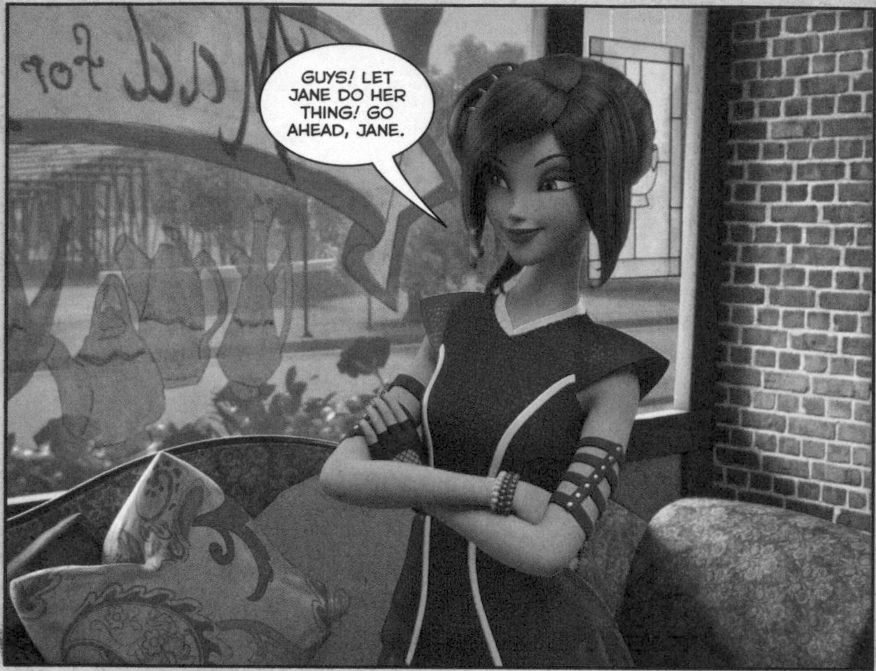
GUYS! LET JANE DO HER THING! GO AHEAD, JANE.

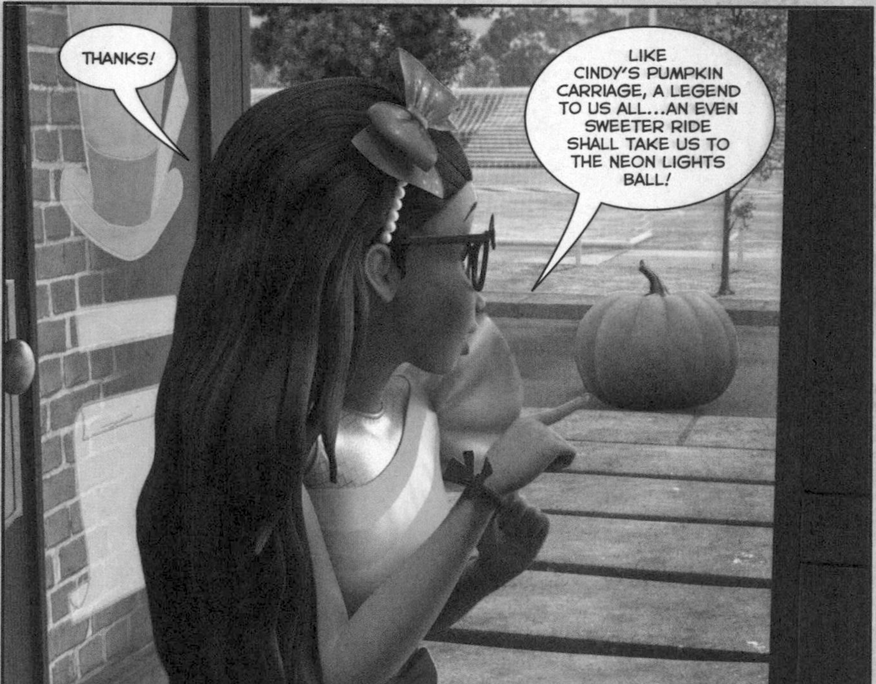
THANKS!
LIKE CINDY'S PUMPKIN CARRIAGE, A LEGEND TO US ALL...AN EVEN SWEETER RIDE SHALL TAKE US TO THE NEON LIGHTS BALL!

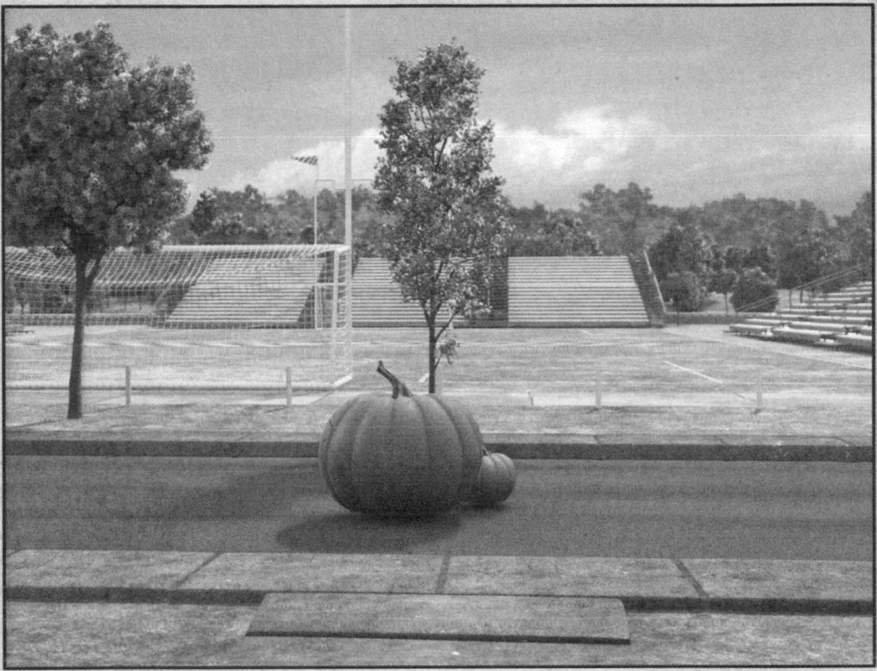

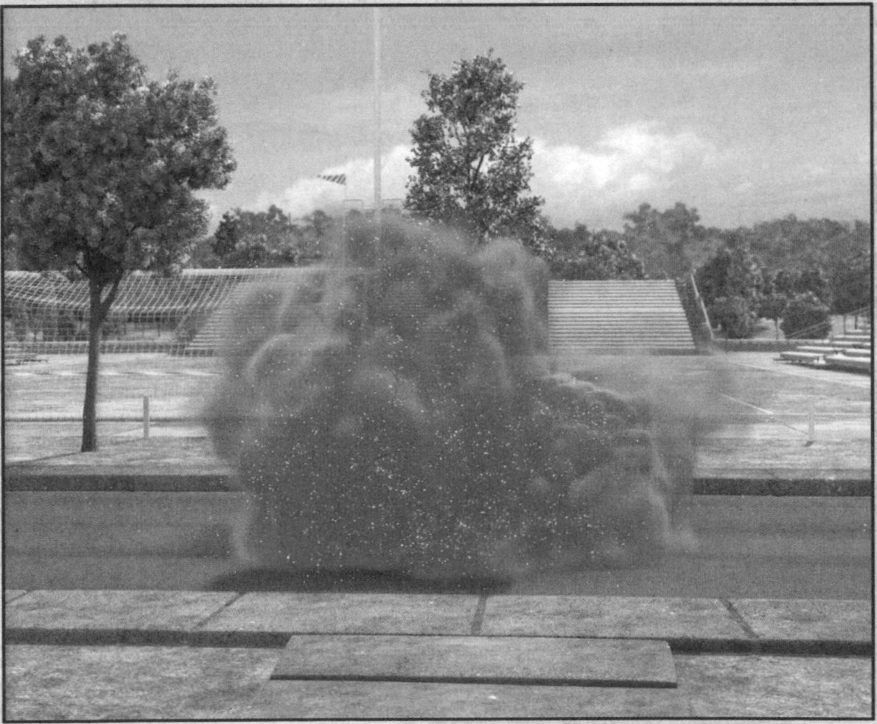

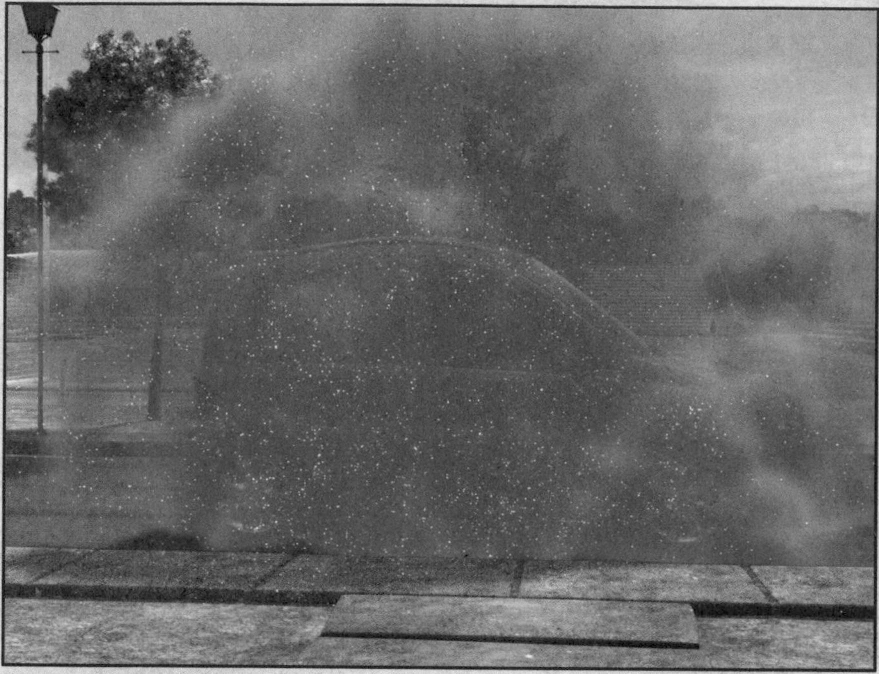

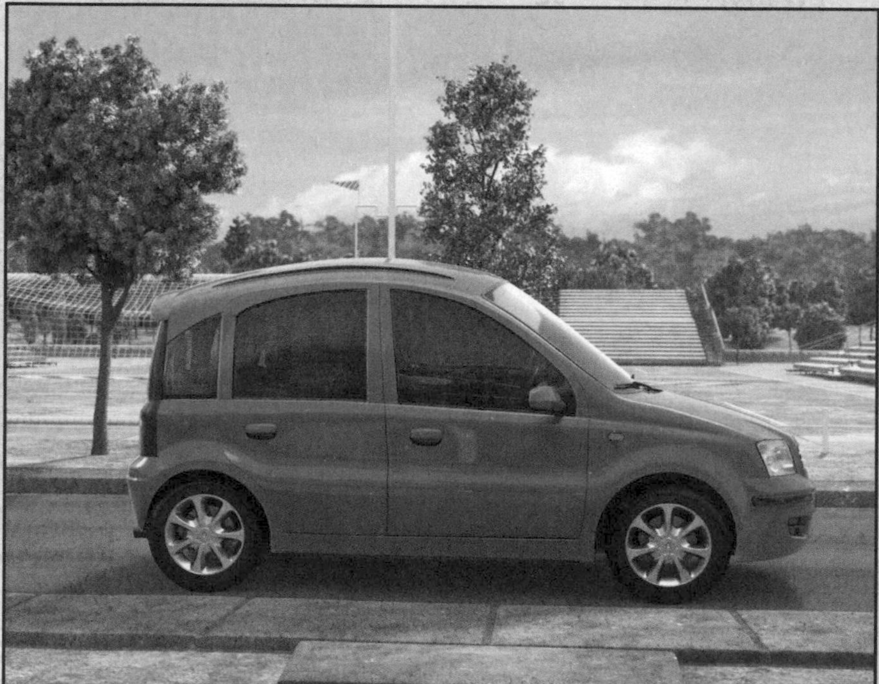

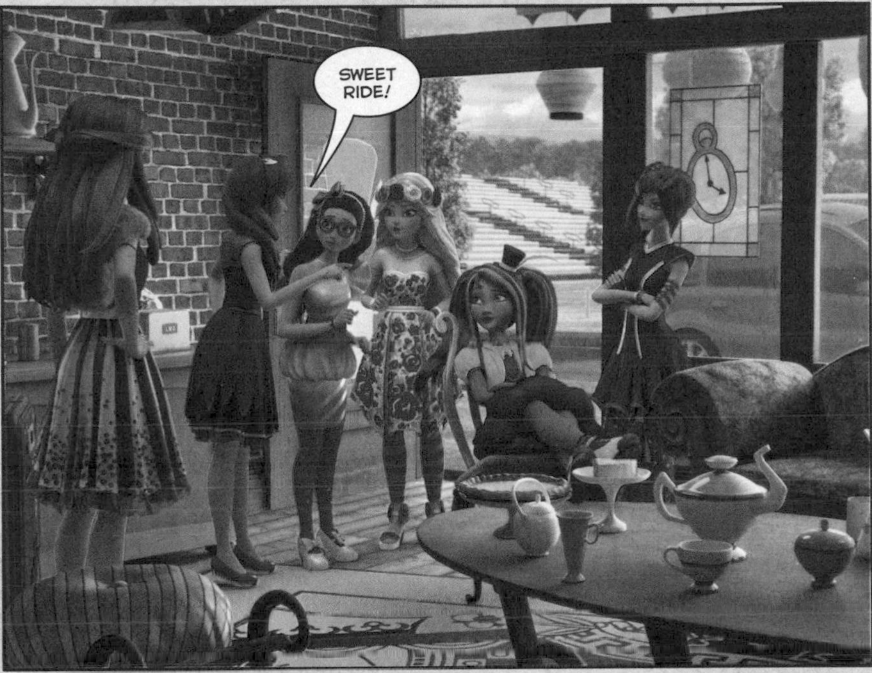
SWEET RIDE!

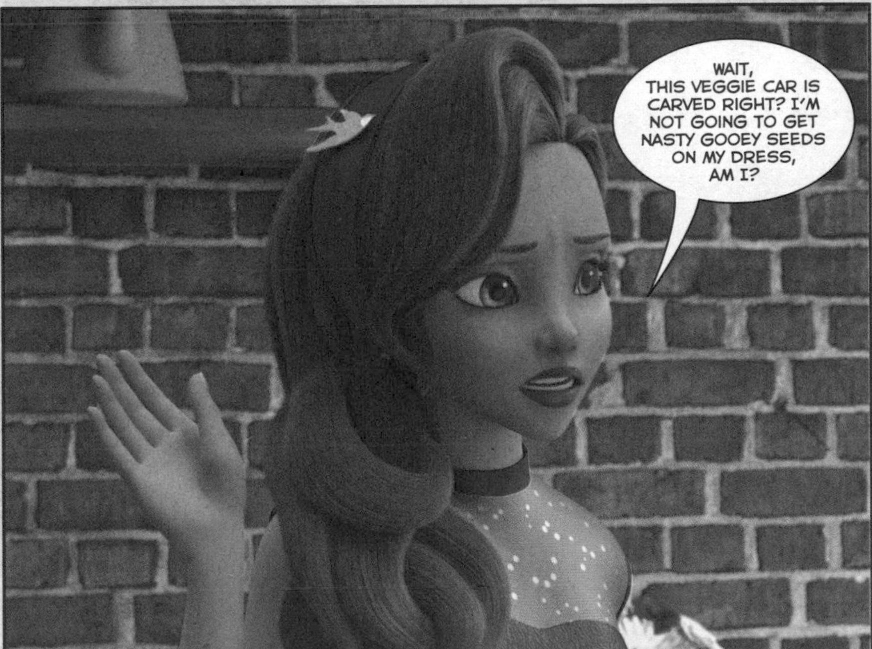
WAIT, THIS VEGGIE CAR IS CARVED RIGHT? I'M NOT GOING TO GET NASTY GOOEY SEEDS ON MY DRESS, AM I?

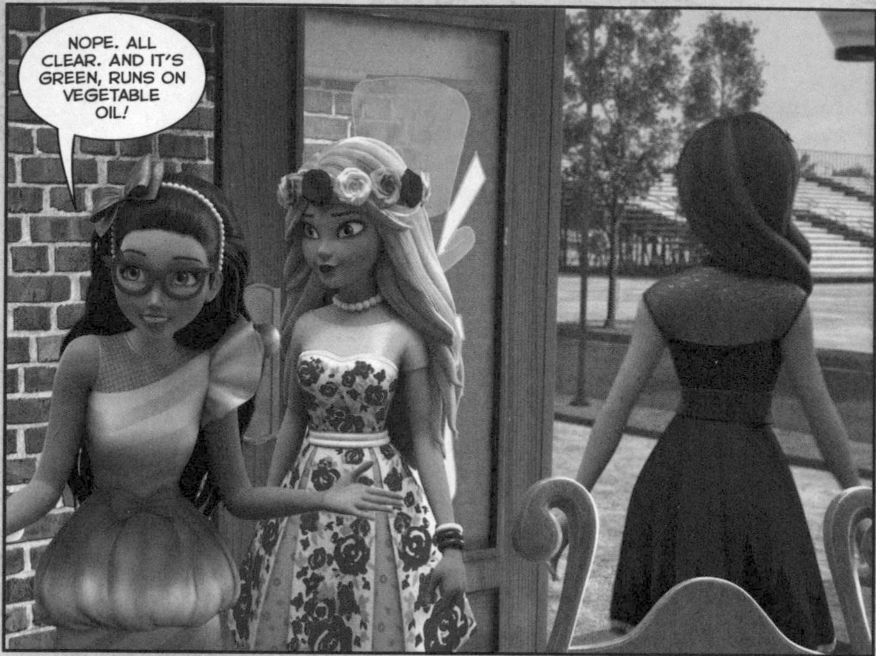
NOPE. ALL CLEAR. AND IT'S GREEN, RUNS ON VEGETABLE OIL!

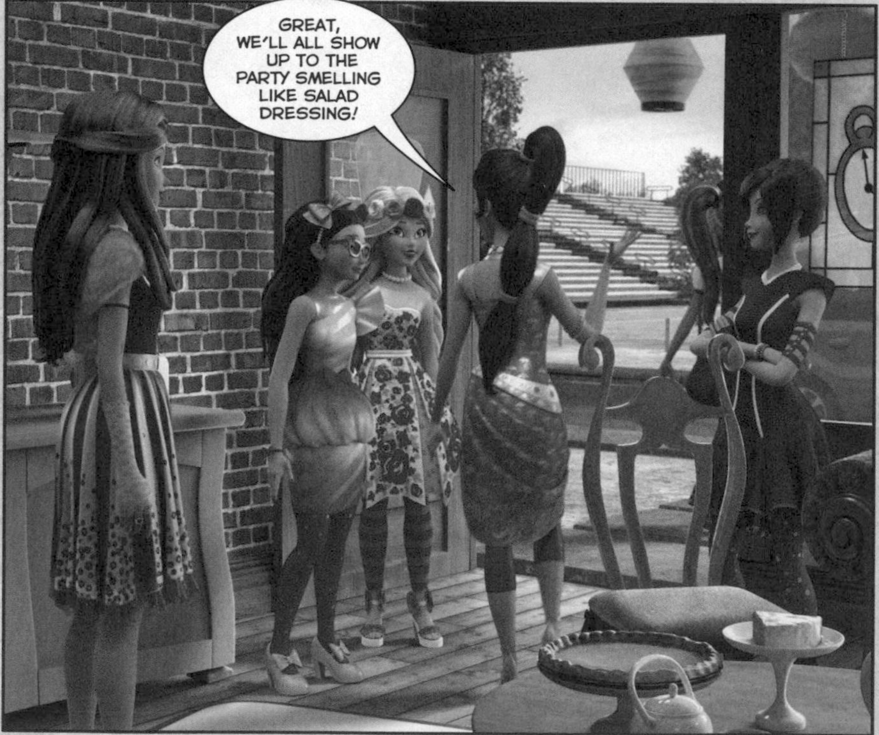
GREAT, WE'LL ALL SHOW UP TO THE PARTY SMELLING LIKE SALAD DRESSING!

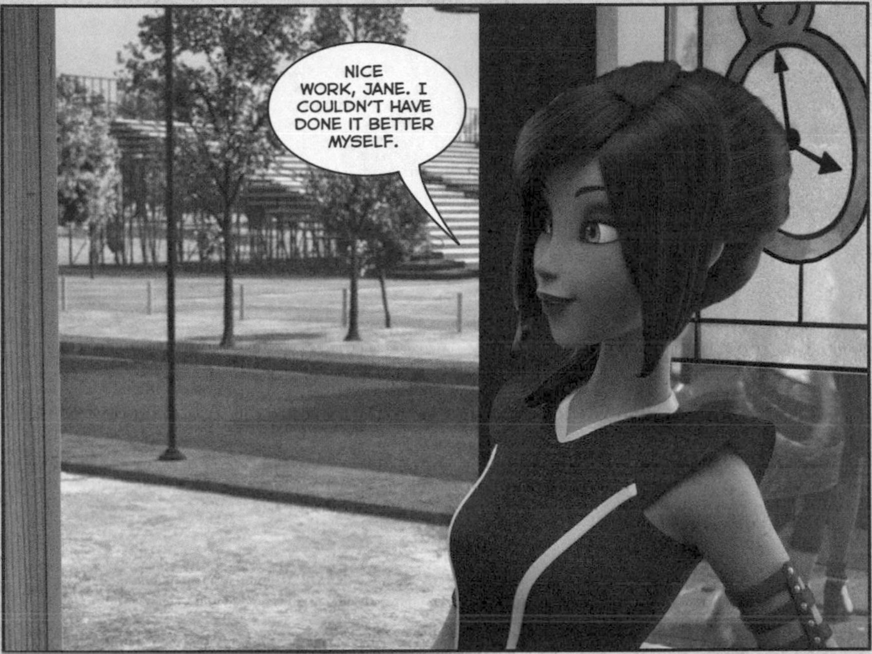
NICE WORK, JANE. I COULDN'T HAVE DONE IT BETTER MYSELF.

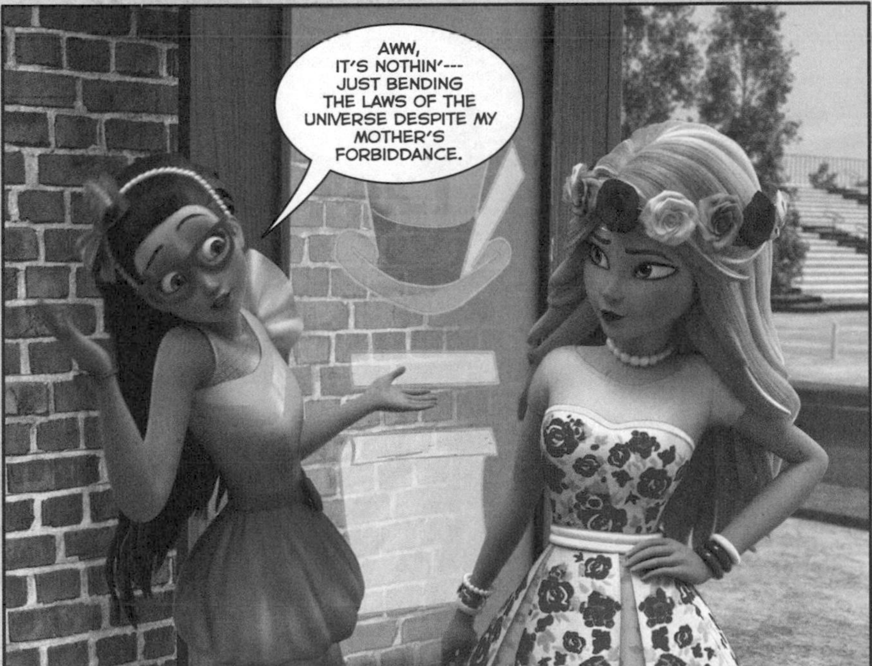
AWW, IT'S NOTHIN'--- JUST BENDING THE LAWS OF THE UNIVERSE DESPITE MY MOTHER'S FORBIDDANCE.

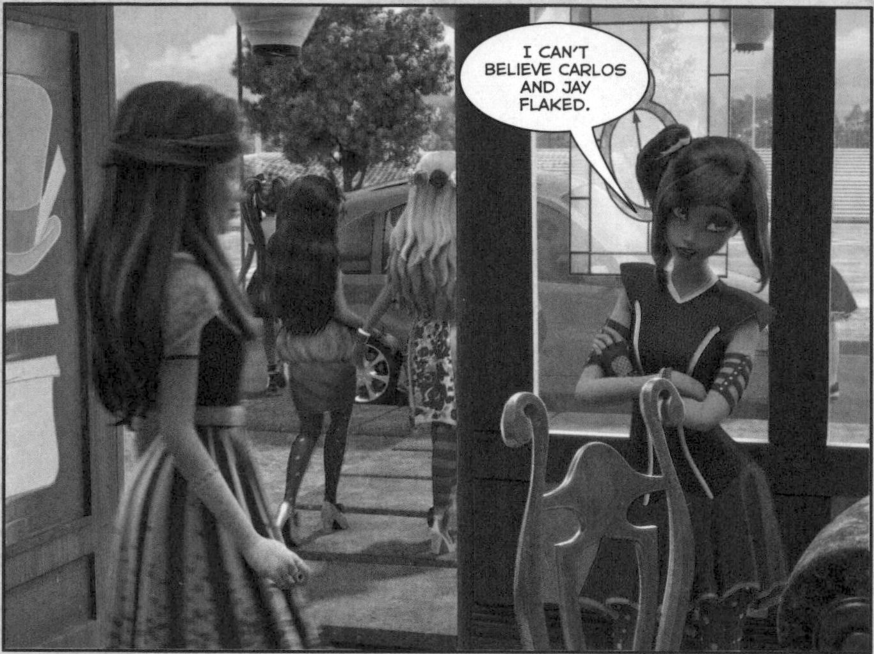
I CAN'T BELIEVE CARLOS AND JAY FLAKED.

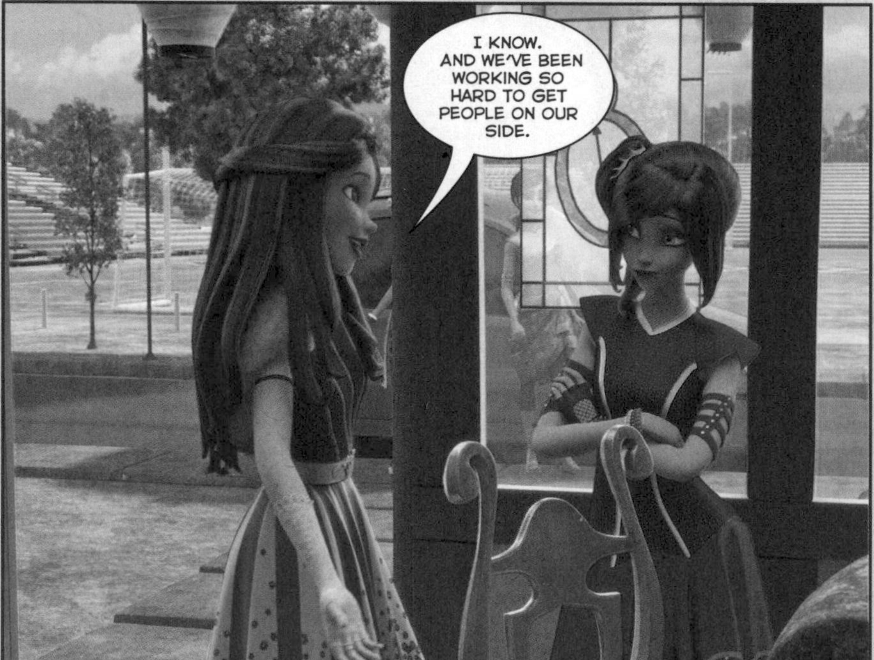
I KNOW. AND WE'VE BEEN WORKING SO HARD TO GET PEOPLE ON OUR SIDE.

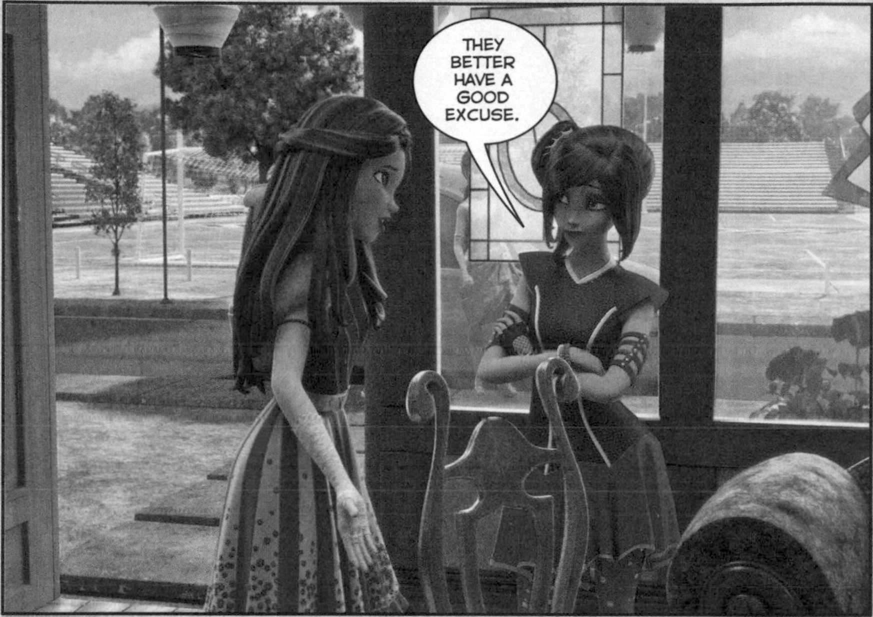
THEY BETTER HAVE A GOOD EXCUSE.

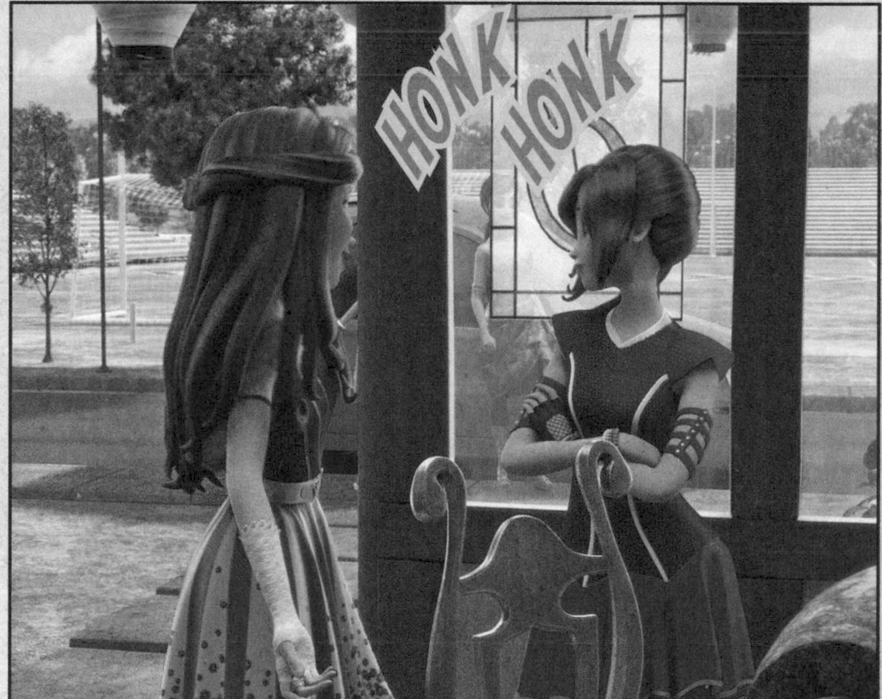
HONK HONK

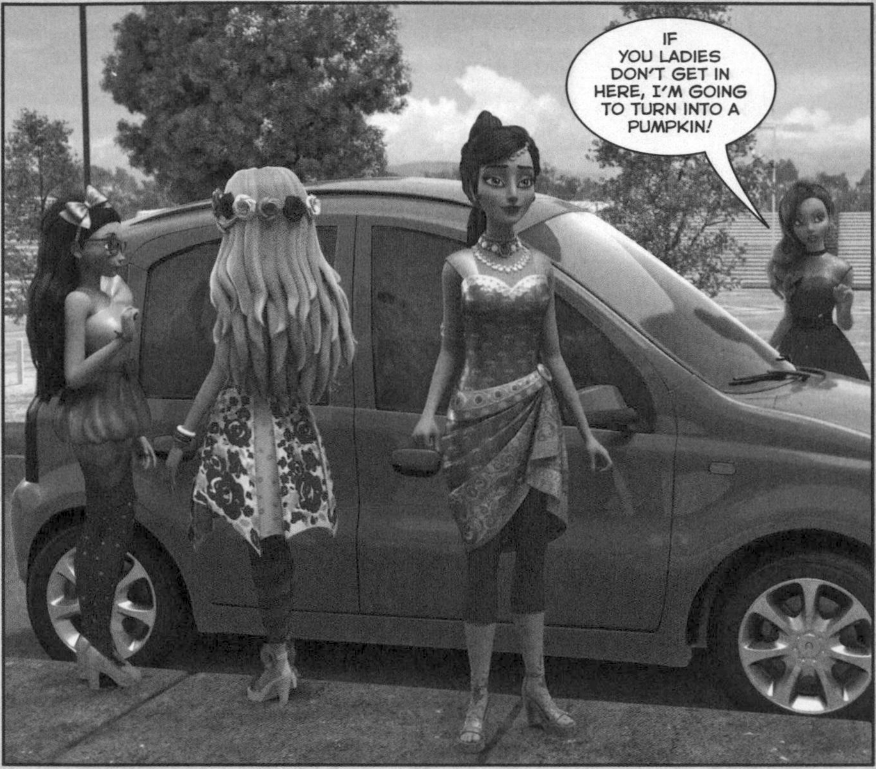
IF YOU LADIES DON'T GET IN HERE, I'M GOING TO TURN INTO A PUMPKIN!

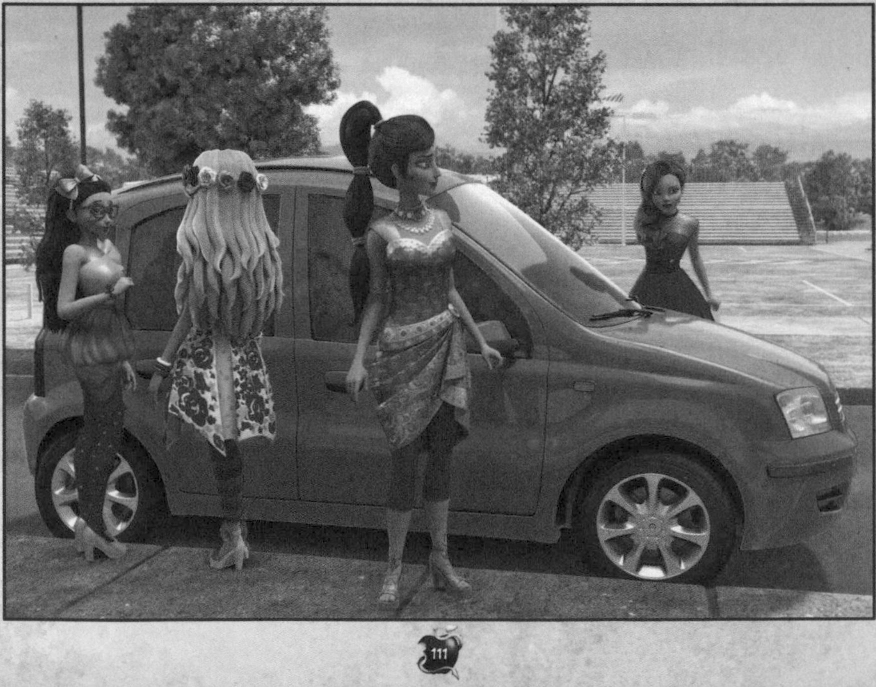

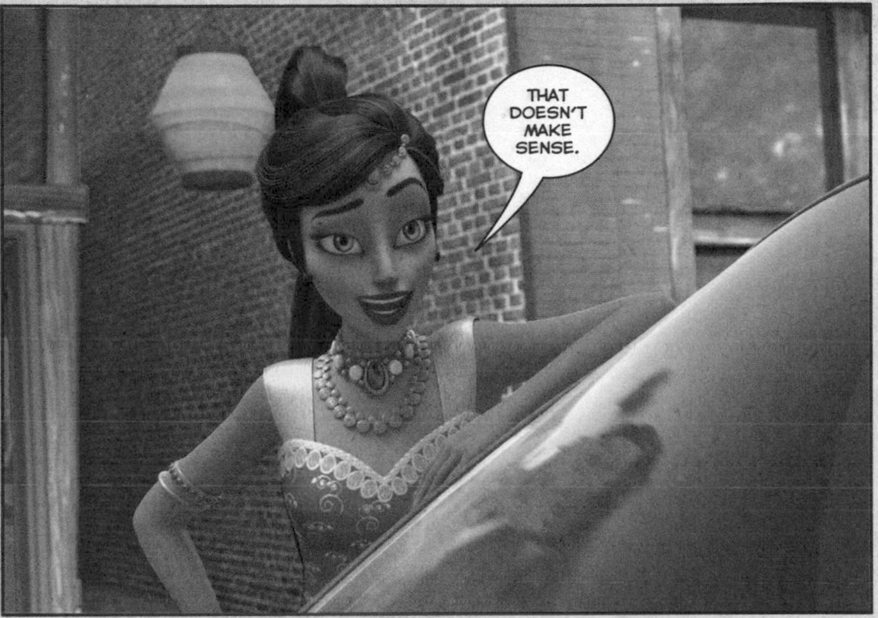
THAT DOESN'T MAKE SENSE.

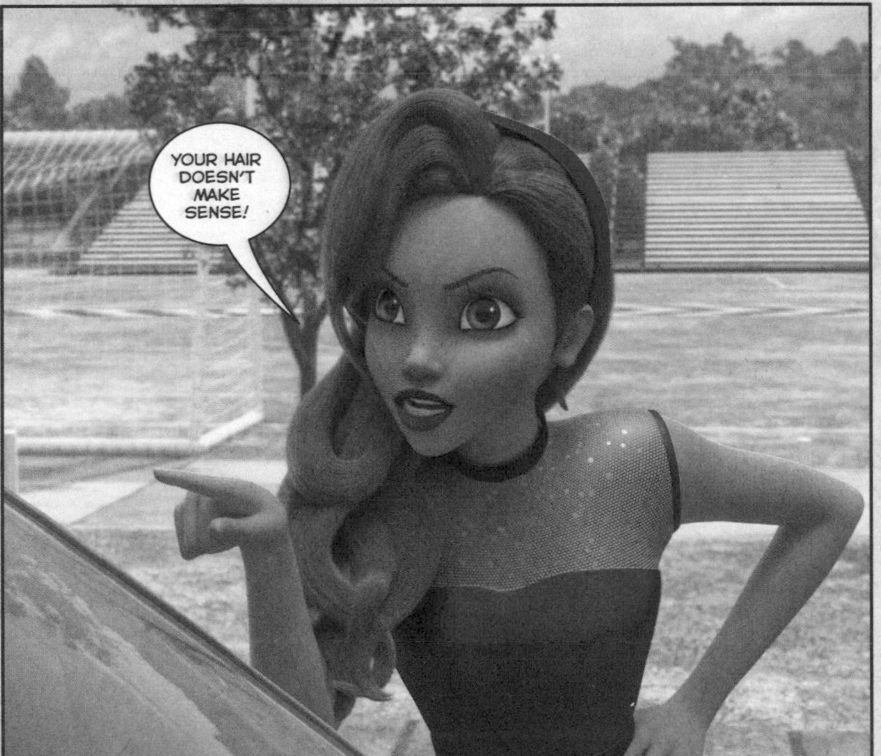
YOUR HAIR DOESN'T MAKE SENSE!

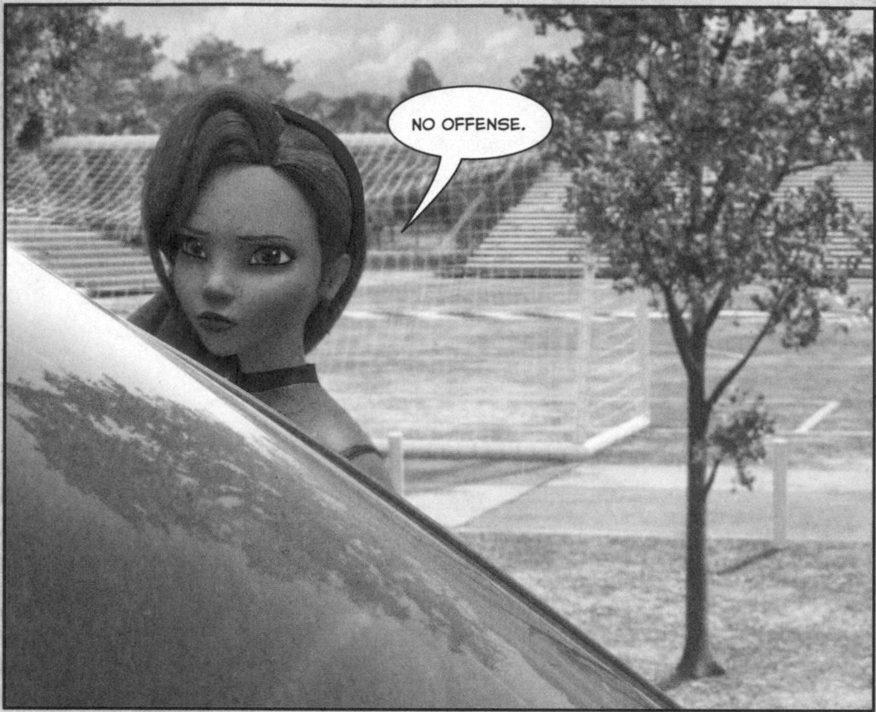
NO OFFENSE.

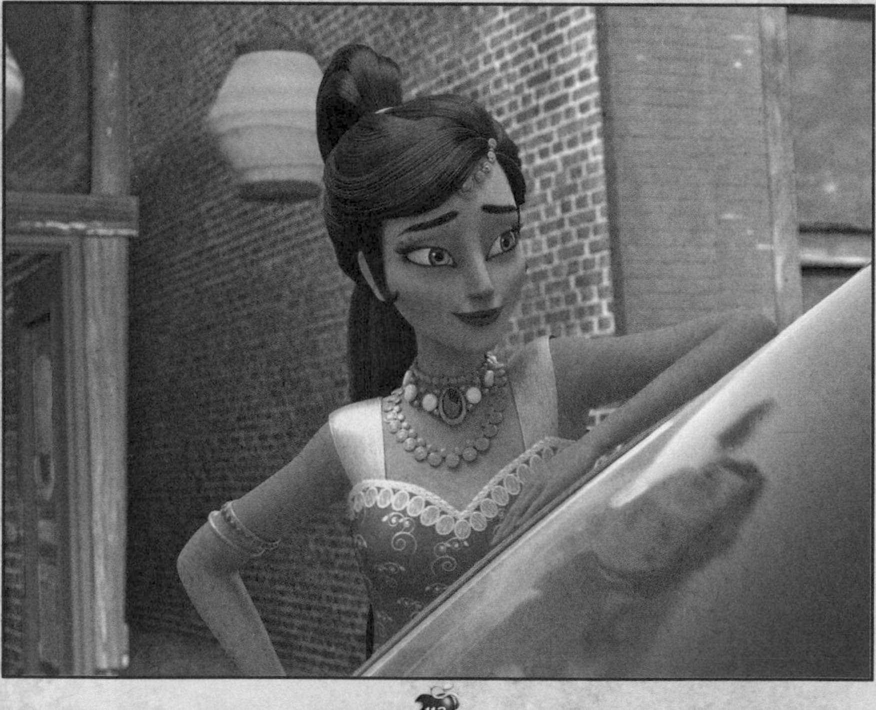

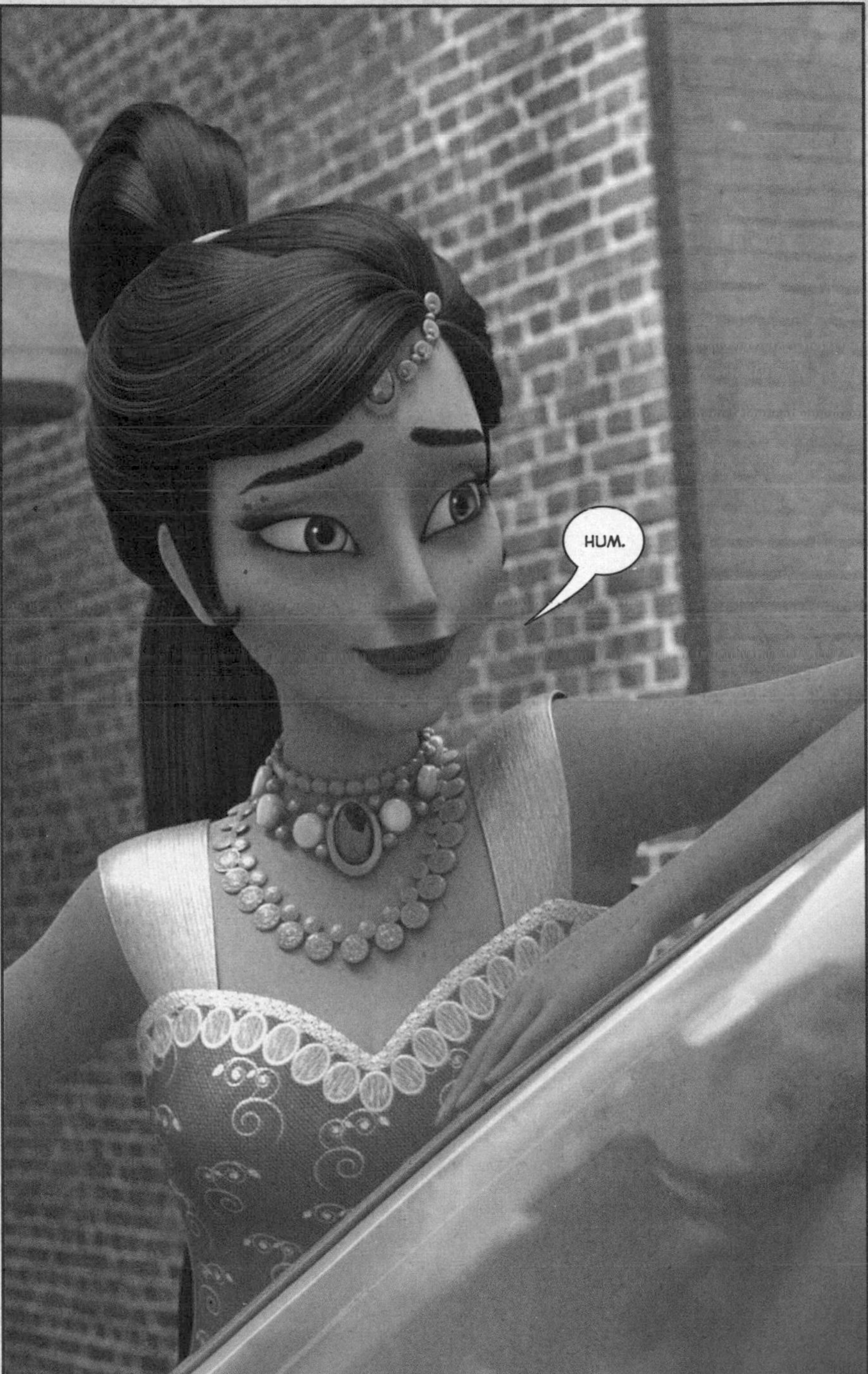
HUM.

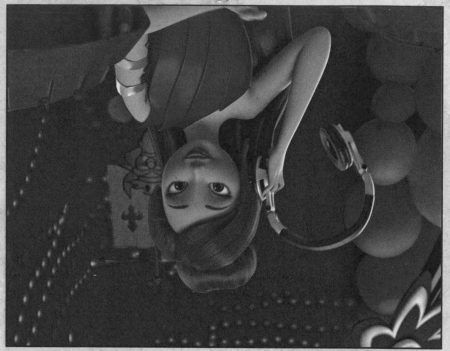

CHAPTER 16: THE
NIGHT IS YOUNG

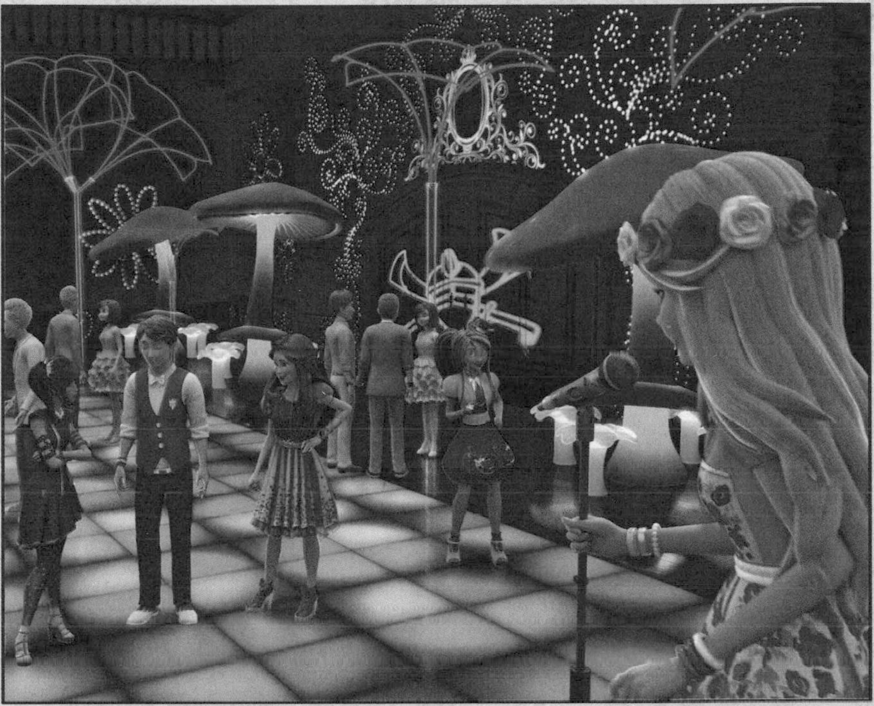

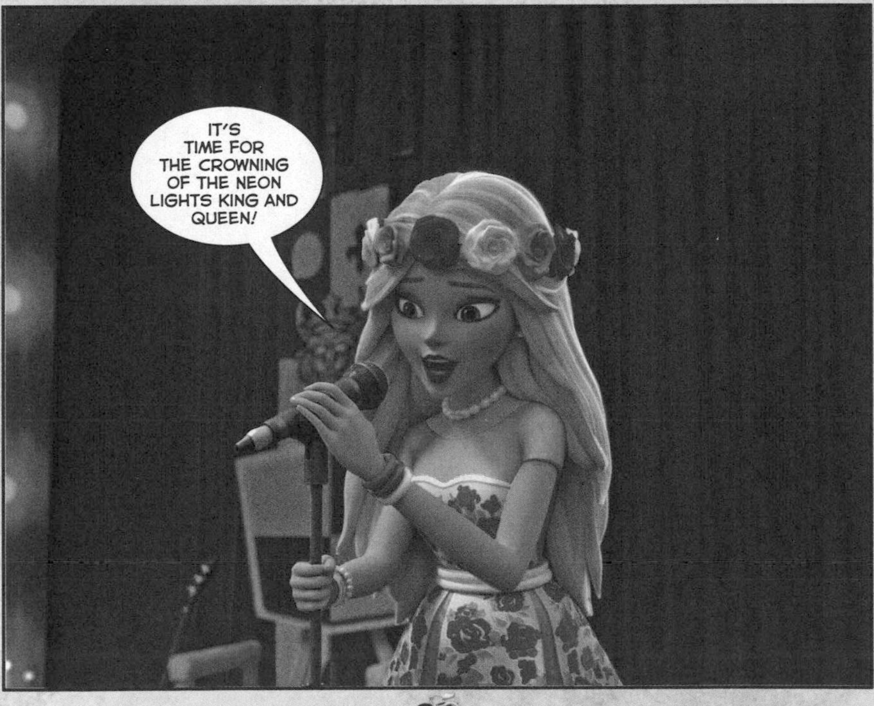
IT'S TIME FOR THE CROWNING OF THE NEON LIGHTS KING AND QUEEN!

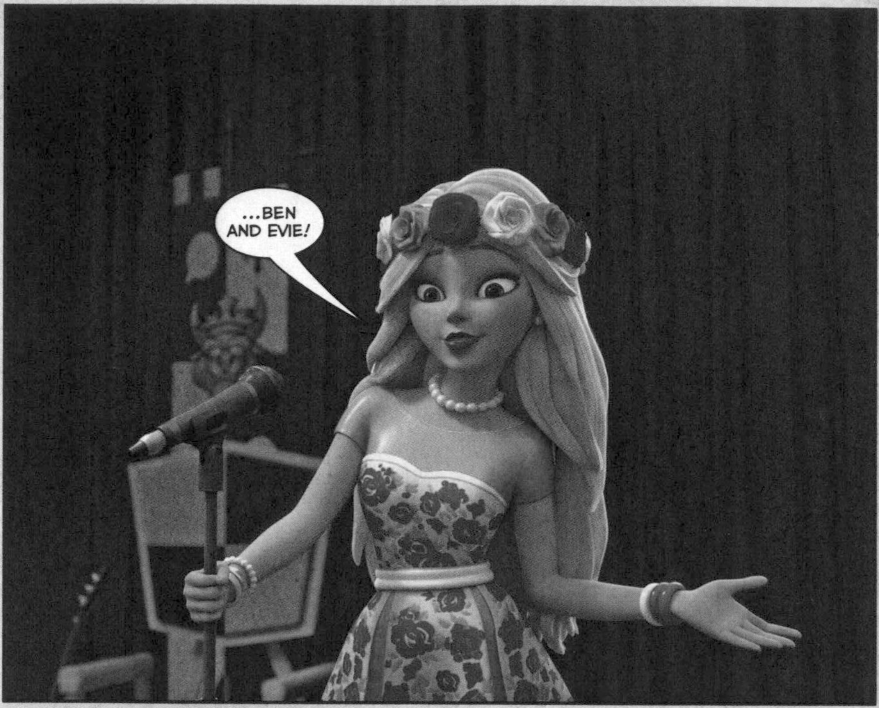
...BEN AND EVIE!

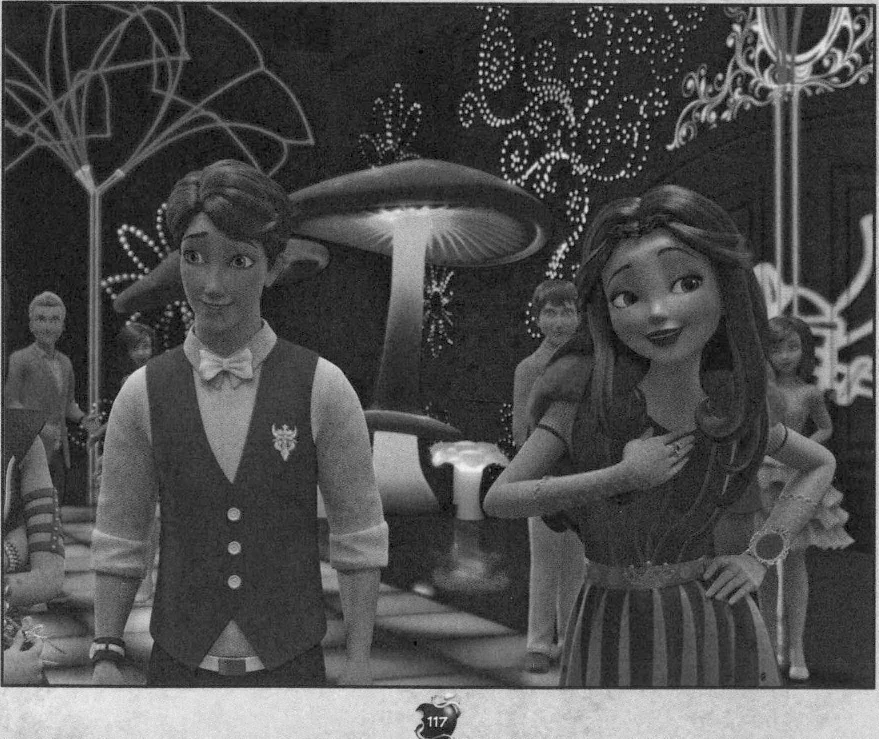

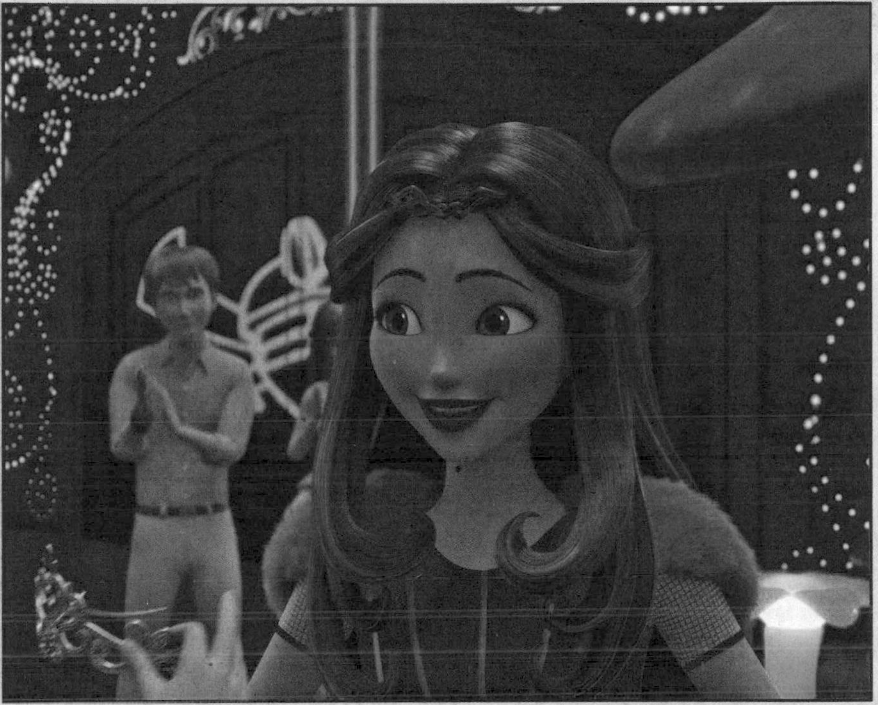

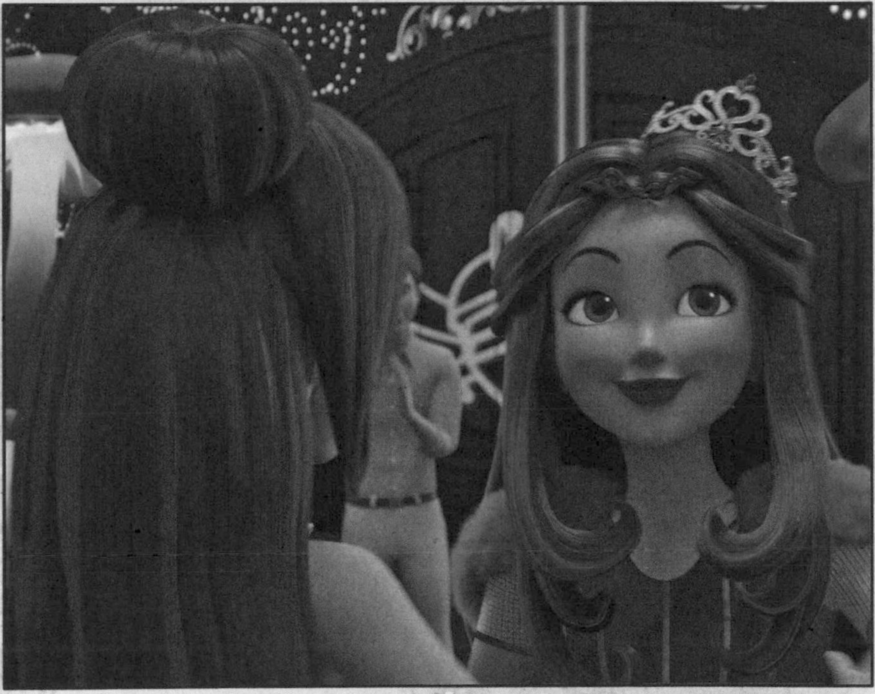

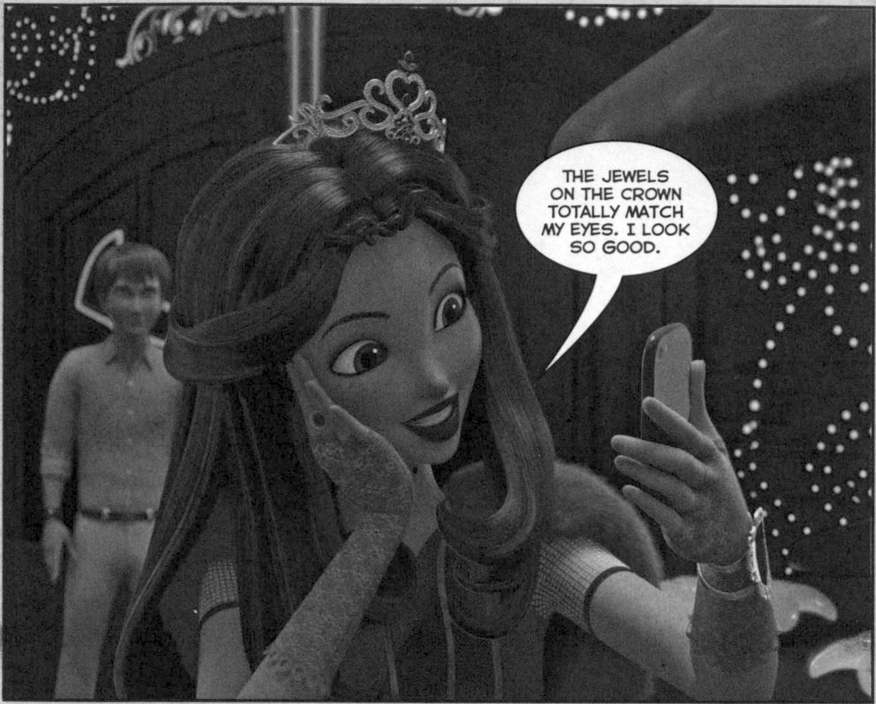
THE JEWELS ON THE CROWN TOTALLY MATCH MY EYES. I LOOK SO GOOD.

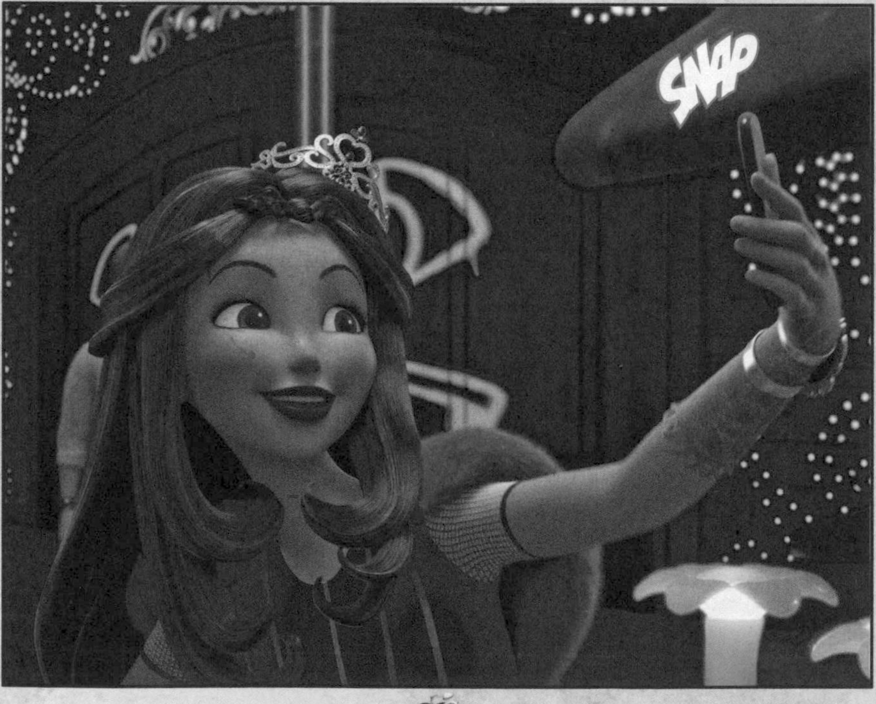
SNAP

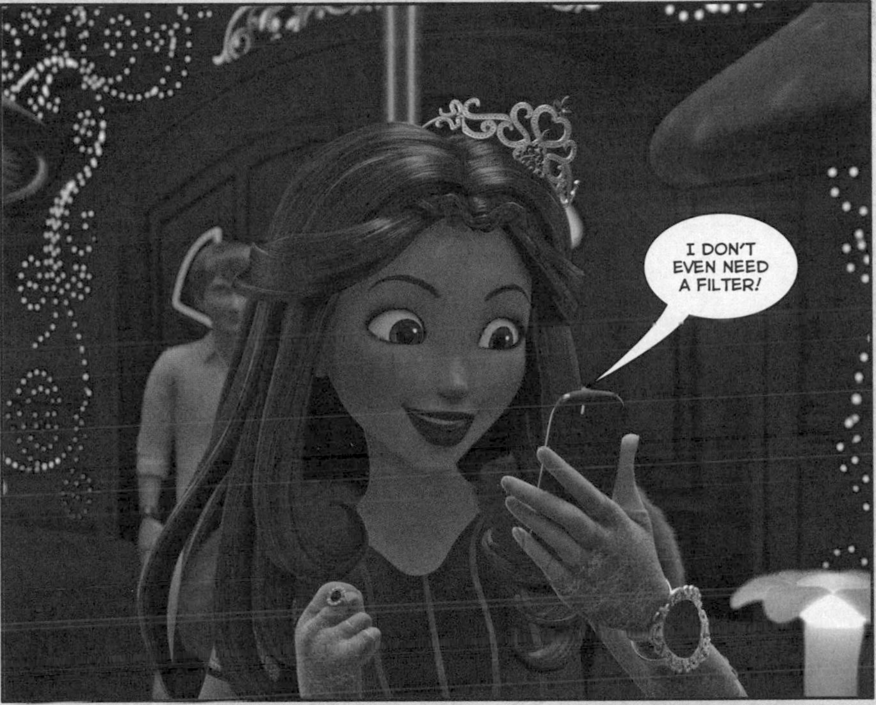
I DON'T EVEN NEED A FILTER!

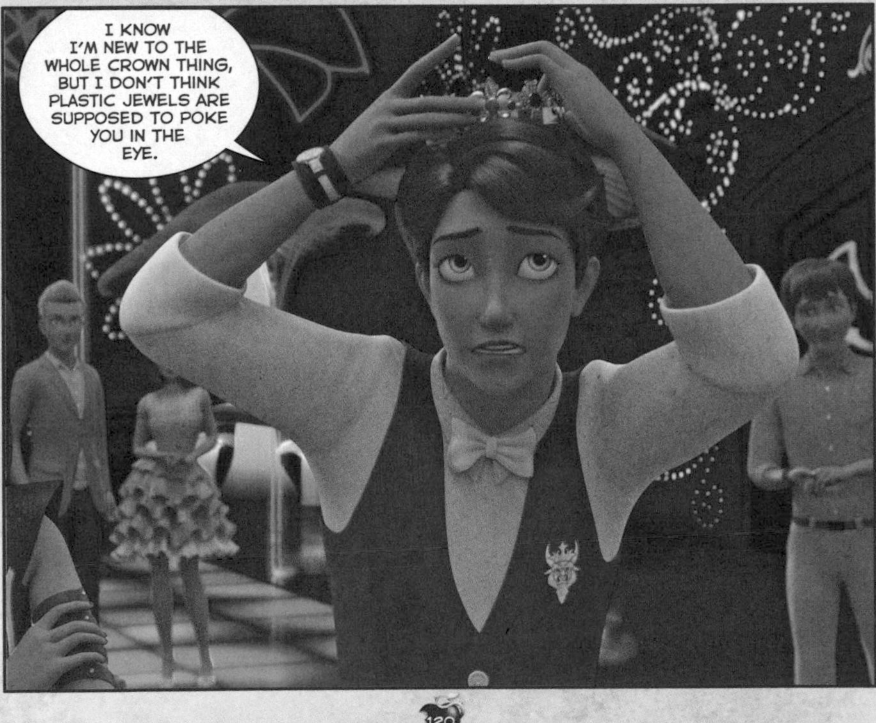
I KNOW I'M NEW TO THE WHOLE CROWN THING, BUT I DON'T THINK PLASTIC JEWELS ARE SUPPOSED TO POKE YOU IN THE EYE.

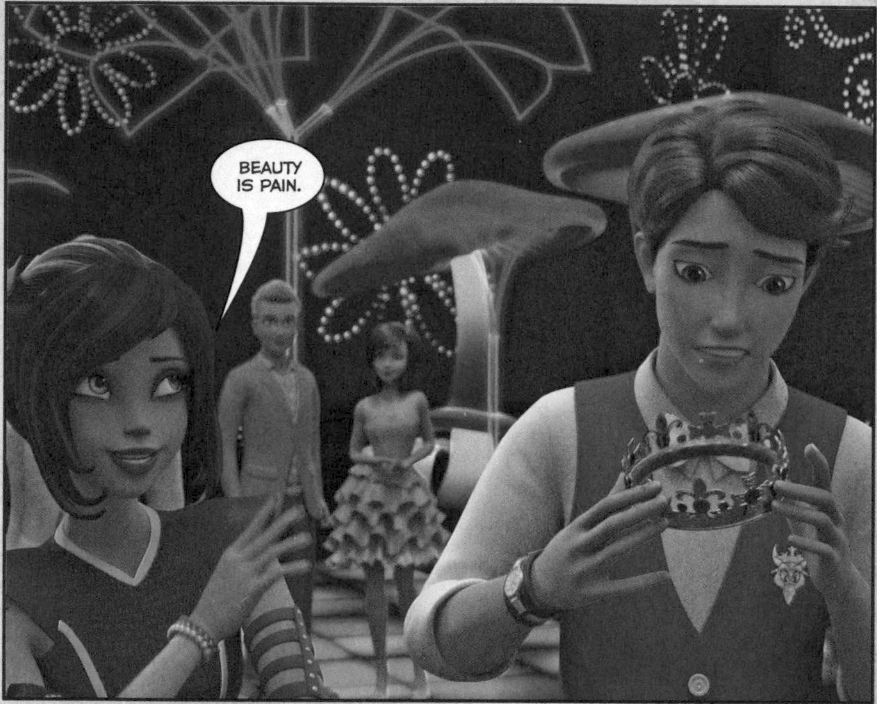
BEAUTY IS PAIN.

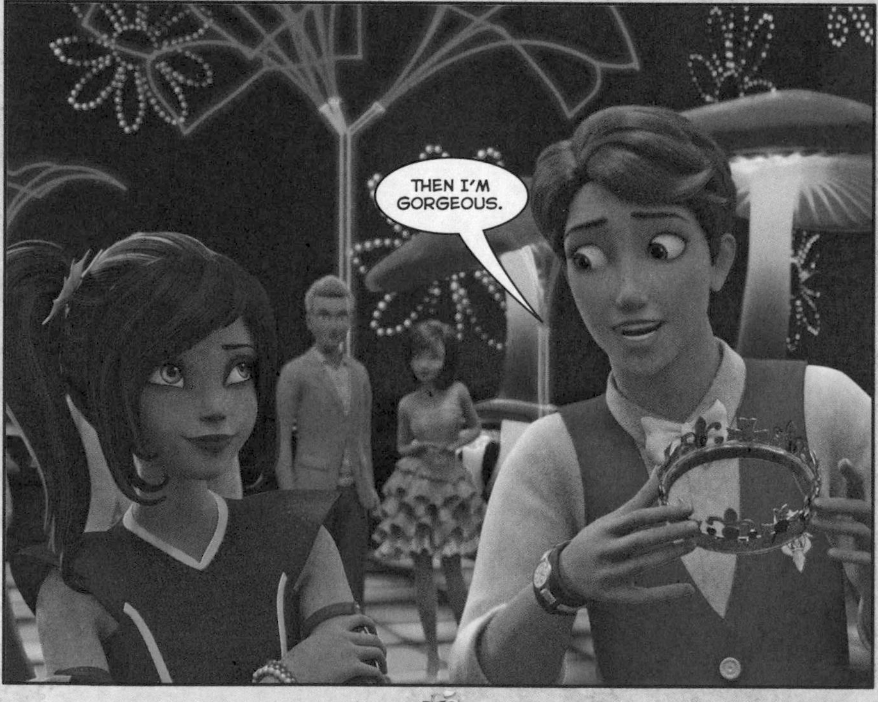
THEN I'M GORGEOUS.

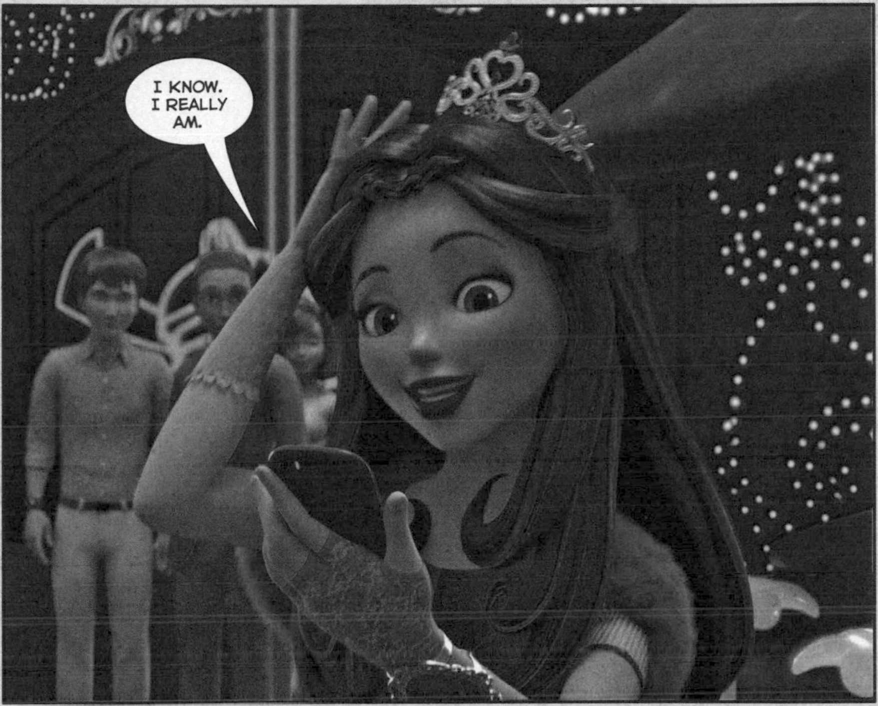
I KNOW. I REALLY AM.

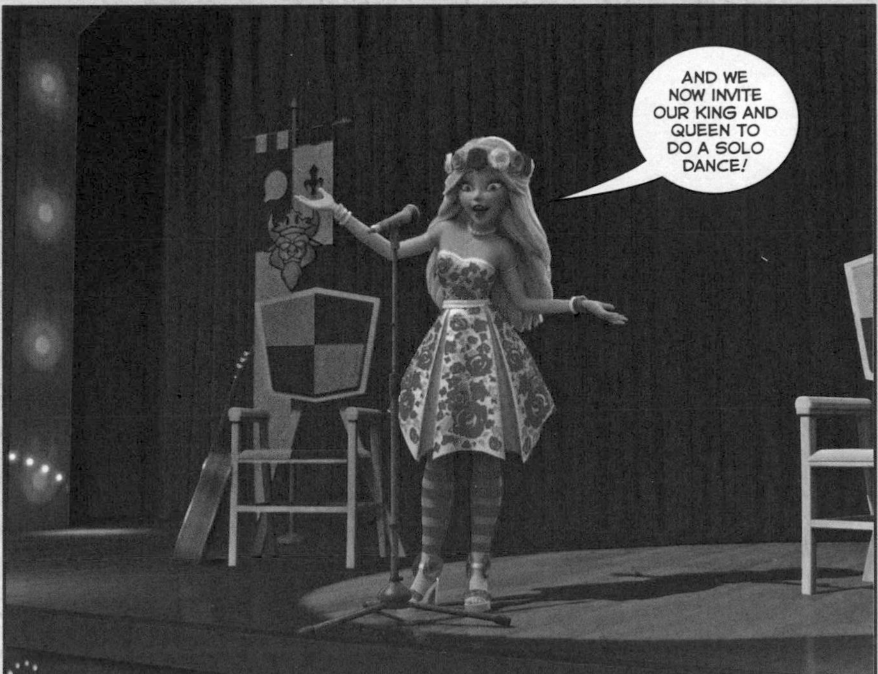
AND WE NOW INVITE OUR KING AND QUEEN TO DO A SOLO DANCE!

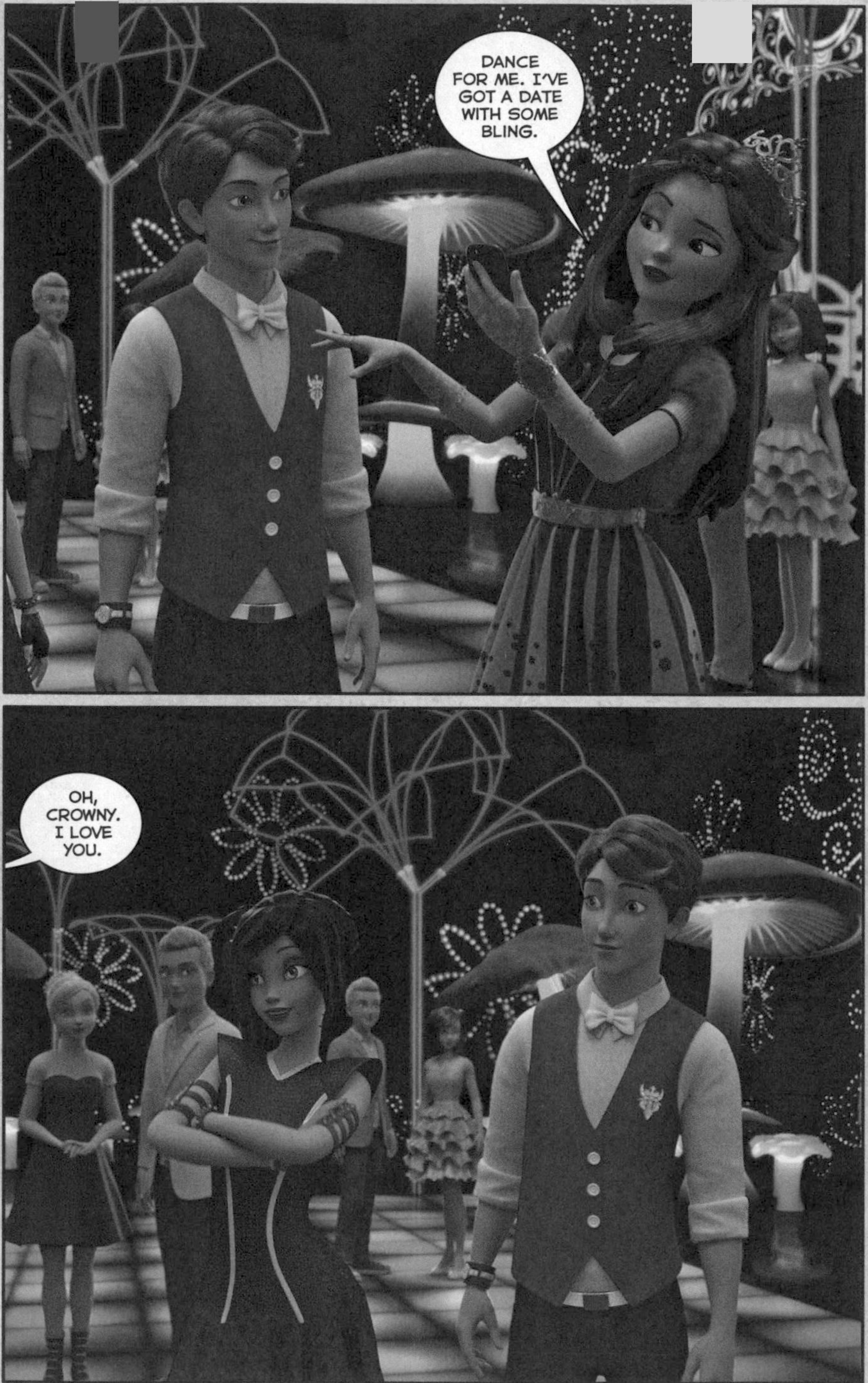
DANCE FOR ME. I'VE GOT A DATE WITH SOME BLING.
OH, CROWNY. I LOVE YOU.

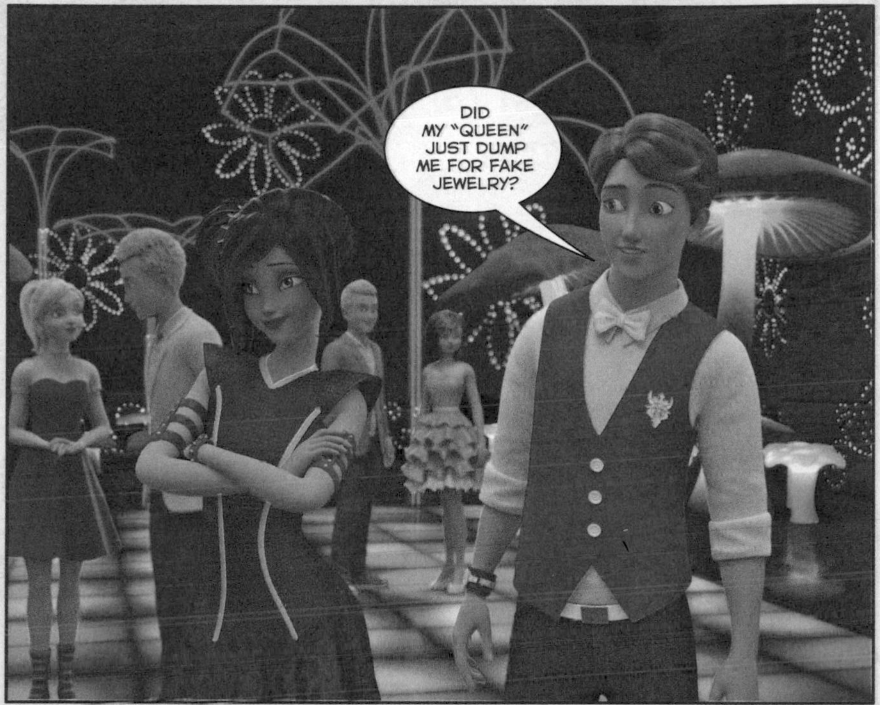
DID MY "QUEEN" JUST DUMP ME FOR FAKE JEWELRY?

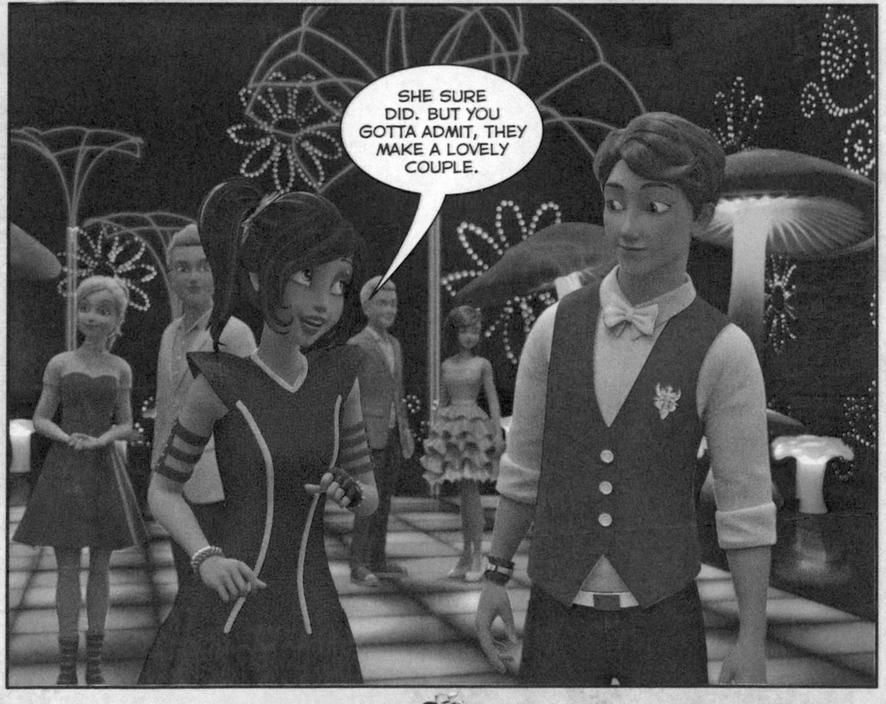
SHE SURE DID. BUT YOU GOTTA ADMIT, THEY MAKE A LOVELY COUPLE.

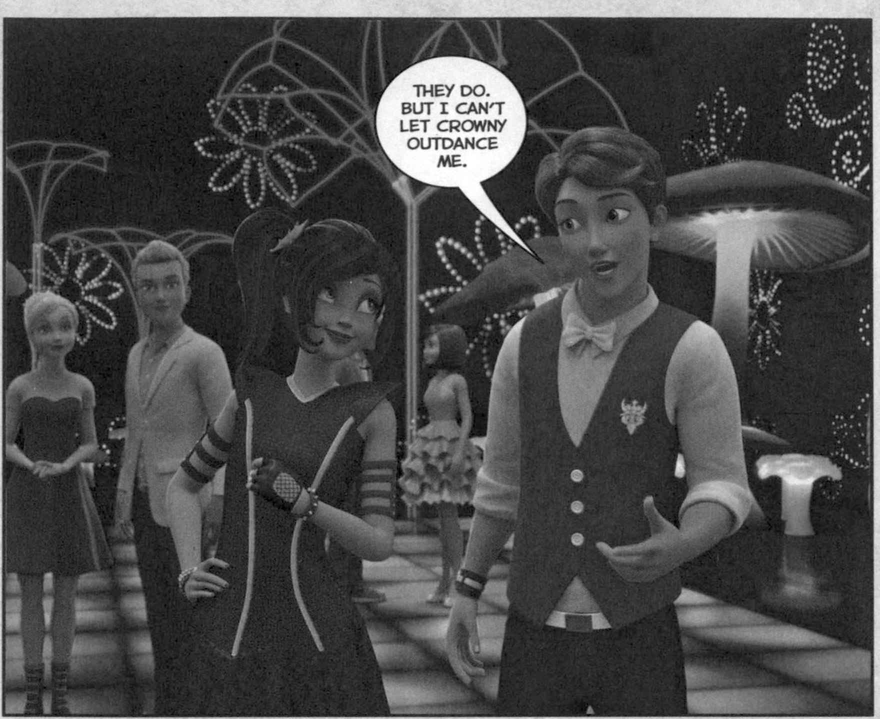
THEY DO. BUT I CAN'T LET CROWNY OUTDANCE ME.

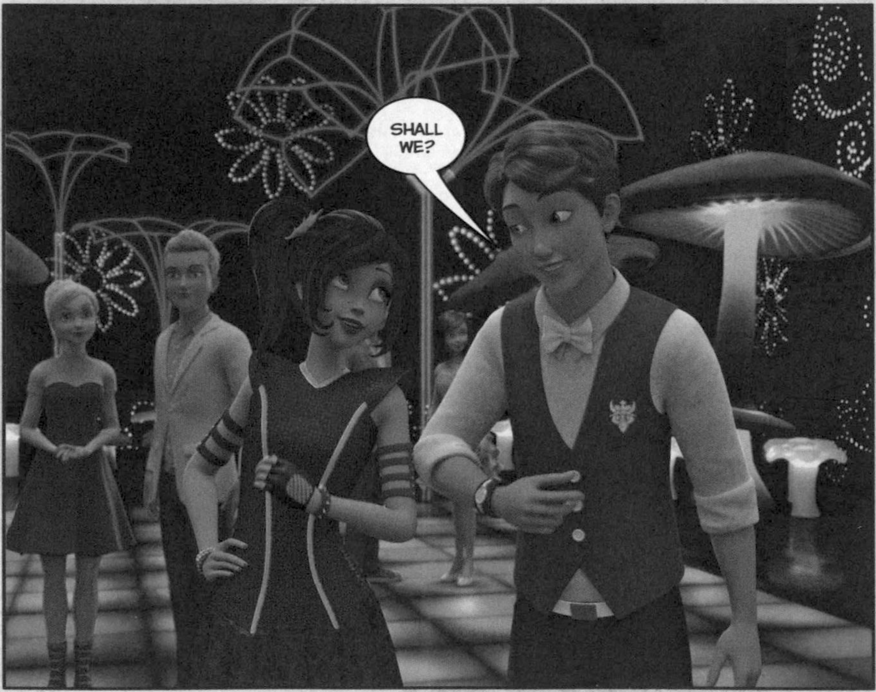
SHALL WE?

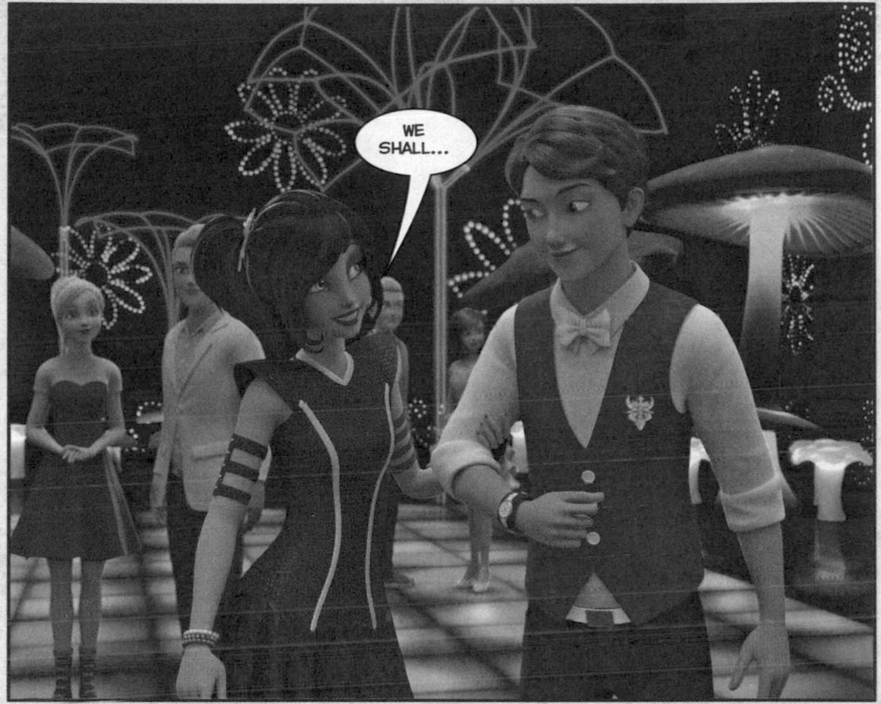
WE SHALL...

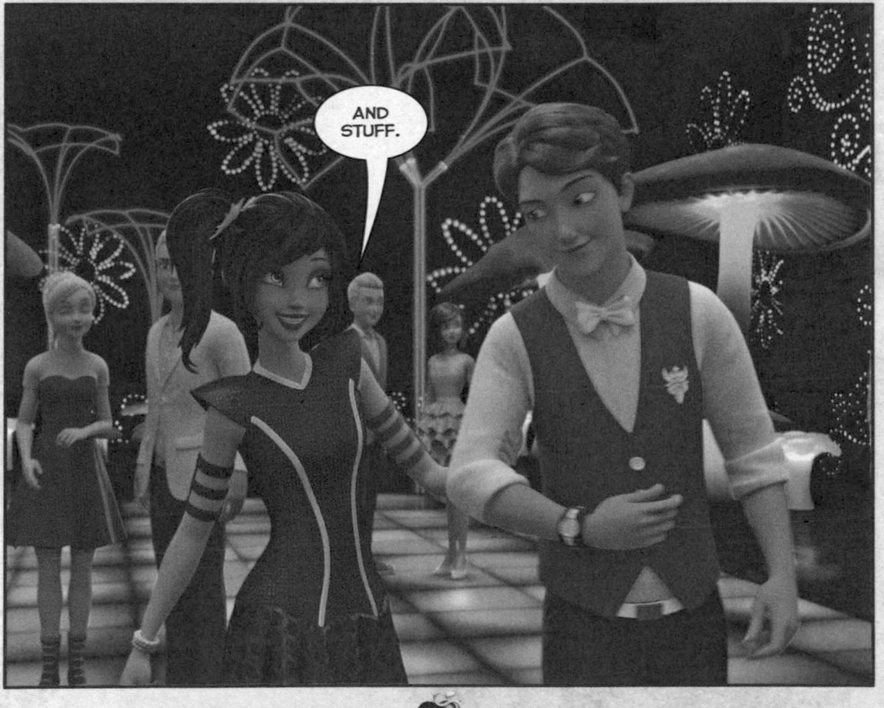
AND STUFF.

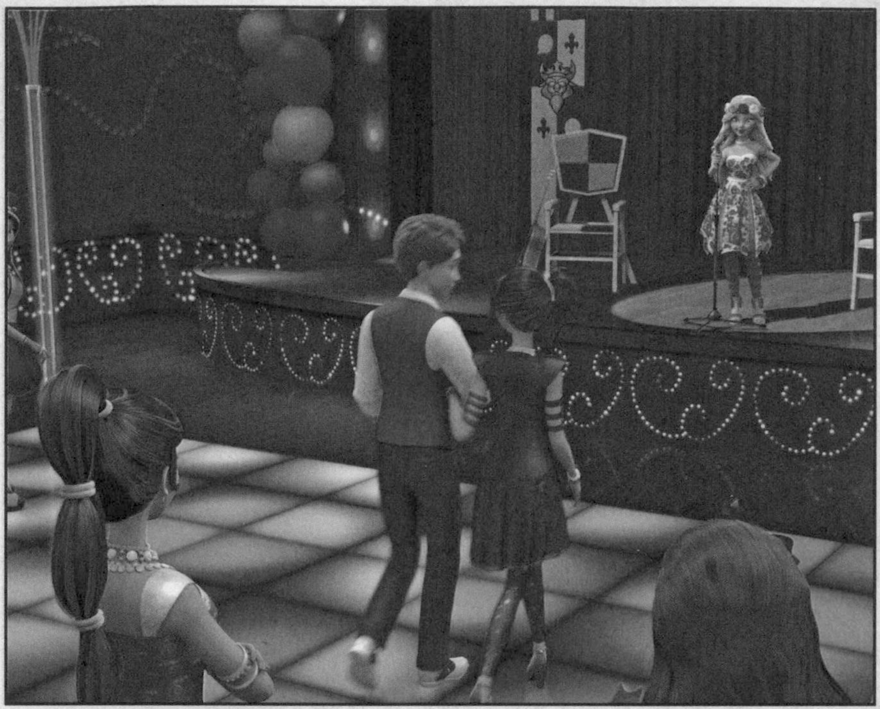

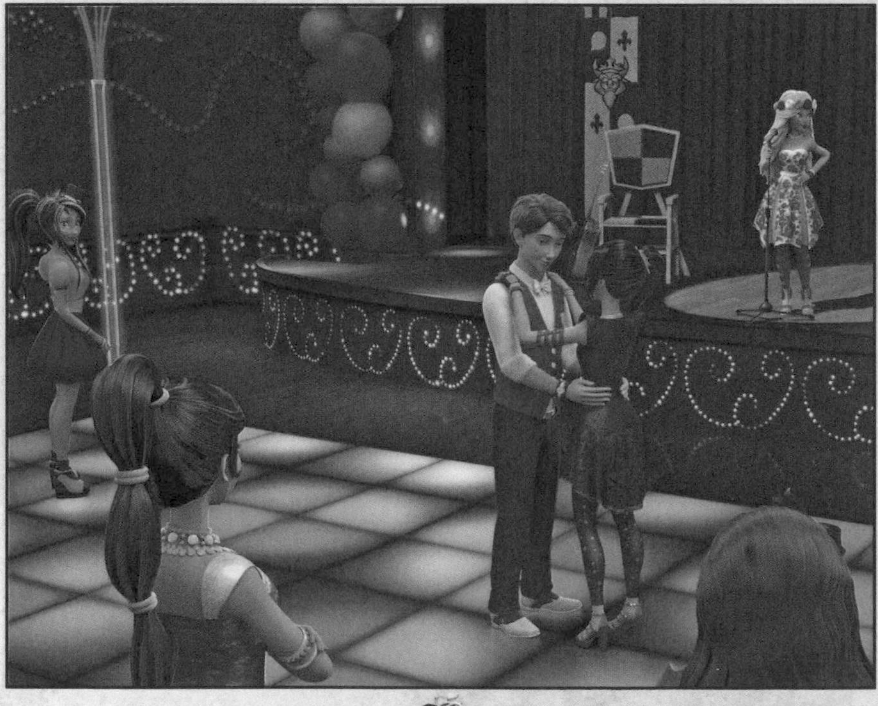

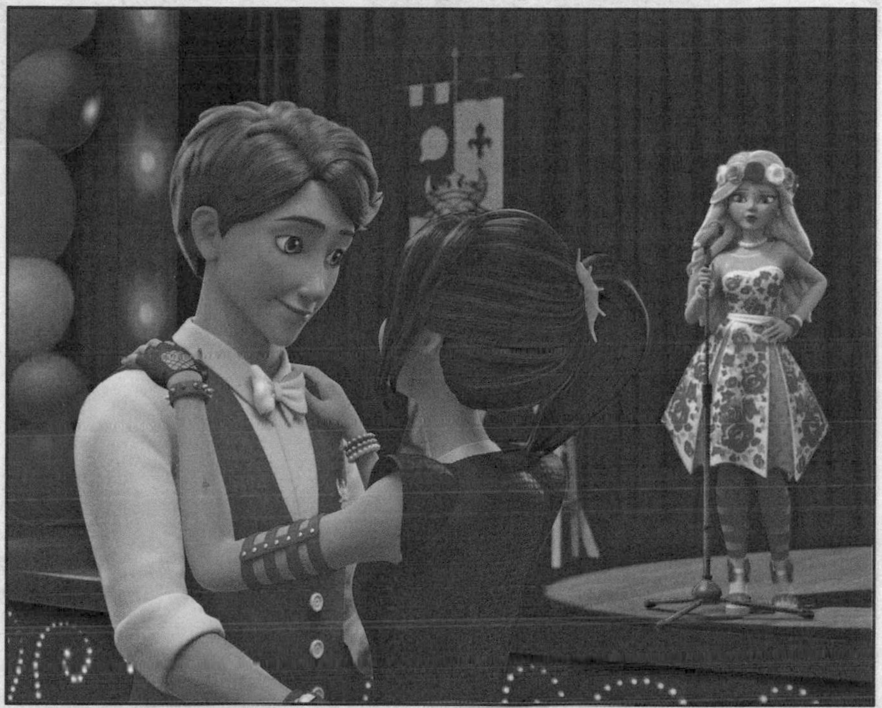

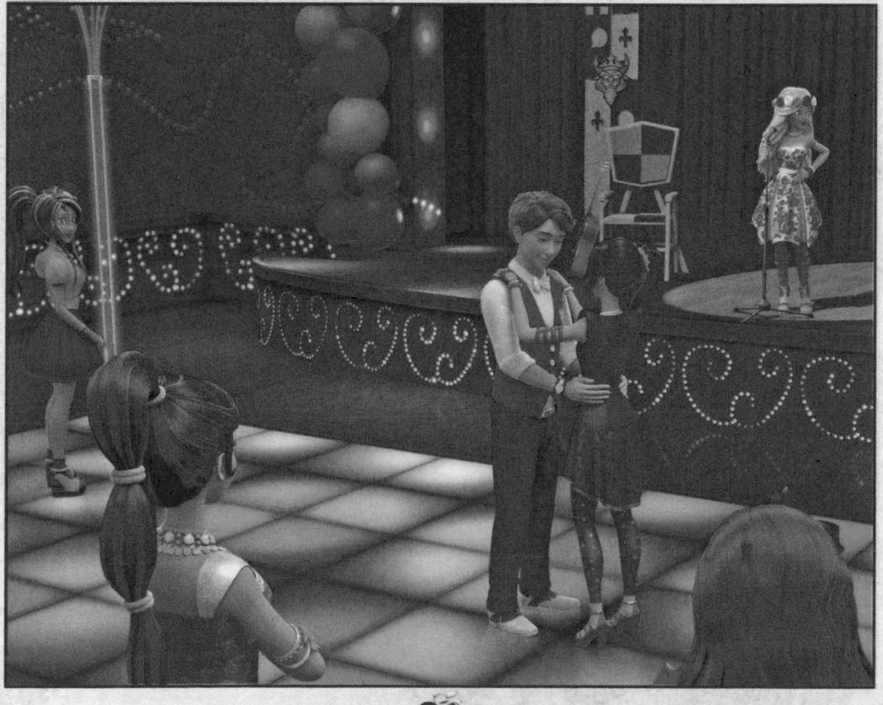

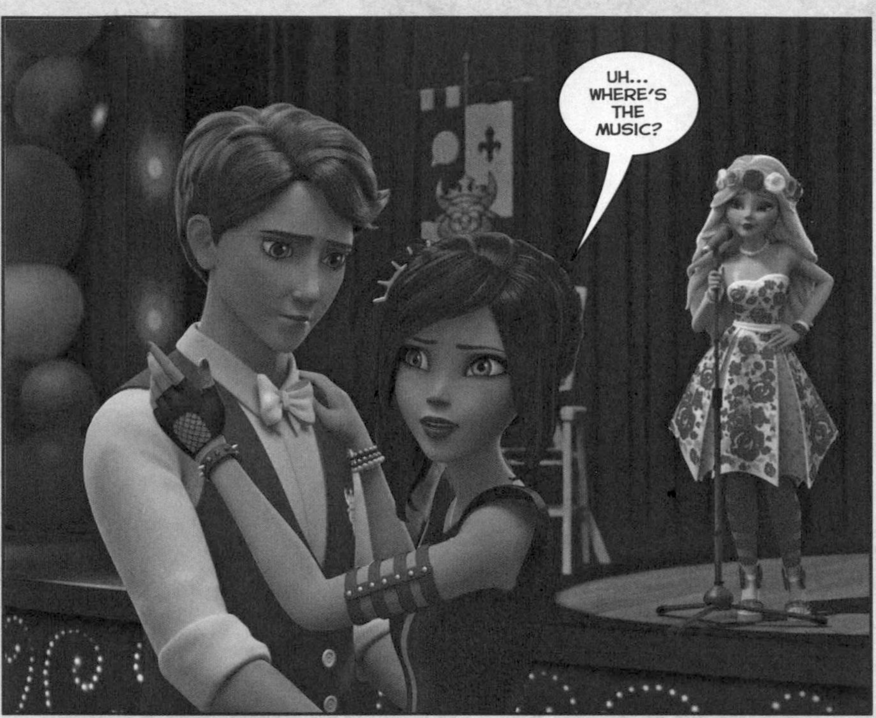
UH... WHERE'S THE MUSIC?

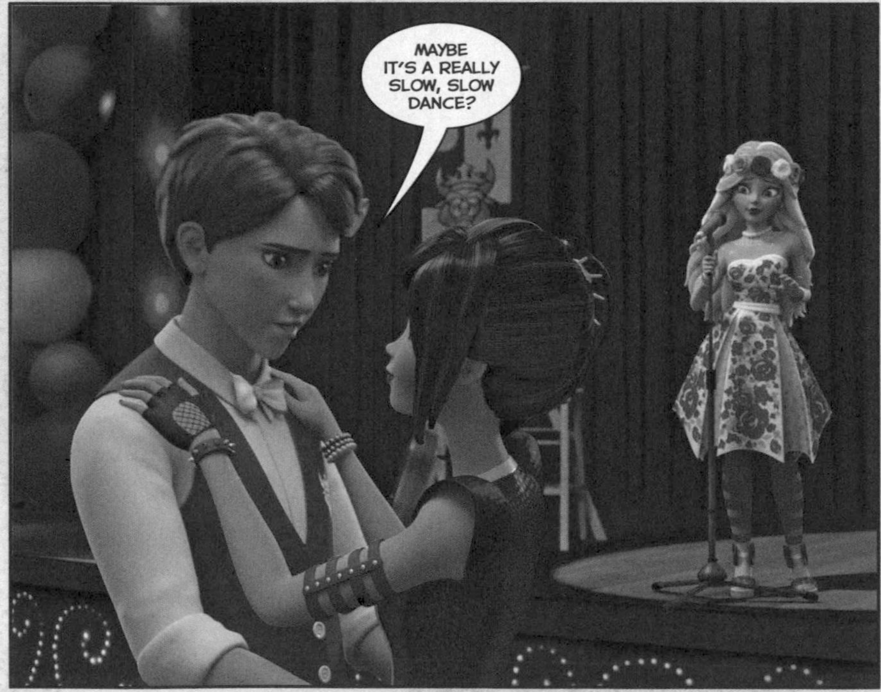
MAYBE IT'S A REALLY SLOW, SLOW DANCE?

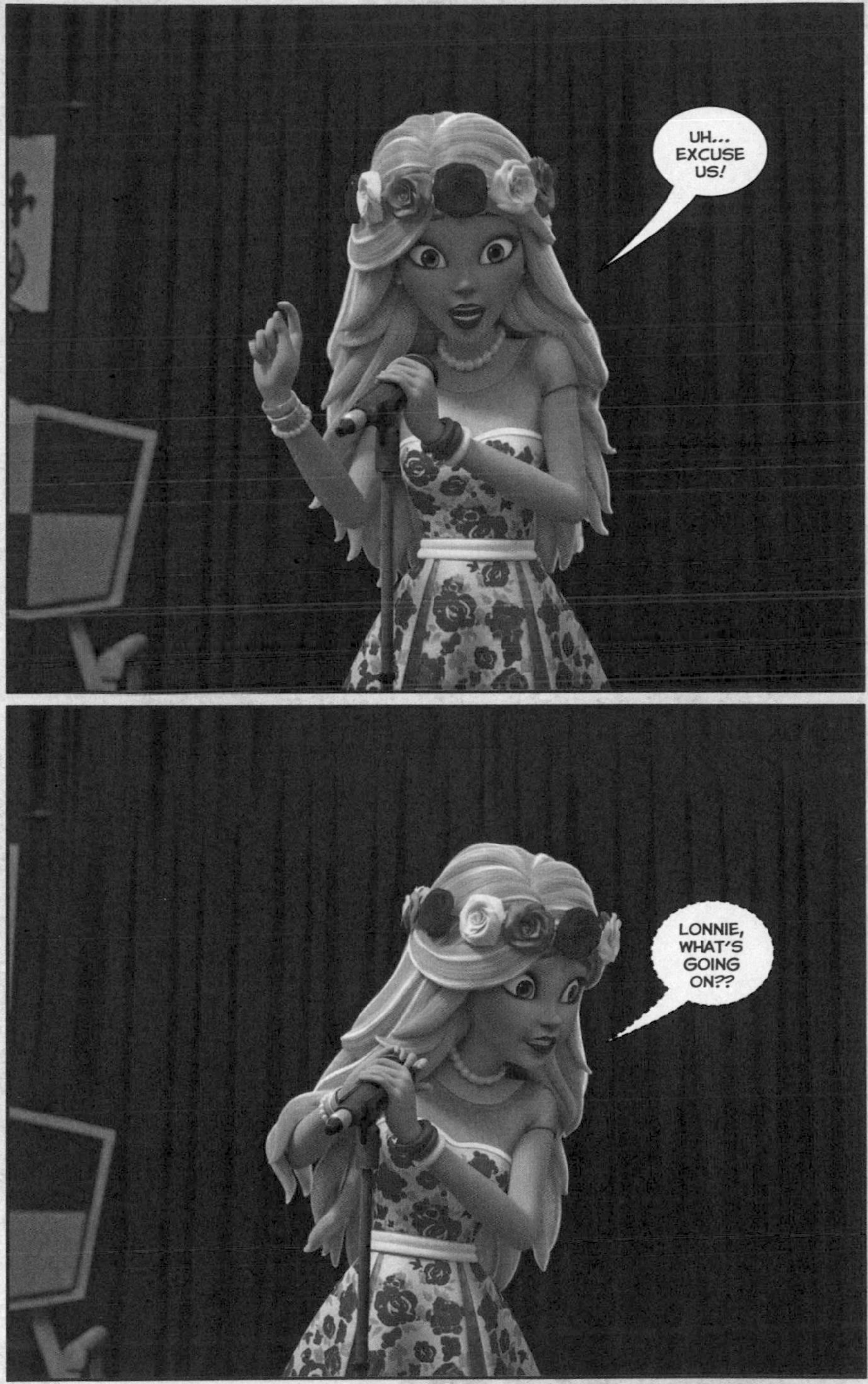
UH... EXCUSE US!
LONNIE, WHAT'S GOING ON??

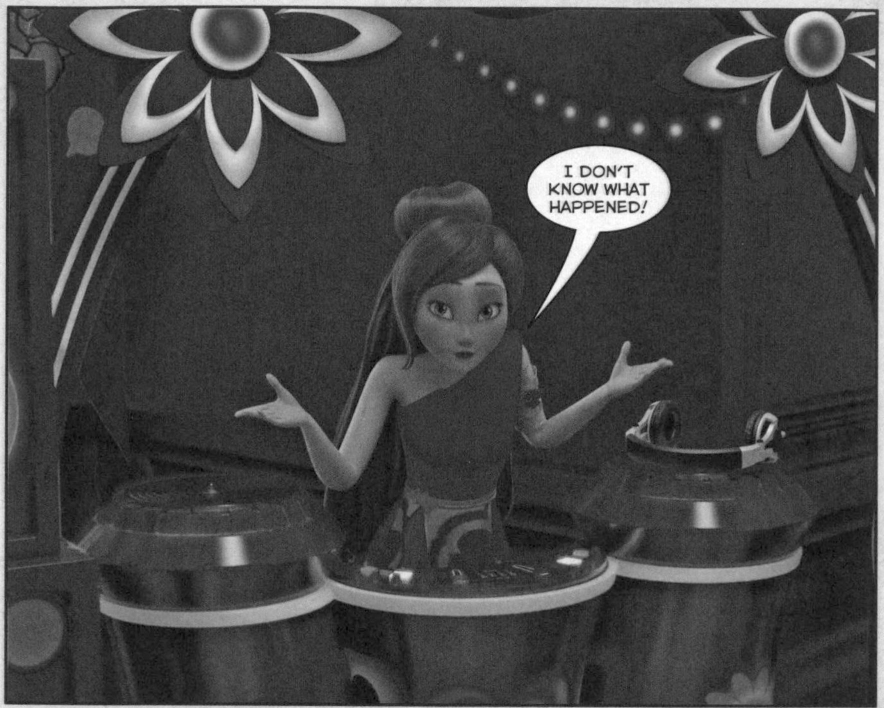
I DON'T KNOW WHAT HAPPENED!

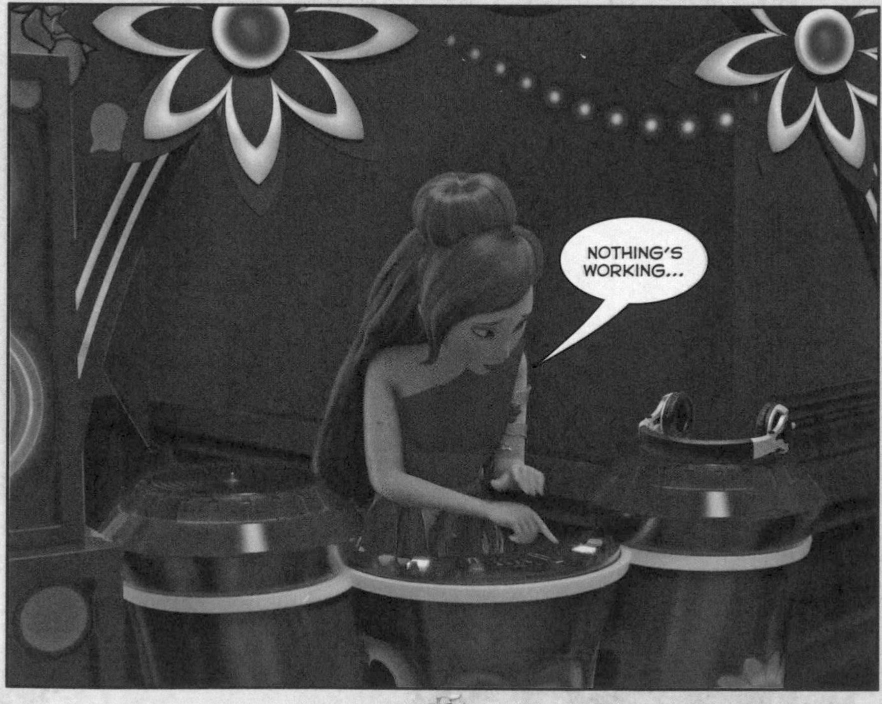
NOTHING'S WORKING...

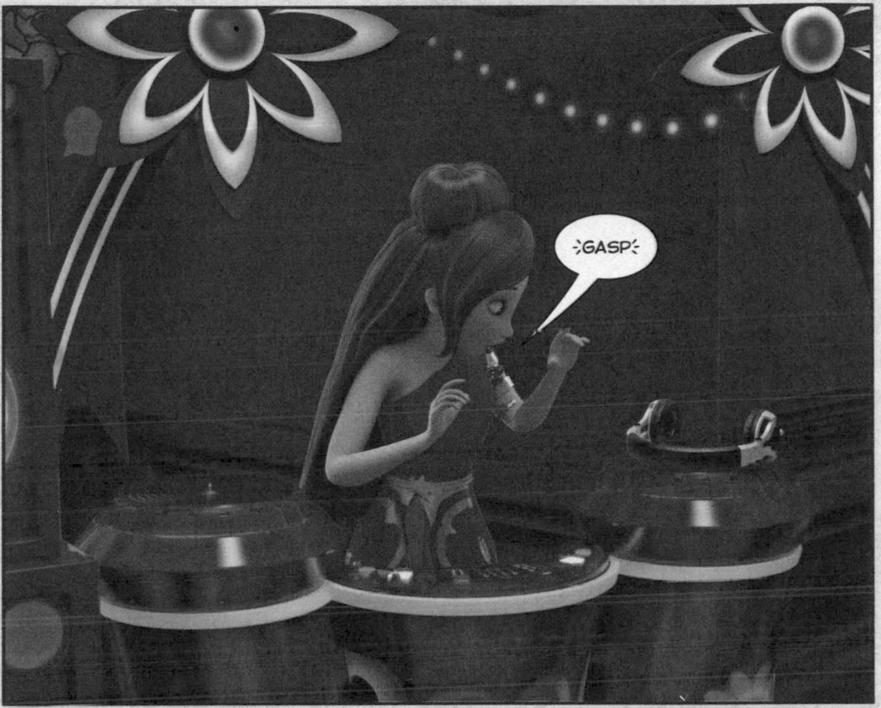
GASP

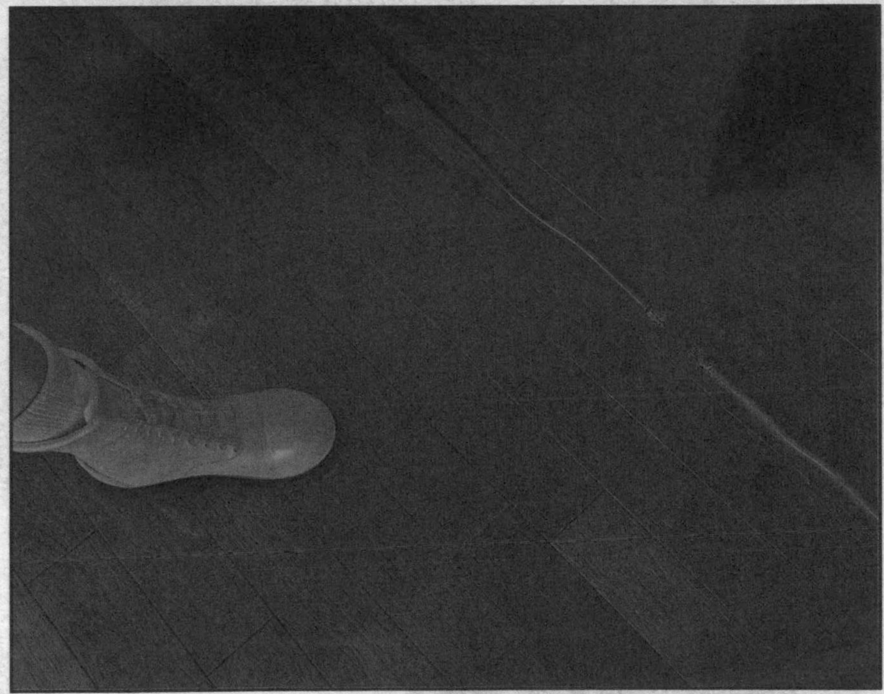

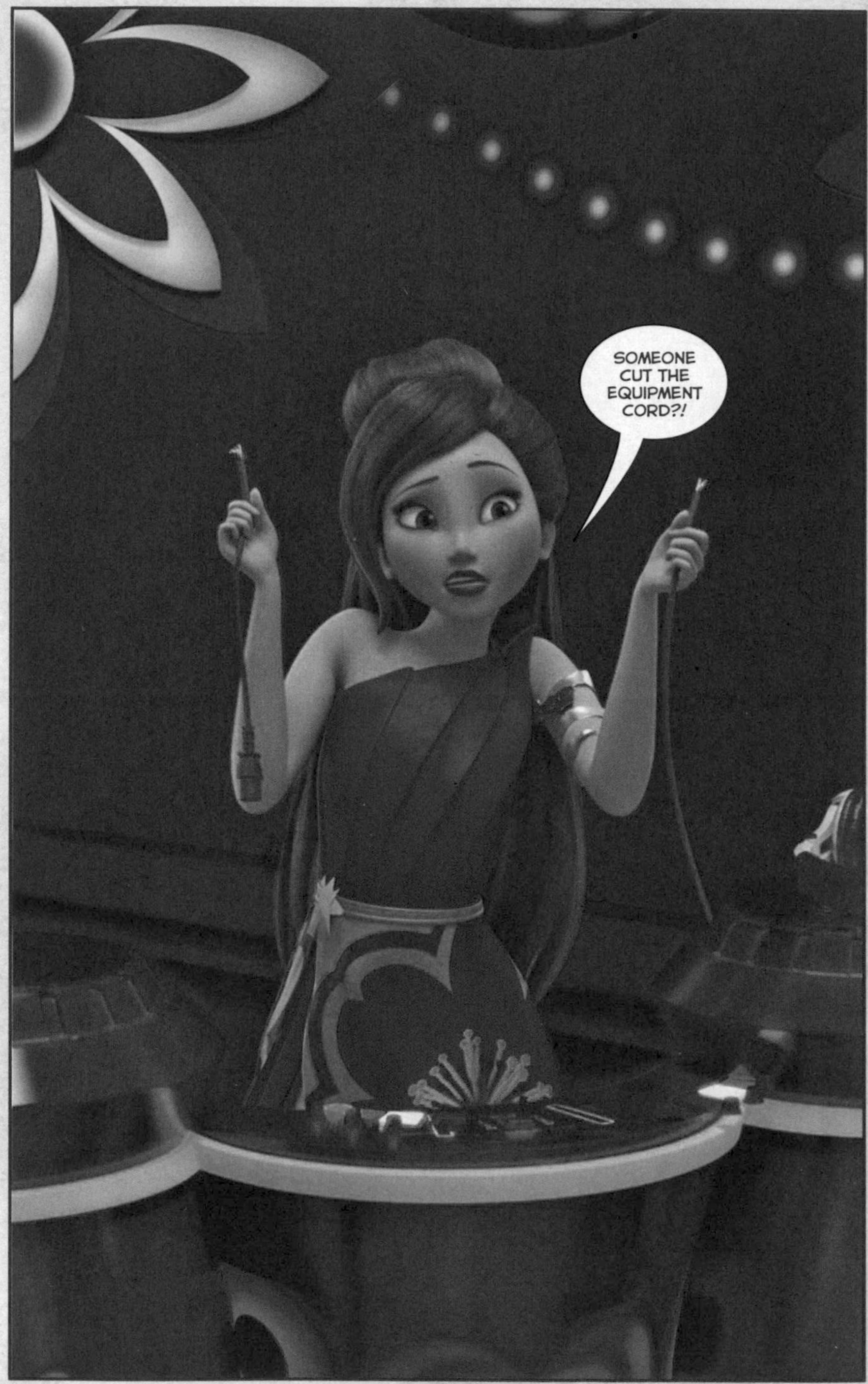
SOMEONE CUT THE EQUIPMENT CORD?!

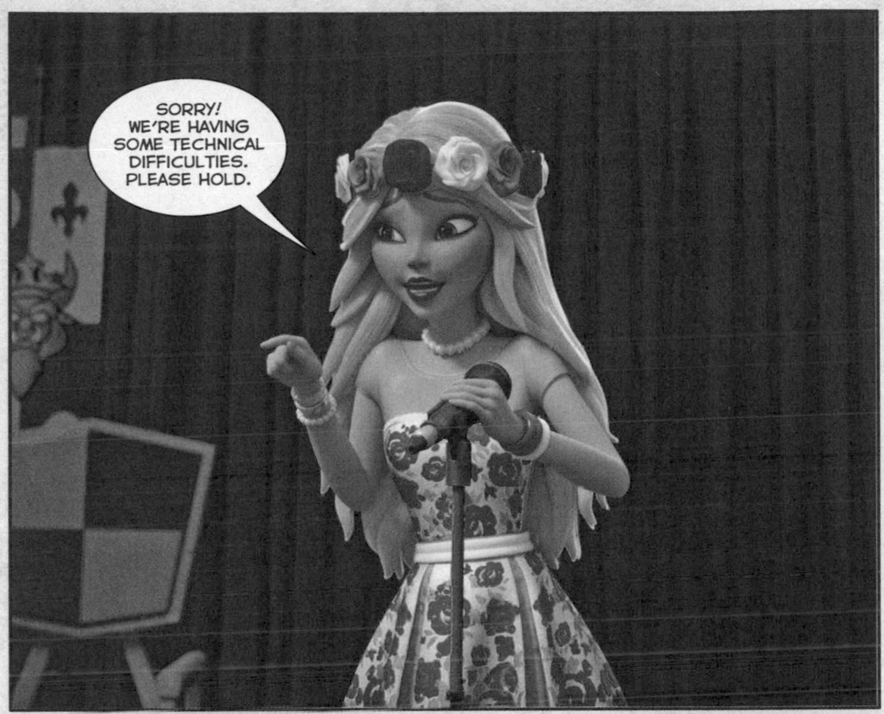
SORRY! WE'RE HAVING SOME TECHNICAL DIFFICULTIES. PLEASE HOLD.

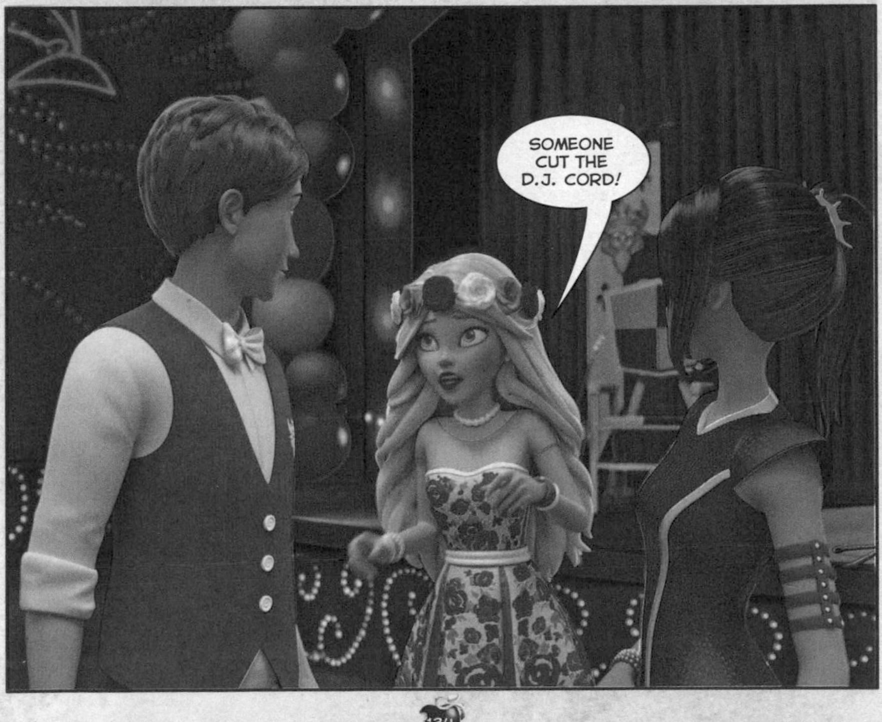
SOMEONE CUT THE D.J. CORD!

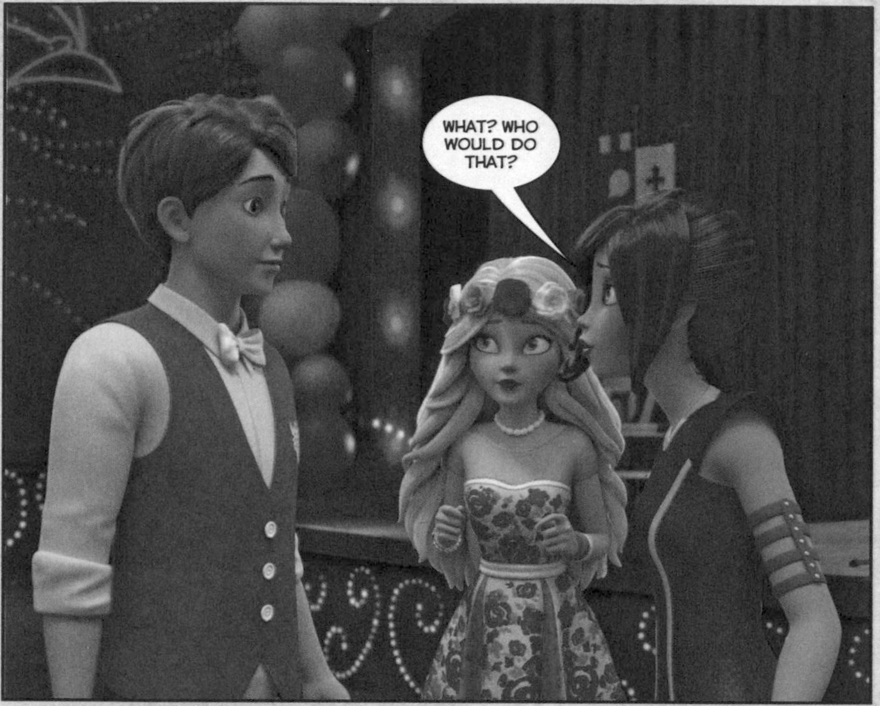
WHAT? WHO WOULD DO THAT?

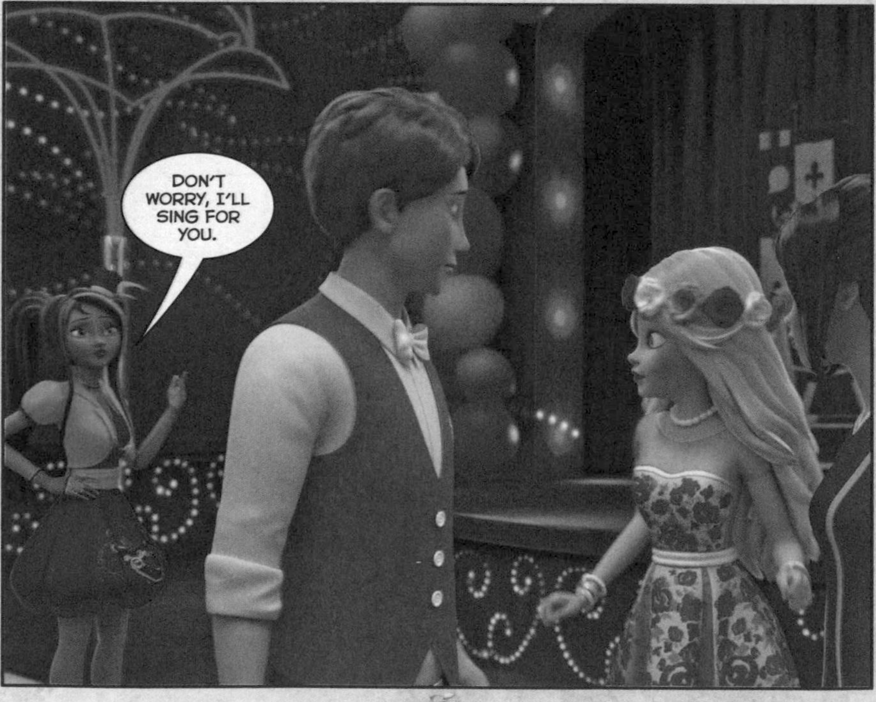
DON'T WORRY, I'LL SING FOR YOU.

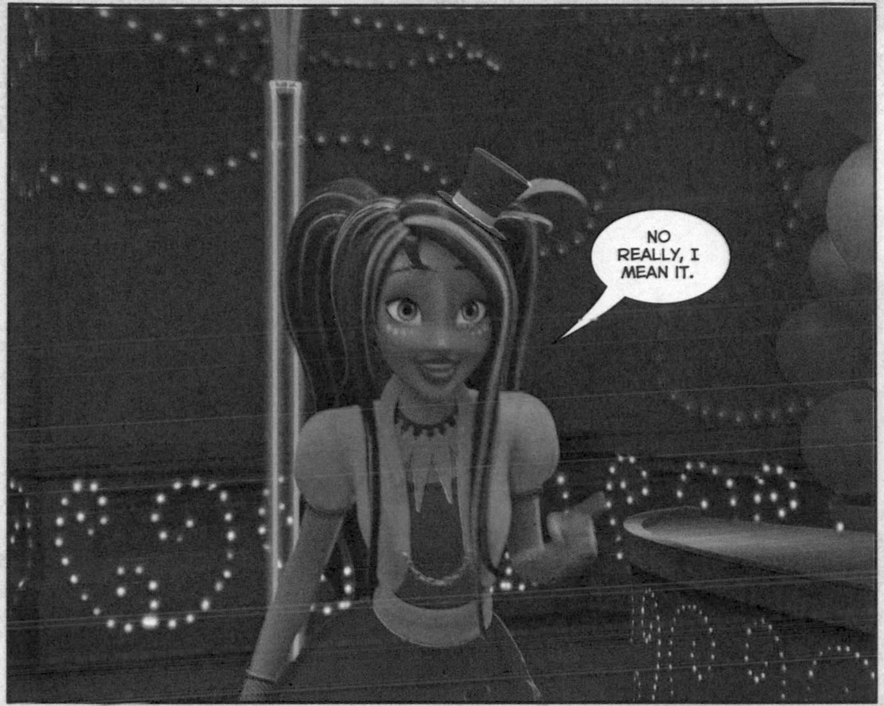
NO REALLY, I MEAN IT.

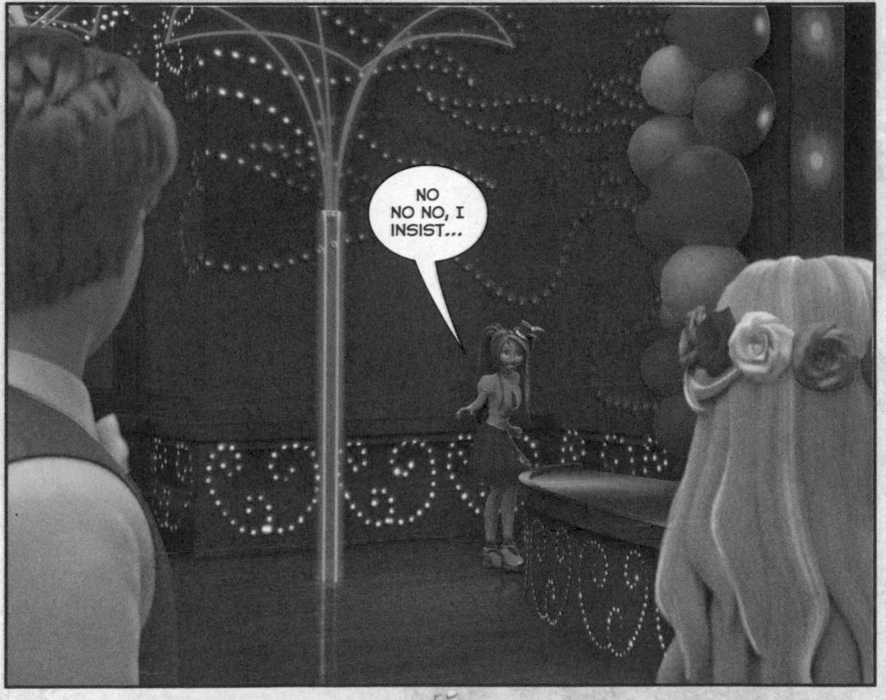
NO NO NO, I INSIST...

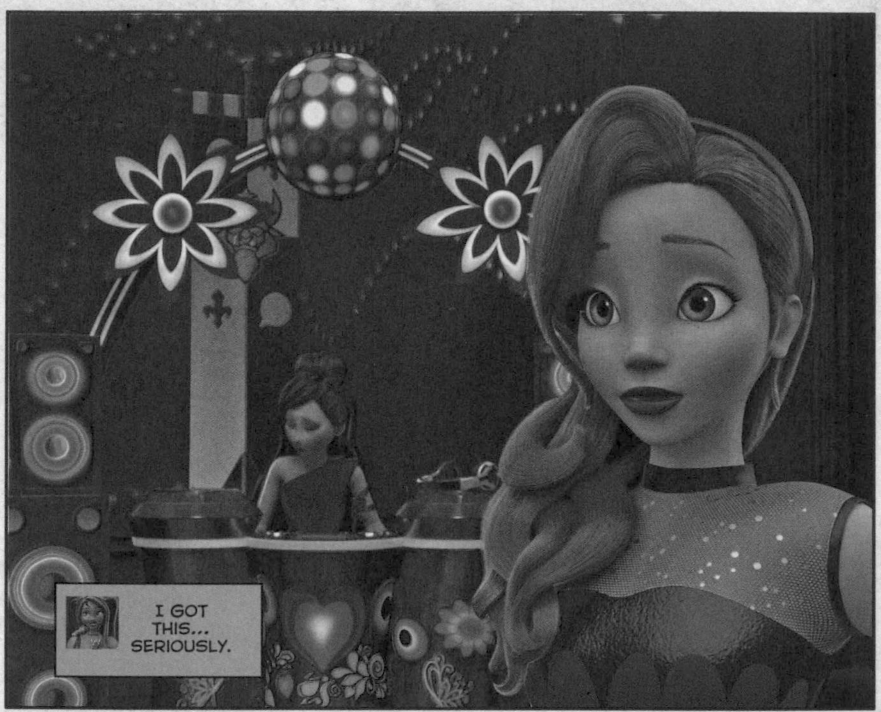
I GOT THIS... SERIOUSLY.

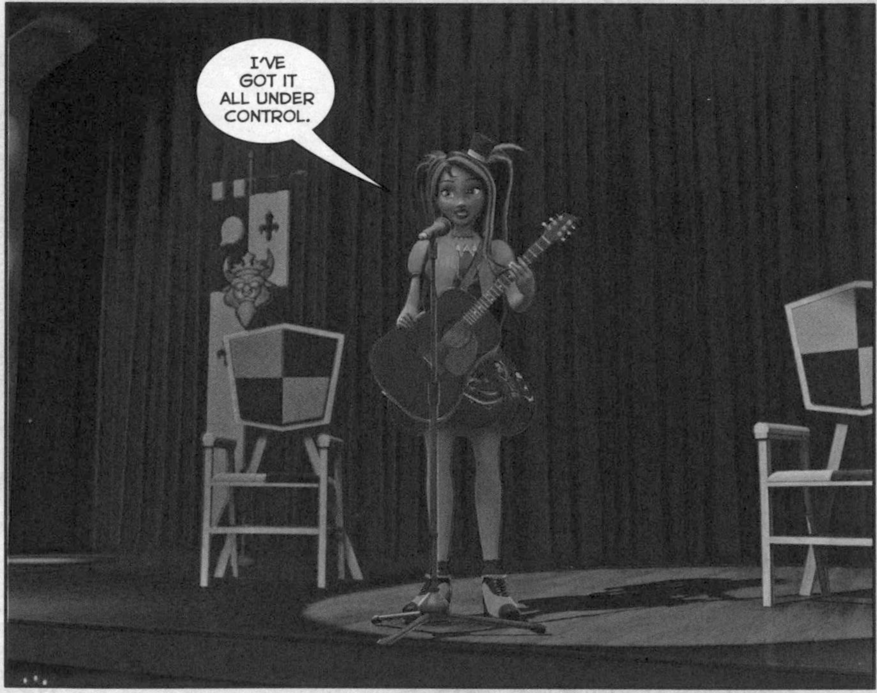
I'VE GOT IT ALL UNDER CONTROL.

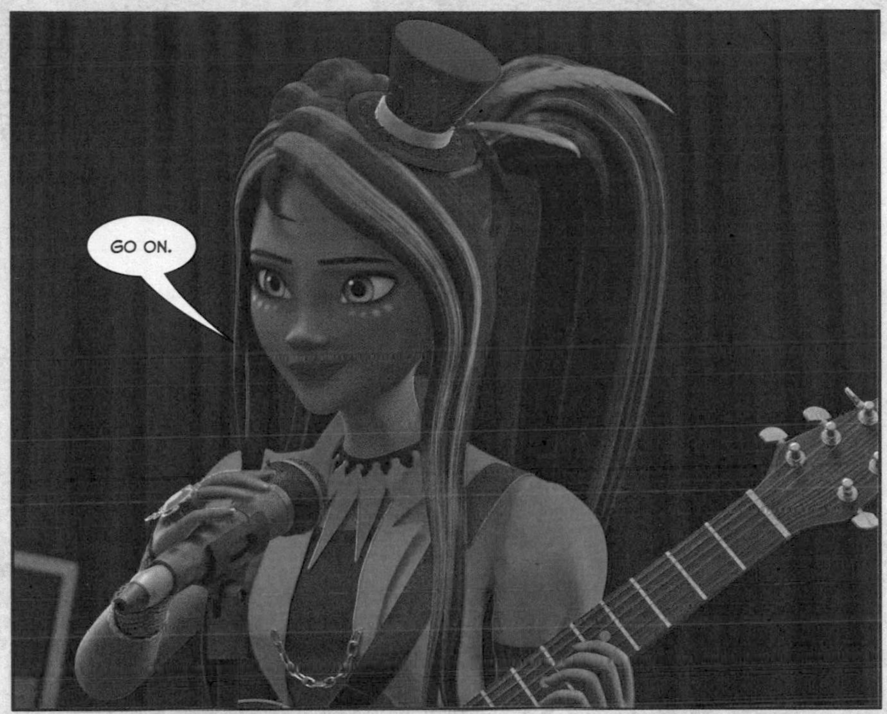
GO ON.

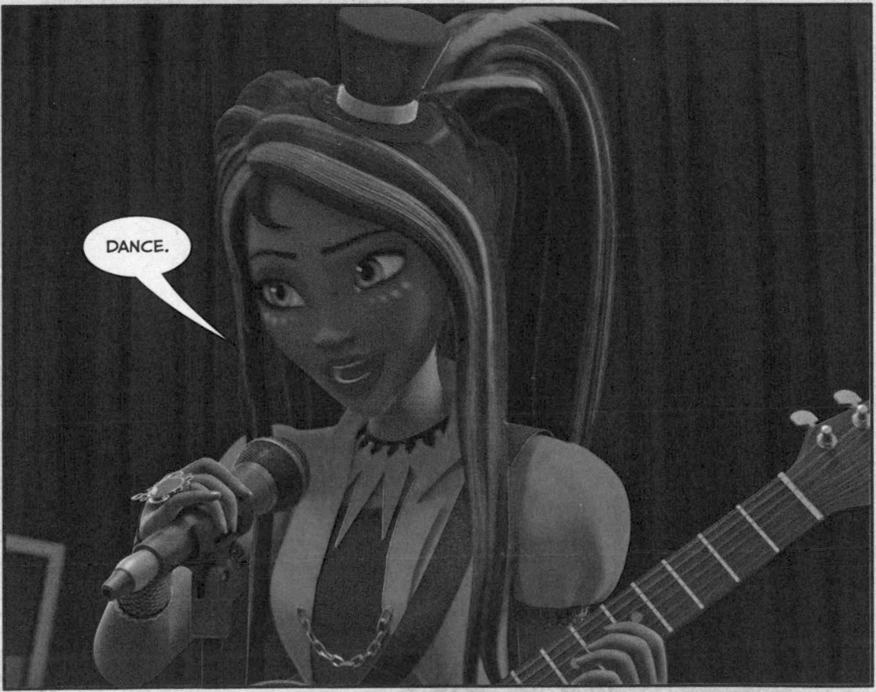
DANCE.

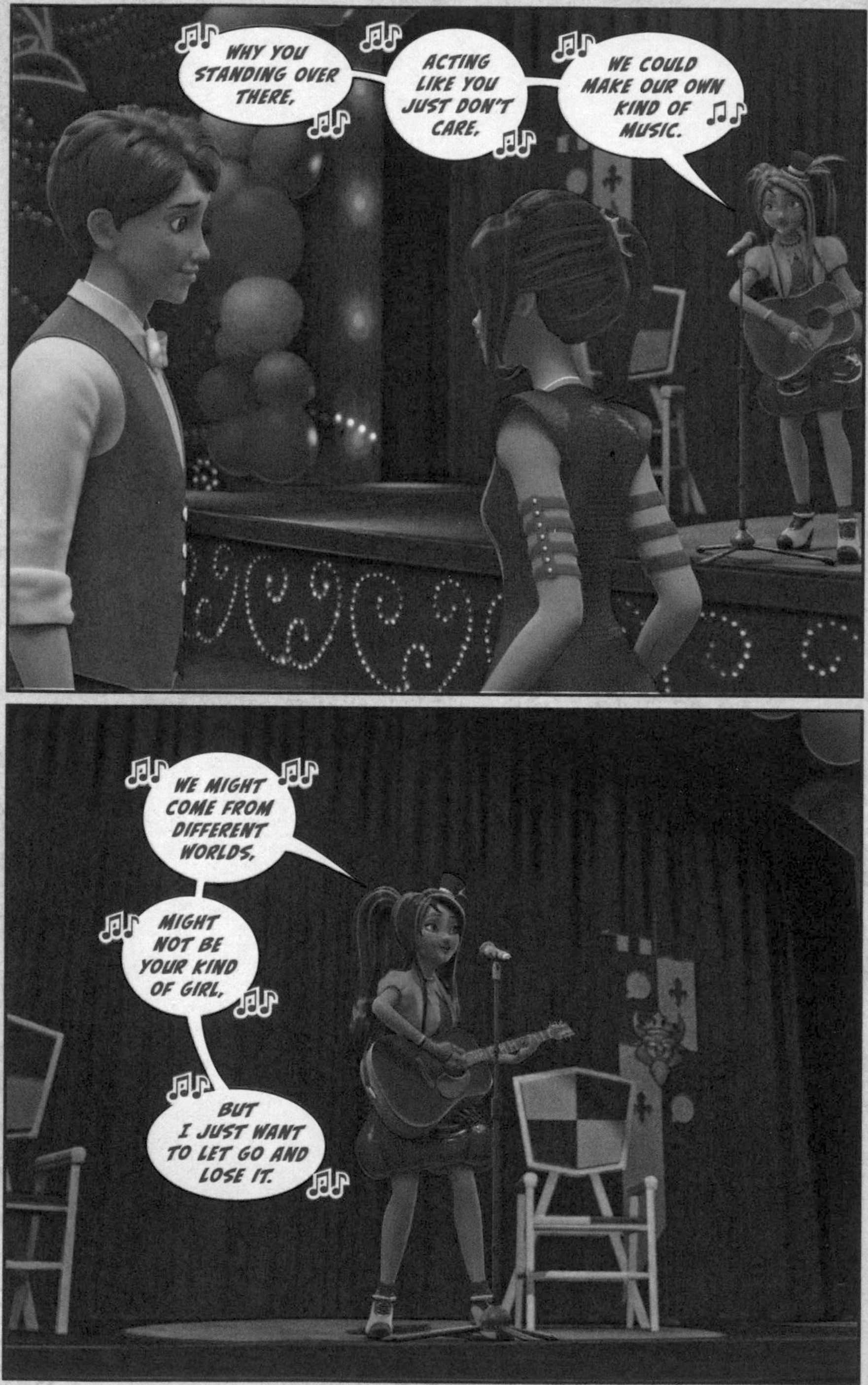
WHY YOU STANDING OVER THERE,
ACTING LIKE YOU JUST DON'T CARE,
WE COULD MAKE OUR OWN KIND OF MUSIC.
WE MIGHT COME FROM DIFFERENT WORLDS,
MIGHT NOT BE YOUR KIND OF GIRL,
BUT I JUST WANT TO LET GO AND LOSE IT.

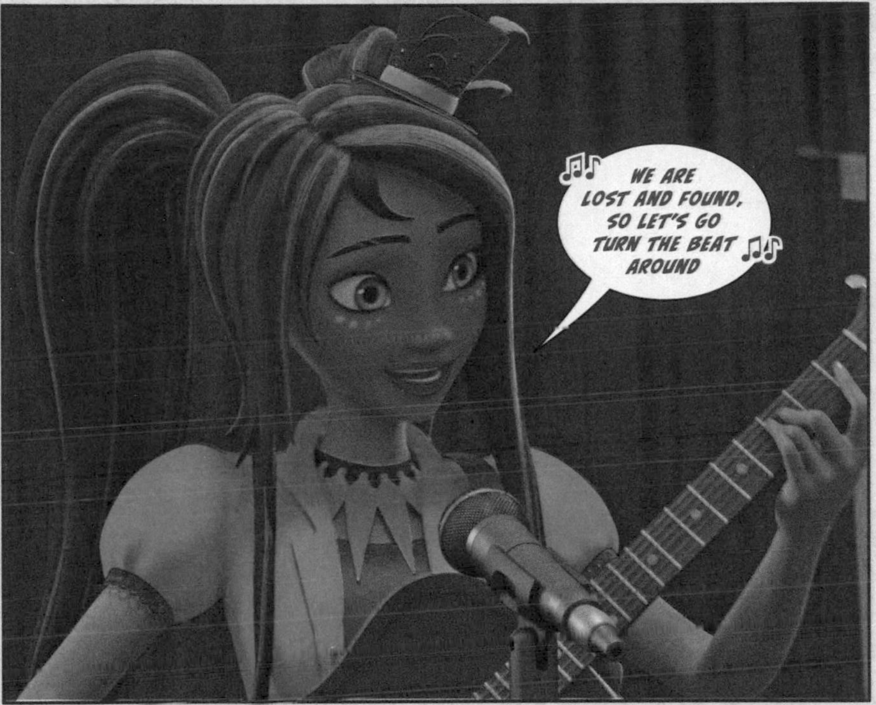
WE ARE LOST AND FOUND, SO LET'S GO TURN THE BEAT AROUND

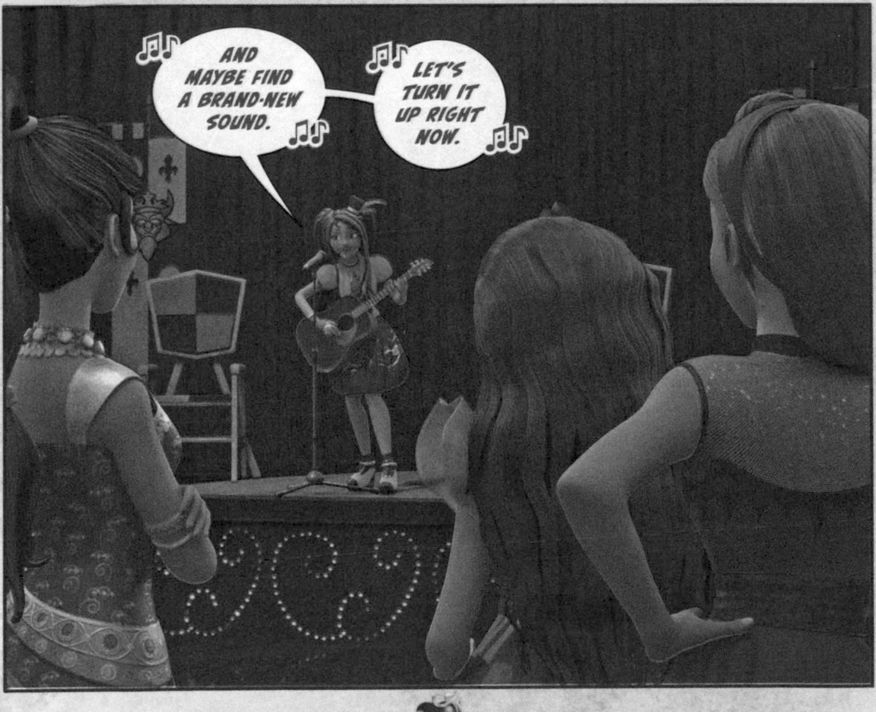
AND MAYBE FIND A BRAND-NEW SOUND.
LET'S TURN IT UP RIGHT NOW.

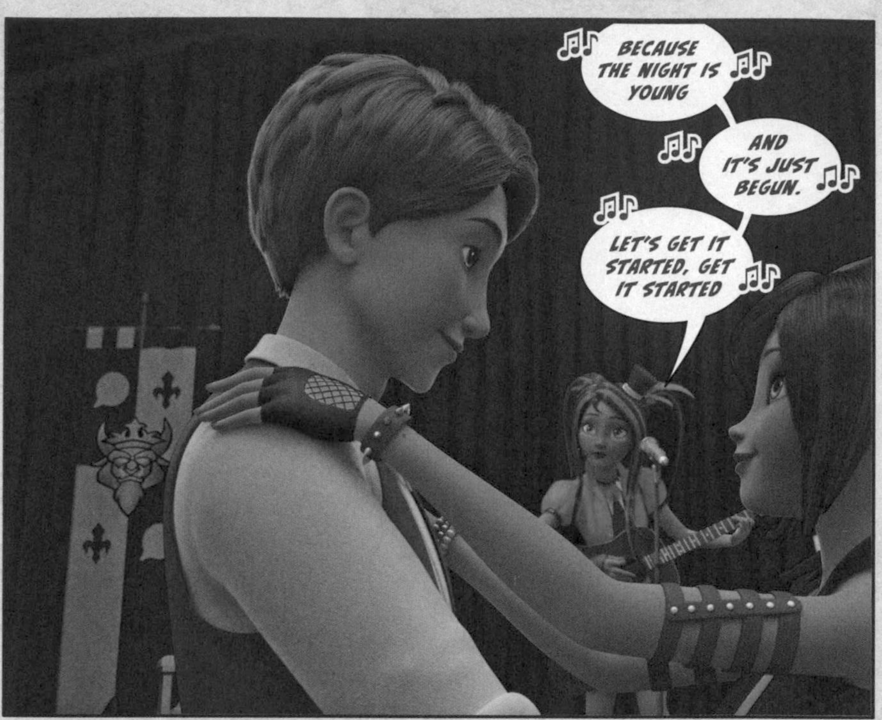
BECAUSE THE NIGHT IS YOUNG
AND IT'S JUST BEGUN.
LET'S GET IT STARTED, GET IT STARTED

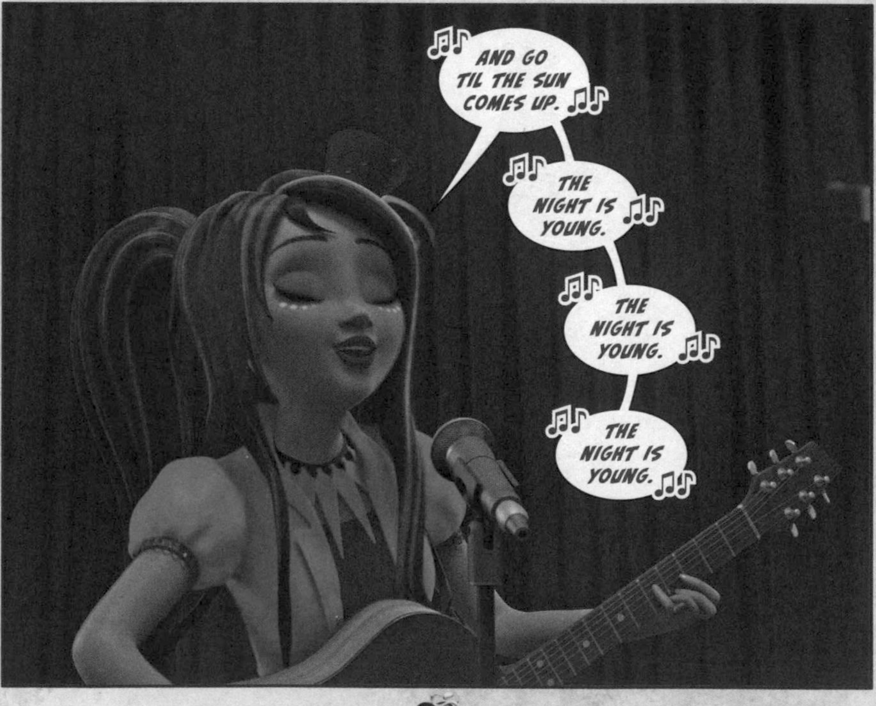
AND GO TIL THE SUN COMES UP.
THE NIGHT IS YOUNG.
THE NIGHT IS YOUNG.
THE NIGHT IS YOUNG.

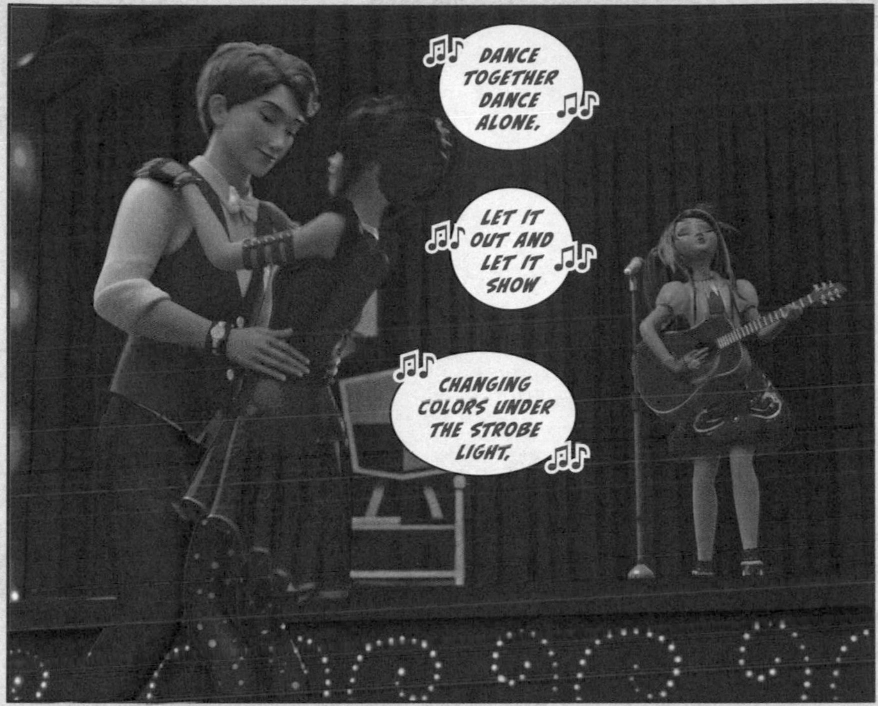
DANCE TOGETHER DANCE ALONE,
LET IT OUT AND LET IT SHOW
CHANGING COLORS UNDER THE STROBE LIGHT,

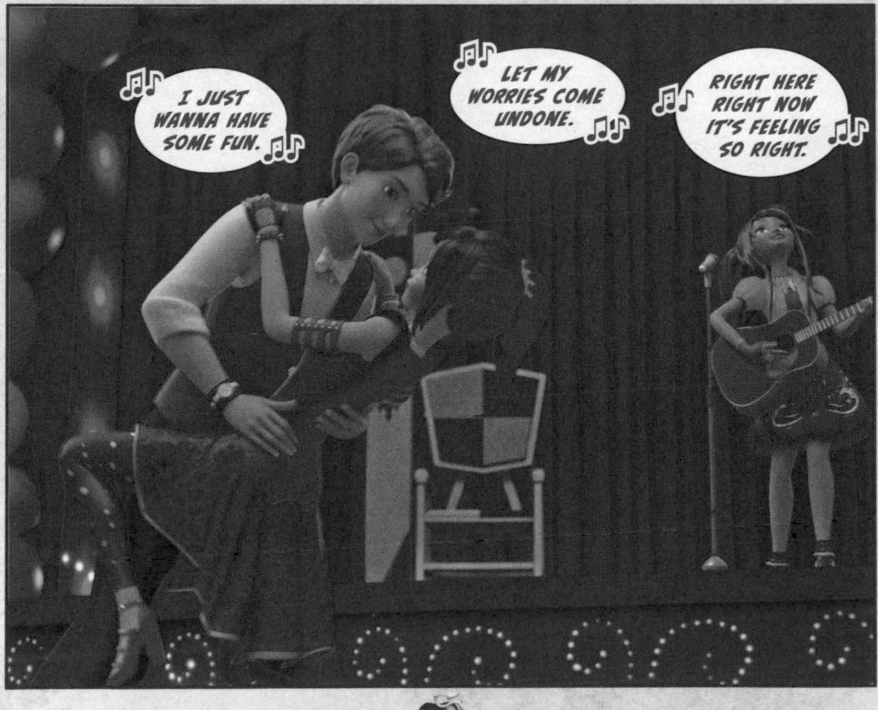
I JUST WANNA HAVE SOME FUN.
LET MY WORRIES COME UNDONE.
RIGHT HERE RIGHT NOW IT'S FEELING SO RIGHT.

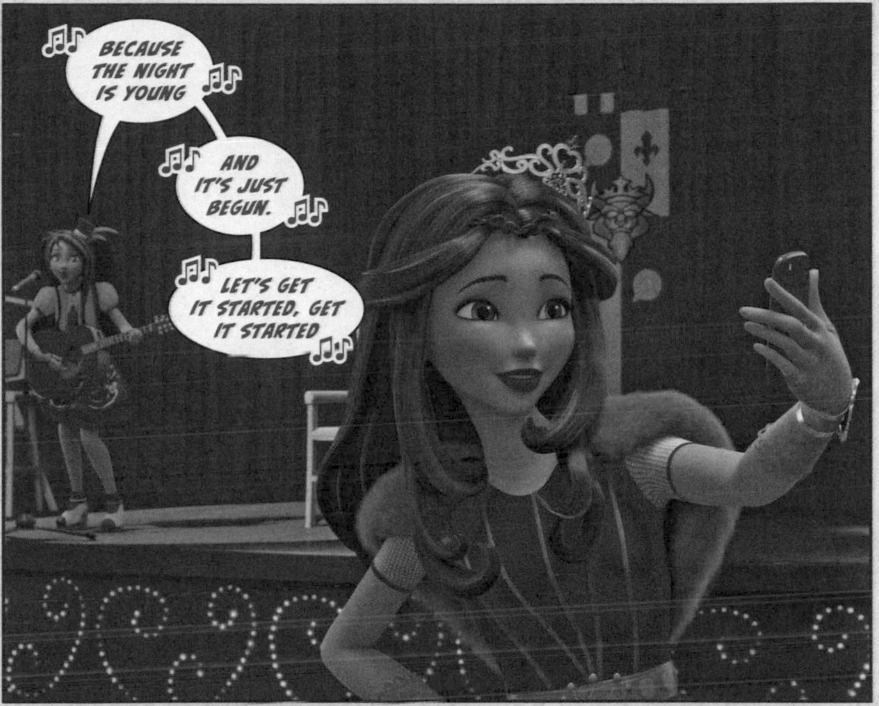
BECAUSE THE NIGHT IS YOUNG
AND IT'S JUST BEGUN.
LET'S GET IT STARTED, GET IT STARTED

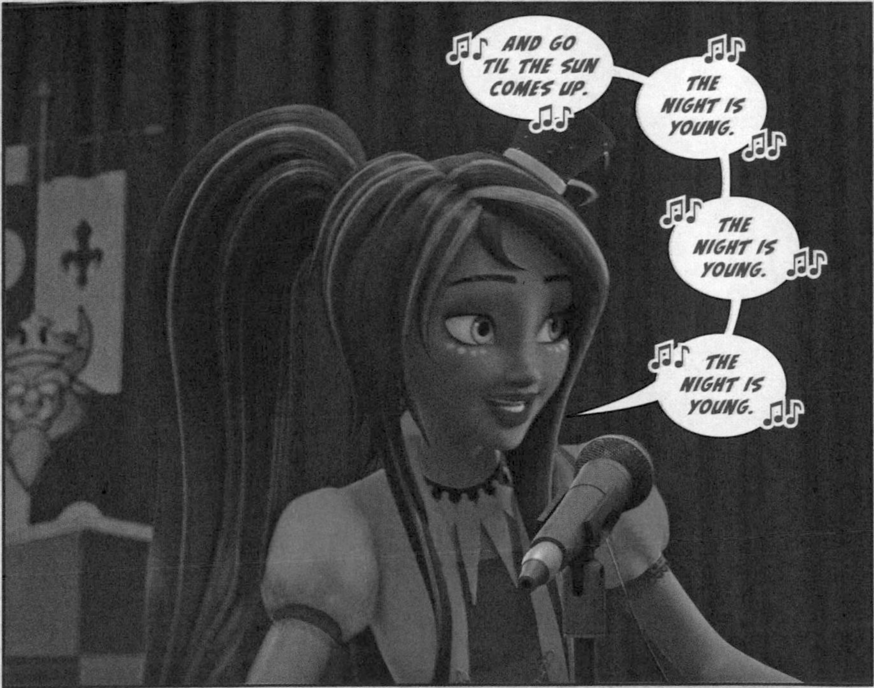
AND GO TIL THE SUN COMES UP.
THE NIGHT IS YOUNG.
THE NIGHT IS YOUNG.
THE NIGHT IS YOUNG.

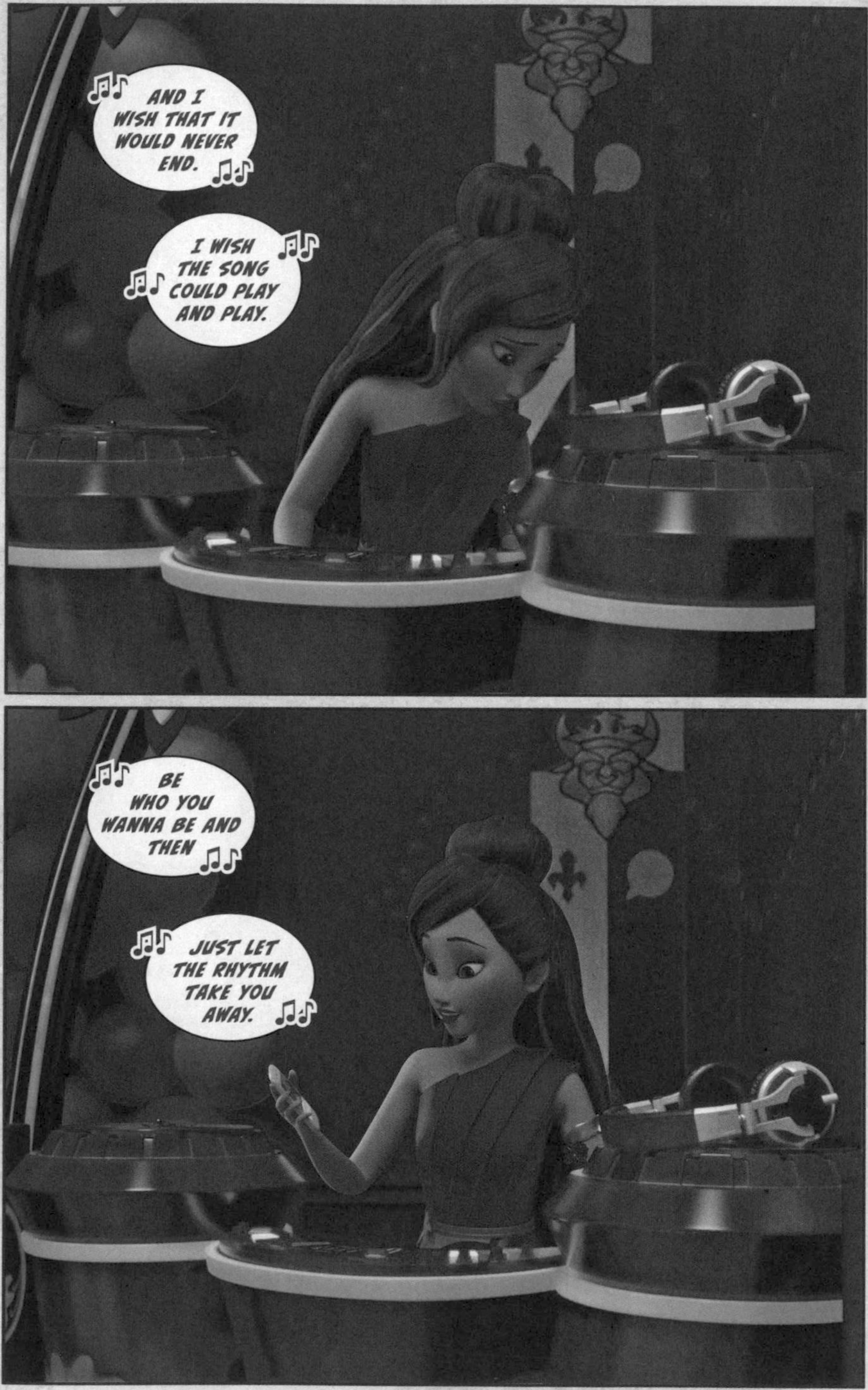
AND I WISH THAT IT WOULD NEVER END.
I WISH THE SONG COULD PLAY AND PLAY.
BE WHO YOU WANNA BE AND THEN
JUST LET THE RHYTHM TAKE YOU AWAY.

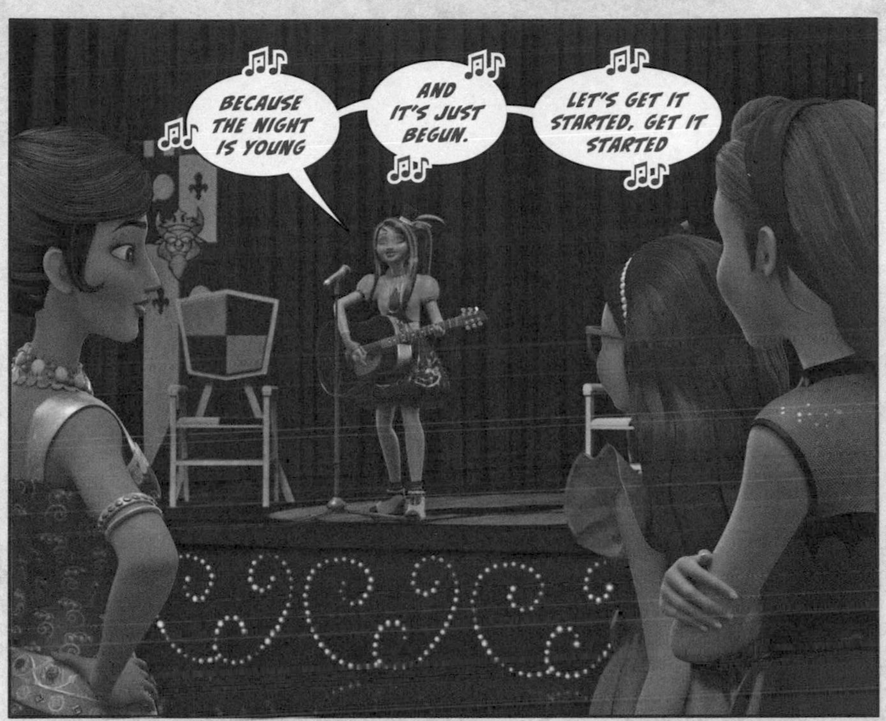
BECAUSE THE NIGHT IS YOUNG
AND IT'S JUST BEGUN.
LET'S GET IT STARTED, GET IT STARTED

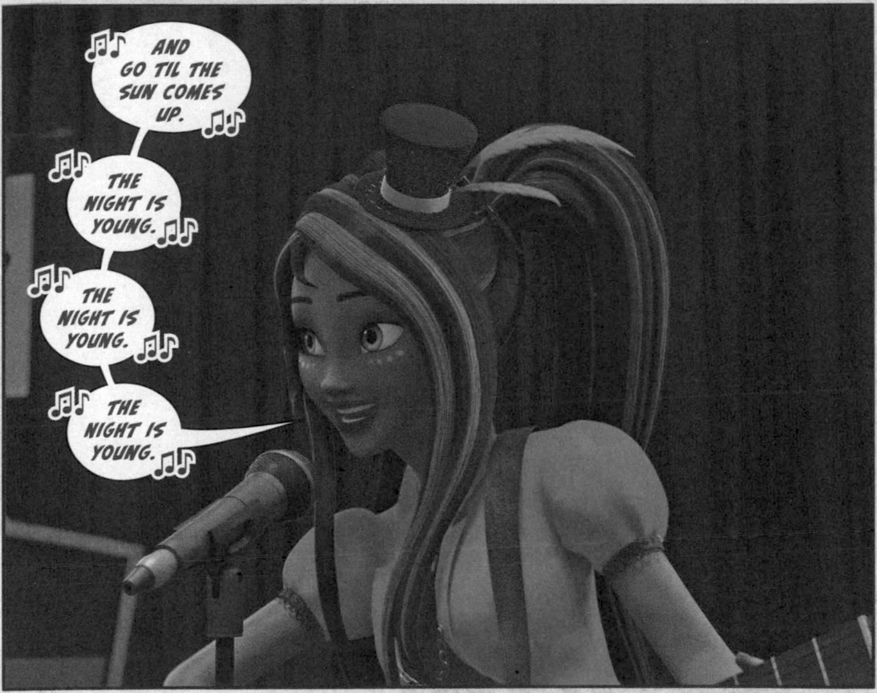
AND GO TIL THE SUN COMES UP.
THE NIGHT IS YOUNG.
THE NIGHT IS YOUNG.
THE NIGHT IS YOUNG.

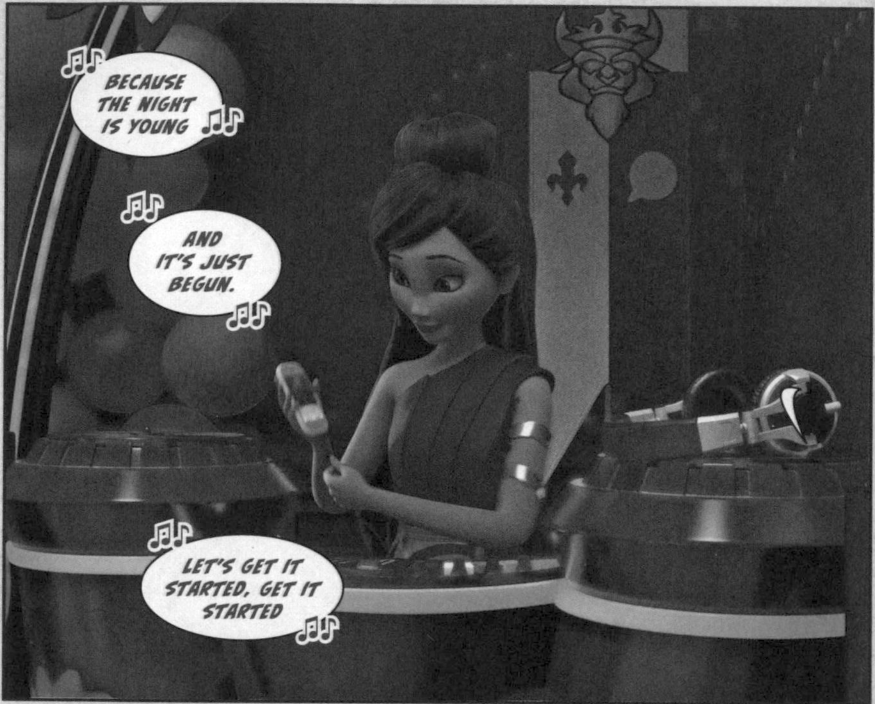
BECAUSE THE NIGHT IS YOUNG
AND IT'S JUST BEGUN.
LET'S GET IT STARTED, GET IT STARTED

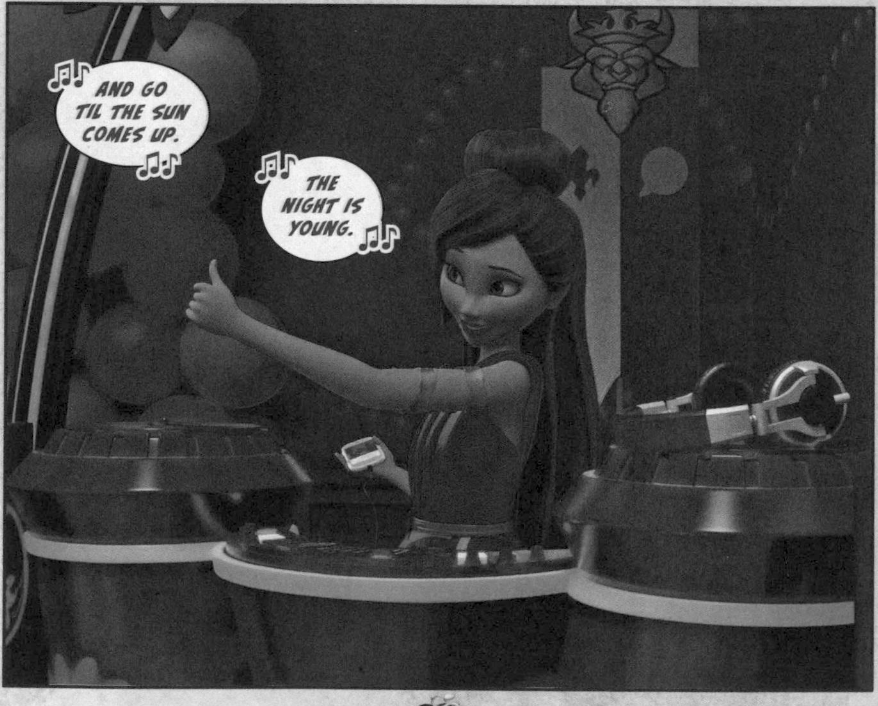
AND GO TIL THE SUN COMES UP.
THE NIGHT IS YOUNG.

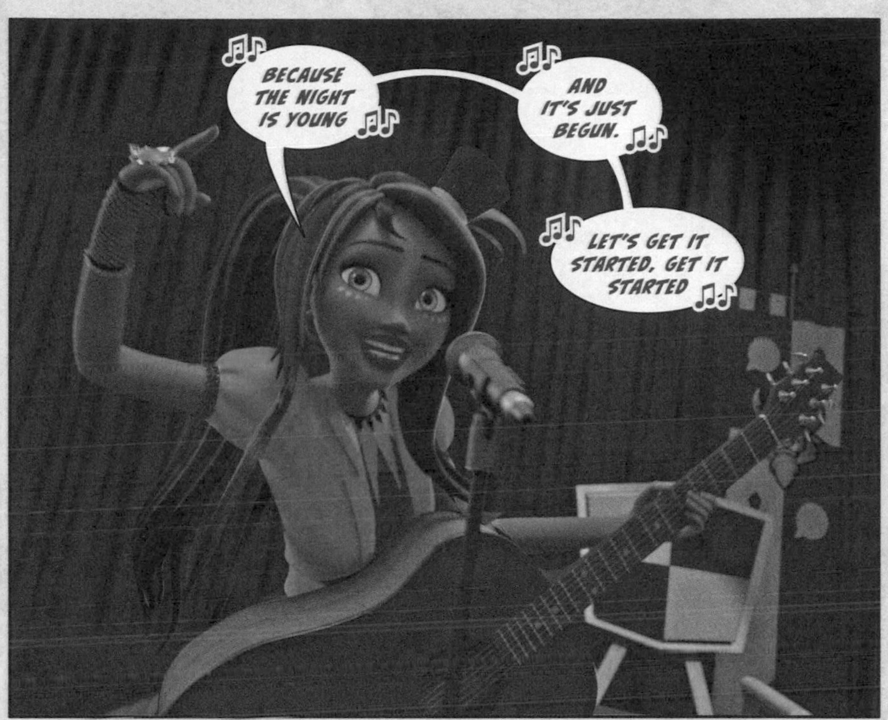
BECAUSE THE NIGHT IS YOUNG
AND IT'S JUST BEGUN.
LET'S GET IT STARTED, GET IT STARTED

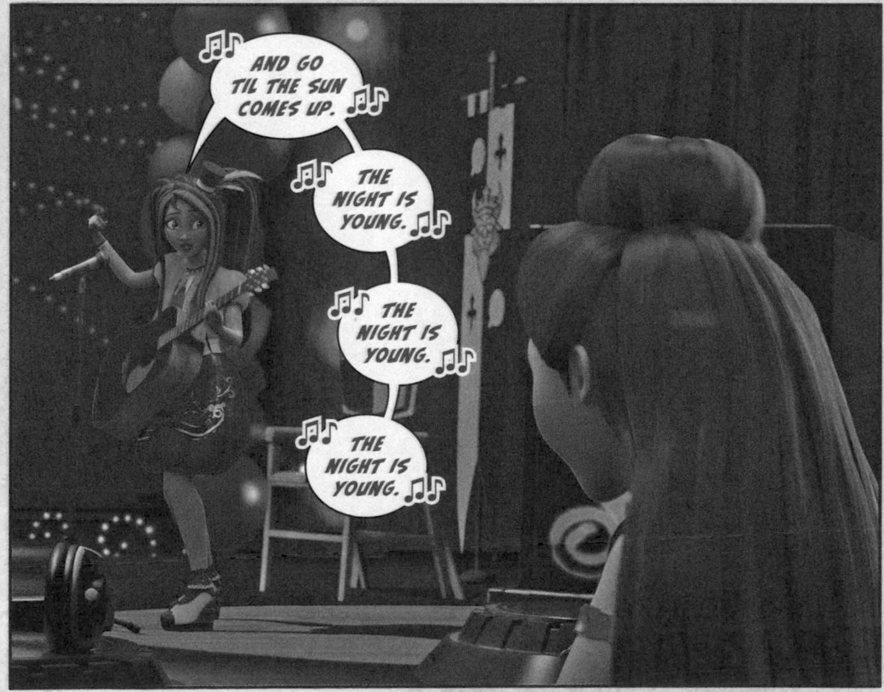
AND GO TIL THE SUN COMES UP.
THE NIGHT IS YOUNG.
THE NIGHT IS YOUNG.
THE NIGHT IS YOUNG.

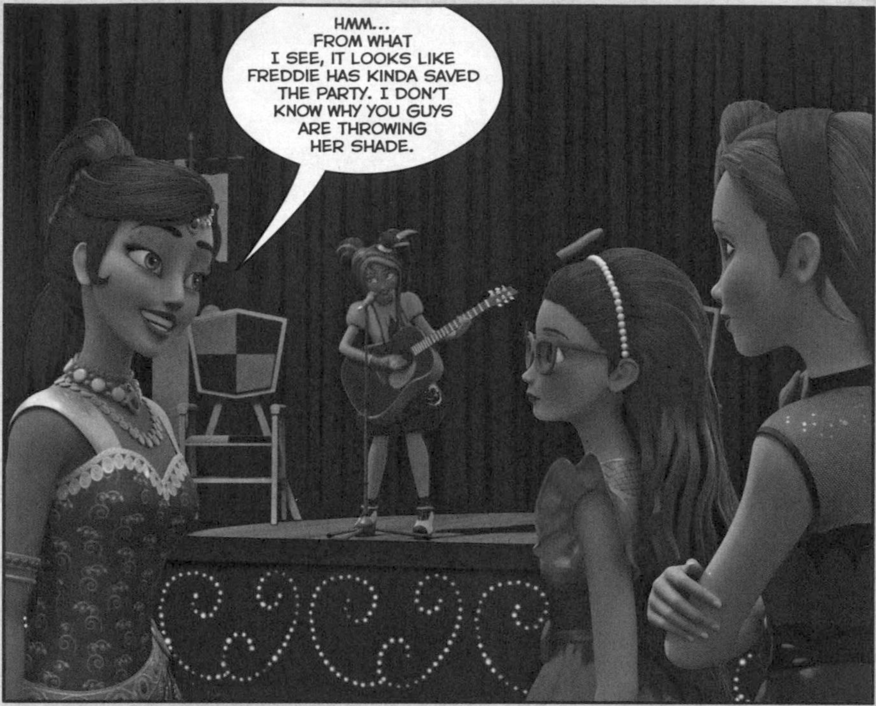
HMM... FROM WHAT I SEE, IT LOOKS LIKE FREDDIE HAS KINDA SAVED THE PARTY. I DON'T KNOW WHY YOU GUYS ARE THROWING HER SHADE.

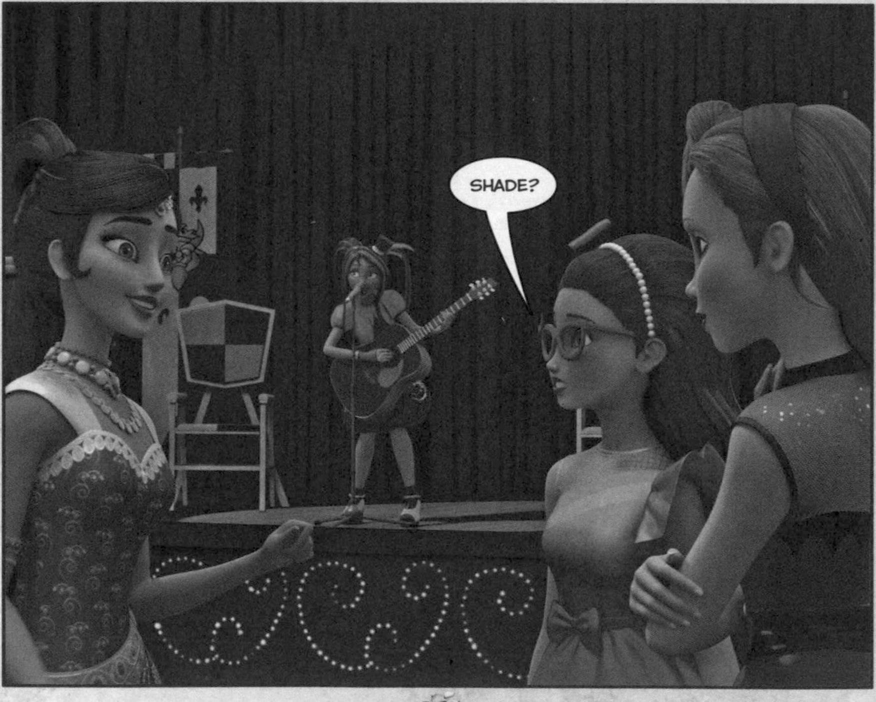
SHADE?

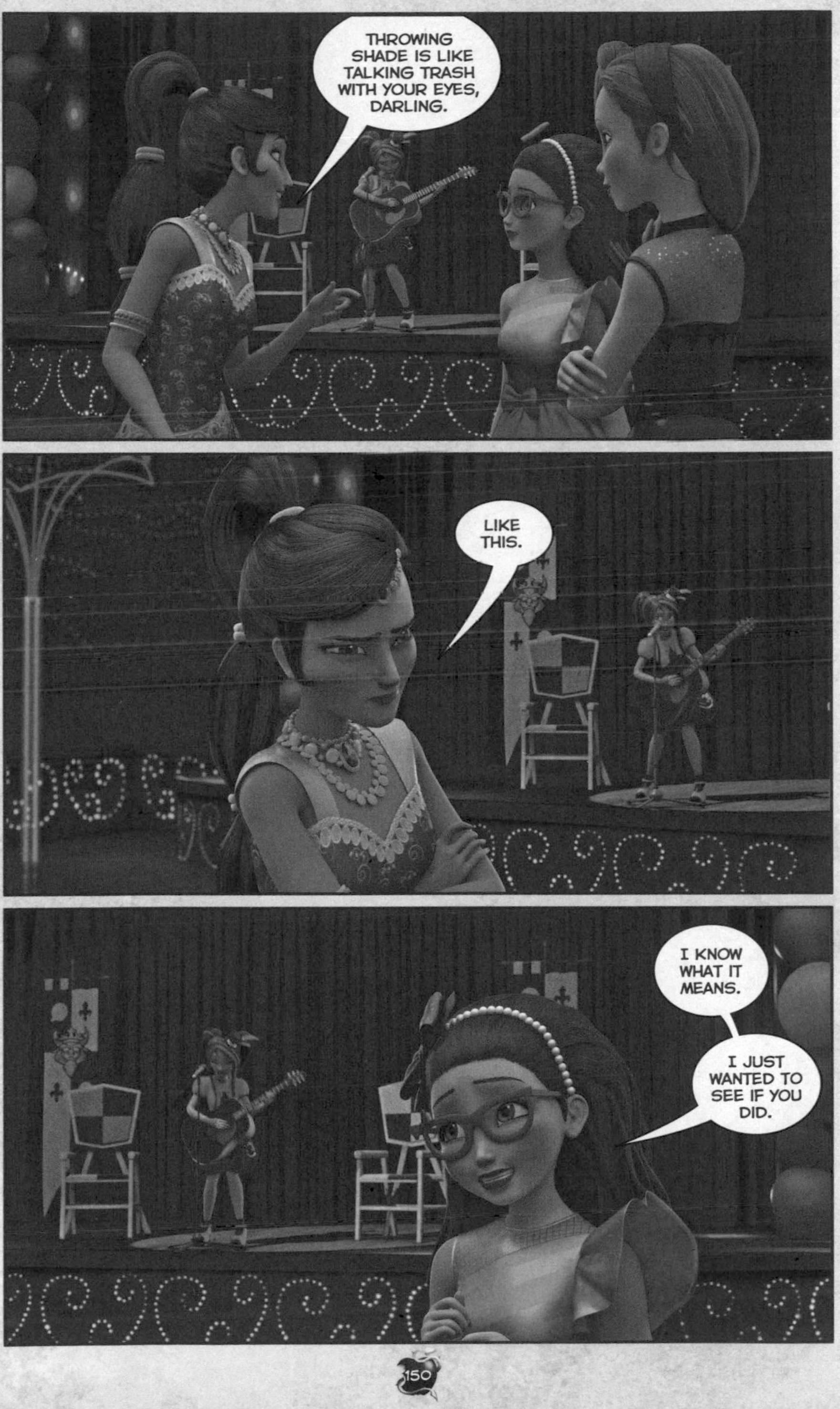
THROWING SHADE IS LIKE TALKING TRASH WITH YOUR EYES, DARLING.
LIKE THIS.
I KNOW WHAT IT MEANS.
I JUST WANTED TO SEE IF YOU DID.

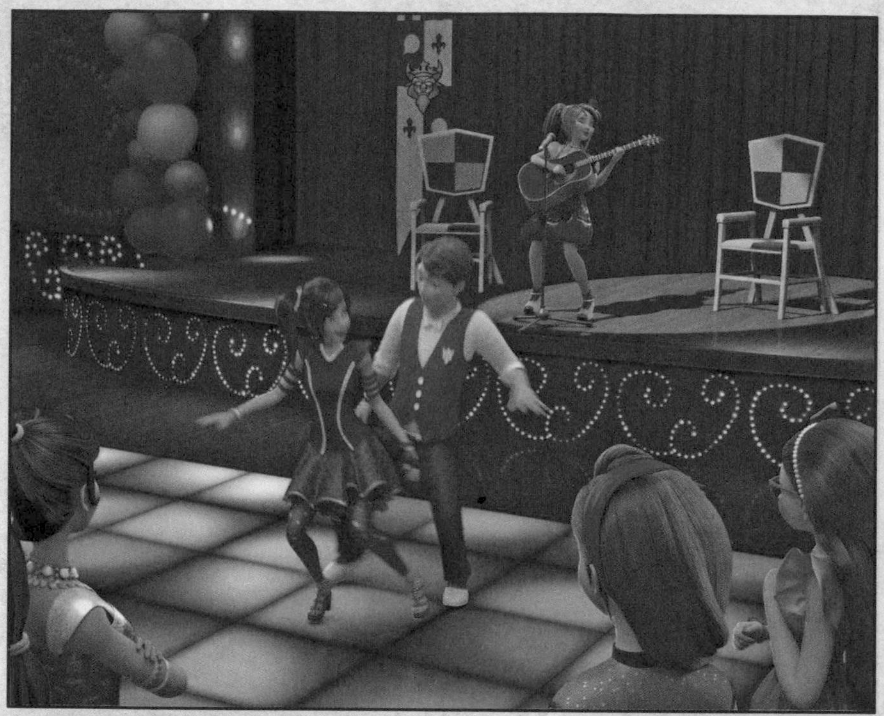

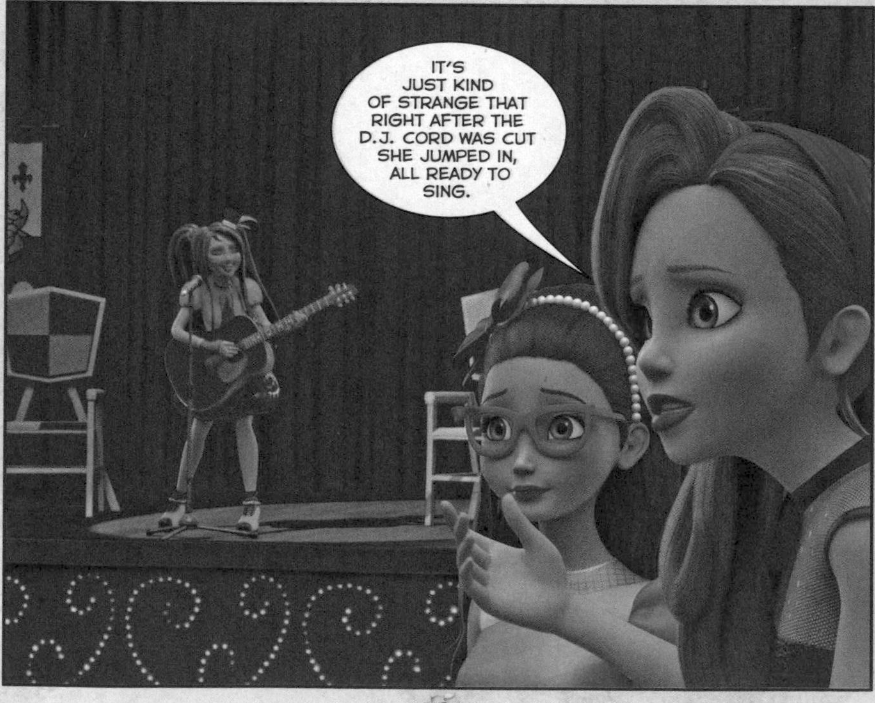
IT'S JUST KIND OF STRANGE THAT RIGHT AFTER THE D.J. CORD WAS CUT SHE JUMPED IN, ALL READY TO SING.

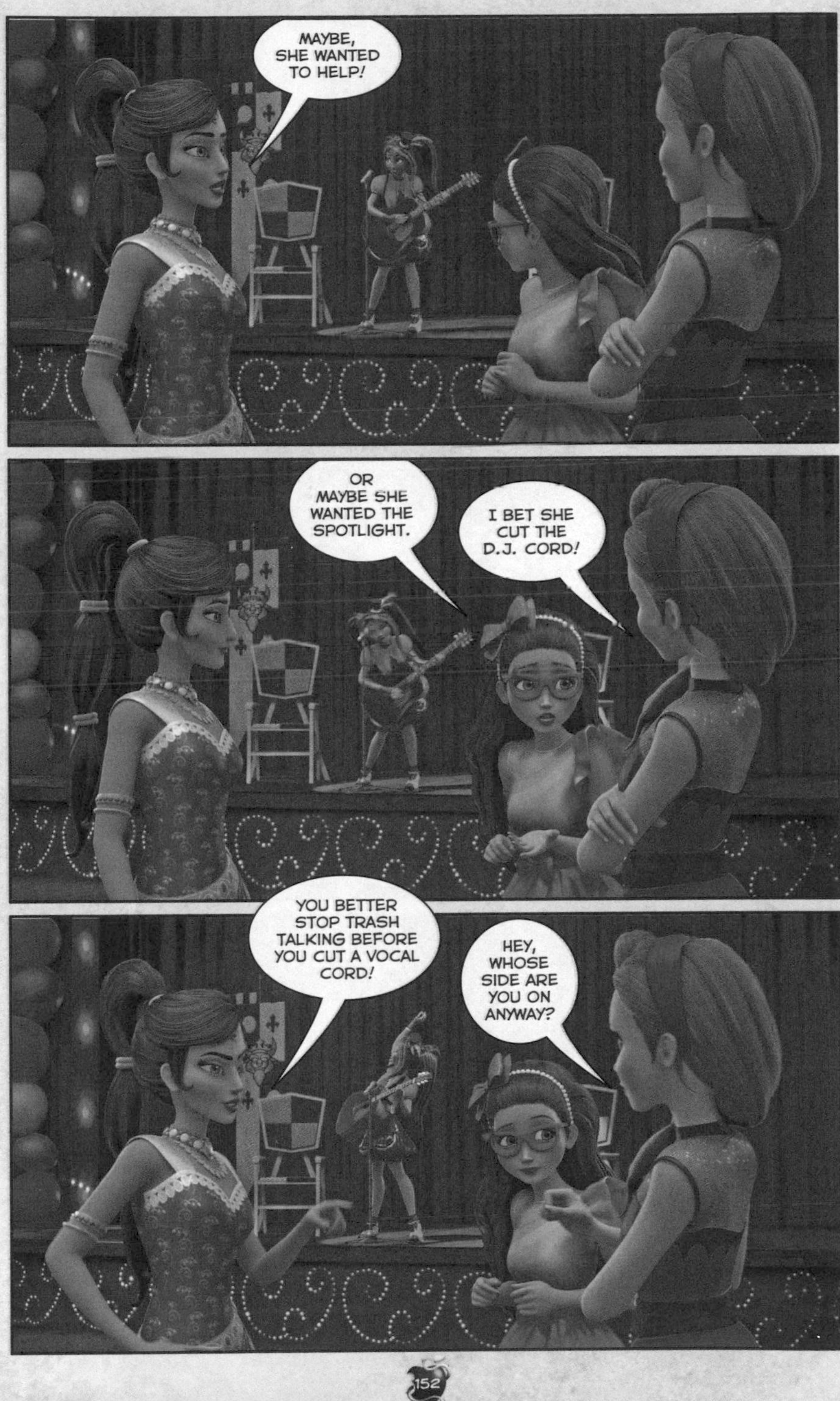
MAYBE, SHE WANTED TO HELP!
OR MAYBE SHE WANTED THE SPOTLIGHT.
I BET SHE CUT THE D.J. CORD!
YOU BETTER STOP TRASH TALKING BEFORE YOU CUT A VOCAL CORD!
HEY, WHOSE SIDE ARE YOU ON ANYWAY?

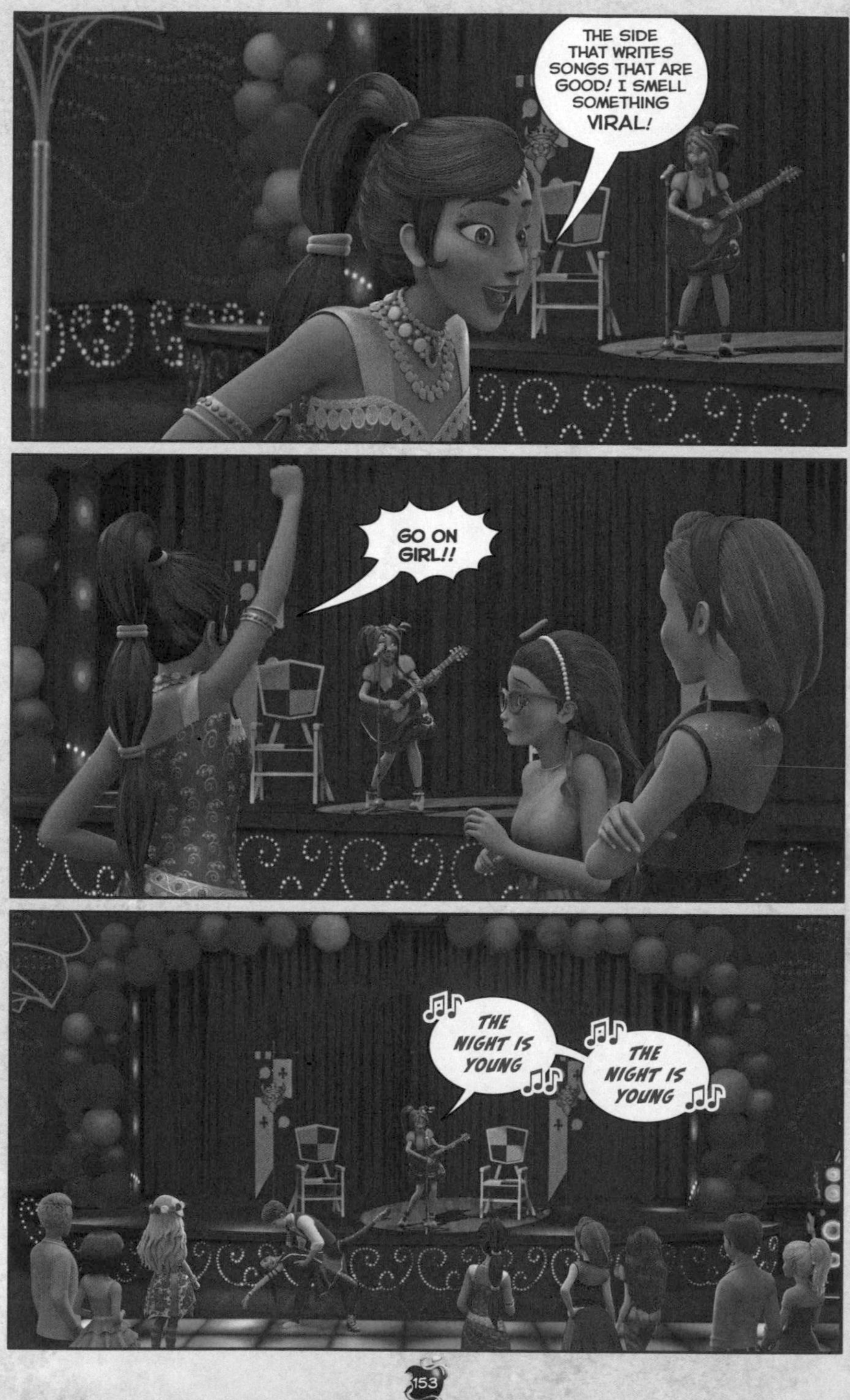
THE SIDE THAT WRITES SONGS THAT ARE GOOD! I SMELL SOMETHING VIRAL!
GO ON GIRL!!
THE NIGHT IS YOUNG
THE NIGHT IS YOUNG

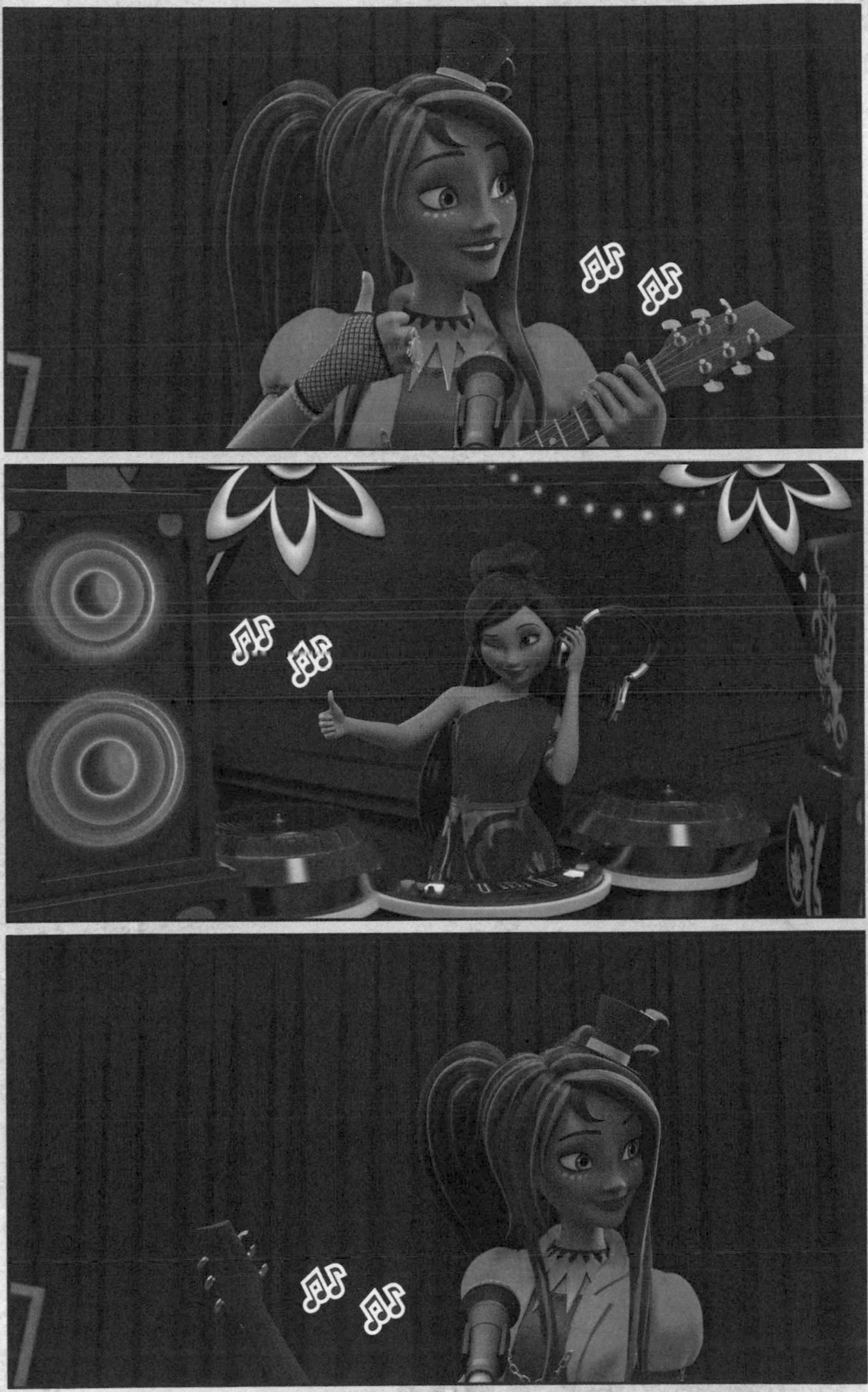

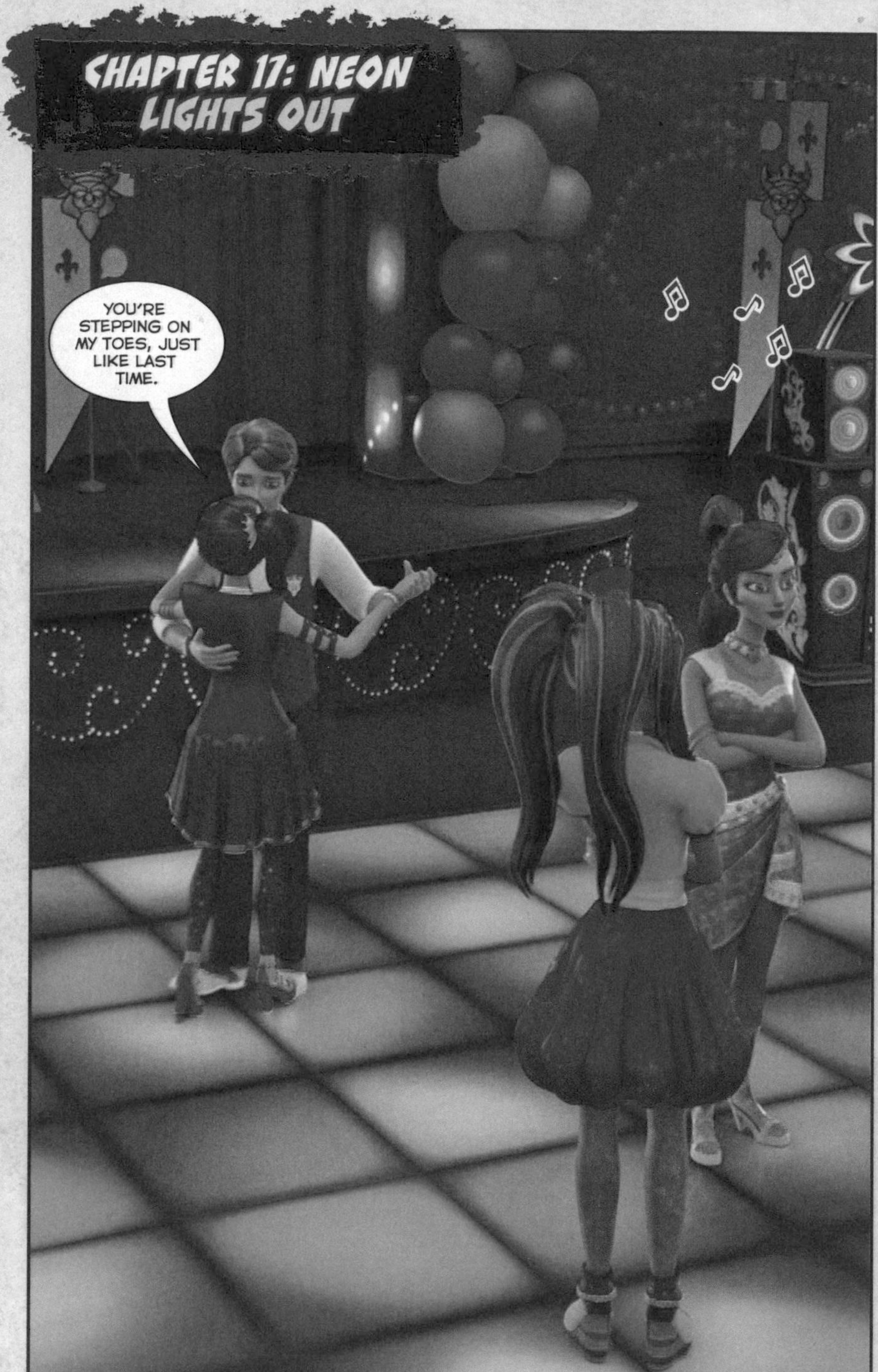
CHAPTER 17: NEON LIGHTS OUT
YOU'RE STEPPING ON MY TOES, JUST LIKE LAST TIME.

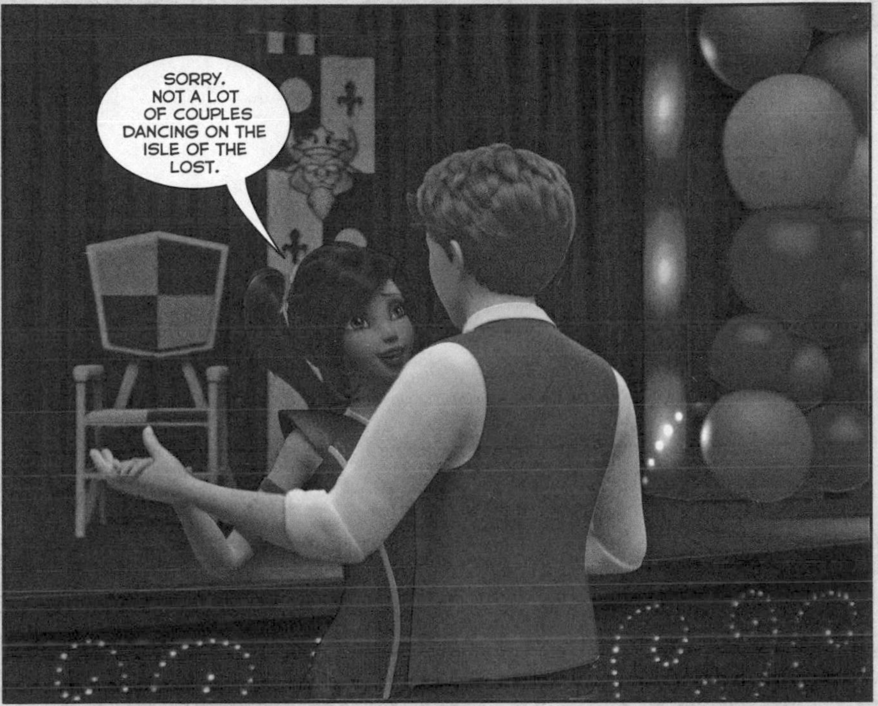
SORRY. NOT A LOT OF COUPLES DANCING ON THE ISLE OF THE LOST.

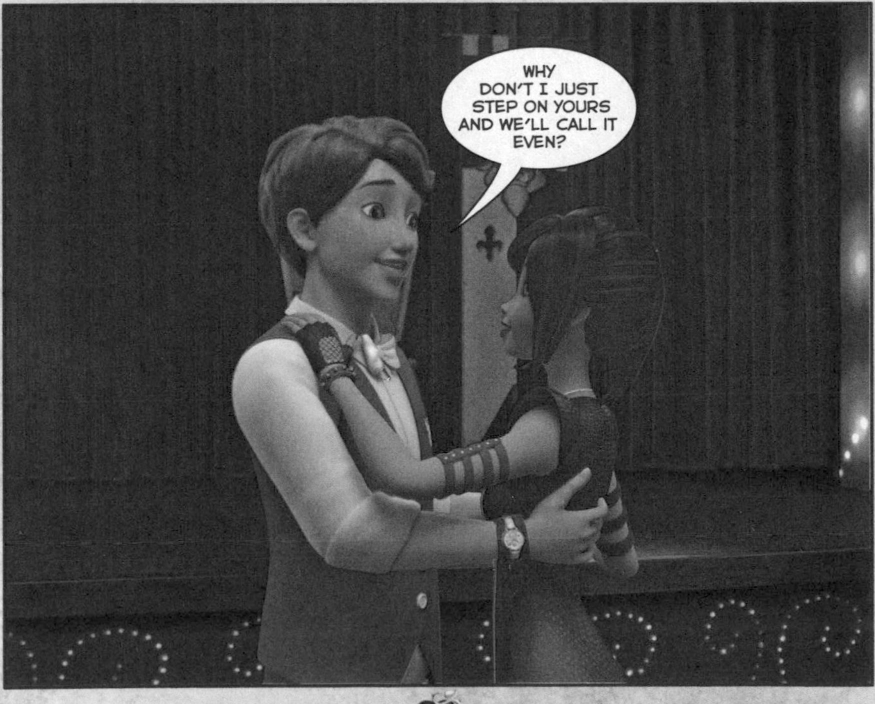
WHY DON'T I JUST STEP ON YOURS AND WE'LL CALL IT EVEN?

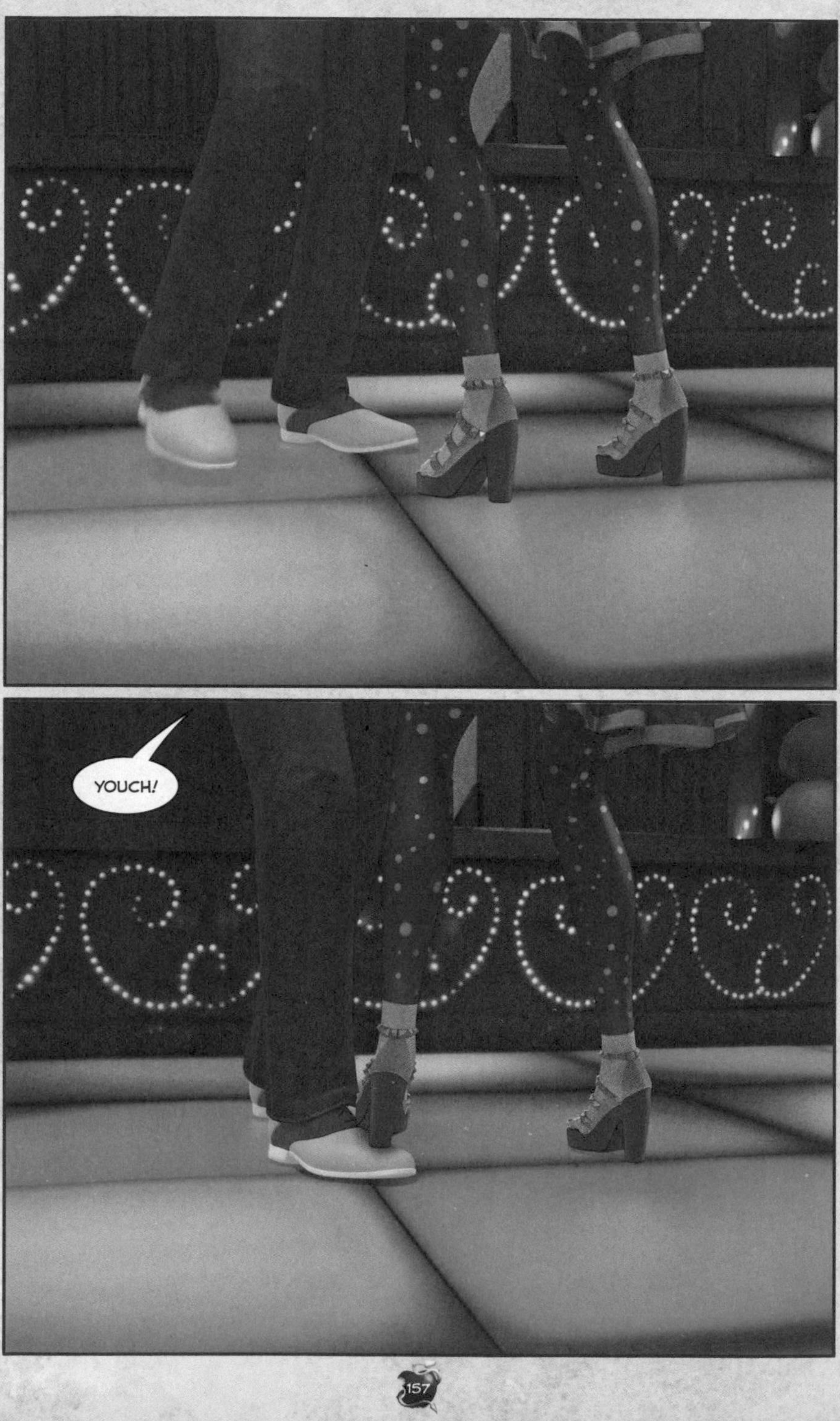
YOUCH!

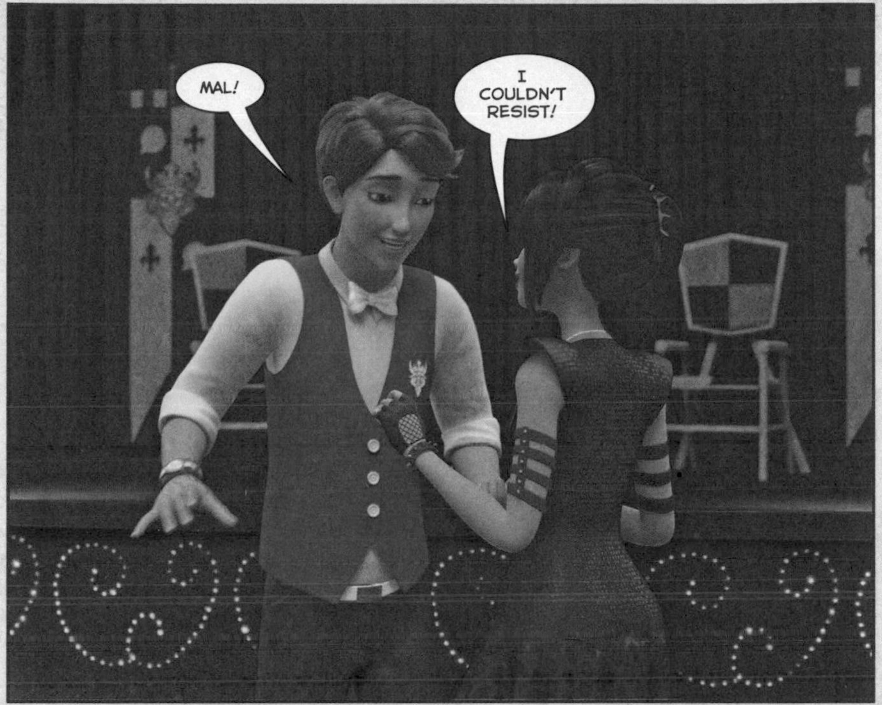
MAL!
I COULDN'T RESIST!

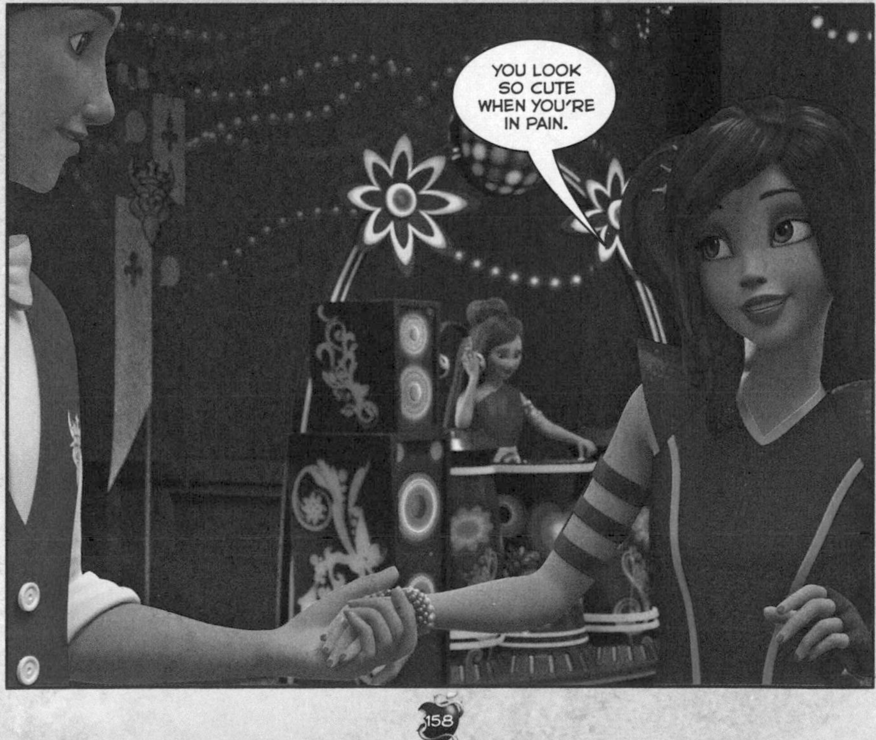
YOU LOOK SO CUTE WHEN YOU'RE IN PAIN.

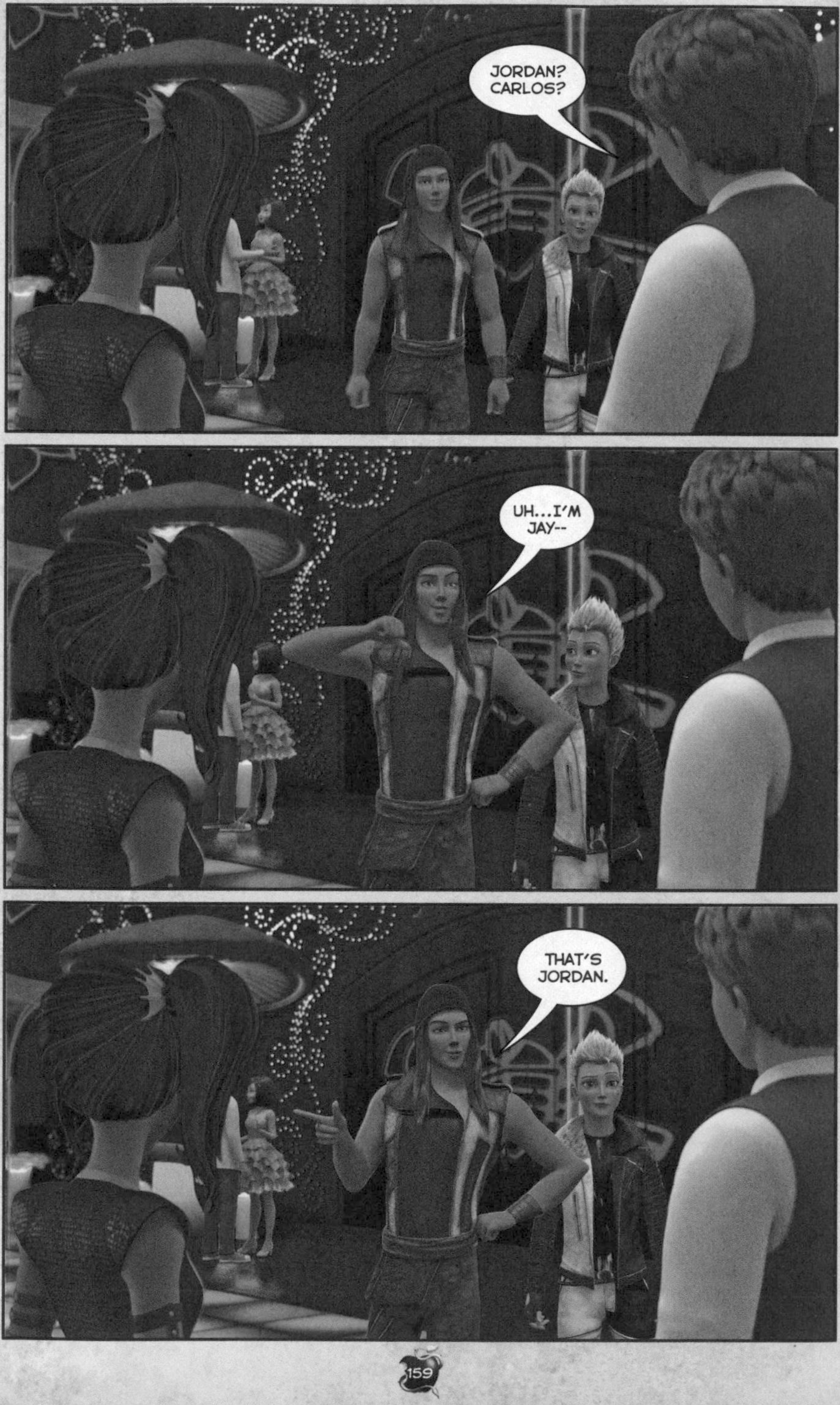
JORDAN? CARLOS?
UH...I'M JAY--
THAT'S JORDAN.

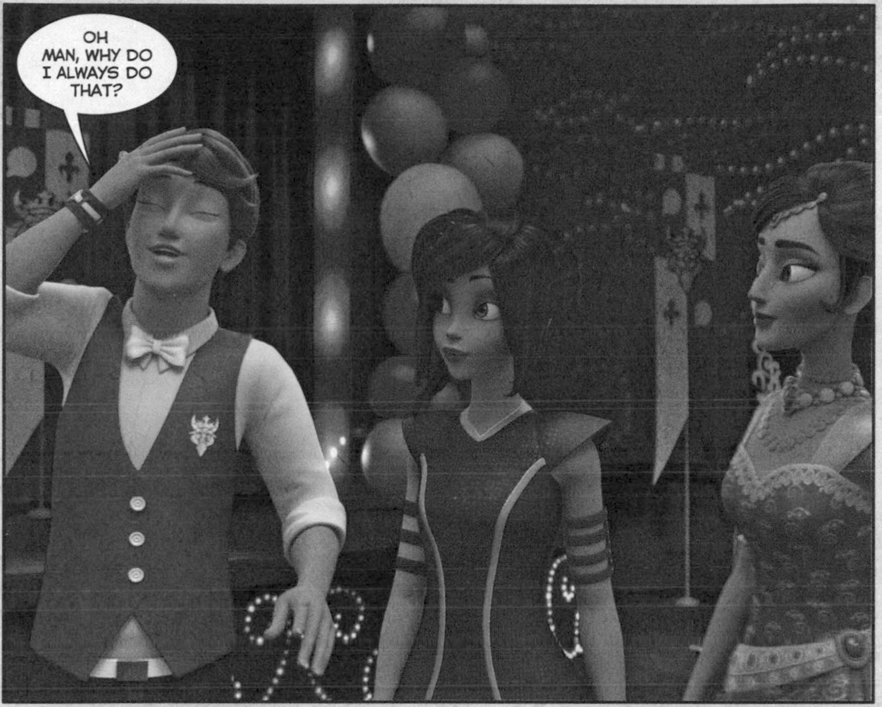
OH MAN, WHY DO I ALWAYS DO THAT?

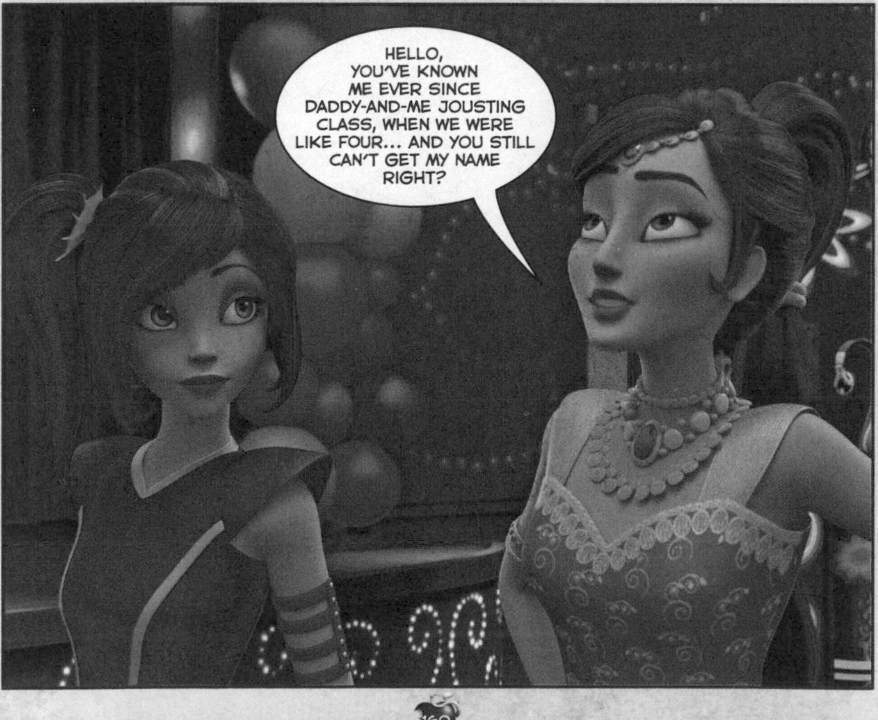
HELLO, YOU'VE KNOWN ME EVER SINCE DADDY-AND-ME JOUSTING CLASS, WHEN WE WERE LIKE FOUR... AND YOU STILL CAN'T GET MY NAME RIGHT?

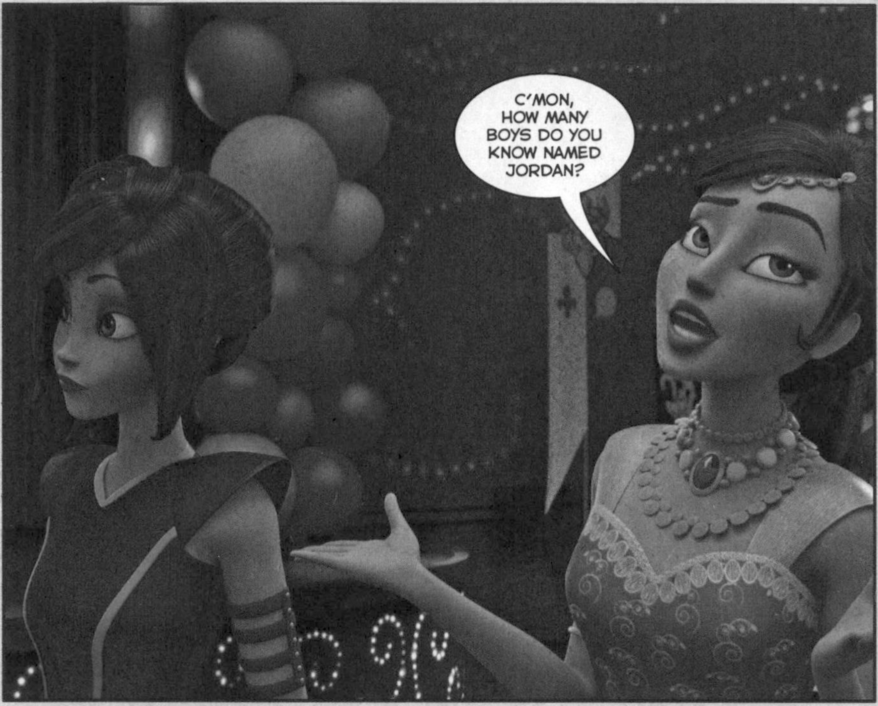
C'MON, HOW MANY BOYS DO YOU KNOW NAMED JORDAN?

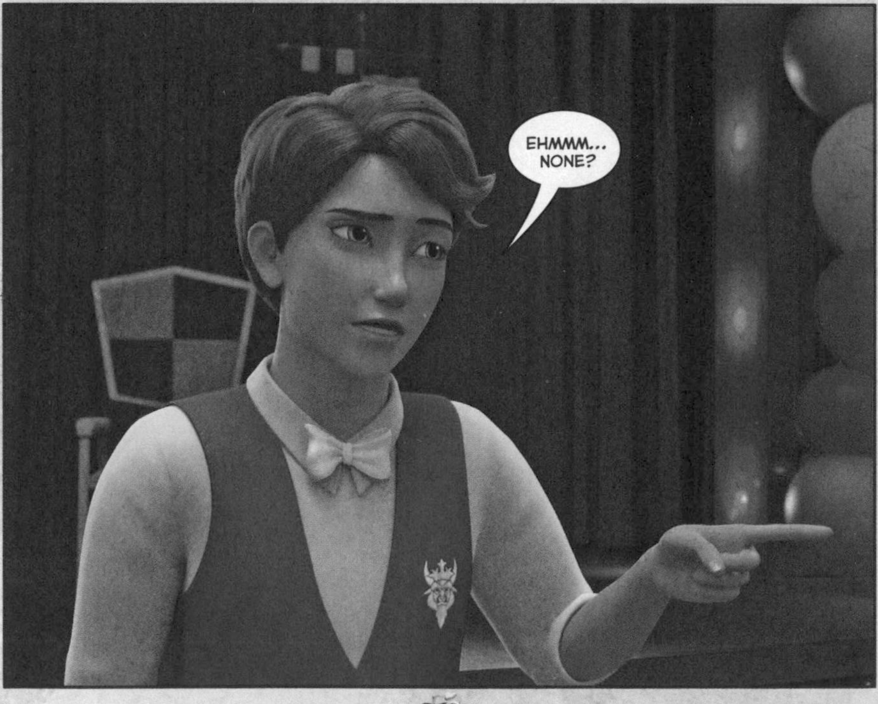
EHMMM... NONE?

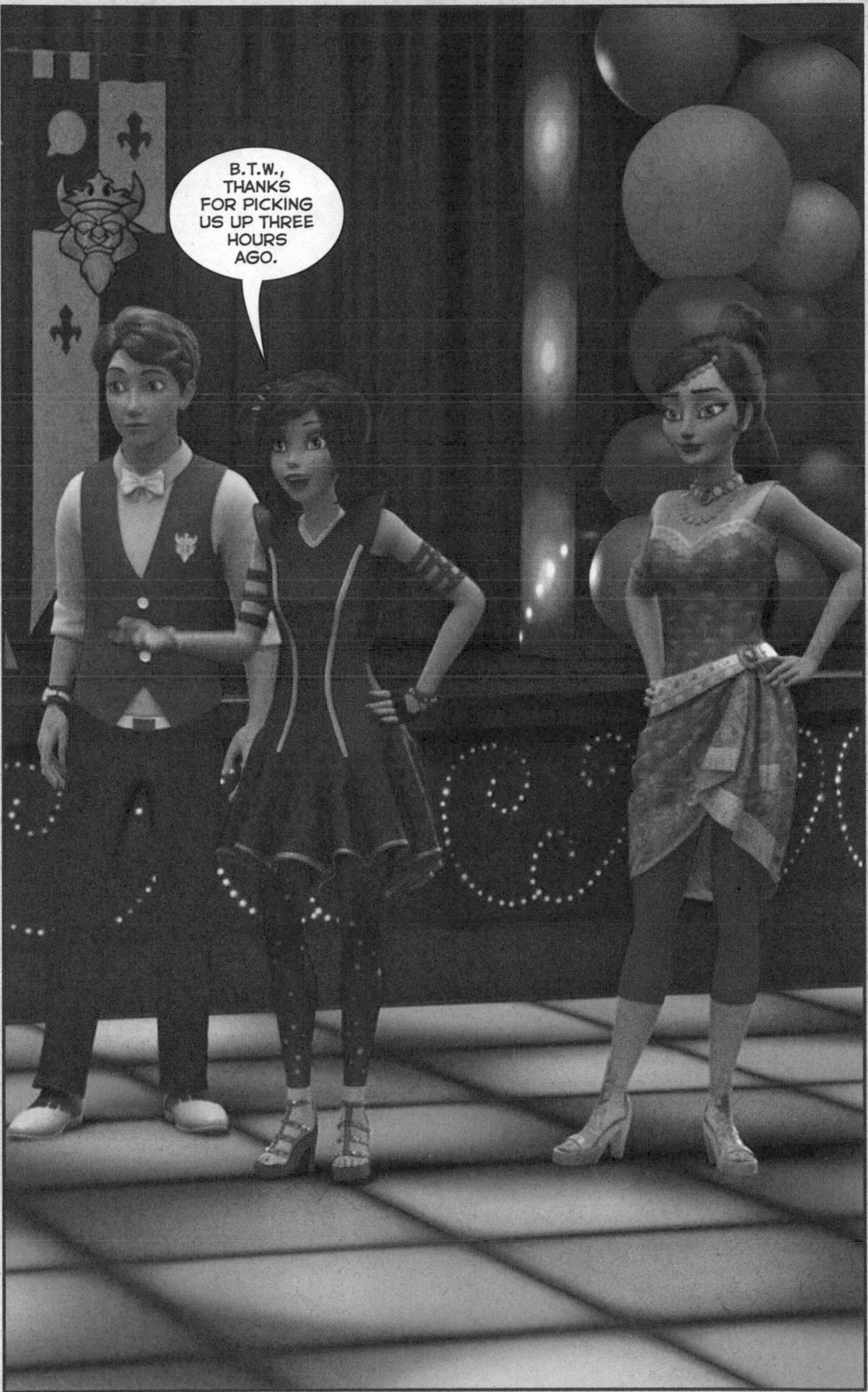
B.T.W., THANKS FOR PICKING US UP THREE HOURS AGO.

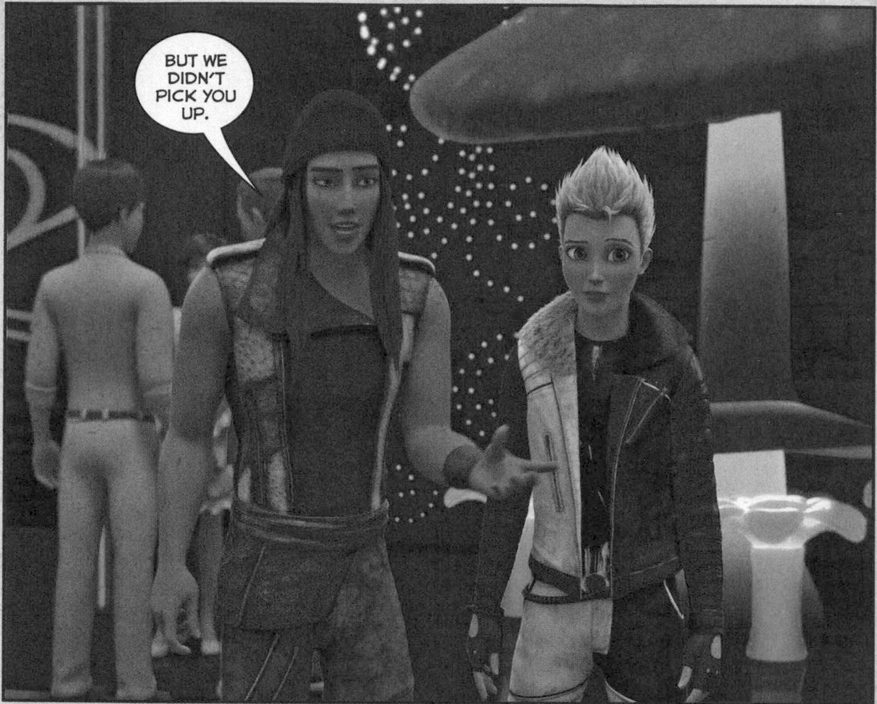
BUT WE DIDN'T PICK YOU UP.

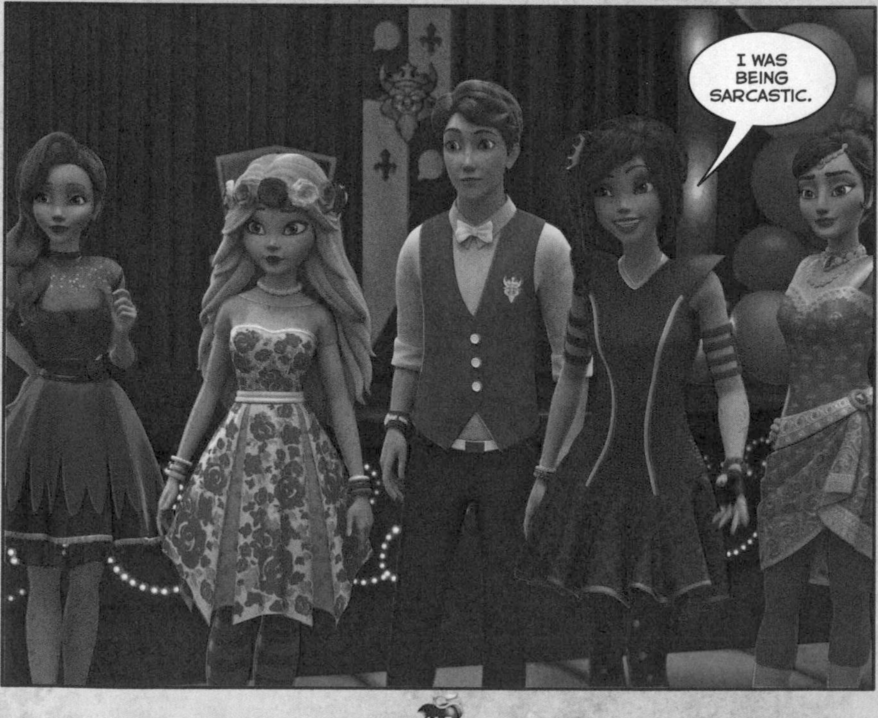
I WAS BEING SARCASTIC.

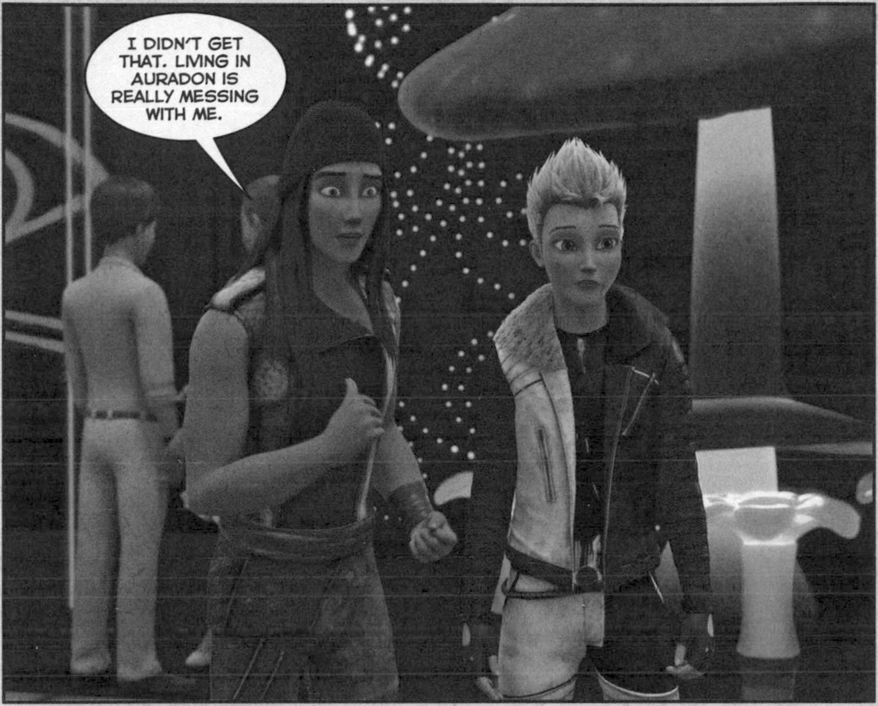
I DIDN'T GET THAT. LIVING IN AURADON IS REALLY MESSING WITH ME.

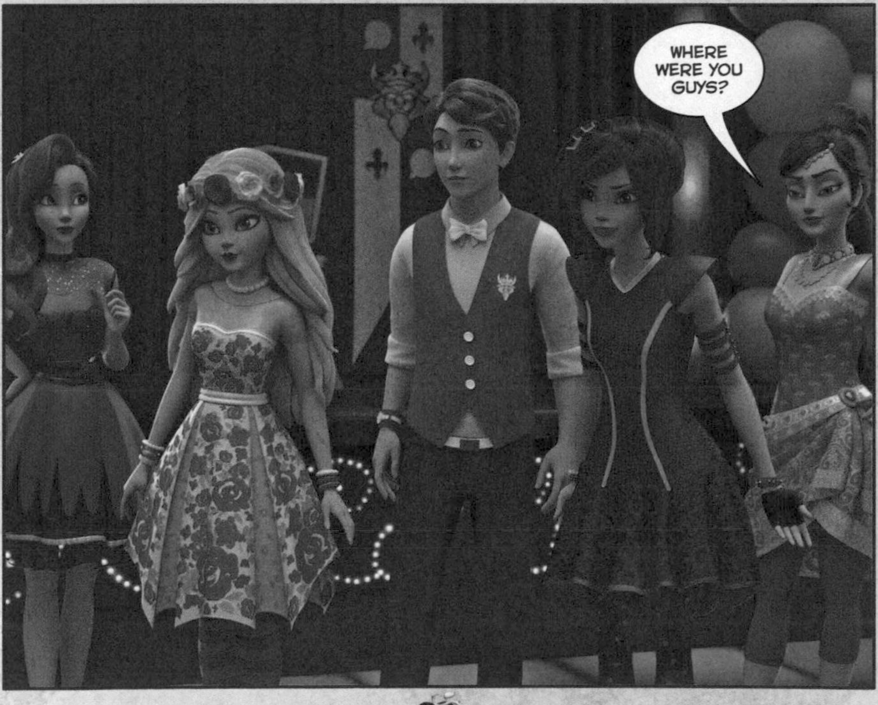
WHERE WERE YOU GUYS?

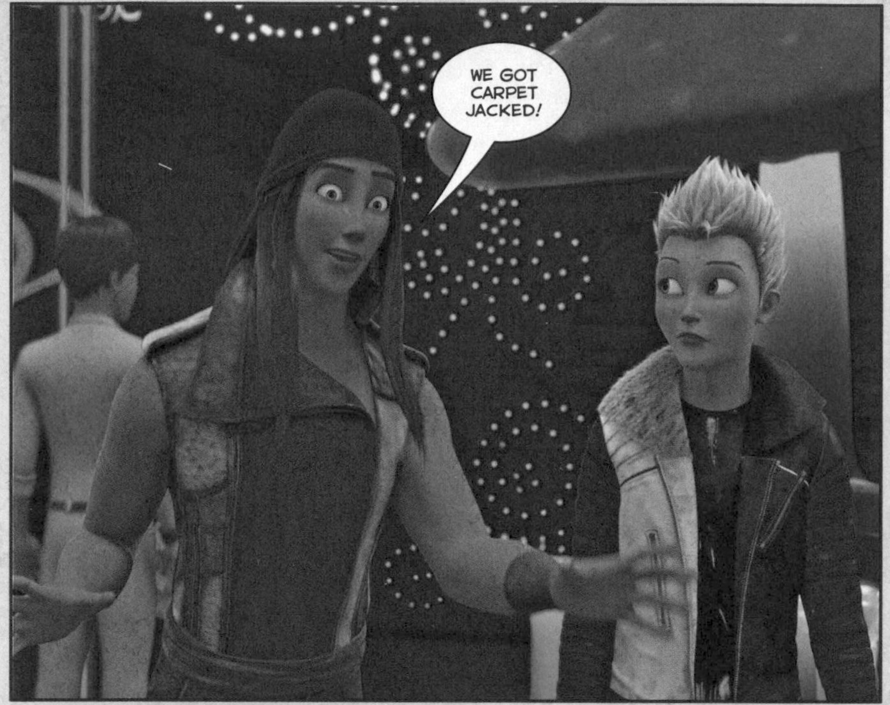
WE GOT CARPET JACKED!

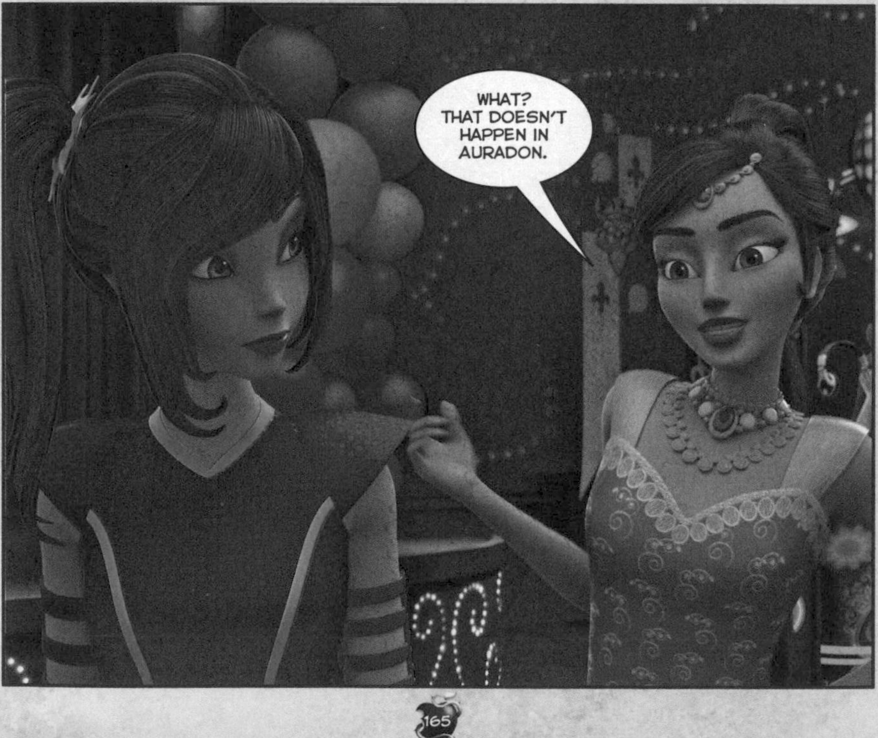
WHAT? THAT DOESN'T HAPPEN IN AURADON.

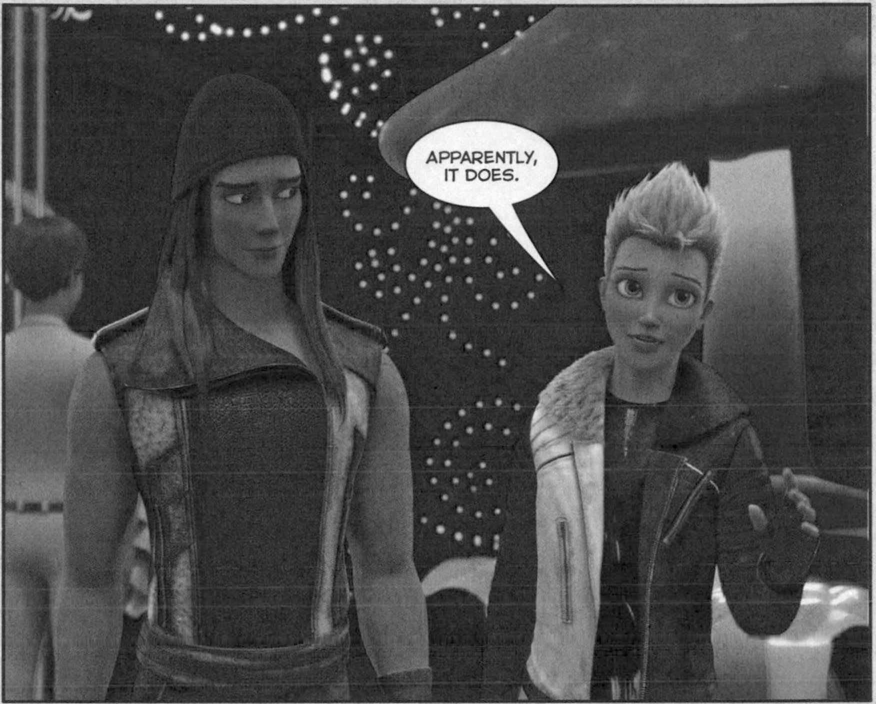
APPARENTLY, IT DOES.

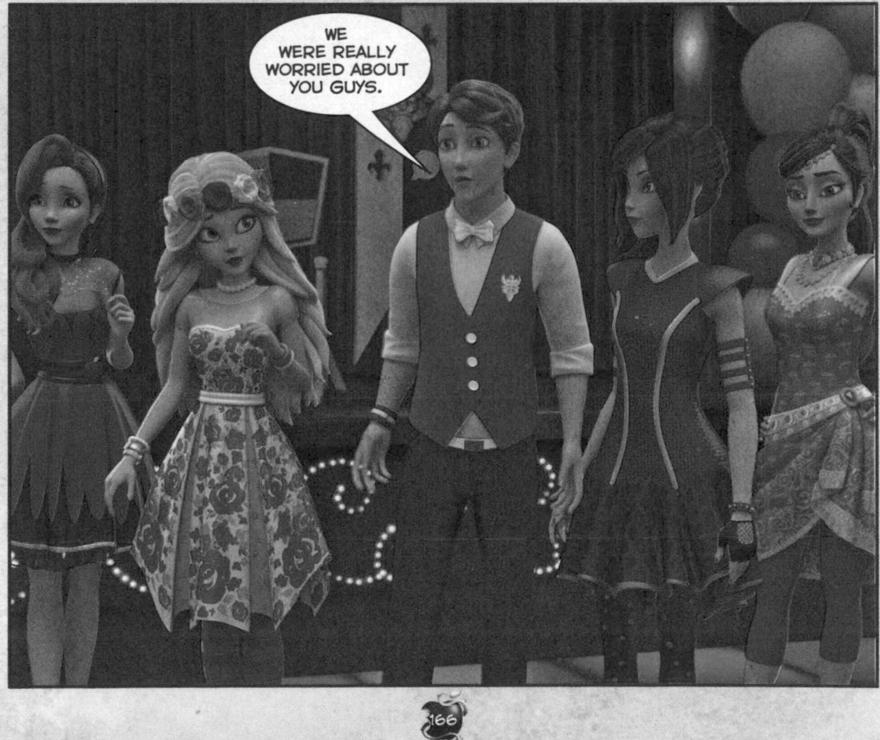
WE WERE REALLY WORRIED ABOUT YOU GUYS.

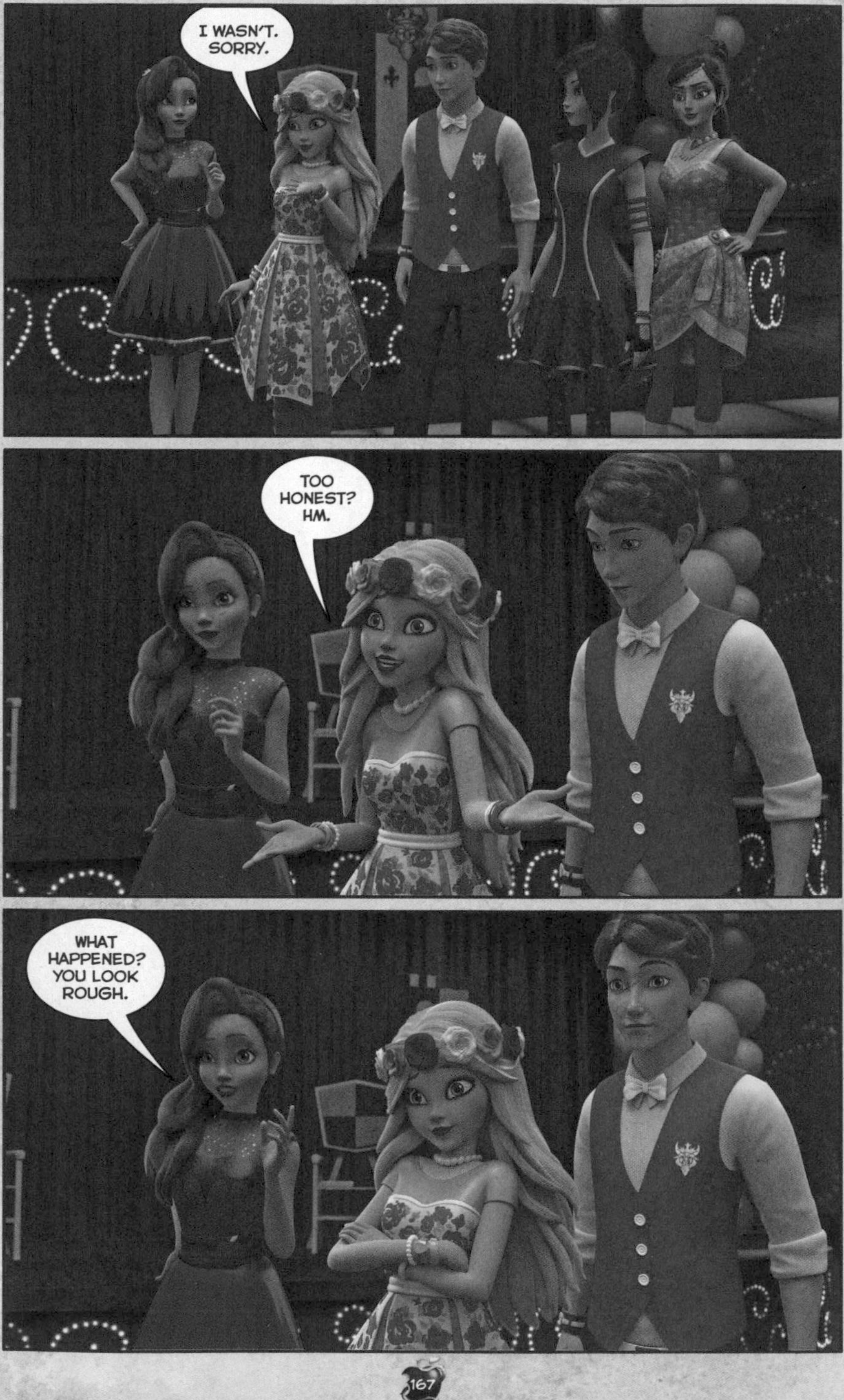
I WASN'T. SORRY.
TOO HONEST? HM.
WHAT HAPPENED? YOU LOOK ROUGH.

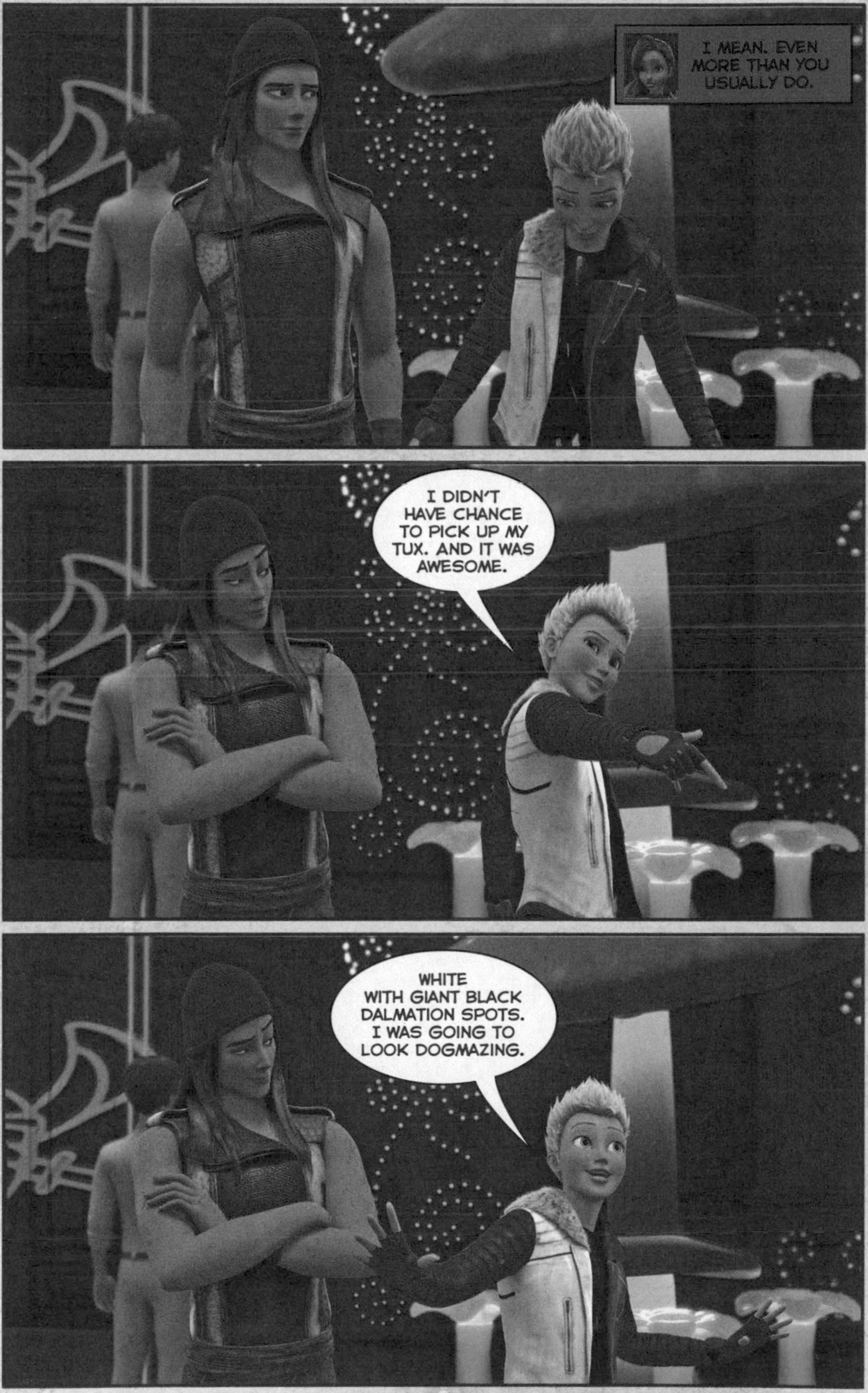
I MEAN. EVEN MORE THAN YOU USUALLY DO.
I DIDN'T HAVE CHANCE TO PICK UP MY TUX. AND IT WAS AWESOME.
WHITE WITH GIANT BLACK DALMATION SPOTS. I WAS GOING TO LOOK DOGMAZING.

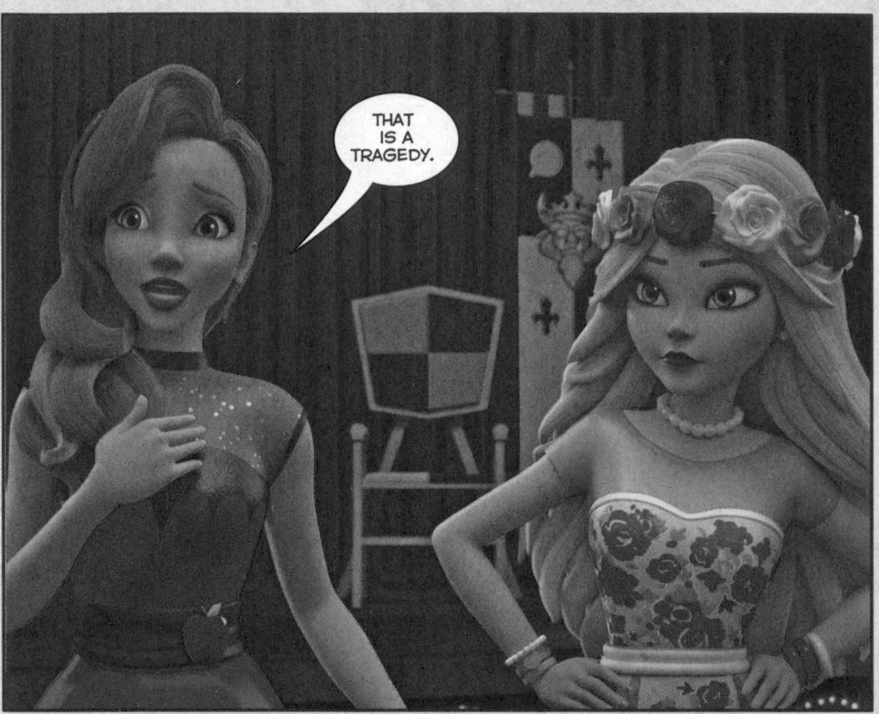
THAT IS A TRAGEDY.

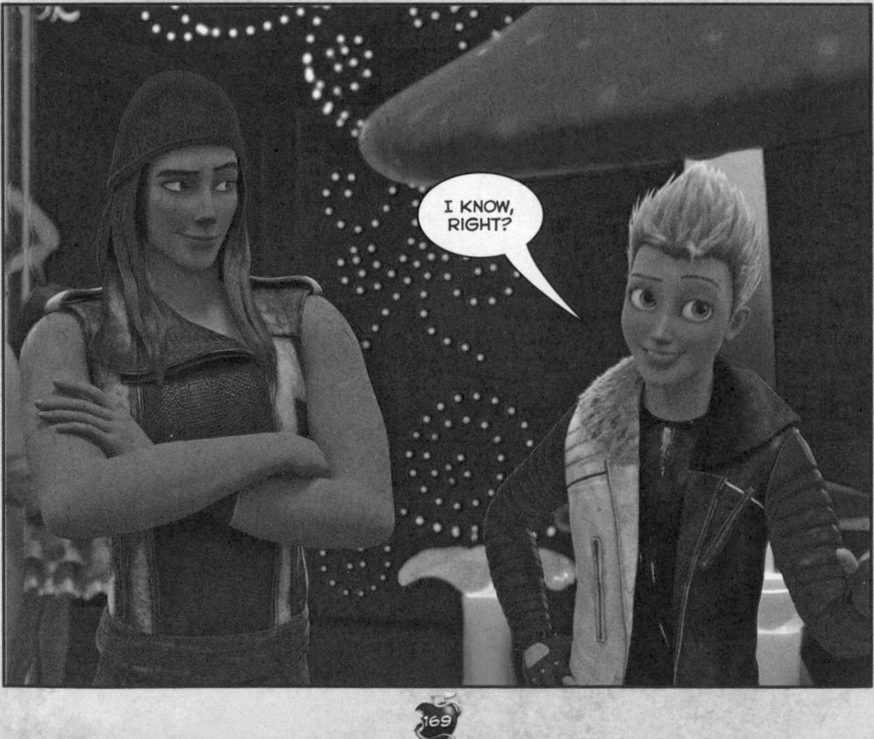
I KNOW, RIGHT?

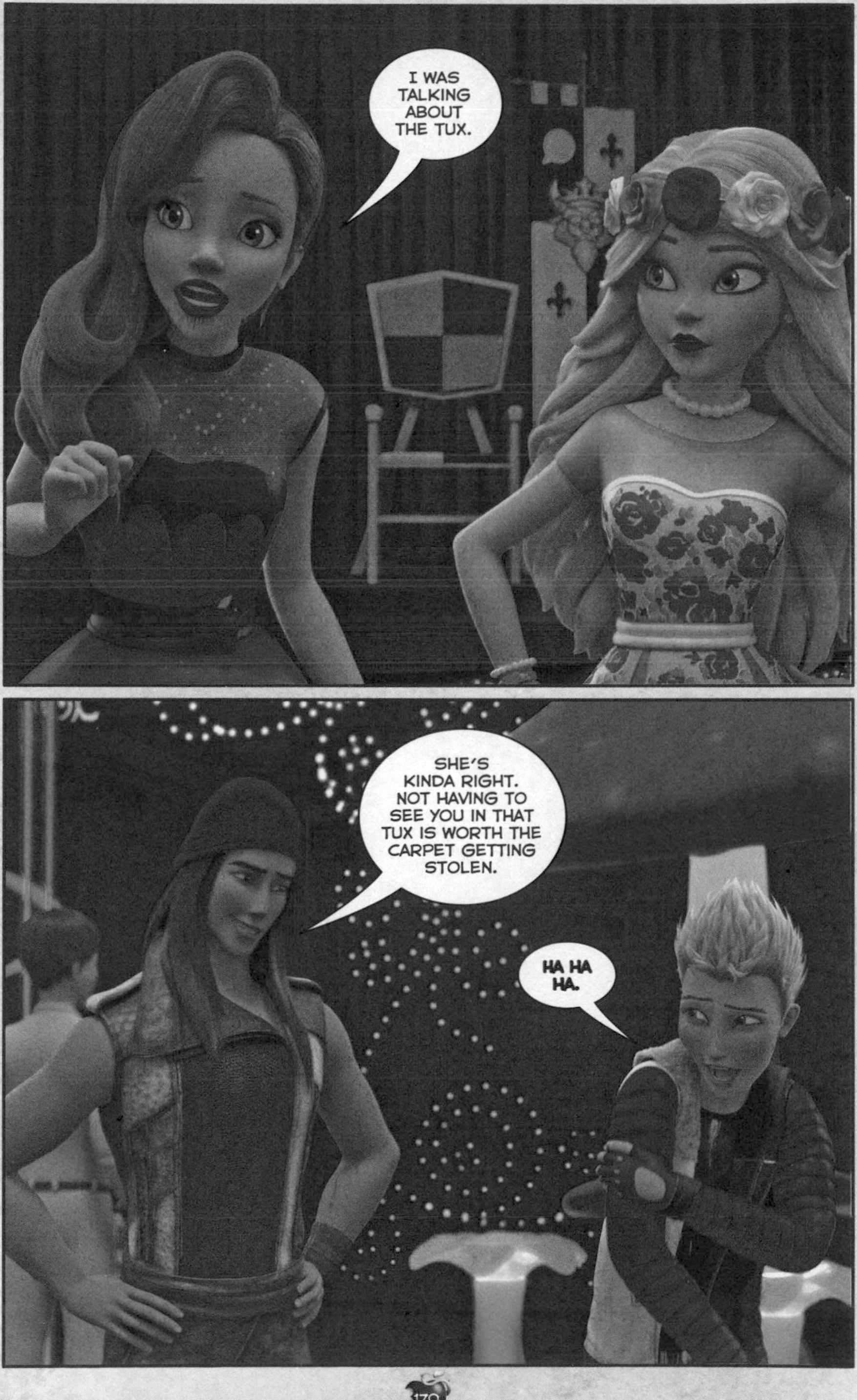
I WAS TALKING ABOUT THE TUX.
SHE'S KINDA RIGHT. NOT HAVING TO SEE YOU IN THAT TUX IS WORTH THE CARPET GETTING STOLEN.
HA HA HA.

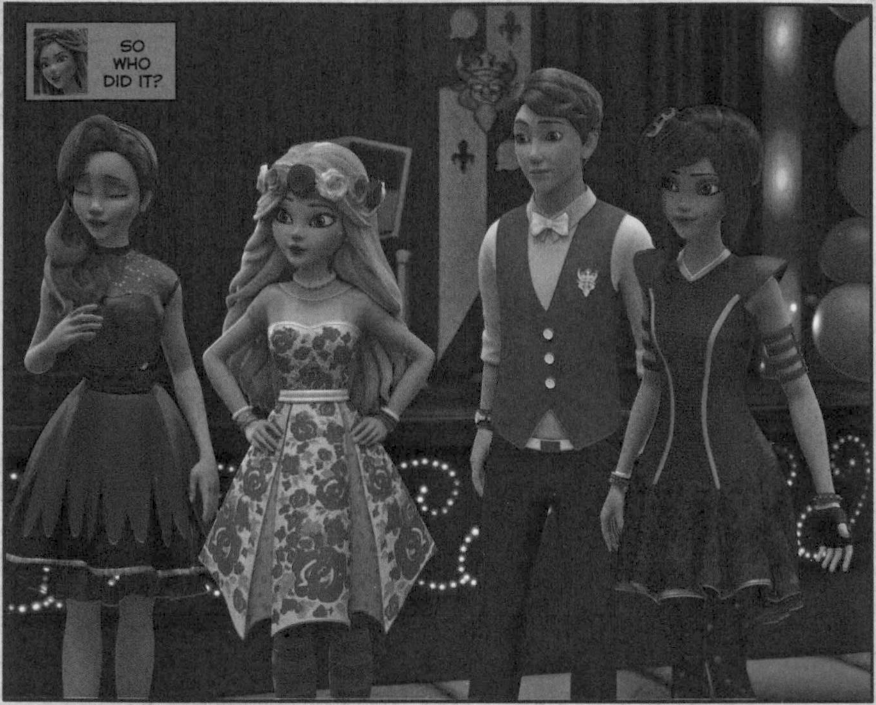
SO WHO DID IT?

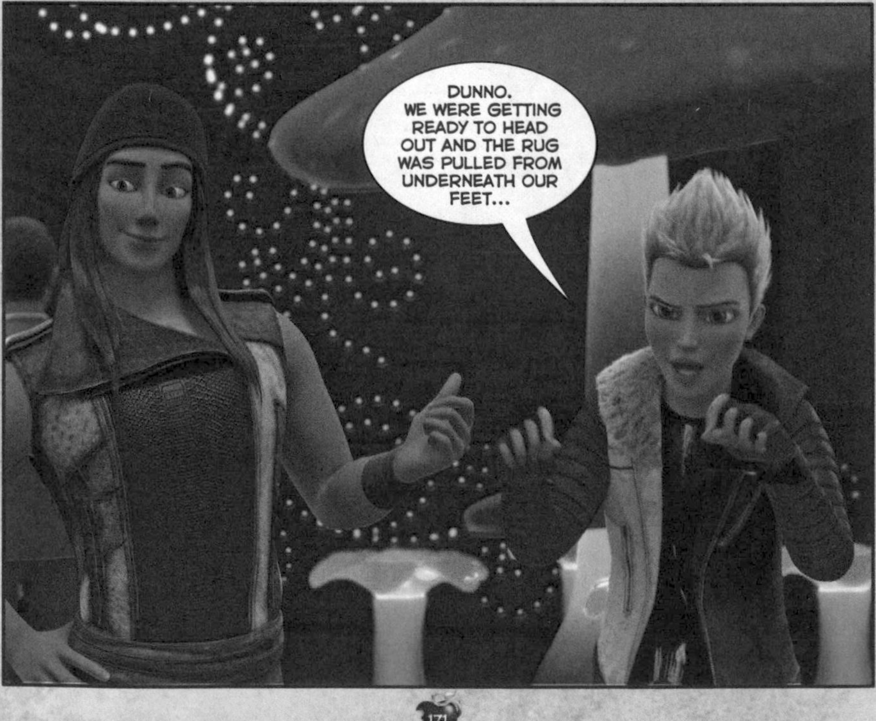
DUNNO. WE WERE GETTING READY TO HEAD OUT AND THE RUG WAS PULLED FROM UNDERNEATH OUR FEET...

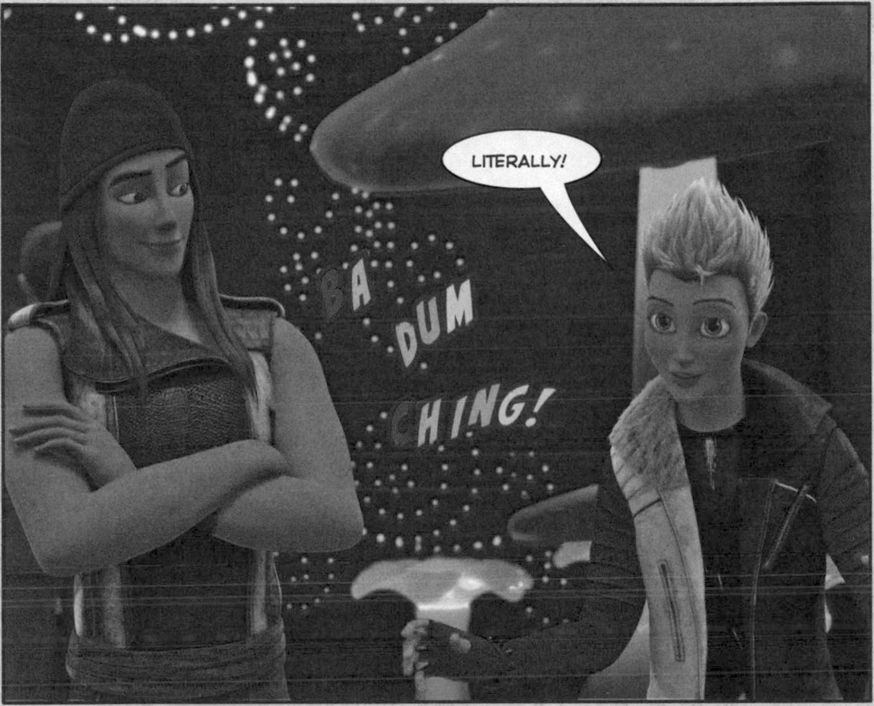
LITERALLY!
BA DUM CHING!

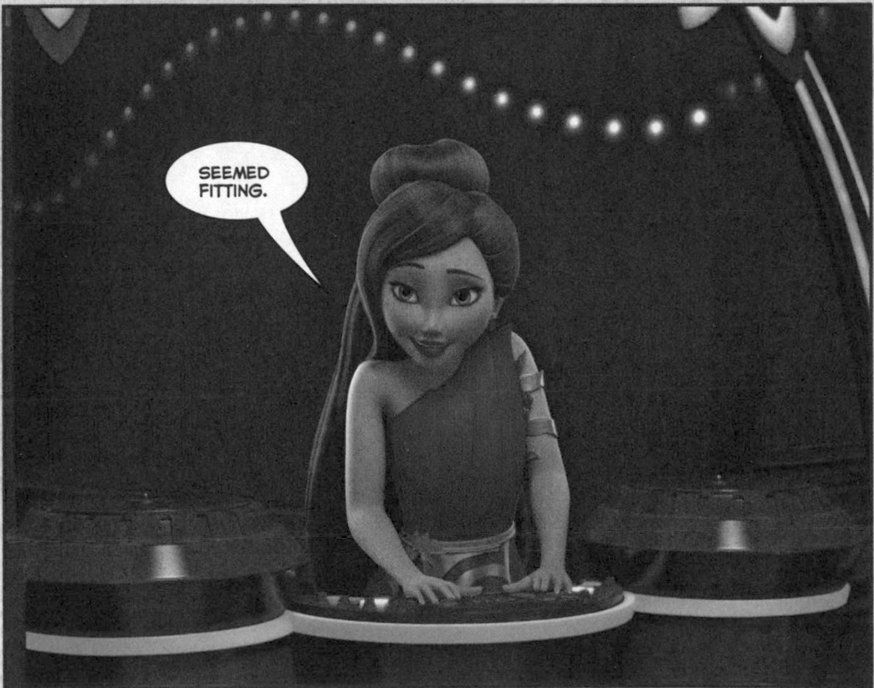
SEEMED FITTING.

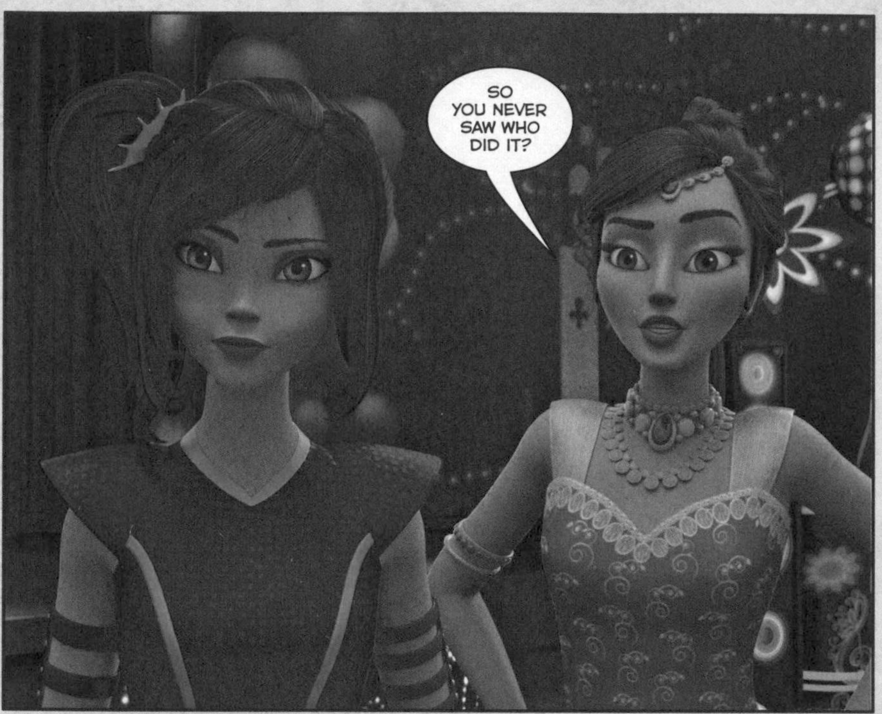
SO YOU NEVER SAW WHO DID IT?

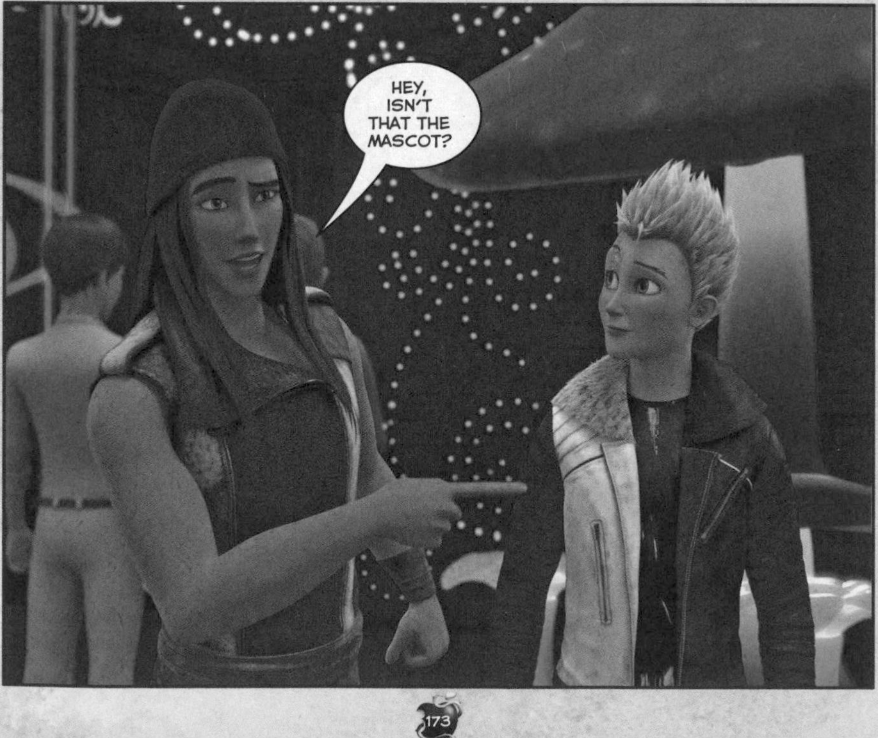
HEY, ISN'T THAT THE MASCOT?

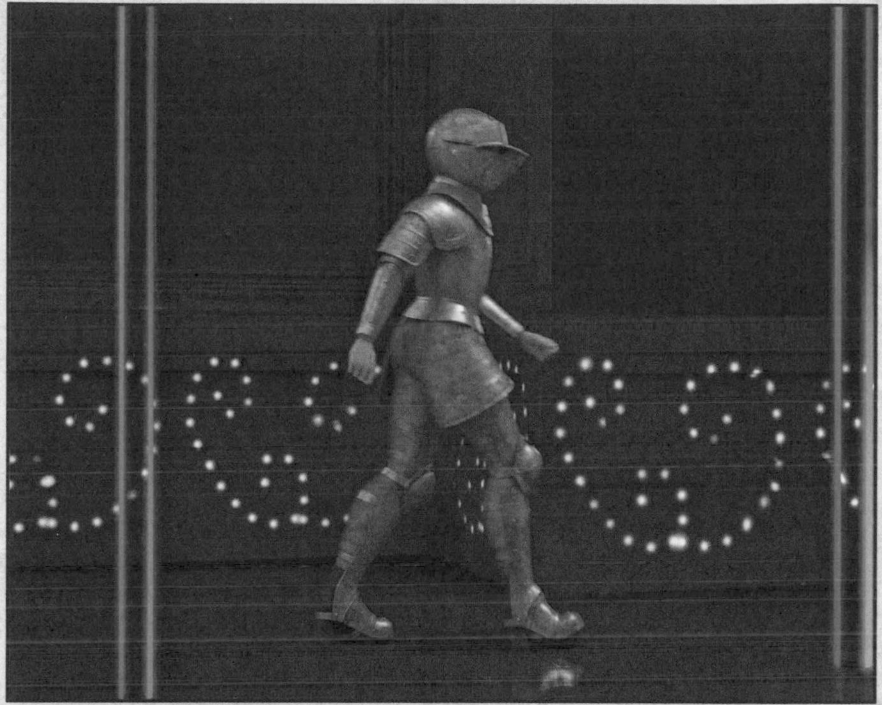

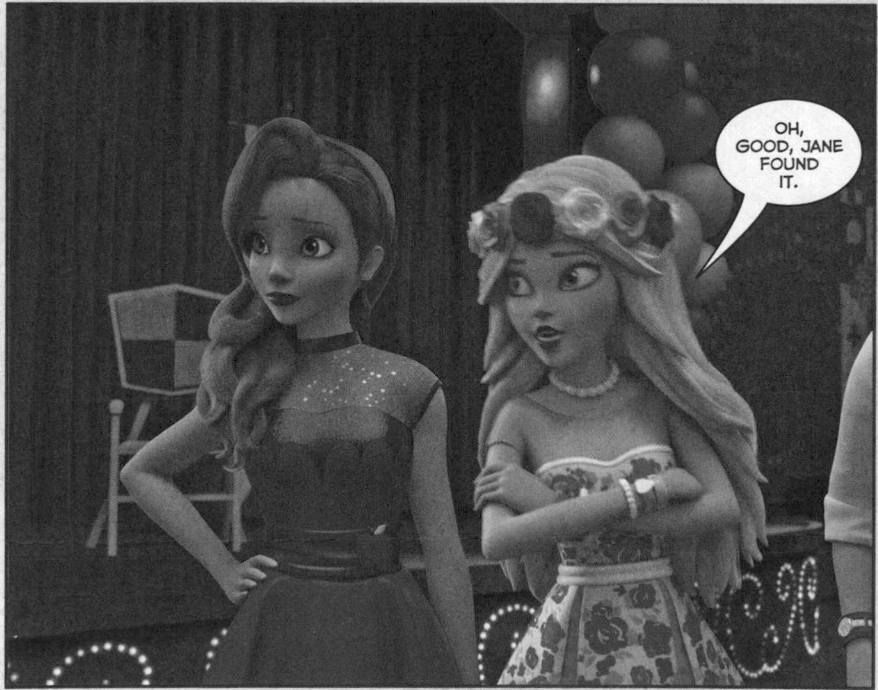
OH, GOOD, JANE FOUND IT.

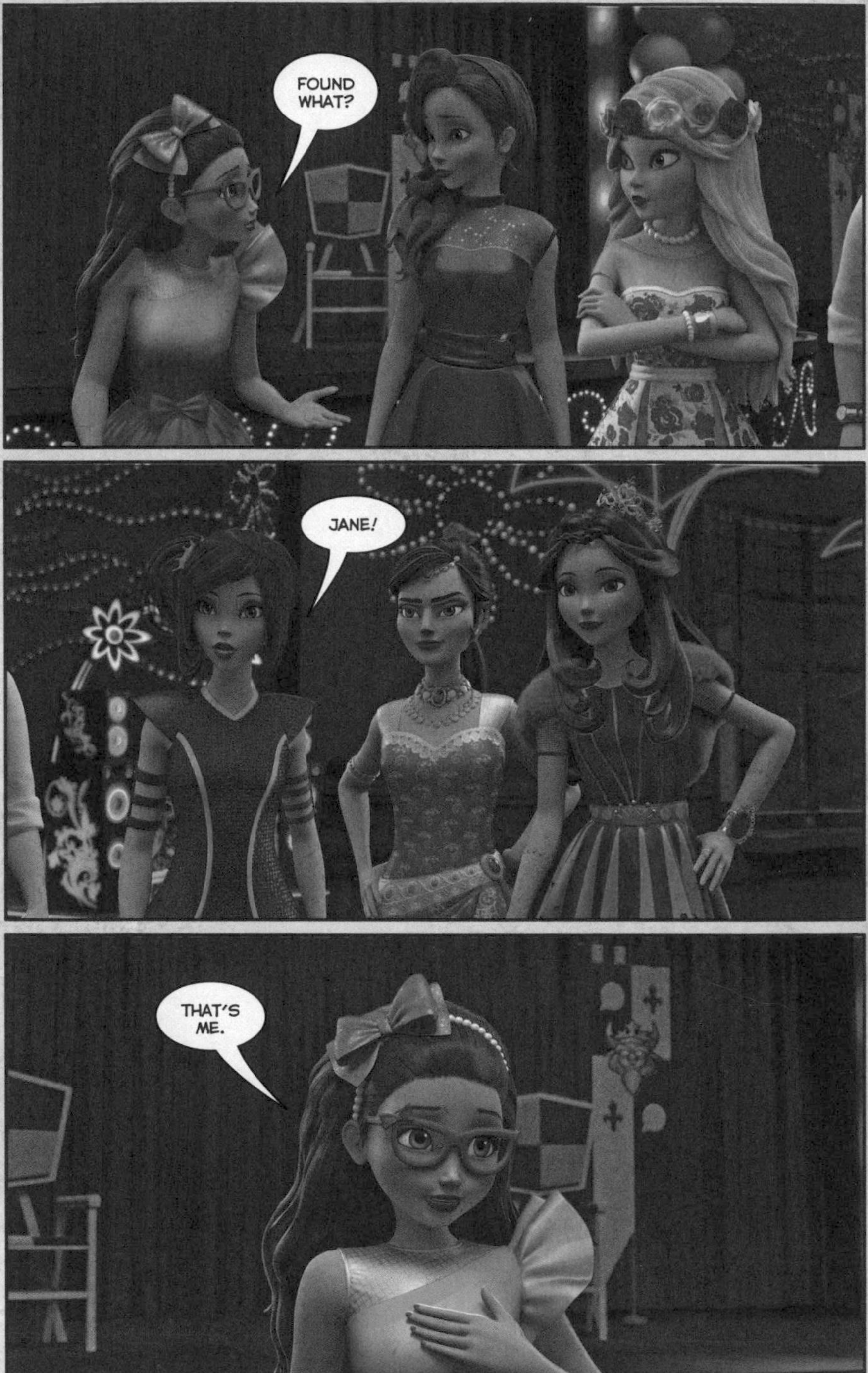
FOUND WHAT?
JANE!
THAT'S ME.

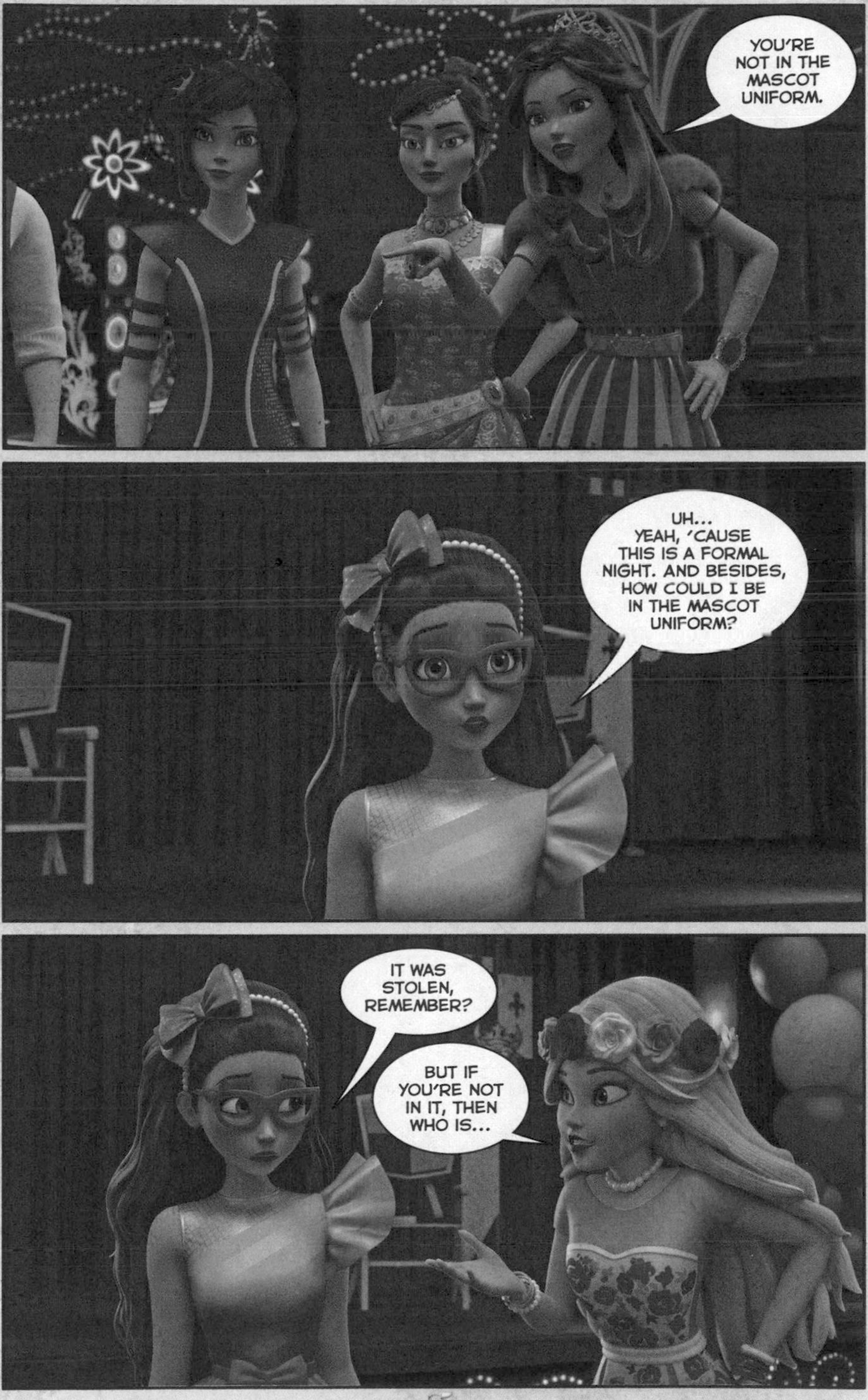
YOU'RE NOT IN THE MASCOT UNIFORM.
UH... YEAH, 'CAUSE THIS IS A FORMAL NIGHT. AND BESIDES, HOW COULD I BE IN THE MASCOT UNIFORM?
IT WAS STOLEN, REMEMBER?
BUT IF YOU'RE NOT IN IT, THEN WHO IS...

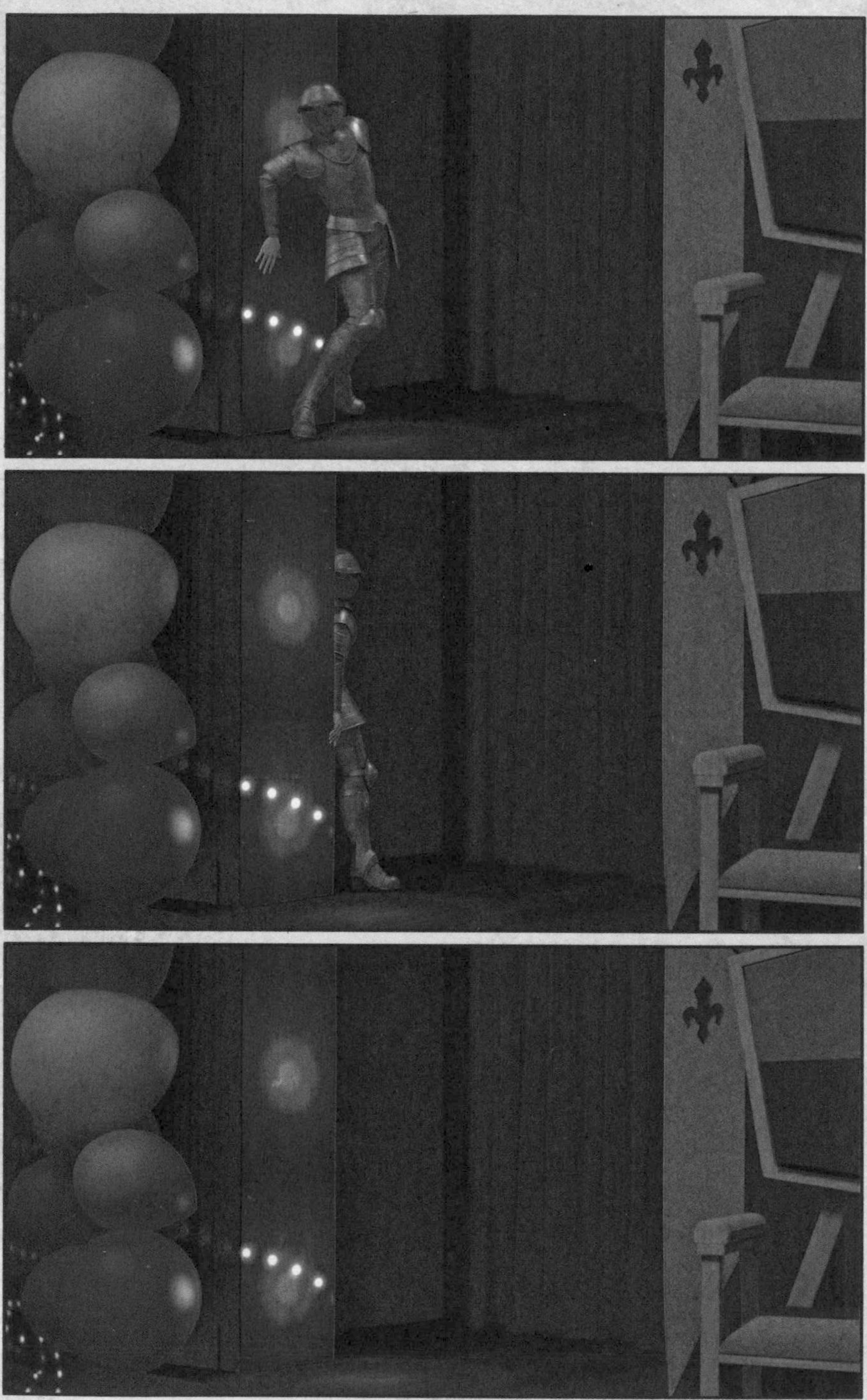

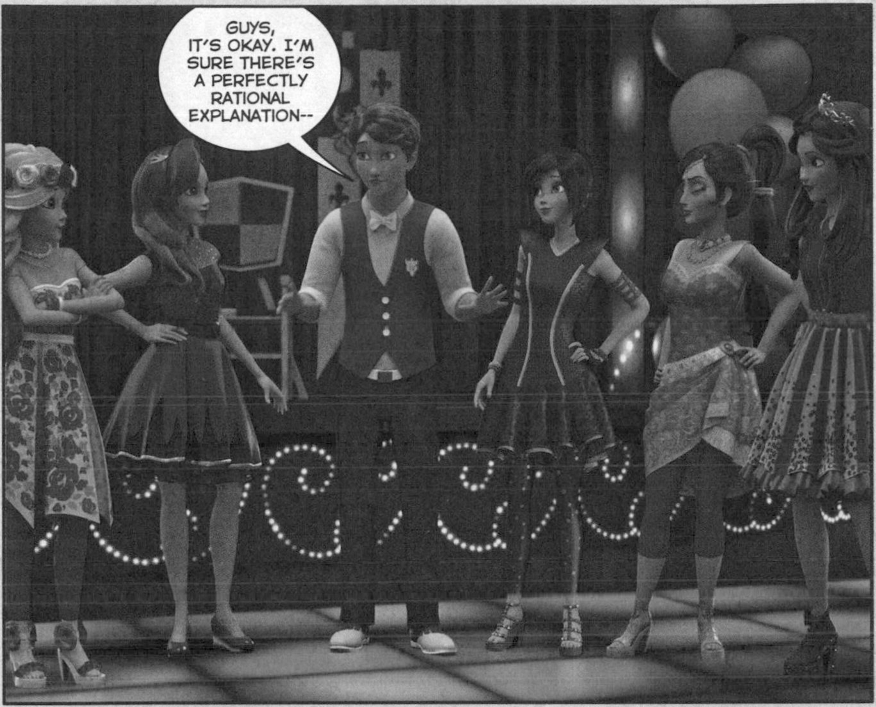
GUYS, IT'S OKAY. I'M SURE THERE'S A PERFECTLY RATIONAL EXPLANATION--

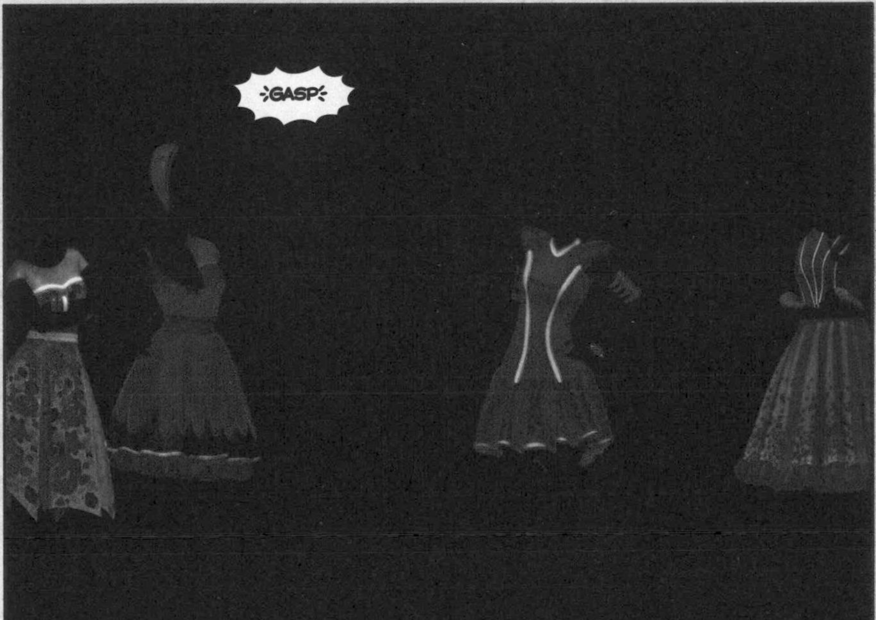
GASP

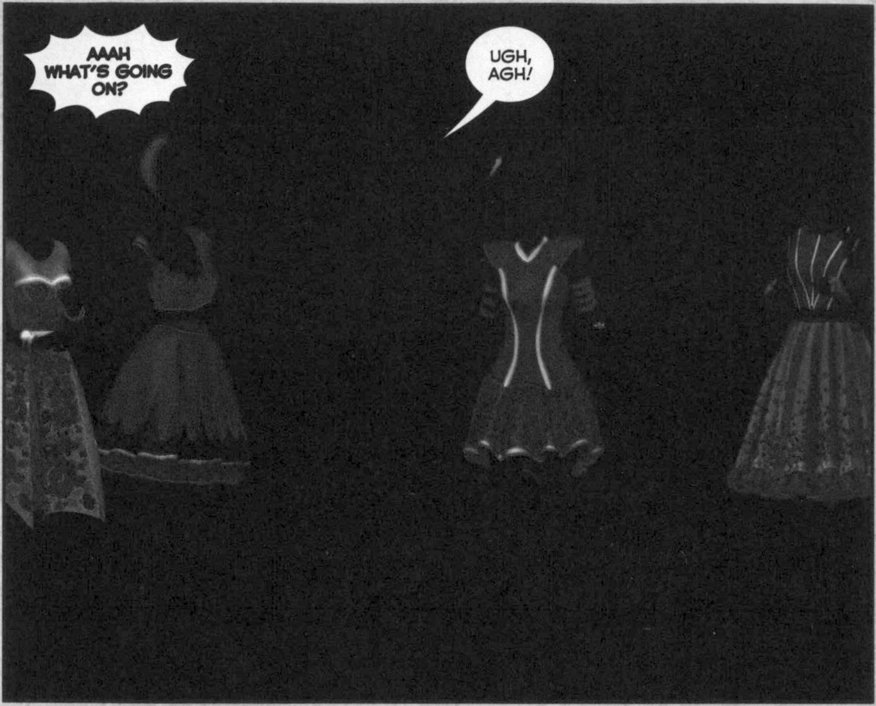
AAAH WHAT'S GOING ON?
UGH, AGH!

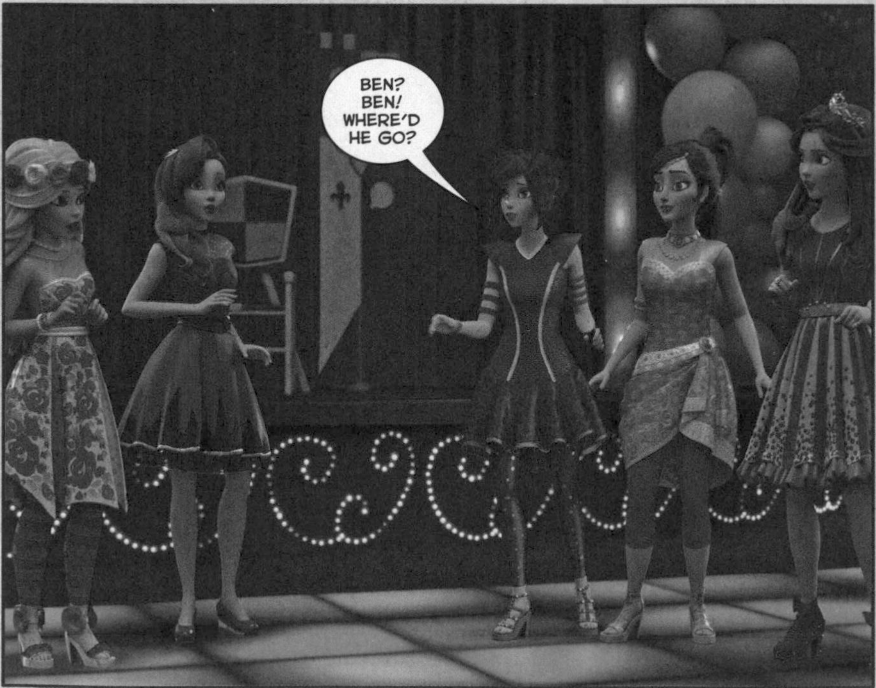
BEN? BEN! WHERE'D HE GO?

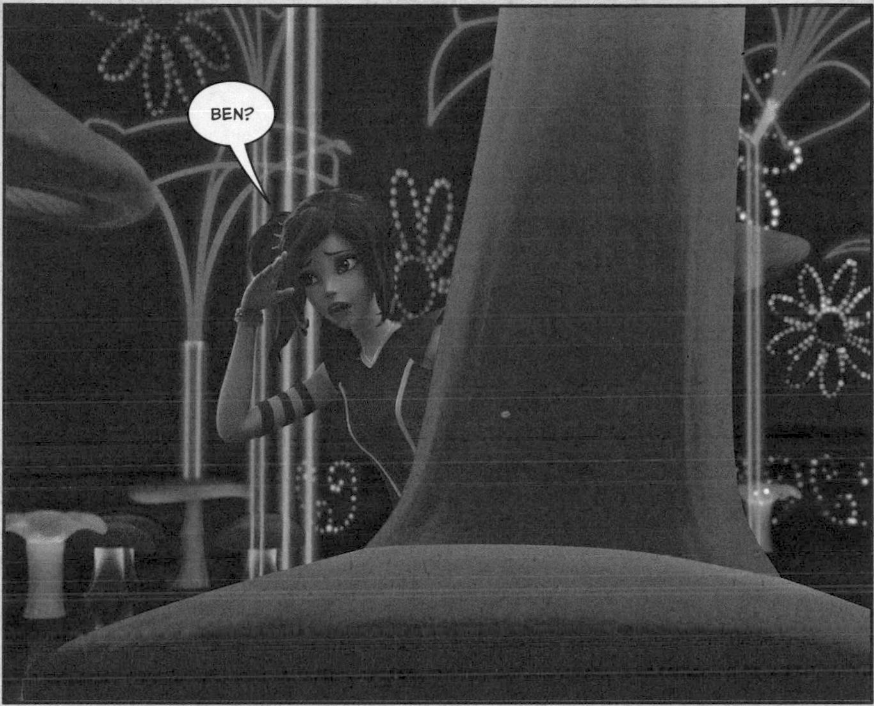
BEN?

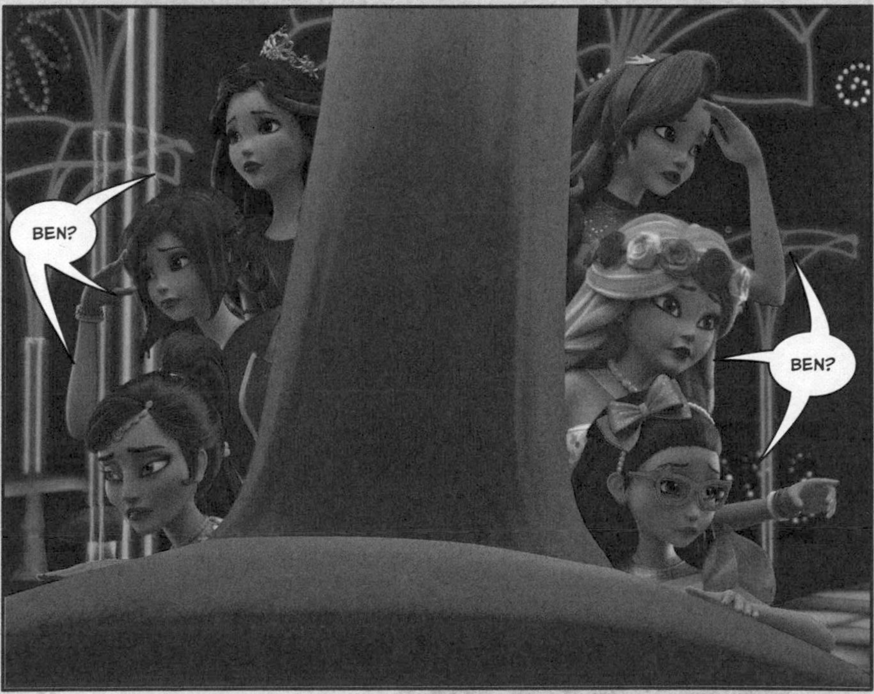
BEN?
BEN?

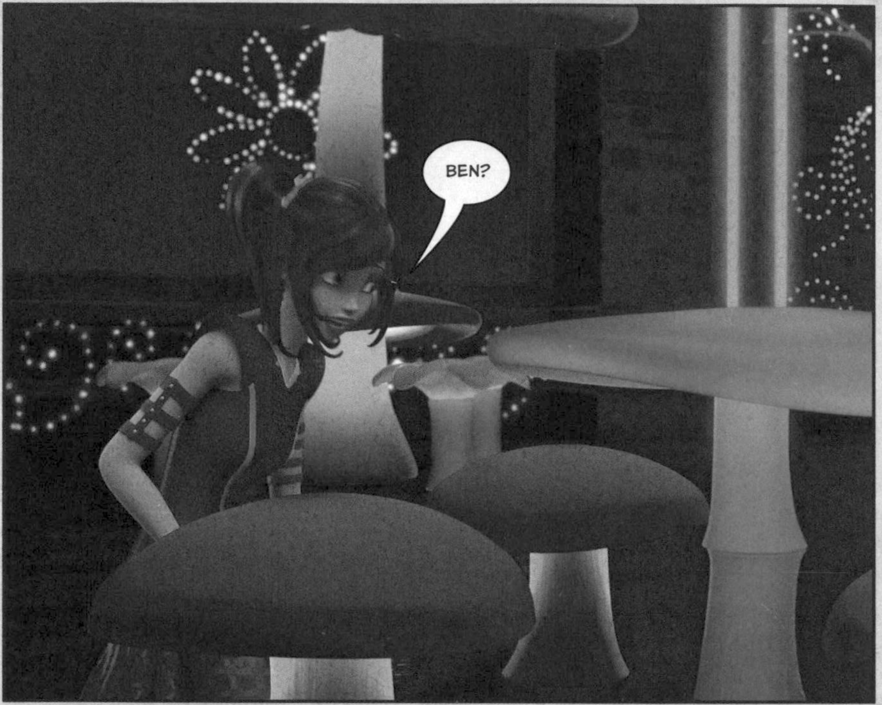
BEN?

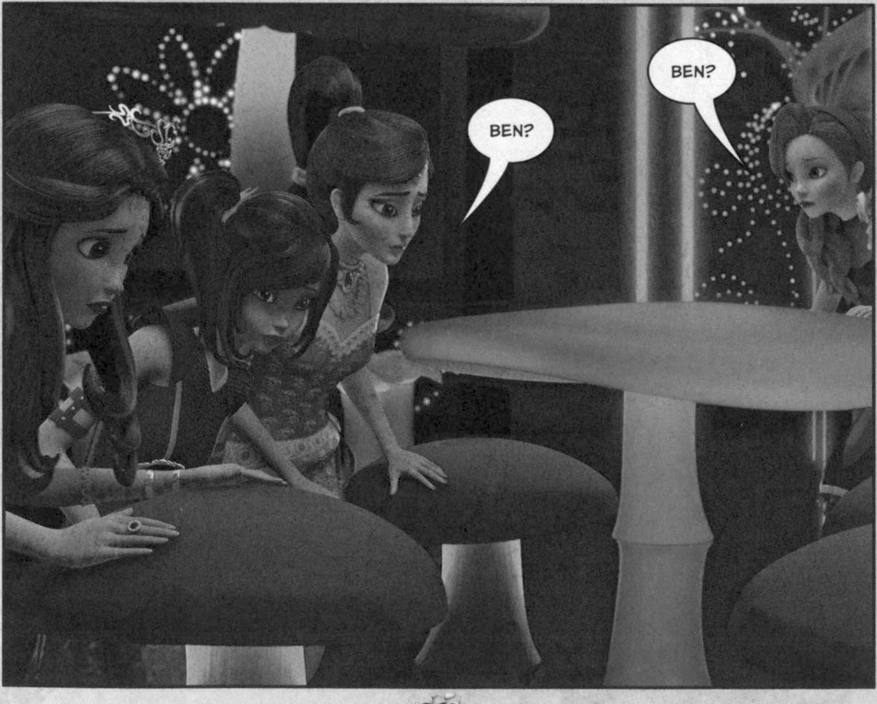
BEN?
BEN?

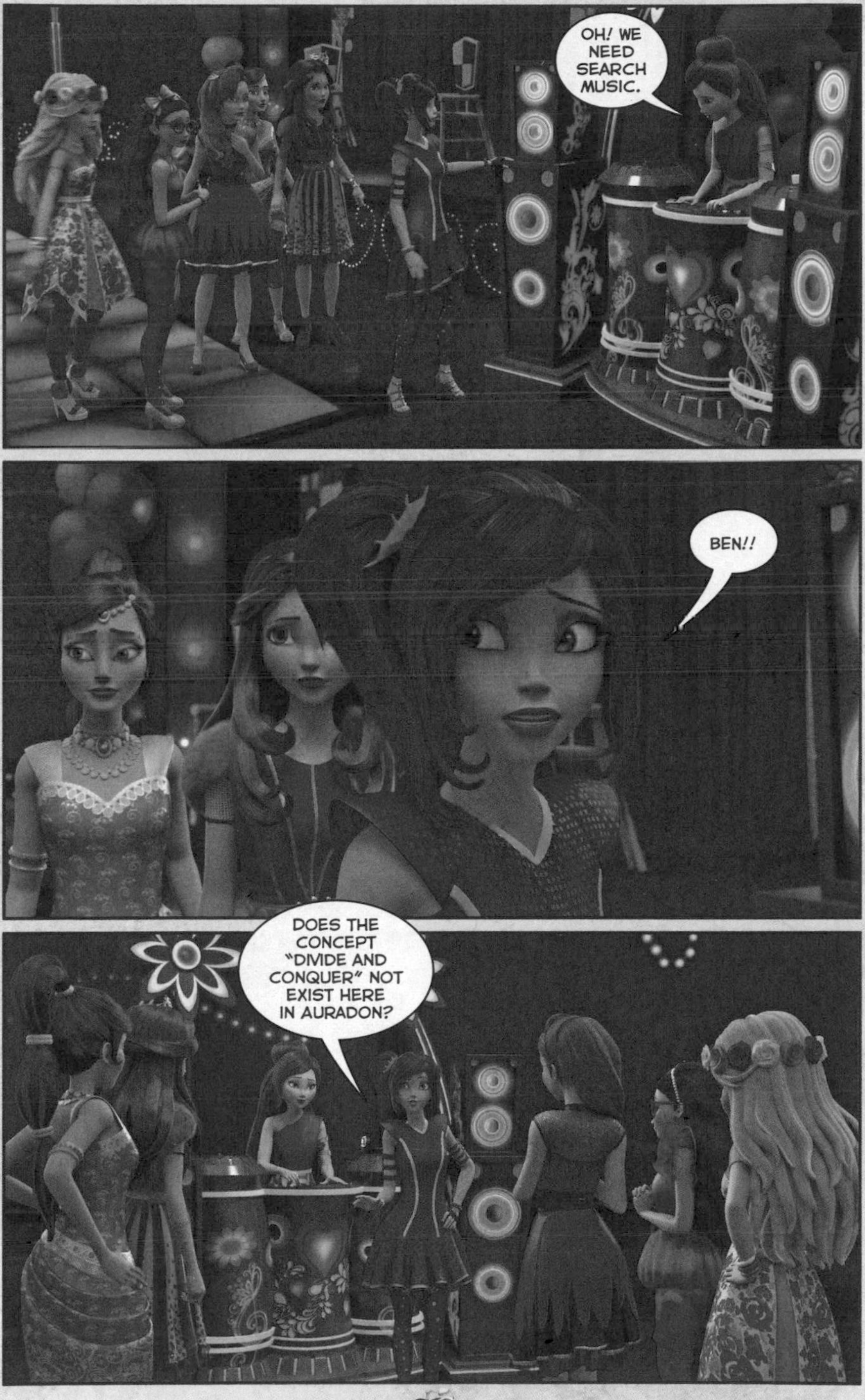
OH! WE NEED SEARCH MUSIC.
BEN!!
DOES THE CONCEPT "DIVIDE AND CONQUER" NOT EXIST HERE IN AURADON?

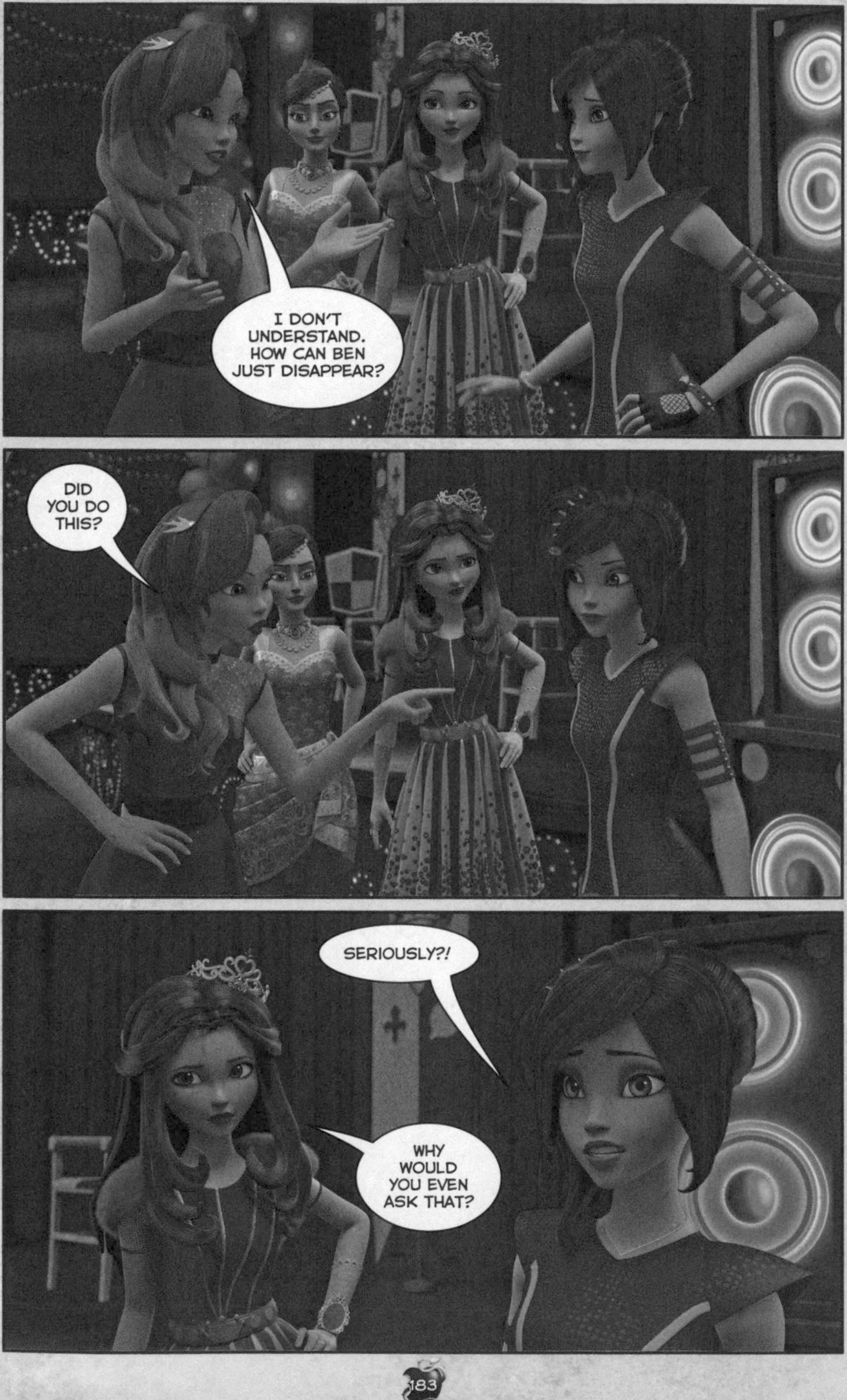
I DON'T UNDERSTAND. HOW CAN BEN JUST DISAPPEAR?
DID YOU DO THIS?
SERIOUSLY?!
WHY WOULD YOU EVEN ASK THAT?

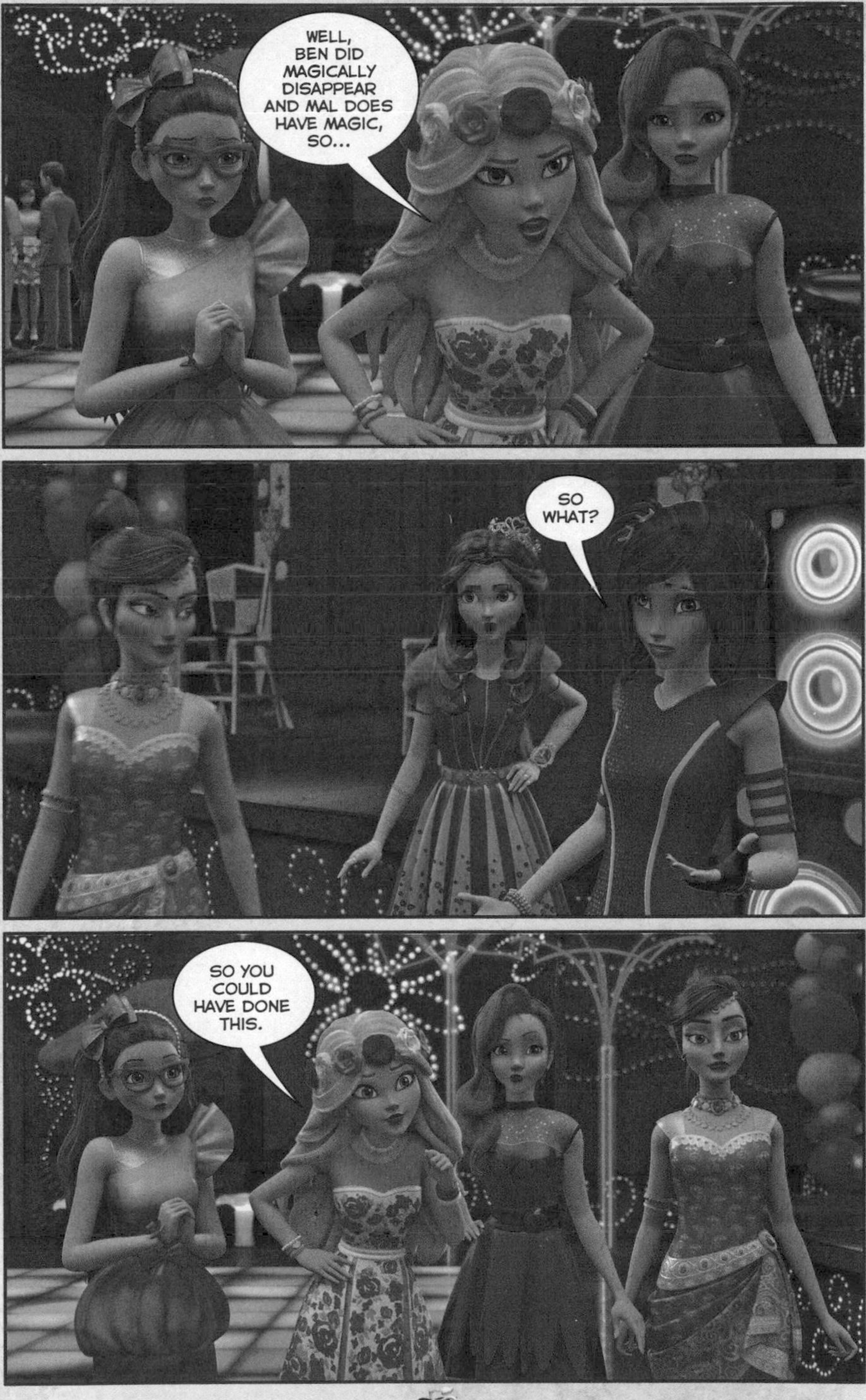
WELL, BEN DID MAGICALLY DISAPPEAR AND MAL DOES HAVE MAGIC, SO...
SO WHAT?
SO YOU COULD HAVE DONE THIS.

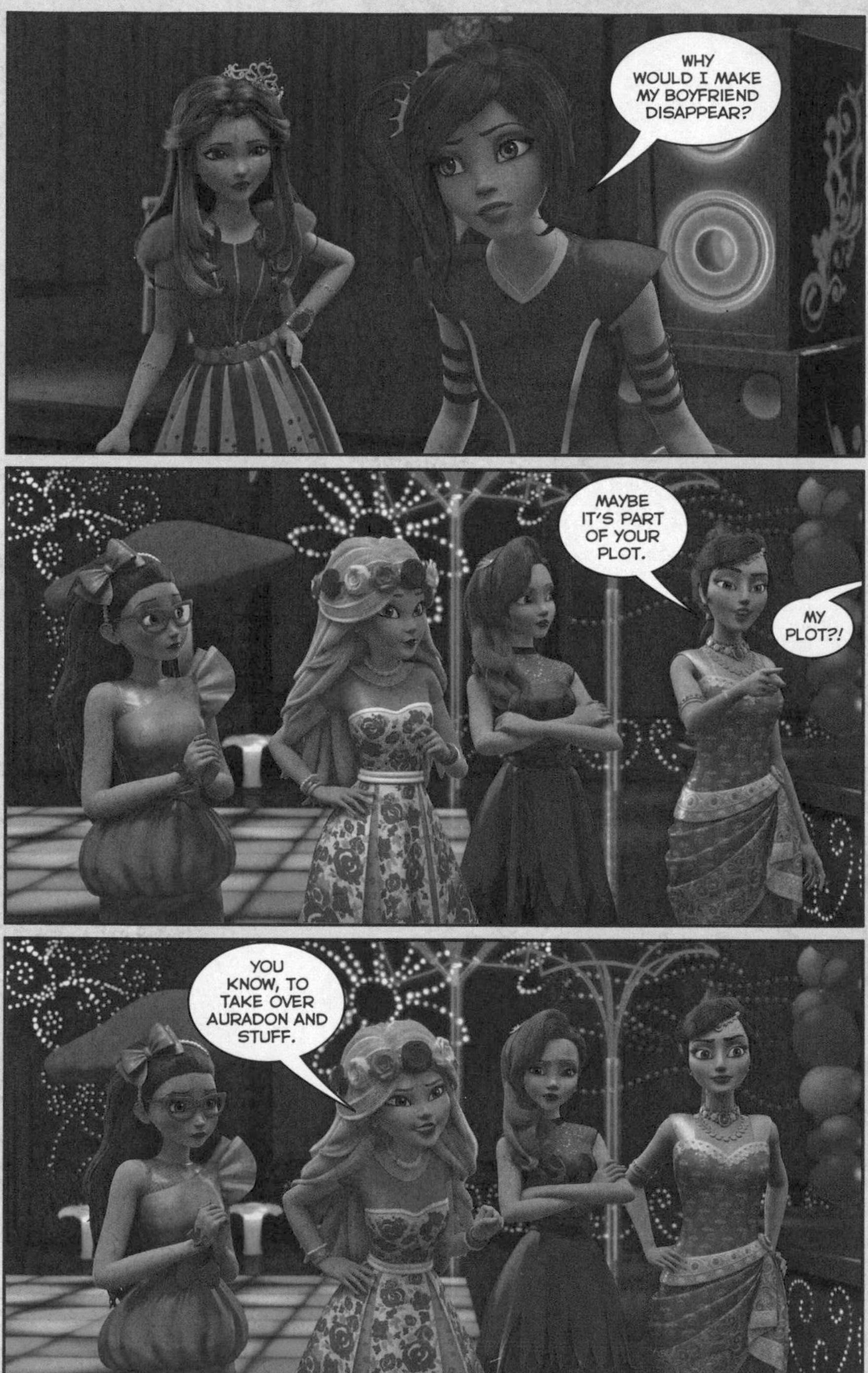
WHY WOULD I MAKE MY BOYFRIEND DISAPPEAR?
MAYBE IT'S PART OF YOUR PLOT.
MY PLOT?!
YOU KNOW, TO TAKE OVER AURADON AND STUFF.

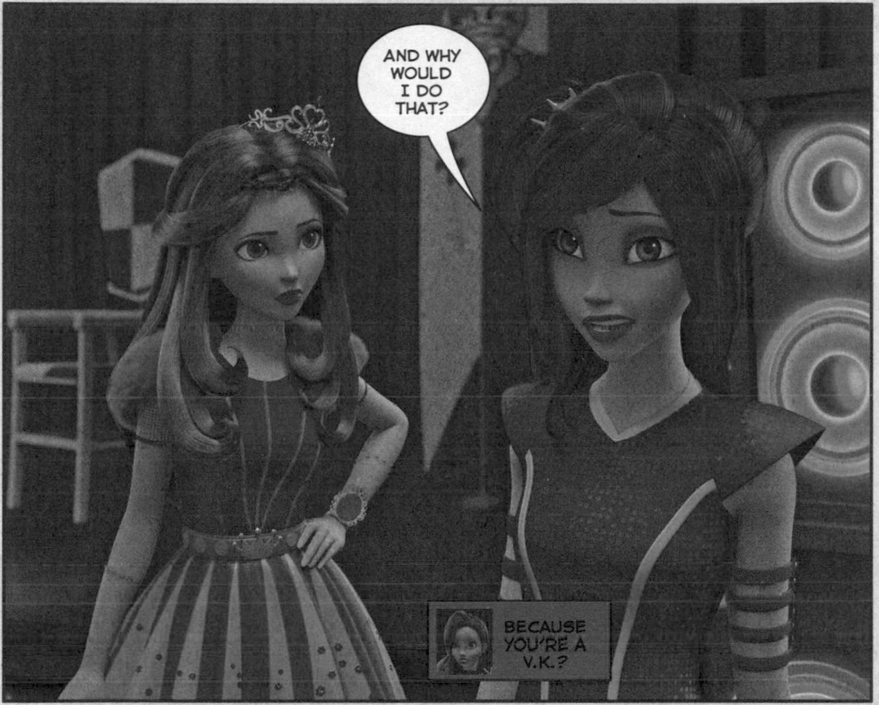
AND WHY WOULD I DO THAT?
BECAUSE YOU'RE A V.K.?

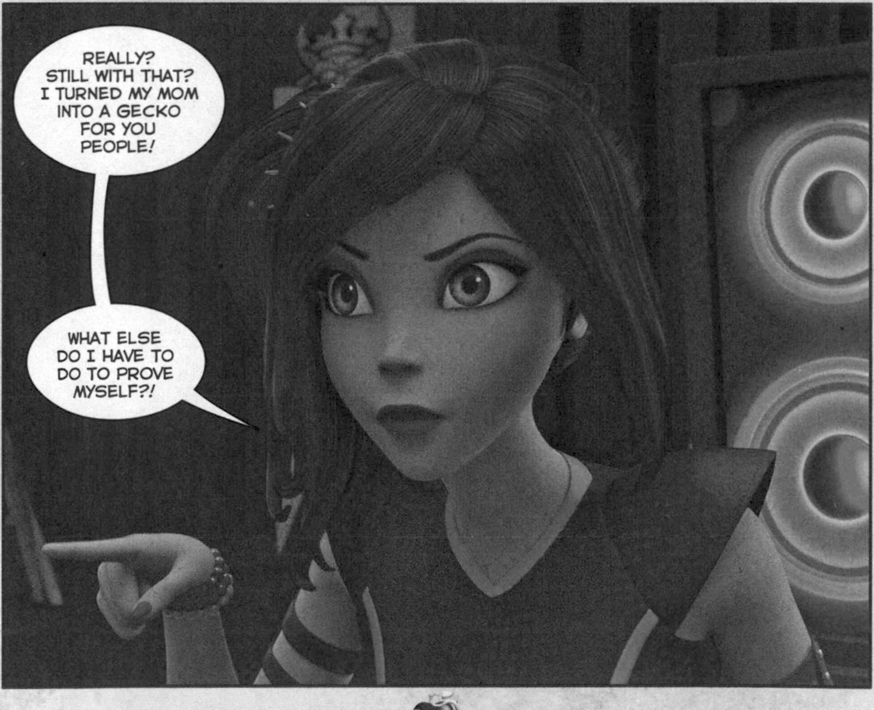
REALLY? STILL WITH THAT? I TURNED MY MOM INTO A GECKO FOR YOU PEOPLE!
WHAT ELSE DO I HAVE TO DO TO PROVE MYSELF?!

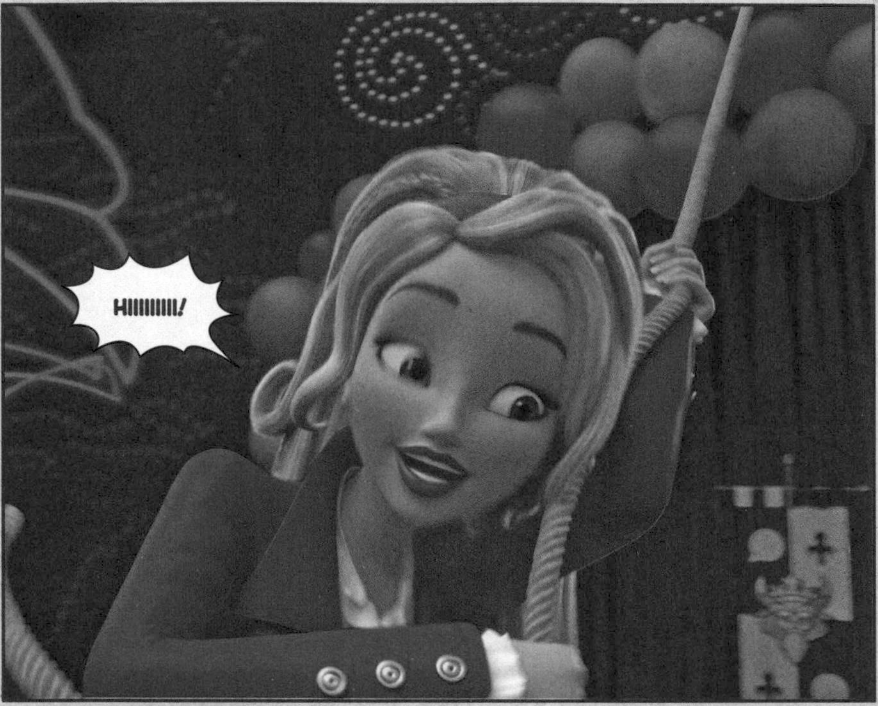
HIIIIIIII!

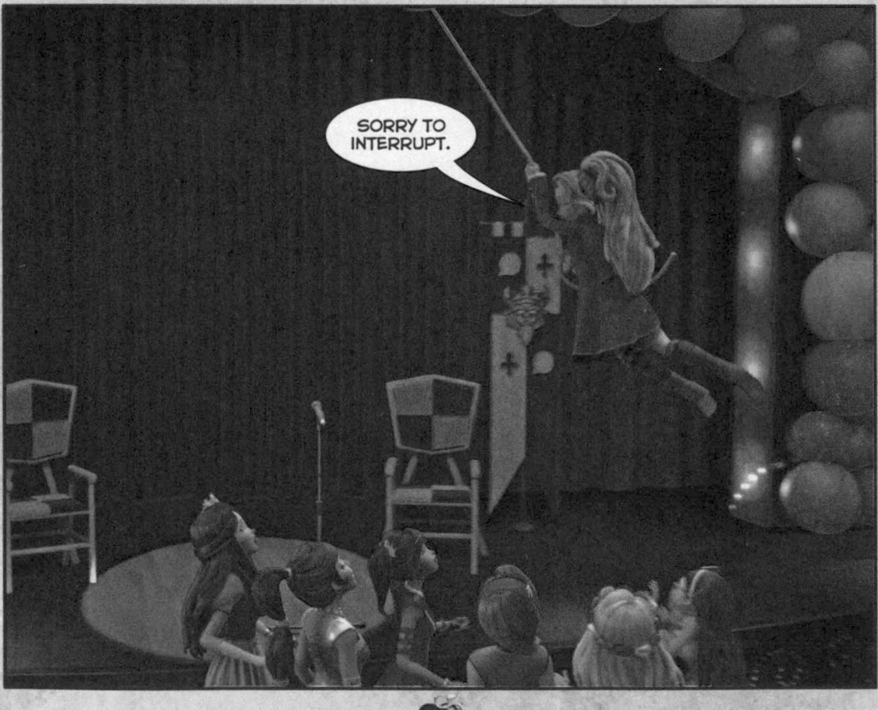
SORRY TO
INTERRUPT.

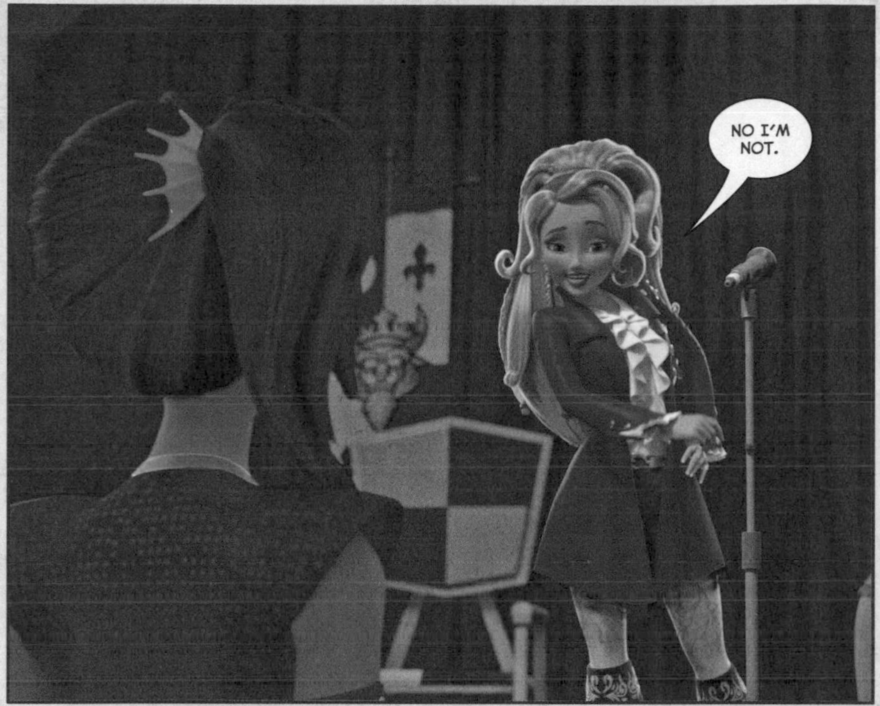
NO I'M NOT.

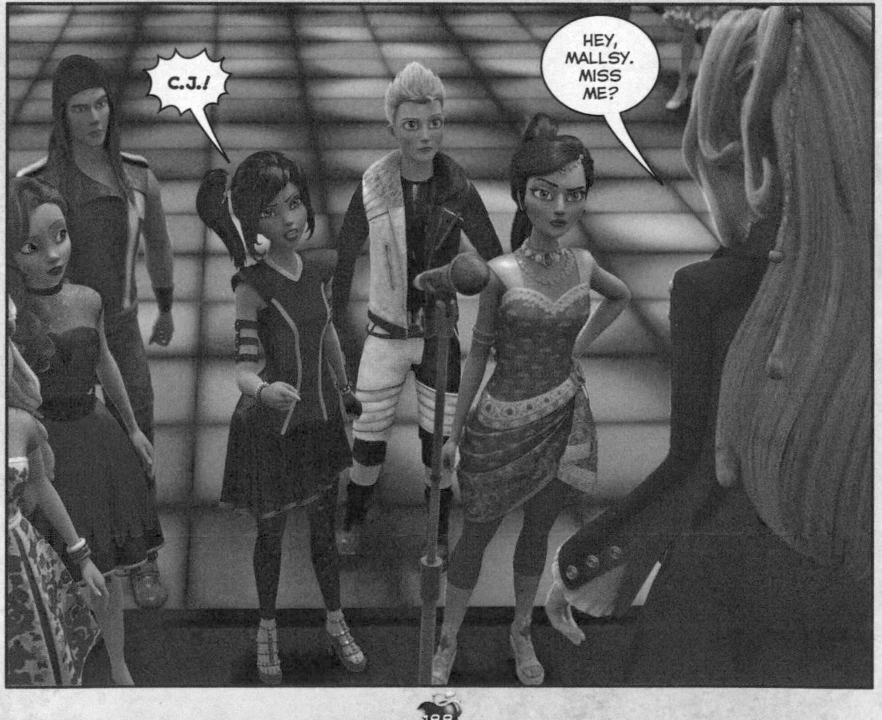
HEY, MALLSY. MISS ME?
C.J.!

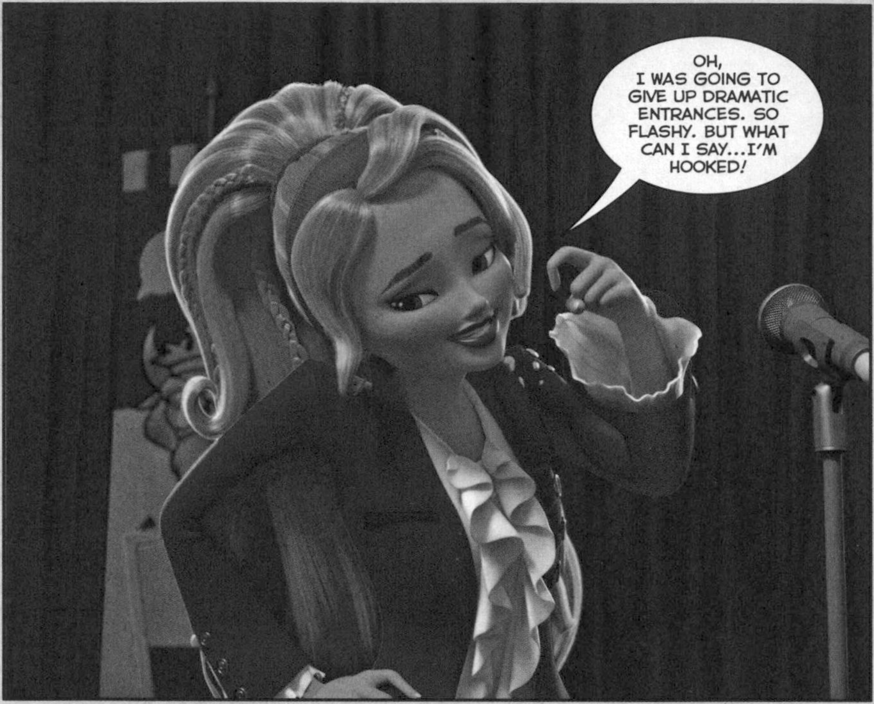
OH, I WAS GOING TO GIVE UP DRAMATIC ENTRANCES. SO FLASHY. BUT WHAT CAN I SAY...I'M HOOKED!

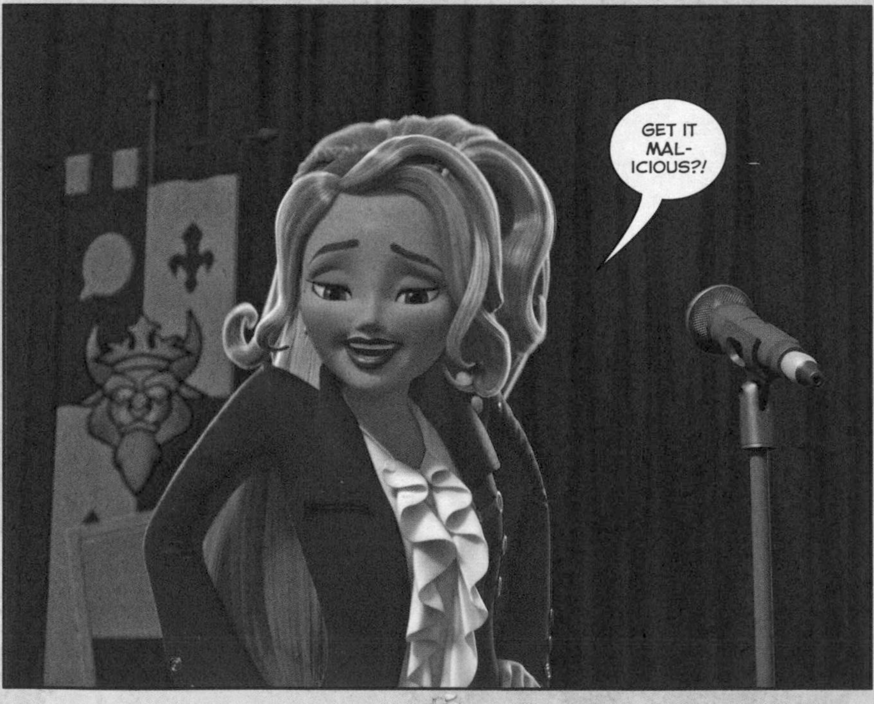
GET IT MAL-ICIOUS?!

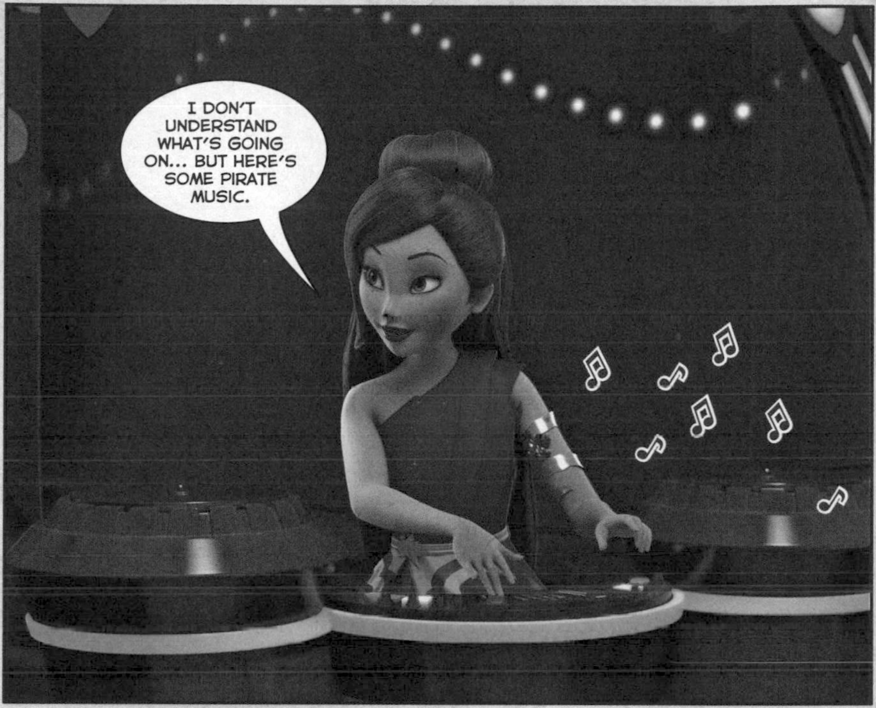
I DON'T UNDERSTAND WHAT'S GOING ON... BUT HERE'S SOME PIRATE MUSIC.

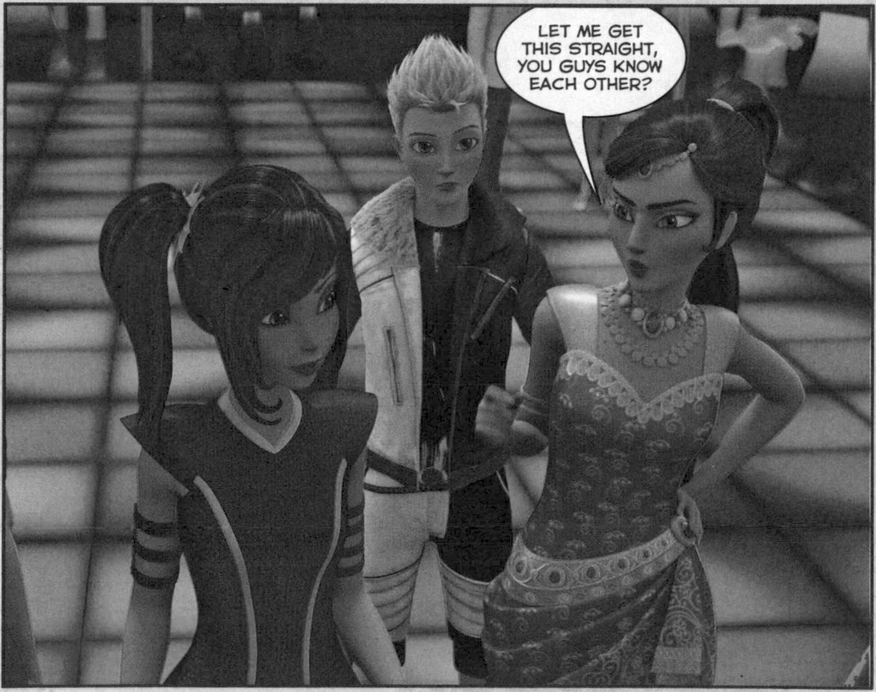
LET ME GET THIS STRAIGHT, YOU GUYS KNOW EACH OTHER?

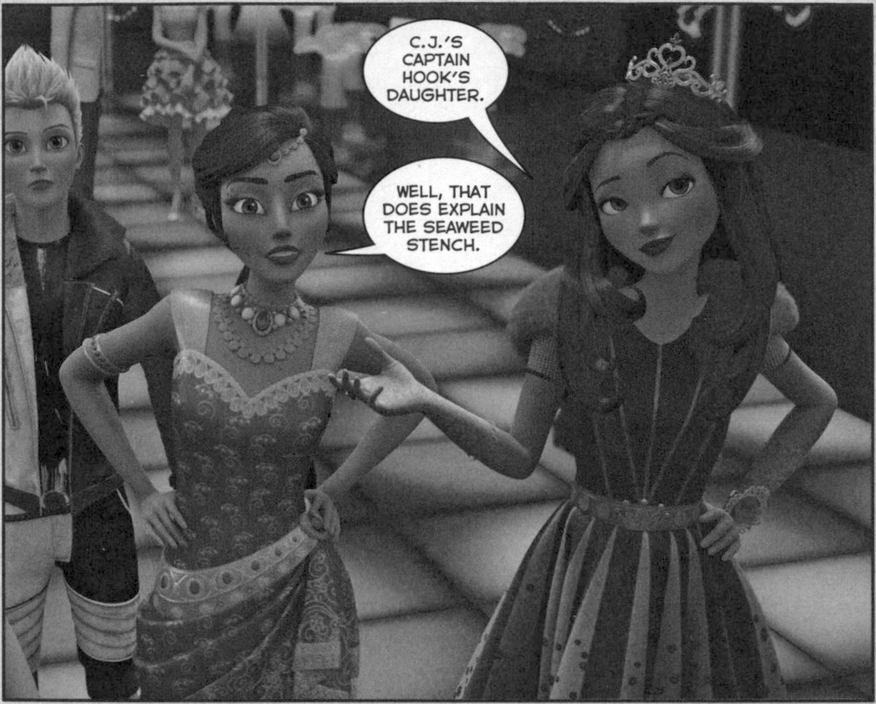
C.J.'S CAPTAIN HOOK'S DAUGHTER.
WELL, THAT DOES EXPLAIN THE SEAWEED STENCH.

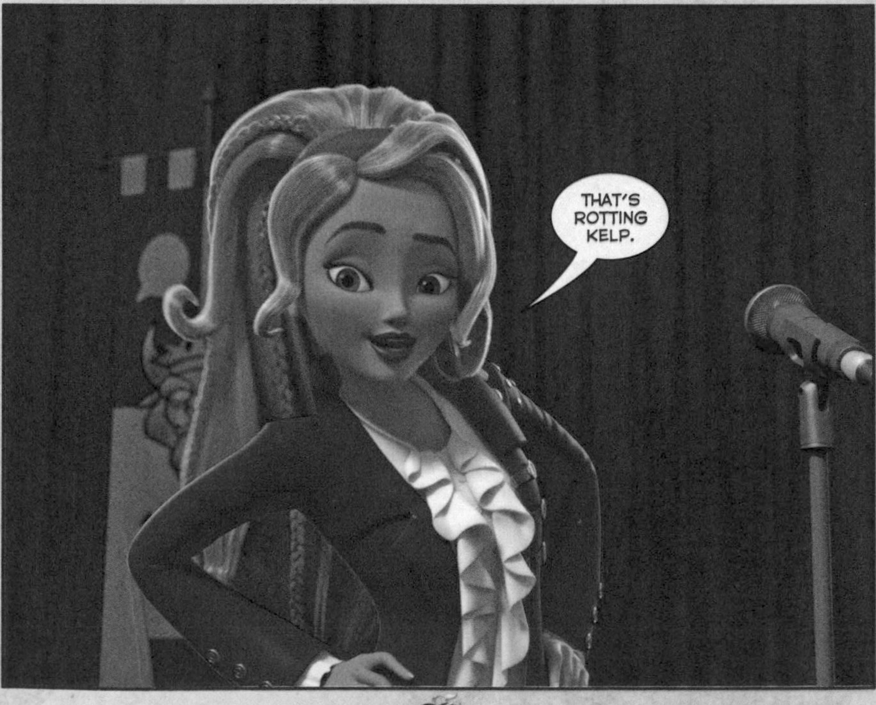
THAT'S ROTTING KELP.

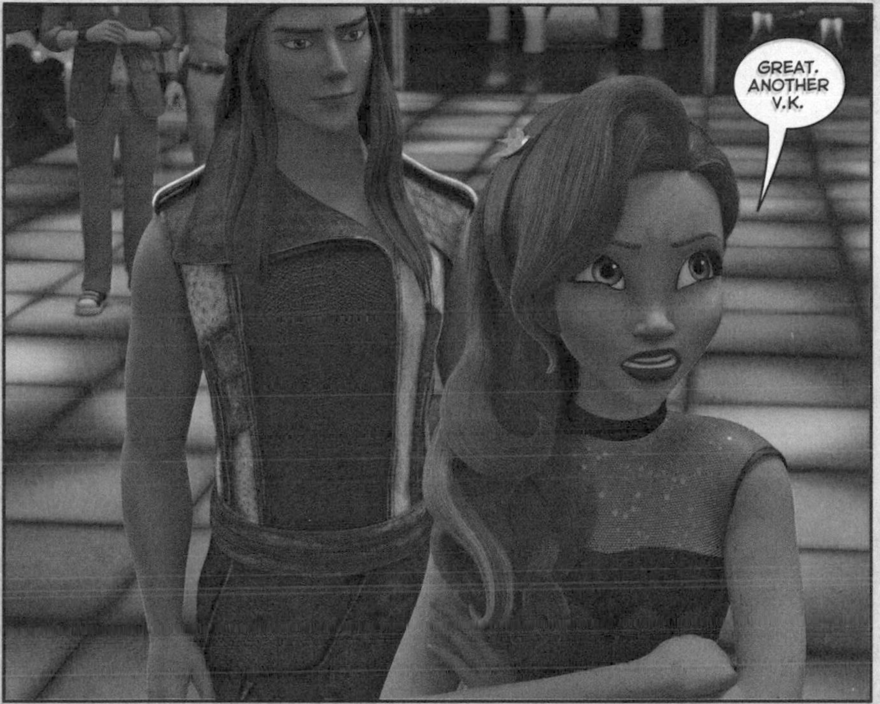
GREAT. ANOTHER V.K.

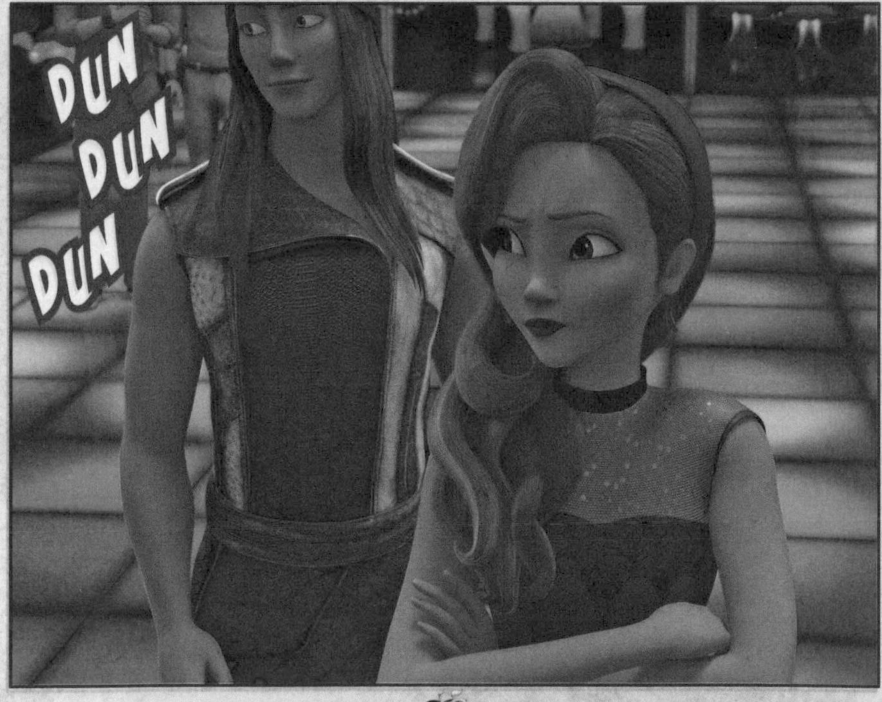
DUN DUN DUN

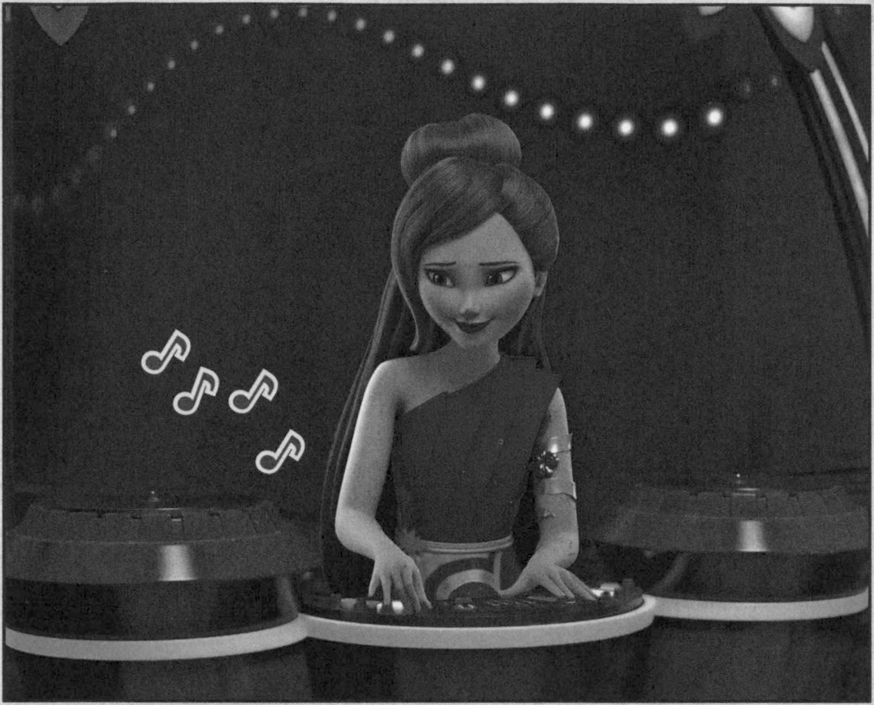

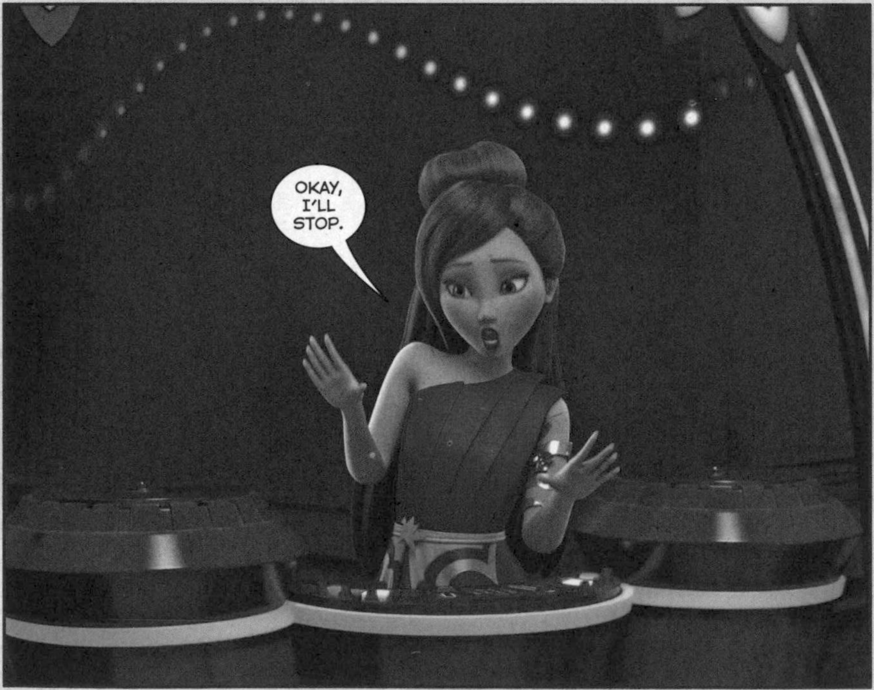
OKAY, I'LL STOP.

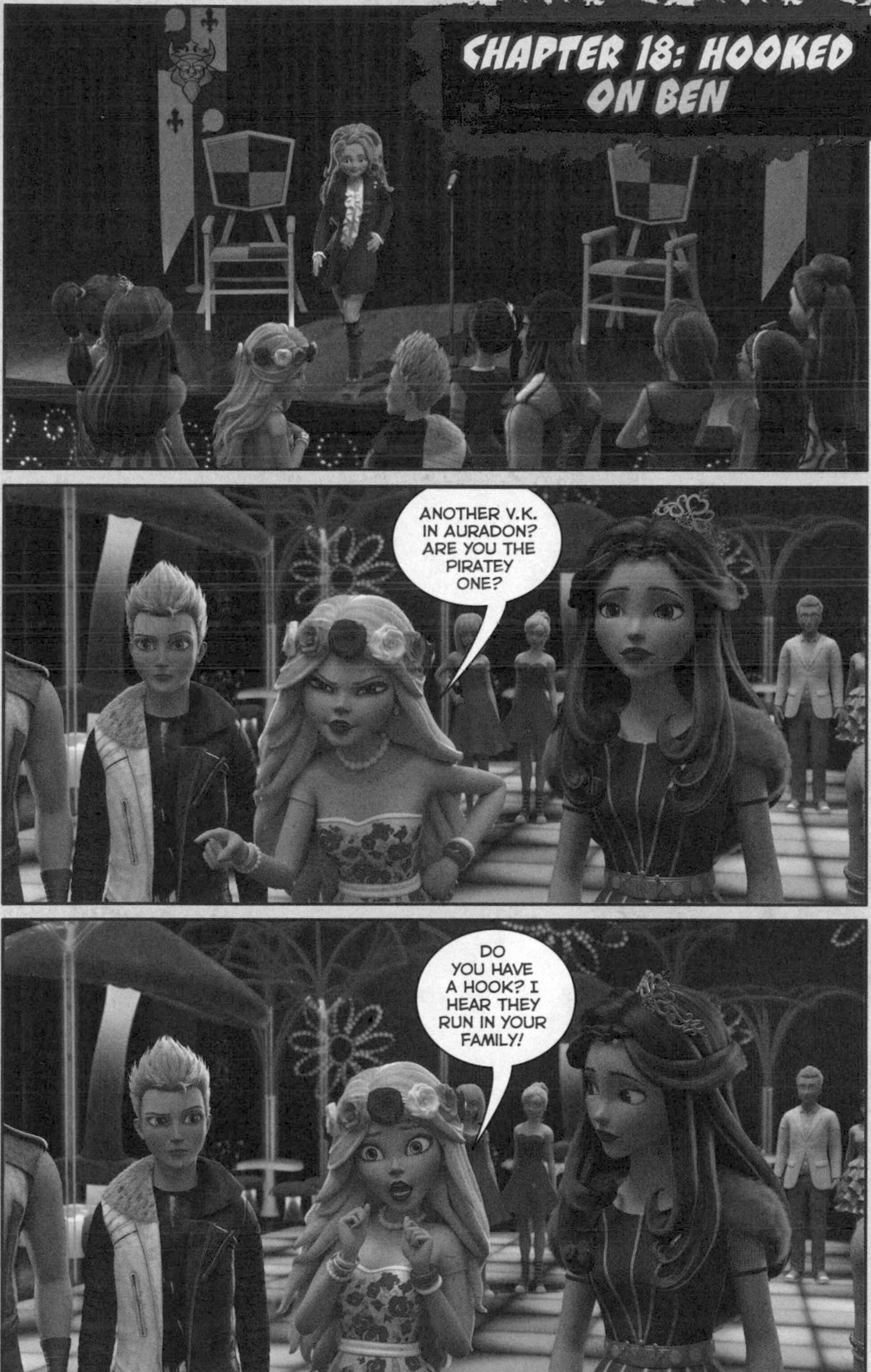
CHAPTER 18: HOOKED ON BEN
ANOTHER V.K. IN AURADON? ARE YOU THE PIRATEY ONE?
DO YOU HAVE A HOOK? I HEAR THEY RUN IN YOUR FAMILY!

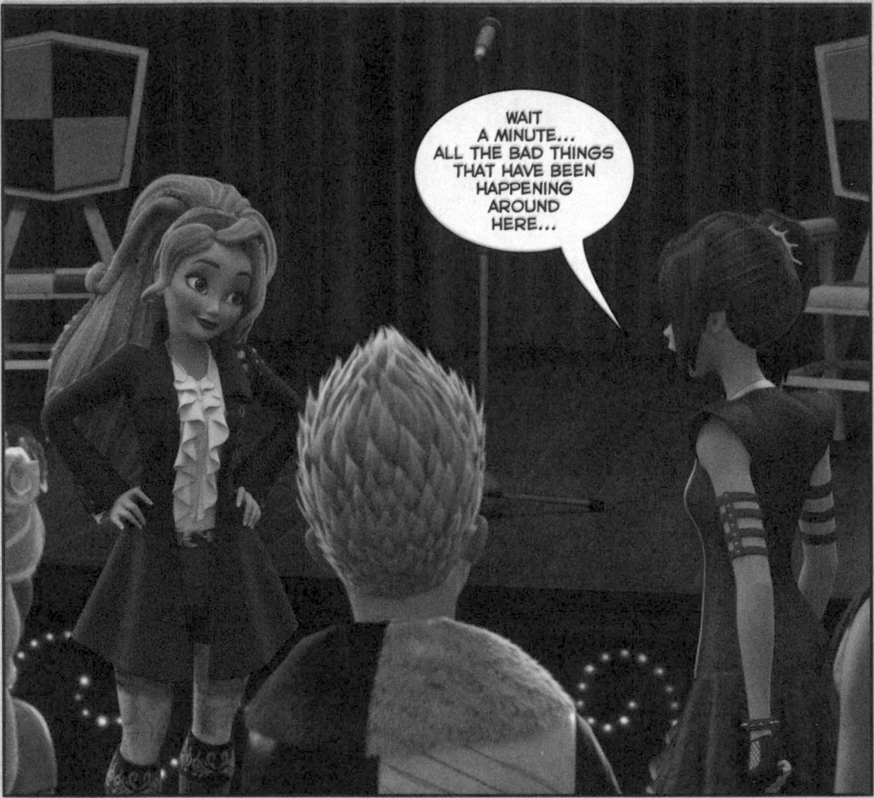
WAIT A MINUTE... ALL THE BAD THINGS THAT HAVE BEEN HAPPENING AROUND HERE...

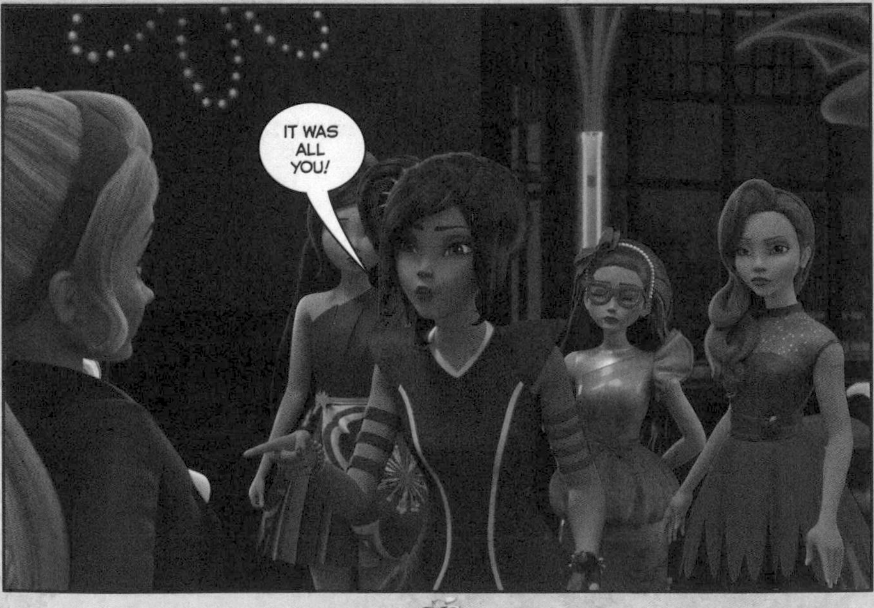
IT WAS ALL YOU!

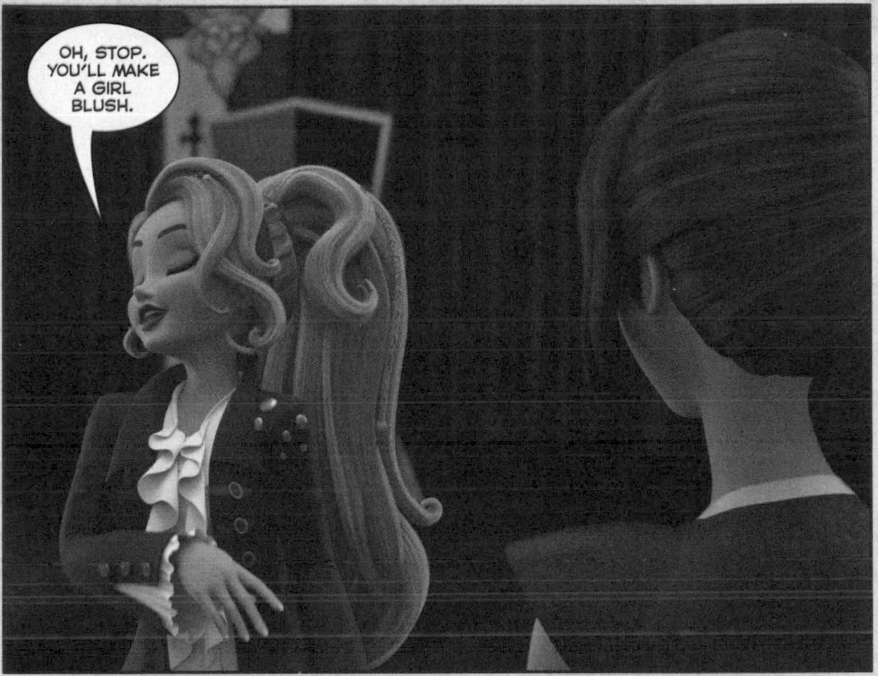
OH, STOP. YOU'LL MAKE A GIRL BLUSH.

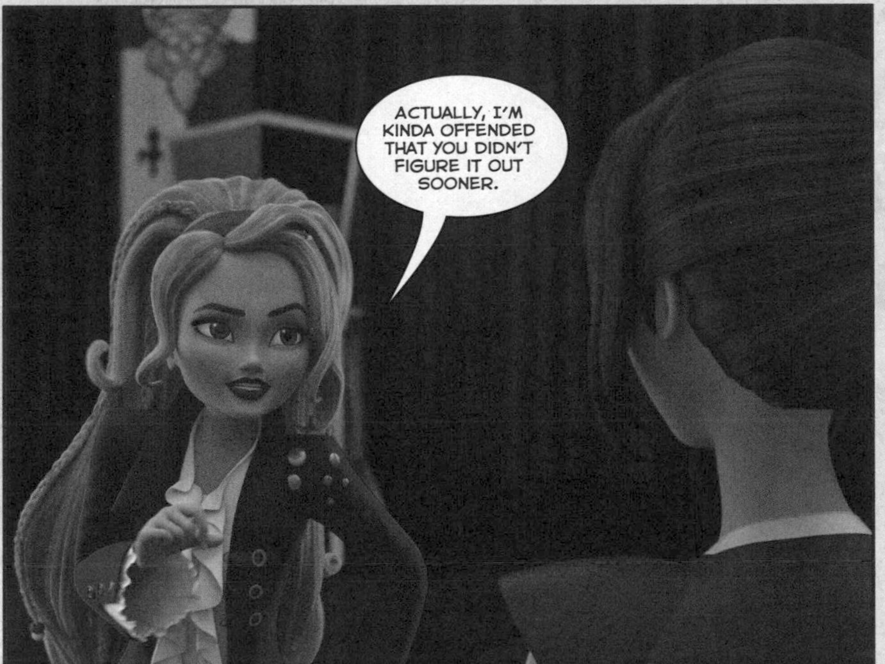
ACTUALLY, I'M KINDA OFFENDED THAT YOU DIDN'T FIGURE IT OUT SOONER.

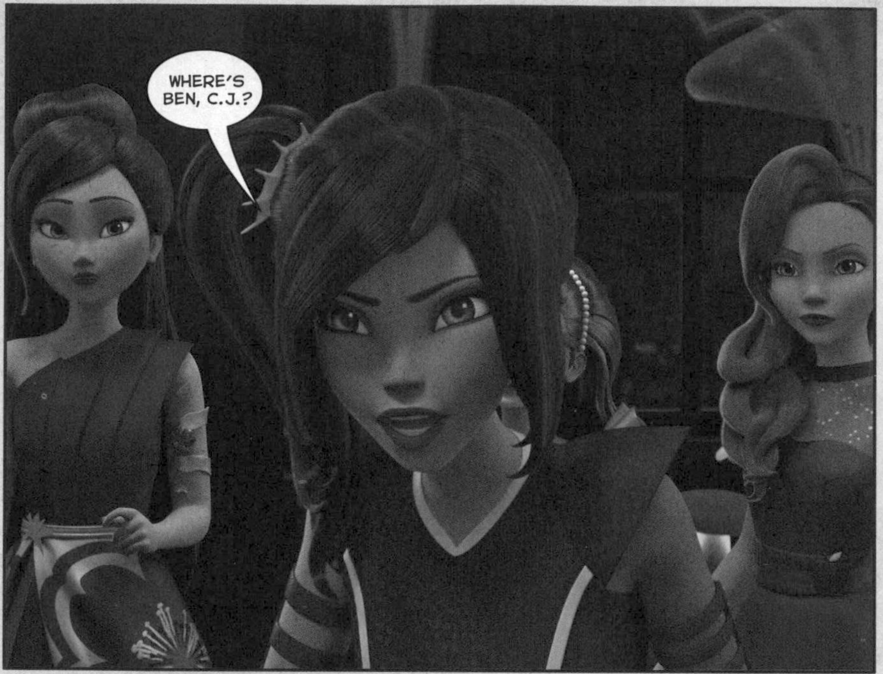
WHERE'S BEN, C.J.?

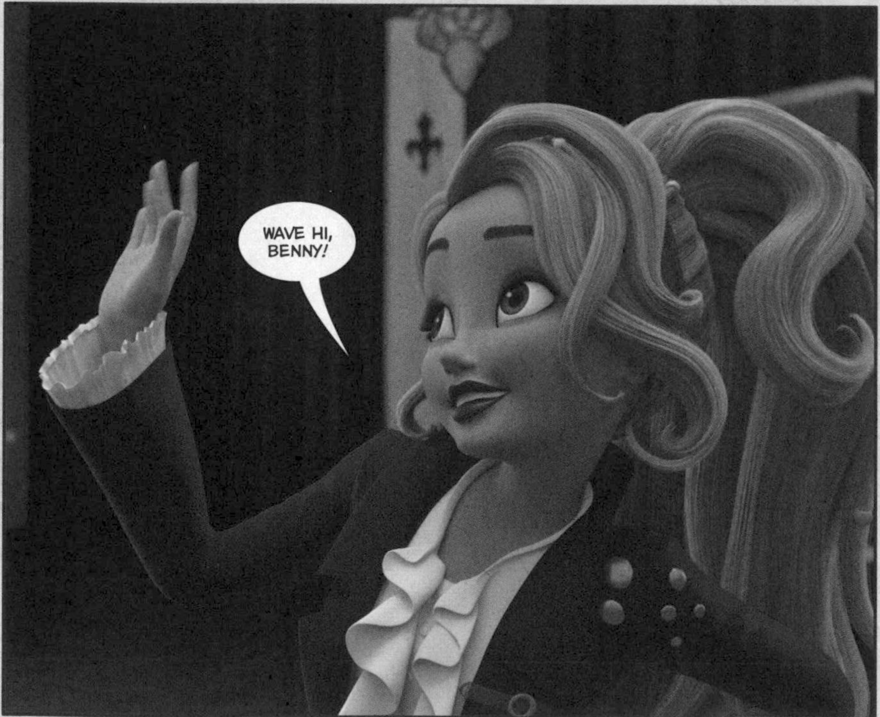
WAVE HI, BENNY!

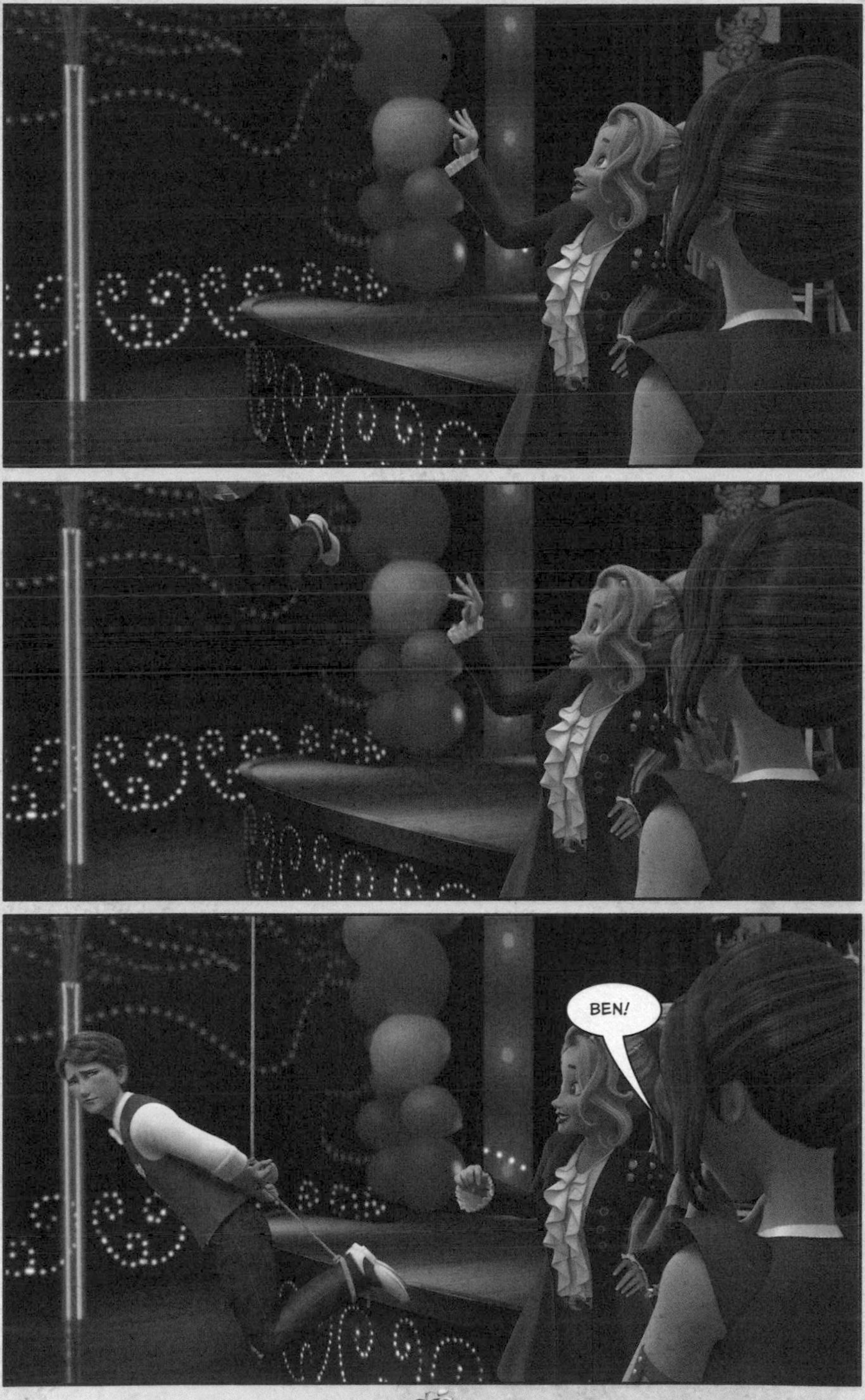
BEN!

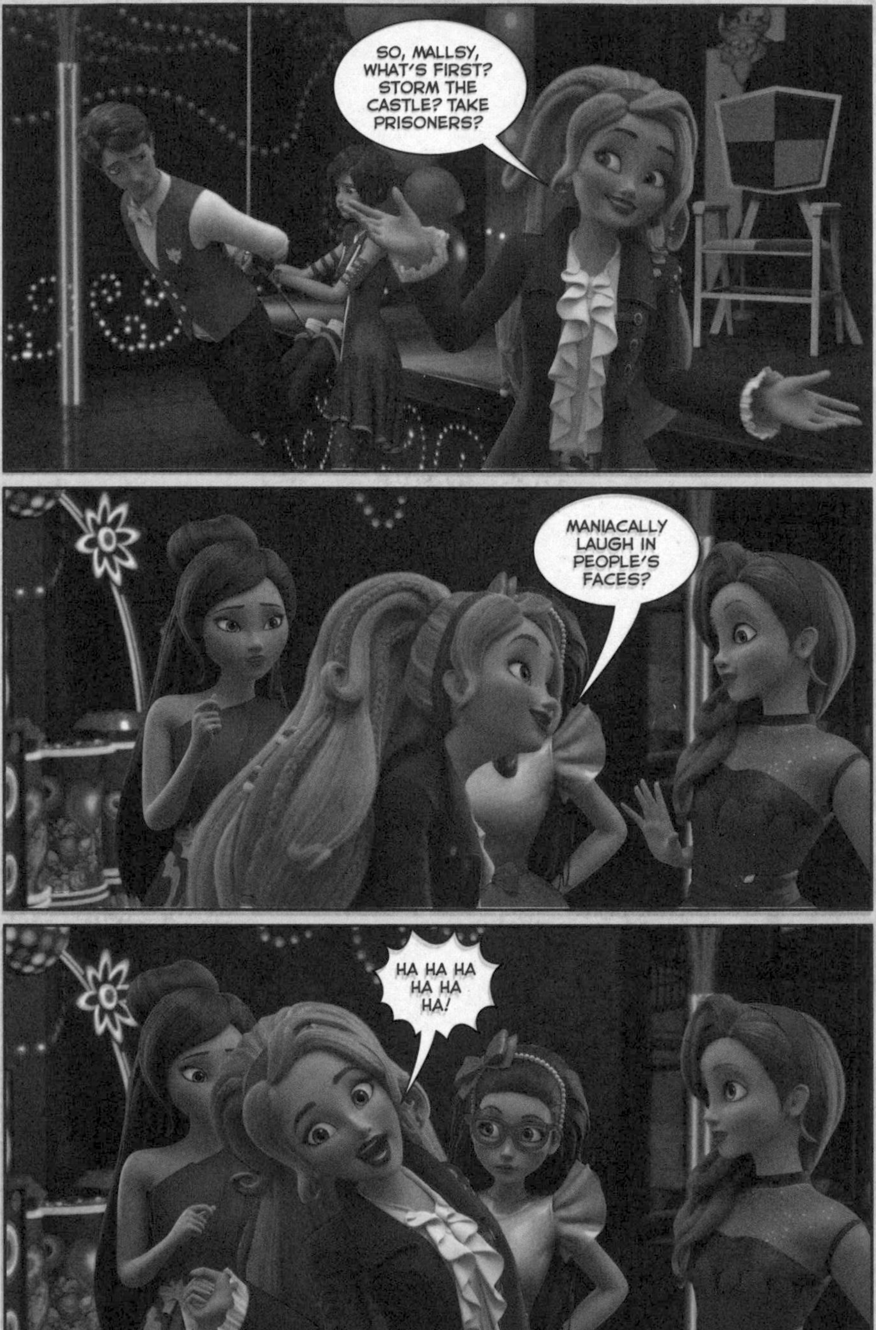
SO, MALLSY, WHAT'S FIRST? STORM THE CASTLE? TAKE PRISONERS?
MANIACALLY LAUGH IN PEOPLE'S FACES?
HA HA HA HA HA HA HA!

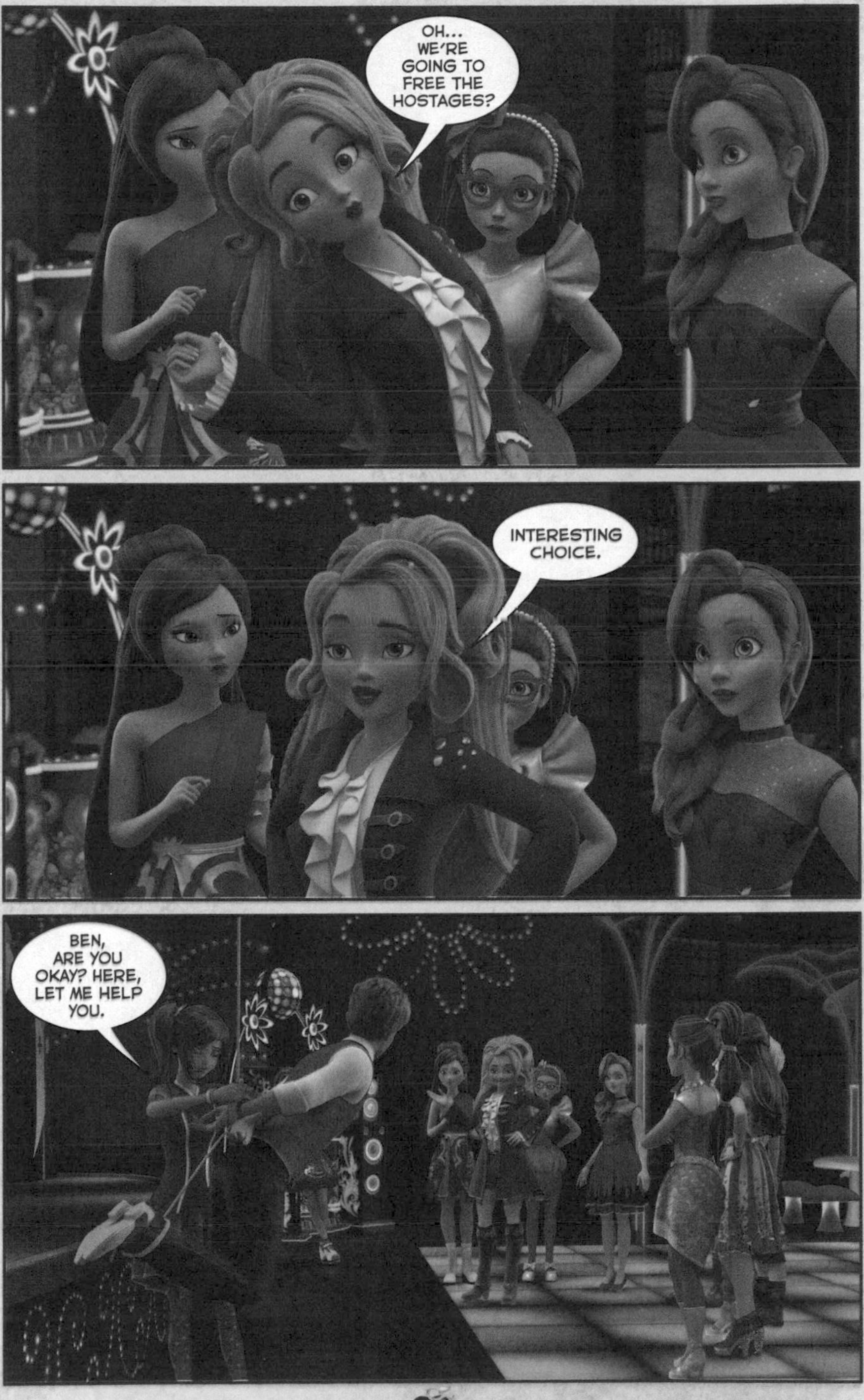
OH... WE'RE GOING TO FREE THE HOSTAGES?
INTERESTING CHOICE.
BEN, ARE YOU OKAY? HERE, LET ME HELP YOU.

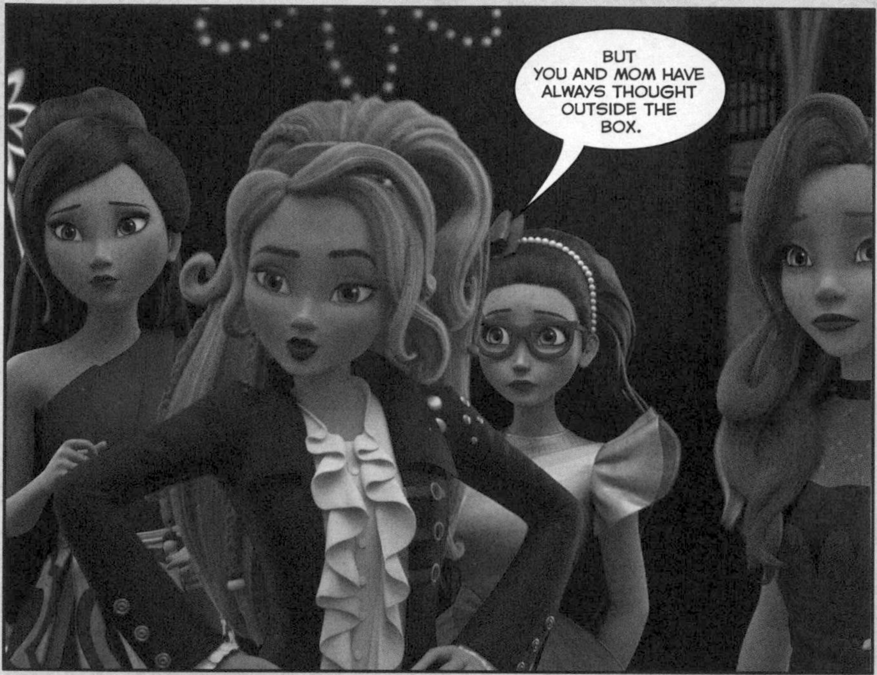
BUT YOU AND MOM HAVE ALWAYS THOUGHT OUTSIDE THE BOX.

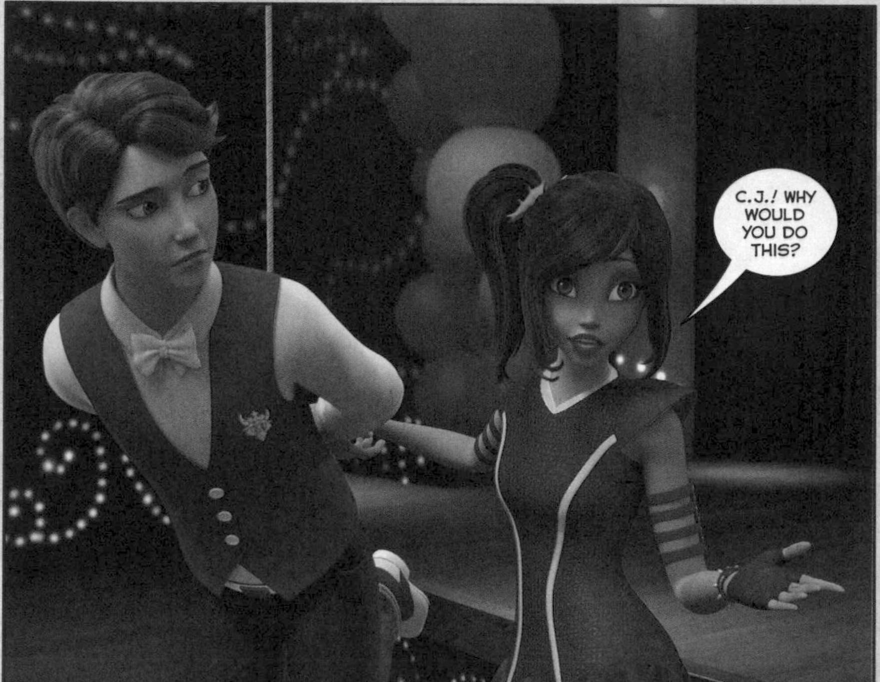
C.J.! WHY WOULD YOU DO THIS?

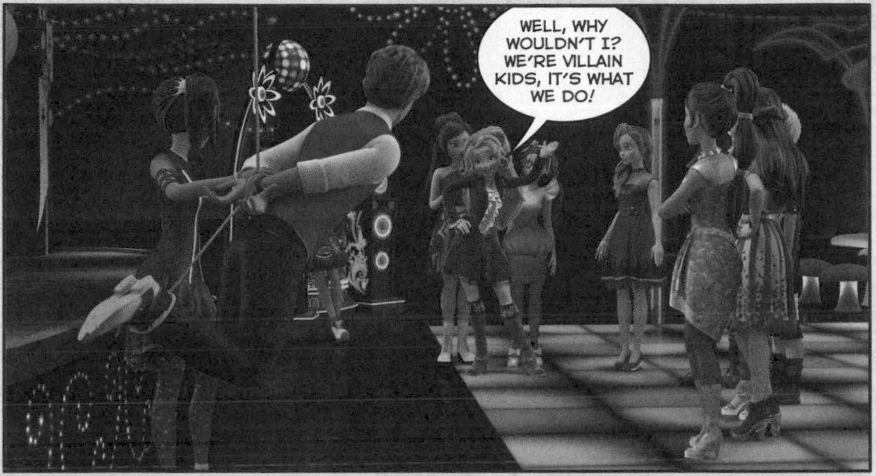
WELL, WHY WOULDN'T I? WE'RE VILLAIN KIDS, IT'S WHAT WE DO!

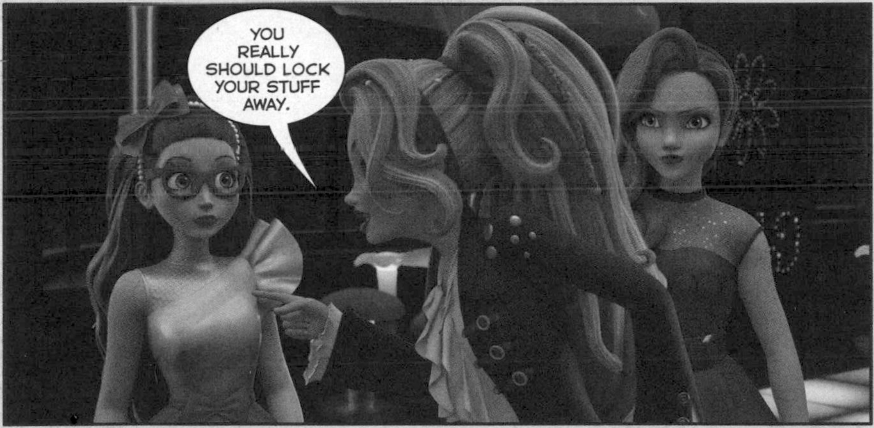
YOU REALLY SHOULD LOCK YOUR STUFF AWAY.

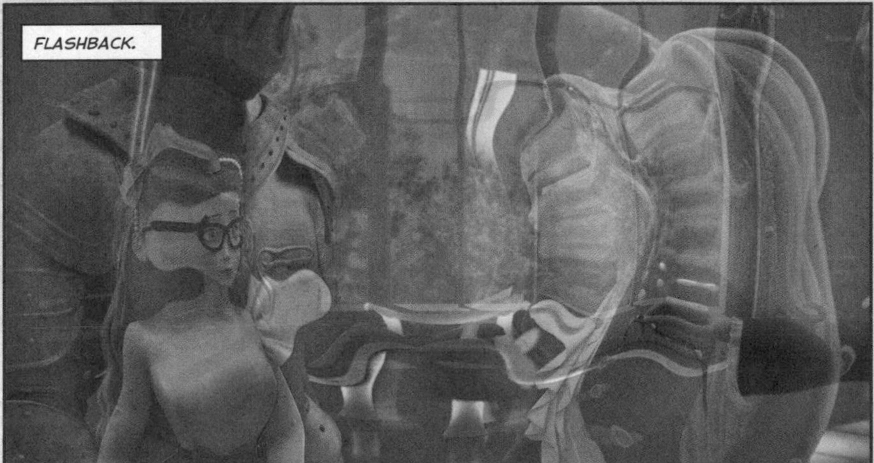
FLASHBACK.

STEALING THAT MASCOT UNIFORM WAS LIKE TAKING CANDY FROM A BABY.

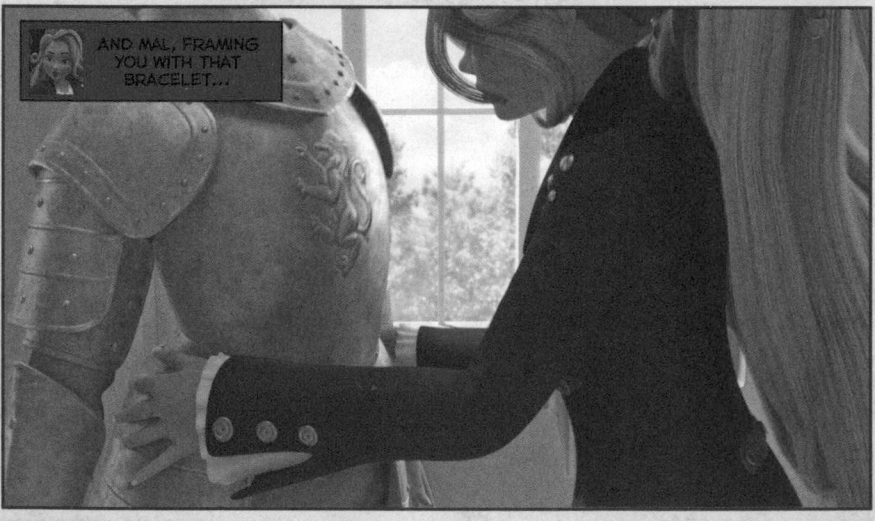

AND MAL, FRAMING YOU WITH THAT BRACELET...

WAS JUST ICING ON THE OLD CAKE.

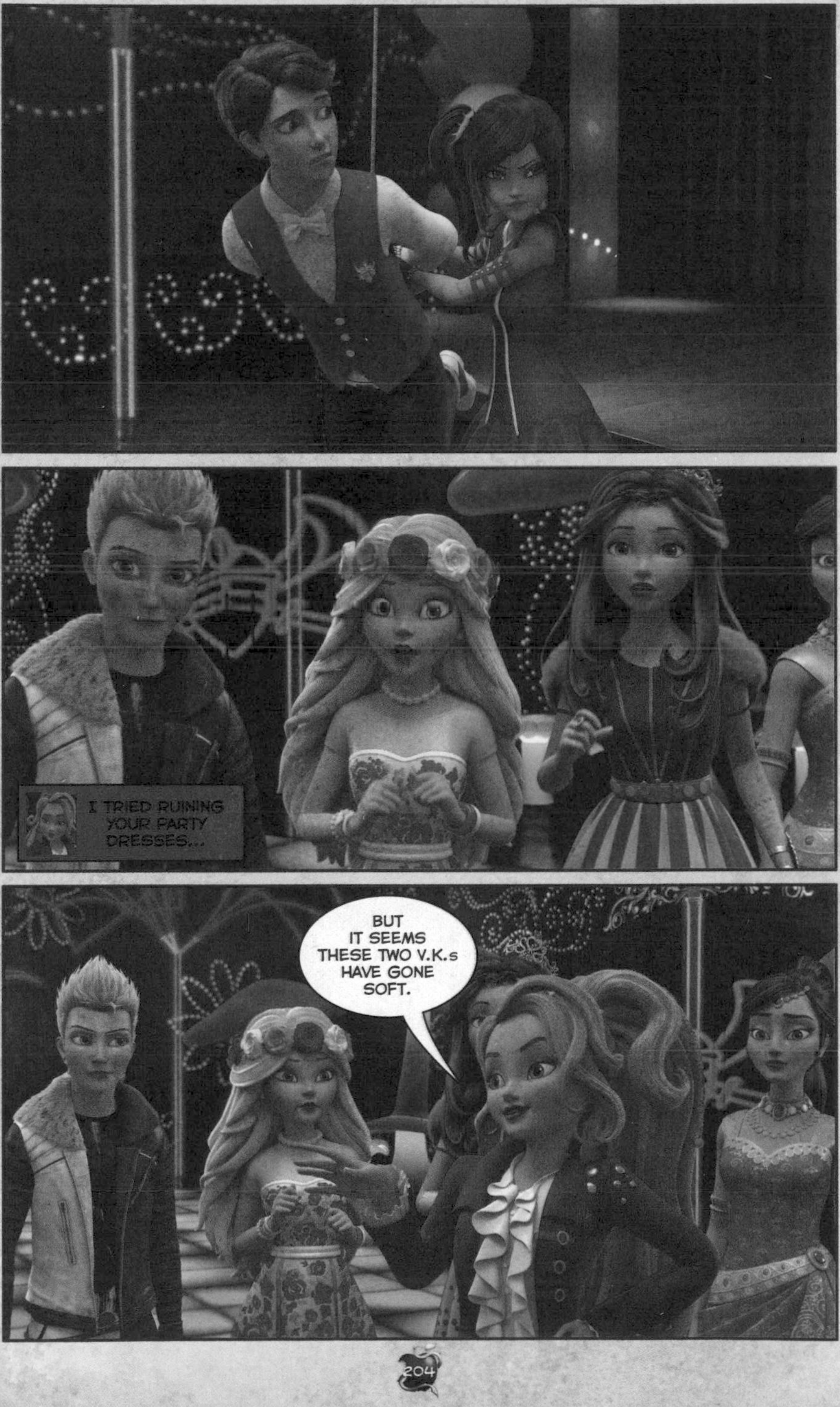
I TRIED RUINING YOUR PARTY DRESSES...
BUT IT SEEMS THESE TWO V.K.s HAVE GONE SOFT.

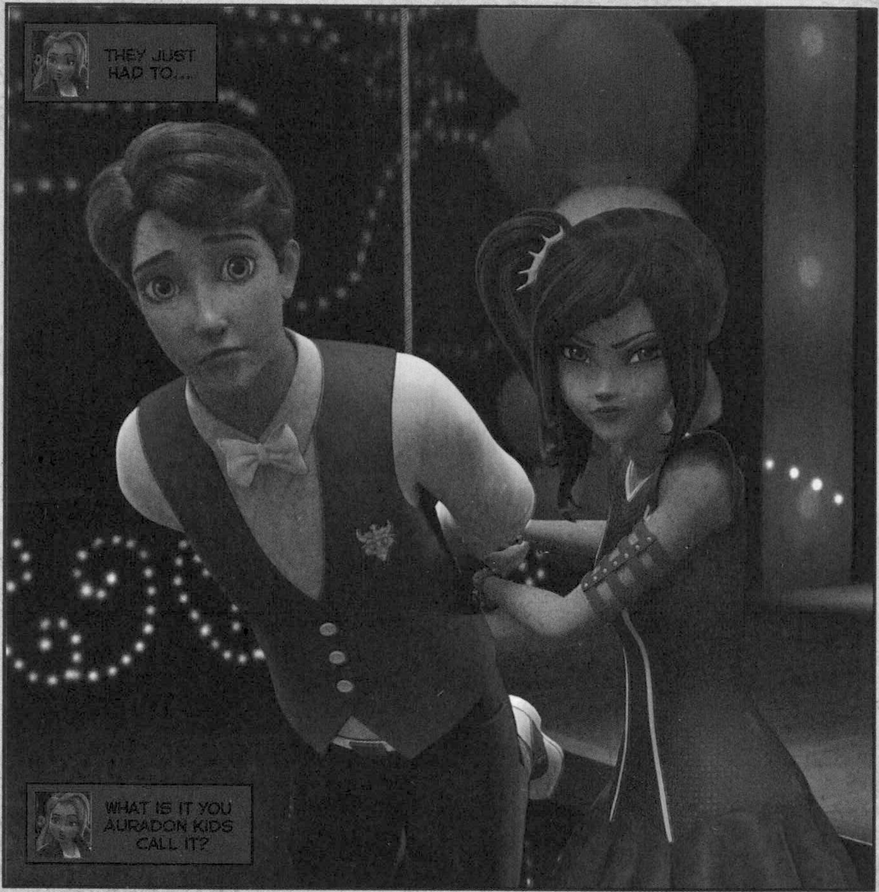
THEY JUST HAD TO...
WHAT IS IT YOU AURADON KIDS CALL IT?

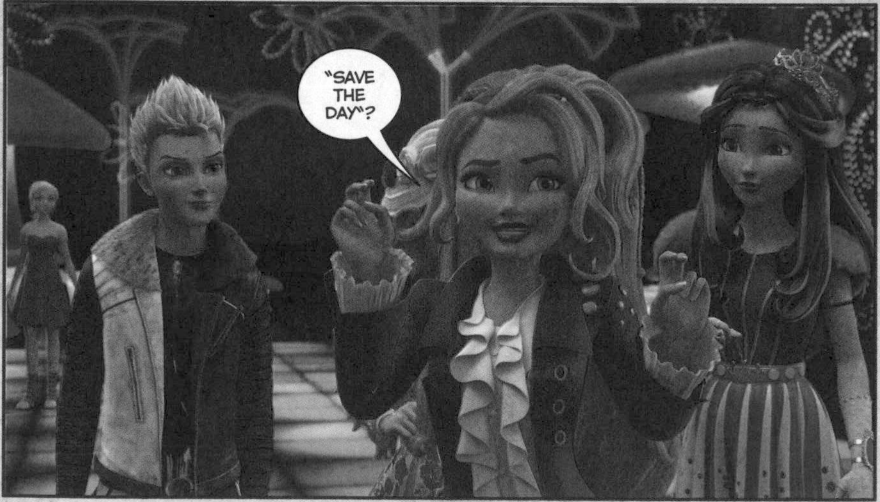
"SAVE THE DAY"?

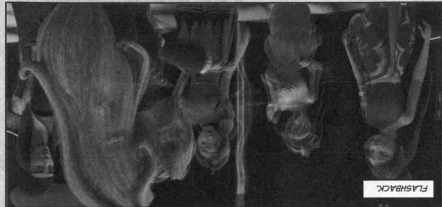

FLASHBACK.

I GOT TO HAND IT TO LITTLE MISS BIPPITY BOPPITY OVER HERE.

OH, AND LET'S NOT FORGET THE NO SHOWS.

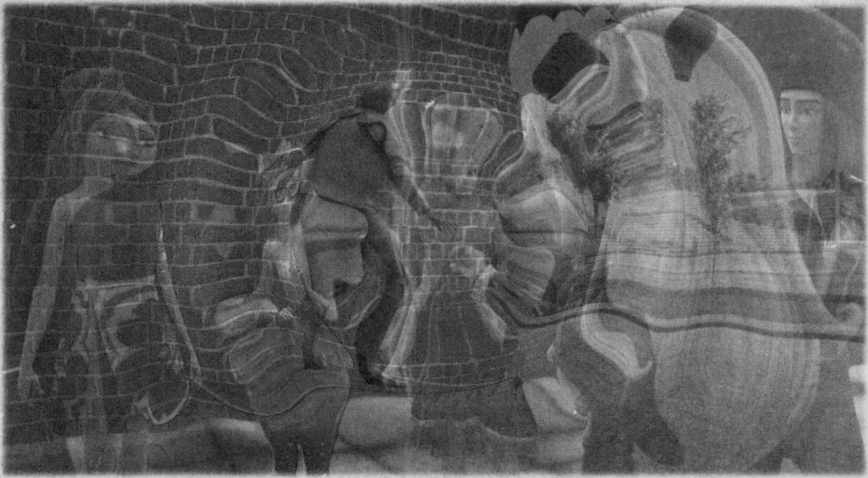

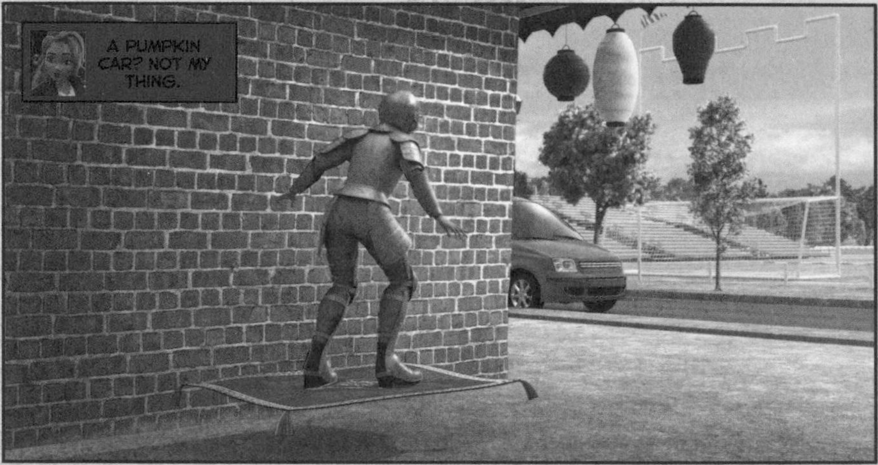
A PUMPKIN CAR? NOT MY THING.

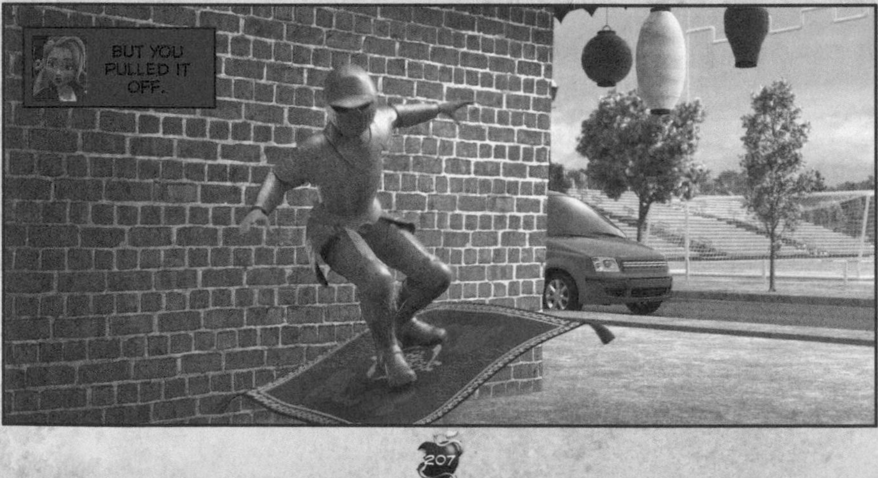
BUT YOU PULLED IT OFF.

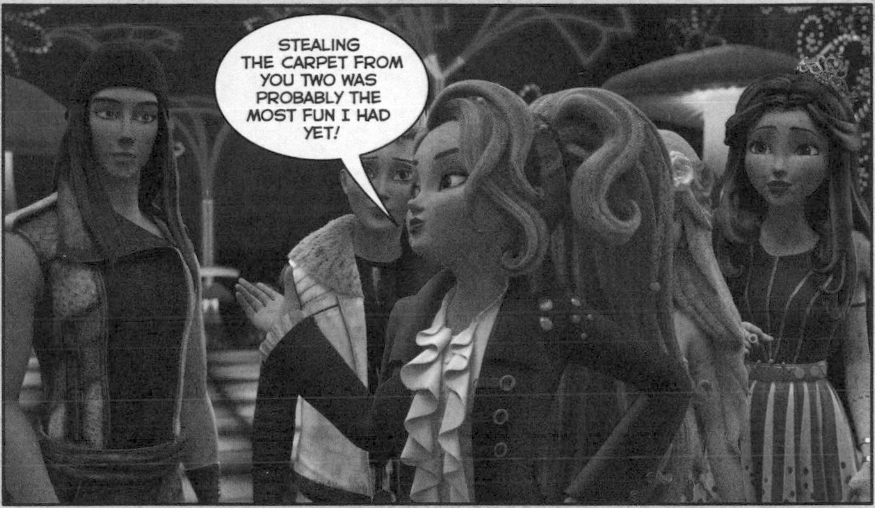
STEALING THE CARPET FROM YOU TWO WAS PROBABLY THE MOST FUN I HAD YET!

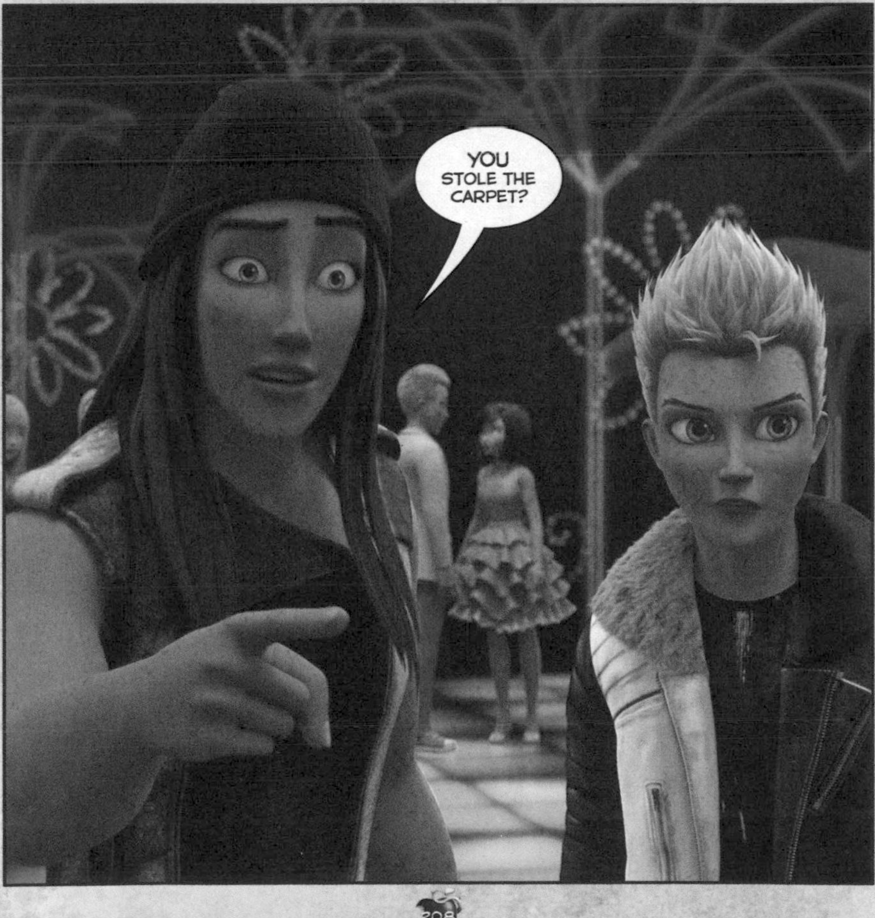
YOU STOLE THE CARPET?

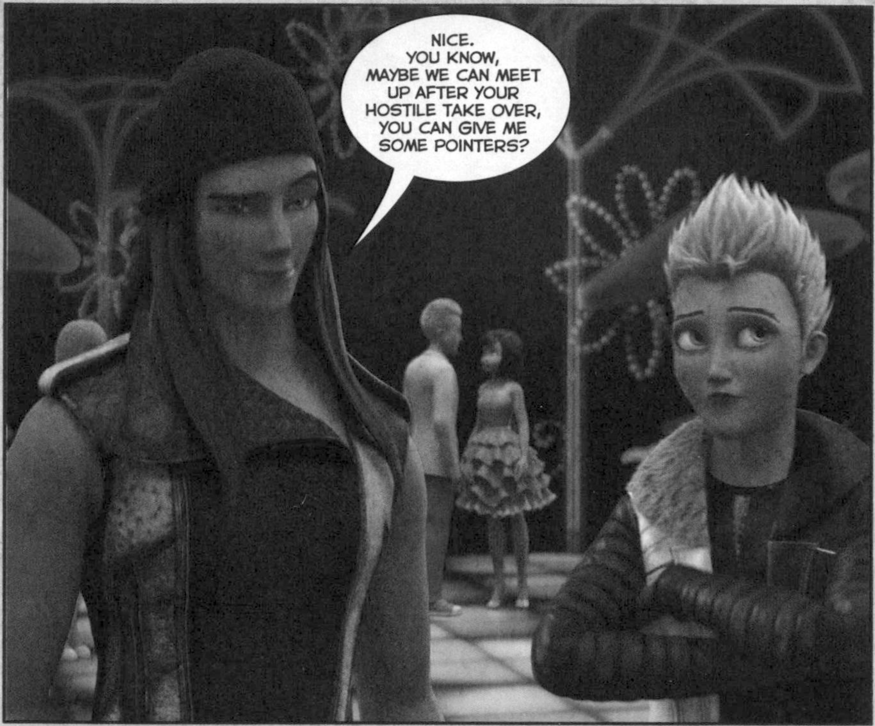
NICE. YOU KNOW, MAYBE WE CAN MEET UP AFTER YOUR HOSTILE TAKE OVER, YOU CAN GIVE ME SOME POINTERS?

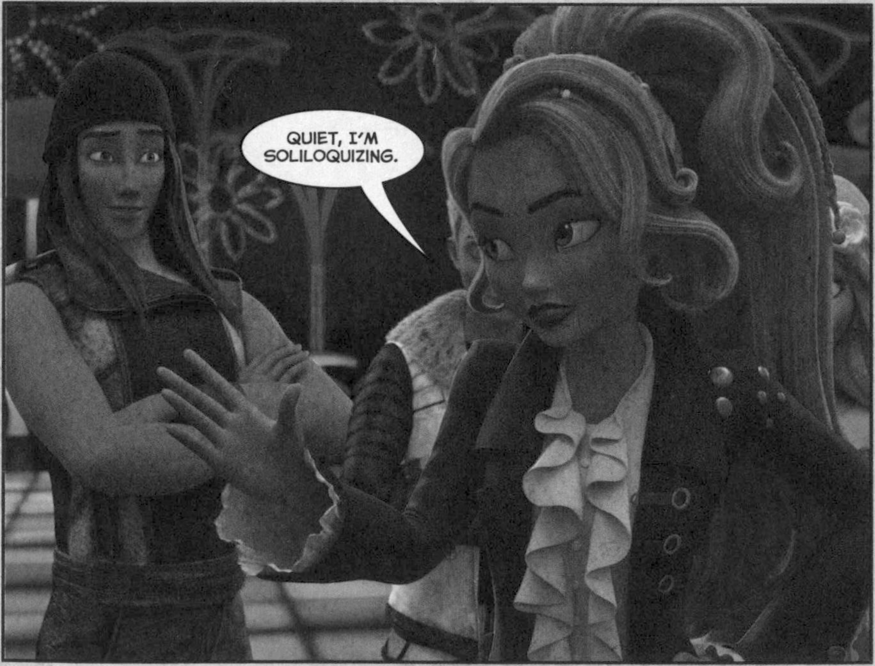
QUIET, I'M SOLILOQUIZING.

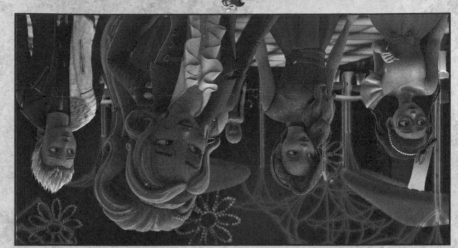

IT WAS THE LEAST I COULD DO AS A THANK YOU FOR SNEAKING ME INTO AURADON.

AND THEN THE GRANDEST OF THEM ALL...CUTTING THAT D.J. CORD SO OUR LITTLE FREDDIE COULD HAVE HER MOMENT IN THE SPOTLIGHT.

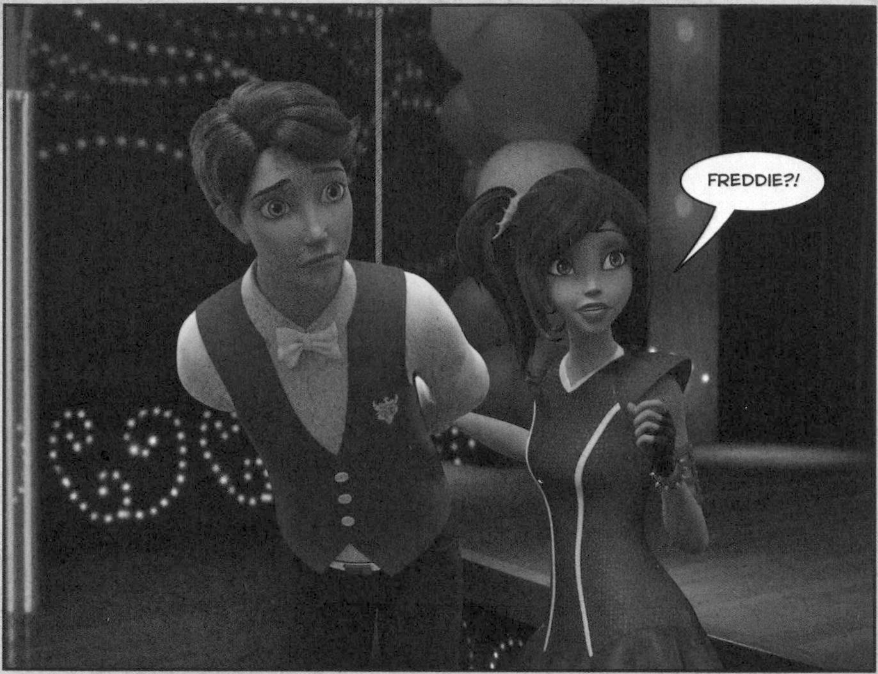
FREDDIE?!

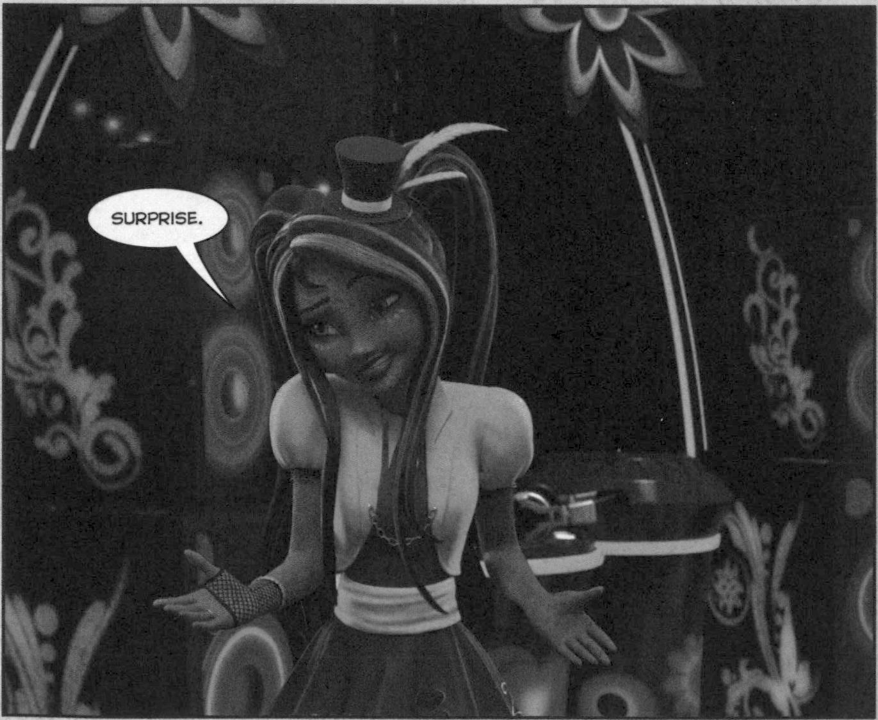
SURPRISE.

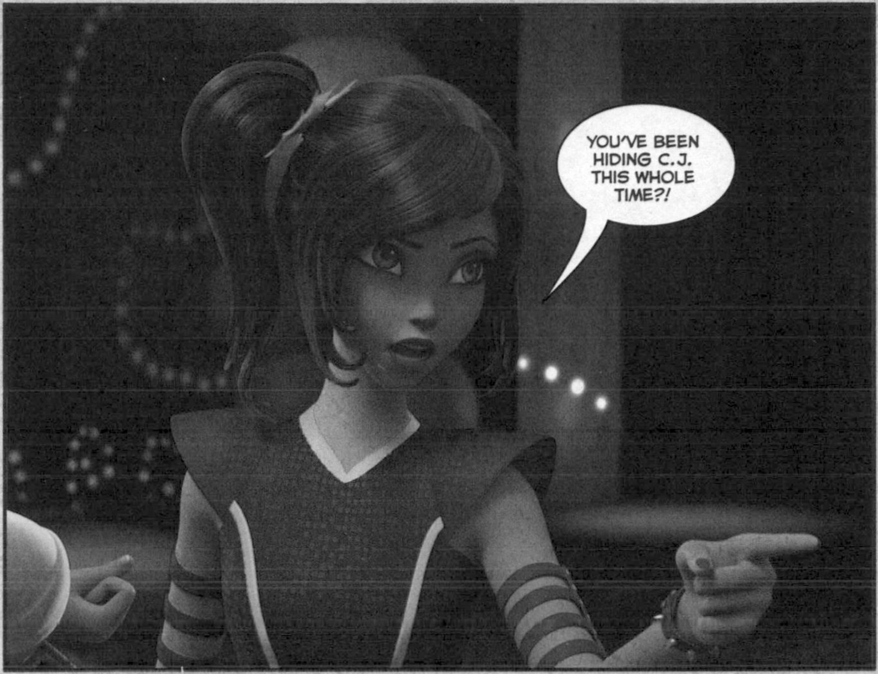
YOU'VE BEEN HIDING C.J. THIS WHOLE TIME?!

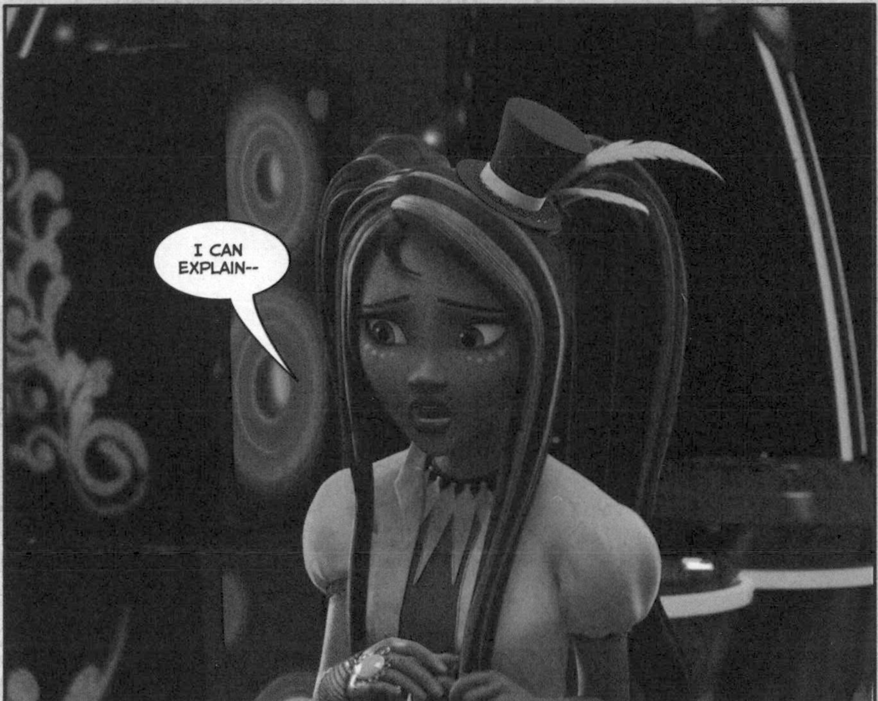
I CAN EXPLAIN--

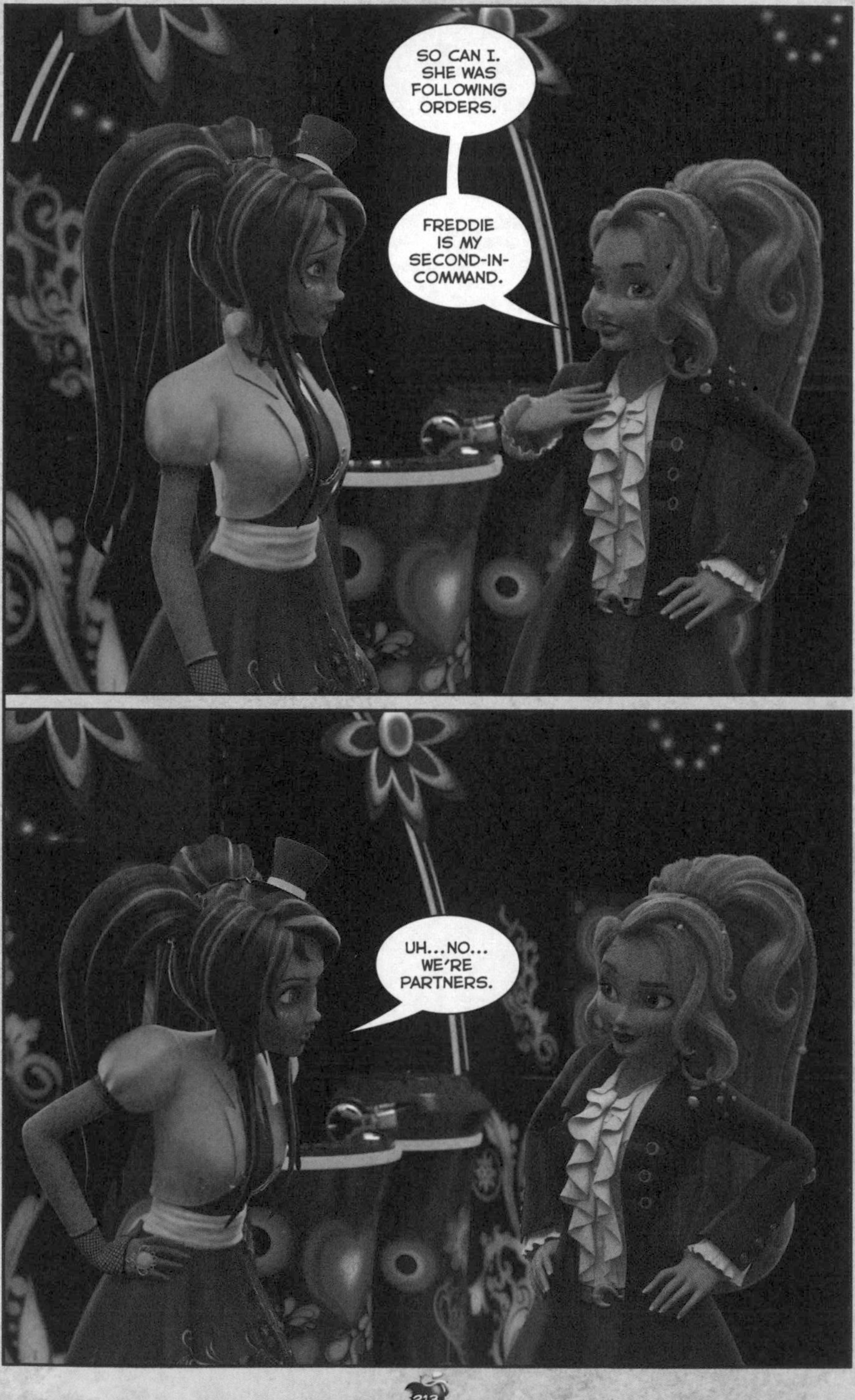
SO CAN I. SHE WAS FOLLOWING ORDERS.
FREDDIE IS MY SECOND-IN-COMMAND.
UH...NO... WE'RE PARTNERS.

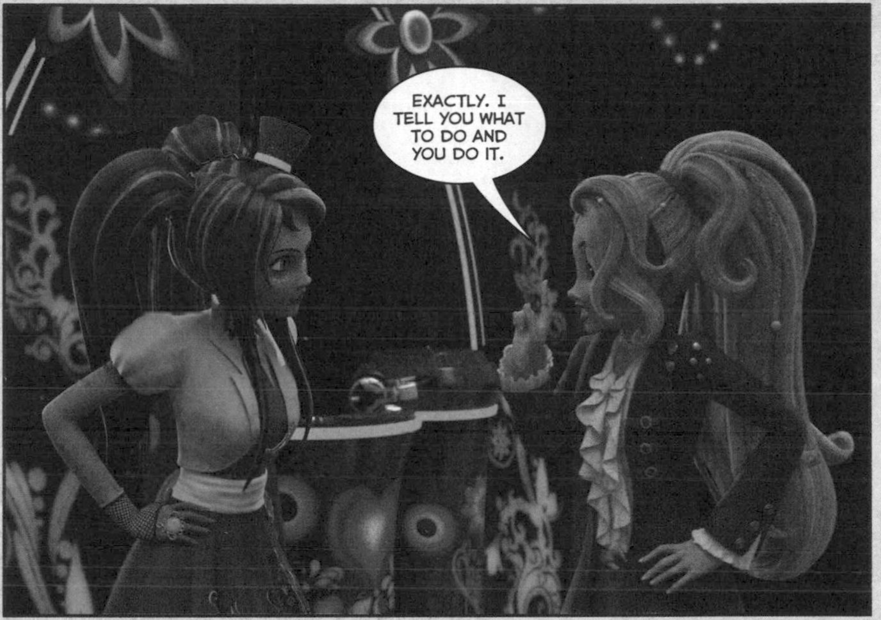
EXACTLY. I TELL YOU WHAT TO DO AND YOU DO IT.

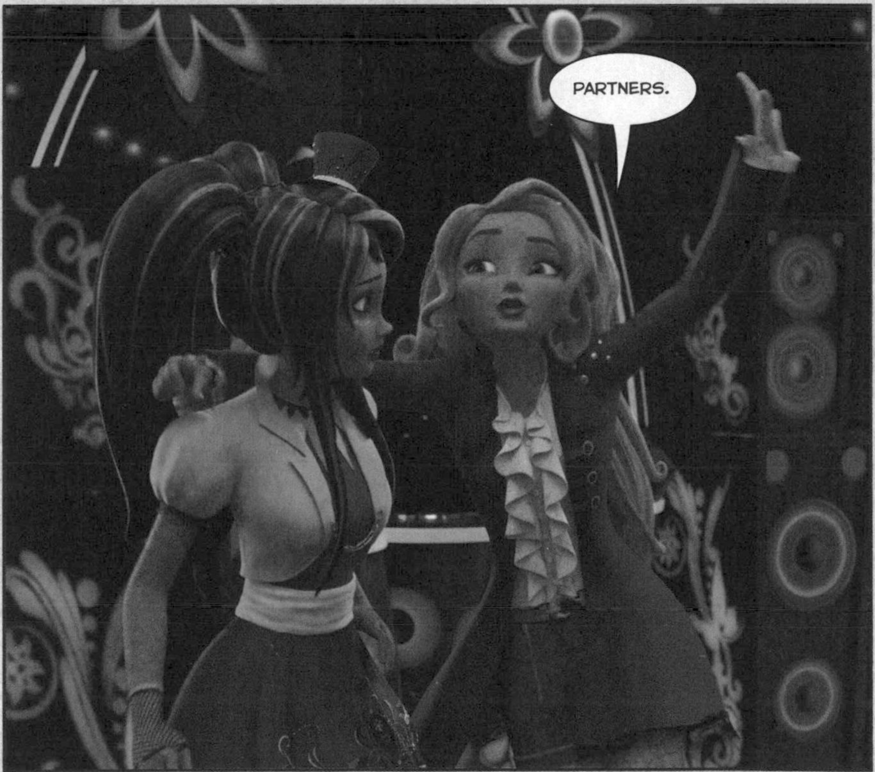
PARTNERS.

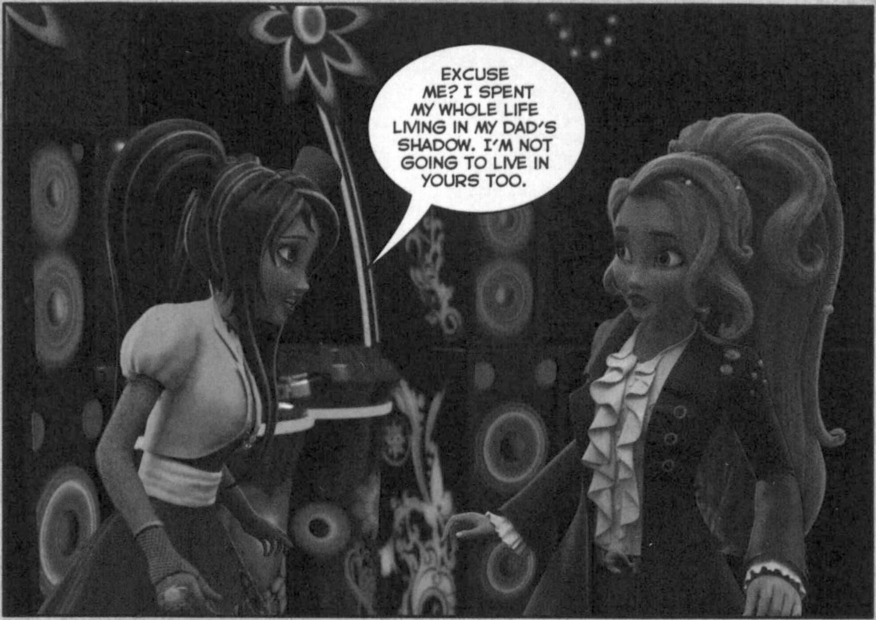
EXCUSE ME? I SPENT MY WHOLE LIFE LIVING IN MY DAD'S SHADOW. I'M NOT GOING TO LIVE IN YOURS TOO.

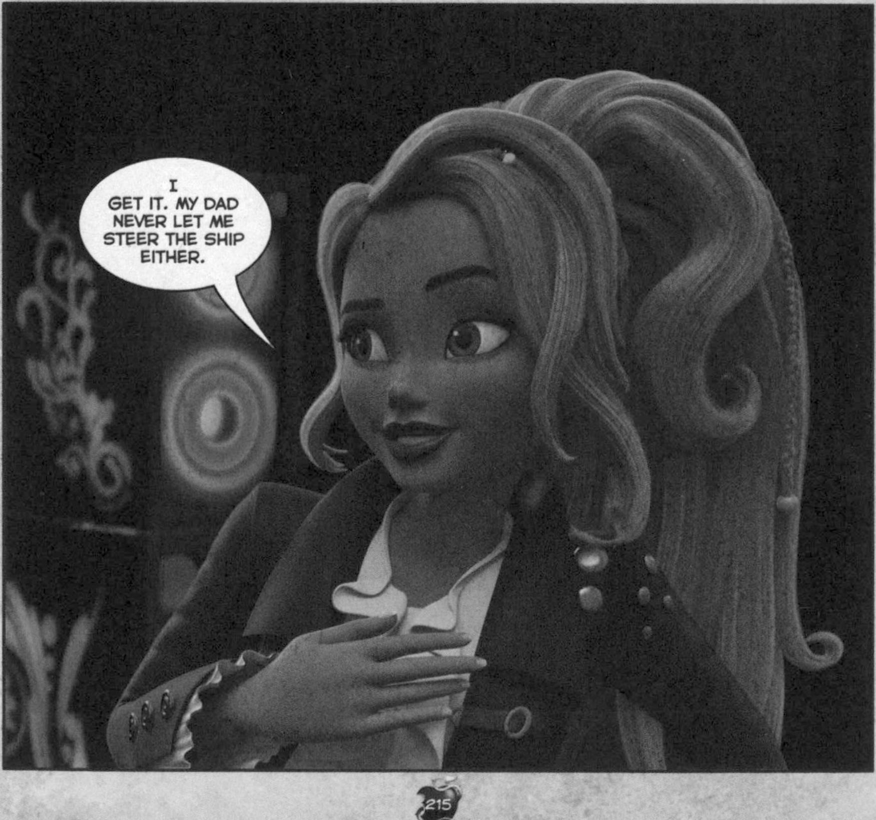
I GET IT. MY DAD NEVER LET ME STEER THE SHIP EITHER.

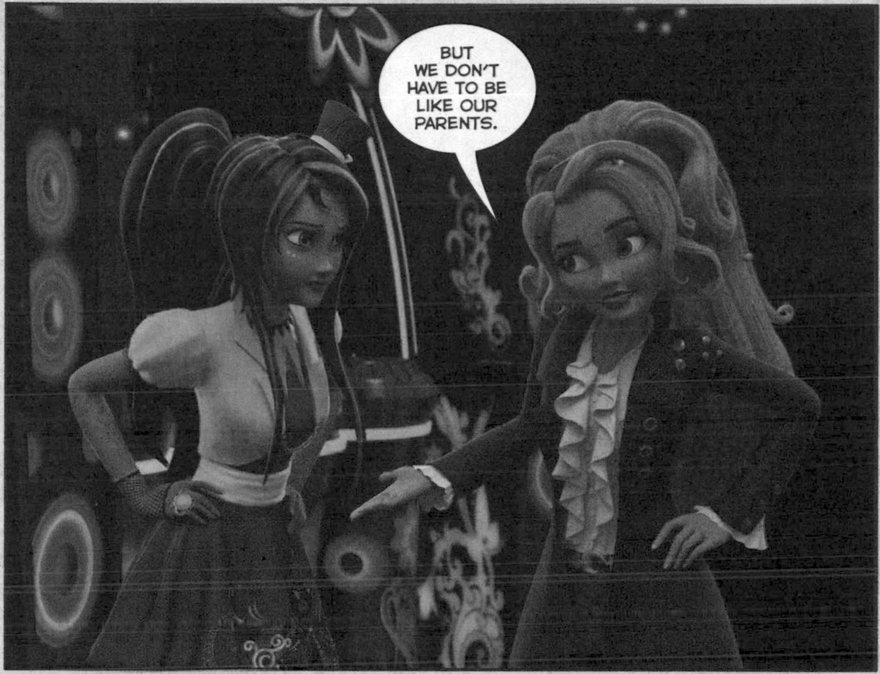
BUT WE DON'T HAVE TO BE LIKE OUR PARENTS.

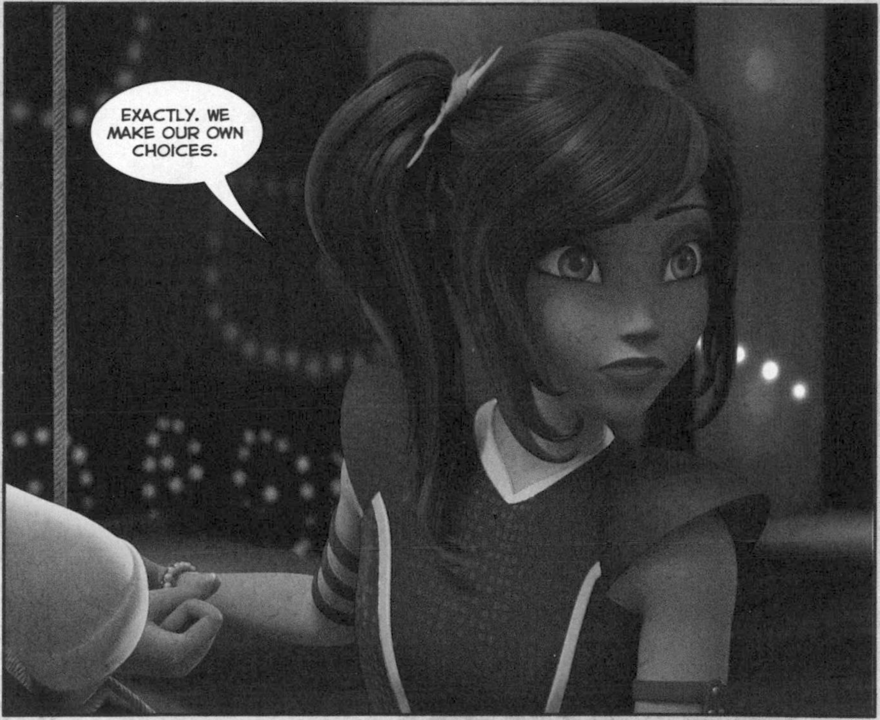
EXACTLY. WE MAKE OUR OWN CHOICES.

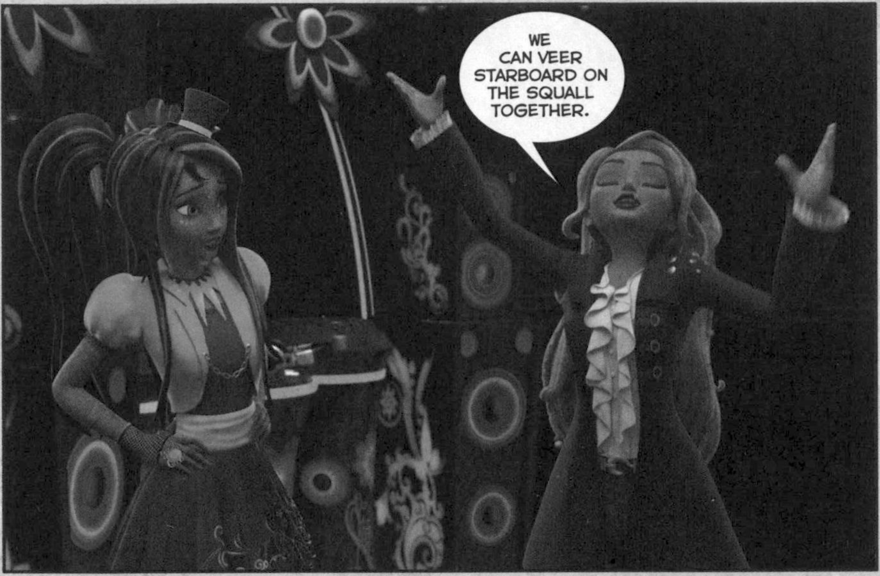
WE CAN VEER STARBOARD ON THE SQUALL TOGETHER.

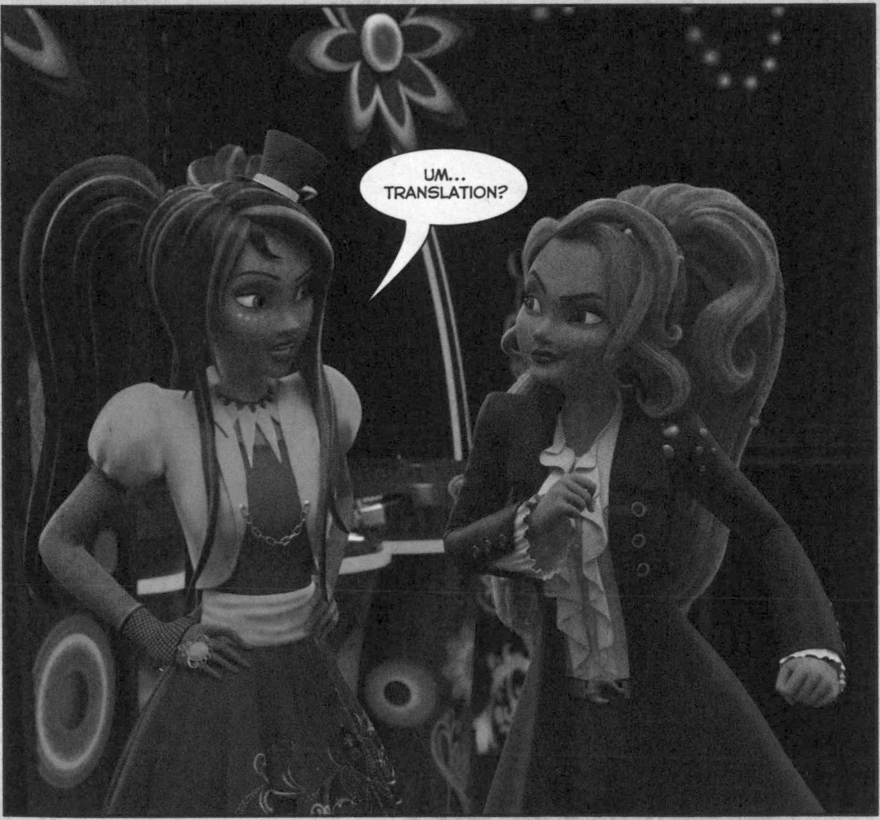
UM... TRANSLATION?

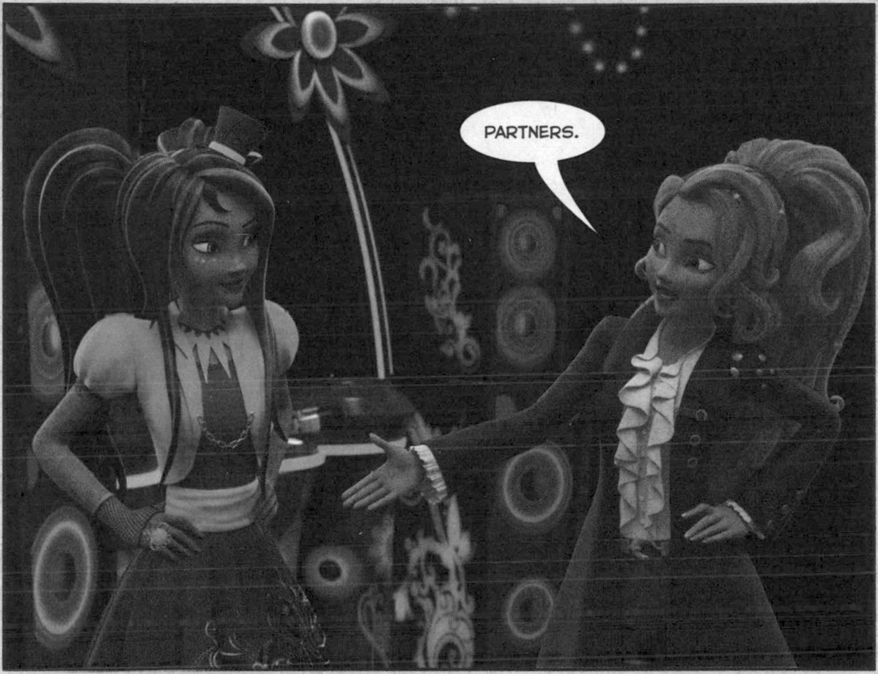
PARTNERS.

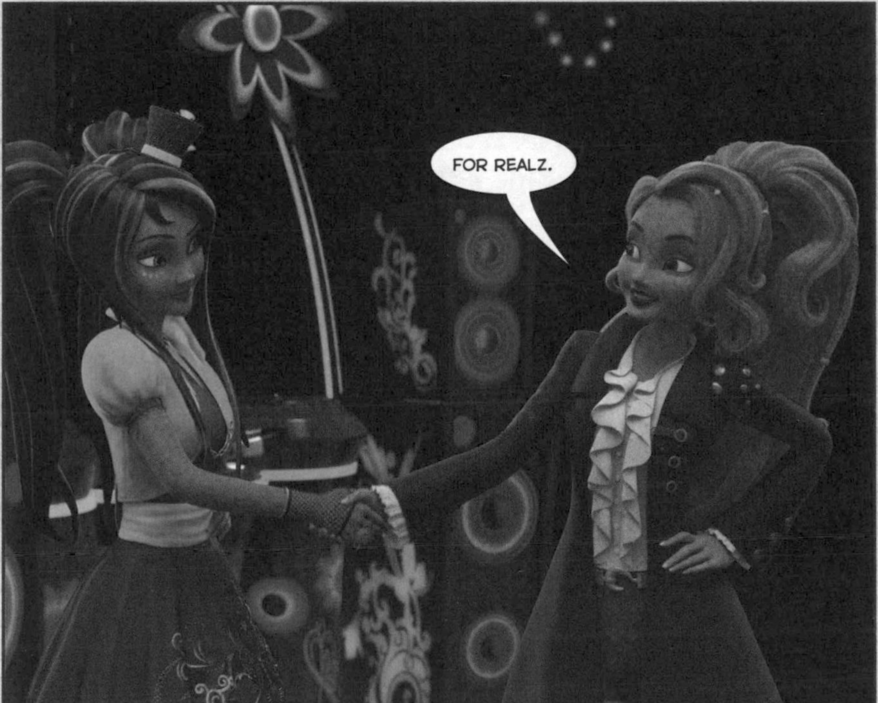
FOR REALZ.

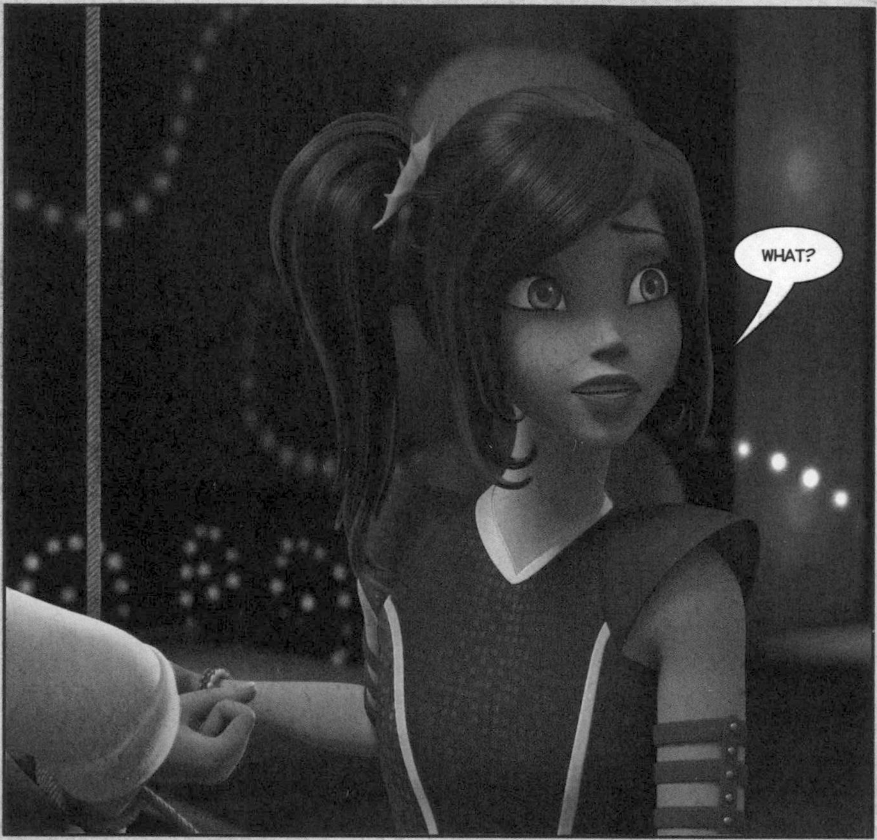
WHAT?

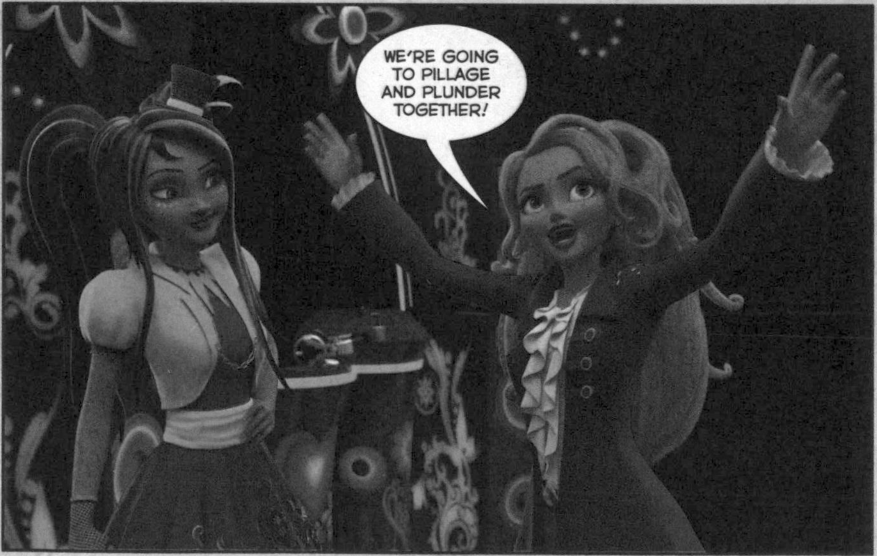
WE'RE GOING TO PILLAGE AND PLUNDER TOGETHER!

FREDDIE, I THOUGHT WE WERE FRIENDS.

WE ARE FRIENDS.

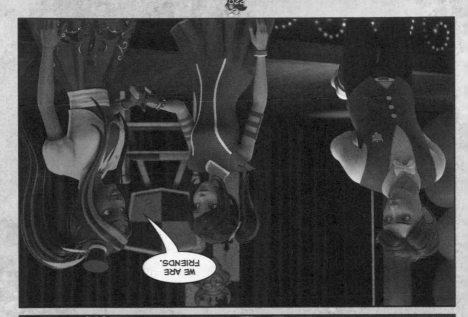

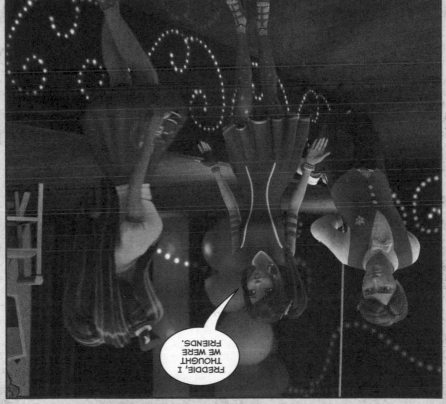

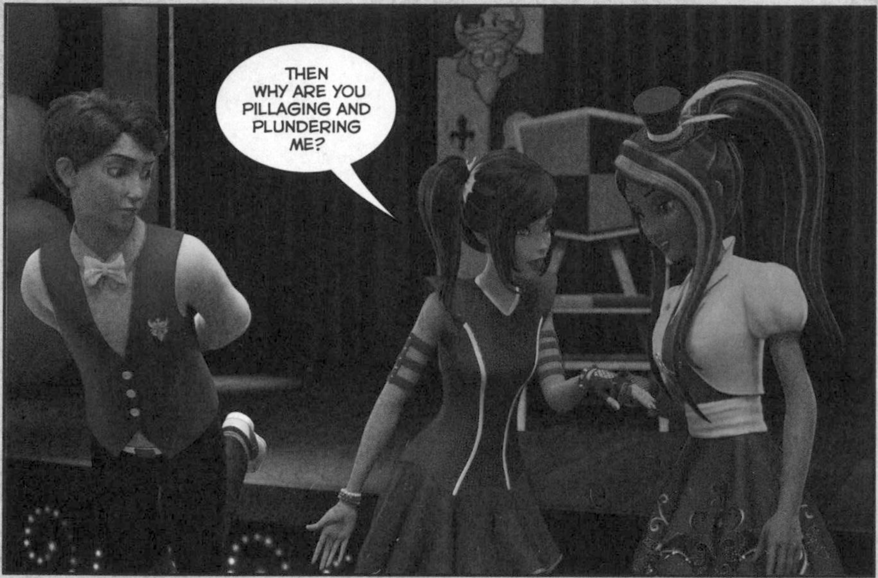
THEN WHY ARE YOU PILLAGING AND PLUNDERING ME?

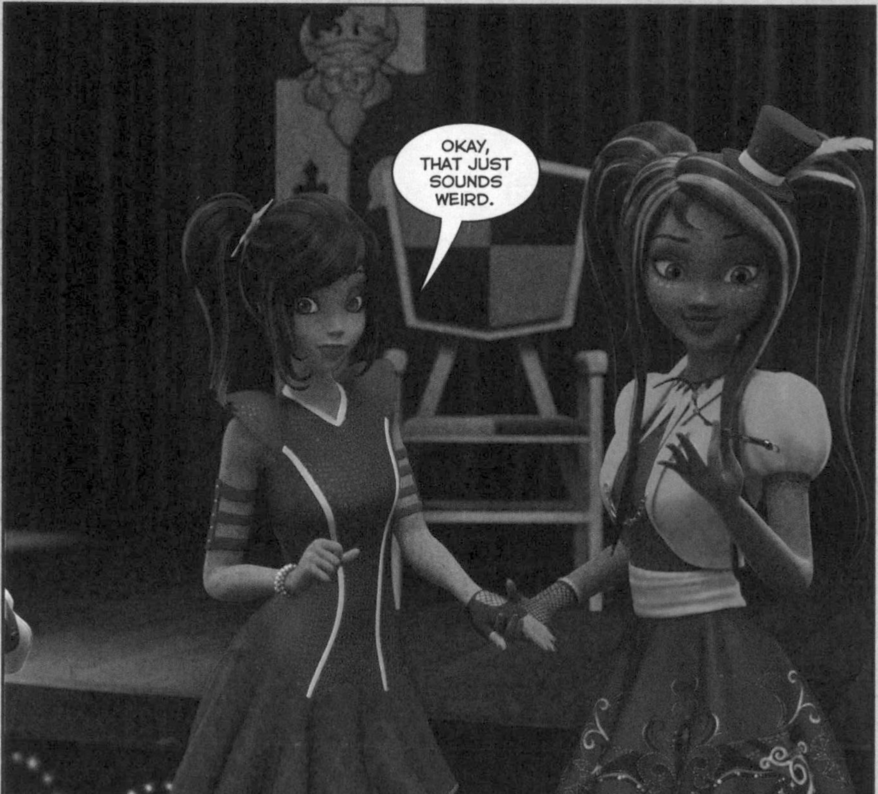
OKAY, THAT JUST SOUNDS WEIRD.

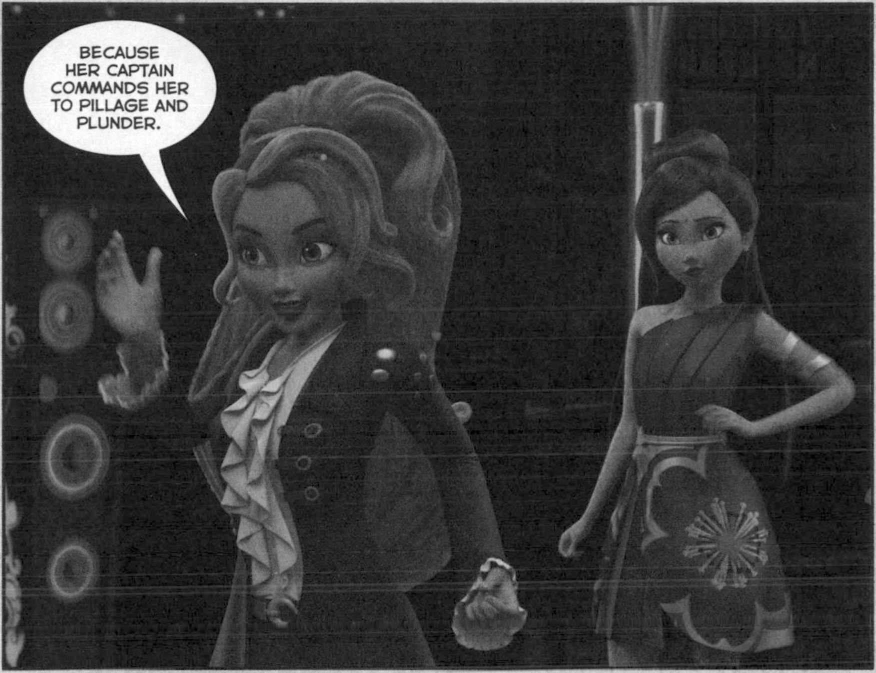
BECAUSE HER CAPTAIN COMMANDS HER TO PILLAGE AND PLUNDER.

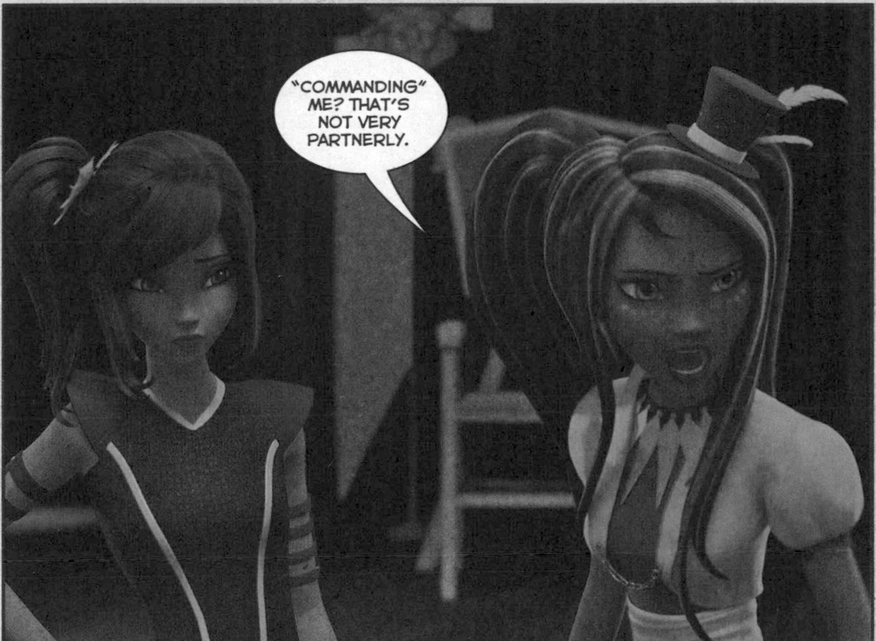
"COMMANDING" ME? THAT'S NOT VERY PARTNERLY.

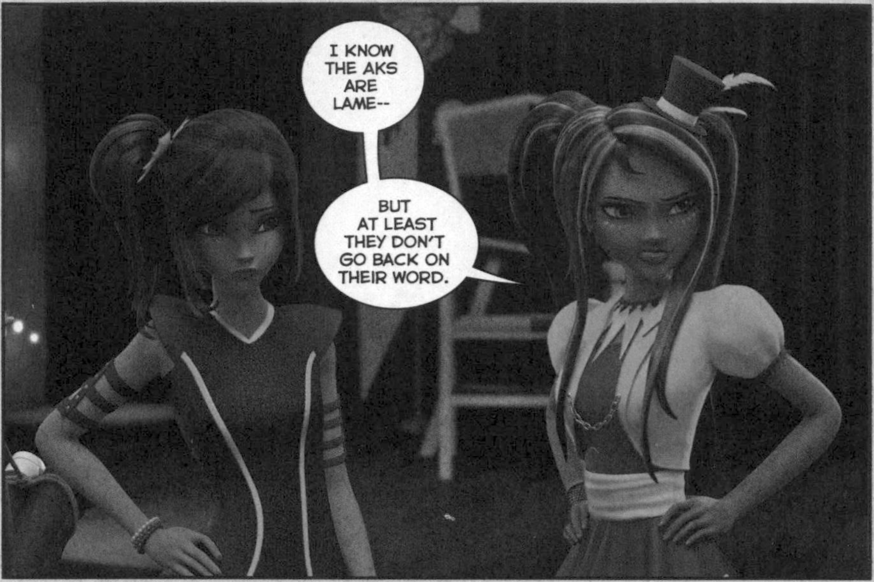
I KNOW THE AKS ARE LAME--
BUT AT LEAST THEY DON'T GO BACK ON THEIR WORD.

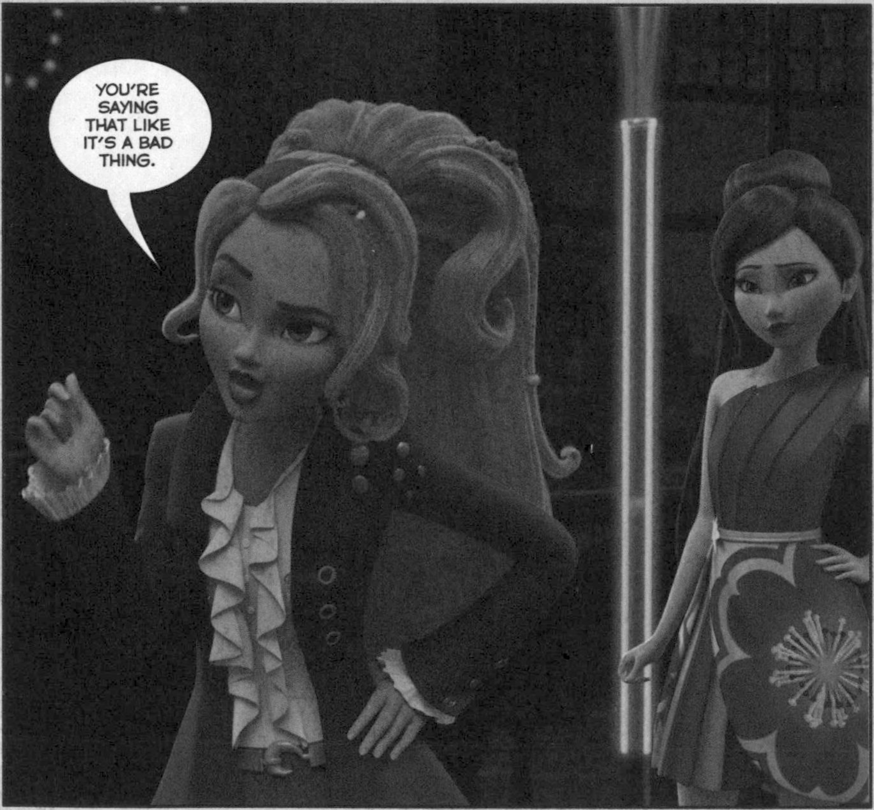
YOU'RE SAYING THAT LIKE IT'S A BAD THING.

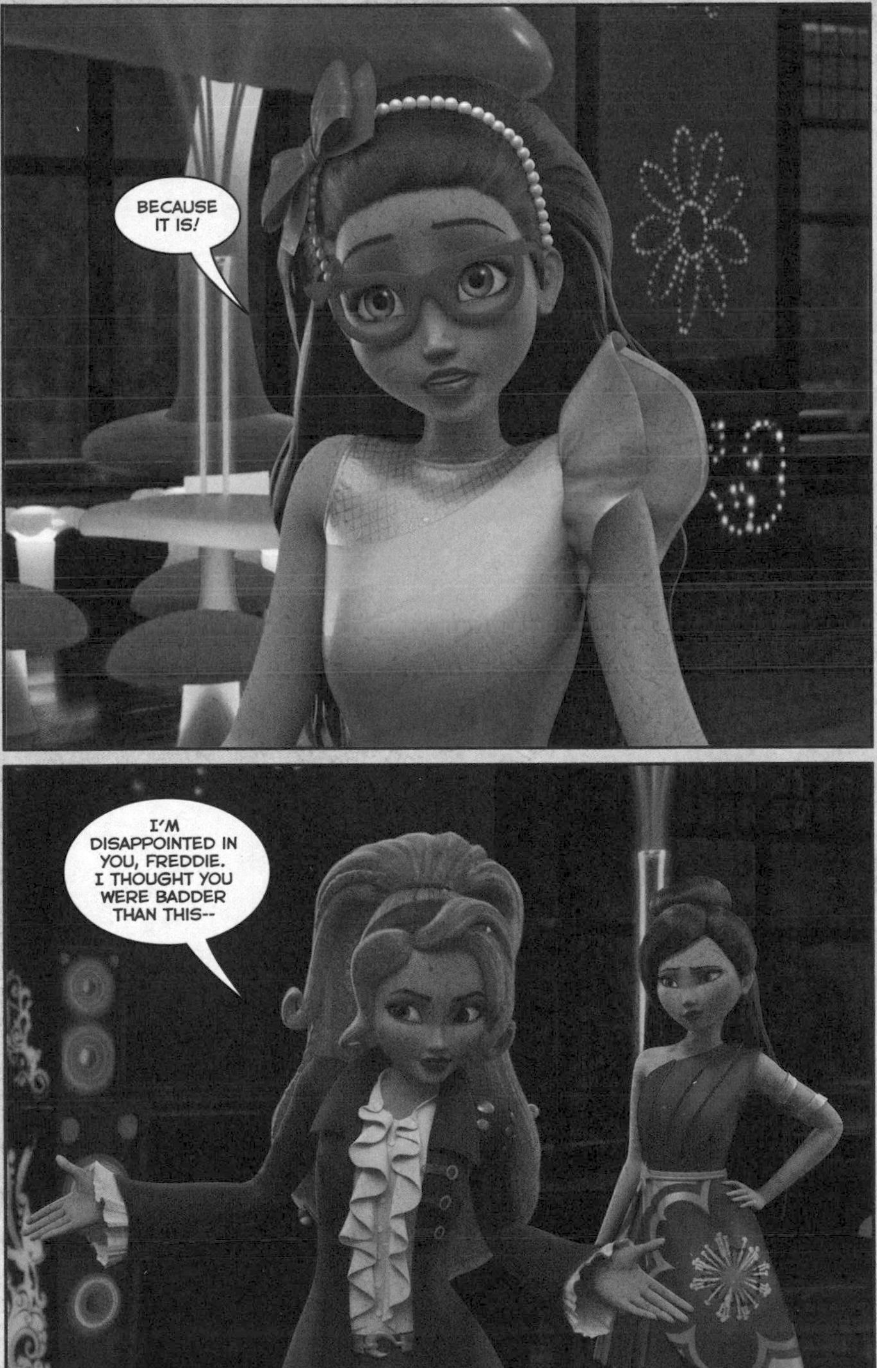
BECAUSE IT IS!
I'M DISAPPOINTED IN YOU, FREDDIE. I THOUGHT YOU WERE BADDER THAN THIS--

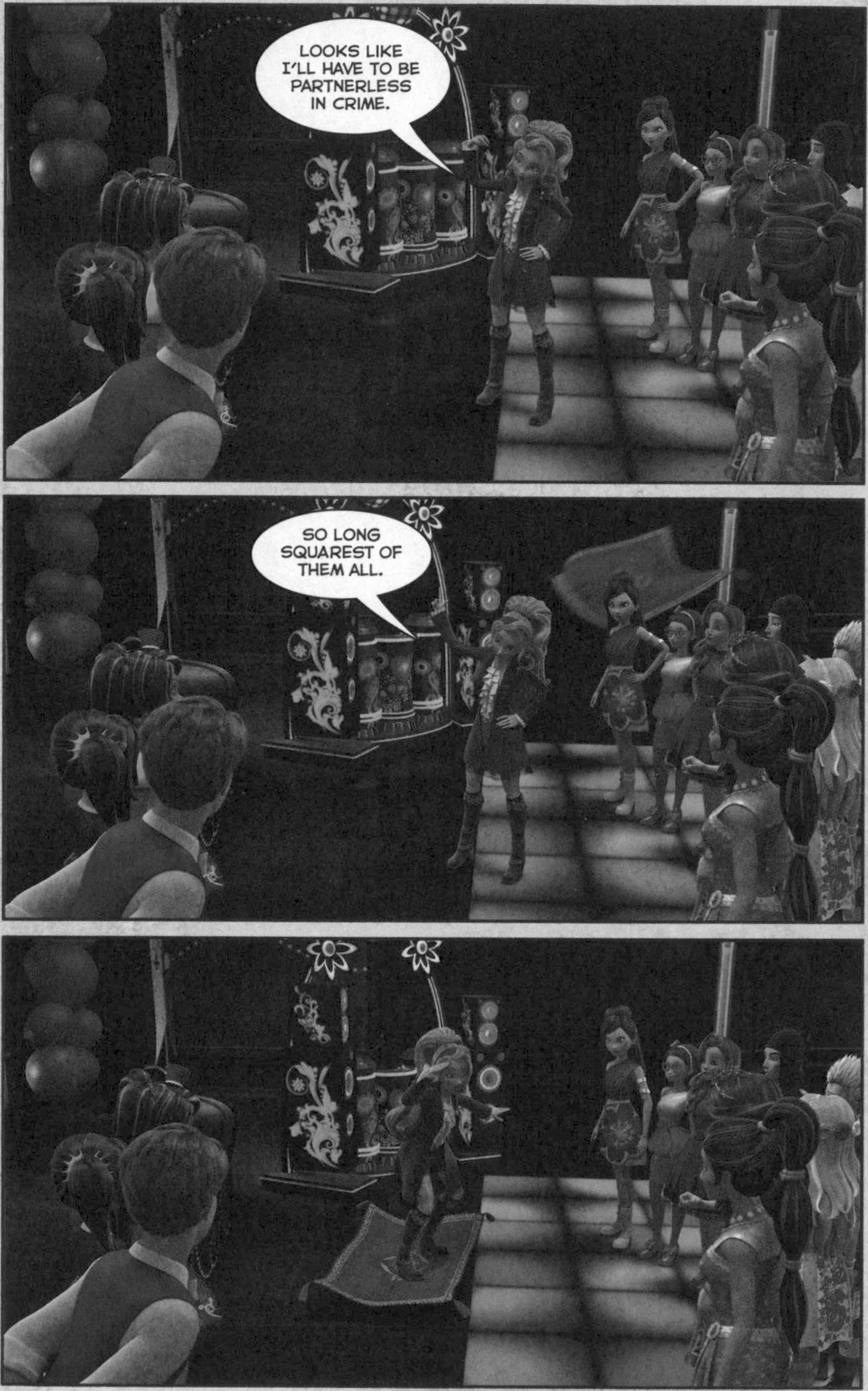
LOOKS LIKE I'LL HAVE TO BE PARTNERLESS IN CRIME.
SO LONG SQUAREST OF THEM ALL.

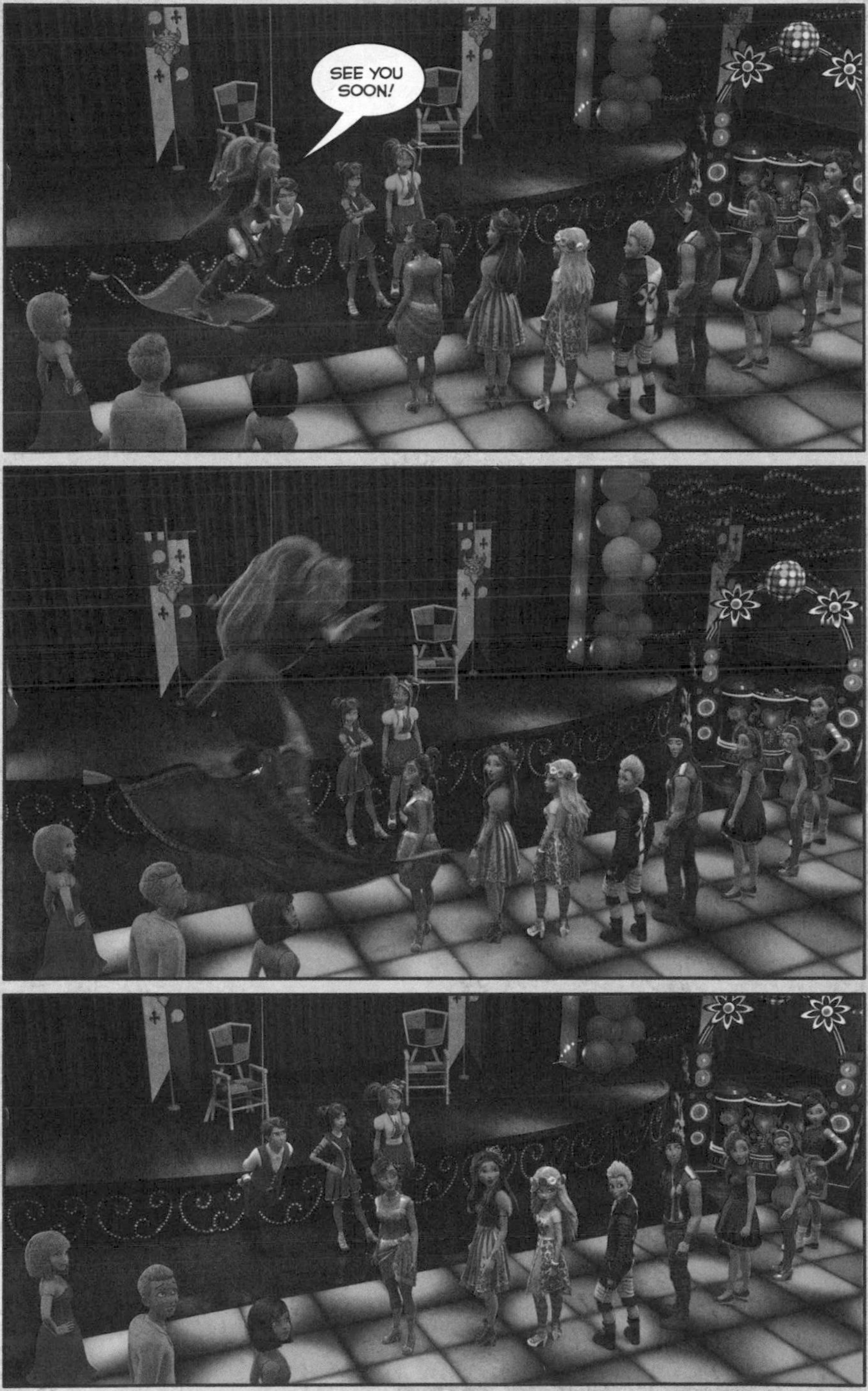
SEE YOU SOON!

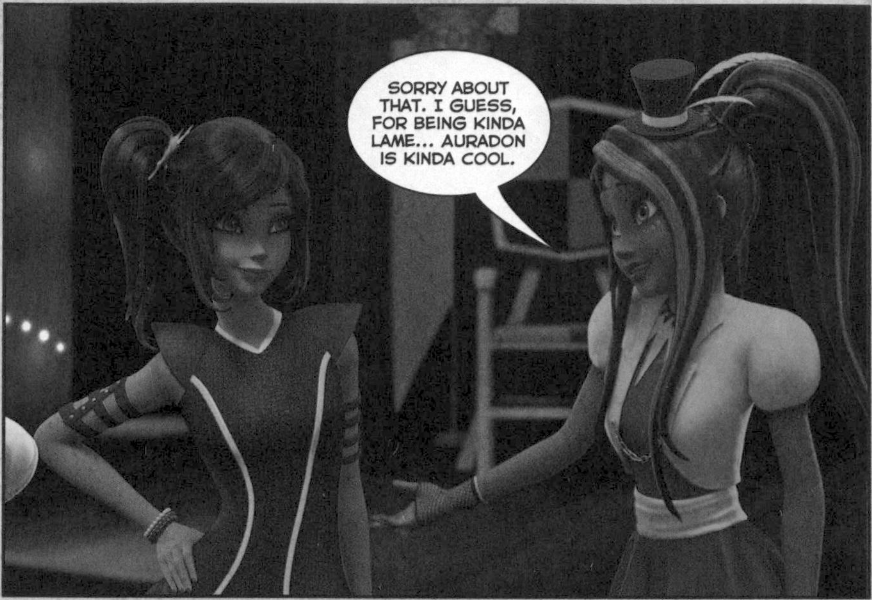
SORRY ABOUT THAT. I GUESS, FOR BEING KINDA LAME... AURADON IS KINDA COOL.

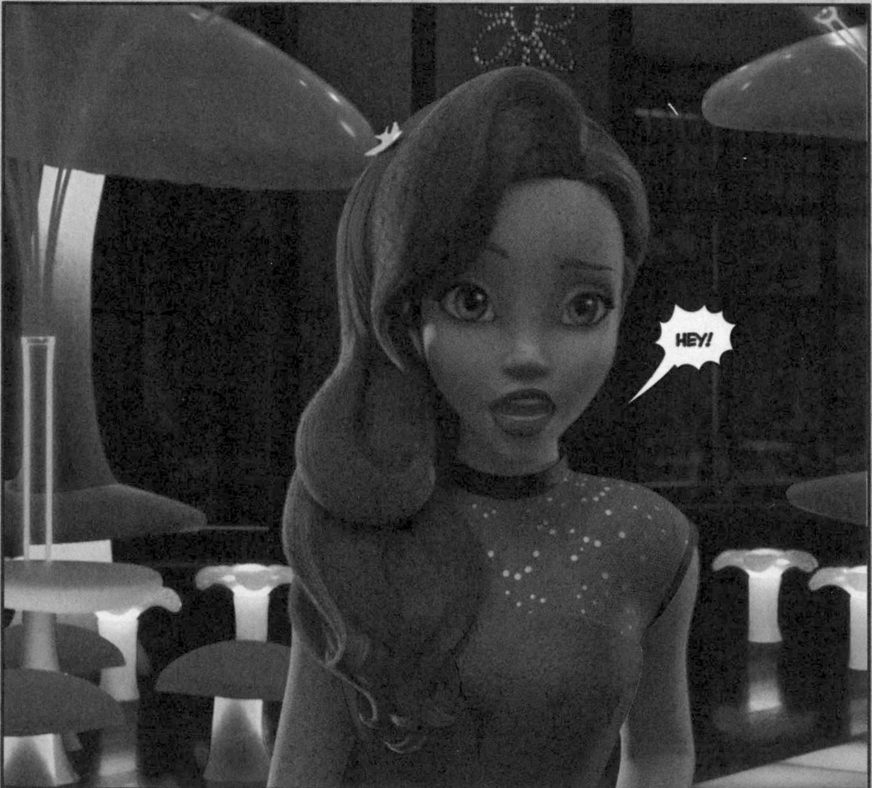
HEY!

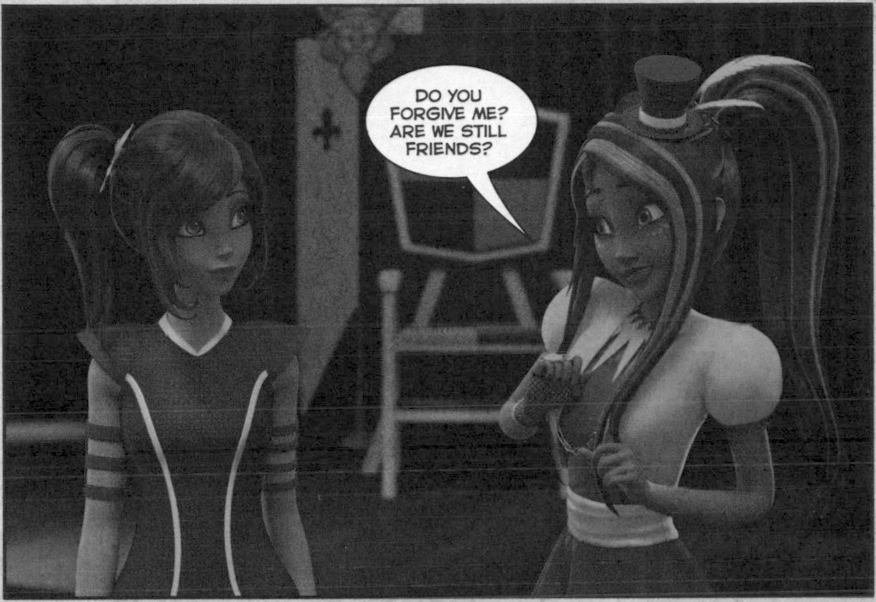
DO YOU FORGIVE ME? ARE WE STILL FRIENDS?

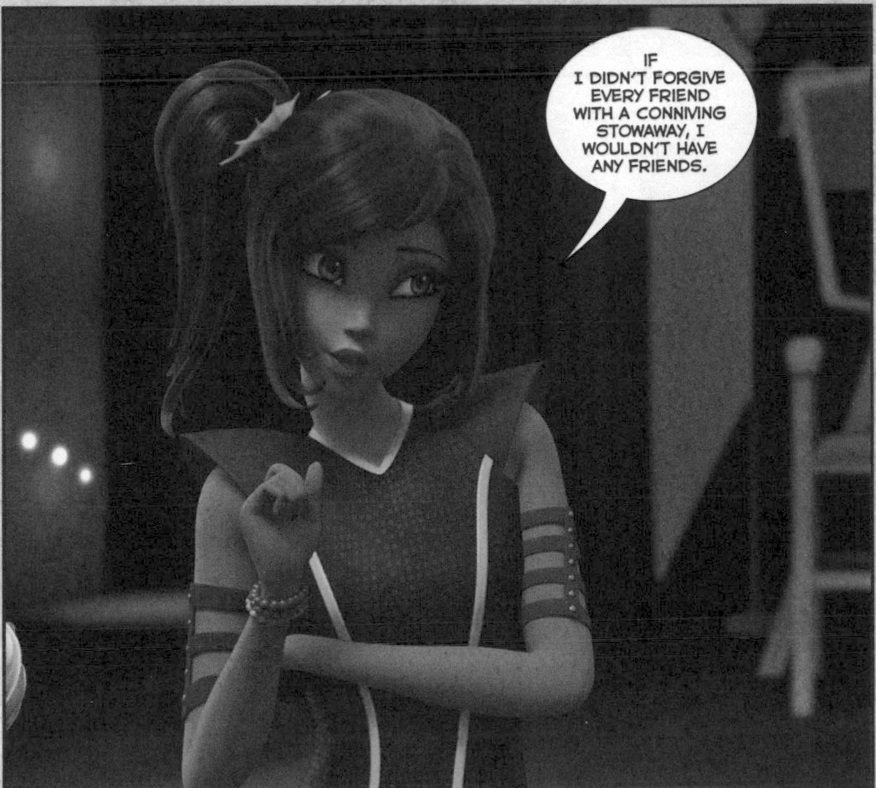
IF I DIDN'T FORGIVE EVERY FRIEND WITH A CONNIVING STOWAWAY, I WOULDN'T HAVE ANY FRIENDS.

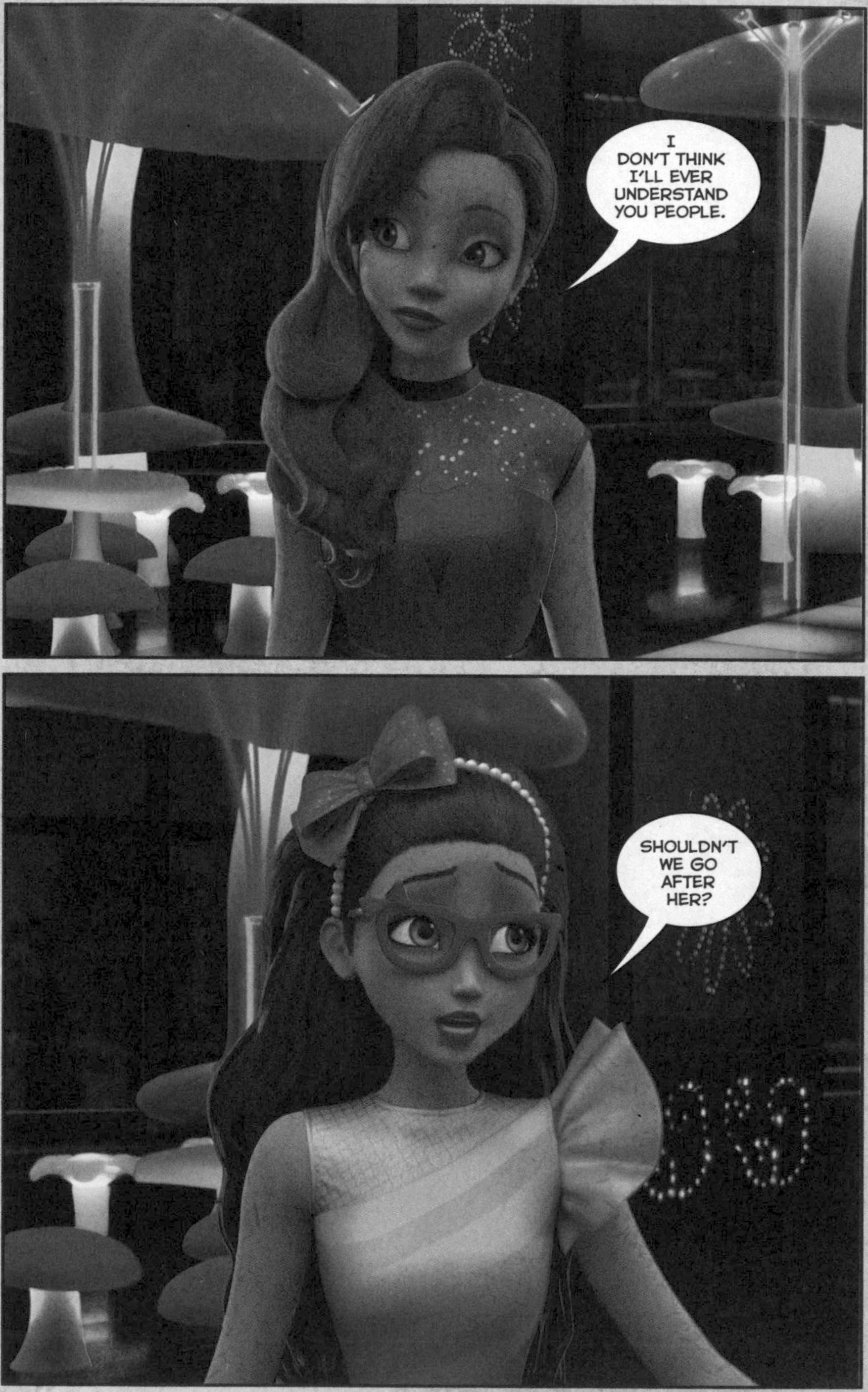
I DON'T THINK I'LL EVER UNDERSTAND YOU PEOPLE.
SHOULDN'T WE GO AFTER HER?

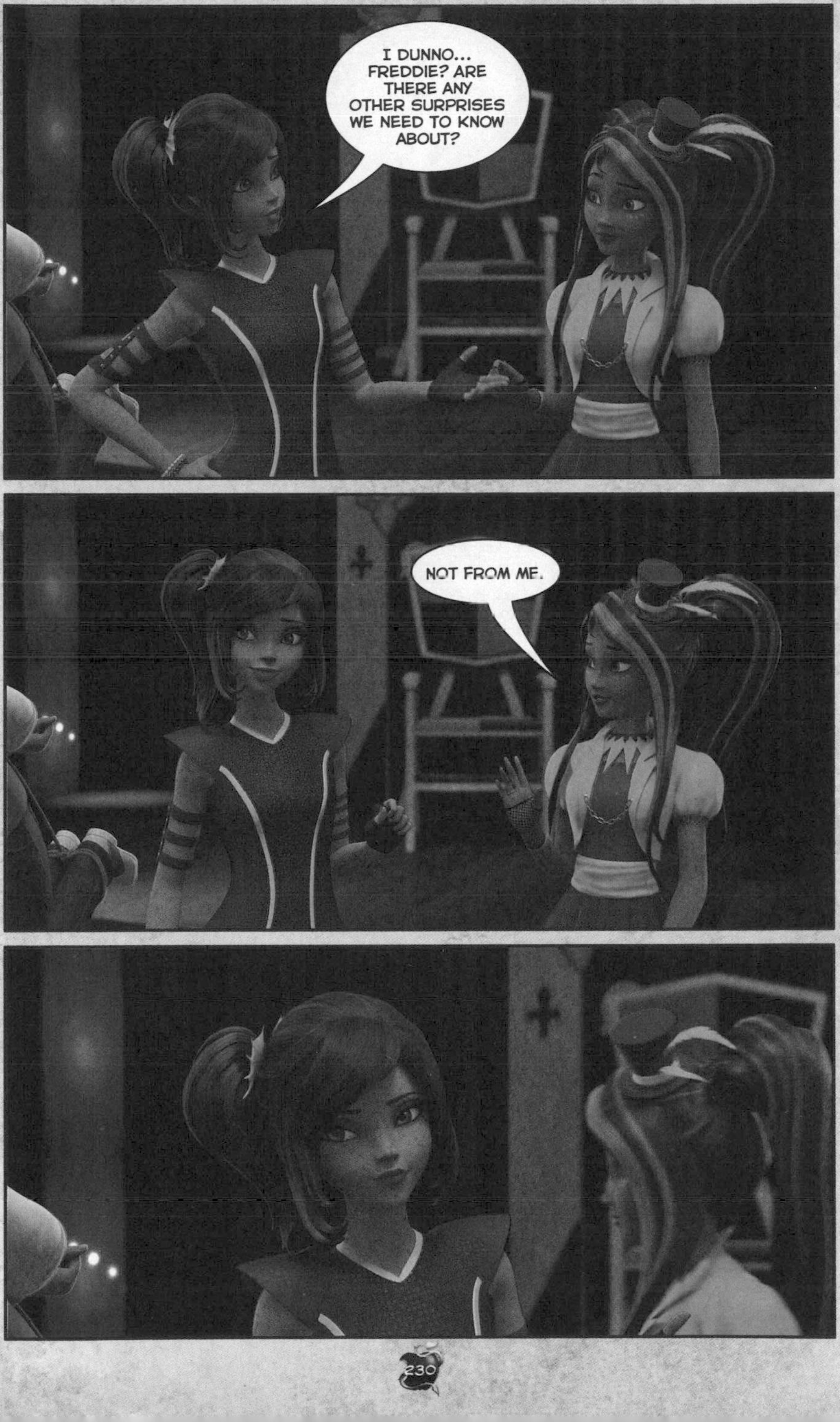
I DUNNO... FREDDIE? ARE THERE ANY OTHER SURPRISES WE NEED TO KNOW ABOUT?
NOT FROM ME.

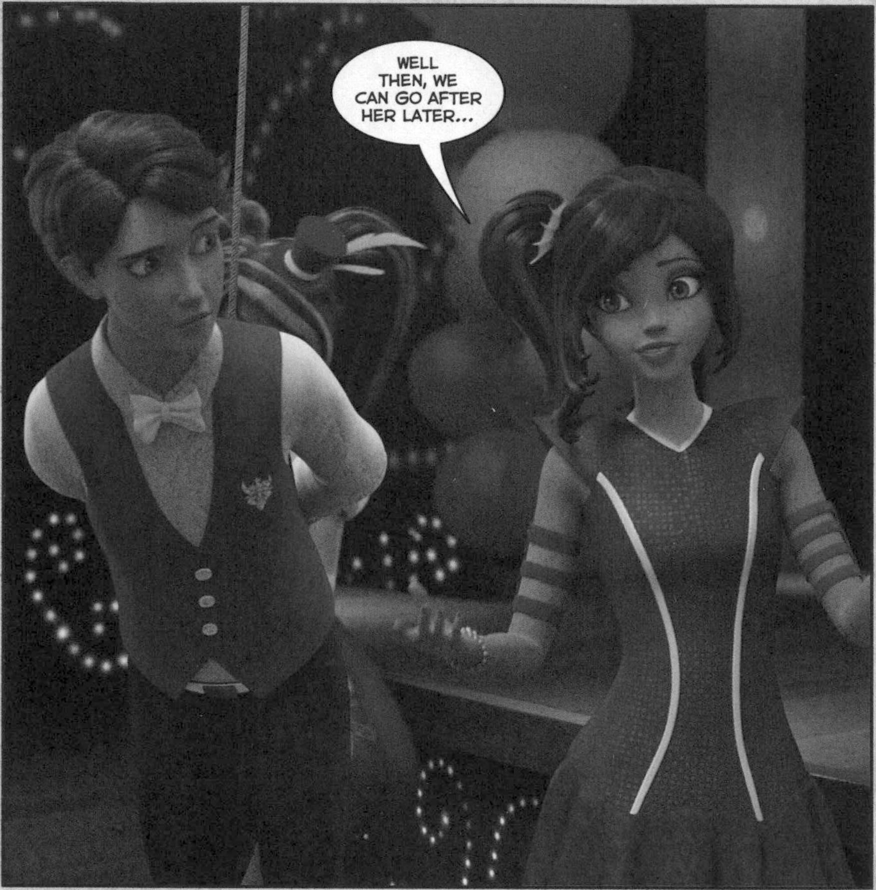
WELL THEN, WE CAN GO AFTER HER LATER...

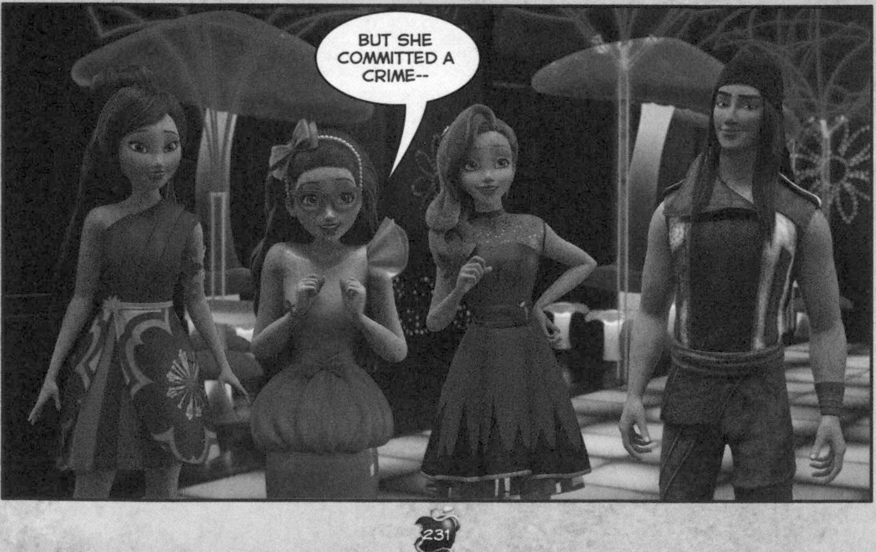
BUT SHE COMMITTED A CRIME--

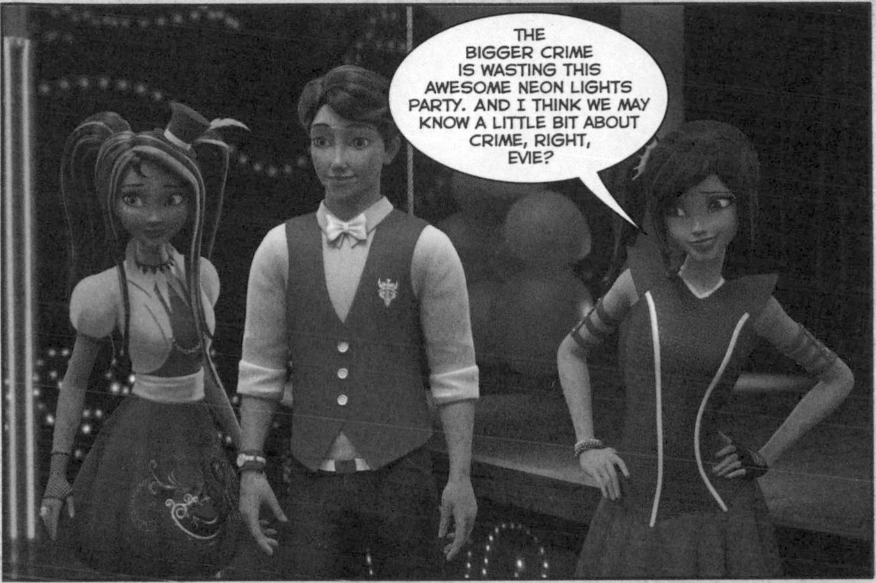
THE BIGGER CRIME IS WASTING THIS AWESOME NEON LIGHTS PARTY. AND I THINK WE MAY KNOW A LITTLE BIT ABOUT CRIME, RIGHT, EVIE?

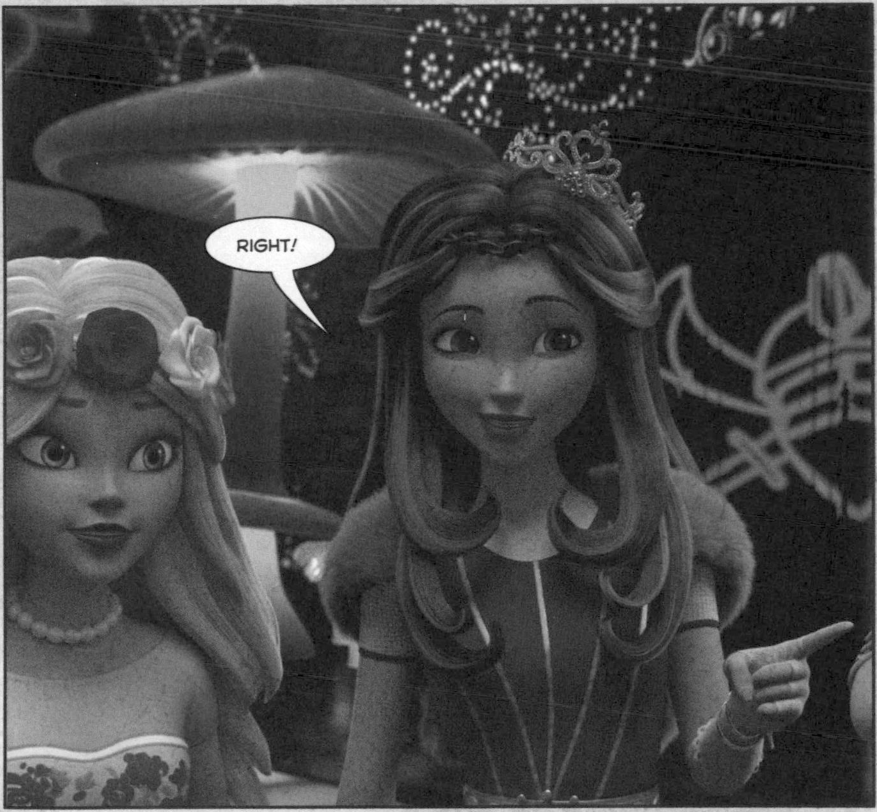
RIGHT!

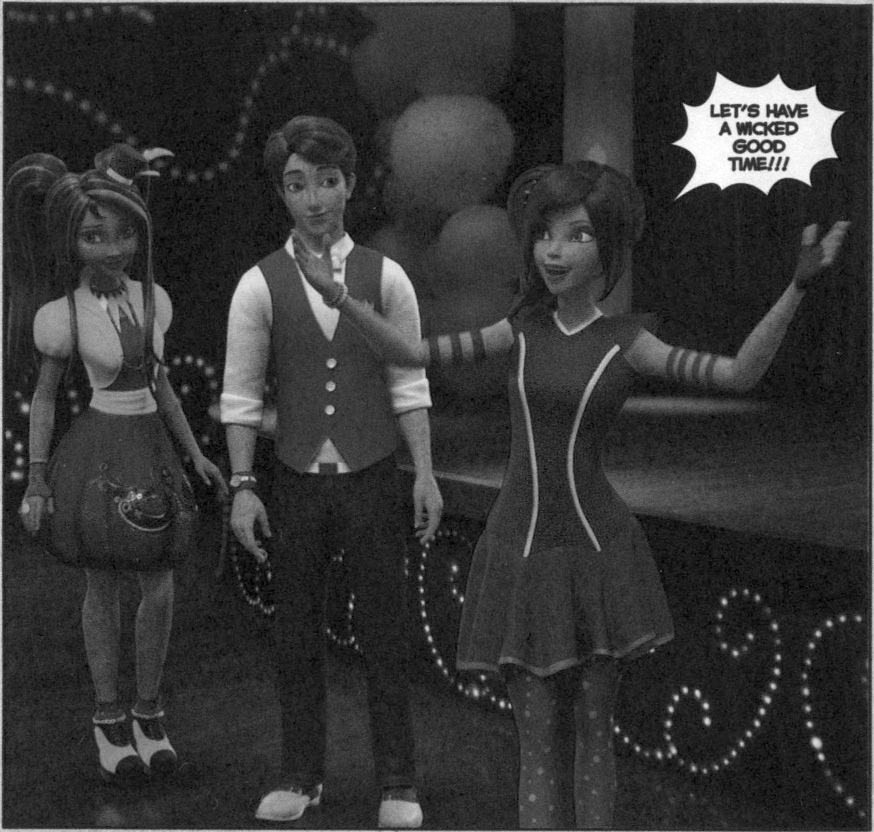
LET'S HAVE A WICKED GOOD TIME!!!

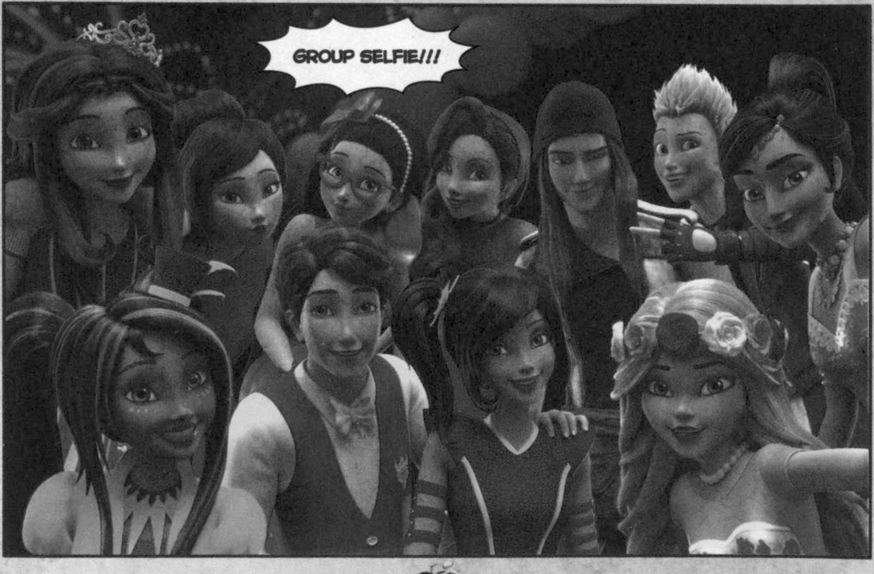
GROUP SELFIE!!!